DAVID GOODIS

DAVID GOODIS

FIVE NOIR NOVELS OF THE 1940s & 50s

Dark Passage
Nightfall
The Burglar
The Moon in the Gutter
Street of No Return

Robert Polito, *editor*

THE LIBRARY OF AMERICA

The paper used in this publication meets the
minimum requirements of the American National Standard for
Information Sciences—Permanence of Paper for Printed
Library Materials, ANSI Z39.48—1984.

Distributed to the trade in the United States
by Penguin Group (USA) Inc.
and in Canada by Penguin Books Canada Ltd.

Library of Congress Control Number: 2011928611
ISBN 978–1–59853–148–0

———

Second Printing
The Library of America—225

Manufactured in the United States of America

David Goodis:
Five Noir Novels of the 1940s & 50s
is published with support from

THE GEOFFREY C. HUGHES FOUNDATION

Contents

DARK PASSAGE

TO MY BROTHER

1

IT WAS a tough break. Parry was innocent. On top of that he was a decent sort of guy who never bothered people and wanted to lead a quiet life. But there was too much on the other side and on his side of it there was practically nothing. The jury decided he was guilty. The judge handed him a life sentence and he was taken to San Quentin.

The trial had been big and even though it involved unimportant people it was in many respects sensational. Parry was thirty-one and he made thirty-five a week as a clerk in an investment security house in San Francisco. He had been unhappily married for sixteen months, according to the prosecution. And, according to the prosecution, a friend of the Parrys came into the small apartment one winter afternoon and found Mrs. Parry on the floor with her head caved in. According to the prosecution, Mrs. Parry was dying and just before she passed away she said Parry had banged her on the head with a heavy glass ash tray. The ash tray was resting near the body. Police found Parry's fingerprints on the ash tray.

That was half the story. The other half meant the finish of Parry. He had to admit a few things. He had to admit he hadn't been getting along with his wife. He had to admit he was seeing other women. The fact that his wife was seeing other men didn't make any difference to the court. Then they got Parry to admit that he hadn't gone to work that day. A sinus headache kept him at home all morning and in the afternoon he had gone for a walk in the park. When he came home he found a crowd outside the apartment house and several police cars, the usual picture. That was what he said. The police said differently. The police said that Parry had hit his wife on the head with the ash tray and then arranged the body so that it would look as if she had tripped, knocking the ash tray off a table as she fell, then knocking her head on the ash tray when she reached the floor. The police said that it was a very clever job and no doubt it would have succeeded except for Mrs. Parry's dying statement.

Parry's lawyer tried hard but there was too much on the other side. There was only one weak link in the prosecution. It involved the fingerprints. When the prosecuting attorney claimed that Vincent Parry was a shrewd, devilish murderer, Parry's lawyer came back with the statement that a shrewd, devilish murderer would have wiped fingerprints from the ash tray. Parry's lawyer said it was no murder, it was an accident.

That was about all, except the character stuff. A lot of people wanted to know why Parry wasn't in uniform. The prosecution played that up big. Parry was a 4-F. The sinus was one reason, a bad kidney was another. Anyway he was a 4-F and added to that was something connected with a stretch in an Arizona reformatory when he was fifteen. He was an only child, an orphan, and his only relative in Maricopa said no and a week later he was hungry and robbing a general store. Then again there was this business of playing around with other women and there was a collection of statements from bartenders and liquor dealers. Parry had a habit of drinking straight gin despite the kidney trouble. The prosecution claimed that the gin was primary cause for the kidney trouble. Connecting the gin with the kidney, the prosecution made another connection and inferred that the 4-F status was attained through excessive gin that made the kidney worse. A few newspapers bit into that and began calling Parry a draft dodger. Other newspapers took it up. There were editorials calling for further examination of the 4-F's who complained of kidney trouble. When Parry was sentenced his picture was in all the papers and one of the papers captioned his picture "Draft Dodger Sentenced."

Just before he was taken to San Quentin, Parry got permission to talk to a friend. This was Fellsinger, who was a few years older than Parry and worked in the same investment security house. Fellsinger was Parry's best friend and one of the persons who believed Parry innocent. Parry gifted Fellsinger with all his possessions. These included a waterproof wrist watch, $63.75, a Packard-Bell phonograph-radio, a collection of phonograph records featuring Parry's assemblage of Count Basie specials and the late Mrs. Parry's assortment of Stravinsky and other moderns. Parry also handed over his clothes, but Fellsinger burned these and also got rid of everything that belonged to Mrs. Parry. Fellsinger was unmarried and he had spent most of his time with the Parrys. He had never liked Mrs. Parry and when he said good-by to Vincent Parry he broke down and cried like a baby.

Parry didn't cry. The last time he had cried was when he was in the reformatory in Arizona. A tall guard had punched him in the face, punched him again. When the guard punched him a third time, Parry went out of his head and put his hands around the guard's throat. The guard was dying and Parry was sobbing with tears as he increased pressure. Then other guards came running in to break it up. They put young Parry in solitary confinement. Later on the brutal guard pulled another rotten trick on one of the kids and the superintendent investigated the situation and had the guard dismissed.

Parry was thinking about that as he entered the gates of San Quentin. He hoped he wouldn't run into any brutal guards. He had an idea that he might be able to extract some ounce of happiness out of prison life. He had always wanted happiness, the simple and ordinary kind. He had never wanted trouble.

He didn't look as if he could handle trouble. He was five seven and a hundred and forty-five, and it was the kind of build made for clerking in an investment security house. Then there was drab light-brown hair and drab dark-yellow eyes. The lips were the kind of lips not made for smiling. There was usually a cigarette between the lips. Parry had jumped at the job in the investment security house when he learned it was the kind of job where he could smoke all he pleased. He was a three-pack-a-day man.

In San Quentin he managed to get three packs a day. He worked as a bookkeeper and he made a financial arrangement with several non-smokers. He got along agreeably with other inmates and the first seven months were no hardship. In the eighth month he ran into the same sort of guard who had punched him during his Arizona confinement. The guard picked on him and finally arranged a situation where it was necessary to exert authority. Parry was willing to take the bawling out but he wasn't willing to take the punch. Then came the second punch. And on the third punch Parry started to sob, just as he had sobbed in Arizona. He put his hands around the guard's throat. Other guards came in on it and broke it up. Parry was placed in solitary.

He was in solitary for nine days. When he came out he was fired from the bookkeeping job and switched to another cell block, much less comfortable than the one he had been in. He learned that the guard had almost died and the episode had reached outside the prison walls and it had been in the papers. He was now doing hard work with a spade and a sledgehammer and at night he was practically out on his feet. He was almost too tired to read the letters he received from Fellsinger. But one night he got a letter from Fellsinger and it told him he was a sap for mixing with that guard. It ruined any chances he might have for a parole. He got a laugh out of that. He knew he was going to spend the rest of his life in this place. He knew what kind of life it was going to be.

It was going to be a horrible life. The food at San Quentin was decent but it wasn't good enough to get along with his condition. And somehow he had the paradoxical feeling that gin had helped his kidney and here he couldn't have gin. He couldn't have women and he couldn't have bright lights and he couldn't have a fireplace. He couldn't have the kind of friends he wanted and he couldn't have streets to walk on and crowds to see. All he had here were the bars on his cell door and the realization that he would be looking at those bars for the rest of his life.

He was sitting on the edge of his cot. He was looking at the bars of the cell door. Like a snake gliding into a pool a thought glided into his mind. He stood up. He walked to the door and put his hands against the steel bars. They weren't very thick but they were strong. He thought of how strong these bars were, how strong was the steel door at the end of corridor D, how ready was the guard's revolver at the end of corridor E, then the two guards at the end of corridor F, and how high the wall was, and how many machine guns were waiting there along the wall. The snake made a turn and started to glide out of the pool. Then it turned again and it began to expand. It was becoming a very big snake because Parry was thinking of the trucks that brought barrels of cement into that part of the yard where they were building a storage house. Parry worked in that part of the yard.

Sleep was a blackboard and on the blackboard was a chalked

plan of the yard. He kept tracing it over and over and when he got it straight he imagined a white X where he was going to be when the truck unloaded the barrels. The X moved when the empty barrels were placed back upon the truck. The X moved slowly and then disappeared into one of the barrels that was already in the truck.

The blackboard was all black. It stayed black until a whistle blew. The motor started. The sound of it pierced the side of the barrel and pierced Parry's brain. There wasn't much air but there was enough to keep him alive for a while. A little while. The sound of the motor was louder now. Then the truck was moving. He knew just how far it had to move until it would be out of the yard. He waited to hear the sound of a whistle. The sound of a siren. He had the feeling that this was nothing more than a foolish idea that would get him nowhere except back in solitary. He shrugged and told himself he had nothing to lose.

There was no whistle. There was no siren. The truck was going faster now. He couldn't believe it. This had been too easy. He told his mind to shut up, because this wasn't over yet. This was only the beginning and from here on it was going to be tough. He had to get out of the barrel and that was going to be a real picnic. He was in one of the bottom barrels and they were stacked three deep. The truck was rolling now. He sensed that it was making a turn. It made another turn and then it rolled faster. He was having trouble drawing air from the black inside of the barrel. He told himself that he had five minutes and no more. Two barrels on top of him, and four rows of barrels between him and the edge of the truck. He took a deep breath that wasn't so deep after all. That scared him. He took another deep breath and that was less deep than the first. He threw his weight against the side of the barrel and the barrel wouldn't budge. He tried again and he made about an inch. He tried a third time and made another inch. He kept on trying and making inches. All at once it came to him that he was battling for his life. It scared him so much that he stopped trying and he decided to start yelling, to start begging them to stop the truck and let him out of the barrel.

Just before he opened his mouth he analyzed the idea. The

gap at the top of the barrel was wide enough for his voice to get through, but if his voice got through it would mean that he would soon be back at San Quentin.

His mouth stayed open but did not release sound. Instead he made another drag at air. He pushed again at the side of the barrel. Now he estimated that three minutes were subtracted from the original five. He had two minutes in which to make good. He kept on dragging at air and pushing at the side of the barrel.

August heat came gushing through the gap at the top of the barrel, mixed with the black thickness in the barrel and the anguish and the effort. Perspiration gushed down Parry's face, formed ponds in his armpits. All at once he realized that more than two minutes had passed, considerably more. Put it at ten minutes. He looked up and through the gap at the top of the barrel he could see yellow sky. He smiled at the sky and now he understood that he had a good chance. Along with the sky a supply of new air was coming through the gap.

Heaving at the side of the barrel, pushing it away from the two barrels on top, he widened the gap to ten inches. He was working on the eleventh inch when the truck hit a bump in the road and the two barrels on top went sliding back to their previous position. He looked up and instead of yellow sky all he could see was black, the black underside of the second barrel. He had lost the gap and he had lost all the air. Now he must start all over again.

He didn't want to start all over again. He wanted to weep. He began to weep and the tears were thick spheres of wet mixing with the wet of increased perspiration. His cramped limbs were giving him pain. He measured the pain and knew that it was bad. And it would get worse, keep getting worse until finally it would blend with the pain in air-starved lungs. Once more he told himself that he was going to die here in the barrel.

Hate walked in and floated at the side of fear. Hate for the bump in the road that had caused the two barrels to slide back. Hate for the two barrels. Hate for the truck. Hate for the prosecuting attorney. Hate for Mrs. Parry. Hate for Mrs. Parry's friend who had entered the apartment that winter afternoon and found the body. Her name was Madge Rapf. Her name was Pest. She had been the Pest from the first moment Parry had known her. She was always in the apartment, butting in. Getting herself invited to dinner and staying late and trying to make time with Parry. Once she had made a certain amount of time with him and he remembered it was on a night when he and Mrs. Parry had engaged in a vicious quarrel. Mrs. Parry had gone into her room and slammed the door. Madge went into the room and stayed there for about twenty minutes. When she came out she asked Parry if he would take her home. He took her home and when she got him inside she started in on him. He didn't want to do anything. She didn't really attract him. She was nothing very special. But he was sick and tired of Mrs. Parry and he didn't particularly care what happened. So he began seeing her and one night it got to a certain point and then he told Madge to lay off, he was going home. She began to pester him. She told him that Mrs. Parry was bored with him but she wouldn't be bored with him. She told him he should split with Mrs. Parry. He told her to mind her own business. But her nature made that impossible and every time she got the chance she told him to split with his wife and pitch in with her. She had been separated from her husband for six years and during all that time he had been trying to get a divorce. She wouldn't give Rapf a divorce because she knew every now and then he had another girl he wanted to marry. She had nobody. She had nothing except the hundred and fifty a month she got from her husband. Now the hundred and fifty a month didn't satisfy her and she wanted somebody. She was miserable and the only thing that eased her misery was to see other people miserable. If they weren't miserable she pestered them until they became miserable. Parry had a feeling that one of the happiest moments in Madge Rapf's life was when the foreman stood up and said that he was guilty.

It was getting awful in the barrel. Parry pushed the hate aside and replaced it with energy. He pushed at the side of the barrel. He made an inch. He made another inch and he had air again. The truck was traveling very fast and he wondered where it was going. He kept pushing at the side of the barrel. The truck hit another bump, hit a second bump, hit a third and a fourth. Parry figured there might be a fifth bump and he advised himself to be ready for it. The four bumps had pushed the two barrels back the way he wanted them to go back. He had about five inches up there. When the fifth bump came he was prepared for it and he heaved hard, going along with the bump, getting the two barrels over to the side, increasing the gap to what he measured as nine inches. He thrust his arms up, pushed at the two barrels, made four more inches. And that was plenty.

Parry pulled himself out of the barrel. He saw the road going away from him, a dark grey stream sliding back between level pale green meadow, sliding toward the yellow horizon. On the left, bordering the pale green, he could see shaggy hills, not too high. He decided to make the hills.

Keeping his head low he weaved his way through the barrels. Then he was at the edge of the truck, figuring its speed at about fifty. It was going to be a rough fall and probably he would get hurt. But if he fell facing the truck, running with the truck, he would be playing along with the momentum and that would be something of a benefit.

He did it that way. He was running before he reached the road. He made a few yards and then went down flat on his face. Knowing he was hurt but not knowing where and not caring, he picked himself up quickly and raced for the side of the road. The pale green grass was fairly high and he threw himself at it and rested there, breathing hard, too frightened to look at the road. But he could hear the truck motor going away from him and he knew that he was all right as far as the truck was concerned. When he raised his head from the grass he saw an automobile passing by. He saw the people in the automobile and their faces were turned toward him and he waited for the automobile to stop.

The automobile didn't stop. Parry stayed there another minute. Before he stood up he took off the grey shirt, the white undershirt. Stripped to the waist he felt the heat of the sun, the thick moisture of deep summer. It felt good. But something else felt bad and it was the pain in both arms, in the elbows. He had fallen on his elbows and the skin was ripped and there was considerable blood. He pulled at grass, kept digging at earth until there was something of a hole, a semblance of mud. He rubbed mud on his elbows and that stopped the blood and formed a protective cake. Then he put the shirt and the undershirt in the hole. He replaced the clods of grass, covering the hole smoothly.

The sun was high, and Parry watched it as he started toward the hills. He guessed the time as somewhere around eleven, and it meant he had been on the truck for almost an hour. It also meant San Quentin had taken a long time to discover his exit. Again he was telling himself it had been too easy and it couldn't last and then he heard the sound of motorcycles.

He threw himself at the grass, tried to insert himself in the ground. As yet he couldn't see the motorcycles, although his eyes made a wide sweep of the road. That was all right. Probably they couldn't see him either. They were coming around a gradual bend in the road. They made a lot of noise, a raging noise as they came nearer. Then he could see them, whizzing past. Two and three and five of them. Just as they passed him they began using sirens and he knew they were going after the truck.

He could picture it. The truck was say three miles down the road. Give them five minutes to search the barrels, to question the driver and helper. Give them another six minutes to come back here, because they would be going slowly, studying the road and the meadow at the sides of the road. All right, wait one more minute and let them make a mile and a third. Let it be two minutes, then take three or four minutes to get to those hills, and pray there wouldn't be any more motorcycles tearing down the road.

2

WHEN HE was in the hills he sat down for a rest. He wondered if it would be feasible to stay here in the hills, give himself a few days here while the search radiated. But if the police couldn't get any leads elsewhere, they'd come back to the road and chances were they'd sift the hills. The more he thought about it the more he understood the necessity for keeping on the move. And moving fast. That was it. Fast. Everything fast.

He got up and started moving in the direction he had first taken. The hills seemed to move along with him. After a while he was tired again but he was thinking in terms of speed and he refused to take another rest. The weariness went away for a time but after some minutes it came back and it was accompanied by thirst and a desire for a cigarette. He couldn't do anything about the thirst but there was an almost empty pack of cigarettes in his trousers pocket. He put a cigarette between his lips and then he searched for a match. He didn't have a match. He looked around, as if he thought there might be a place where he could buy a book of matches. He puffed at the cigarette, trying to imagine that it was lit and he was drawing smoke. He didn't have any matches. He began to think of the things he didn't have.

He didn't have clothes. He didn't have money. He didn't have friends. No, he was wrong there. He had a few friends and one friend in particular. And it was a cinch that Fellsinger would go to bat for him. But Fellsinger was in Frisco and Frisco was going to be a very hot place aside from the heat of August. Nevertheless it was practical for him to see Fellsinger. The next move was Frisco. The police wouldn't watch Fellsinger. Or maybe they would. Or wouldn't.

As an hour passed the hills gave way to another stretch of pale green. There were no roads, there were no houses, nothing. Parry negotiated the pale green, moved toward dark green. It was heavily wooded area and he tried to guess what was on the other side. He looked back, knowing that the division of terrain would be a decent sort of guide, preventing him from traveling in a circle. He entered the woods.

He was in the woods for more than an hour. He was moving fast. Then he could see a lot of bright yellow breaking through the dark green. It meant that he was about to come out on the other side of the woods. Already he could see a band of white-yellow out there and he knew it was a road.

At the side of the road he leaned against a tree, waiting. He wanted to see a truck or an automobile and at the same time he was afraid to see anything of that sort. He kept sucking at the unlighted cigarette. He looked at the other side of the road and saw a continuation of the woods. All right, let an automobile come by. Let something happen.

Nothing happened for about forty minutes. Then Parry heard a sound coming down the road and it belonged to an automobile. There was an instant of animal fright and he was turning to dart back into the woods. A spurt of gambling spirit pushed aside the fright and Parry ran out to the center of the road. He saw the automobile coming toward him. It was a Nash, a 36 or 37, he wasn't sure but he didn't particularly care either. It was something that might take him to Frisco, if it was going to Frisco. He was out there in the center of the road, waving his arms beseechingly. The Nash was going rather fast and it didn't look as if it was going to stop. It increased speed as it closed in on Parry. There was only one person in the car and it was a man. It was a very pleasant man who was using this method to tell Parry that he would either get out of the way or get hit.

Parry got out of the way and the Nash went ripping down the road. Another fifteen minutes came in and went out again. Parry was leaning against the same tree. He wanted a match badly. He wanted water badly. He wanted a lift badly. He wished it wasn't August. He wished he had been born somewhere up in the Arctic Circle where these things didn't happen to a man. He heard another automobile.

This was a Studebaker. It was from way back. It was doing about thirty and Parry had an idea it couldn't do any more no matter how hard it tried. Again he was out in the center of the road, waving his arms.

The Studebaker stopped. Its only occupant was the driver, a

man in old clothes, a man who looked Parry up and down and finally opened the door.

Parry stepped in. He closed the door and the man put the car in gear and got it up to thirty again. Parry had already noticed that the Studebaker was a coupé and the man was about forty or so and he was about five eight and he didn't weigh much. He wore a felt hat that had been dead for years.

For a few minutes there was no talk. Then the man half looked at Parry and said, "Where you going?"

"San Francisco."

The man looked at him directly. Parry looked straight ahead. He was thinking that approximately four hours had passed since he had stepped into the barrel. Perhaps by this time it was already in the papers. Perhaps the man had already seen a paper. Perhaps the man wasn't going to San Francisco. Perhaps anything.

"Whereabouts in Frisco?" the man said. He pushed the hat back an inch or so.

Parry was about to say Civic Center. Then he changed his mind. Then he took another look at the man and he came back to Civic Center. It really didn't make much difference what he said, because he was going to get rid of this man and he was going to take the car.

He said, "Civic Center."

"I'll get you there," the man said. "I'm taking Van Ness to Market. How come you're using this road?"

"Fellow gave me a lift. He said it was a short cut."

"How come he left you off back there?"

"We had an argument," Parry said.

"What about?"

"Politics."

"What are you?"

"Well," Parry said, "I'm non-partisan. But this fellow seemed to be against everything. He couldn't get me to agree with him and finally he stopped the car and told me to get out."

The man looked at Parry's bare ribs. The man said, "What did he do—steal your shirt?"

"No, I always dress this way in summer. I like to be comfortable. You got a match?"

The man fished in a coat pocket and two fingers came out holding a book of matches.

"Want a cigarette?" Parry said as he scratched a match.

"I don't smoke. Mighty funny looking pants you got there."

"I know. But they're comfortable."

"You like to be comfortable," the man said, and then he laughed, and he kept on looking at the grey cotton pants.

"Yes," Parry said. "I like to be comfortable."

"You can keep the matches," the man said. He kept on looking at the grey cotton pants. He dragged the Studebaker back to twenty-five, then to twenty. His eyes went down to Parry's heavy shoes.

Parry said, "How come you got matches if you don't smoke?"

The man didn't answer. Parry kept his face frontward but his gaze was sideways and he could see the man's weather-darkened features and the short thin nose and the long chin. He got his gaze a little more to the side and he could see the ear and the mixture of black and white hair beneath the rippling brim of the felt hat. The right temple, he was thinking. Or maybe just under the right ear. He had heard somewhere that just under the ear was the best place.

"Where you from?" the man said.

"Arizona."

"Whereabouts in Arizona?"

"Maricopa," Parry said truthfully.

"Hitched all the way from Maricopa, eh?"

"That's right," Parry said. He eyed the rear-view mirror. The road back there was empty. He got ready. His right hand formed a fist and he tightened it, making it hard. His right arm quivered.

The man said, "Why Frisco?"

"What?"

"I said why are you going to Frisco?"

Parry rubbed the fist against his thigh. He turned his body and leaned against the door as he looked at the man. He said, "Mister, you get on my nerves with all these questions. I don't need to be bothered with you. I can get another ride."

The man frowned, deepened it and then let it break and

shape itself into a weak grin. He said, "What you getting excited about? All I did was——"

"Forget it," Parry said angrily. "I'll pick up the kind of a ride where I don't have to tell my life history. How far am I from Frisco?"

"No more than fifteen miles," the man said. "But you're being foolish. I'm trying to help you out and you're——"

"Stop the car, mister. And thanks for taking me this far."

The man shrugged. He lifted a foot from the accelerator, brought it over to the brake. The car moved to the side of the road and as it came to a stop Parry leaned forward and sent his right arm toward the man's head. His fist landed on the upper part of the man's jaw, just under the ear. The aim was all right, but Parry didn't have much of a punch and the man let out a yell and clutched Parry's arm as the fist went forward again. Parry squirmed and tried to use his left. The man was stronger than Parry had supposed, and mingled fear and desperation increased the strength and tripled Parry's trouble. The man brought up a knee and tried to put it against Parry's groin. Parry managed to send a straight left into the man's face and the man let out another yell. The knee made another try at Parry's groin. Parry tried to stand up, but the knee was in his way. The man began to shout for help. Parry put another left in the man's face, followed it with a straight right that landed against the man's temple. The man was all fear now and he stopped shouting and he began to plead. As Parry hit him again he begged Parry to lay off. He said he didn't have much money on him but he'd hand it over if Parry would only leave him alone and allow him to go on his way. Parry again banged him on the temple, banged him on the jaw and on the temple again. The man's head went back and Parry punched him under the right ear and knocked him out.

Parry was very tired. He blew air out of his mouth and rested his head back against torn upholstery. Through the sound of the idling Studebaker he could hear another sound, the sound of an automobile coming down the road. It was coming from the Frisco direction. Straight ahead down the road it was a shining grey convertible coupé that was growing too quickly. Parry wanted to throw the whole thing away. He wanted to open the door and leap out into the woods and keep going.

He called that a bright idea and told himself that another
bright idea was to try hiding on the floor of the Studebaker.
They were wonderful, these bright ideas. He saw smoke coming up from the floor, coming from the half-smoked cigarette.
He reached down, picked up the cigarette, brought it toward
the face of the unconscious man. He had his hands cupped
around the end of the cigarette. He had his eyes on the grey
convertible coupé coming down the road. Let them think
there had been three in the Studebaker and the Studebaker
was stopping here so that one of them could go into the woods
for something and the other two were waiting here and having
a smoke.

The grey convertible rushed in and went past. Parry blew
more air out of his mouth. There would soon be another car
coming down the road. Now the road seemed to average a car
every four or five minutes. Let the next car think there was
only one in the Studebaker, and the Studebaker was parked
here while the driver went into the woods for something. Parry
opened the door, pulled the unconscious man out of the car
and quickly dragged him into the woods. He undressed the
man and he was putting on the man's clothes when the man
opened his eyes and started to open a bleeding mouth. Parry
bent low and chopped a right to the side of the head. The man
went out again and Parry went back to his dressing.

It wasn't a bad fit. The felt hat was the best item. It had a
fairly wide brim that would shadow his face to a great extent.
There was a dirty checkered shirt and a purple tie with orange
circles on it. There was a dark-brown coat patched in half a
dozen places and a pair of navy-blue trousers rounding out
their first decade.

He had the clothes on and he was going back to the Studebaker. Nearing the edge of the woods he stopped and put fingers to his chin. He saw the Studebaker and the grey convertible
coupé parked directly behind the Studebaker. The grey convertible was a Pontiac. He saw grey-violet behind the wheel.
Grey-violet of a blouse belonging to a girl with blonde hair.
She was sitting there behind the wheel, waiting for Parry to
come out of the woods. He decided to go back into the woods
and keep on going. As he turned, he saw the girl open the
door and step out of the Pontiac.

She saw him. She beckoned to him. There was authority in the beckoning and Parry was very frightened. He completed the turn and he started to run.

It was hard going. There were a lot of trees and twigs in his way. He could hear footsteps back there, the breaking of foliage, and he knew the girl was coming after him. Once he looked back and he saw her. She was about twenty yards behind him and she was doing her best. The snake came gliding into the pool. He would get her about fifty yards deep in the woods and then he would knock her unconscious and go back and grab the Studebaker. The snake made a turn and started gliding out of the pool. He didn't need to knock her unconscious. He didn't need to be afraid. The whole thing was very simple. The girl was lost on the road. Her Pontiac had passed the Studebaker and gone down the road maybe a half mile and when she knew she was lost she made a U-turn. She remembered the parked Studebaker and she came back to ask directions. That was all. He had only imagined the authority in that beckoning. It was curiosity and perhaps a stubborn decision to get her bearings that made her chase him through the woods.

Anyway he was now fifty yards deep in the woods and either way there was nothing to worry about. He stopped and turned and waited for her.

She came running up to him. The grey-violet blouse was supplemented by a dark grey-violet skirt. She was little. She was about five two and not more than a hundred. The blonde hair was very blonde but it wasn't peroxide. And there was a minimum of paint. A trace of orange-ish lipstick that went nicely with genuine grey eyes. She was something just a bit deeper than pretty, although she couldn't be called pretty. Her face was too thin.

He said, "What's on your mind?"

"I had a look at the fuel gauge. It shows almost empty." Her voice harmonized with the grey eyes and the lack of peroxide in her hair.

Parry said, "Where do I come in?"

"I don't know this road. I'd hate to be stuck here."

"So would I." Parry examined the grey eyes and couldn't find anything.

She was looking at the old clothes. She said, "Could you spare a few gallons? I'd pay a dollar a gallon."

It was an equation and it checked. The thing to do was to get rid of her in a hurry. Parry said, "Let's go back to the road and we'll talk it over."

They started back to the road. Parry waited for something but it didn't happen. He guided her away from the spot where he had left his man, and yet he had a feeling that she had already seen the man. He had a feeling that the gasoline story was just a story. Maybe this girl was lonely and she wanted a friend. Maybe this girl was starved for excitement and she wanted action. There were a lot of maybes and none of them went anywhere.

He got another good look at her. She was twenty-seven if she was a day. Give her a big break and call her twenty-six. He saw lines under her eyes that told him she didn't get much sleep. The way her lips were set told him she didn't get much out of life. One thing, she had money. That grey-violet outfit was money. The Pontiac was money. He looked for something on her hands and the only thing he saw was a large pale amethyst on the ring finger of her right hand.

They came to the edge of the road. She turned to him and said, "All right, let's get in my car and get out of here fast."

3

PARRY TOOK a step away from her. He said, "I don't get you."

She gestured back to the woods. "I saw the body."

"He isn't dead. He gave me a lift and he tried to take my wallet. I knocked him out and then I got scared and took him into the woods. I'm not scared now. I'm going to take his car. Don't you try to scare me."

"I'm not trying to scare you," she said. "I'm trying to help you." She started toward the Pontiac and gestured for him to come along. She said, "Come on, Vincent."

He stood there with his eyes coming out of his face.

She said, "Please Vincent—we don't have much time."

He stabbed a glance at the idling Studebaker. Then he remembered that the Studebaker couldn't do better than thirty. The Pontiac could do plenty. It was a 1940 and it had good tires. He could use something like that. He looked at the girl. He looked at the point of her chin.

He took a step toward her.

She didn't budge. She said, "It won't get you anywhere, Vincent. If you're alone in that car you'll be picked up. If you come with me I'll hide you in the back seat. I've got a blanket there."

"You're with the police."

"If I was with the police I'd be carrying a gun. Look, Vincent, you've got a chance here, and if you don't take it——"

"I'm going to take it." He took another step toward her.

This time she cowered. Backing away from him she pleaded, "Don't do it, Vincent. Please don't. I'm for you. I've always been for you——"

It stopped him. He said, "What do you mean—always?"

"From the very beginning. From the day the trial opened. Come on, Vincent—please? Stick with me and I won't let them get you."

The way she said it brought tears to his eyes and out of his eyes, brought the thought from his brain and out of his mouth and he said, "I don't know what to do—I don't know what to do——"

She put a hand on his wrist and took him to the Pontiac. She opened the door, pulled up the front seat. He got in the back and crawled under the blanket.

The door slammed. The motor started and the Pontiac began to roll.

He got his head out from under the blanket and he said, "Where are we going—Frisco?"

"Yes. You'll stay at my place. Keep under that blanket. We're due to be stopped. They've got all roads blocked. We're lucky they're not probing this road."

"You're in on it. I know you're in on it." He couldn't get the quiver out of his voice. The tears kept coming out of his eyes.

The Pontiac was doing forty. It made a turn and Parry felt a sudden decrease in speed. Then he heard the sound of motors —sharp little motors—motorcycles. His body started to shake. He tried to stop the shaking. He bit deep into the back of his hand. The motorcycles were coming from up front, closing in, getting louder. The Pontiac went down to twenty—fifteen—it was going to stop.

He could hear her saying, "Don't move, Vincent. Don't make a sound. It's going to be all right."

The Pontiac stopped. The sound of motorcycles came close, broke like big waves nearing a beach, then became little waves coming up on the beach. The motorcycles were idling now. Parry pictured them parked at the side of the road. All he could see was the black inside of the blanket that was even blacker than the inside of the barrel. And yet he got his mind past the blanket and he could picture the police walking over to the parked Pontiac.

Then he didn't need to picture it any more because he was hearing it.

A motorcycle policeman said, "Got your license, miss?"

He could hear the sound of a panel compartment getting opened. He begged himself to stop the shaking.

"Where are you going, miss?" The same voice.

"San Francisco."

"I see you live there." The same voice.

"Yes." It was her voice. "What's the matter, officer? Have I done something wrong?"

"I don't know yet, miss." The same voice.

Then another voice. "Carrying anything?"

Then her voice again. "Yes."

"What have you got?" The first voice. "What have you got there in the back!"

Her voice. "Old clothes. I'm making a collection for China War Relief."

The first voice. "We'll have a look, if you don't mind."

Her voice. "Go right ahead."

The sound of the door opening. The sound of the blonde girl moving over so that the policemen could gain access to the back seat. He started to picture it again. They were looking at the blanket. They were going to lift the blanket. Then he could feel it—their fingers touching the blanket, lifting the edge of the blanket. He pulled his hand inside the sleeve of Studebaker's coat. They could see the sleeve now, but they couldn't see his hand. And they could see part of the coat and that was as far as they got. They took their fingers away from the blanket.

The first voice. "Well, I guess it's all right, miss. Sorry to have troubled you, but we're checking every car on this road."

Her voice. "Perfectly all right, officer. Will there be anything else?"

"No. You can drive on now."

The sound of the door closing. The sound of the motor rising. The Pontiac rolled again. Parry felt a wetness against his lips and it was blood coming thickly from the back of his hand, getting through the place where his teeth had penetrated the sleeve.

The Pontiac made a turn. It picked up speed and it went more smoothly now. Parry knew they were on another road. He got his head halfway out of the blanket.

He said, "You told them to go ahead and look."

"I had to," she said. "I knew they would look anyway. I had to take the chance."

"Do you think we'll be stopped again?"

"No. From here on it's going to be all right."

"Everything's going to be all right," Parry said. He looked

at the back of his hand. His teeth had gone in deep. The blood wouldn't stop. And his elbows were beginning to hurt again. And he wanted a drink of water. He wanted a cigarette. He wanted to go to sleep.

He closed his eyes and tried to get comfortable. Maybe he could fall asleep.

She said, "How's it going?"

"Dandy. Everything's going to be all right and everything's dandy."

"Stop it, Vincent. You're free."

"Free as the breeze. I don't have a worry in the world. I'm doing great and everything's dandy. Look, if you're not the police, who are you?"

"I'm your friend. Is that enough?"

"No," Parry said. "It's not enough. If they catch me they catch me, but in the meantime I want to stay out as long as I can. And I won't stay out long if I make mistakes. I want to be sure this isn't a mistake. How did you know I was on that road?"

"I didn't. That is, I wasn't sure. But I had a feeling——"

"You had a feeling. So you went to a fortune teller and he told you Vincent Parry broke out of San Quentin and was going into the hills and through the woods and getting a lift in a Studebaker."

"Don't make fun of fortune tellers." Her voice was light. He wondered if she was smiling.

He raised his head a few more inches from the blanket. He could see her blonde hair above the grey velour upholstery. All he had to do was get hold of her hair and pull her head back to get a crack at her jaw.

"How did you know I broke out of San Quentin?" he asked.

"The radio."

He brought his head up another inch. He said, "All right, that passes. Let's try this one—how did you know I was on that road?"

"I know the section."

"What are you giving me?"

"I'm telling you I know the section." Her voice was no longer light. "I know all the roads around here. The first radio announcement said you got away. The second announcement said you got away in a truck. They gave the location where police stopped the truck. I know the section very well. I used to paint."

"You used to paint what?"

"Water color. Landscape stuff. I used to hang around there and paint those meadows and hills. Sometimes I'd go into the hills and I'd get a slant on the woods. Then sometimes I'd use the road to get another slant on the woods. That's how I knew about the road. I had a feeling you'd be on that road."

"I'm supposed to believe that."

"Don't you want to believe it? Then don't believe it. Do you want to get out?"

"What?"

"I said do you want to get out? I got you past the police. If you had taken that Studebaker you'd be on your way back to San Quentin by now. That's one thing. And if they had pulled back that blanket another few inches I'd be letting myself in for a few years of prison. That's another thing. Right now I'm letting myself in for a broken jaw."

"What do you mean a broken jaw?"

"You're all set to clip me one, aren't you?"

Parry said, "Now I know why you stick up for the fortune tellers. You're a fortune teller yourself. You're a mind reader."

"Please, Vincent. Please wait it out."

"Wait for what?"

"For the chance. A real chance. There's going to be a real chance for you. I have the feeling——"

"Let's try a hard one," Parry said. "Tell me the date of my birth."

"April first, the way you're acting now. Do you want to get out?"

"You want to get rid of me, don't you?"

"Yes."

"Why?"

"I'm beginning to feel afraid."

"Sister, I don't blame you. The law——"

"I'm not afraid of the law, Vincent. I'm afraid of you. I'm sorry I started this. I'm sorry I threw the blanket in the back of the car and went out to find you. Now I've found you and I'm stuck with you. I didn't know it would be this way."

"What way?"

"You. The way you're carrying on. I thought it would be very different from what it is. I thought you'd be soft. And kind. And very grateful. Very grateful for every little thing. That's the way I always imagined you. That's the way you were at the trial."

"You attended the trial?"

"Yes. I was there almost every day."

"How come?"

"I was interested."

"In me?"

"Yes."

"Sorry for me."

"Yes. At the trial. And after you were sentenced. And earlier today. Now I'm no longer interested. I did something I wanted to do very badly. I did my little bit for you. And it hasn't turned out the way I thought it would turn out. You're not soft, Vincent. You're mean—and I'm stuck with you."

"You're not stuck with me," Parry said. "I'm getting out here. And I'm not doing what I did to Studebaker. All I'm doing is saying good-by and good luck."

The Pontiac went over to the side of the road and came to a stop.

"How is it?" Parry said.

"It's clear."

"Any place I can duck?"

"Take a look."

He brought his head up and gazed through all the windows. Directly ahead the wide white road sliced through a narrow valley devoid of houses. On the right side the valley widened and on the left side there was a patch of woodland going level for a few hundred yards and then climbing up a mountain.

"This will be all right," Parry said. He put his hand on the door handle. He tilted the back of the empty front seat, quickly opened the door and leaped out. Running toward the patch of woodland he heard the Pontiac going away.

He was twenty yards away from the woodland when he heard a motor grinding and without looking he knew that the Pontiac was in reverse and coming back. He turned and raced toward the road.

The door was open for him.

She said, "Get in."

He jumped in, closed the door and got under the blanket as if it were home and he had been away from home for a long time.

The Pontiac started forward and went into second and moved up to third and did forty. She held it there.

Parry said, "Why did you come back?"

"You looked lonely out there."

"I felt lonely."

"How do you feel now?"

"Better."

"Much better?"

"Much."

For a while they didn't say anything. Then Parry asked her if it was all right to smoke and she opened both side windows and tossed a book of matches over her shoulder. She asked him to light one for her. He lit two cigarettes, reached up and gave her one, then got down under the blanket and pulled smoke into his mouth. The smoke aggravated the heat that was already in the blanket. He didn't mind. He found that the thirst was going away and going along with it was the pain in his elbows and the back of his hand had stopped bleeding.

She said, "I forgot something."

"You mean you left something with the police?"

"No, I forgot something when I said you weren't soft, the way I'd expected you'd be. When I said you were mean. I forgot that you were in a prison for seven months. Of course you're mean. Anyone would be mean. But don't be mean to me. Promise me you won't be mean to me."

"Look, I told you before—you're not stuck with me."

"But I am, Vincent. I am."

Parry took the cigarette from his mouth, put it in again and took a long tug. He got the smoke out and then he sighed. He said, "It's too much for me."

She didn't answer that. Parry felt the car turning, going slower, heard the sound of San Francisco coming in and getting under the blanket. The sound of other automobiles and the honking of horns, the hum of trade and the droning of people on the streets. He was frightened again. He wanted to get away from here and fast. He began remembering pictures he had seen in travel folders long ago. Places that looked out upon water. Lovely beaches. One was Patavilca, Peru. Another was Almeria, Spain. There were so many others, it was such a big world.

The Pontiac came to a stop.

4

PARRY GOT his head past the edge of the blanket. He said, "What's the matter?"

"We're at my place. It's an apartment house. We're on Geary, not far from the center of town. Are you ready?"

"Ready for what?"

"You're going to get out of the car. You're going to stay at my place."

"That's no good."

"Can you think of anything better?"

Parry tried to think of something better. He thought of the railroad station and he threw it away. He thought of hopping a freight and he knew they'd be watching the freight yards. They'd be watching every channel of possible getaway.

He said, "No."

"Then get ready, Vincent. Count up to fifteen. By that time I'll be in the apartment house and the elevator will be set to go up. When you reach fifteen get out of the car and walk fast but don't run. And don't be scared."

"What's there to be scared about?"

"Come on, Vincent. Don't be scared. It's all right now. We've reached home."

"There's no place like home," Parry said.

"Start counting, Vincent," she said and then she was out of the car and the door closed again and Parry was counting. When he reached fifteen he told himself that he couldn't do it. He was shaking again. This wasn't her apartment house. This was her way of getting rid of him. What did she need him for? What good could he do her? She had the keys to the car and now she was taking a stroll. When he got out of the car he would see there was no apartment house and no open door and nothing. He told himself that he couldn't get out of the car and he couldn't remain in the car.

He got out of the car and faced a six-story yellow brick apartment house. The front door was halfway open. He closed the door of the Pontiac. Then he walked quickly across the pavement, up the steps of the apartment house.

Then they were in the elevator and it was going up. It stopped at the third floor. The corridor was done in dark yellow. The door of her apartment was green. The number on the door was 307. She opened the door and went in and he followed.

It was a small apartment. It was expensive. The general idea was grey-violet, with yellow here and there. Parry reached for a ball of yellow glass that had a lighter attachment on top. He lighted a cigarette and tossed the empty pack into a grey-violet wastebasket. He looked at a yellow-stained radio with a phonograph annex. Then he found himself glancing at the record albums grouped in a yellow case beside the yellow-stained cabinet.

"I see you go in for swing," he said.

From another room she said, "Legitimate swing."

He heard a door closing and knew she was in the bathroom. All he had to do now was open the door that faced the corridor. Then down the corridor and out by way of the fire escape. And then where?

Dragging at the cigarette he stooped over and began going through the record albums. When he came to Basie he frowned. There was a lot of Basie. The best Basie. The same Basie he liked. There was *Every Tub* and *Swinging the Blues* and *Texas Shuffle*. There was *John's Idea* and *Lester Leaps In* and *Out the Window*. He took a glance at the window. He came back to the records and decided to play *Texas Shuffle*. He remembered that every time he played *Texas Shuffle* he got a picture of countless steers parading fast across an endless plain in Texas. He switched on the current and got the record under the needle. *Texas Shuffle* began to roll softly and it was very lovely. It clicked with the fact that he had a cigarette in his mouth, watching the smoke go up, and the police didn't know he was here.

Texas Shuffle was hitting its climax when she came out of the bathroom. Parry turned and looked at her. She smiled at him.

She said, "You like Basie?"

"I collect him. That is, I did."

"What else do you like?"

"Gin."

"Straight?"

"Yes. With a drink of water after every three or four."

She stopped smiling. She said, "There's something odd about that."

"Odd about what?"

"I also go for gin. The same way. The same chaser schedule."

He said nothing. She went into another room. The record ended and Parry got Basie started with *John's Idea*. The idea was well under way and Basie's right hand was doing wonderful things on the keys and then she was coming in with a tray that had two glasses and two jiggers, a bottle of gin and a pitcher of water.

She poured the gin. Parry watched her while he listened to the jumping music. She gave him some gin and he threw it down his throat while she was filling her jigger. He helped himself to a second jigger. He lit another cigarette. She put on another record, and sat down in a violet chair, leaning back and gazing at the ceiling.

"Light me a cigarette," she said.

He usually smoked a bit wet but he lighted her cigarette dry. As she took it from him she leaned over to lift the needle from the finished record.

"More?" she said.

"No. Let's talk instead. Let's talk about what's going to be."

"Do you have plans already?"

"No."

"I do, Vincent. I think you should live here for a while. Live here until the excitement dies down and an opening presents itself."

Parry picked himself up from the floor. He walked to the window and looked out. The street was almost empty. He saw smoke coming from a row of stacks beyond rooftops. He took himself away from the window and looked at a grey-violet wall.

He said, "If I had a lot of money I could understand it. The way it is now I don't get it at all. There's nothing in this for you. Nothing but aggravation and hardship."

He heard her getting up from the chair, walking out of the room. From another room he heard a sound of a bureau drawer getting opened. Then she was coming back and saying, "I want to show you something."

He turned and she handed him a clipping. He recognized the print. It was from the *Chronicle*. It was a letter to the editor.

> There's a great deal to be said in behalf of Vincent Parry, the man now on trial for the murder of his wife. I don't expect you to print this letter, because the issue will be ultimately settled in court and from the looks of things it is a fair trial and Parry has his own lawyer. And yet the prosecution has steadily aimed at getting away from the technical aspects of the case and attempted to picture Parry as a combination of unfaithful husband, killer and draft dodger. I am not acquainted with Parry's marital difficulties. As for the killer angle, the case is not yet completed and further testimony will no doubt bring up new facts that will decide the matter one way or another. However, I am certain that Vincent Parry is not a draft dodger. I happen to know that Parry made several attempts to enter the armed forces even though he had been rejected previously because of physical disability.

The letter was signed—Irene Janney.

Parry said, "Is that you?"

"Yes."

"It's not much of a letter. It hardly says anything."

"It's not the entire letter. The *Chronicle* couldn't print all of it. They'd have to use a couple of columns. But they tried to be fair. They included that contradiction of the draft-dodging angle."

"How did you know I tried to get in?"

She pressed her cigarette in a yellow glass ash tray. "I have a friend who works at your draft board. He told me. He said you were called up twice and rejected. He said you kept pestering the draft board for another chance to get in."

"Is that what got you interested in the case?"

"No," Irene said. "This friend knew I was interested. He called me up and told me what had happened at the draft board. He told me you really wanted to get in. It checked with the way I felt about the entire affair. Sometimes I get that way. I get excited about something and I give it everything I have."

"I think I'll clear out," Parry said.

"Sit down. Let's keep talking. Let's tell each other about ourselves. How's the kidney trouble?"

"I've been feeling better," Parry said. He lit another cigarette.

"It's odd about the kidney trouble."

"Why?"

"I have it also. Not serious, but it bothers me now and then."

"Look, I think I'll clear out. How's the fire escape?"

"Stay here, Vincent."

"What for?"

"Stay until it's dark at least."

He looked at the stained-yellow cabinet, the unmoving shining black record on the phonograph disc. He said, "It's this way. I've got to keep moving. And moving fast. Like this it's no good. The police will be working while I'm doing nothing. They're running after me and if I don't run I'll be caught."

"There's a time to run."

He was about to say something but just then the phone rang. It was a French phone, yellow. It was on a yellow table beside the grey-violet davenport. Irene picked up the phone.

"Hello—oh, hello Bob. How are you—yes, I'm fine—tonight? Oh, I'm sorry, Bob, but I won't be able to make it tonight—no, no other commitments, but I just don't feel like going out. —Oh yes, I'm quite all right, but I'm in the mood for a quiet evening and reading and the radio and so forth all by myself—no, I just feel that way—don't be silly—oh, don't be silly Bob—well, maybe tomorrow—oh, Bob don't be silly—stop it, Bob, I don't like to hear you talk that way. Call me tomorrow—yes, tomorrow about seven. —Of course not. How's your work coming along—that's fine—all right, Bob—yes, tomorrow at seven I'll expect to hear from you. Good-by——"

Parry walked toward the door.

She stood up and stepped between Parry and the door. She said, "Please, Vincent——"

"I'm going," he said. "That phone call did it."

"But I didn't want to see him anyway."

"All right, but there will be times when you'll want to see him. And times when you want to be at certain places. Doing certain things. And you won't be able to, because you'll be stuck with me."

"But I said only for tonight."

"Tonight will be a beginning. And if we let it begin it will keep on going. You're trying to help me but you won't be helping me. And I certainly won't be helping you any. We'll only get in each other's way. I'm going."

"Just until tonight, Vincent. Until it gets dark."

"Dark. They won't see me when it's dark." He stood there staring at the door as she stepped away from him and went into another room. He didn't know what she was doing in the other room. When she came back she had a tape measure in her hand. He looked at the tape measure and then he looked at her face.

She said, "I'm going to buy you some clothes."

"When?"

"Right now. I want the exact measurements. I want the fit to be perfect. And it's got to be expensive clothes. I know a place near here——"

She took his measurements. He didn't say anything. She took the measurements and then she made notes in a small memo book. He watched her going into another room. Again he heard the sound of a bureau drawer getting opened. As she came out again she was counting a roll of bills. A thick roll.

"No," Parry said. "Let's forget about it. I'm going now——"

"You're staying," she said. "I'm going. And I'll be back soon. While you wait here you can be doing things. Like getting rid of those rags you're wearing. All of them, even the shoes. Take them into the kitchen. You'll find wrapping paper there. Make a bundle and throw it into the incinerator. Then go into the bathroom and treat yourself to a hot shower. Nice and hot and plenty of soap. And you need a shave." A little laugh got out before she could stop it.

"What's the laugh for?"

"I was thinking you could use his razor. It's a Swedish hollow-ground safety razor. I used to be married and I gave it to my husband for a Christmas present. He didn't like it. I used it every now and then when I went to the beach. I stopped using it when someone told me depilatory cream was better."

"What happened to your husband?"

"He took a walk."

"When was this?"

"Long, long ago. I was twenty-three when we married and it lasted sixteen months and two weeks and three days. He told me I was too easy to get along with and it was getting dull. I just remembered there's no shaving soap. But I've got some skin cream. You can rub that in and then use the ordinary soap and you won't cut yourself. The incinerator is next to the sink. Don't forget to get every stitch of those clothes into the bundle. Maybe you better make two bundles so you'll be sure they get down."

"All right, I'll make two bundles."

She was at the door now. She said, "I'll be back soon. Is there anything special you want?"

"No."

"Will you do me a favor, Vincent?"

"What?"

"Will you be here when I come back?"

"Maybe."

"I want to know, Vincent."

"All right, I'll be here."

"What colors do you like?"

"Grey," he said. "Grey and violet." He wanted to laugh. He didn't laugh. "Sometimes a bit of yellow here and there."

She opened the door and left the apartment. Parry stood a few feet away from the door and looked at the door for several minutes. Then he walked back to the tray where the gin was and he poured himself two shots and got them down fast. He took a drink of water, went into the kitchen and found the wrapping paper. He undressed, slowly at first, then gradually faster as he realized he was getting rid of Studebaker's clothes and they were dirty clothes. For the first time he was aware that they had a smell and they were itchy. It was a pleasure to take them off and throw them away. Now he was naked and he was making two bundles. He got a ball of string from the kitchen cabinet, tied the bundles securely, then let them go down the incinerator. He heard the swishing noise as the bundles dropped, the vague thud that told him they had reached bottom. Knowing that Studebaker's clothes and the prison shoes were going to burn and become ashes he felt slightly happy.

He walked into the bathroom. It was yellow tile, all of it. There was a glassed-in shower and he got it started and used a rectangle of lavender soap. He made the shower very hot, then soaped himself well, got the hot water on again, switched to full cold, let it hit him for the better part of a minute. Then he was out of the shower, using a thick yellow towel that he could have used as a cape.

The skin cream mixed well with the soap, resulting in a decent lather that gave the razor a smooth ride. He shaved in three minutes and then he went into the parlor and lit a cigarette. He had the yellow towel wrapped around his middle and tucked in. He looked over the Basie records and decided to play *Shorty George*.

He let the needle go down and just as it touched the black he felt something coming into the apartment. It was only a noise but to him it had form and the ability to clutch and rip at his insides.

It was the buzzer.

Parry lifted the needle and stopped the phonograph. He waited.

The buzzer sounded again. Parry slowly lifted the cigarette to his lips and took a long haul. He sat down on the edge of the davenport and waited. He gazed at the phone attachment beside the door and as the buzzer hit him again he decided to lift the phone and tell the person down there to go away and leave him alone. He let his head go into cupped hands.

Then the buzzing stopped.

The tears started again, coming into his eyes, collecting there, ready to gush. He told himself that he had to stop that sort of thing. It was bad because it was soft and if there was anything he couldn't afford now it was softness. The lukewarm and weak brand of softness. Everything had to be ice, and just as hard, and just as fast as a whippet and just as smooth. And just as accurate as a calculating machine, giving the buzzer a certain denomination. Now that the buzzer had stopped a key was clicking into position and crossing off the denomination. The buzzer had stopped and it was all over. The person down there had gone away. Check that off. Then check off all the other things that needed checking off. Get another key in position and check off San Quentin. Go back further than that and check off the trial. Come back to San Quentin, go ahead of San Quentin and check off the barrel and the truck, the pale-green meadow, the hills and the dark-green woods. Check off the Studebaker, the man in the Studebaker, the ride to San Francisco and the motorcycle cops. Check off Studebaker's clothes. Get started with now and keep going from now. Check off the buzzer. Start *Shorty George* again.

He turned the lever that started the phonograph running. The black record began to spin. He put the needle down and *Shorty George* was on its way. Parry stood a few feet away from the phonograph, watching the record go round and listening to the Basie band riding into the fourth dimension. He recognized the Buck Clayton trumpet and he smiled. The smile was wet clay and it became cement when he heard knuckles rapping against the apartment door.

All of him was cement.

The rapping was in series, going against *Shorty George*. The first series stopped and Parry tried to get to the phonograph so he could cut off the music that wasn't music any more, only a lot of noise telling the person out there that someone was in the apartment. He couldn't get to the phonograph because he couldn't budge. The second series of raps came to him, stopped for a few moments and then the third series was on and he counted three insistent raps.

Then he knew it was impossible to check off all those things. They were things to be remembered and considered. This thing now rapping at the door was the police. It was logical that they hould be here. It wasn't logical for them to have slipped up on that blanket episode. Then again it was logical for them to have taken the Pontiac's license number as the car went away from them. It was easy to sketch—them talking it over, telling each other they should have looked further under the blanket to see what was in those old clothes for China, then congratulating each other on their brains in taking the license number, and now coming here to have a talk with Irene Janney.

He turned and looked around the room and tried to see something. The window was the only thing he saw. *Shorty George* was rounding the far turn and coming toward the homestretch, but he didn't hear it, he was staring at the window.

The fourth series of raps got through the door and bounced around the room, and following the raps a voice said, "Irene—are you there?"

It belonged to a woman. Then it couldn't be the police. And yet there was something about the voice that was worse than the police.

"Irene—open the door."

The music was music again. Parry figured if he made the music louder he wouldn't hear the voice.

It was a voice he knew and he was trying to place it and he didn't want to place it. He made the music louder.

"Irene—what's the matter? Let me in."

Shorty George was coming down the homestretch. The voice outside the door was louder than *Shorty George*.

"Irene—I know you're in there and I want you to let me in."

The voice was getting him now, closing in on him, forceps of sound that was more than sound, because now he recognized the voice, the pestering voice that belonged to Madge Rapf.

5

IT WAS as if the door was glass and he could see her standing out there, the Pest. His eyes made a turn and looked at the ball of yellow glass with the lighter attachment. All he had to do was grab hold of that thing and open the door, go out there and start banging her over the head to shut her up. This wouldn't be the first time he had liked the idea of banging her over the head.

"Irene—I don't think this is a bit funny and I want you to open the door."

Parry reached over and picked up the heavy ball of yellow glass.

"Irene—are you going to open the door?"

Parry tested the weight of the ball of yellow glass.

"Irene—you know I'm out here. What's the matter with you?"

Parry took a step toward the door. He wasn't shaking and he wondered why. He wasn't perspiring and he wasn't shaking and the ball of yellow glass was steady and all set in his right hand. He wondered why he felt so glad about this and all at once he understood he was about to do mankind a favor.

"Irene—do you intend to open the door?"

Shorty George crossed the finish line and the glazed center spun soundlessly under the needle.

Rapping again. Angry, puzzled rapping.

"Irene—open the door."

Parry took another step toward the door and he began to shake. He began to perspire. His teeth were vibrating. A grinding noise started deep in his belly and worked its way up toward his mouth.

"Irene——"

"Shut up," Parry yelled, realized that he was yelling, tried to hold it, couldn't do anything about it. "For God's sake— shut up."

"What?"

"I said shut up. Go away."

He knew that she was stepping back and away from the door, looking at the number to see if she had the right apartment.

Then she said something that was Madge Rapf all over. She said, "Irene, is someone in there with you?"

"Yes, someone's in here with her," Parry said. "Now go away."

"Oh, I didn't know."

"Well, now you know. So go away."

She went away. Parry had an ear next to the door crack and he could hear her footsteps going down the corridor toward the elevator. He moved to the phonograph and picked up the needle from the silent record. He lit another cigarette and then took a position near the window and waited there. He estimated two minutes and it was slightly under two minutes when he saw Madge Rapf getting past the partition of yellow brick. He knew she was going to turn and have a look at the window and he ducked just as she turned. When he came up she was on her way again and he watched her crossing the street. He figured she had to cross the street but when she got to the other side he knew that was wrong. She was there because she wanted to get a better view of the window.

He kept one eye past the limit of the window. He didn't know whether or not she could see that half of his face. But even if she could see that one half of face she wouldn't be able to recognize it. Now she came walking down the other side of the street and stopped when she was directly across from the apartment house. She stood there and looked at the window. Her head went low and that meant she was looking at the grey Pontiac. Then the window again. Then the Pontiac. Then the window. Then she started on down the street. Then she stopped and took another look at the window. She took a few steps in the direction of the apartment house. She hesitated, then came on.

"For God's sake—" Parry murmured.

She stopped again. This time she made a definite about-face and walked on and kept on walking.

Parry looked at the door and he was about to make a go for it when he remembered that his attire consisted of a yellow towel and nothing more. He sucked at the cigarette and walked without meaning in a small circle and then he went back to the window. No Madge Rapf. But something else. This time it was a policeman on the other side of the street. The policeman didn't look at the apartment house. Parry crossed to the davenport and sat on the edge, the cigarette burning furiously as he gave it the works.

Something pulled him up from the davenport and he went into the kitchen. It was small and white and spotless. He put his hand on a solid bar of glass, the handle of the refrigerator. He opened the door and looked at the food without knowing why he was looking at it. He looked at a neat row of oranges and then he closed the door. He looked at the kitchen cabinet, the sink, the floor—the incinerator. He opened the metal cap of the incinerator and gazed into the black hole. He closed the incinerator, went out of the kitchen and into the bathroom. When he came out of the bathroom he went into the one room that was left, the bedroom.

The bedroom was all yellow. Pale yellow broadloom rug and furniture and dark yellow walls. Four water-color landscapes that weren't bad. They were signed "Irene Janney." He recognized the pale-green meadow and the hills. And again he saw the dark-green woods and the road. He wanted another cigarette and he went into the parlor.

When he came back to the bedroom he stood in front of the bureau and ran his fingers across the shining yellow wood. He puffed hard at the cigarette and then he opened the top drawer. It was divided in two sections. There was a big bottle of violet cologne that would follow the half-filled bottle on top of the bureau. There was a carton of Luckies, two jars of skin cream, a pile of handkerchiefs wrapped in a sachet-scented fold of grey-violet satin. There was a box filled with various sorts of buttons. That was about all for the top drawer.

The second drawer had underthings and more handkerchiefs and three handbags. They were expensive. Everything was expensive. Everything was neat and clean. The third drawer was about the same. The fourth drawer was heaped with papers and note-books and text-books. Parry examined the papers and books. He found out that Irene Janney had attended the University of Oregon, had majored in sociology, had graduated in 1939. There were considerable examination papers and theses and most of them were marked B. There was a record book from the Class of '39 and he followed the alphabetical order until he came to her picture and write-up. Her picture was nothing special. She was even thinner then than now, and she was plenty thin now. She looked uncertain and worried, as if she was afraid of what would happen to her after graduation.

There was something at the bottom of the drawer peeping out from the edge of a textbook. It was from a newspaper. It became a clipping as Parry took it out. He saw the picture of a man who looked something like Irene. The picture was captioned "Dies in Prison." Underneath the picture was the name Calvin Janney. Alongside the picture was an article headed "Road Ends for Janney."

> Calvin Janney, sentenced four years ago to life imprisonment for the murder of his wife, died last night in San Quentin prison. He had been ill for the past several months. Officials said Janney made a death-bed statement claiming his innocence, the same claim he made during the sensational trial in San Francisco.
>
> Janney, a wealthy real-estate broker, was accused of killing his bride of a second marriage, less than a week after they had celebrated their first wedding anniversary. Death was attributed to a skull fracture caused by a heavy blow with an ornamental brass jar. The body had been found at the foot of a staircase in the Janney home. Janney stated that his wife had fallen down the stairs, had knocked the brass jar from the base of the banister in her descent, then had struck her head on the jar. This statement was disproved by the prosecution. It was established that Janney had charged his wife with infidelity and had threatened on several occasions to kill her. Janney's fingerprints on the brass jar was a primary factor in the guilty verdict.
>
> Efforts to obtain a new trial proved fruitless. In recent months Janney's attorneys made another plea founded on new developments, the result of continued investigation during the past four years. The plea made no headway due to lack of witnesses.
>
> Janney was 54. He is survived by a son, Burton, a chemical engineer in Portland. Also a daughter, Irene, a grade-school student in the same city.

There was a date at the top of the clipping. It said February 9, 1928. Parry kept looking at the date. On the basis of the date and the record-book date, she was nine when her father died and she was five when the trial took place. He read the clipping again. Then again. He decided she ought to be coming back soon and maybe he ought to get the clipping and the papers and books back in the drawer. He started to handle the clipping and he was getting it back in the textbook when he heard the door opening into the parlor and footsteps coming into the apartment, going through the parlor, coming into the bedroom.

She looked at him. She looked at the clipping half in his hand and half in the textbook. Her arms were filled with paper boxes and she put these on the bed and kept on looking at Parry, looking at the clipping, then back to Parry.

"Did you get rid of the clothes?" she said.

"Yes. I made two bundles and threw them down the incinerator."

"How was the razor?"

"Fine."

"That shower and shave did you a world of good. How do you feel?"

"Fine," Parry said.

She pointed to the open drawer. "What's the big idea?"

"I didn't have anything to do."

"All right, let's close the drawer, shall we?"

Parry got the clipping into the textbook, got the textbook back in the drawer along with the other books and papers. He closed the drawer.

She pointed to the closed drawer. "Anything happen while I was away—outside of that?"

"You had a caller." He wondered why he was telling her.

Irene frowned. "I hope you didn't answer the buzzer."

"No, I didn't answer the buzzer. But she came up and she knocked on the door."

"A she?"

"Yes. She talked to you through the door. I stayed there and let her talk. It would have been all right except I had the phonograph going and she could hear it. She kept asking you to open the door. Finally I told her to go away."

The frown went deeper. "That wasn't such a bright idea."

"I know. It got out before I could stop it."

"Did she argue with you?"

"No. She went away. Does that close it?"

"I hope so."

"What do you mean you hope so?" Parry asked.

"Well, my friends know I don't go in for that sort of thing. Now they'll think——"

"All right, let me get into those clothes and scram out of here."

"Wait," Irene said. "I didn't mean that. I don't care what they think. I'm only trying to be technical. And very careful."

"Let's see the clothes."

She sat down on the edge of the bed and looked at him. Then she blinked a few times and lowered her head. She put a forefinger to the space between her eyes and pressed there and took it around in little circles.

Parry leaned back against the bureau. He said, "You're tired, aren't you?"

"Headache."

"Got any aspirins?"

"In the bathroom cabinet."

He went into the bathroom, came back with two aspirins and a glass half-filled with water. She smiled at him. She took the aspirins and drank all the water. He took the glass back to the bathroom. When he came back to the bedroom she was opening the paper boxes.

It amounted to almost a wardrobe. Four shirts, three white and one grey. Five neckties, three grey and two on a grey-violet theme. Five sets of underwear and a stack of handkerchiefs. Six pairs of grey socks. A grey worsted suit with a vertical suggestion of violet. A pair of tan straight-tipped blucher shoes. And grey suspenders.

There were other things. A military brush and a comb. A toothbrush and a jar of shaving cream and a safety razor.

She arranged the things neatly on the bed and then she went out of the room. Parry got started with the clothes. Everything fitted perfectly. His hair was still damp from the shower and it moved nicely under the brush and comb. He had on one of the white shirts and a grey-violet tie and he put a white handkerchief in the breast pocket of the grey worsted suit. He felt very new and shining.

He walked into the parlor.

Irene was sitting on the davenport and when she saw him she smiled and said, "Well—hello."

"Okay?"

"Very okay."

"I bet you paid plenty."

"I like to spend money for clothes."

"What did you tell them?"

"I said I had a boy friend just discharged from the Army and I wanted to surprise him with a complete new outfit. They're a small, exclusive store and they don't like to be hurried. But it was a big order and they didn't want to lose it, and anyway there wasn't much work to be done on the suit."

"How's the headache?"

"Better."

"That's good. Thanks for the clothes."

"You're welcome, Vincent. You're really very welcome. And I've got something else for you." She opened a handbag, took the wrapping from a flat white case. She handed it to him.

It contained a round waterproof-type wrist watch, chromium plated with a grey suede strap.

Parry looked at the wrist watch. He said, "Why this?"

"You'll need a watch. That's one of the things you'll really need."

He put the watch on his wrist. He said, "You're laying out a lot of money. Can you afford it?"

"What do you think?"

"I've got an idea you can afford it."

"You've got the right idea," she said. "Now tell me where you got it."

"From the clipping."

Her eyes were soft. Her lips weren't curved but it was a smile anyway. She said, "Vincent, will you always be that way with me?"

"What way?"

"Honest."

"Yes. I'll be that way with you until we say good-by. It's getting dark now. It's almost time to say good-by."

She stood up. She said, "Let's have dinner. I'm not a bad cook. Do you like fried chicken?"

"Better than anything."

"Same here," she said, and then they were looking at each other. She started a smile, started to lose it, got it again when he smiled at her. They stood there smiling at each other. He reached toward the cigarette box and she said, "Light one for me," and then she went into the kitchen.

He lit two cigarettes, went into the kitchen, saw her putting on an apron. She was tying the apron strings. She gestured with her lips and he put the cigarette in her mouth and walked out of the kitchen.

"Let's have some music," she said.

"Radio?"

"Yes, put the radio on."

He got the radio working. A small studio orchestra was trying to do something with *Holiday for Strings* but there weren't enough strings. Toward the middle most of the orchestra seemed to be taking a holiday. Parry went over to a circular mirror at the other side of the room and looked at himself and admired the grey suit. He fingered the necktie and then he touched the smoothness of the suede wrist-watch strap. Looking at the wrist watch he told himself it was fast. It couldn't be eight already. He turned toward the window. The San Francisco sky was greying.

Irene came in and said dinner was ready. She really knew how to fry a chicken. She opened a bottle of Sauterne and he knew before he took the first taste it was high-priced wine. He told her she was a good cook. She smiled and didn't say anything. For dessert they had butterscotch pudding. She told him she had a weakness for butterscotch pudding and made it three times a week. He asked her if she ate out much and she said no, she liked her own cooking and besides restaurants these days were an ordeal.

They had black coffee and then they sat there smoking cigarettes. He offered to help her with the dishes and she said no, she could do them in a jiffy. He went into the parlor and she did the dishes in a jiffy. Parry took another look at the sky and it was getting dark. He was watching it get darker as Irene came into the parlor. She followed his gaze out the window. She followed his gaze to the wrist watch.

She said, "Don't go. Stay here tonight. You can sleep on the davenport."

"That's out. We've got maybe thirty minutes and then I'm on my way. And now I want to ask you something. Where is your brother?"

"Dead. He was in a terrible automobile accident six years ago. What you really want to know is how I got my money. And that's how. My father willed it to Burton, and then in the hospital, just before he died, Burton willed it to me. It amounts to a couple hundred thousand dollars."

"That's a lot of cash."

"It's good to have. It's the only thing I have."

"What about your husband?"

"I received the final decree a few months ago. I don't know where he is. Do you want the name?"

"Why should I want the name?"

"Why should you want to know where I got my money?"

"Curious. You didn't get it with water colors. I knew that. And you didn't get it through sociology. I knew that. So I went back to the clipping and I wanted to check on it and I wanted to know why you had it and not your brother. Was this where you lived with your husband?"

"No."

"What kind of guy was your husband?"

"A louse."

"When did you find it out?"

"The first week."

"Why didn't you leave?"

She said, "I had the money and I had me and I had him. I wasn't much interested in the money. That left me and him. He liked to drink, but that was all right, so did I. And he liked to gamble and that wasn't so good, because he had an idea he knew poker and he didn't know the first thing about poker. Even nights when we stayed home together he wanted to play poker and one night I took him for every cent he made that month. I think that was the only thing he liked about me—the fact that I could make him look sick when it came to poker."

"What was his line?"

"All right, Vincent, I'll tell you about him. His name is George Hagedorn and I met him three years ago. We knew each other four months and then we got married. We were a couple of lonely people and I guess that was the only reason we married. He didn't know I had money. I told him a few days after the wedding and it didn't seem to make much difference. I guess that was one of the very few things that was good about him. He had a lot of pride. Maybe too much. I think that was why he gambled. I think that was the only way he reasoned he could get money with his own hands. He hadn't tried many other ways because he was very lazy. One of the laziest men I've ever seen. When we married he was thirty-two and a complete failure. A statistician making forty-five a week in an investment security house."

"What house?"

"Kinney."

"I know that firm," Parry said. "They're big. Offices in Santa Barbara and Philly. I can't figure Santa Barbara."

"He tried to get transferred down to Santa Barbara but they didn't need him there. He wouldn't have lasted at the office here but he had asthma and it kept him out of the Army and I guess they figured they might as well keep him for the duration. Besides, they had him broken in. But he was late and absent a lot and I guess they finally got fed up with him. About a year ago I tried to get in touch with him and I called Kinney and they said he didn't work there any more. They didn't know where he was."

"Why did you want to get in touch with him?"

"I was lonely. I wanted a date."

"What about Bob?"

"I had an idea you'd remember that. You remember things, don't you."

"Certain things stick in my mind. What about Bob?"

"That was during a time when I wasn't seeing Bob. Every now and then it happens that way."

"What way?"

"Well, I get afraid. Or maybe it's my conscience, because he's married. Not really married. He's separated, but his wife won't give him a divorce. She doesn't want him and at the same time she won't let anyone else have him. She gets a kick out of it. But I don't have to tell you, Vincent. You know what she is. You know who she is."

6

PARRY LOOKED at the window. Now it was dark grey out there and getting darker. He said, "I better be going."

"She worked against you at the trial, Vincent. She works against everybody. She has a way about her. She won't leave people alone. And the way she pesters me——"

"The way she pesters you has nothing to do with me," Parry said. He got up and moved toward the door. "All I know is she couldn't see me through the door and she didn't see me through the window. That's all I want to know. You've been good to me. I won't forget it but I want you to forget it. Being good to people sounds nice but it's hard work. From here on there's only one person you'll need to be good to. That's yourself. Good-by, Irene."

"Good-by, Vincent. Wait, you've got things here. I'll put them in a grip——"

He opened the door and walked out. He looked up and down the corridor and then he stepped quickly to the elevator. When he reached the street he saw it was even darker than it had looked from the window. He walked quickly, walked south, searching for a drugstore. Three blocks and then he saw a drugstore and instinctively his hand went into the right side-pocket of the grey worsted trousers, groping for change. His fingers touched paper and he was taking bills from the pocket. All new bills, crisp and bright. It amounted to a thousand dollars. Eight one-hundred dollar bills. Two fifties. The rest in tens and fives. He wondered how she knew he kept his money in the right side-pocket of his trousers. He started toward the drugstore, then told himself a telephone call was out. A taxi made a turn and started slowly up the street. Parry stepped to the curb and raised his arm.

The taxi came to a reluctant stop. The driver was a thick-faced man close to forty. The driver said, "How far? I'm on my way to a fare."

"It's not far."

The driver examined the grey worsted suit. "North?"

48

"Yes. A couple miles. Just keep going north and I'll tell you how to get there."

"All right, hop in. Mind a little speed?"

"I like speed."

The taxi went into a sprint, made a lot of wracking noise as it turned a corner to get on a wider street. Parry sat low, trying to get his face away from the rear-view mirror because he sensed the driver was studying the mirror. He wondered why the driver was studying the mirror.

"That's a nice suit you're wearing," the driver said.

"I'm glad you like it. What are we doing?"

"Forty. Another turn and we'll do fifty. On this kind of a deal I usually take her up to sixty."

"What do you mean this kind of a deal?" He could see the driver grinning at him in the rear-view mirror. He wondered why the driver was grinning.

"A double job," the driver said. "Two fares on one trip. Is your trip really necessary?"

"Sort of," Parry said.

"It's crazy the way they get these slogans out," the driver said. "What they do with words. Take *necessary*, for instance. It means different things to different people. Like me. What's necessary to me?"

"Passengers," Parry said. "And I'll tell you what's necessary to passengers—getting where they want to go without a lot of talk."

He thought that would make the driver shut up. The driver took the taxi up to fifty and said, "I don't know. Some passengers don't mind talk."

"I do."

"Always?"

"Yes, always," Parry said. "That's why I don't have many friends."

"You know," the driver said, "it's funny about friends——"

"It's funny the way you can't take a hint," Parry said.

The driver laughed. He said, "Brother, you never drove a cab. You got no idea how lonely it gets."

"What's lonely about it? You see people."

"That's just it, brother. I see so many people, I take them to so many places. I see them getting out and going in to places.

I pick up other people and I hear them talking in the back seat. I'm up here all alone and I get lonely."

"That's tough," Parry said.

"You don't believe me."

"Sure," Parry said. "I believe you. My heart goes out to you. All right, turn here, to the left. Stay on this street."

"Where we going?"

"If I give you that you'll ask me why I'm going there and what I'm going to do there. After all, a guy gets lonely driving a taxi."

"That's right, lonely," the driver said. "Lonely and smart."

Parry noticed that the driver was no longer watching the rear-view mirror. Parry said, "Smart in what way?"

"People."

"Talking to people?"

"And looking at people. Looking at their faces."

Parry started to shake. He glanced at his shaking hand. He measured the distance from his hand to the door handle. He said, "What about faces?"

"Well, it's funny," the driver said. "From faces I can tell what people think. I can tell what they do. Sometimes I can even tell who they are."

And now the driver again watched the rear-view mirror.

Parry reached over and put his hand on the door handle. He told himself he had to do it and do it now and do it fast. And not sit here and hope he was wrong, because he couldn't be wrong, because it was an equation again and it checked. The evening papers were out long ago and the taxi driver had to read one of those papers, had to see the picture that had to be on the front page. The taxi driver had time to read the write-up. Front-page stories were made to order for taxi drivers who didn't have time to read the back pages.

"You, for instance," the driver said.

"All right, me. What about me?"

"You're a guy with troubles."

"I don't have a trouble in the world," Parry said.

"Don't tell me, brother," the driver said. "I know. I know people. I'll tell you something else. Your trouble is women."

Parry took his hand from the door handle. It was all right.

He had to stop this business of worrying about things before they happened.

He said, "Strike one. I'm happily married."

"Call it a two-base hit. You're not married. But you used to be, and it wasn't happy."

"Oh, I get it. You were there. You were hiding in the closet all the time."

The driver said, "I'll tell you about her. She wasn't easy to get along with. She wanted things. The more she got, the more she wanted. And she always got what she wanted. That's the picture."

"That's strike two."

"That's the picture," the driver said. "She never made much noise and she was always a couple steps ahead of you. Sometimes she wasn't even there at all. That gave her the upper hand, because she could keep an eye on you and you didn't know it."

"Strike three."

"Strike three my eye. You were a rubber band on her little finger."

"All right, make a left-hand turn. Go right at the next light."

"So finally—" The taxi made a wide, fast turn. "So finally it was up to your neck and you couldn't take it any more. You were tired of boxing with her—so you slugged her."

Parry was shaking again. He had his hand going toward the door handle. He said, "You know, you ought to do something with that. You could make money at carnivals."

"It's a thought."

Parry put his hand on the door handle.

The taxi made a right turn. Two neon signs flashed past, one yellow, the other violet. It was a market section. It was busy. There were people, too many people. But he didn't care. He started to work the handle.

"Yep," the driver said. "She gave you plenty of trouble. I don't blame you. I don't blame you one bit."

The handle was halfway down. Perspiration dripped onto grey worsted. The handle was almost all the way down.

"Not now," the driver said. "And not here. There's too many cops around."

7

Parry let go of the handle. He sagged. He started to breathe as if he had just finished a two-mile run and the officials said it didn't count and wanted to get another race going immediately.

The driver said, "Is it far from here?"

"I'll give you five hundred dollars," Parry blurted. "I'll give you——"

"Don't give me anything," the driver said. "Just let me know where it is and I'll pick out a dark street that's empty and you can walk the rest of the way. And don't try hitting me on the head or I'll run us up on the pavement and into a wall."

Parry had his head almost to his knees. He made fists and pressed them against his forehead. He said, "The hell with it, the hell with it. Take me to a police station."

"Don't be that way. You're doing all right. You're doing fine."

"No," Parry groaned. "It's no go. It was easy for you to see. It'll be easy for others to see."

"Now that's where you're wrong," the driver said. He twisted the taxi into a sharp turn and sent it sliding down a narrow street that was empty and very dark. Halfway down the street he brought the taxi to a smooth stop. He rested his arm on the back of the seat and turned and faced Parry. He said, "And here's why. I'm out of the ordinary. Not my eyes, but the way I stick things on my brain and keep them there. And the way I put things together. I get five or six little things and I put them together and I get one big thing."

"What's the difference?" Parry said. He wasn't talking to the driver. "The worst I can get is a week in solitary. And no privileges. And no chance of a parole. But there wasn't a chance anyway. They told me I was lucky I didn't get the chair. That's something I've got to remember—I'm lucky. I'll always be lucky because I didn't get the chair." He looked up and saw the driver watching him. He said, "Go on—take me to a police station."

"I don't see no sense in that," the driver said. "Unless you think you'll be happier in Quentin."

"Sure," Parry said. "I'll be happier there. That's why they send us there. To keep us happy."

The driver brought up a forearm, put most of his weight on the elbow, leaning his face against a big hand. "I got a better idea for you. Let me take you over to the Bridge. You can jump off and it'll be over in no time."

"The Bridge?"

"Sure. All you gotta do is step off and you faint on the way down. It's like going to a painless dentist."

"I'm young," Parry said, again talking aloud to himself. "There's a lot of years ahead of me."

"Why spend them in Quentin?"

"What else can I do?" Parry asked.

"I want to know something," the driver said. "Did you really bump her off?"

"No."

"That's not the way I figure it," the driver said. "I figure she made life miserable for you and finally you lost your head and you picked up that ash tray and slugged her. I know how it is. I live with my sister and my brother-in-law. They get along fine. They get along so fine that once he threw a bread knife at her. She ducked. And that's the way it goes. Maybe if your wife ducked there wouldn't be any trial, there wouldn't be any Quentin. But that's the way it goes. You want a smoke?"

"All right," Parry said. He accepted a cigarette and a light.

The driver filled his lungs with smoke, sent the smoke out through the side of his mouth. He said, "Let me find out something, just to see if I got it right. What was she like?"

"She was all right," Parry said. "She wasn't a bad soul. She just hated my guts. For a long time I tried to find out why. Then it got to a point where I didn't care any more. I started going out. I knew she was going out so it didn't make any difference. We hardly ever talked to each other. It was a very happy home."

"What made you marry her in the first place?"

"The old story."

"I almost got roped in a couple times," the driver said.

"If you find the right person it's okay," Parry said.

Then they were quiet for a while. They sat there blowing smoke. After a time the driver said, "Where we going?"

"I don't know," Parry said. "What should I do?"

"You won't listen."

"I'll listen," Parry said. "I want ideas. That's what I need more than anything else. Ideas. Look, I didn't kill her. Why should I go back to San Quentin and stay there the rest of my life if I didn't kill her?"

The driver shifted his position so that he faced Parry directly. He beckoned to Parry. He said, "Come up a few inches. Let's see if he can do anything with your face."

"Who?"

"A friend of mine." The driver was studying Parry's face. The driver said, "This guy's good. He knows his stuff."

"What would he want?"

"What do you have?"

"A thousand."

"To spend?"

"No," Parry said. "A thousand's all I have."

"He'd take a couple hundred."

"What would he want afterward?"

"Not a cent. He's a friend of mine."

"What do you want?"

"Nothing." The driver got paper and a stub of pencil from an inside pocket and he was writing something.

"How long will it take?" Parry asked.

"Maybe a week if he doesn't touch your nose. I've seen him work. He's good. I don't think he'll touch your nose. I think he'll fix you up around the eyes. But you can't stay there. You got a place to stay?"

"I think so," Parry said.

The driver handed Parry a slip of paper. Parry folded it and put it in his coat pocket.

"I'll call him tonight," the driver said. "Maybe he can do it tonight. Maybe I better call him right now. You got the cash with you?"

"Yes, but I'm not sure about tonight. Let's work it this way —you call him and say there's a good chance I'll be there at two in the morning. Or better make it three. Are you sure this guy's okay?"

"He's okay as long as he knows you're okay. That good enough?"

"I'll gamble," Parry said. "How do I get in?"

"It's an old building on Post. One of them dried-up places filled with two-by-four offices. He's got his office on the third floor. There's an alley on the left side of the building. There's a back door and he'll have it open for you. He works fast and you'll be out of there before it gets light."

"What do I do after I get out? I can't walk the streets all bandaged up."

"Don't worry about it," the driver said. "I'll be there. I know the section and I got the whole thing mapped out already. The alley cuts through to a second alley. I'll have the taxi parked there at the end of the second alley."

"Suppose he can't make it tonight."

"We'll take the chance. I think we better shove now. I don't want any cops to see me parked here. Where do we go?"

"Make a right hand turn at the end of the block," Parry said.

The taxi went down the street, made a right turn, made another right turn, then a third, then down four blocks and a left-hand turn.

"Stop alongside that apartment house," Parry said.

The taxi went halfway down the street and came to a stop.

"What'll it be?" Parry said.

"An even two bucks."

Parry handed the driver a five-dollar bill. He said, "Keep it."

The driver handed Parry a dollar bill and a dollar in silver. "You need some silver," he said. "Besides, you don't want to go throwing your money around like that. Now what's it going to be?"

"Three on the dot."

"All right. I'll call him. And you be there. And listen, keep telling yourself it'll work out okay. Keep telling yourself you don't have a thing to lose."

"But you," Parry said. "You've got plenty to lose. You and your friend."

"Don't worry about me and my friend," the driver said. "You just be there at three. That's all you got to worry about."

Parry opened the door and stepped out of the taxi. He walked toward the entrance of a third-rate apartment house.

He heard the taxi going away and he turned and saw the tail light getting smaller in the blackness down the street.

The lobby of the apartment house was dreary. People who stayed in this place were in the forty-a-week bracket. The carpet was ready to give up and the wallpaper should have given up long ago. There were three plain chairs and a sofa sinking in the middle. There was a small table, too small for the big antique lamp that was probably taken at auction without too much bidding. Parry had been here before and every time he came here he wondered why George Fellsinger put up with it. He looked at it through the window of the door that kept him in the vestibule. He sighed and wanted to go away. There was no other place to go. He gazed down the list of tenants, came to Fellsinger and pressed the button. There wasn't any voice arrangement. There wasn't any response to the first press. Parry pressed again. There wasn't any response. Maybe the Bridge was better after all. It didn't pay to keep up with this, all this vacuum in the stomach, going around, going up to his brain and going back to his stomach and coming up again and eating away at his heart. He pressed the button again, and this time he got a buzz and he opened the door, quickly crossed the lobby, saw that the elevator was right there waiting for him. Maybe the police were waiting upstairs. Maybe they weren't.

The elevator took him to the fourth floor. He hurried down the corridor, knocked on the door of Fellsinger's apartment.

The door opened. Parry stepped into the apartment. The door closed. George Fellsinger folded his arms and leaned against the door and said, "Jesus Christ."

George Fellsinger was thirty-six and losing his blonde hair. He was five nine and he had the kind of build they show in the muscle development ads, the kind of build a man has before he sends the coupon away and gets the miracle machine. Fellsinger had blue eyes that were more water than blue and the frayed collar of his starched white shirt was open at the throat.

The apartment was just like Fellsinger. It consisted of a room and a bath and a kitchenette. The davenport was set with pillow and sheets and there were six ash trays stocked with stubs, a magazine on the floor, an empty ginger-ale bottle resting on the magazine. Parry knew Fellsinger had fallen asleep on the davenport after having finished the magazine and the ginger ale and the cigarettes. There was a trumpet on one of two chairs.

"Jesus Christ," Fellsinger said again.

"How've you been, George?"

"I've been all right. Jesus, Vincent, I never expected anything like this—" Fellsinger ran to a small table, opened a drawer, took out a carton of cigarettes. With a thumbnail he slit the carton, extracted a pack, and with the same thumbnail he opened the pack, with the same thumbnail got a match lit. He ignited Parry's cigarette, ignited his own and then went back to the door and leaned against it.

"You saw the papers?"

"Sure," Fellsinger said. "And I couldn't believe it. And I can't believe this."

"There's no getting away from it, George. I'm here. This is really me."

"In that brand-new suit?"

Parry explained the suit. From the suit he went back to the road, told Fellsinger how she had picked him up, told Fellsinger everything.

"You can't work it that way," Fellsinger said. "What you've got to do is take yourself out of town. Out of the state. Out of the country."

"That's for later. What I need now is a new face."

"He'll ruin you. I tell you, Vince, you're working it wrong. Every minute you waste in town is——"

"Look, George, you said I was innocent. You always kept saying that. Do you still believe it?"

"Of course. It was an accident. Nobody killed her."

"All right, then. Do you want to help me?"

"Of course I want to help you. Anything, Vince. Anything I can do. For Christ's sake——"

"Look, George, have there been any big changes in your life since they put me away?"

"I don't know what you mean."

"I mean, you never used to have any visitors. You were always alone up here. Is it still that way?"

"Yes. I lead a miserable life, Vince. You know that. You know I have nobody. You were my only friend." A suggestion of tears appeared in Fellsinger's eyes.

Parry didn't notice the tears. He said, "I'm mighty glad nobody comes up here. That'll make it easy. And it won't be more than a week. Do it for me, George. That's all I'm asking. Just let me stay here for a week."

"Vince, you can stay here for a year, for ten years. But that's not the point. You said she gave you money. That's half the battle already. With money you can travel. Here you'll only run into the police. Maybe even now——"

"I can't travel with this face. It needs to be changed. I'm going there tonight. Maybe the police will be here when I get back. Maybe not. It's fifty-fifty."

Fellsinger took a key case from the back pocket of his trousers. He unringed a key and handed it to Parry. "It's good for both doors," he said. "I still think you're working it wrong, Vince."

"Got anything to drink?"

"Some rum. It's awful stuff, but that's all I can get these days."

"Rum. Anything."

Fellsinger went into the kitchen, came out with a bottle of rum and two water glasses. He half filled both glasses.

They stood facing each other, gulping the rum.

"I still can't believe it," Fellsinger said.

"I was lucky," Parry said. "I got breaks. If I had planned it for a year it couldn't have worked out any better. The truck was right where I wanted it to be. The guards were nowhere around. It was all luck."

"And that girl," Fellsinger said.

Parry started to say something, then found his lips were closed, found the words were crumbling up and becoming nothing. He didn't want to talk about her. He was sorry he had told Fellsinger about her. He couldn't understand why he had told Fellsinger everything, even her name and her address and even the number of her apartment. He was very sorry he had done that but he didn't know why he was sorry. He knew only that now and from now on he didn't want to talk about her, he didn't want to think about her.

Fellsinger made himself horizontal on the davenport. He finished the rum in his glass, got the glass half filled again. Parry brought a chair toward the davenport and sat down.

"And Madge Rapf," Fellsinger said. "You sure that's who it was?"

"That's who it was."

"All my life I've tried to keep from hating people," Fellsinger said. "That's one of the people I hate. I remember once I was at your apartment with you and Gert, and Madge walked in. I saw the way she was looking at you. I remember what I was thinking. That she was out to get you and once she had you she'd rip you apart and throw the pieces away. Then she'd go out and look for the pieces and put them together and rip you apart again. That's Madge Rapf. And how come she's connected with this Janney girl? What takes place there?"

Parry thought he had already told Fellsinger what took place there. Wondering why he kept it back now, he said, "I don't know."

"Sure you don't know?"

"George, I've told you everything, I'm depending on you now. I wouldn't keep anything from you."

Fellsinger took a long gulp of rum. He said, "I wish I could sleep with Madge Rapf."

"Are you out of your mind?"

"You don't get me," Fellsinger said. "I wish I could sleep with her provided I was sure she talked in her sleep. I think she'd say the things I want her to say. I think she'd admit Gert never made that dying statement. Jesus Christ, if we could only prove that was a frame."

"I don't think it was a frame," Parry said. "I think Madge was telling the truth."

"Maybe she thought she was telling the truth. Maybe she drilled it into herself that Gert really said that. People like Madge make a habit of that sort of thing. It becomes part of their make-up."

"Gert hated me."

"Gert didn't hate you. Gert just didn't care for you. There's a difference. Gert would have walked out on you only she had no one else to go to. No one."

"There were others."

"They weren't permanent. She would have walked out if she could have found something permanent. And she wouldn't frame you, Vince. She was no prize package, but she wouldn't frame you. Madge framed you. Madge wanted to hook you. When she couldn't hook you one way, she hooked you another way. Madge is a fine girl."

"Maybe one of these days she'll get run over by an automobile."

"It's something to pray for," Fellsinger said. He took a thick watch from the small top pocket of his trousers. "What's your schedule?"

"I want to be there at three."

"Plenty of time," Fellsinger said.

"How's the job going?"

"The same job," Fellsinger said. "The same rotten routine. Sometimes I feel it getting the best of me. Last week I asked for a raise and Wolcott laughed in my face. I wanted to spit in his and walk out. One of these days I'm going to do just that. I can't stand Wolcott. I can't stand anything about that place. Thirty-five dollars a week."

"What are you kicking about? That's a marvelous salary."

"I talked to my doctor a few months ago. I asked him if I could stand a manual job. He said the only kind of job I could stand was a job where I sit in one place all day and don't use my muscles. I had no idea I was in such awful shape. He gave me a list of rules to follow, diet and cigarettes and liquor and all that. Rather than follow those rules I'd throw myself into the Bay."

"You mean jump off the Bridge?"

"What?"

"Nothing."

"Not nothing. Something. You've been thinking in terms of the Bridge. You got to get rid of that, Vince. That's no good."

"I'm all right. And everything's going to be all right. With a new face I won't need to worry. At least I won't need to worry so much. As long as I'm careful, as long as I keep my wits about me, as long as I have something to hold on to I'll be all right."

They sat there talking about themselves, the things that had once amounted to something in common. Fellsinger's amateur status with the trumpet. Fellsinger's refusal to go professional. Fellsinger's ideas in regard to sincere jazz. Fellsinger's interest in higher mathematics, and his lack of real ability with higher mathematics, and his feeling that if he had real ability he could make a lot of money in investment securities. Fellsinger's lack of real ability with anything. Parry's claim that Fellsinger had real ability with something and as soon as he found that something he would start getting somewhere. Their vacation at Lake Tahoe a few years back. Fishing at Tahoe and the two girls from Nevada who wanted to learn how to fish. Empty bottles of gin all over the cabin. What a wonderful two weeks it had been, and how they agreed that next summer they would be there again at Tahoe. But they weren't there the next summer because Parry was married that next summer and Gert wanted a honeymoon in Oregon. She wanted to see Crater Lake National Park. She was interested in mineralogy. She collected stones. She claimed there was flame opal to be found in Crater Lake National Park. She liked opal, the flame opal, the white opal with flames of green and orange writhing under the glistening white. She was always asking Parry to get her something in the way of flame opal. He couldn't afford flame opal but he got her a stone anyway. He went to a credit jewelry store downtown and said he wanted a flame-opal ring. They said they didn't have any flame opal in stock but if he came back in a few days they would have something. He didn't tell Gert about it. He wanted to surprise her. She would have a birthday in four days and he would have that flame opal in three. When he went back to the credit jewelry store they had the flame opal, a fairly large stone set in white gold with a small diamond on each side. They wanted nine hundred dollars. Parry had figured on about four hundred dollars and he was telling himself his only move was to turn and walk out of the store. Then he was thinking the flame opal would make Gert very happy. She hadn't found any flame opal in Crater Lake National Park. It ruined the honeymoon. She was always saying how badly she wanted flame opal. Parry made a down payment of three hundred dollars, which reduced his bank account to one hundred dollars. He told them to wrap the ring nicely. He took the ring home and on the following day, which was Gert's birthday, he presented her with the flame opal. She snatched it out of his hand. She broke a fingernail tearing off the wrapping. Parry was in the room but Gert was all alone in the room with her flame opal and she had a magnifying glass and she studied the stone for twenty minutes. Then when she saw Parry was there she asked him how much he had paid for the stone. He told her. She asked him where he had bought the stone. He told her. She started to carry on. She said he didn't have any sense. She said the credit jewelry store was a gyp joint and anybody with half a brain wouldn't put out nine hundred dollars for a flame opal in a place of that sort. She told him to take the ring back and demand his money. She said the flame opal was full of flaws and the diamonds were chips and at the very most the ring was worth two hundred dollars. She hopped up and down and made a lot of noise. He asked her to quiet down. She threw the ring at him and it hit him in the face and cut his cheek. Gert started to sob and yell at the same time and Parry begged her to quiet down. He said he would take back the ring and try to regain his down payment. She laughed at him. On the following day he took the ring back but they wouldn't return the down payment. When he became insistent they told him to get a lawyer. He said the ring wasn't worth nine hundred dollars. They told him to go get a lawyer. He walked out of the store and he was very weary and he knew he was out three hundred dollars. He wanted to go home and tell Gert he had regained the three hundred and put it back in the bank. He knew that wouldn't work. He had never been much good at putting a lie across. He told himself Gert was right. He didn't have any sense. He should have used his head and taken her with him when he went to purchase her birthday gift. She was absolutely right. He didn't have any sense. It was for his own good she had carried on like that. She wanted him to be something, not a nothing. She wanted him to be something she could respect. He put his hand to the cut on his cheek. She hadn't meant to do that. She hadn't meant to hurt him. It was for his own good. Maybe this would be the beginning of a change in his life. Maybe from here on he would start to use his head and make something of himself, climb out of that thirty-five-a-week rut in the investment security house. Maybe this was all for the best. He went to the bank and took out fifty of the remaining hundred. He went into a large, dignified jewelry store and asked if they had anything in the way of flame opal. A man wearing white and black and grey looked Parry up and down and said they didn't have anything under six hun-

dred dollars. Parry walked out of the store. He went into another store and they didn't have anything under seven hundred
dollars. He went into a third store and a fourth and a fifth. He
was forty minutes past his lunch hour and he hadn't eaten yet
and he was getting a fierce headache. He made up his mind he
wouldn't go back to the office until he had a flame opal for his
wife. He went into a sixth store. A seventh and an eighth. The
headache was awful. He went into the ninth store and it was a
small establishment that seemed sincere, that also seemed as if
it was having a hard time staying on its feet. A man well past
seventy showed Parry a ring set with a rather small flame opal,
a sterling silver setting. The ring looked as if it had been in the
store since the store was founded, and the store looked as if it
had been founded a hundred years ago. But it was a flame opal
and Gert wanted a flame opal, and when the man said $97.50 it
became a sale. Parry threw a milkshake down his throat and
sprinted back to the office. When he arrived at the office the
headache was taking his head apart and Wolcott was telling
him this sort of thing would never do, and besides his work
lately had been anything but satisfactory, and he had better
wise up to himself before he found himself out on the street
looking for another job. When Parry got home that night he
tried to kiss Gert but she turned away from him. He handed
her the small package and said happy birthday. She opened the
small package and looked at the small flame opal. She looked
at it for a while and then she let it fall to the floor. She put on
her hat and coat. Parry asked her where she was going. She
didn't answer. She walked out of the apartment. Parry heard
the door slamming shut. He reached down, picked up the ring.
He looked at the closed door, then looked at the flame opal,
then looked at the closed door and then looked at the flame
opal.

8

Fellsinger tilted the bottle, poured rum into the two glasses.

"What time is it?" Parry asked.

Fellsinger glanced at his wrist watch. "One thirty."

"I better be going." Parry downed the rum.

"When will you be back?"

"I'd say around five or five thirty." Parry reached in his coat pocket, took out the key Fellsinger had given him. "Got one for yourself?"

"Yes. I've always kept two keys, although I don't know why."

"Should I wake you up when I come in?" Parry asked.

Fellsinger grinned. "Do that. I want to see what you look like."

"I'll be all bandaged up. I'll be a mess."

"Wake me up anyway," Fellsinger said.

"I hate to walk out of here," Parry said. "I hate to go down that elevator and out on that street."

"You don't need to go. You can stay here. I'm telling you you're better off if you stay. Once you walk out——"

"No. I'll have to do it sooner or later and I might as well do it now. Can you spare a pack of cigarettes?"

"Absolutely not." Fellsinger took a pack from the carton, took another pack and handed the two packs to Parry. He was up from the davenport as Parry got up from the chair. He hit Parry on the shoulder and said, "For Christ's sake, Vince—be careful."

"Careful," Parry said. "Careful and lucky. That's what it's got to be. You better go to sleep now, George. You got a day of work ahead of you tomorrow."

"Be careful, Vince, will you?" Fellsinger walked Parry to the door. He put his hand on the knob. He tried to keep his hand steady but his hand shook. He said, "Be careful, Vince."

Parry opened the door and went down the corridor. He pressed the elevator button and stood there waiting. The elevator came up for him and just before he stepped in he turned and saw Fellsinger standing beside the open door. Fellsinger was smiling. Fellsinger was giving him a little wave of encouragement. He smiled and waved back and entered the elevator. As the elevator took him down he extracted the folded slip of paper from his coat pocket. He looked at the name, *Walter Coley*, and the address on Post Street, and *third floor—room 303*. The elevator came to a stop and Parry walked out of the apartment house, walked for two blocks and saw a wide street that had car tracks. A streetcar was approaching but he knew he couldn't take a streetcar. He had to depend on another taxi. He opened one of the cigarette packs, realized he had no matches, put the pack back in his pocket. He looked up and down the street and there was nothing resembling a taxi. He walked down the wide street, telling himself that he needed a smoke, needed it badly. He walked into a small confectionery store. There was an old woman behind the counter.

"A book of matches," Parry said.

The old woman put two books of matches on the counter and said, "A penny. Anything else?"

"No," Parry said. He was handling some of the silver the taxi driver had given him. The old woman was looking at him. He put a nickel on the counter.

"You don't have any pennies?" the old woman said.

He didn't like the way she was looking at him. She seemed to be examining his face. Then she was turning her head slowly and her eyes were going to another part of the small store and Parry's eyes went along with her eyes, following her eyes, then frantically leaping ahead of her eyes and getting there first, getting to the stack of newspapers beside a candy counter, getting to the front page and the big photograph of Vincent Parry on the front page. Automatically he sucked in his cheeks and frowned and tried to change the set of his face, and as the eyes of the old woman came back to his face he made an abrupt turn and he was going out of the store.

"You got change coming," the old woman said.

Parry was out of the store and walking fast down the street. As he neared the end of the block he started to run. He had a picture of the old woman at a telephone, a picture of a police sergeant at the other end of the line. He ran fast, and faster, as fast as he could go. The empty pavement went sliding toward

him, dim white in the lateness of empty night, then gave way
to black street. In the middle of the street he told himself he
ought to turn here, he ought to get off the wide street. As he
turned he saw two headlights coming at him and he heard a
horn honking and he tried to get out of the way. The horn
honked again and with the horn Parry heard the brakes fighting with momentum, fighting with the street and trying to do
something for him. Then the automobile hit him, and as he
went down under the bumper, going around in the big circle
that was a preliminary to sleep, he told himself this was the first
time in his life he had ever been hit by an automobile.

9

SOMEONE WAS saying, "—turned and came right at me."

Someone else said, "You should have full control of your car at all times. Your speed——"

"Officer, I swear I wasn't doing more than twenty-five."

"That's what you say. Now we'll see what he has to say. He's coming to."

Parry raised his head, lifted himself on his elbows. He saw the big face in front of his own face, the shield on the cap, the bright buttons on the coat. There were other faces surrounding the big face but he wasn't paying attention to them. He kept staring at the big face of the policeman.

Someone was saying, "Officer, I should drop down dead if I was doing more than twenty-five. As true as there's——"

"All right, save that for later," the policeman said.

Parry said, "I'm all right, officer." He stood up. There was a pain in the back of his head. There was a pain in his right knee. He put a hand to the back of his head and felt the bump. He took a couple of steps forward and people were stepping back to give him room.

The policeman had a long rounded nose and a rounded chin. The policeman put a huge arm around Parry's middle and said, "Sure you're all right?"

"Perfectly sure," Parry said, squirming away from the policeman's arm. "Just had the wind knocked out of me."

"Thank God," someone said, and Parry turned and saw a little man who had a bald head and a moustache that was too big for his little face.

The policeman faced the little man and said, "Cards."

"Sure, officer. Right here." The little man tussled with a back pocket and took out a wallet. It was an overloaded wallet and as the little man hurried to open it a collection of cards and papers fluttered out and showered to the street.

Parry said, "I'm all right, officer. No damage at all."

"He hit you, didn't he?" the policeman said.

The little man was on his knees, picking up the papers and

cards. The little man looked up and said, "I'm telling you, officer, I wasn't doing more than——"

"Aw, keep quiet, will ya?" the policeman said impatiently. "All I want from you is your cards."

"Yes, sir," the little man said. He went on picking up the papers and cards.

Someone said, "Better call an ambulance."

"I don't need an ambulance," Parry said. He wondered if there was a chance to make a break. He estimated nine people in this bunch. Out of nine maybe there were none who could run as fast as he. Undoubtedly he could run faster than the big policeman.

"Got any pain?" the policeman said.

"None at all," Parry said. "I'm perfectly all right."

"You sure?" the policeman said.

The little man was up with the papers and cards, saying, "If he says he's all right then he must be all right."

Turning to the little man, the policeman said, "What are you, master of ceremonies? Let's see those cards."

"Yes, sir," the little man said. He was extending cards. "My driver's license, and here's my owner's——"

"All right, I got eyes," the policeman said. He studied the cards. He looked at the little man.

Parry said, "It wasn't his fault, officer. I ran right in front of his car."

"That's right, officer," the little man said. "That's just the way it was. I was——"

"Let's take this step by step," the policeman said. He pushed the cap back on his head. He looked at Parry. "You say it wasn't his fault?"

"That's right. It wasn't his fault at all."

"That's right, officer," the little man said. "I was——"

"Now look, Max—" the policeman pushed the cap forward again. "I'm in charge of this deal and it's going to be handled my way. Is that clear, Max?"

"Sure, officer," the little man said. "You're in charge. Anything you say goes. All I want to do is——"

"Max," the policeman said, "all you want to do is keep that mouth of yours quiet so's I can get this matter straightened out." He turned to Parry. "Now look, mister, are you sure you're all right?"

Someone said, "I'd call an ambulance. If it's a skull fracture——"

"It aint no skull fracture," the little man said loudly.

"How do you know it aint?" the other man said.

The little man faced the big policeman and gestured toward Parry. He said, "The man's got a bump on the head and already they got him dead and buried."

"If it was up to me I'd get an ambulance," the other man said.

The policeman turned and faced the other man. The policeman said, "It aint up to you. I'm in charge here, unless you want to argue about it."

"I'm not arguing about anything," the other man said aggressively. "All I say is you ought to get an ambulance."

The policeman took a step forward while pointing back to Parry and saying, "Do you know that man?"

Parry was telling himself all he had to do was get past the policeman because there was a gap to the left of the policeman and if he could get through the gap he would be on his way.

The other man was saying, "No."

"All right then," the policeman said. "If you don't know him it aint none of your business."

"I'm a citizen," the other man said. "I've lived in this city for thirty-seven years."

"I don't care if you were one of the founders," the policeman said.

"I've got certain privileges," the other man said.

The policeman took another step forward. He said, "Look, friend, it's a late hour. Why don't you go home and get a good night's rest?"

It got a few laughs. The man didn't like being laughed at. He pointed a long arm at Parry. He said, "That man—" and Parry was all set to run "—that man might have a skull fracture. And I say it's your official duty, as a sworn servant of the law, to protect the citizens of this city. It is your official duty to call an ambulance."

"I said I was all right," Parry said.

The policeman turned to Parry and said, "Mister, what's your name?"

Parry looked at the policeman. He said, "Studebaker."

"What's that again?"

"Studebaker," Parry said. "George Studebaker."

"Does it make any difference what his name is?" the little man said. "If he's not going to prefer charges——"

"God damn it, I'm handling this," the policeman said.

"You're handling it all wrong," said the man who had lived in San Francisco for thirty-seven years.

"Now listen here, you," the policeman said. He pushed the cap back on his head. "You keep that up and I'll run you in for interfering with an officer in the performance of his duty."

"You won't do anything of the sort," the man said. "I'm a citizen. I'm a respectable member of this community. I've got a clean record and I own my own home. I've got a wife and four children. I've worked in the same plant for thirty-two years."

"And never been late or absent," someone said.

"Absent once," the man said. "I fell down a flight of stairs and broke my left leg."

"That's too bad," the policeman said. "How's the leg now?"

"It's all right now."

"That's fine," the policeman said. "That means you can walk. So go ahead and walk."

"Sure," the little man said, coming up to stand beside the policeman. "Go home already."

"Nobody asked you," the other man said. "You're just one of these wise little Jews."

The little man was stiff for a moment, then he bent back, like a strip of flexible steel, and sprang forward with both fists slashing at the other man's face, but before he could reach the other man the policeman grabbed him. He tried to get away from the policeman. He tried to get to the other man and he said, "You can't talk like that any more. We don't take it any more. We're through taking it. If my boy in the South Pacific was here now he'd tear you apart with his bare hands. You got to realize you can't talk like that any more. Let go of me, officer. I won't let him get away with that. I won't let any of them get away with thàt. I don't care if they're eight feet tall——"

"All right, Max," the policeman said soothingly. "Take it easy."

"We don't take it easy any more," the little man said. "We don't let them talk like that any more."

The crowd was looking at the other man. The other man was backing away. The policeman looked at the other man and said, "That's right, take a walk, because I got a good mind to let Max loose, and once he gets loose you're gonna regret the whole thing. It happens I also had a boy in the South Pacific."

The man who had lived in San Francisco for thirty-seven years was backing away, gradually turning, so that at last he had his back to the crowd and was walking quickly down the street.

"Now I don't care what happens," the little man said. His whole body was shaking. "You can call the ambulance, you can call the wagon. I don't care what you do. I don't care."

Someone said, "Why don't we just break it up already?"

The policeman pushed the cap farther back on his head, turned to Parry and said, "Look, Studebaker, are you sure you're all right?"

"I'm absolutely sure, officer," Parry said. "You'd be doing me a favor if you let it ride."

The policeman pushed the cap farther back on his head, stood there with uncertainty all over his face, rubbed a big hand across his big chin. Then he pushed the cap forward on his head, glared at the crowd and said, "All right, let's break it up."

The crowd moved back as the policeman walked forward. The crowd radiated.

Parry told himself to wait, to hold it until the policeman crossed the street. The little man came over to Parry and said, "Thanks, mister. You could have said it was my fault."

"It's all right," Parry said. He was watching the policeman.

"Maybe you ought to see a doctor after all," the little man said. "Can I take you any place?"

"No," Parry said. "Thanks anyway. Wait. You going toward Post?"

"Sure," the little man said. "I'm not going there but I'll go there anyway. Any place you want to go."

They stepped into the car. Both doors closed. The little man was still shaking and he stalled the car twice before he really got it going. The car made a turn. Parry took out a pack of cigarettes.

"Smoke?"

"Thanks," the little man said. "I need it."

Parry gave him a light, lit his own, leaned back and watched the street lamps parading quickly toward the car.

"Sometimes I just get burned up," the little man said.

"I know."

"I get so burned up I don't know what I'm doing," the little man said. "And it's not good for me. I got high blood pressure. I've had it for years."

Parry was watching the rear-view mirror.

The little man was taking something from his pocket.

Parry tugged hard at the cigarette and wondered if the single light he saw back there was the headlamp of a motorcycle.

"Here, take this," the little man said, handing Parry a card. "I'm nobody important, but any time I can do you a favor——"

Parry looked at the card. Glow from the street lamps showed him *Max Weinstock, Upholsterer.*

"Sure you feel all right?" the little man said.

"I'm fine," Parry said. "I wasn't hurt at all."

"But maybe you should see a doctor just to make sure."

"No, I'm all right," Parry said.

The little man looked at him.

Parry looked at the rear-view mirror.

The car made another turn, stopped for a light, went down three blocks, stopped for another light, made another turn and the little man said, "Whereabouts on Post?"

Parry took the folded slip of paper from his pocket, studied it for a few moments. He directed the little man to let him off at a street that was one block away from the address on the paper.

The car made another turn, going left on Post.

"Do you have the time?" Parry said, forgetting the watch on his wrist.

The little man glanced at a wrist watch. "Two-thirty."

"Too early," Parry said.

"Early?"

"Nothing," Parry said. "I was just thinking."

The little man was looking at him. As the car stopped for another light the little man leaned forward slightly so he could get a better look at Parry's face. Parry took out the pack, lit another cigarette, sustaining the match and holding his left hand in front of the left side of his face. Glancing sideways, he knew the little man was still looking at him. He had a feeling it was going to happen now, while they were waiting for this light to change. He told himself Post was reasonably empty and he could handle the little man as he had handled Studebaker. The little man was still looking at him and now he had his cigarette going and the match was going to burn his fingers. He blew out the match, his hand came down. The little man was still looking at him. Parry's teeth clicked, his head turned mechanically, he stared at the little man, his stare went past the eyes of the little man and he was staring at a police squad car parked there beside the little man's car.

The light changed. The police squad car went forward.

"The light changed," Parry said.

The little man turned and looked at the light. He made no move to get the car going.

"The light changed," Parry said.

"Yes," the little man said. "I know." He made no move to get the car going.

"What's the matter?" Parry said.

The little man looked at him.

"Can't we get started?" Parry said.

The little man was leaning back now, his head was down, he was looking at nothing.

"Won't the car go?" Parry said.

"The car's all right," the little man said.

"Then what's the matter?" Parry said. "Why are we standing here?"

The little man looked at Parry. The little man said nothing.

"I don't get you," Parry said. He looked at the rear-view mirror. He put fingers on the door handle. He said, "We can't stay here in the middle of the street. We're blocking traffic."

"There's no traffic," the little man said. It was under a whisper.

"Well, why don't we move?" Parry said. He gripped the door handle.

The little man said nothing. He was leaning back again. His head was down again. He was looking at nothing again.

"What's the matter with you?" Parry said. "Are you sick or something?"

"I'm not sick." It was way under a whisper.

"Then what's the matter? What are you sitting there like that for? What's wrong with you? What are you doing sitting there like that? What are you doing? Answer me, what are you doing? What are you doing?"

The little man raised his head slowly and he was gazing straight ahead and still he looked at nothing. Then he said, "I'm thinking."

10

THE LIGHT changed again.

Parry tried to put pressure on the door handle. He couldn't collect any pressure.

The motor stopped.

Parry wanted to hear the motor going. He said, "Start the car."

The little man pressed his foot against the starter. The car jumped forward and stalled. The little man started the motor again, the car inched forward.

"Don't go against the light," Parry said. "Wait for the light to change."

The little man crossed his arms on the steering wheel, leaned his head on his arms. Parry got some pressure on the door handle, got the door handle moving, then took his hand away, wondered why he was taking his hand away, wondered why he was staying in the car.

The light changed.

"All right," Parry said. "The light changed. Let's go."

The little man brought his head up, looked at the light, looked at Parry. Then he had the car in first gear and he was letting the clutch out. He was driving the car across the intersection, turning the wheel slowly, bringing the car to a stop at the curb.

Again Parry had his fingers on the door handle. He looked at the little man and said, "What are we stopping for?"

"Let me look at you," the little man said.

"What?"

"Let me take a good look at you."

They faced each other and Parry had his right hand hardening slowly, shaping a fist. And the fist trembled. He wondered if he had the strength to go through with it.

The little man said, "Are you sure you're all right?"

"I didn't do it," Parry said. "I didn't do it and I won't go back."

"You won't go back where?"

"I won't go back."

The little man put a hand to his forehead, rubbed his forehead, rubbed his eyes as if he had a headache. He said, "Nobody claimed it was your fault. It was just one of those things. It was an accident."

"That's right," Parry said. "That's what I told them. It was an accident."

The little man brought his face closer to Parry's face and said, "You don't look so good to me."

Parry was trying to make his way through a huge barrel that rolled fast and messed up his footing. He heard himself saying, "What are you going to do about it?"

And he heard the little man saying, "I think you better let me take you to a hospital."

The barrel stopped rolling. Parry said, "Stop worrying about it."

"I can't help worrying," the little man said. "Will you do me a favor? Will you let a doctor look you over?"

Parry was working the door handle. He had it down now and he was getting the door open. He said, "I'll do that," and then the door was open and he was out of the car, the door was closed again, the light was changing and the car was going away from him.

He got his legs working. The pain in his head was going away, and he found it easy to breathe, easy to walk, easy to think. The whole thing was beginning to lean toward his side of it. He really had a grip on it now and it was going along with him. Everything was going along. And everybody, so far. Beginning with Studebaker, although with Studebaker it was involuntary. With the policeman who had looked under the blanket it was sheer carelessness. With Irene it was her own choice and the reason for that choice was an immense question mark despite the things she had told him. With the taxi driver it was human kindness. With George Fellsinger it was friendship. With the old woman in the candy store it was bad eyesight, because if her eyes were halfway decent she would have checked his face with that picture on the front page. And he knew she hadn't checked it, because if she had it would have brought a parade of police cars to the scene of the accident a few blocks away from the candy store. With Max it was as Max had put, just one of those things. He had to forget about it, because it didn't matter now and he had to check off everything that didn't matter. He remembered his wrist watch and the hands showed him 2:55.

The slip of paper came out of his pocket and he glanced at the address, pushed the paper back in his pocket and walked faster. In a few minutes he was there. He looked up along the windows of a dilapidated four-story building. The windows were dark, except for reflected light from dim street lamps that showed dirt on the glass. The alley bordering the building was very black and waiting for him. He walked down the alley.

The alley branched off to the right at the rear of the building. He went that way, came to the door. He touched the door. He touched the knob. He handled the knob, turned it. He opened the door.

He went in and closed the door. Weak greenish light from one of the upper floors came staggering down a narrow stairway. The place was very old and very neglected. Parry went over to the stairway and let some of the greenish light get on the wrist-watch dial. The hands said 2:59. He was on time. He was all set. He started up the stairway.

The greenish light didn't come from the first floor. It didn't come from the second floor. It came from a hanging bulb on the third floor, and it illuminated several of the mottled glass panels in splintered doors. There was an advertising specialty company and a firm of mystic book publishers and an outfit that called itself Excelsior Enterprises. Parry walked down the corridor. He came to a glass panel that had the words—*Walter Coley.* And underneath—*Plastic Specialist.* A suggestion of yellow glow came from the other side of the glass.

Parry tapped fingers against the glass.

There were footsteps from inside, a trading of voices. Then more footsteps, and then the door opened, and the taxi driver stood there. The taxi driver had a half-smoked cigar between his teeth.

"How's it going?" the taxi driver said.

"It's going all right," Parry said.

The taxi driver stepped back. Parry walked in and the taxi driver closed the door. This room was trying to be a waiting room. It was nothing more than an old room with a few chairs

and an old rug and sick wallpaper. The yellow glow came from
the other room. The taxi driver went forward, opened the door
leading to the other room, walked in and Parry followed.

It was another old room. It was very small. There was a single
secondhand barber's chair from about fifteen years back. There
was a big sink and three glass cabinets stocked with scissors,
knives, forceps and other instruments designed to get through
flesh. There was a short thin man, seventy if he was a day, and
his hair was white as hair can be, and his skin was white kidskin,
and his eyes were a very pale blue. He wore a white sport shirt,
open at the throat, and white cotton trousers held up by a
white belt. He looked at Parry's face and then he looked at the
taxi driver.

The taxi driver chewed on the cigar and said, "Well, Walt—
what do you think?"

Coley put a hand to the side of his jaw, supported his elbow
with the other hand. He got his eyes on Parry's face again and
he said, "Around the eyes, mostly. And the mouth. And the
cheeks. I'm going to leave the nose alone. It's a nice nose. It
would be a shame to break it."

"Will I need to come back again?" Parry asked.

"No. I wouldn't want you to come back again anyway. I'm
taking a big enough chance as it is." He turned to the taxi
driver. He said, "Sam, I won't need you in here. Go into the
other room and read a magazine."

The taxi driver walked out and closed the door.

Coley pointed to the ancient barber's chair. Parry sat down
in it and Coley began working a pedal and the chair began going
down. The chair went down to a shallow oblique and Coley
pulled a lamp toward the chair, aimed the lamp at Parry's face
and tugged at a short chain. The lamp stabbed a pearly ray at
Parry's face.

Parry closed his eyes. The towel-covered headrest felt too
hard against his skull. The chair was uncomfortable. He felt as
if he was on a rack. He heard water running and he opened his
eyes and saw Coley standing at the sink and working up a
lather on white hands. Coley stood there at the sink for fully
five minutes. Then he waved his hands to get some of the water
off and he held his hands up in the air with the fingers droop-

ing toward him as he came back to the chair and looked at Parry's face.

"Will it take long?" Parry said.

"Ninety minutes," Coley said. "No more."

"I thought it took much longer than that," Parry said.

Coley bent lower to study Parry's face and said, "I have my own method. I perfected it twelve years ago. It's based on the idea of calling a spade a spade. I don't monkey around. You have the money?"

"Yes."

"Sam said you can afford two hundred dollars."

"You want it now?"

Coley nodded. Parry took bills from his pocket, selected two one-hundred dollar bills, placed them on the top of a cabinet neighboring the chair. Coley looked at the money. Then he looked at Parry's face.

Parry said, "I'm a coward. I don't like pain."

"We're all cowards," Coley said. "There's no such thing as courage. There's only fear. A fear of getting hurt and a fear of dying. That's why the human race has lasted so long. You won't have any pain with this. I'm going to freeze your face. Do you want to see yourself now?"

"Yes," Parry said.

"Sit up and take a look in that mirror." Coley pointed to a mirror that topped one of the cabinets.

Parry looked at himself.

"It's a fairly good face," Coley said. "It'll be even better when I'm done with it. And it'll be very different."

Parry relaxed in the chair. He closed his eyes again. He heard water running. He didn't open his eyes. He heard the sound of metal getting moved around, the sound of a cabinet drawer opening and shutting, the clink of steel against steel, the water running again. He kept his eyes closed. Then things were happening to his face. Some kind of oil was getting rubbed into his face, rubbed in thoroughly all over his face and then wiped off thoroughly. He smelled alcohol, felt the alcohol being dabbed onto his face. Then water running again. More clinking of steel, more cabinet drawers in action. He tried to make himself comfortable in the chair. He decided it was impossible for Coley to do this job in ninety minutes. He decided it was impossible for Coley to change the face so that people wouldn't recognize it as belonging to Vincent Parry. He decided there wasn't any sense to this, and the only thing he would get out of it was something horrible happening to his face and he would be a freak for the rest of his life. He wondered how many faces Coley had ruined. He decided his face was going to look horrible but people would recognize him anyway and he wondered what he was doing up here in this quack set-up in San Francisco when he should be riding far away from San Francisco. He decided his only move was to jump out of the chair and run out of the office and keep on running.

He stayed there in the chair. He felt a needle going into his face. Then it went into his face again in another place. It kept jabbing deep into his face. His face began to feel odd. Metal was coming up against the flesh, pressing into the flesh, cutting into the flesh. There was no pain, there was no sensation except the metal going into his flesh. Different shapes of metal. He couldn't understand why he preferred to keep his eyes closed while this was going on.

It went on. With every minute that passed something new was happening to his face. Gradually he became accustomed to it—the entrance of steel into his flesh. He had the feeling he had gone through this sort of thing many times before. Now he was beginning to get some comfort out of the chair and there was a somewhat luxurious heaviness in his head and it became heavier and heavier and he knew he was falling asleep. He didn't mind. The manipulation of steel against his face and into his face took on a rhythm that mixed with the heaviness and formed a big, heavy ball that rolled down and rolled up and took him along with it, first on the top of it, on the outside, then getting him inside, rolling him around as it went up and down on its rolling path. And he was asleep.

He had a dream.

He dreamed he was a boy again in Maricopa, Arizona. A boy of fifteen running along a blackened street. He was running alone and eventually he came to a place where a woman was performing on a trapeze. From neck to ankles the woman was garbed in a skin-tight costume of bright orange satin. The woman's hair was darkish orange. The woman had drab brown eyes and her skin was tanned. It was the artificial tan that came from a violet-ray lamp. The woman was about five feet four inches tall and she was very thin and she was not at all pretty but there was nothing in her face to suggest ugliness. It was just that she was not a pretty woman. But she was a wonderful acrobat. She smiled at him. She took the trapeze way up high and sailed away from it. She described three slow somersaults going backwards, going up, going over and coming down on the trapeze again as it whizzed back. Elephants in the three rings far below lifted their trunks and lifted their eyes and watched her admiringly. The trapeze whizzed again and she left the trapeze again, going up and up and up, almost to the top of the tent until she described the wonderful series of backward somersaults that brought her down again to the trapeze. She was tiny way up there and then she grew as she came down. She stepped off the trapeze and came sliding down a rope. She bowed to the elephants. She bowed to everybody. She came over to him. He told her she was wonderful on the trapeze. She said it was really not at all difficult and anyone could do it. He could do it. He said he couldn't do it. He told her he was afraid. She laughed and told him he was silly to be afraid. She took his arm and led him toward the rope. The bright orange satin was flesh of flame on her thin body. She opened her mouth to laugh at him and he saw many gold inlays among her teeth. He pleaded with her to take him away from this high, dizzy place, this swirling peril. The trapeze came up to the limit of its whizzing arc and she left the trapeze, took him with her and they went up, somersaulting backward together, going up and over and he fought to get away from her and she laughed at him and he fought and fought until he got away from her. He went down alone. Down fast, face foremost, watching the sawdust and the faces and the colossal dull green elephants coming toward him. Down there they were attempting to do something for him. They were trying to arrange a net to catch him. Before they could get the net connected he was in amongst them, plunging past them and landing on his face. He felt the impact hammering into his face, the pain tearing through his face, hitting the back of his head and bouncing back and running all over his face. He was flat on his back, his arms wide, his legs spread wide as he looked up at the faces

looking down on him. The pain was fierce and he moaned and
the mob stood there and pitied him. He could see her high up
there. The orange satin twirled and glimmered as she went away
from the trapeze in another backward somersault. She came
down wonderfully on the trapeze and although she was way
up there her face was very close to his eyes and she was laughing at him and the gold inlays were dazzling in her laughing
mouth.

The pain was fierce. It was a burning pain and there was
something above the pain that felt very heavy on his face. He
opened his eyes. He looked up at Coley.

"All over," Coley said.

The taxi driver was standing beside Coley working on a new
cigar.

Coley had his arms folded and he looked down at Parry and
said, "Stay there for a while. Don't try to talk. Don't move
your mouth. I've got you all taped up. I've left a small space in
front of your mouth so you'll be able to take nourishment.
You'll use a glass straw and you can have anything liquid. If
you want to smoke you can use a cigarette holder. But I don't
want you to move your mouth and I don't want you to try
talking. The bandages can come off after five days. When the
bandages come off you'll look in the mirror and you'll see a
new face. It'll be all healed by then and you can shave."

Parry's eyes talked to Coley.

Coley said, "There won't be any scars. I did a sensational job
on you. I think it's the best job I've ever done. And I've done
a lot of exciting things to people's faces. I've got it down pat,
hiding those scars."

The pain was digging and tugging and digging. It was burning there in Parry's face and gradually he began to feel it in his
arms. He looked at Coley. His eyes asked another question.

Coley answered, "I took off your coat and rolled up your
shirtsleeves. I worked on your arms. The upper part of the under-
arm. Up near the armpit, where you can spare the flesh. I used
that flesh on your face. Now I'm going to ask you a question
and if the answer is yes I want you to nod very slowly. Do you
have a place to stay?"

Parry nodded slowly.

"Do you have someone to help you?"

Parry nodded again.

"All right," Coley said. "When you get there you can talk to that person with paper and pencil. Now here's the ticket. You're to sleep flat on your back. Have this person tie your hands to something so you won't be able to turn over. During the day I want you to take it easy. Sit in one place most of the time and read or listen to the radio or play solitaire. Keep your mind off your face and above all keep your hands away from your face. In another day or so it's going to start itching but no matter how bad it is I want you to keep your hands off those bandages. I guess you can get up now."

Parry sat up. He took himself off the chair. His shirt was open a few buttons down from the collar and his sleeves were rolled up high. The upper parts of his arms were bandaged. He looked at his arms, he looked at Coley and Coley nodded. Parry rolled his sleeves down and buttoned them. He buttoned up his shirt and put on his necktie and got into his coat. Then he walked over to the mirror and took a look at himself.

He saw his eyes and his nose and a small hole in front of his mouth. He saw most of his forehead and his ears and his hair. The rest was all white bandage, the white gauze padded thickly on his face, the criss-cross of adhesive going back along with the bandage around the back of his head. The bandage went under his chin and around his jaws and slanted down around his neck.

Coley came over and stood beside him. He said, "There's a lot of wax and goo under that bandage. It's hard now but in a couple of days it'll be soft and part of it will become part of your new face."

Parry glanced at his wrist watch. It said 4:31. He looked at Coley.

Coley said, "Ninety minutes. Just like I told you."

The taxi driver said, "We better get moving."

Parry was looking at Coley and holding out his hand. Coley took the hand. Coley said, "Maybe you did it and maybe you didn't. I don't know. Sam claims you didn't do it and I've known Sam a long time. I have a lot of faith in his ideas about things. That's the main reason I took this job. If I thought you were a professional killer I wouldn't have any part of it. But the way it is now I've given you a new face and you've given me two hundred dollars and that's as far as it goes. I never keep records of my patients and I never make an effort to remember names. When you walk out of here you're through with me and I'm through with you."

Parry looked at the taxi driver. The taxi driver walked to the door, opened it, went to the other door, opened it and stood there looking up and down the hall. Then he turned and beckoned to Parry, and Parry went out there with him and they went down the hall and down the stairs. They were out in the alley and down a second alley that led to a small side street. The taxi was parked there. They got in and the two doors closed and the motor started.

The taxi driver used side streets, used them deftly, making good time without too much speed. Parry leaned back and closed his eyes. He was very tired. He was very thankful he had a place to go to and a friend to help him. The pain kept digging into his face and banging away at his arms but now he didn't mind. He had a place to stay. He had Fellsinger. He had a new face. Now he really had something that amounted to a chance.

The taxi came to a stop.

Parry looked out the window. They were home.

The taxi driver turned and looked at him and said, "How is it?"

Parry nodded.

"Think you can make it alone?"

Parry nodded again. He took bills from his pocket, picked out a fifty dollar bill and handed it to the driver. The driver looked at the bill and then offered it back. Parry shook his head.

The taxi driver said, "I'm not doing this on a cash basis."

Parry nodded. The taxi driver made another attempt to return the bill. Parry shook his head.

The taxi driver said, "Now you're sure you can make it?"

Parry nodded. He started to open the door. The taxi driver touched his wrist. He said, "You don't know me. I don't know you. You'll never see me again. I'll never see you again. You don't know the name of the men who fixed your face. Or put it this way. You always had the face you have now. You were never in a courtroom. You were never in San Quentin. You were never married. And you don't know me and I don't know you. How does that sound?"

Parry nodded.

The taxi driver said, "Thanks for the tip, mister."

Parry stepped out of the taxi. The taxi went into first gear and went on down the street. Parry walked up to the door of the apartment house, went in, and from his coat pocket he took the key that Fellsinger had given him. He opened the inner door.

In the elevator he wondered if Fellsinger had a cigarette holder up there. He was in great need of a cigarette. The elevator climbed four floors and came to a stop. Parry walked down the hall. He wondered if Fellsinger had a glass straw in there. He wondered how it would be to take rum through a glass straw. He wished Fellsinger had some gin around. He wanted gin and he wanted a cigarette. He had a feeling that falling asleep tonight would be hard work. He was at the door of Fellsinger's apartment and he put the key in the door and turned it and opened the door and went in.

It was dark in there, but light from the hall showed Parry the switch on the wall near the door. He flicked the switch and closed the door, facing the door as he closed it and then turning slowly and facing the room. He looked at Fellsinger.

Fellsinger was on the floor with his head caved in.

11

THERE WAS blood all over Fellsinger, blood all over the floor. There were pools of it and ribbons of it. There were blotches of it, big blotches of it near Fellsinger, smaller blotches getting even smaller in progression away from the body. There were flecks of it on the furniture and suggestions of it on a wall. There was the cardinal luster of it and the smell of it and the feeling of it coming up from Fellsinger's busted skull and dancing around and settling down wherever it pleased. It was dark blood where it clotted in the skull cavities. It was luminous pale blood where it stained the horn of the trumpet that rested beside the body. The horn of the trumpet was slightly dented. The pearl buttons of the trumpet valves were pink from the spray of blood.

Fellsinger was belly down on the floor, but his face was twisted sideways. His eyes were opened wide, the pupils up high with a lot of white underneath. It was as if he was trying to look back. Either he wanted to see how badly he was hurt or he wanted to see who was banging on his skull with the trumpet. His mouth was halfway open and the tip of his tongue flapped over the side of his mouth.

Without sound, Parry said, "Hello, George."

Without sound, Fellsinger said, "Hello, Vince."

"Are you dead, George?"

"Yes, I'm dead."

"Why are you dead, George?"

"I can't tell you, Vince. I wish I could tell you but I can't."

"Who did it, George?"

"I can't tell you, Vince. Look at me. Look what happened to me. Isn't it awful?"

"George, I didn't do it. You know that."

"Of course, Vince. Of course you didn't do it."

"George, you don't really believe I did it."

"I know you didn't do it."

"I wasn't here, George. I couldn't have done it. Why would I want to kill you, George? You were my friend."

"Yes, Vince. I was your friend."

"George, you were my best friend. You were always a real friend."

"You were my only friend, Vince. My only friend."

"I know that, George. And I know I didn't kill you. I know it I know it I know it I know it I know it."

"Don't carry on like that, Vince."

"George, you're not really dead, are you?"

"Yes, Vince. I'm dead. And it's real, Vince, it's real. I'm really dead. I never thought I'd be important. But now I'm very important. They'll have me in all the papers."

"They'll say I killed you."

"Yes, Vince. That's what they'll say."

"But I didn't do it, George."

"I know, Vince. I know you didn't do it. I know who did it but I can't tell you because I'm dead."

"George, can I do anything for you?"

"No. You can't do a thing for me. I'm dead. Your friend George Fellsinger is dead."

"George, who do you think did it?"

"I tell you I know who did it. But I can't say."

"Give me a hint. Give me an idea."

"Vince, I can't give you anything. I'm dead."

"Maybe if I look around I'll find something."

"Don't do that, Vince. Don't move from where you are now. If you step in the blood you're going to make footprints."

"Footprints won't make any difference one way or another. As soon as they find you here they'll say I did it."

"Yes, Vince. That's what they'll say. You can't do anything about that. But if you give them footprints you'll be throwing everything away. What I mean is, if they have the footprints they'll have more than a conclusion. They'll have you, because they have means of tracing footprints, tracing right through to the store where the shoes were bought. When they get that they'll get her. And if they get her they'll get you, because you can't operate without her."

"George, I can't go back to her."

"What do you mean, you can't go back? You've got to go back. You can't go anyplace else. Where else could you go?"

"I don't know, George. I don't know. But I can't go back to her."

"Jesus Christ."

"I can't help it, George. I can't go back to her. I can't bring her back into it now."

"But she wants to help you, Vince."

"Why, George? How do you make it out? Why does she want to help me?"

"She feels sorry for you."

"There's more to it than that. There's much more. What is it?"

"I don't know, Vince."

"I can't go back to her."

"You've got to go back. You've got to stay there for five days. You need someone to take care of you until those bandages come off. Then when you go away you can really go away. You'll have a new face. You'll have a new life. You always talked about travel. Places you wanted to see. I remember the things you said. How grand it would be to get away. From everybody. From everything. How I felt bad about it when you said that, because I figured our friendship was one of those very valuable things that don't happen very often between plain guys like you and me. How I hoped you'd include me in your plans to go away. You knew that. You knew how I felt. And I had an idea that when you finally went away you would take me with you. To that beach town in Spain. Or that place in Peru. Was it Patavilca?"

"Yes, George. It was Patavilca."

"Patavilca in Peru. Jumping out of our cages in an investment security house. Jumping out of our cages in dried-up apartment houses. Going away, going away from it, all of it, going to Patavilca, in Peru. With nothing to do down there except get the sun and sleep on the beach. They showed that beach in the travel folder. It was a lovely beach. And they showed us the streets and the houses. The little streets and the little houses under the sun. I was waiting for you to say the word. I was waiting for you to say let's pack up and go."

"Why didn't you say the word, George? Why didn't you take the bull by the horns? There wouldn't have been any trial. This trouble would have never happened."

"You know why I didn't say the word. You know me. Guys like me come a dime a dozen. No fire. No backbone. Dead

weight waiting to be pulled around and taken to places where
we want to go but can't go alone. Because we're afraid to go
alone. Because we're afraid to be alone. Because we can't face
people and we can't talk to people. Because we don't know
how. Because we can't handle life and don't know the first
thing about taking a bite out of life. Because we're afraid and
we don't know what we're afraid of and still we're afraid. Guys
like me."

"You had ideas, George."

"I had ideas that I thought were great. But I was always afraid
to let them loose. Once you were up here and I put my entire
attitude toward life into a trumpet riff. You told me it was
cosmic-ray stuff. Something from a billion miles away, bouncing off the moon, coming down and into my brain and coming
out of my trumpet. You told me I should do something with
ideas like that. And I agreed with you but I never did anything
because I was afraid. And now I'm dead."

"I think I better be going now."

"Yes, Vince. You go now. You go to her."

"George, I'm afraid."

"You go to her. Stay there five days. Then go to Patavilca, in
Peru. Stay there the rest of your life."

"I can't see myself going away."

"You've got to see that. You've got to do that. You've got to
go far away and stay there."

"I wish I knew who killed you."

"It doesn't make any difference. I'm dead now."

"And that's why it makes a difference. Because you're dead.
And they'll say I killed you, just as they said I killed her. And I
said I didn't kill her. I said it was an accident. All along I said it
was an accident and that's what I believed. I always believed she
fell down and hit her head on that ash tray. I don't believe that
any more. I know someone killed her and that same someone
killed you."

"You're curious, Vince. And you're getting angry. That won't
do. You can't be curious and you can't be angry. You've got to
think in terms of getting away, and only that. And now you
better go."

"Good-by, George."

Parry switched off the light. He stepped out of the apartment and closed the door slowly. There was a stiffness in his legs as he walked down the corridor. In the elevator he had a feeling he was going to faint. He sagged against the wall of the elevator and he was going to the floor and as his knees gave way he put his hands on the wall and braced himself and made himself stay up.

On the street he tried to walk fast but his legs were very stiff and he couldn't get any go into them. The pain in his face mixed with the pain in his arms and he wanted to get down on the pavement and sleep. He kept walking. He looked at his wrist watch and it said a few minutes past five and he looked up and saw the beginnings of morning sifting through the black sieve. He walked down the empty quiet streets.

He walked a mile and knew he had another mile to go. He didn't think he could make it. A taxi came down the street and he turned and saw the driver looking at him. He was tempted to take the taxi. But he knew he couldn't take a taxi. Not now. Not at this stage. The taxi slowed down and the driver was waiting for him to make a move. He kept walking. He faced straight ahead, knowing that the taxi driver was regarding his bandaged head with increasing curiosity. He kept walking. The taxi picked up speed and went down the street and made a turn.

A glow came onto the pavement, dripping from the grey light getting through the black sky. Parry walked past a cheap hotel and stopped and looked back at the sign. He was tempted to go in and take a room. He was so tired. The pain was so bad. He was so very, very tired.

He kept walking. Now he was going faster and he knew he was racing the morning. He knew he couldn't keep it up like this, and if he didn't get there soon he was going to go out cold. He knew he couldn't afford to go out cold and he kept walking fast. He was getting there. He was almost there. He measured the streets. He told himself it was three blocks. He knew it was more than three, more on the order of six or seven. He didn't think he could last out seven blocks. They were long blocks. The morning was getting a lead on him. He tried to walk faster. He tried to run and his legs became cotton fluff under him and he went to the pavement. He stayed there on his knees, feeling a wetness flowing all over his body, and for a few moments he thought it was the blood from his face getting out through the split flesh and pouring down under the bandage and down through his collar and going all over him. He put his hand to the under-edge of the bandage. His hand came away moist. He looked at his hand. It glistened with perspiration. He stood up and started to walk. He asked the blocks to come toward him, slide toward him and go away behind him. He kept walking. Then he could see it, the apartment house. He started to open his mouth to let out a cry and a dreadful pain spread out from his lips and went up to his eyes and came down to his lips again. He closed his mouth, and his eyes were jammed with tears. He looked at the apartment house coming toward him as he went toward it. He was about sixty steps away from the apartment house. He didn't think he could cover those sixty steps. He covered five of them and ten of them and thirty of them. He was ahead of the morning now and he was going to make it and he knew it. And as he knew that he knew it he saw something on the other side of the street, almost at the end of the block, parked there and waiting there and it was the Studebaker.

12

IT WAS the same Studebaker. It was the very same, the same Studebaker from way back. The same hunk of junk that had picked him up on the road. It couldn't be. It just couldn't be. And yet it was. There it was, parked across the street. There it was. Waiting there. The same Studebaker.

Parry came toward the apartment house, not knowing he was going toward the apartment house, knowing only that he was going toward the Studebaker, wanting to make sure that it was the same car and knowing it was the same car and not believing it was the same car and knowing it anyway. There was nobody in the car. It couldn't be the same car.

It was the same car.

He didn't want to start asking himself why. And how. And why and how and when and how and why and how and why. He asked and he couldn't answer. If there was any answer at all it was coincidence. But there was a limit to coincidence and this was way past the limit. This neighborhood aimed toward upper middle class, anywhere from fifteen thousand a year on up. Or give Studebaker a break and make it ten thousand. Even seventy-five hundred and still Studebaker didn't belong around here. Studebaker was way down in the sharecropper category. And the car was parked in front of an apartment house that wouldn't rent closet space for less than one ten a month. It couldn't be the same car.

It was the same car.

All right, Studebaker worked there as a janitor. No. All right, Studebaker had a wealthy brother living there. No. All right, Studebaker was driving down the street and he ran out of gas and had to park there. No. No and no and no.

It wasn't the same car. It couldn't be the same car.

It was the same car.

The morning light came down and tried to glimmer on the Studebaker. There was no polish on the Studebaker and very little paint, therefore very little glimmer. There was only the old Studebaker coupé, dull and quiet there on the other side of the street, waiting for him.

Parry turned and went toward the apartment house. He was staggering now. On the steps he stumbled and fell. In the vestibule his finger went toward the wrong button and he veered it away just in time and got it going toward the right button and pressed the button.

He got a buzz. He went through the lobby and entered the elevator. He pressed the 3 button. The elevator started up and Parry felt himself going down. As the elevator went up he kept going down and his eyes were closed now. He saw the black wall of his shut eyelids and then he saw the bright orange and the trapeze again and he saw the gold inlays in the laughing mouth and then he saw the black again just before everything became bright orange and after that it was all black and he was going in there in the black and he was in there. He was in the black.

Gradually the black gave way and its place was taken by grey-violet and yellow. He was on the sofa. He looked up and he saw her. She was standing beside the sofa, watching him. She smiled.

She said, "I didn't think you'd come back."

She was wearing a yellow robe. Her yellow hair came down and sprayed her shoulders.

She said, "When I heard the buzzer I was frightened. When nobody came up I was terribly frightened. Then after a while I went out in the hall and I saw the light from the elevator. I went down there and I opened the elevator and I saw you in there. I was so very frightened when I saw the bandages but I recognized the suit and so I understood the bandages. I'm lucky you're not heavy, because otherwise I couldn't have managed it. Tell me what happened to you."

Parry shook his head.

"Why not?"

He shook his head.

"Why can't you tell me?"

He pointed to his mouth. He shook his head.

"Can you talk?"

He shook his head.

"Can I do anything for you?"

He shook his head. Then he nodded. With an imaginary pencil he scribbled on a palm. She hurried out of the room. She came back with a pad and a pencil.

Parry wrote——

> A taxi driver recognized me. He offered to help me. He took me to a plastic specialist who operated on my face. Then he brought me back and left me off a few blocks from here. The bandages must stay on for five days. I can eat only liquids and I've got to take them through a glass straw. I can smoke cigarettes if you have a holder. I've got to sleep on my back and to keep from turning over on my face I've got to have my wrists tied to the sides of the bed. My face hurts terribly and so do my arms where he had to cut to get new skin for my face. I'm very tired and I want to sleep.

She read what he had written. She said, "You'll sleep in the bedroom. I'll sleep here on the sofa."

He shook his head.

"I said you'll sleep in the bedroom. Please don't argue with me. I'm your nurse now. You mustn't argue with the nurse."

She led him into the bedroom. She stayed out while he undressed. When he was under the covers he knocked on the side of the bed and she came in. She used handkerchiefs to tie his wrists to the sides of the bed.

"Is that too tight?"

He shook his head.

"Are you comfortable?"

He nodded.

"Anything more I can do?"

He shook his head.

"Good night, Vincent."

She switched off the light and went out of the room.

In a few minutes Parry was asleep. He was up a few times during the night, coming out of sleep when he tried to turn over and his tied wrists held him back. Aside from that he slept the full sleep of fatigue, the heavy sleep that got him away from shock and pain. He slept until late in the afternoon, and when he awoke she was in the room, waiting for him with a breakfast tray. There was a tall glass of orange juice. There was a bowl of white cereal, very soft and mostly cream, so that it could be taken through a glass straw. There was a pot of coffee and a glass of water. There were three glass straws, new and glinting, and he knew she had gone out in the morning to buy them. He thanked her with his eyes. She smiled at him. She reached for something on the bureau and when she held it up he saw a long cigarette holder, new and glinting. It was yellow enamel and it had a small, delicately shaped mouthpiece.

She said, "Did you sleep well?"

He nodded. She untied the handkerchiefs and he started to get out of the bed and then he looked at her. She walked out of the room. He went into the bathroom. When he was finished in the bathroom he took his breakfast through the glass straws. Basie music came from the phonograph in the other room, then she came in from the other room and lighted a cigarette and watched him sip his meal through the straws. She looked at the empty glasses, the empty bowl and the empty cup.

She smiled and said, "That's a good boy. And now would you like a cigarette?"

He nodded.

She placed a cigarette in the holder and lighted it for him.

She said, "Does your face feel better today?"

He nodded.

"Much better?"

He nodded.

"What would you like to do?"

He shrugged.

"Would you like to read?"

He nodded.

"What would you like to read?"

He shrugged.

"A magazine?"

He shook his head.

"The paper?"

He looked at her. She wasn't smiling. He tried to get something from her eyes. He couldn't get anything. He started a nod and then he stopped it and he shrugged.

She went out of the room and came back with an afternoon edition. She gave it to him and he held it close to his eyes and saw that in San Francisco a man named Fellsinger had been murdered in the early hours of the morning and police said it was the work of the escaped lifer from San Quentin. Police said Parry's fingerprints were all over the place, on the furniture, on the cellophane wrapping around a pack of cigarettes, on a glass, on practically everything except the murder weapon, which was a trumpet. Police put it this way—they said Vincent Parry had gone to his friend George Fellsinger and had demanded aid in his effort to get away. Fellsinger no doubt refused. Then Fellsinger tried to call the police or told Parry he would eventually call the police. In rage or calm decision Parry took hold of the trumpet forgetting his other fingerprints throughout the room and knowing only that he mustn't get his fingerprints on the trumpet. And so he must have used a handkerchief around his hand as he wielded the trumpet and brought it down on Fellsinger's head. Again and again and again. The only fingerprints in the place were those of Fellsinger and those of Parry. There was positively no doubt about it. Parry did it.

Parry looked up. She was watching him. He pointed to the story.

She nodded. She said, "Yes, Vincent. I saw it."

He made a gesture to indicate that she should offer a further reaction.

She said, "I don't know what to say. Did you do it?"

He shook his head.

"But who could have done it?"

He shook his head.

"You were there last night?"

He nodded. Then he made the pad and pencil gesture. She brought him the pad and the pencil and he wrote it out for her, as it had happened. She read it slowly. It was as if she was studying from a textbook.

When she finally put the pad down she said, "In that statement you wrote this morning you said nothing about Fellsinger. Why?"

He shrugged.

"Is there anything else you didn't tell me?"

He shook his head. He thought of the Studebaker. He thought of Max. And the Studebaker. And he shook his head again.

She said, "I know there's something else. I wish you'd tell

me. The more you tell me the more help I can give you. But I can't force you to tell me. I only ask if it's important."

He shook his head.

She went to the door and there she turned and faced him. She said, "I have work to do this afternoon. Settlement work. I devote a few hours every day to it. I'll be back at six and we'll have dinner. Promise me you'll stay here. Promise me you won't answer the buzzer and no matter what takes place and no matter what thoughts get into your head you'll stay here."

He nodded.

She said, "There are cigarettes in the other room and if you get thirsty you'll find oranges in the refrigerator and you can make juice."

He nodded.

She walked out. He leaned over the newspaper and a few times more he read the Fellsinger story. He heard her going out of the apartment. He went through the newspaper. He tried to get interested in the financial section and gradually he succeeded and he was going through the stock quotations, the Dow-Jones averages, the prices on wheat and cotton, the situation in railroads and steel. He saw a small and severely neat advertisement from the firm where he had worked as a clerk, where Fellsinger had worked. He began to remember the days of work, the day he had started there, how difficult it was at first, how hard he had tried, how he had taken a correspondence course in statistics shortly after his marriage, hoping he could get a grasp on statistics and ultimately step up to forty-five a week as a statistician. But the correspondence course gave him more questions than answers and finally he had to give it up. He remembered the night he wrote the letter telling them to stop sending the mimeographed sheets. He showed the letter to Gert and she told him he would never get any-where. She went out that night. He remembered he hoped she would never come back and he was afraid she would never come back because there was something about her that got him at times and he wished there was something about him that got her. He knew there was nothing about him that got her and he wondered why she didn't pick herself up and walk out once and for all. She was always talking in terms of tall bony men with high cheekbones and hollow cheeks and very tall. He was bony and very thin and he had high cheekbones and hollow cheeks but he wasn't tall. He was really a miniature of what she really wanted. And because she couldn't get a permanent hold on the genuine she figured she might as well stay with the miniature. That was about as close as he could come to it. She was very thin herself and that was the way he liked them, thin. Very thin. She had practically no front development and nothing in back but that was the way he liked them and the first time he saw her he concentrated on the way she was constructed like a reed and he was interested. He disregarded the eyes that were more colorless than light brown, the hair that was more colorless than pale-brown flannel, the nose that was thin and the mouth that was very thin and the blade-line of her jaw. He disregarded the fact that she was twenty-nine when she married him and the only reason she married him was because he was a miniature of what she really wanted and she hadn't been able to get what she really wanted. She married him because he came along at a time when she was beginning to worry about it, to worry that she wouldn't be able to get anything. There were times when she told him the only reason he married her was because he was beginning to worry, because he couldn't get what he really wanted and he supposed he might as well take this colorless reed while the taking was good, and before years caught up with him and he wouldn't be able to get anything at all. He said that wasn't true. He wanted to marry her because she was something he really wanted and if she would only work along with him they would be able to get along and they would find ways to be happy. He tried to make her happy. He thought a child would make her happy. He tried to give her a child and once he got one started but she went to a doctor and took pills. She said she hated the thought of having a child.

Parry turned the pages of the newspaper and came to the sports section. Basketball was scheduled for tonight. He remembered he had always liked basketball. He remembered he had played basketball while he was in the reformatory in Arizona, and later he had played on a Y.M.C.A. team when he was living alone in San Francisco and working in a stock room for sixteen a week. He remembered he went to the games every now and then and one week end he went up to Eugene in Oregon to see a great Oregon State team play a great Oregon team. He remembered how he wanted to see that game, and how happy he was when finally he was in there with the crowd and the teams were on the floor and the game was getting under way. He remembered once he took Gert to a game on a Saturday night and it was after they were married four months. She kept saying she wasn't interested in basketball and she would rather see a floor show somewhere. He kept saying she ought to give basketball a chance because it was really something exciting to see and after all it was a change from floor shows. She said it was because seats for the basketball game were only a buck and a half or somewhere around that and he just didn't want to put out nine or ten or eleven in a night club. He said that wasn't a fair thing to say, because he was always taking her wherever she wanted to go on Saturday night, and she always wanted to go to night clubs, and it wasn't nine or ten or eleven anyway, it was more on the order of sixteen and seventeen and nineteen, because they both did considerable drinking. He didn't say the other things he was thinking then, that when she was in the night clubs she kept looking at tall, bony men, always kept looking at them, never looking at him, never listening to him, always kept turning her head to look at tall, bony men with high cheekbones and hollow cheeks. How he would finally stop talking and she wouldn't even realize he had stopped talking. Yet that night she had finally condescended to go to the basketball game with him. And it was an exciting game, it was very close, getting hotter all the time, and he was all pepped up and he was happy to be here. She was sitting there beside him, he remembered, not saying anything, not asking him about the game, not curious about the way it was played, but interested nonetheless. Interested in the tall bony boys who ran up and down the floor. Interested in their tall bony bodies, their long arms, their long legs glimmering in the bright light of the basketball court as they ran and stopped and ran again. And when she had seen all of them that she could see, she said she was fed up looking at all that nonsense down there, a bunch of young fools trying to cripple each other so they could throw a ball through a hoop. She said she wanted to leave. He asked her to stay with him until the game was over. She said she wanted to leave. She said if he didn't leave with her she would go alone. She was talking loud. He begged her to lower her voice. She talked louder. People around them were telling them to keep quiet and watch the game. She talked louder. Finally he said all right, they would leave. As they got up and started to leave he could hear other men laughing at him.

Parry turned the pages and arrived at the woman's section. Somebody was telling the women how to cook something. He remembered she hated to cook. They ate out most of the time. There were nights when he came home very tired and he cringed at the thought of going out and standing in line at the popular and expensive restaurants she liked, and how he wished she would learn to cook, because even on the few nights when they ate at home she gave him uncooked food, cold cuts or canned fish and the only thing hot was the coffee. Once he tried to talk to her about it and she started to yell. She took the percolator and poured the coffee all over the floor.

He remembered she took two thirds, more than two thirds of the thirty-five a week he made. He remembered she hardly ever smiled at him. When she did smile it wasn't really a smile, it was because she was amused at something. She never told him what amused her. And things that amused her didn't amuse him. He remembered once they were walking down the street and there was a traffic jam and one car bumped into another and they locked bumpers. She said, "Good." She started to laugh. He tried to see something funny in it. He tried to laugh. He couldn't laugh.

Once they were walking toward the apartment house and a delivery boy passed them on a bicycle, with the wire tray heaped with packages on the handle bars. The bicycle hit a bump and turned over. The boy fell on his face and the packages went flying all over the street. The boy had a cut on his face and he was sitting there in the street and putting a handkerchief to the blood on his face. She started to laugh. He asked her what she was laughing at. She didn't answer. She kept on laughing.

He was beginning to feel tired again. The pain in his face was dull now, and he was getting accustomed to it. But as he sat there measuring the pain he gradually realized there was something else besides the pain. Like little feathers under the

bandage. That was the itch Coley had talked about. The healing process, the mending was under way. He welcomed the
itch. He told it to get worse. He turned the pages of the newspaper and saw nothing to catch his interest, and besides he was
very tired. He pushed the newspaper aside and let his head go
back against the pillow. He closed his eyes, knowing he
wouldn't sleep, knowing he would just stay there, resting.
Feeling the pain, feeling the itch under the bandage, flowing
into the pain, then crawling under the pain. Once he opened
his eyes and looked toward the window. There was going to be
rain in San Francisco. The sky was a heavy, muttering grey,
getting ready to let loose. He closed his eyes again. He didn't
care if it rained. He was here, he was in here, he was all right in
here. And in less than five days he would be out of here and he
would be going away with his new face and everything would
be all right. And the buzzer was sounding and everything
would be all right. And the buzzer was sounding.

He sat up.

The buzzer was sounding again. Then it stopped. He sat
there waiting. It sounded again. It was a needle going into him.
And then it stopped.

He waited. He wondered who it was down there. He took
himself off the bed and walked to the window and waited
there. Then he saw someone going away from the apartment
house and walking across the street, walking toward the Studebaker that was parked on the other side of the street. And it
was the man who had given him the lift. It was Studebaker.

It was really Studebaker, with different clothes, new clothes
and no hat, and really Studebaker. And Studebaker was looking for him. Studebaker alone. No police. Parry couldn't get
that, couldn't get anywhere near it.

The sky gave way. Rain came down.

Parry stood there at the window and watched Studebaker
getting into the car. The car crawled, jolted, went forward, went
on down to the corner and made a turn. Parry began to quiver.
Studebaker was going to the police. But why now? Why not
before? Why now? If Studebaker hadn't talked to the police
until now, why was he going to see them now?

The rain came down hard and steadily. Parry went away from
the window, went toward the bed, then stopped and went

toward the dresser and stood before the dresser, looking in the mirror. He decided to take off the bandage and get out of the apartment before Studebaker came back with the police. He brought his hands to his face and his fingers came against the adhesive. He tugged at the adhesive. A tremendous burst of pain shot across his face and went leaping through his head. His fingers came away from the adhesive. He told himself that he mustn't be afraid of the pain. He must try again. He must get out of here, and he couldn't afford to be wearing the bandage when he went out. He got his fingers on the adhesive and once more he tugged at it and once more the pain slashed away at him. He knew he wouldn't be able to stand any more of it. He decided to stay here and let them come and get him. He went into the living room and seated himself on the sofa and looked at the floor. He sat there for a while, and then he got up and went into the bedroom and got the cigarette holder. He returned to the living room and picked up a pack of cigarettes.

He sat there looking at the floor and smoking cigarettes. He smoked nine cigarettes in succession. He looked at the stubs in the ash tray. He counted them, saw them dead there in the heaped ashes. Then he wondered how long it would take until the police arrived. He wondered how long it would be until he was dead, because this time he wouldn't be going back to a cell. This time they had him on a charge that would mean the death sentence. He looked at the window and saw the thick rain coming out of the thick grey sky, the broken sky. He decided to take a run at the window and go through the glass and finish the whole thing. He took a step toward the window and then stopped and turned his back to the window and looked at the wall. He stood there without moving for almost a full hour. He was going back and taking chunks out of his life and holding them up to examine them. The young and bright yellow days in the hot sun of Maricopa, always bright yellow in every season. The wide and white roads going north from Arizona. The grey and violet of San Francisco. The grey and the heat of the stock room, and the days and nights of nothing, the years of nothing. And the cage in the investment security house, and the stiff white collars of the executives, stiff and newly white every day, and their faces every day, and their voices every day. And the paper, the plain white paper, the pink paper, the pale-green paper, the paper ruled violet and green and black in small ledgers and larger ledgers and immense ledgers. And the faces. The faces of statisticians who made forty-five a week, and customers' men who sometimes made a hundred and a half and sometimes made nothing. And the executives who made fifteen and twenty and thirty thousand a year, and the customers who sat there or stood there and watched the board. The customers, and some of them could walk out of that place and get on their yachts and go out across thousands of miles of water, getting up in the morning when they felt like getting up, fishing or swimming around their grand white yachts, alone out there on the water. And in the evening they would be wearing emerald studs in their shirt-fronts with white formal jackets and black tropical worsted trousers with satin black and gleaming down the sides, down to their gleaming black patent-leather shoes as they danced in the small ballrooms of their yachts with tall thin women with bared shoulders, dripping organdie from their tall thin bodies as they danced or held delicate glasses of champagne in their thin, delicate fingers. And when these customers came back to the investment security house they came in their gleaming black limousines and they came in very much tanned and smiling and he would be there in his cage, looking at them, thinking it was a pity such fortunate people had to eventually die, because it was really worthwhile for them to live on and on, they had so much to live for, they had so many things to enjoy. He liked to see them coming in wearing their expensive clothes, smoking their expensive cigars, talking with their expensive voices. He was so very glad when they came in, when they stood where he could see them, because he got a lift just looking at them. There were times when he wished he could talk to them, when he wished he had the nerve to start a conversation with one of them. If he could only have a talk with one of them so he could hear all about the wonderful things, the wonderful houses they lived in, the wonderful trips they made, the wonderful wonderful things they did. As he looked at them, as he thought of the lives they led, the luxuries they enjoyed, he decided that if he used his head and had some luck he might be able to climb up toward where they were. That was all it really was, a matter of using his head and having a little luck, and he decided to get started. And that was about the time when he decided to take the correspondence course in statistics.

He went into the living room and put another cigarette in the holder. He put himself on the sofa and rested there, sucking at the holder. He tried to build a mental microscope to deal with these tiny things he had on the table of his mind. He came to a point that became a wall and he couldn't slide under or climb over. He had to stay there. Now he was getting tired again. He took the stub out of the holder, crushed it in a tray. He let his head go back against the softness of the sofa. His eyes closed and the thoughts circled his brain, circled more slowly, and slowly, and then he was asleep.

The door opening pulled him away from sleep. He sat up and looked at her. She was closing the door. Her arms were heaped with packages. Now she came toward him. She said, "How do you feel?"

He nodded.

"Everything all right?"

He nodded.

She said, "Punctual, am I not? It's exactly six. And now we'll have some dinner. Feel hungry?"

He nodded.

She went into the kitchen. He could hear her moving around in there. He waited on the sofa, waited for dinner, waited for the buzzer to sound again, waited for Studebaker to come up with the police.

The dinner tasted fine, even though it went in through the glass straw. There was beef broth, there was the tan cream of a vegetable-beef stew, there was a butterscotch pudding thinned down to liquid. He gestured his willingness to help her with the dishes. She told him to go into the other room and play some records. He went in and got a Basie going under the needle. It was *Sent For You Yesterday And Here You Come Today*. And Rushing was beginning to yell his heart out when the telephone rang.

Parry stood up. He looked at the telephone. It rang again just as Rushing repeated his cry that the moon looked lonely.

She came out of the kitchen, looked at the phone, looked at Parry. She took a step toward the phone. It rang again. Parry lifted the needle from the record.

She looked at Parry as the phone rang again. She said, "There's nothing to worry about. I know who it is."

She picked up the phone.

"Hello? Oh, yes, hello, yes—yes?—oh, I've just had dinner—no, thanks anyway—well—well—all right, when can I expect you?—all right—right."

She put down the phone and looked at Parry. She said, "That was Bob Rapf. He'll be here in an hour."

13

PARRY RAISED his arms to indicate that he did not understand.

She said, "It'll be all right. You stay in the bedroom. He won't know you're here."

Parry gestured toward the bedroom, then raised his arms again.

She said, "He won't look in the bedroom."

Parry lowered his head and shook it slowly.

"Please don't worry about it," she said. He looked up. She was smiling at him.

He shrugged.

She went back in the kitchen. When she was finished with the dishes she came in and straightened the living room. As she emptied an ash tray she said, "I know you think it's a mistake, letting him come here. But it can't be any other way. I've known him for so long, I've been seeing so much of him lately, it's got to a point where I have a definite hold on him. I wish it wasn't that way. But as long as it is that way, I've got to go along with it. I know what happens to him when I refuse to see him. I wish I knew some way to break it without ripping him apart. But there doesn't seem to be any way to break it. All I can do is wait for it to die out."

She emptied another ash tray. She looked at him and saw that he was looking at her.

She said, "It's not physical. It never was. It never will be. It can't be. What he likes about me is the things I say, and the things he thinks I think about, the feelings he thinks I have. All he wants to do is be with me and talk to me and look at me and get a picture of the things I'm thinking. Even when I have nothing to say he just likes to be there with me. I don't know why I started it. I guess perhaps I started it because I felt sorry for him. He had no one to really be with."

All the ash trays were now emptied into one big tray. She took the tray into the kitchen. Then she came out, she said, "I guess that's what it was. I was sorry for him. I still feel sorry for him. But I can't let it go on much further. Have you ever seen him?"

Parry shook his head.

"He's a good-looking man," she said. "He's thirty-nine now, but he looks older. You can't see the grey in his hair because he's blond, but you can see the lines in his face. He has mild blue eyes, and that's the way all of him is, very mild, even though he's built heavy. And he's not very tall. He's a drafts-man and he works at a shipyard. He likes expensive clothes. He likes to spend money. He and Madge had a baby but it died when it was less than a year old. Did she ever tell you about that?"

He nodded.

"Did she ever tell you about him?"

He nodded.

"I imagine she must have painted him badly. She did that when she spoke to me about him. That was after she knew I was seeing him. She didn't try to block it. She just struck up a close friendship with me, much closer than I liked, and she began to tell me things about him. She wasn't very clever about it, for instance she said he was cheap and of course she should have known that I knew differently. She said he was selfish and he isn't that way at all. What she wanted me to do was give him walking papers, not because she wanted him back, but because she wanted him to lose me. She still wants that. She wants him to lose everything. She keeps telling me I'd be doing myself a big favor if I closed the door on him."

Parry nodded.

"You mean you agree with her?"

He shook his head.

"Oh, you mean she told you the same thing. I suppose she tells everyone that. I can't understand her. She ought to realize she'll never be happy as long as she keeps interfering with him. Or maybe that's the only thing that gives her happiness. Interfer-ing."

The buzzer sounded.

She frowned. "That can't be Bob. Much too early."

Parry stood up. It had to be Studebaker. And the police.

She said, "Go in the bedroom. I'll find out who it is."

Parry went into the bedroom and closed the door. He sat on

the edge of the bed and he was hitting the joints of his fingers together. The itching under the bandage was beginning to grow, to spread, and he wanted to get at it. He sat there, hitting the joints of his fingers together. He heard a door opening. He heard voices and they were both feminine, and one of them belonged to Madge Rapf.

"But that's ridiculous," Irene was saying.

"Honey, honey, you've got to help me. I'm scared out of my wits," Madge said.

"Ridiculous."

"Why is it ridiculous?" Madge said. "Look what he did to George Fellsinger. You surely read about it. Why, he went up there and—it gives me the shakes just to think of it. And if he did that to George he'll do it to me. He's got it in for me, you know that. You've got to let me stay here, honey. Let me hide here. Oh, let, let me——"

"Want a drink?"

"Yes, please honey, let me have a drink. Oh, my God, I'm in terrible shape. I haven't been able to eat a thing all day."

"Can I fix you something?" Irene said.

"No, I'm not hungry. How can I be hungry? He's going to kill me. He's going to look me up and when he finds me he'll—oh, God Almighty, what am I going to do?"

"Pull yourself together," Irene said. "They'll catch him."

"They haven't caught him yet. Listen, honey, as long as they haven't caught him I've got to hide. It was my testimony that sent him up. I tell you I'm so scared I don't know whether I'm coming or going."

"Sit down, Madge. Sit down and relax. You can't let yourself go to pieces like this."

Parry heard a series of dragging, grinding sobs.

Between the sobs, Madge was saying, "Let me stay here."

"I can't."

"Why not?"

"Well, I—I fail to see the necessity of it."

"Oh, I see. You don't want to be put out."

"It isn't that, Madge. Really, it isn't."

"Well, what is it, then? This place is big enough to hold two. It's——"

"It's this—I'm expecting Bob here any minute."

"All right, I'll hide. I'll go in the bedroom."

"No," Irene said. "Don't do that."

"Why not?"

"Well, it's—it's sort of cheap. You have nothing to hide. You have nothing to be ashamed of."

"That's one way of looking at it," Madge said. "And then of course there's another way." Now she sounded as if she was talking between puffs at a cigarette. "Of course, there's a chance he'd walk into the bedroom."

"Do you think he does that?"

"I don't know."

"If you don't know, why do you insinuate? I think we ought to understand each other, Madge. You can't make statements like that and expect me to take it without a whimper. You've said things on that order before, little needles here and there and every now and then, and I tried to think you didn't mean anything by it. But this time the needle's gone in just a bit deeper. And I don't like it. I want you to know I don't like it."

"Honey, you needn't get all excited. It wouldn't make any difference to me even if——"

"Please, Madge."

"Let me stay here, honey. I tell you I'm afraid to go out of here alone."

"This is silly."

"All right, it's silly, but that's the way it is with me and what can I do about it? For God's sake, honey, try to understand what a fix I'm in. You've got to let me stay here or else you've got to stay with me wherever I go. Oh, come on, honey, let's pack up——"

The buzzer sounded.

"You better go now, Madge."

"For God's sake——"

"Look, Madge. You go down the hall. Wait there until you hear the door closing. Then leave."

The buzzer sounded.

"But I'm afraid——"

"Madge, I don't want you to be here when he comes in."

"Why not?"

"Let's not start that again."

The buzzer sounded.

Parry stood up and looked at the window. He wondered if the window offered a way of reaching the fire escape. He knew it was Studebaker down there. It wasn't Bob Rapf. It was Studebaker. And the police.

"Go on, Madge. Go now."

"Oh, I'm so afraid."

"Go now, Madge."

The buzzer sounded.

"I won't go. I won't go out alone. I can't. Parry will find me. I know he'll find me. Oh, God, I'm so terribly afraid. Please, Irene—oh, honey, why won't you help me?"

The buzzer sounded and kept sounding.

"Look, Madge——"

"No, I won't go. No—I won't leave here alone." Madge was sobbing again, the grinding dragging sobs that dragged along with the buzzer as it kept sounding.

"All right, Madge. I'm going to let him come up."

The buzzer stopped sounding.

Parry walked toward the window, walked softly, slowly, came to the window and looked through the wet glass, wet on the other side where the rain was hitting. The rain was rapid and thick, racing down from the broken sky, dark grey now and mottled dark yellow and fading blue. Parry put his fingers on the window handles and started to bring pressure. The window wouldn't give. He stepped away from the window and watched the rain running down, oblique toward him, coming against the glass and washing down.

He heard the door opening.

He heard a man saying, "For Christ's sake——"

He heard Madge saying, "Hello, Bob."

He heard the man saying, "What takes place here?"

"Raining hard, Bob?" It was Irene.

"Pouring," Bob said. "But what I want to know is what takes place."

"Nothing very special," Irene said.

"I don't go for these deals," Bob said. "This looks as if it's been arranged."

"Why should anything be arranged?" Irene said.

"I don't know," Bob said. "For Christ's sake, Madge, what's wrong with you?"

"I'm scared," Madge said. "Honey, should I tell him?"

"Tell me what?" Bob had a mild voice, trying to get away from mildness.

"Sure," Irene said. "Go on and tell him."

Madge said, "It's Vincent Parry. I'm scared he'll find me. He'll kill me."

"If he does," Bob said, "I'll look him up and shake his hand."

Madge let out a howl.

"Bob, that wasn't necessary," Irene said.

"I can't stand it," Madge sobbed. "I can't stand it any more."

"Neither can I," Bob said. "Why don't you leave people alone? Why do you go around finding excuses to come up here? Irene doesn't want you here. Nobody wants you. Because you're a pest. You're not satisfied unless you're bothering people. You got on your family's nerves, you got on my nerves, you get on everybody's nerves. Why don't you wise up already?"

"Do you know what you are?" Madge said. "You're a hound. You have no feeling."

"No feeling for you," Bob said. "No feeling at all, except I'm annoyed whenever I see you."

"You married me," Madge said. "You're still married to me. Don't forget that."

"How can I forget it?" Bob said. "You see these lines on my face? They're anniversary presents. Irene, will you do me a favor? Will you ask her to please leave?"

"I won't go out of here alone," Madge said.

"She thinks Parry's looking for her. That's all he's got to do, look for her. Listen, Madge, if there's anyone Parry wants to avoid more than the police, it's you." Bob's voice was getting louder. "You're the last person he wants to kill. You're the last person he wants to see. And you know why. And you know I know why."

"What kind of a riddle is this?" Irene said.

"She pestered him," Bob said. "She kept pestering him until she had a hold on him. That's why he killed Gert."

"You're a liar," Madge said. "He killed Gert because he hated her. And that's why he'll kill me. He hates me."

"He doesn't hate you," Bob said. "Nobody hates you. You're not the type that makes people hate. You only make people annoyed. He didn't know he was annoyed. He didn't have the

brains to see it. He was ignorant and he's still ignorant. If he
wasn't ignorant he wouldn't have killed Fellsinger. He wouldn't
have come to San Francisco in the first place. Now it's a cinch
they'll give him the chair."

"That's what makes me scared," Madge said. "He knows he's
going to get the chair. He knows he has nothing to lose now.
When it gets like this they go out of their mind. They don't
care what they do. That's why I'm afraid to be alone. He'll find
me. He'll look for me until he finds me."

"He won't look for you," Bob said. "I know how it is with
him."

"How is it with him?" Irene said.

"It's a matter of psychoanalysis," Bob said. "The power of
suggestion, and a bit of the identification process. Like this—
she managed to get a hold on him, and she increased that hold
to the point where he thought he wanted her more than anything else. Because he was weak and ignorant, he looked for
the easiest way to get rid of Gert. He thought the easiest way
was murder. Now he identifies her with trouble. He'll stay
away from her."

"What do you know about psychoanalysis?" Madge said.
"What do you know about these things? You never had any
brains yourself. All you know is T squares and drawing boards
and you don't even know much about that. What are you?
You're nothing."

"Yes, I know that," Bob said. "We've been through that before. A couple hundred thousand times. A couple hundred
thousand years ago, when I was a monkey and I didn't know
that the only way to stop hearing that voice of yours was to
walk so far away that I wouldn't be able to hear it."

"I could say plenty," Madge said.

"That's very true," Bob said. "Your mouth is the greatest
piece of machinery I've ever seen. Even if Parry is already out
of his mind he'll have enough sense to stay away from that
mouth of yours. You'd not only talk him out of killing you,
you'd talk him into taking up with you again."

"You're a dirty liar," Madge said. "He never had anything to
do with me."

"And Santa Claus has nothing to do with Christmas," Bob said.
"Listen, Madge, I got out of kindergarten a long time ago.

And I only sleep eight hours a day. The rest of the time my eyes are wide open. And my hearing is perfect. Put it together and what have you got?"

"Either you're lying," Madge said, "or someone was lying to you."

"Gert wasn't a liar," Bob said. "She was many other things but she wasn't a liar."

"She lied," Madge said. "She lied, she lied——"

"Every word she said was God's honest truth," Bob said. "And don't sit there with your eyes bulging out as if you can't make head or tail of it. Will you deny that he went to your apartment?"

"What?"

"What. What. What. Listen to her."

Irene's voice came into it, part confusion, yet somewhat firm. "Bob, please—don't be a cad."

"I want her to know, Irene. I want her to know I'm not the fool she thinks I am. She thinks I was in the dark all the time she was hiring someone to watch me."

"I never did that," Madge said.

"All right, you never did that. Except if I wanted to go to the trouble I could prove that you did. Because I got hold of the little rat you hired. And I asked him what you were paying. And I offered him double the amount to keep an eye on you. The very next day he made good. He came back and told me there was a man in your apartment the night before. He told me the man stayed about four hours."

"He's a liar, you're a liar——"

"Everybody's a liar," Bob said. "But it's amazing the way all these lies fit together and click, like a key opening a lock. Because he told me he followed the man from your apartment. He followed the man home. And home was the apartment house where the Parrys lived. If you want me to go further I'll go further. He gave me a description of the man. I had never seen Parry but Gert told me what Parry looked like. And you know what I did? I put it down in black and white, with the date and the time and everything. And I had this little rat sign a statement, and if I wanted to I could have used that statement. But I didn't and I'll tell you why. I felt sorry for Parry. I even felt sorry for Gert."

"You kept that signed statement?" Irene asked.

"Yes."

"Why didn't you bring it up at the trial?" Irene asked. "Why didn't you give it to Parry's lawyer?"

"I don't see what good it would have done," Bob said. "It would have only made things worse for him. And it would have implicated me. I didn't want any part of it. I knew Parry was guilty anyway and I knew he didn't have a chance to prove otherwise."

"It's all a lie," Madge said. "The whole thing is one big lie. Don't fall for it, honey. He's only trying to paint me bad."

"Madge, you're not bad," Bob said. "You're just a pest."

Madge began to sob.

Irene said, "Bob, you shouldn't say things like that."

Madge said, "What he says doesn't bother me. It's just that I'm so scared."

Irene said, "I think you ought to go now, Madge."

"I won't go home alone."

"Take her home, Bob."

"Not me. I don't want to have anything to do with her."

Madge was sobbing loudly.

Irene said, "Madge, I'm going to call a taxi."

"All right," Madge said, and she stopped sobbing. "Call a taxi. And after I'm gone you can turn on the phonograph." Her voice was stiff now, with all the sobbing out of it, with something else in it that had the shape in sound of a blade. "Turn it on loud so you can hear it in the bedroom."

Then everything was quiet. And everything was waiting.

It lasted for the better part of a minute.

Then Bob said, "Would you mind explaining that last remark?"

"Does it need explaining?" Madge said. She put something of a laugh into it.

"I think so," Bob said. "Because I haven't the faintest idea of what you're talking about."

"Your memory can't be that bad," Madge said. "Don't tell me you can't remember back to yesterday afternoon."

"What about yesterday afternoon?" Bob said.

"I came here to see Irene. I might as well get this out here and now. I came here to see her. She wouldn't answer the buzzer. I knew she was home. I was curious. So I used the fire-escape exit and came up here and knocked on the door. There wasn't any answer and I was ready to think I had made a mistake and she wasn't home after all. But I could hear the phonograph going. That meant she was in and she didn't want to answer the door. She was in here with you. Yesterday afternoon."

Everything was quiet again.

It lasted for a good ten seconds.

Then Bob said, "It wasn't me, Madge."

"Then it was someone else," Madge said.

Bob laughed. It was a mild laugh yet it was sort of twisted. He said, "Of course it was someone else. You know that. You made sure of it yesterday afternoon when you called up the place where I work, when you asked to speak to me. You must have called from the drugstore on the corner, right after you left here. And as soon as I got on the phone and you heard my voice you hung up. I was wondering about that call. I've been wondering about it until now."

"But someone was up here," Madge said. "I heard the phonograph going."

"That's very true," Irene said. "The phonograph was going and someone was in here with me."

"A man?" Bob said.

"Yes, Bob. It was a man."

"Who was it?" Bob said. His voice was all twisted.

Seconds dragged through quiet. Then Irene said, "Vincent Parry."

14

PARRY WAS standing near the door. His eyes were taking his body through the door but his feet were staying where they were and pulling his body back. The itching under the bandage was a moist itching that made little pools of itching all over his face. And the little pools became jagged here and there and they had facets that contained more itching. He couldn't feel air going through the hole in the bandage in front of his mouth and he couldn't feel himself breathing. The quiet from the other room got through the door and shaped itself around him and began to crush him. He thought it was because he wasn't breathing. He knew he could breathe if he wanted to but he didn't want to because he knew, if any air came into his mouth and down into his lungs he was going to let it out in a shout. This thing happening now was what he had expected, what he had expected would happen sooner or later, when she finally realized she couldn't keep it up, so sooner or later she must come out with it. So now she was out with it, taking herself away from it as it came out. And now he was alone again, and he couldn't take himself away from it as she could. He was alone with it, and she was going away from it, and it was part of the quiet that crushed him now. And he was alone, crushed by it. And he knew as long as he was alone he mustn't be alone here. Turning and staring at the window he could see the roof tops of San Francisco forming a high, jagged wall that stared back at him and solemnly dared him to get past, and telling him what a difficult time it would be, what a complex time, what a lonely time he would have of it. Sliding back at him now, coming back like a wheeled thing on greased rails, bouncing away from a cushioned barrier, was the memory of a night when Madge had almost captured him, when her arms were tight around his middle and he was standing there looking past her shoulder at the window and a San Francisco night beyond. And wanting to twist away from her but not being able to twist away, and he had to stand there and listen as she told him that he was not happy with Gert, he

would never be happy with Gert. With Gert his life amounted
to one agony after another, with Gert he was only a tool that
Gert picked up at widely spaced intervals, but with Madge he
would be a permanent necessity and why couldn't he understand that he was fortunate to be wanted so badly. While she
talked he talked silently back to her, admitted to her that she
was gradually selling him a carload of merchandise, talked to
himself and asked himself what he was going to do with that
merchandise once he had it. She talked on, throwing arguments at him, and they were sound arguments, anyway they
sounded sound, and he was telling himself that he might as
well go ahead and try it out, he didn't have anything to lose.
His life with Gert was one big headache, and if Madge lived up
to a fraction of the things she was promising now, it might be
a good idea to take the gamble and let her complete the sale.
And then he wanted to get his hands free so he could light a
cigarette, and as he pulled his arms away from Madge he heard
a grinding gasp and it was Madge, gasping again, backing away
from him, asking him why he had pulled away like that. He
said he only wanted to light a cigarette. She hurled herself at a
sofa, sobbing loudly, saying that a cigarette was more important to him than a woman who wanted him more than she
wanted to breathe. She wriggled convulsively on the sofa and
all at once she sat up and showed him a wet face and she
wanted him to tell her why so many other things were more
important to him than herself. He found himself trying to explain that these so many other things weren't really more important, they were merely little conveniences that a man had
to have every now and then. Every now and then a man had to
take time out to light a cigarette or grab a drink of water or
walk around the block or stand alone in a dark room.

Madge refused to accept that. Madge said it wasn't fair for
him to go for that cigarette just when they were about to put
their two lives together and make one out of it. And just then
he realized what a great mistake it would be to go along with
Madge. They would never get in step because she would never
allow him to follow his own plans. She had to be in on everything. She had to be the captain, and even if he went ahead
and handed her the captaincy she would find something wrong
with that. She would turn the captaincy over to him and when

he took it she would find something wrong with that and she would take a jump at the sofa and start that wriggling and sobbing. He told himself she really wasn't such a bad person, she was just a pest, she was sticky, there was something misplaced in her make-up, something that kept her from fading clear of people when they wanted to be in the clear. He felt uncomfortable just looking at her there on the sofa. That was it precisely. In the same room with her he would never be comfortable.

He told her that. He put the blame on his own shoulders, saying he was one of these selfish specimens and he could never give her the attention she was looking for. She came leaping from the sofa, crying loudly he was all wrong, they would really click, they really would, and let them have the courage to take a shot at it, and please, Vincent, please, and she had her arms around him again, and his resistance was flowing away. If she wanted him that badly maybe he ought to give it a try despite all the reasons against it. He wanted to smoke a cigarette and think it over and again he tried to get free of her arms and the feel of her arms was like a chain and frantically he wanted to get away.

His head turned and again he was looking at the window. He knew he had to take a chance with that window. He moved toward it.

He heard Bob Rapf saying, "You're very funny, Irene."

Irene said, "What's funny about it?"

Madge said, "What was Vincent Parry doing here?"

"He came here to kill me," Irene said.

"Hilarious," Bob said.

"Well," Madge said, "what happened?"

"I talked him out of it," Irene said.

"Aw," Bob said, "for Christ's sake."

"I'm afraid to be alone," Madge said.

"Keep quiet, Madge." Again Bob's voice was twisted. "Listen, Irene, I think before I go you should tell me who was really here yesterday."

"I told you."

"All right," Bob said. "I think I understand. This is the final stop, isn't it?"

"I'm afraid so," Irene said. "I should have told you before.

But I didn't think it was serious with him. Yesterday he said it was serious. I don't know yet how it is with me. But I keep thinking about it and at least that's something. I think I ought to give it a chance."

"Who is he?" Bob said.

"Just another man. Nothing extraordinary."

"What does he do?" Bob said.

"He's a clerk in an investment security house."

"That's what Parry was," Madge said.

"Madge, why don't you keep quiet?" Bob said. "Irene, I want you to know I valued our friendship. I valued it highly. I hope things work out nicely for you."

"Thanks, Bob."

"Good-by, Irene."

"Are you going to call a taxi?" Madge said.

"No," Bob said. "We'll get a taxi outside. Where's your car?"

"It's getting fixed," Madge said. "Maybe we won't see a taxi."

"Keep quiet," Bob said. "Come on, I'll take you home."

"Good night, honey." Madge was starting to sob again. "I'll call you tomorrow morning."

"I'm going to be rather busy," Irene said.

"When should I call you?" Madge said.

"Well," Irene said, "I'm going to be rather busy from now on."

"Oh," Madge said. "Well, I'll get in touch with you in a couple of days. Or maybe I'll call you up tomorrow night."

Bob said, "I'll tell you what to do, Irene. You pick up the sofa and throw it at her. Maybe that would make her understand. Come on, Madge."

The door opened and closed. The place was quiet. Parry leaned against a wall and looked at the floor. Minutes were sliding past and he was waiting for the bedroom door to open. He heard the sound of his breathing and it was a heavy sound. He was trying to get it lighter and he couldn't bring it down from the heaviness.

The bedroom door opened. Irene came in and walked to the window. She said, "They're going down the street. They'll probably go to the traffic light intersection and get a taxi there." She turned and looked at Parry. She said, "Well?"

He shook his head slowly.

"If you were in there," Irene said, "if you had seen their faces, you'd know I handled it right. I had to be funny. I couldn't work on Madge alone. And I had to be delicate with Bob. Now he won't bother me and he won't let her bother me."

He kept on shaking his head. And he was waiting for the buzzer to sound again. He was waiting to hear the voice of Bob Rapf, demanding to see the bedroom, to search the place. He was waiting for Studebaker and the police. He was waiting to hear the voice of Madge Rapf, asking if it was really Parry who had been here yesterday afternoon.

Then yesterday was yesterday no longer. Yesterday was two days ago.

And yesterday was three days ago. He went through four magazines and dreadful itching under the bandage and waiting for her to come in, and taking the food through the glass straws. And smoking up pack after pack of cigarettes.

And yesterday was four days ago and the itching was unbearable and the waiting was without time, without measurement. There were no calls. There were no visitors, no buzzing, nothing, only the food through the glass straws and the itching, the endless itching, and his wrists tied to the bedposts at night, and orange juice through the glass straws in the morning, and the waiting, and alone in the afternoon waiting for her to arrive with the food and the magazines and the cigarettes and the papers. In the papers, it was no longer on the front page. The column was shrinking. The headline was in smaller face type now, and they were saying they were still looking for him but that was all. And she had a new dress. And he wondered why there was no buzzing, why there were no visitors. He wondered what happened to Studebaker. He couldn't see any car out there now. He wondered why he was still afraid of Studebaker when there was no Studebaker out there now.

Then yesterday was five days ago.

It was raining again.

It was raining very hard, and he heard the rain before he opened his eyes. As he knocked his fist against the side of the bed to bring her in so she could untie his wrists, he was turning his head and looking at the rain coming down. The door opened and she was in the doorway, saying good morning and asking him if he had slept well, then putting a cigarette in the holder, lighting a match for him.

The itching under the bandage was a soggy itching, and it remained that way all through the day, and in the early evening it was a flat itching, without the burning, as if it was going away, as if it was smoothing out and going away from itself. The bandage felt very loose, getting looser every hour, and it was as if the bandage was telling him now it was ready to come off, now he didn't need it any more.

He was glad the time had come to take the bandage off, he was afraid to take the bandage off, he was anxious to take the bandage off, he sensed the itching going away finally and completely, actually felt it walking away as he sat there on the sofa a few hours after dinner, as he sat there with a cigarette in the holder and the holder in his mouth, as he looked at Irene sitting across the room. She was reading a magazine, and she looked up and looked at him. He looked at his wrist watch. It said ten twenty. Coley had said five days. And at four thirty it would be exactly five days. He had six hours to go until it would be five days. He was sitting there wearing the grey worsted suit with the suggestion of violet in it and he was waiting for another hour to go by. Then the hour was behind him and it was five hours to go until it was five days. Under the bandage his face felt dry and flat and smooth. He picked up a magazine. It was a picture magazine and it showed him a girl in a bathing suit, on tiptoe with her arms flung out toward the sea, with the waves rolling in toward the smooth beach where she stood, and his face felt smooth like the beach looked, and the girl wore a flower in her hair which was blond, very blond though not as blond as the hair Irene wore sort of long so that it sprayed her shoulders, where it was very yellow against the yellow upholstery of the chair on the other side of the room. The girl in the bathing suit was slim but not as thin as Irene, who was very thin there on the other side of the room where she sat wearing a yellow dress, light and loose, and yet not as light and loose as the bandages on his face.

He closed his eyes. He let his head sag, let the magazine slide from his fingers, and he knew he was going to stride halfway toward sleep and stay there, dangling at the halfway point, and she couldn't wake him up. She would let him stay there, half asleep until it was four thirty, until it was time to get the bandage off. Now he could feel his face separated from the bandage, knowing it was new and ready under the bandage, all ready with the bandage so loose and air in there and everything dry and fresh and ready. And clean, like the clean shirt he wore, and new, like the new tie, and ready as his body was ready, ready to get moving and go away. And he thought of Patavilca, and he thought of George Fellsinger and he thought of the money remaining in the pocket of the grey worsted suit. Almost eight hundred dollars, and it was enough, very much enough. It was enough for food and lodging and railroad tickets. Down through Mexico, down through Guatemala, Honduras, Nicaragua, Costa Rica. Down through Panama. Or perhaps he could fly. It would be better to fly. It would be swift and luxurious. Down through Mexico. Past them all and down through Colombia and Ecuador. Down to Peru, landing in Lima, then going up to Patavilca, staying in Patavilca, staying there for always. And the things he had seen in the travel folder were spreading out, going out very wide, and now immense, and moving in all the dimensions, the water purplish out there away from the bright white beach, the water moving, the waves coming in, smooth under the sun, smooth as his face was smooth, smooth under the bandage.

He wondered who had killed George Fellsinger.

The money would last long in Patavilca. American money always lasted long down there in those places, and after he made certain arrangements with papers he would find work and gradually he would learn to speak Spanish, learn to speak it the way they spoke it down there and would have something to start with, something to build from, something that would grow by itself even as he kept building it.

He wondered about his health. The kidney trouble. The sinus.

He would be all right if he watched himself, and if he did have attacks now and then he knew how to handle these attacks and he would be all right. He would be all right in Patavilca. He would be fine down there, and he wondered if they had cigarettes down there, and he wondered what Peruvian cigarettes tasted like, and wondered if he would see a woman down there who would be very thin, very graceful with the thinness.

He decided that after a while when his Spanish was all right he would open up a little shop and sell the things they needed down there. He could make trips to Lima and buy things and bring them up and sell them in the shop. He wouldn't work hard. He wouldn't need to work hard. He would have everything he needed and would really have everything he wanted. And it would be delightful down there in Patavilca.

He wondered why anyone would want to kill George Fellsinger.

If there was anything wrong with the Patavilca idea, it was only that he would be alone down there. But wherever he went he would be alone because he couldn't afford to take up with anyone. Sooner or later that someone would begin asking questions that had no direct answer and it would lead to a puzzle and that someone would want to solve the puzzle. So Patavilca was logical after all, and he was glad it was logical because it was the place where he wanted to be, because he so much liked what he had seen in the travel folder, and he had seen many travel folders, many pictures of many places and he had never seen anything quite like Patavilca. So he was glad it was going to be Patavilca after all, and when he was down there for a while maybe he wouldn't be alone after all because then he would be speaking Spanish and he would get to know Peruvians and there would be things to talk about and places to see and he would have everything he wanted in Patavilca. He wouldn't get too friendly with anyone, but he would know just enough people to prevent himself from getting lonely.

He wondered if things had happened in the Fellsinger case that weren't in the papers.

And in Patavilca they would never get him. For the rest of his life he would be away from them. He saw something that had happened long ago. It was when he was in Oregon to see that basketball game. That day when he arrived up there it was snowing in Eugene. He was in his room in a little hotel and outside it was gradually clearing but there was much snow. A little bus came down the street. There were some children playing on the sidewalk and they were making snowballs. As the bus passed them they threw snowballs at the windows. He remembered one of the children was wearing a bright green sweater and a bright green wool cap. And the bus was bright orange, and as the snowballs hit the windows the driver let loose with the exhaust that caused a minor explosion, a spurt of black smoke that frightened the children and sent them scampering away. But they were away and that was what they wanted. And he would be away and that was what he wanted. The spurt of black exhaust smoke was the futile attempt to grab him, but it wasn't enough to grab him and in Patavilca he would be away. He would be away from everything he wanted to be away from.

He wondered why someone had killed Gert. He wondered why that someone had killed George Fellsinger.

In Patavilca he would be under the sun most of the time, letting the sun pour down on him, on the beach under the sun, walking into the purplish water. Perhaps it was really and fully as purplish as it had looked in the travel folder.

A hand nudged his shoulder. He looked up. He saw her.

She said, "Vincent—it's time."

He brought his head back. She was smiling.

She said, "It's four thirty. It's time to take the bandage off."

He looked at his wrist watch. It said four thirty.

She went into the bathroom. She came out with a pair of scissors. He began to quiver. His face felt very dry and flat and smooth and ready under the bandage. The bandage was soggy and old and his face felt new.

She started to cut the bandage. She worked slowly. She sat there with his face brought forward a little so she could get at the bandage better. Now the bandage was coming off. It came off smoothly, easily, and she unwrapped the gauze until she came to more adhesive tape, then she went through that with the scissors and unwrapped more gauze. He watched her. She didn't see his eyes. She had her attention centered on the bandage, getting it away from his mouth, now going up past his cheeks and his nose, and he watched her, and her face wouldn't tell him anything, and she had it coming away from the upper part of his face and then she took hold of it where it was caked and very slowly she pulled it away so that now she had the entire bandage off. And she had it in her hands, with the scissors and she was looking at him. She was looking at his new face.

And then she fainted.

15

IT WAS quiet and very slow, the way she went down, the way she subsided on the floor. She looked tired and little there, and now he was not yet starting to wonder why she had fainted. He only felt sorry for her because she had fainted. He went into the bathroom and took hold of a glass and turned on the cold water faucet. Then he realized there was a mirror in front of him, level with his face. And he looked up.

And he saw his new face.

He frowned.

It was very difficult to believe that he was actually looking at himself. This was not himself.

This was new and different and he had not expected this. The shape of his face was changed. The aspect of his face was all changed. He still had the same eyes and nose and lips, unchanged, but they seemed to be placed differently.

There was nothing dreadful about it. There was everything remarkable and fascinating about it. The man who had fixed his face was a magician. He wondered why Irene had fainted. He leaned toward the mirror. There were no scars, except when he made extremely close study he could see the faint outlines. Only five days ago, and it was astounding. There was nothing in the mirror to indicate that he had been given a new face, but his former face had undergone an operation and new flesh had been added and steel had gone into the flesh and his face had been changed. There were no signs of damage, there was nothing except the new face. He could see it under the five-day beard, the pale, scattered growth.

And he wondered why she had fainted.

He leaned even closer toward the mirror. And he examined his new face. He twisted his features and his features twisted nicely, as if he had always owned this face. He put his hands to his face and it was really his face. In the mirror he saw his hands on his face and on his face he felt the pressure of his hands and there was no pain, there was no special feeling. Only his hands on his new face.

Perhaps the beard had something to do with it. But he didn't have much of a beard, and his face was distinct under what beard there was. The beard hadn't caused it. He wondered what had caused it, what had caused her to faint.

He filled the glass with cold water, went into the living room. He dipped fingers into the glass, flicked water on her face. She opened her eyes. She started to sit up. She looked at his face and shuddered and closed her eyes again. He flicked more water, and she opened her eyes, sat up fully. She looked at him. Her eyes stretched up and down.

He said, "Is it as bad as that?"

His voice was different.

He said, "It's all right with me. And if it's all right with me it ought to be all right with you."

His voice was very different. It had always been a light voice. Now it was even lighter, and it was somewhat hollow.

She stood up. She was looking at him. She said, "I expected to see something very dreadful."

"Is that why you fainted?"

She nodded. She couldn't stop the up-and-down stretching of her eyes. She said, "I guess it was everything, added up. I'm sorry."

He didn't know what to say. He mumbled, "I guess these things happen sometimes."

"Take the whiskers off," she said. "Maybe I'm imagining things."

He went into the bathroom. He looked at the face again. Then he prepared it for shaving. The skin cream felt all right, the soap felt all right. Even the razor felt all right. And afterward the cold water felt like cold water always feels. He mopped the towel against the face and then he looked at the face. It was bright and new and clean. He wondered what had happened to the flesh that had been taken from his arms. He couldn't see any sign of it on his new face. And on his arms the cuts had healed, had been healed now for two days. And he had a new face, and already he was beginning to feel that he had always owned this face. And it was magic.

He went into the living room, buttoning his shirt.

She looked at him. Now he was arranging his tie. She said, "Yes, it's unbelievable."

"Are you going to let it get you?"

"I don't know what I'm going to do."

"You have no problem," he said. "I'm all right now. I can go now. You don't need to worry about it any more."

She looked at the window. Out there it was coming down from overturned tubs. The wind was hitting it and throwing it all around out there and it was one of those very big rains that come down now and then from the north, pushed by a wild and warm wind.

She said, "When are you going?"

"Now."

"No."

"I can't stay here."

"Where will you go?"

"I don't know."

"I can't stay here either," she said.

"Why not?"

"I just feel that I can't, that's all."

"I don't get this."

"Neither do I. But it's the way I feel. I just can't stay here. I've got to go away somewhere."

He picked up a pack of cigarettes. She wanted one. He lit her cigarette and lit his own. He looked at the window. He said, "All right, Irene. Give me it. All of it."

"Beginning with what?"

"Your father." He walked toward the window. He examined the thickness and speed of the rain. He turned and looked at her.

She said, "He didn't kill my stepmother. It was an accident. That's what he said. That's what I believed and what I'll always believe. And I'll always believe that you didn't kill your wife and you didn't kill George Fellsinger."

"With Gert and Fellsinger it was no accident. Somebody killed them."

"It wasn't you."

"Then who was it?"

"I don't know."

He sat on the sofa and made little burning orange circles with the end of the cigarette. He said, "Maybe it was Madge."

"Maybe."

"Maybe it was Bob Rapf."

"Maybe."

He stopped playing with the cigarette. He put it in his mouth and gave it a pull. He let the smoke come out slowly and he looked at her and he said, "Maybe it was you."

She came over to the sofa and sat at the other end. She leaned back and her eyes went toward the ceiling. She said, "Maybe."

Parry took another pull at the cigarette. He said, "I don't know why I'm trying to figure it out. I don't see what difference it makes now. I don't want to get even with anybody. All I want is to get away. I've got my new face and nobody will recognize me, and I ought to be getting on my way while the getting is good."

"But you're curious, aren't you?"

"I guess that's it," he said. "I guess I'm beginning to get curious."

"And angry."

"No," he said. "No, I'm not angry. I thought all along it was an accident that killed Gert. Now that I know it was murder I ought to be angry. But I'm not. I'm not even angry about Fellsinger. I'm sort of sad about Fellsinger but not too sad because he didn't have much to live for anyway. What I can't understand is why anyone would want to kill him."

"And your wife?"

"That's easier."

"Well," she said, "that's something. Start from there."

"No. I'll let it stay where it is and I'll go away from it. I've had enough of it. I've got to get away."

"Maybe if you tried you could find something."

He looked at her. He studied the grey eyes and said, "Do you really want me to try?"

"If you think it's worth it, yes. If you think you've got something to start with, a place to start, and a time, and if you can work from there——"

"Yes," he said, still studying the grey eyes. "I've got a place and a time. The place was that road. The time was the moment you followed me into those woods."

"Take it back further. Take it back to the trial. Do you see any logic in the fact that I was more than a little interested in the trial?"

He looked at the floor. "How sure are you that your father was innocent?"

"Just as sure as I know you're innocent. Just as sure as I know there's a world and a sun and stars. I reacted normally when I recognized the similarity between your situation and what happened to my father. I couldn't get in on your trial but I knew it was an accident, just as my stepmother's death was an accident. All I could do was write crazy letters to the *Chronicle*."

He nodded. "That was all right then." He shook his head. "Now there's no similarity. There's a killer in this somewhere."

"You're not a killer, Vincent."

He frowned. "That can't be the only reason you're going to bat for me. There's another reason dancing around in the middle of all this and now that we're having a showdown you might as well hand it over."

She didn't reply to that immediately.

He watched her.

A good fifteen seconds went by. Then she said, "I'm helping you because I feel like helping you. Do you mind?"

"No," he said. "I'm too tired to mind. I'm too tired to coax it out of you. But every now and then I'll think about it. Maybe I'll even worry about it. I don't know. Let's play some Count Basie."

"Nothing doing." Abruptly her voice was firm. "You don't want to hear Basie just now. You want to hear all about the hook-up. Madge, and myself—and Bob."

He remembered a phrase used by the little man, Max Weinstock, the upholsterer. He said, "Just one of those things."

"No, Vincent. Not just one of those things. San Francisco is a big city. When the trial ended I wasn't satisfied. I knew there were things that hadn't come out in the courtroom. I wanted to get at those things. There's a certain gift some people have for getting to meet people and striking up friendships. I'm either blessed or damned with that gift, because only a few weeks after the trial ended I was friendly with Madge Rapf."

"Did she know what you were after?"

"If she did, if she had the slightest idea, she ought to get an

Academy Award. No, Vincent, I'm sure I managed it all right. We were seeing a lot of each other, lunch and shopping and movies and so forth, and it got to the point where I could write her biography if I wanted to."

"Would there be a chapter on me?"

"Not more than a paragraph, if Madge had her way. She painted you as a liar and a rat and a murderer. She said you made a tremendous play for her and not only her but anything you came across in a cocktail bar."

"Well?"

"It's all right, Vincent. I'm pretty sure I know the way it was. She pestered you and you didn't want any part of her so she finally gave it up. That's what I got from Madge, even though she put it the other way around. I guess we really shouldn't blame her too much. The old pride angle. When a woman loses everything else she can keep on going as long as she holds onto her pride. Or spirit. Or whatever you want to call it."

"Okay," Parry said. "Let's sit here and feel sorry for Madge."

Irene smiled. "You know, it's odd. I ought to get irritated. I ought to get irritated at a lot of things you say. Or maybe it's because I know what you really mean to say. You say we should sit here and feel sorry for Madge and what you really mean is we should sit here and check Madge off the list and get onto Bob."

Parry started toward the window, changed his mind, went over to the radio-phonograph and ran fingers along the glazed yellow surface. He said, "When does Bob come into it?"

"About a month or so after I became friendly with Madge. Of course she told me all about him, what a cad he was, what a beast, what a skunk, and I think she went at least halfway through the zoo. I saw a way of maneuvering the situation and when I saw his name in the telephone book I did a very rotten thing. I called him up and told him I was a friend of Madge's and I was curious to see what he looked like and what he amounted to. He was peeved at first but I put some comedy into it and after some twenty minutes of fencing he agreed to give me a dinner date. I told Madge about it and she got a kick out of it and later I told her about the dinner date and she got a kick out of that, too. But then when there were more dates and she walked in on one of them she stopped getting a kick out of it. She saw I was having a definite effect on Bob and that was when she began to bother me. You know, the subtle approach. An insinuation here and there, a dig, a statement that I could take two ways. She never came out in the open and demanded that I stop seeing Bob. That isn't her method. When I told Bob about it he said I shouldn't give it another thought. He said Madge is happy only when she is pestering people. He told me to get into the habit of shutting a door in her face, but I couldn't get myself to do that."

"Did Bob ever talk about Gert?" He wasn't sure why he was asking that.

"He said she was a plague. He said he pitied you."

"How did he know she was a plague? Did Madge tell him that?"

"No. That was his own opinion."

"Based on what? Maybe I'm going to find out something. I didn't know Bob was closely acquainted with Gert."

"He was seeing her."

"Oh. So he was seeing her. You mean he admitted that?"

Irene nodded. "He was seeing a lot of her."

"Because he wanted to?"

"I can't say for sure. He didn't go into it with me."

"What do you think?"

"I think Gert was trying to lasso him."

"Let's come back to Madge. Did Madge know about Gert and Bob?"

"I asked Bob about that and he said no. He said he wasn't seeing Gert during the time Madge had that man watching him. There was no way Madge could know. They were meeting each other in out-of-the-way places. They were very careful."

"You mean Bob Rapf admitted that to you?"

"He admitted the technical side of it."

"The technical side," Parry murmured. "And did it give you anything to work with?"

"No," Irene said. "There wasn't enough of it. And it was only one side. Anyway, by that time I wasn't working on it any more. I was beginning to feel that there wasn't any way I could help you."

"Only one side," Parry murmured, again looking at the floor. "—only one side, and it's the technical side. All right, let's stay technical. Let's put it in numbers. Did he say how many times a week he was seeing Gert?"

"I didn't ask him that. I didn't see where it mattered."

"I don't see either. But I'm trying to see. During those last two months before she died she was out three or four nights a week. I never asked where she went, because by that time I didn't give a hang where she went. I don't know, there could be an opening here. Three or four nights a week, and if I could know definitely she was spending all those nights with Bob Rapf I might have something."

"And what would you do with it?"

"I don't know. This sort of thing is out of my line. Those last two months. You see what I'm getting at? I want to know what she was doing those last two months. That's the keyhole, and now all I need is the key."

"I'm afraid that's out, Vincent. It's too late for the key."

"Because I'm in no position to go hunting?"

"Because the key is Gert. Only Gert could tell you what she was doing those last two months, those three or four nights a week when she was out. You can't build anything from what you've got now. You have no way of knowing there was anything important between Gert and Bob. Or Gert and anyone. So you can't do anything with that. You've got to find something else. Maybe if you could take yourself back to those last two months you could find something."

"Make it four months. The last four months. But there's nothing in that except trouble and heartache, knowing everything was ruined, the way she wouldn't let me touch her, the way she made me sleep in the living room those last four months. Were you there that day when they got that out of me?"

"Yes," she said. "I was there every day."

"And you remember when they asked me about other women? You remember the way my lawyer objected and the prosecution claimed it was necessary to establish the factor of other women or perhaps one woman in particular, and you remember what I said?"

"I remember you said there was nobody special. You said you were with other women now and then. They asked you for the names of those other women and you said you didn't remember. The prosecution said it was impossible for you not to remember at least one or two of those names and you said you didn't even remember one. I knew you were lying. Everybody in that courtroom knew you were lying. You made a big mistake there, Vincent, trying to protect those other women, because you should have been thinking only of your own case. What you should have done was to say that you remembered but refused to give those names in public."

"I know," Parry said. "My lawyer bawled me out for it afterward. But afterward was too late. Anyway, it wouldn't have mattered. I didn't have a chance, no matter which way you look at it. And if I start with the what I should have dones and the what I should have knowns all I'll get out of it is a bad headache. My whole case was built around the theory that it was an accident, that she fell and hit her head on the ash tray. That was really the big mistake. But why go back to it? Why try to do anything about it? It's too late. It's much too late. I can't hang around even though I've got this new face, and besides I don't have the brains for that sort of thing. I don't know how to go about it. There's only one thing for me to do, and that's to get out of this town as fast as I can."

"You'll need more money."

"What you've given me already is plenty."

"Where will you go?"

"I told you I don't know."

"You do know but you won't tell me."

"All right, I do know. Why should I tell you?"

She got up from the sofa. She walked across the room, turned when she came to the wall. She leaned against the wall. She said, "Do you think I'd ever change my mind? Do you think I'd ever let them know where you were?"

"You might."

"And that's why you won't tell me?"

"That's why."

"That's not why. You won't tell me because you think I'll come there. You think I'll follow you."

"You'd be crazy to follow me."

"Was I crazy to pick you up on that road? Was I crazy to let you stay here?"

"Yes."

"And if I was crazy enough to do that, I'd be crazy enough to follow you. Isn't that it?"

"I guess so. I don't know." He glanced at the wrist watch.

She took herself away from the wall. She folded her arms, as if she was standing in the cold. She looked very little, standing there. She said, "You do know. You know you could trust me. You know I'd never say anything. But you have a feeling I'd follow you if you told me where you were going. And you don't want me to do that. You don't want me there. You don't need me there. Isn't that the way it is?"

"I guess that's the way it is."

She smiled. She went into the bedroom. When she came out there was money in her hand. She gave the bills to him, one at a time, and it added up to a thousand dollars.

He stood there with the money in his open hand. He said, "I really don't need this."

"You've got to have something. What you have isn't enough."

"All right, thanks." He put the money in his pocket.

She said, "Shall I call a taxi?"

"Please."

He felt light, he felt unfettered. She was going to call a taxi and he could walk out of here and get in a taxi and go wherever he wanted to go. He had his new face. He could do whatever he wanted to do. It was as if he had been stumbling along a clogged and muddy uncertain road, and all at once it branched off to become a wide and white concrete road, smooth and clean, and stretching away and away and away.

She was calling a taxi. He lit a cigarette.

She put the phone down. "Forty minutes," she said. "We'll have time for breakfast."

He smiled at her. She was a very dear friend. She was going to make breakfast for him. He said, "That'll be fine. I'm anxious to see."

"To see what?"

"How it feels to eat with a knife and fork."

She laughed brightly and went into the kitchen. He opened the lid of the phonograph. The black roundness was there, waiting for the needle. It was Basie again, the same Basie he had been using for the past four days, concentrating on the trumpet take-off, the wailing. It was *Sent for You Yesterday And Here You Come Today*. He turned the lever, lowered the needle, and there was the melancholy beginning, the rise of reeds and brass and the continued rise and the sudden break and Basie's right hand touching against not many keys but just the right keys. And he had almost eighteen hundred dollars in his pocket and he was very rich and he had this new face. And he was going to have a nice breakfast and then he was going to get in a cab and go wherever he wanted to go. And Basie was giving him just the right notes and everything was just right.

The record was ended. He played it again. He played it a third time. He selected another Basie. He kept on playing Basies until she called from the kitchen, telling him that breakfast was ready.

It was a very nice breakfast. The orange juice was just right, the scrambled eggs were just right, and the coffee. And he enjoyed using a knife and fork again. He enjoyed chewing on food, and the feeling of his new face.

He insisted on helping with the dishes. She let him dry them. They had cigarettes while they worked on the dishes. And when they were in the living room again they had more cigarettes. They were talking about Basie, they were talking about Oregon. She liked Oregon. She said the grass was a special shade of green up there. And she liked the lakes up there, the canoeing and the fishing and the hiking through country where there were no houses and everything was quiet and green for miles and miles. She had made many water colors of the Oregon country. She asked him if he would like to see some of her work. He said yes, and she went into the bedroom and he heard her searching for the paintings. Then she was coming into the living room and she had a large packet tied with string. She started to untie the string and the buzzer sounded.

She looked up. She said, "Your taxi."

"Yes."

The buzzer sounded again.

She said, "It sounds very final, doesn't it?"

"Yes."

"You're all right now, Vincent. They can't get you now."

"I'll need a new name."

"Let me give you a name. Even though you'll change it later let me give you one now. To go with your new face. It's a quiet face. Allan is a quiet name. Allan and—Linnell."

The buzzer sounded.

"Allan Linnell," he said.

"Good-by, Allan."

He was going toward the door. He turned and looked at her. She was all alone. He had a feeling she would always be alone. She would always be starved for real companionship.

The buzzer sounded again.

She would be all alone here in her little apartment. Her father was dead, her brother was dead, she really had nobody.

The buzzer sounded.

"Good-by," he said, and he walked out of the apartment.

The rain was flooding the street as he hurried toward the taxi. His eyes were riveted to the open door of the taxi. That was all he wanted to see. And when the door closed all he wanted to do was sit back and shut his eyes and shut his mind. But as the taxi started down the street he turned and looked through the rear window. He looked at the apartment house, at the third row of windows. And he saw something at one of the windows. He saw her standing there at the window, watching him go away.

The taxi took him to Civic Center. He got off on Market, went into an all-night diner and asked for a cup of coffee. He stayed with the coffee for twenty minutes. Last night's newspaper was on the counter and he picked it up and glanced at the front page. He began to turn the pages. He asked for another cup of coffee. He was on page seven. They were still wondering where he was. They gave him three inches and a single small headline that simply said he was still on the loose. There were no further developments. He looked at his wrist watch and it said six forty. He turned and looked through the grimy window of the diner. It was still raining very hard.

He felt uncomfortable. He told himself there was no reason why he should feel uncomfortable. All he had to do was wait around until nine o'clock, when the stores would open. Then he could go buy himself some clothes and things, and a grip, and he would be ready to check in at a hotel and make his arrangements from that point. Maybe by tonight he would already be on a train, or even a plane. He wondered why he was uncomfortable. He took his glance away from the newspaper and noticed there was a man sitting beside him. He remembered the man had been in the diner when he had come in. The man had been there at the far end of the counter. Now the man was sitting beside him.

The man was rolling a cigarette. He wore a swagger raincoat and a low-crown hat with a fairly wide brim. The cigarette wasn't rolling very well and the man finally gave it up and let the tobacco spill on the counter. Parry looked at the tobacco.

The man turned his head and looked at Parry.

It was time to go. Parry started to slide away from the counter.

"Wait a minute," the man said.

Parry looked at the man's face. The face was past thirty years old. It featured a long jaw and not much eyes and not much nose. There was a trace of moustache.

"What's the matter?" Parry said. He kept going away from the counter.

"I said wait a minute," the man said. It wasn't much of a voice. There was a crack in it, there was alcohol in it.

Parry came back to the seat. He looked at the spilled tobacco. He said, "What can I do for you?" He wondered if his face was changed sufficiently.

"Answer a few questions."

"Go ahead," Parry said. He tried a smile. It didn't give. He said, "I've got plenty of time." He wondered if that was all right. The man's face didn't tell him whether or not it was all right.

The man said, "What are you doing in this weather without a raincoat?"

"I'm absent-minded."

The man smiled. He had perfect teeth. He said, "Nup. Let's try it again."

"All right," Parry said. "I don't have a raincoat."

"That's better. We'll go on from there. Why don't you have a raincoat?"

"I'm absent-minded."

The man laughed. He played a forefinger into the spilled tobacco. He said, "That's okay. That's pretty good. What are you doing up so early?"

"I couldn't sleep."

"Why not?"

"I'm not well. I have a bad kidney."

"That's tough," the man said.

"Yeah," Parry said. "It's no picnic. Well—" He started to get up.

"Wait a minute," the man said.

Parry settled himself on the seat. He looked at the man and he said, "What hurts you, mister?"

"My job," the man said. "It's a rotten job. But it's the only thing I know how to do. I've been at it for years."

"Are you on it now?"

"That's right."

"What do you want with me?"

"That depends. Let's have a few statements."

"All right," Parry said. "My name is Linnell. Allan Linnell. I'm an investment counselor."

"In town?"

"No." He grabbed at a town. He said, "Portland."

"What are you doing here?"

"Hiding," Parry said.

"From what?"

"My wife. And her family. And her friends. And everybody."

"Come on, now. It can't be that bad."

"I'll tell you what you do," Parry said. "You go up there and live with her for seven years. And then if you're still in your right mind you come down here and tell me all about it."

The man shook his head slowly. He said, "I'm sorry, bud. I don't want to bother you like this, but it's my job. This town is very hot right now. All kinds of criminals all over the place. We got orders to check every suspicious personality. I'll have to see your cards."

"I don't have anything with me."

The man kept shaking his head. "You see? I've already started with you. I can't let it pass now. I'll have to take you in."

"I've got my wallet at the hotel," Parry said. "Couldn't we go over there? I'll give you all the identification you need."

"All right," the man said. "That'll make it easier. Let's go to the hotel."

Parry took some change out of his pocket, laid it on the counter.

They walked out of the diner, stood waiting under the sloping roof that kept the rain away from them.

"Where you staying?" the man said.

Parry tried to think of a place. He couldn't think of a place. He thought of something else. He looked at the man and he said, "I just remembered. The wallet's not there. I never keep my money in the wallet. The only thing I took with me was money. All my available cash."

"How much?"

"Close to two thousand."

The man tapped a forefinger against his thin moustache.

Parry said, "I don't want to go back to Portland. It's bad enough the way it is now. I'm just about ready to crack. I almost cracked a year ago and if I crack now I'll never get over it. And here's another thing. My name's not really Linnell. It's a new name because I'm trying to make a new start. I'll never make it if you take me in."

"You working now?"

"I only checked in last night," Parry said. "I'll find work. I know investments backwards and forwards."

The man folded his arms and watched the rain ripping down. He said, "What's the offer?"

"A hundred."

"Make it two."

Parry took bills from his pocket and began counting off fifties. He put four fifties in the man's hand.

The man studied the money and pocketed it and walked away.

Parry waited there for ten minutes. He saw an empty taxi, waved to it. The driver beckoned.

The taxi took him to Golden Gate Park, took him around the park and back to Civic Center. He went into a hotel lobby and bought a magazine and used up an hour. Then he went through the revolving door and stood under an awning and watched the rain weaken. When the rain had stopped altogether he walked down the street, kept walking until he came to a department store.

He bought a grip, a good-looking piece of yellow calf. He paid for it and told the salesman to hold it for him. Then he went over to the men's furnishings department and bought a suit and a thin raincoat. He bought shirts and shorts and ties and socks. He bought another pair of shoes. He was enjoying himself. He went into the toilet goods department and bought a toothbrush and a tube of toothpaste. He bought a razor and a tube of brushless shaving cream.

When he came back to the luggage department he told the salesman he wanted to put his purchases in the grip. He said it would be easier to carry them that way. The salesman said that was all right, as long as he had the receipts.

As he was leaving the department store a man came up to him and politely asked him if he had made any purchases. He said yes, and he showed the receipts. The man thanked him politely and told him to come again. He said he would, and he walked out of the store.

He looked for a hotel. He selected the Ruxton, a small place that wasn't fancy but was clean and trim. They gave him a room on the fourth floor. He was registered as Allan Linnell, and his address was Portland.

The room was small and very clean and neat. He gave the bellhop a quarter and when he was alone in the room he opened the grip, took out the packages and began to unwrap them.

The phone rang.

He looked at the phone.

The phone rang again.

He decided to let it ring.

It kept on ringing.

He sat down on the edge of the bed and stared at the phone.

The phone kept ringing and ringing.

He got up and walked across the room and picked up the phone.

He said, "Yes?"

"Room 417?"

"Yes?"

"Mr. Linnell?"

"Yes?"

"There's someone here to see you. May I send him up?"

It was a him. Then it had to be the detective. It had to be more money. The detective had trailed him, so it had to be more money or else the detective had changed his mind about taking the money and was going to take him in. He turned and saw three doors. One was a closet door, one was for the bathroom, one was for the corridor. He thought of the corridor, the fire escape. But if it was more money it would be all right. He thought of the fire escape. It was no good. It brought things back to a chase basis. He had to get rid of that. He had to end it before it became a chase.

"Mr. Linnell?"

"Yes, I'm still here."

"Shall I send him up?"

"Don't hurry me," Parry said, and he meant it. Again he thought of the fire escape. He told himself to stop thinking of the fire escape.

"Mr. Linnell?"

"Who is it wants to see me?"

"Just a moment, please."

Parry heard dim voices. The name wouldn't help, except that this gave him a few more seconds to think it over even though he knew there was nothing to think over.

"Mr. Linnell?"

"Yes?"

"It's a Mr. Arbogast."

Arbogast. It sounded hard, just as hard as the detective's face was hard. It had to be more money. And more money was all right and it had to be all right.

"Mr. Linnell?" The voice down there was impatient.

"All right," Parry said. "Send him up."

He put the phone down and went back to the bed and leaned against the post. It had to be more money, maybe another three hundred. And he could spare that. He told himself it would be all right after he gave the detective another three hundred and then he told himself it wouldn't be all right because this was the second time. And as long as there was a second time there was the possibility of a third time. And a fourth and a fifth. And after his money ran out the detective would take him in. Again he began to consider the fire escape and this was the best time for the fire escape because the detective was already in the elevator and the elevator was going up. To use the fire escape he must use it now and right now.

Then he was moving toward the door, going slowly, telling himself to go faster, telling himself it was already a chase even though a chase was the last thing he wanted. He was trying to go faster and his legs wouldn't play along and he begged himself to go faster, to open the door and get out of here and give himself a lead and build the lead. He was almost at the door. He heard sounds in the corridor, footsteps coming toward the door. He felt empty and worn out, and he knew it was too late. If he ran now he would be up against a gun. All these detectives carried guns. A good idea for a novelty song. All detectives carry guns.

This was the end of it, because it couldn't be money, because it was a matter of plain reasoning, because the detective had already taken a big risk, taking that two hundred, and the detective had no intention of taking a bigger risk now. The detective was here to work, to give back the two hundred and take him in. There was a weakness in the wife in Portland story and the detective had snatched at the weakness before letting him get out of sight, and had trailed him and had him now and would take him in. And this was the end of it and it had to end this way, it had to end here, and what he had sensed all along was reality now, there was really no getting away, they had to grab him sometime, an ostrich could stick its head in the ground, stop seeing everyone else but that didn't mean they wouldn't see the ostrich. As he stood there listening to the footsteps coming toward the door he thought of how easy it had been at the beginning, how convenient everything had been, the way the truck was placed, the empty barrels in the truck, the guards away from the truck and the open gate and the truck going through. It had been very easy but it was ended now, and the ending of it was reasonable even though it wasn't fair, because now they would kill him, and he didn't deserve death.

The footsteps came closer and he wondered why it was taking so long for the footsteps to reach the door.

The sound of the footsteps was a soft mallet sound, softly tapping at the top of his skull, and slowly.

The sound of the footsteps took form and became a mallet. The mallet was a weapon. He ought to defend himself against a weapon. He had that right. It was proper and it was just that he should defend himself now. The mallet was the beginning of death and he had a right to defend himself against death.

The sound of the mallet was louder now, closer now, the feeling of it was heavier, and now it was fully upon him and it was hurting and he ought to think in practical terms, think of a way to defend himself. The detective was a fairly big man and the detective had a gun and fists wouldn't be sufficient. There was Patavilca to think of, there was getting away from here and going to Patavilca to think of, and the detective was trying to keep him away from that, trying to take him away from life and the delight of Patavilca and he had a right to defend himself, to hold onto life. He was looking at the door, listening to the footsteps coming toward the door, listening to the mallet, feeling the mallet, knowing that as each blow of the mallet came against him it was doing something to his brain, knowing he had to stop that, knowing he couldn't stop it, knowing he had a right to defend himself, listening to the footsteps, feeling the mallet, knowing it wasn't fair that they should kill him, knowing that soon it would be too late, he would be dead, and he was alive now, and he should be preparing to defend himself, knowing he was going to do something to defend himself, knowing he didn't hate the detective and he really didn't want to hurt the detective but he had to do something to defend himself and what he had to do was grab something. He turned his head and on the dresser across the room he saw an ash tray.

It was a glass ash tray.

It was fairly large.

It was heavy. A very heavy ash tray had killed Gert. This one was very heavy.

He stared at it.

The mallet was banging now, banging hard on his skull. He got up from the bed and went over and picked up the ash tray and he was thinking that he would open the door for the detective and hide the ash tray behind his back and manage to get behind the detective and then hit him with the ash tray, hit him hard enough so he would go down, hard enough so he would stay down, but not too hard, because too hard would kill the detective and he didn't want to kill the detective. He didn't want to but he wanted to hit the detective hard enough to put him down and keep him down long enough for the negotiation of the fire escape and the complete beginning of a complete getaway, but not too hard, of course not too hard. But hard enough. That would take measuring and he wondered if he would be able to measure it correctly. And he knew he wouldn't be able to measure it. He knew he was going to bring it down too hard because he was so anxious to get away, because now he was at a point where he was more afraid of bringing it down too lightly than too hard. And now that he had it in his hand and his mind was made up to use it he could not put it down and he was going to do something now that he didn't want to do, that he never expected he would do, and he didn't want to do it, and he pleaded with himself not to do it, and he knew he would always regret doing it, and he was sick and he was tired, every part of him was so tired except his right arm and his right hand and the fingers that had a firm hold on the heavy glass ash tray. He pleaded with himself to drop it, to let his fingers go limp, to let the ash tray go to the floor. His grip tightened on the ash tray, the mallet crashed down on him, the door became liquid, flowing toward him, flowing back, the floor was liquid, the door flowed in again, the mallet crashed down again, he saw it happening, just as if it was already happening he saw the detective coming in and the perfect teeth smiling at him and the forefinger tapping against the thin moustache and he heard the detective telling him it was tough and it was too bad but it was necessary to take him in and he could hear himself saying something about the offer of an extra three hundred and he could see the detective shaking a head and saying no, it was tough, it was too bad and it was a rotten job but it was a job all the same and it was necessary to take him in. And the detective was asking him to come along and he said all right, he would come along and then he was getting around and sort of behind the detective and the heavy glass ash tray was a part of his fingers, a part of his arm as he brought up his arm, brought it up high as the detective started to turn to look at him to see what he was doing and then he brought it down, swinging it down, the heavy glass ash tray, very heavy, very hard and thudding so horribly hard against the detective's head. And the detective stood there looking at him. And he wanted the detective to go down. And he brought the ash tray down again, and the head began to bleed. The blood came running out but the detective wouldn't go down so he hit the head again and still the detective wouldn't go down and he hit the head once more. And the detective refused to go down even though the blood was running very thickly now, very fast, and the ash tray came against the head and against the head again and the blood washed down over the detective's face and the perfect teeth were smiling and very white and glistening until the blood dripped down over the teeth and made them very red and glistening and the detective stood there with his head of blood and he wouldn't go down.

The blood dripped onto the detective's shoulders, down over the detective's shoulders, down the arms, dripped off the ends of the fingers, dripped onto the floor, collected and pooled on the floor, rose up and clung to the detective's shoes, came up along the detective's trousers as more blood came down over the detective's chin, dripped onto the shirtfront and the detective was wearing a very red and glistening shirt and then a very red and glistening suit. All of the detective was red and glistening and the redness gushed from the black and deep openings in the detective's head and added to the glistening and the red. And the detective wouldn't go down. The detective was a glistening and red statue, all red, standing there and refusing to go down, and now it was impossible to use the ash tray again because the arm was tired, too tired to lift the ash tray again, and the detective stood there smiling with his perfect red teeth, and then there was a knocking on the door.

The redness stood there.

The knocking came again.

The redness vanished as Parry opened his eyes. Then he closed his eyes again, closed them tightly and tried to see redness or anything near redness and all he got was black. He opened his eyes and he heard the knocking, and he walked over to the dresser and put the ash tray back where it belonged.

Then he walked back across the room toward the door, and with the inside of his head a spinning vacuum he put a hand on the knob, knowing a crazy, careening joy as he anticipated the living face of the detective.

He opened the door and saw the face of Studebaker.

16

THERE WAS no hat this time. There was grey hair, very thin on top. There was a new suit, a new shirt and a new tie. And new shoes. And Studebaker was smiling as he stood there in his new clothes. He put a hand in his coat pocket. He took out a small pistol and he pointed it at Parry.

He said, "Walk backward. Keep walking with your hands up until you hit the wall."

Parry walked backward. His shoulders came against the wall and he bounced a little and then he stood still with his hands up.

Studebaker was in the room now and he was closing the door. He had the pistol pointed at Parry's stomach. He said, "I could shoot you now and make myself five thousand dollars."

"I didn't know they were offering anything," Parry said.

"That's what they're offering," Studebaker said. "They're stumped."

"Have you talked to them?"

"No," Studebaker said. "If I was a dope I would've talked to them. I'm not a dope. In old clothes I know I look like a farmer but I'm not a farmer. Just stand there with your hands up and I'll stand here and we'll talk it over."

"What do you want?"

"Money."

"How much?"

"Sixty thousand."

"I can't afford that. I can't come anywhere near it."

"She can."

"Who?"

"The girl."

"What girl?"

"Irene Janney."

"Who's she?"

"Look, Parry. I told you I'm not a dope. And I'm not a farmer. I know she's worth a couple hundred thousand. She can spare sixty of it."

"She's out of it. You can't do a thing."

"Except turn you in. And that brings her in. That makes her an accessory to the Fellsinger job. It's twenty years off her life."

"They wouldn't give her that."

"All right, let's give her a break. Let's make it ten. It's still worth sixty thousand. That leaves her a hundred and forty thousand. With that hundred and forty she can get back the sixty in no time. And then we'll all be happy."

"No."

"You sure?"

"Yes," Parry said. "I'm sure." He watched the pistol. The pistol remained pointed at him but it was moving. Because Studebaker was moving, because Studebaker was going toward the phone.

Studebaker took hold of the phone and lifted it from the hook.

"Put it down," Parry said.

Studebaker smiled. He put the phone down. He said, "You'll play?"

"I'll think about it."

"That's okay. Think about it all you want to. Look at it up and down and sideways. You'll come to the same thing. You'll see it's the best way. What you've got to do now is shake me. I'm a big stone in the road and you've got to get rid of the stone to keep on going. So what you've got to do is talk to her and show her what her only move is. You got plenty on her."

"You too. You seem to know plenty."

"Not as much as you. If I went to her alone I wouldn't have much to back myself up. What I want to do is go there with you and have her see you with me so she'll know I'm not kidding. Then and there I want her to write me out a check for sixty thousand. That's the way we work it. We go there together."

"You've done this sort of thing before, haven't you?"

"Nup. This is the first time. How am I doing?"

"You're doing fine. Tell me, Arbogast, what are you?"

"I'm a crook."

"Small time?"

"Until now."

"In old clothes you don't look like a crook."

"In old clothes I look like a farmer."

"What will you do with the sixty thousand?"

"Probably go to Salt Lake City and open up a loan office. There's a fortune in it. People are crazy these days. People are always crazy but these days they're especially bughouse. They're making money but they want more. They're spending like lunatics. With a loan office I'll clean up. The way I got it figured out, sixty thousand gives me a perfect start."

"You won't keep bothering her, will you?"

"I tell you sixty thousand is just the right amount. I'll have it doubled and redoubled inside a couple years."

"Okay if I light a cigarette?"

"No. Keep your hands up."

"You're a careful guy."

"Sure I'm careful. I'm no dope. I'm careful and I'm smart. I'll give you a slant on how smart I am. I'll tell you the way I handled it, and then you'll know just how much of a chance you've got to put something over on me. Now you remember when I picked you up on that road, you remember you were wearing a pair of grey cotton trousers and heavy shoes and nothing more."

"You knew who I was right away."

"I didn't know anything of the kind," Arbogast said. "You had Quentin written all over you, but that was all. So I said to myself here's a fellow making a break from Quentin. I said to myself I'll pick up this fellow and see what he has to offer."

"That," Parry said, "I don't get."

"I'll tell you how it is with me," Arbogast said. "I'm always on the lookout for an opportunity. Anything that comes along with a possibility tag on it I grab. Here you were, out on the road, a fellow running away from Quentin. Maybe you had connections. Maybe you'd be willing to pay for a lift and a hiding place. Maybe I could stretch it out long enough to get something on you and shake you down later. That's the way I figured it. We'll say it was twelve to five I could make myself some heavy money on the deal. Twelve to five is always good enough for me, especially when my only bid is picking you up and having a talk with you. Now let's be agreeable and keep our hands up."

"They're up."

"Get them up higher and keep them that way. And maybe you better turn around. Yeah, I think you better turn around and face the wall and I'll see what you got."

Parry turned and faced the wall, holding his hands high. Arbogast came over and in four seconds checked him for a gun.

Then Arbogast stepped back. "So that was what I had in mind. But you pulled something I wasn't ready for and that made things tough for me. Not too tough, because I wasn't out cold when you got in the car with that girl. I saw the car going away and at first I didn't know what to make of it. But I'm no dope. That was a classy-looking car and there had to be money behind it. So I took the license number in my head. I got a good head for that sort of thing. You beginning to see the way I had it laid out?"

"I'm beginning to see you're a man who plans for the future."

"Always," Arbogast said. "Anything that looks like it might lead to something. A fellow's got to be a few moves ahead of the game. It's the only way to get along in this world. Well, I had that license number in my head but I was in my underwear and I knew I couldn't go far that way. But you left your grey pants there and they fitted all right and I was wearing a sleeveless jersey and I still had my socks and shoes so that was all right, too. So I got in the car with that license number in my head and I made a U-turn and went back down the road aways and took another road. There was nothing for me to worry about because all my cards were in the Studebaker and if they stopped me and asked questions I could tell them I had a fall and banged up my face. But it didn't matter, I wasn't stopped. I took a roundabout way to Frisco and when I got in town I made a telephone call."

"Oh," Parry said. "There's another party in on it."

"No," Arbogast said. "You don't need to worry about that. It's just that I belong to an automobile club. It's not a big club but it's convenient and it has a knack of getting a line on people. So here's what I did. Now get this, and you'll see how it happens that a guy can go along for years living on breadcrumbs and out of a clear blue sky a jackpot comes along and hits him in the face. I called up this automobile club and told them a grey Pontiac convertible slammed into me and busted my car and made me a hospital case and then kept on going on a hit-run basis. I gave them the license number and I wanted to know if it was worth my while to start action. They told me to wait there and they'd call back in ten minutes. When they called back they said I should go get myself a lawyer because I really had something. They said she was a wealthy girl and they gave me her name and address. They said she was listed for a couple hundred thousand at the inside and I ought to collect plenty. You staying with me?"

"I'm right alongside you."

"That's dandy," Arbogast said. "Now stay with me while I go out of that telephone booth telling myself I'm in for a thousand or two. Or maybe four or five if I can rig up a good story. Stay with me while I walk down the street and while I pass a newsstand. Then I'm walking away from that newsstand and then I'm spinning around and running back to that newsstand and throwing two bits into the tin box and forgetting to pick up change. And there I am, looking at that front page, looking at those big black letters and looking at your face."

"You must have been glad to see me."

"Was I glad to see you? You asking me was I glad? I'm telling you I almost went into a jig. Then I pulled myself together and I started to think. What I don't understand was how she got connected with you at that particular place in the road. But I'm no dope. She must have seen you getting out of the car or else you waved to her when she passed in the Pontiac. Something like that, but I wasn't bothering myself about it. All I had to do was keep my eyes open and my head working and stay with her. So I did that. I had some money from a job I did in Sacramento and I got myself some clothes. I really splurged, because I knew I'd soon be coming into some high finance. But I didn't think in terms of a room. No, because I knew the Studebaker was going to be my home for a while, parked outside the apartment on the other side of the street. So there I am, parked there on the other side of the street and playing it conservative and taking my time. I saw her Pontiac parked outside the apartment and that was fine, but I wanted to make sure you were still with her. Late that night I saw you coming out of the apartment and that was what I'd been waiting for. I saw you getting into a taxi."

"You followed me."

"No. I'm no dope. I knew you'd come back."

"Who told you?"

"Nobody told me. Just like I say, I had my head working. That's all I need. That's why I always work alone. All I need is my head. I knew you'd come back because she was in on it with you and you had to come back sooner or later. So I stayed there and early in the morning I was there in the Studebaker and I was watching that street with both eyes. And I saw you coming down the street."

"You couldn't know it was me. My face was all bandaged."

"Look." Arbogast sounded like a patient classroom instructor. "I recognized that brand new grey suit. I checked the suit and your build and I figured it out in no time at all. You had something done to your face and that's no new story with fellows in your position. I knew you were going to lamp the Studebaker and I wasn't worried about that but I didn't want you to lamp me. Not yet, anyway. So I ducked and stayed on the floor. When I got up I saw you going into the apartment house. Then I knew I had to keep you guessing, the two of you, I had to handle it like a spider, getting you in, not too fast, nothing hurried about it, just coaxing you in. I took the Studebaker down a block and parked it there so you couldn't see it from the window. And from there I watched the apartment house. And the only thing that bothered me then was maybe when you came out with your new face you wouldn't be wearing that grey suit. But I couldn't do anything about that. So I waited and then along comes another jackpot when I buy a paper from a boy and I read all about that Fellsinger job. And that doubled the pot, because now she wasn't only tied in with a jailbreak, she was connected with a murder. You see what I had on her?"

"But I didn't do it."

"I don't care whether you did it or not. The cops say you did it. That's enough for me. Anyway, I was still sort of bothered about that business of you coming out of the apartment wearing a different suit, so I decided to have a talk with you before anything like that could take place. I went up to the apartment and I rang the buzzer. That was during one of those times after she went away in the Pontiac to go shopping. You see I used to watch her going away and coming back with packages and I knew you were going to be there for a while. So there you have me ringing the buzzer and then changing my mind, saying to myself to hold off for a while, play it the way I'd been playing it, taking it slow. How did I know there wasn't a third party up in that apartment? Or a fourth party? Or a mob? What I had to do was take my chances with that suit situation and wait it out until I could get you alone and away from the apartment. With all that money involved I could afford to stay in with those aces back to back and just waiting there for somebody to raise. And that raise came this morning when the grey suit came out of the apartment house. I wasn't even looking at the face. I followed the grey suit. I followed the taxi. Downtown the grey suit got out of the taxi and the whole thing was going nicely until that dick got hold of you in the diner. I saw you give him a bribe. How much did you give him?"

"Two hundred."

"You see what I'm getting at? If you could afford two hundred she must have handed you at least a couple thousand. Whoever she is, she's got feeling for you. She'll do what you say. That's why I'm arranging it the way I am. That's why we'll go there together and you'll do the asking. Now look, don't get smart."

"What's the matter?"

"You just keep your hands up, that's what's the matter. You're not dealing with no dope. I played it shrewd all the way and I aim to keep on playing it shrewd. I didn't miss a trick. I followed you from the diner and I followed you on that taxi ride to and from Golden Gate Park and I followed you on that department-store trip and I followed you here. At the desk I said I had a message for the man who just came in wearing a grey suit and they asked did I mean Mr. Linnell and I said yes. That puts us here together where I wanted us to be. So now you can turn around and we'll talk it over face to face and we'll see what we got."

Parry turned and faced Arbogast and said, "You've still got that question of a third party or even a mob."

Arbogast smiled and shook his head. "You wouldn't be checking in here alone if there was a mob. You'd either want someone with you or if there was a boss the boss would want someone with you. I know how these things go. Let's call it the way it is. It's you and the girl and me and nobody else."

"I won't argue with you."

Arbogast widened the smile. "That kind of talk is music to me. Who did that job on your face?"

"I'm not saying."

"It's high-class work."

"What good is it now?"

"Don't talk like a dope," Arbogast said. "You're going to be better off now than you ever were. As soon as I get the sixty thousand I'll be clearing out and you'll be set. All right, what do you say?"

"You're holding the gun."

"Now you're using your head. I'm holding the gun. I'm holding the high cards. And as soon as I rake in the chips I walk out of the game."

"You make it sound simple."

"Sure, because that's the way it is. It's simple. Why make it complicated?"

Parry wanted to think that it was simple. He wanted to conclude that once she gave Arbogast the sixty thousand everything would be all right. And yet he knew that once Arbogast got the sixty thousand he would ask for more and keep on asking. The man was made that way. This was the first real money Arbogast had ever come up against. For Arbogast it was a delicious situation and Arbogast would want it to remain that way.

Parry told himself what he had to do. He looked at Arbogast and he told himself he had to get rid of Arbogast. He had foxed Arbogast once and maybe he could do it again.

"No," Arbogast said.

"No what?"

"Just no, that's all. The only way you get rid of me is sixty thousand. That's the only way. Look at the gun. If you try to take it I put a bullet in you. If you try to run away I put a bullet in you. And I make myself five thousand. Either way you die and either way I make money."

Parry told himself he had to get rid of Arbogast because Arbogast would keep on bothering her. Arbogast wasn't interested in him. He wished Arbogast was interested in him and only him.

Arbogast said, "All right, what do we do?"

"We'll go there," Parry said.

"That's fine," Arbogast said. "You'll stay just a bit ahead of me and you'll remember there's a gun behind you."

They walked out of the room. In the elevator Arbogast remained slightly behind Parry. In the lobby Arbogast was walking at the side of Parry and half a step behind. On the street it was the same way. The street was bright yellow from hot August sun following the heavy rain. The street was crowded with early morning activity and horns were honking and people were walking in and out of office buildings and stores.

"Let's turn here," Arbogast said.

They turned and walked up another street, then down a narrow street and Parry saw the Studebaker parked beside a two-story drygoods establishment.

"You drive," Arbogast said. He took keys out of a pocket and handed them to Parry.

Parry got in the car from the pavement side and Arbogast came sliding in beside him. Parry started the motor and sat there looking at the narrow street that went on ahead of him until it arrived at a wide and busy street.

"The whole thing won't take more than an hour," Arbogast said.

The car moved down the narrow street.

"And remember," Arbogast said, "I've got the gun right here."

"I'll remember," Parry said.

The car made a turn and it was on the wide street. Parry took it down three blocks and turned off.

"What are you doing?" Arbogast said.

"Getting out of heavy traffic," Parry said.

"Maybe that's a good idea."

"Sure it's a good idea," Parry said. "We can't afford to be stopped now. As long as we're started on this thing we might as well do it right."

The car made another turn. It was going past empty lots. There were old houses here and there. The sun was very big and very yellow and it was very hot in the car.

"I can't start worrying about her," Parry said.

"You gotta be selfish," Arbogast said. "That's the only way

to get along. Even if she means something to you. Does she mean anything to you?"

"Yes."

"How bad is it?"

"It's not too bad. I'll manage to forget about her."

"That's what you gotta do," Arbogast said. "You gotta go away and forget about her. She'll be all right. I won't keep after her. Once I get that sixty thousand I'll leave her alone. You don't need to worry about anything. Hey, where we going?"

"We'll go down another few blocks and then we'll circle around and get up there from the other side of town."

The street was neglected and bumpy and the car went slowly and there were empty lots and no houses now and it was very hot and sticky and quiet except for the motor of the car.

"You do that," Arbogast said. "You go away and forget about her."

"She helped me out and I thanked her," Parry said. "I can't keep on thanking her."

"What you gotta do is get away," Arbogast said. "You got that new face and it's a dandy. All you gotta do is fix up some cards and papers for yourself and you'll be in good shape. Where do you figure on going?"

"I don't know."

"Mexico's a good bet."

"Maybe."

"You won't have any trouble in Mexico. And if you use Arizona you won't have any trouble at the border. How much did she give you?"

"I've got about fifteen hundred left. Close to sixteen hundred."

"That's plenty. Tell you what you do. You use Arizona and when you get down there buy yourself a car in Benson. That's about thirty miles from the border. Once you got some papers arranged you won't have any trouble buying the car. They'll be only too happy to sell you one. And once you have the car you'll have the owner's card and that's all you'll need. Do you know where you can get papers arranged?"

"I guess I can find a place."

"Sure, it's not hard. There's guys with printing presses who specialize in that sort of thing. Once you get to Benson and buy that car you'll be all right."

"They'll ask questions at the border."

"Sure they'll ask questions. Don't you know how to answer questions?"

"They'll ask me why I'm going to Mexico."

"And you'll tell them you're going there to mine silver. Or you're going there to look for oil. Or you just want a vacation. It don't make any difference what you tell them. All you gotta do is talk easy and don't worry about anything and don't get yourself mixed up. Didn't you learn all these things when you were in Quentin?"

"I didn't mix much in Quentin."

"You should of mixed. It's always a good idea to mix. That's the only way to learn things. Especially in a place like Quentin. And you don't need to tell me anything about Quentin. They put me in there twice. And I learned things I never knew before. I learned tricks that got me out of more jams than I can count. You got some shrewd boys in Quentin."

"Where can I get the papers arranged?"

"Well," Arbogast said. "Let's see now. There's a guy I know in Sacramento but that won't do because you'd have to give my name and I can't act loose in Sacramento for a while yet. Then there's a guy in Nevada, in Carson City, but I did a job in Carson City a few weeks ago so I'm still hot there so that lets Carson City out. So let's see now. Las Vegas is out because I'm wanted there and let's see, maybe if we come back to California, but, no, I'm still hot in Stockton and Modesto and Visalia, it was all little jobs but these small town police are terriers, that's exactly what they are. And don't go thinking they're dumb, because they're anything but dumb. Don't go calling them dopes. Especially in some of these little California towns. I tell you California is plenty mean and the sooner I get out when I get the cash——"

"Get what cash?"

"The two hundred thousand, I mean the sixty."

"You mean the sixty thousand dollars."

"Sure, that's what I mean. The sixty. What did you think I meant?"

The car was going very slowly now and the lots were very empty. There was thin wooded area going away from the lots on the left and on the right the nearest houses were away past low hills and almost at the horizon. In front the bumpy road was all yellow dirt going ahead slowly as the car went slowly, going ahead toward more stretches of empty lots. The sun was banging away a hard and bright yellow steadiness that seemed to splash and throw itself around, thick and wriggling and squirming in its hot stickiness.

"I figured you meant the sixty," Parry said. "We'll turn soon. There's an intersection down ahead."

The car crawled. Under the hot sun the empty lots were very bright and yellow and quiet. The grinding motor was a sphere of sound complete in itself and apart from the quiet of the empty lots.

"Where's that intersection you were talking about?"

"We'll come to it." He wondered how long he could stretch this out.

"I don't see anything out there," Arbogast said.

"It's there," Parry said. He half-turned and saw Arbogast sitting beside him, leaning forward and looking ahead and trying to see an intersection. Then Arbogast was looking at him and waiting for him to say something and he said, "I wish you could think of a place."

"What kind of a place?"

"A place where I could get those papers arranged."

"Yeah," Arbogast said. "That's something you'll need to do. You can't overlook that. You'll need papers and cards. Let's see now, let's see if I can help you out. You'll be going through Nevada by train or maybe bus is better. Yeah, that's what you better do. You better use one of those two-by-four bus companies. Let's see if I can think of a place. You can't do anything in California and I can't think of any place in Nevada. Let's see, you'll be buying that car in Arizona, in Benson, so let's see what's north of Benson. Yeah, there's a place. There's a guy I know in Maricopa."

"Maricopa?"

"Yeah. You ever been there?"

"I was born and raised there."

"Come to think of it, you did tell me. Yeah, that day I picked you up you said Maricopa when I asked you where you came from. It's funny, aint it?"

"It's one of those things."

"It just goes to show you we're always going back. You went away from Maricopa and now you gotta go back there. How long since you left there?"

"About seventeen years."

"And now you're going back. Out of all the places you could go it's gotta be Maricopa. That's really something."

"Who do I see?"

"Well, this printer I know. He did a few license jobs for me and some guys I sent to him. He knows his work and he's tight as a rivet. He'll remember my name. It's been more than a year now but he'll remember. He'll give you what you want and he'll take your money and that's as far as it goes. You look him up when you get to Maricopa. His name's Ferris."

"What?"

"Tom Ferris."

"That name's familiar," Parry said.

"What?"

"That's right," Parry said. "Tom Ferris, the printer. I remember him."

Arbogast slapped a hand on a knee. "Now what do you think of that?" he said. "You know him. That takes it. I tell you, that takes it. You're gonna go back to Maricopa and you're gonna see your old friend Ferris. Good old Ferris is gonna fix up those papers for you. Well, I'll tell you something. That takes it."

"Tom Ferris." Parry smiled. He shook his head slowly.

"And he prints fake cards and papers for guys on the run," Arbogast said. "He prints the town paper and people think he's as straight as they come. You'd never believe it, would you?"

Parry stopped smiling. He said, "How do I work it?"

"It's easy," Arbogast said. "You just go there and look him up. Get him alone and tell him Arbogast sent you. Tell him what you want and the price you're willing to pay. That's all he wants to know. It's gonna cost you about three hundred for a license and a few other cards and papers that you'll need to have. He knows all about it. He knows just what you need. He's been doing this work for years."

"How long will it take?"

"Maybe an hour. He'll go to work right away. You can't tell me it aint worth a few hundred."

"It's worth every cent of that," Parry said.

"Sure. Well, I'm telling you, that takes it. Now where's that intersection?"

"Right up ahead."

"I don't see it."

"It's there."

"I tell you I don't see it," Arbogast said. "There's no intersection. What are you trying to pull?"

"We've got to stay away from traffic."

"That don't mean we gotta go to the South Pole. I'm telling you there's no intersection up ahead."

"I'm telling you there is." He brought the car to a stop, readied himself.

"And I say no," Arbogast said. "And I've got the gun. Look. Go on, look at it."

"All right," Parry said, "it's your car. It's your gun." He reached forward to release the emergency brake and then without touching the emergency brake, he sent his hands toward the wrist of the hand that held the gun. Arbogast was raising the gun to fire but Parry had hold of the wrist and was twisting it. Arbogast wouldn't let go of the gun and Parry kept twisting and Arbogast let out a yell. And Parry kept twisting and Arbogast let out another yell and then he dropped the gun and it fell on the space of empty seat between Parry and Arbogast. With his free hand Arbogast grabbed at the gun and Parry kept twisting the wrist of the other hand and Arbogast's head went back and he yelled and kept on yelling and forgot about taking the gun. Parry released Arbogast's wrists and snatched at the gun and took it. He got his finger against the trigger and he pointed the gun at Arbogast's face.

17

ARBOGAST LOOKED at the gun. He started to go back. He kept going back until he came against the door and then he tried to push himself through the door.

"Just stay where you are," Parry said.

"Don't shoot me in the face," Arbogast said.

Parry lowered the gun and had it aimed at Arbogast's chest.

"How's that?" Parry said.

"Look," Arbogast said. "Let me go now and I promise you I'll keep on going and I'll never bother you again."

Parry shook his head.

"Please," Arbogast said.

Parry shook his head.

"I had an idea you were going to pull something like this," Arbogast said.

"Why didn't you do something about it?" Parry asked.

"Why did I have to start with you in the first place?" Arbogast said.

"I can answer that," Parry said. "You're a crook."

"There's honor among crooks," Arbogast said. "Believe me, there is. And if I give you my word I'll go away and won't bother you——"

Parry shook his head.

"Are you going to shoot me?" Arbogast said.

Parry shook his head.

"What are you going to do?" Arbogast said.

Parry gazed past Arbogast's head. He saw the stretch of empty lot very yellow under the bright yellow sky and beyond the lot the beginnings of woodland. He said, "Get out of the car."

"What are you going to do with me?"

"Open the door and get out," Parry said.

"Please——"

"Do as I tell you or I'll be forced to shoot you."

Arbogast opened the door. As he stood there on the side of the road he looked up and down and he saw nothing but emptiness. Then Parry was turning off the motor and coming out there with him and closing the door. And they stood out there together and Parry had the gun pointed at Arbogast's chest.

"Let's take a stroll," Parry said.

"Where are we going?"

"Into the woods."

"Why?"

"I want us to be alone. I don't want any interference."

"You're going to shoot me," Arbogast said.

"I won't shoot you unless you make a try for the gun," Parry said.

They were walking across the empty lot, and Parry had the gun aimed at Arbogast's ribs.

They weren't saying anything as they walked across the lot. Then they were past the lot and they were going through the woods. It was moist in the woods, very sticky and very hot. They were going slowly.

They went about seventy yards into the woods and then Parry said, "I guess this is all right."

Arbogast turned and looked at the gun.

Parry looked at the place on Arbogast's middle where the gun was aiming. Parry said, "Did you kill Fellsinger?"

"No."

"Did you follow me to Fellsinger's apartment?"

"No."

"But you knew Irene Janney had money. You knew she had two hundred thousand dollars."

"Yes, I knew that. I told you."

"And you wanted to get your hands on that cash."

"I'll admit that."

"All right then, it checks. Part of it, anyway. Two hundred thousand is something out of the ordinary. You could have figured it this way—you could have said to yourself she'd get a year or two for helping me get away. But if I killed somebody while I was loose then she'd be in real trouble and she'd get maybe ten years or even twenty. And you had your mind set on that two hundred thousand. So maybe you followed the taxi when I left her apartment."

"No."

"Maybe you followed the taxi and when I went in there you followed me and you were hiding in the vestibule and watching to see what button I pressed. Then after I left you pressed that same button. And here's what you could have been thinking—that the taxi driver would be a witness. At least when the police gave him my description he'd say I was the man who came to the apartment house at a certain hour that night. So the taxi driver would be one thing and my fingerprints here and there would be another. You knew I wasn't going up there to kill Fellsinger and you knew I was going up there to see somebody who would help me. You didn't know it was Fellsinger but you knew it was a friend of mine. And you knew the police would tie me in and when they got my fingerprints and when they got a statement from the taxi driver they would come right out and say I did it. You knew all that. So maybe you went up there and killed Fellsinger."

"No."

"It's got to be. You admit you were watching her apartment house. You admit you were waiting for me to come out. That checks. You had your car there. And that checks. And you could have followed me to Fellsinger's apartment. And you had a reason for killing Fellsinger. Because you knew I'd be blamed and that would bring her in on it. So that checks."

"No," Arbogast said. "I didn't kill Fellsinger."

"Then who did? Somebody did, and it wasn't me. So who was it if it wasn't you?"

"I don't know."

"Whoever killed Fellsinger followed me there, went up and killed him after I went away. I know that much. So let's go back. You were outside her apartment house. You saw me get in a taxi. You saw the taxi going down the street. Did the taxi pass you?"

"Yes."

"Did you follow the taxi?"

"No. I told you no."

"You just stayed there and watched the taxi going away?"

"That's right."

"You're a liar. I walked three blocks before I got in that taxi."

"And I followed you for three blocks," Arbogast said.

"You said you stayed there."

"I said I stayed at the place where I saw you getting in the taxi. That was as far as I wanted to go. Look, here's what I did. I saw you walking down the street. You made about a block, and then I put the car in gear and followed you. I stayed about half a block behind you and I had the car in second and I was just creeping along and watching you. Then you were about three blocks away from the apartment house and you were getting in that taxi."

"What did you do?"

"I pulled up at the curb."

"And then what did you do?"

"I stayed there. I watched you going away in the taxi."

"And then what?"

"I made a turn and went back to the apartment house. I parked on the other side of the street, far down the block."

"You say you made a turn. What kind of a turn? Around the corner?"

"No," Arbogast said. "It was a U-turn."

Parry examined Arbogast's eyes. Parry said, "You're sure it was a U-turn?"

"I'm giving it to you straight. I made that U-turn and went back and parked across the street from the apartment house. I knew you'd come back."

"How did you know?"

"I'm no dope. You had a perfect set-up there. You got new clothes out of it, and I knew you were getting money out of it. And when they gave me the lowdown on her they told me she was single and that meant you were alone with her up there so it was perfect for you and you'd be a dope to walk out on it. What I figured was you'd stay there until things calmed down and then you'd make a break out of town."

"Now you're sure you made a U-turn? You're sure you didn't go around the corner and up the next block and then down?"

"Look," Arbogast said. "If I made a turn around the corner and up the next block and then down it would've brought me on the same side of the street as the apartment house. You lamped the car, didn't you?"

"Yes."

"You saw it was on the other side of the street?"

"Yes," Parry said.

"The front of the car was facing you, wasn't it?"

"Yes."

"All right, that proves I made a U-turn. And what's all this about a U-turn?"

"Two U-turns."

"Well, sure it was two U-turns," Arbogast said. "I was parked on the other side of the street when I saw you coming out of the apartment house. I had to make a U-turn to follow you, didn't I? And I had to make another U-turn to come back."

"You made the first U-turn right away?"

"No," Arbogast said. "I told you I waited until you were about a block away."

"You had your headlights off?"

"They were off. I'm not a dope."

"That second U-turn. Tell me about it."

"What's there to tell about a U-turn? You turn the steering wheel and you turn the car around and that's all there is to it."

"That second U-turn. Did you make it right away?"

"No. Like I told you I stayed there and watched the taxi going away."

"You're trying to tell me you saw the taxi going away and you just stayed there and watched it go away. That doesn't make sense."

"My car can't do more than thirty."

"All right, that does make sense," Parry said. "But you didn't know the taxi would go past thirty. So again it doesn't make sense. There was a reason why you didn't follow that taxi and I know what it is and you know I know what it is. You saw a car going after that taxi."

"What do you mean a car?"

"A car. A machine. An automobile. You saw it following the taxi. That's why you waited there. You saw that car going down the street with its headlights turned off. You didn't know who it was but you knew it was going after the taxi. So here's what you thought. You thought it could be the police. Then again maybe it wasn't the police. And as long as you weren't sure you decided to make a U-turn and go back and watch the apartment house and wait for me. You figured maybe the taxi would shake the car and maybe I'd come back and even if I didn't come back there was a chance I'd stay on the loose. And even though I was on the loose you had something on her. And as long as you had something on her you were going to stay in the neighborhood and watch the apartment house. So that night you were playing for say ten or fifteen thousand. The next morning when you saw me coming back with the bandages on my face you knew you were still in it for ten or fifteen. Later that day you were patting yourself on the back and saying I'm no dope because a morning paper told you of a man murdered the night before and the police said I did it. So then you knew you were in it for all she had. You saw yourself with every cent of her two hundred thousand. Now all you see is a gun. And all you know is you've got to tell me about that car."

"I didn't see any car."

"Tell me or I'll shoot you above the knee. I'll keep on shooting until I tear your leg off."

"There wasn't any car," Arbogast said.

"There had to be a car. And it had to be a certain kind of a car. You got a chance to walk away from here with both legs if you tell me what kind of a car it was and if it's the same car I'm thinking of."

Arbogast looked at Parry's face.

Parry stood there waiting. He knew he had thrown everything into that one. That was the big one. That was the big bluff.

Arbogast looked at the gun.

"I don't have a thing to lose," Parry said.

Arbogast took a lot of air in his mouth and swallowed it.

"I can see it's no use," Parry said. "You won't tell me. And if you do tell me you won't be telling the truth. You've tried to make things miserable for her and for me and now I'm going to make things miserable for you."

"I'll tell you," Arbogast said.

"Tell me and make it good the first time, because there won't be a second time."

"It was a roadster," Arbogast said. "It had a canvas top and it was a bright color. I think it was orange."

"Bright orange," Parry said.

"A bright orange roadster," Arbogast said.

"And who was in it?"

"I couldn't see."

"All right," Parry said. "I guess that doesn't matter. I guess I got everything I need now."

"What happens to me?"

"That's not my worry."

"What are you going to do with me?"

"Nothing. I'm going to leave you here. What do I need you for? You're out of it now."

"If I'm out of it, let me go."

"Sure," Parry said. "You can go. Just turn around and start walking."

"Let me take my car."

"No," Parry said. "I'm taking that."

"You can't take my car."

"And you didn't think I could take your gun either but I took it."

"You won't get away."

"I'm not trying to get away," Parry said. "Not any more. I've got the big lead now. You handed it to me on a silver platter. You followed me and kept on following me until finally you gave me exactly what I needed. Maybe that's the way things are arranged. I don't know, do you?"

"I'm not out of it yet," Arbogast said.

"Maybe it's got to be that things always turn out this way," Parry said. "Maybe there's a certain arrangement to things and even if it takes a long time it finally has to work itself out."

"You're not taking that car."

"You can't tell me what I can take and what I can't take. All you can do is stand there and tell yourself you've lost a couple hundred thousand dollars. You know it's wonderful when guys like you lose out. It makes guys like me believe maybe we got a chance in this world."

"I tell you I'm not out of it yet."

"Take a walk, mister. Turn around and take a walk."

"I'm not through yet," Arbogast said. "I started out to get something and I'm gonna get it."

And he came leaping at Parry. And Parry lifted the gun and fired in the air hoping to scare Arbogast but Arbogast was beyond scaring and came slamming into Parry and they went down together with Arbogast trying for the gun. Parry stretched his arm back to get the gun away from Arbogast's hand. The weight of Arbogast was heavy on Parry and Arbogast went sliding forward to get the gun and Parry tried to slide away and Arbogast kept on sliding forward. Parry twisted and rolled but Arbogast was there now with the gun and trying with both hands to get the gun out of Parry's hand. Parry held onto the gun. Arbogast used his knees to keep Parry down and he was still going forward and making noises down in his throat as he tried to get the gun out of Parry's hand. Parry wouldn't let go of the gun and Arbogast kept going forward until he got a knee against Parry's throat and when he knew he had the knee there he pressed with the knee. Parry's head went back as the knee went jamming against his throat and hurting and blocking the air and the knee pressed harder and already it was bad and then it was very bad and it was getting worse but he wouldn't let go of the gun. And he had a feeling that his hand had become part of the gun and it was impossible for anything to get the gun away from his hand and he had a feeling that Arbogast knew that also because now the knee was taking everything away from him because the knee was so heavy and fierce against his throat and taking everything away from him and now the pain in his throat was a long tube of pain that went out from both ends, went up to his eyes and down to his stomach and twirled itself and kept twirling as the knee pressed harder. And he wouldn't let go of the gun as the pain went driving into him and going up and down the tube and in his stomach the tube was glossy and purple and in his brain the tube was black and burning and somewhere in the middle the tube was clear and it was a glass tube and he could see into it and know that Arbogast was no longer trying hard for the gun but trying hard to kill him with the knee in the throat. He could see it in the glassy clear middle of the tube, Arbogast burying him here and then going back to her and getting sixty thousand from her and going away and getting twenty more thousand from her and going away and coming back and getting thirty more thousand, forty more thousand, going away, coming back, going away and coming back and he could see her giving the money to Arbogast and he could get the sound of her asking Arbogast where he was and what had happened to him and Arbogast telling her he was somewhere around and what difference did it make where he was and what he was doing as long as she gave the money when she was asked for it. And the pain came slashing into his throat and pouring into the tube, going up and down, going fast now and it was killing him. Outside the pain he felt something on his hand, like a little warm breeze warmer than the warm yellow air, and he knew it was the breath of Arbogast, coming from the face of Arbogast close to his hand as Arbogast kept jamming the knee into his throat. He twisted his hand and, bringing it up as he twisted it, bringing the gun up, far outside the tube of pain he heard the scream of Arbogast and then he pulled the trigger.

18

ALL OF the tube was black and it was thick now, filling his throat, and in his head it was a big ball of black nothing. He could feel it up there and he knew it was getting bigger and he wondered if it was going to get too big. He could hear the sound of his dragging breath, and it was as if his breath was cinders grinding across more cinders.

Then it began to go away, the black and the cinders. He had his eyes closed as he reached up and loosened his tie and unbuttoned his collar. Now the air was going in smoother and faster and the tube was getting thin and then it was melting and then it was gone.

He opened his eyes. He saw dark brown branches and bright green leaves against the heavy hot yellow. He closed his eyes and told himself it would be nice to sleep for a while.

Gliding into sleep was very nice, and staying in sleep was soft and light and proper, because it was not a full sleep and he sensed the comfort of it as he rested there with his eyes closed, taking in the air and getting rid of the shock and the hurt.

Then when he opened his eyes again he knew he had slept there for a couple of hours at least and he knew he was much better now and he could get up. He got up slowly. He wondered if he could stand without leaning against anything. He could stand all right. He could move his legs. He felt his throat and it seemed to feel swollen but there was no pain now, only a heaviness on the outside. He turned and looked at Arbogast.

He saw Arbogast resting face down. The back of the head bulged out.

He went over and rolled the body face up. He looked at the face.

The eyes were open and wrenched loose, and there was blood where the flesh was split. The nose was torn apart and the hole was big and black and green and yellow, going up and going deep and going through the head and making the bulge. There was blood all over the mouth and all over the chin. There was dried blood in the ears and clotted blood on the coat and the shirtfront.

There was blood all over the gun where it rested near the body.

Without sound the body said, "I started out to get something."

Without sound Parry said, "You got it."

He stooped to pick up the gun and he saw the sticky blood all over his hand. He took out a handkerchief and wiped off the blood. Then he examined himself for more blood. He couldn't see any blood on his clothing and he knew the body had fallen away from him when the bullet went in.

He picked up the gun, keeping the handkerchief between his hand and the gun so as not to stain his hand with more blood. Then he walked deeper into the woods and established a hole for the gun. He covered the hole and smoothed it carefully. Then he walked away several yards, made another hole and buried the blood-stained handkerchief. Then he came back to the body and looked at it.

Without thinking of it, he reached in a coat pocket, took out a pack of cigarettes and a book of matches. He put a cigarette in his mouth as he looked at the body. Standing there and looking at the body he lit the cigarette.

He stood there smoking the cigarette and looking at the body.

He was puzzled.

He couldn't understand why he felt no regret, why he felt no horror at the sight of this dead thing on the ground, this thing he had killed. It had always seemed impossible that he would ever kill anyone, that he would ever have either the cause or the impulse.

Wondering about it, he knew he wasn't glad. At the same time he wasn't sorry. It was something mechanical and as he stood there looking at the body he knew it was one of those logical patterns. It was geometry. He was alive and the thing on the ground was dead. It had to be that way and the pattern was expanding now, taking in Irene, because he knew now he had wanted to stay with Irene, and he knew now every time he had gone away from her he had wanted to go back. And each time he had managed to hurdle that want as it came rolling toward him. Now it was with him again, greater than ever before, and there was no need for hurdling it, because he knew the identity of the murderer. He knew how and why Gert and Fellsinger had been killed, and he knew what he had to do now. He was building the method, telling himself how he could prove the guilt of the other person, forcing the showdown that would display and clarify his own innocence. And the pattern kept expanding, showing him the simple and ordinary happiness he had always wanted, the happiness he had expected to find with Gert, the clean and decent happiness of a little guy who wasn't important and had no special urge to be important and wanted nothing more than a daily job to do and someone to open a door for him at night and give him a smile.

It kept expanding. It began to glow. He would get a confession from the murderer after showing the murderer the absence of any loophole. And then his girl would be waiting for him. He had tears in his eyes, knowing she was waiting for him even now, knowing she wouldn't need to wait much longer. The happiness flowed from the pattern and flowed over him. A job in a war plant, and Sundays with his girl, and every morning and every night with his girl, his little girl.

He was telling himself that everything was all right now.

He walked away from the body. He walked through the woods, came out on the empty lot, walking slowly. He walked across the empty lot, slowly working on the cigarette as he told himself what he had to do. He crossed the road and got in the car and turned on the motor. Before he released the brake he turned his head and looked across the empty lot, across the yellow emptiness broken by the line of green woodland. And the woodland seemed very quiet and passive.

Then the car was moving. He took it into a U-turn and started back toward the city. His wrist watch was still working and it showed him two forty-five.

Coming into the city he parked the car on a narrow side street three blocks away from a busy section. He was feeling hungry and the pain of his throat had gone away completely. He told himself there was no reason why he shouldn't eat something. He got out of the car and walked toward the busy section. Then he was in a restaurant and he had pork chops and vegetables, a cup of coffee and a piece of pie. He sat there with another cup of coffee and a cigarette. He had another cigarette and then he walked out of the restaurant and went down the street and stood on a corner waiting for a taxi. Three taxis went past without paying any attention to him. The fourth taxi picked him up.

The taxi moved slowly through heavy traffic.

Parry looked at his trousers, his sleeves. He looked all over and there was no blood. The taxi was making a turn. He lit another cigarette. The taxi was getting away from the center of town. He moved across the seat so he could see himself in the rear-view mirror. He arranged his tie and smoothed his hair. He leaned back and breathed the heat that gushed in through open windows. The taxi made another turn. It was going faster now.

The taxi went up a steep street, then down, then up again. Then the taxi was going through a section devoted to apartment houses. The taxi came to a light and stopped and there was a drugstore on the corner.

"I'll get out here," Parry said.

"You said——"

"I know, but I'll get out here. It's only a couple blocks away."

"You're the doctor."

Parry paid his fare and walked into the drugstore. He picked up a telephone book and his forefinger ran down a line of names. He closed the book, went over to the counter and made change, getting two dimes and a nickel for a quarter. He went into a telephone booth and dialed a number.

Someone said, "Hello."

"Mrs. Rapf?"

"Yes?"

"How are you, Madge?"

"Who is this?"

"A friend of your husband."

"I don't have a husband. Anyway, I don't live with him."

"I know, that's why I'm calling."

"What do you want?"

"I'd like to meet you."

"Say, what is this?"

"Nothing very special, except I just started working here a

few weeks ago and I don't know many people. I met your husband and he told me about you. He gave you a nice build-up."

"Oh, he did, did he? What are you, a leper or something?"

"I told him I'd like to meet you and he gave me your number. I hope you don't mind."

"I think you got a lot of crust."

"May I see you?"

"You may not."

"Look, Madge, I think you'd like me."

"Who gave you permission to call me Madge?"

"When you see me you'll give me permission."

"Oh, I will, will I?"

"I think so. From what your husband said, I think you're the type I like. And I'm sure I'm the type you like."

"I don't like the fresh type."

"I'm not really fresh. Just sort of informal."

"What do you look like?"

"I'm good looking."

"How tall are you?"

"Average."

"Thin?"

"Yes."

"How old are you?"

"Thirty-six."

"How come you're not married?"

"I was. Twice. They weren't the type I was looking for. I'm looking for a certain type."

"You don't mince words, do you?"

"What's the use of mincing words?"

"What's your name?"

"Allan."

"Allan what?"

"Just call me Allan."

"What did my husband say?"

"I'll tell you when I see you."

"How do you know you're going to see me?"

"I don't know, because that's up to you. But if you're at all curious, I'm right here in the neighborhood. I could drop in and say hello. When we see each other we'll know if it's worthwhile getting started. And if it is we'll have dinner tonight."

"I'd like to know what he said."

"I'll tell you."

"Tell me now."

"I'd like to, but that might spoil my chances of seeing you."

"You putting a sword over my head?"

"Not because I want to. But I'm very anxious to meet you."

"I'm not dressed. I was in the bathtub. It's such a hot day."

"There's no hurry."

"I'll tell you what. I'll slip something on. Be here in fifteen minutes, make it twenty."

"All right, twenty minutes," he said, and he hung up. He walked out of the booth and went over to the counter and asked a clerk for a pack of cigarettes and the clerk handed them to him. Then he glanced at his wrist watch. The clerk asked him if there was anything else. He said he didn't think so. Then he saw boxes of candy stacked in pyramid fashion and he asked the price and the clerk said two dollars and he asked the clerk if there was something more expensive. The clerk ducked under the counter and came up with a violet box with violet satin ribbons all around it and said four and a half. Parry said that was really expensive and it ought to be something special. The clerk said it was really something special, all right, it was continental style chocolates and there wasn't much of that stuff around any more and this was the last box in the store and if he wanted something really special he ought to take this while the taking was good. He bought the box for four dollars and fifty cents plus tax and he told the clerk to wrap it up fancy and the clerk smiled knowingly and went to work on the box. Parry took the package and walked over to the magazine stand and stood there looking at the covers. A woman came in and bought a hot-water bottle. A little boy came in and bought a bar of candy. A man came in holding a hand to a swollen jaw with a prescription in the other hand. Parry glanced at his wrist watch. A young woman came in and asked for something and the clerk tried to make a date with her and she asked the clerk why wasn't he wearing a discharge pin. He said he had a double hernia and he'd show her if she wanted to see and she walked out. The clerk came out from behind the counter and came over to Parry and said things like that burned him up. He opened his shirt and showed Parry an awful looking scar that

ran from his chest down along his ribs and he said he got that
at Kasserine Pass. Parry glanced at his wrist watch. The clerk
said it burned him up the way people went around making remarks and he said he was good and fed up with people anyway.
He was buttoning his shirt and saying one of these fine days he
was going to haul off and punch somebody in the mouth. The
owner of the store came out of a small side room and stood in
the center of the store looking out through the open doorway
at the black street turned yellow by the sun. A little girl came
in and said she forgot what her mother sent her for and went
out again. The owner of the store put his hand in front of an
electric fan and shook his head and walked across the store and
turned on another electric fan. A sailor came in and sat down
at the soda fountain and asked for a peach ice-cream soda. The
clerk said there wasn't any peach. The sailor took strawberry
and sat there mixing the ice cream with the soda and said that
was the only way to enjoy an ice-cream soda. An old woman
came in and bought a bottle of mineral oil and walked out.
The sailor said it was sure a hot day and the clerk said it sure
was and the sailor asked for another strawberry ice-cream soda.
Parry glanced at his wrist watch and walked out of the store.

He walked down the street, turned, went down another
street, turned and he was on the street that was all apartment
houses. He knew the street. He knew the apartment house,
the white brick structure with the black iron gate and the black
window frames. He lit a cigarette, crossed the street and went
through the open gate. He glanced at his wrist watch as he
entered the vestibule. Then he looked at the listing and he saw
her name and he pressed the button. There was a buzzing response. He opened the door and went into the lobby.

In the elevator he dropped the cigarette and stepped on it.
The elevator took him to the fifth floor. He walked down the
hall. He remembered the hall, everything about it. He told
himself there was a certain way he had to go about this, and
what he ought to do was stand here a moment and itemize the
things he had to say and the order in which they were to be
said. Then he was thinking that it might not be a good idea to
rehearse it this way because that would be mechanical and he
had to avoid the mechanical now. He remembered the way
he had pulled it out of Arbogast, the way he had hammered

away at the U-turns to get Arbogast's mind back to that night and specific moments of that night, getting Arbogast to see it again, going back to the first U-turn, the waiting before the first U-turn, the waiting before the second U-turn, seeing that Arbogast wasn't really back there yet and drilling the U-turns into Arbogast, keeping Arbogast there with the U-turns, keeping Arbogast on that street in those moments, then the first U-turn, and then the second U-turn, and the interval again between the first and second U-turn so that Arbogast would stay there and be there long enough to remember. He had not planned that and he knew that if he had planned something it would not have been the U-turns. And it was only because of the U-turns that he had managed to get it out of Arbogast. It was a spontaneous maneuver and there was nothing mechanical in it and there must be nothing mechanical in this.

He was at the door now.

He knocked on the door.

19

THE DOOR OPENED.

She stood there looking at his face. Then she was looking him up and down. Then again she was looking at his face.

She was thin. She was about five feet four and she didn't weigh much more than a hundred.

She had an ordinary face without anything pretty in it. She had eyes the color of an old telegraph pole. Her nose was short and wide at the base and too wide for her face and her mouth was too large. But she wasn't really ugly. It was just that she wasn't pretty. She was tan and there was something artificial about the tan, as if she got it from some kind of a lamp. Her hair was dyed darkish orange. She wore it parted in the center and brought back with her ears showing. She was wearing a bright orange house coat and pale orange slacks and she wore sandals that showed her toenails painted bright orange. She had a cigarette in her hand and the smoke came up and rolled slowly over her head.

"Come in," she said.

Parry walked in and closed the door. He stood on a dark orange broadloom carpet. It was fairly new. Everything in the apartment was changed and fairly new. Everything was orange or leaned toward orange. There were orange lines running down and crossways on the frames of the big window. There was a big vase of glazed orange on the left side of the window and on the right side there was a conference of Indian pottery all white except for zigzag orange lines around the middle.

She seated herself in a low and rounded chair of pale orange and indicated the dark orange sofa.

Parry sat down. He was looking at her. He put the package on the sofa.

She said, "I don't think I should have let you come here."

"Don't you like what you see?"

"That's not the point. I don't usually do things this way."

"Well, I'm glad I came."

"Would you like a drink?" She was looking at the package.

"Please. Something cold."

She got up and went into the kitchen. She came out with a tray that had two tall glasses half-filled with ice, a dish of sliced limes and a bottle of carbonated water. She opened a pale orange cabinet and took out a bottle of gin. She mixed the drinks.

Parry sipped his drink and looked at the carpet.

She said, "What did my husband say?" She glanced at the package.

Parry looked up. She was opening her mouth to get at the drink. He saw gold inlays glimmering among her teeth.

He said, "Gave me a description."

"Accurate?"

"Yes."

She took a big drink. "What else?" She glanced again at the package.

"He said you weren't easy to get along with."

"Maybe I'm not."

"Maybe that's what I like."

"Are you easy to get along with?"

"Sometimes. It depends."

She smiled at him. Her mouth was open and he saw the gold inlays again. She said, "What else?"

"About me?"

"No. What my husband said about me." She looked at the package.

"He said you almost drove him out of his mind."

"And what else?" She had her mouth open wide as she smiled.

He looked at the gold inlays. He said, "Well, your husband claimed you had a habit of putting on the act."

"What kind of an act?"

"Acting as if you didn't have much brains, merely an ignorant sort of pest."

"Is that what he really said?"

"Yes, and he said you were really a shrewd manipulator and when you were out to get something you stopped at nothing. He said he left you because he was afraid of you."

"And what do you think?"

"I think he had something there."

"Do you think you'd be afraid of me?" She looked at the package.

"Every now and then. And that's where you'd have a problem. You'd have to guess when."

She laughed. The gold inlays caught some of the sun and juggled it. She said, "What do you do?" And she laughed again.

"I work in an investment security house."

She stopped laughing. She looked at him. She said, "What do you do there?"

"I'm a customer's man."

"What house?"

"Kinney."

"How long have you worked there?"

"Only a few weeks. I told you I just got in town."

"How did you meet my husband?"

"He came in to make an investment."

"Where's he getting the money to make investments?"

"He didn't invest much."

"How much?"

"I'm not saying."

She stood up. She said, "Are you going to tell me?"

"No."

"All right then, get out of here."

"Okay." He got up and he was going toward the door.

She started to laugh. He turned and looked at her. The gold inlays seemed magnified. She said, "You were really going to go, weren't you?"

"Yes."

"And would you have gotten in touch with me again?"

"No."

"Why not?" She looked at the package on the sofa.

"You'd start asking questions about him. You've got him on your mind."

"Don't be silly."

"All right, then, you've got his money on your mind."

"You don't go for that, do you?"

"Part of it I don't go for. I don't care what you've got on your mind. But when I'm around I don't want to hear questions about him or his money."

"Who said you were going to be around?"

"I didn't. Neither did you. But we both know."

"Don't tell me what I know." She looked at the package.

"All right, I won't. There's no point in my telling you if you know already."

She looked at the package. She said, "Is that for me?"

"Yes."

She went over and opened the package. She untied the violet satin ribbons and opened the box and looked at the chocolate candy.

She smiled. She was very pleased. She said, "This is lovely."

"I'm glad you like it."

She put a piece of chocolate in her mouth and he saw the gold inlays again. She munched the chocolate and said, "It's very delicious."

She sat down in the low rounded chair with the box of candy in her lap. Her mouth was soft with contentment and her eyes glittered with anticipation. She was stimulated now and that was what he wanted to see.

She said, "Thank you for the candy, Allan. Allan what?"

"Linnell."

She was looking at his mouth. She said, "When I looked at the candy I knew I was going to like the taste of it." She kept on looking at his mouth.

He said, "Well, what do you think? Do you think we've got something here?"

She leaned back and lifted another piece of candy. She smiled and said, "Allan Linnell." Then she put the candy in her mouth and bit into it.

And that told him he was ready.

He said, "I should have brought the candy in an orange box."

She watched him gazing at the dark orange carpet. She said, "Yes, it's my big weakness."

"I bet everything you own is on the orange side."

"Just about." She was looking at his mouth.

"Even your car?"

"Even my car. It's bright orange. And my jewelry is orange beryl. And my favorite drink is an orange blossom, just because of the color."

"Yes," he said. "I guess certain colors appeal to certain people."

She was looking at his mouth as he said that, and when it got through her ears and into her head her gaze dropped and she was looking at his suit. Then her eyes came up again and she was looking at his eyes. Then her gaze dropped once more and she was looking at the grey worsted fabric and the violet stripe. And she looked at the violet box of candy. And she looked at the violet lines in the grey suit. And she looked at his eyes.

Then she shuddered and closed her eyes.

Then she opened her eyes and looked at him.

Without moving from the chair she was trying to take herself out of the room.

He said, "You know. You recognize the suit. You got a good look at it that night. Now you're looking at my face and you don't believe it but there's nothing else for you to do and no other way for you to take it. You've got to believe it."

She was trying to get out of the chair and she couldn't move.

He said, "It's really me."

"Go away," she said. "Go away and leave me alone."

"I can't do that, Madge. I can't do that now. I'm the Pest now. You've always been the Pest but now I'm the Pest. I've got to be. It's this way, Madge, I've got to stay here with you and I've got to pester you because I know you killed Gert and you killed Fellsinger and I've got to make you own up to it."

"Go away."

"You can't send me away, Madge. You did that once but you can't do it now. You're very clever, Madge, but you're not an enchantress. In a dream I had you were a bright orange enchantress on a high trapeze, and you got me to go up there with you on the trapeze, and once you had me up there you let me drop. I was broken and dying and everyone was sorry for me. And you were up there on the high trapeze, laughing at me and showing your gold inlays. But I got away from the dream. And you can't get away. You're still up there on the high trapeze and you're all alone."

"Go away, Vincent. Please go away. If you go away now they'll never find you."

"Now I want them to find me."

"They'll kill you."

"Do I look worried?"

She shuddered again. She stared at him.

He said, "No, Madge, I'm not worried. I know you did it and I know I can convince them you did it. I've got facts to prove you followed me from Irene Janney's apartment the night Fellsinger was murdered. That's the first thing I'm going to give them. Then I'll take them back to the day you killed Gert. I'll tell them why you killed her and I'll show them how you killed her. You killed her because you were on the trapeze and you were alone. You wanted me up there with you. I never realized how badly you wanted me. It must have been awful, knowing that the only way to get me was by getting rid of Gert. So you put on a pair of gloves and you picked up that ash tray and you killed her. And you had me. You had me up there on the trapeze but once you had me you didn't want me any more. So you threw me away. You told the police Gert said I did it. At the trial you testified cleverly, giving them all the reasons why I would want to kill Gert, drilling it into them that I killed her. They had my fingerprints on the ash tray and they had your story and that was enough for them. And I had nothing. Because I knew nothing. I thought it was an accident that killed her and I didn't know how badly you had wanted me."

"You can't take them back."

"But I can, Madge. The other night when you and Bob were in Irene's apartment you made certain statements and Bob made certain statements and I can take them back with that."

Her gaze drifted past him. She said, "You've got Bob with you."

"He doesn't know it yet, but he's with me. And you're alone. And when I take them back to the day Gert was killed I'll have all of them with me and you'll remain alone. When you come right down to it, Madge, you've always been alone—"

"Give it up, Vincent. Walk away from it. You can't go out selling when you have nothing to sell."

"—because you wanted to be alone. Because whenever you got what you wanted you were anxious to get rid of it. But when you saw someone else get hold of it you couldn't stand that. You knew Irene Janney wanted me and you killed Fellsinger because it was your best way of making sure she'd never get me. You knew they'd give me the chair for the murder of Fellsinger. That was the big thing in your mind when you killed him, when you told yourself you were rid of me once and for all and no one else would have me. It was more important than any other thing, even your practical reasons for killing him."

"Take my advice, Vincent, and give it up. There's no way you can build a case against me."

"You see, Madge? Even now you're still trying to make sure she doesn't get me. You're really a specimen, Madge. It's almost impossible to figure you out. But it just happens bright orange shows up against a dark street."

"That's no evidence. You don't have anything there. What you need is a confession. That's what you're trying to get, isn't it?"

"Well, it would simplify matters, anyway. As things stand now I know what you did, the reasons and the methods. And the problems you faced. Your first real problem came when you knocked on the door of Irene's apartment and then you heard the phonograph going and then you heard me telling you to go away. You had a feeling that wasn't Bob's voice and when you were outside you kept looking at the window. And then you checked up on Bob, and meanwhile you learned I was loose from San Quentin. And here's where you get that Academy Award, because you knew she was interested in me, you had it analyzed from the very beginning, and underneath that mask of an ignorant pest you were laughing at her, because here she was, in there pitching for me and I didn't even know there was such a person as Irene Janney."

"She told you that. She told you to come here."

"No. You're not even warm. I'm the banker now. I've got all of it. I can see you with your problems. I can see you thinking it over, telling yourself I was on the loose, and as long as you knew and I knew I didn't kill Gert, it was possible I'd use my freedom to try and find out who did kill her. Then you were worried about it, you knew you had to do something definite and drastic. There was that very big surprise, that Irene Janney had more brains than you gave her credit for and she was hiding me in her apartment. So you knew you had to begin with keeping an eye on the apartment. Then when I came out you followed me. Your bright orange roadster followed the taxi to Fellsinger's place. You watched when I pressed the button. When I went up you came in and saw Fellsinger's name alongside that particular button. You knew it was only a question of time before the police would visit Fellsinger and ask him if I had tried to make contact. That time element was important. You wanted me to hurry and come down, and when I came down you slipped out from wherever you were hiding and you went in and pressed that same button. You were planning it then, as you went upstairs. And what you wanted most of all was to make sure that Irene Janney would never get me. Next to that you wanted to make sure Fellsinger wouldn't help me to find out who killed Gert. Then again you knew if you killed Fellsinger every finger would point at me because the police knew of my friendship with Fellsinger and you were certain they'd find my fingerprints in the room and that was all they needed. So you went in there and killed Fellsinger. You got talking to him and you got him off guard and you did away with him. Didn't you?"

"Yes."

"Will you tell that to the police?"

"No."

"They'll get it out of you anyway. Because they'll have facts to work with. They'll have that motivation aspect. Don't forget the big item about Bob. He'll be with me."

She smiled. "That's no good. Bob would be recognized as a prejudiced witness. Besides, what could he say? He'd say I wanted you. What tangible proof would he have?"

"A signed statement from the man you hired to follow him. The man who turned right around and played both ends against the middle and followed me to your apartment. That signed statement, Madge, that does it."

She stopped smiling. She said, "All right, that's concrete in itself, but it isn't sufficient. The jealousy factor isn't strong enough."

"Then let's make it stronger. Let's bring in a nasty bit of gossip concerning Bob and Gert."

"Bob. And Gert. Bob and Gert. No. No, don't try that on me. That's not possible."

"But that's the way it is. And when Bob gets up and admits his connection with Gert it bursts the whole thing wide open."

"I'll tell them I never knew anything like that was going on. And I'll be telling the truth."

"They won't believe you, Madge. You hired that man to follow Bob. That's an act of frenzy and it establishes motivation. You're afraid now. And I'll tell you this—as soon as you knew I was here in town you were really scared stiff. Otherwise you would have found a way to tip off the police and let them know I was hiding at Irene Janney's apartment. But you were really scared by that time, whereas before that you were only uncomfortable. And now you couldn't bring the police in on it because you thought Irene Janney and I were working on something and maybe we had it at a point where we were just about ready to hand it over to the police. The only way you could bust that up was to bring in a second killing, to kill Fellsinger. That's where the practical side comes in, but it wasn't practical enough. You overlooked a big issue. If I had facts to prove I hadn't killed Gert, why would I want to kill Fellsinger?"

"You know, I thought of that."

"You thought of it when it was too late. Fellsinger was already dead. You had slipped up on that and maybe you had slipped up on other things, so you were still afraid to give it to the police. The night you came to Irene's place you weren't putting on any act. You were really in bad shape. You were hoping I wouldn't be there and it would mean I had skipped town and I was running way from the whole thing. That was what you wanted, because then you'd know for sure the Fellsinger investment was paying dividends your way, and you could finally talk to the police. But here it comes, trouble again. Irene says Bob will be arriving any minute now and she won't let you hide in the bedroom. So you know I'm in that bedroom. Then you're sick. You're going around on a spinning wheel and you can't get off. What's Vincent Parry up to? What's keeping him here in San Francisco? Why doesn't he run away? What is he waiting for? And how long is he going to wait? I'm afraid—I'm afraid. Right, Madge?"

She ran thin forefingers up and down the creases of the pale orange slacks. She looked at her knees, then she arranged the violet box of candy in the middle of her lap and studied the contents.

Parry folded his arms and watched her.

She selected a chocolate and brought it up slowly toward her mouth and when she had it halfway there she stopped its progress, she let it come into her palm and her hand closed on it and she squeezed it. The chocolate surface broke and white butter cream came gushing out between her fingers. Her head swayed from side to side and she opened her mouth as if in a frantic need for air. She kept squeezing the mashed candy and then all at once snapped her hand open and looked at what she had done. There was a mess of chipped chocolate and butter cream all over her palm and dripping between her fingers. She let out a grinding noise of disgust and rubbed the stuff on her slacks. Then she rubbed her hand on the bright orange house coat, kept rubbing until her hand was clean again. Then she looked at the mess on her slacks and her house coat and she raised her head and her mouth remained open, wide open now in a loose, sagging sort of way.

She said, "I want you, Vincent. At night I've cried in my want for you."

He unfolded his arms and held them stiff, away from his sides.

"All right, Vincent. Let's examine it. She's got you now. She's got you and you've got me. But if you don't hold onto me it means they're still after you. And as long as you don't have me it means you can't prove anything because I won't be there to admit anything. Motivation alone isn't enough. They'll want certain facts."

"You'll be there," he said. He took a few steps backward so that he was between the low rounded chair and the door.

"You're wrong, Vincent. You'll never be able to prove it because I won't be there. You need evidence, you need something concrete, you need a witness. And you don't have a witness, do you? No. Of course you don't."

He watched her. She began to laugh lightly and with enjoyment.

The various shades of orange were merging and melting and flowing toward him.

She kept laughing. She said, "You don't have a witness—no witness."

"I've got the facts and I've got you and that's all I need."

"The facts aren't enough. You can't prove them without me."

"But I've got you."

"No, Vincent. You don't have me." She stood up. She smiled at him.

He said, "Do you think I'm going to stand here and let you get away?"

She took a long breath and he could hear the dragging in her throat. She said, "They'll always be looking for you. She wants you very badly. And that's why she'd be willing to run away with you and keep on running away and always scared, always running away. And it would ruin everything for her but she wouldn't care because she'd be with you and that's all she wants. And you know that and that's why you won't take her. That's why she doesn't have you now and she'll never have you and nobody will ever have you. And that's the way I wanted it. And that's the way it is. And it will always be that way."

She laughed at him and he saw the gold inlays. He saw the bright orange going back and away from him, going too fast. She was running backwards, throwing herself backwards as he went after her but she was too fast and he saw the gold inlays glittering and the bright orange flaring as her arms went wide as the gold inlays flashed as she hit the window and the window gave way and the cracked glass went spraying and she went through.

He was at the window. He leaned through the broken window and he saw her going down, the bright orange acrobat falling off the trapeze. And it was as if she was taking him with her as she went down, the bright orange rolling and tossing and going down and hitting the pavement five stories below. He saw two baby carriages and two women and he heard the women screeching.

Then he saw the upturned faces of the women. And he knew they were staring at the face of the man up there, framed in broken glass. They screeched louder.

He ran out of the apartment, thinking of Irene, darted toward the elevator, thinking of Irene, knew he couldn't use the elevator or the front entrance. He ran down the corridor and took the fire escape. He was thinking of Irene. He used an alley and a narrow street and another alley and finally a street with car tracks. He waited there, thinking of Irene and then a street car came along and took him to the center of town. He ran to the hotel, his brain jammed with Irene. He went up to his room and got into the new clothes and packed his things. Then he was downstairs and paying for one day and saying he was called out of town unexpectedly and he was thinking of Irene and he was seeing her alone in her little apartment and at the window as he went away and wanting him to come back, wanting him to take her with him. And he was trying to tell her how much he wanted to take her with him but he couldn't take her with him because now there was no way to prove his innocence and they would always be running away and even though the road was wide it was dark, frantic, and there was no certainty. There would be a haven now and then but no certainty and he couldn't do that to her. He told himself she was all alone and he would always think of her as all alone and he told himself to go back there and take her with him. He told himself he couldn't do that to her. Here she had a home and she was safe. With him she would never be safe and she would never have a home because a home was never a home when it was a hideaway and he knew what it was to hide and run and hide again. He couldn't ask her to share that even though he knew she would leap at sharing it. And he knew once she had it, once it hit her, she wouldn't say anything and she would cover up and smile and say everything was all right. That was Irene. That was his girl. That was the happiness, the sweet purity he had always wanted and wanted now more than anything. And he could hear her pleading with him to come back and take her. He could hear himself pleading with himself to go back and take her. And under flashing sunlight the road remained dark.

He walked out of the hotel and kept walking until he found a two-by-four bus depot. He went in and a lot of people in low-priced clothes were sitting on a bench facing a splintered counter. He went up to the counter and a young man behind the counter asked him where he wanted to go and he said

Patavilca and the young man said what was that again and he said Arizona and the young man asked where in Arizona and he said Maricopa.

The young man picked up a route map and asked him if he was going alone and he nodded. Then he had his ticket and he found a place on the bench and sat down to wait. It was very warm and sticky in there. He began to think of Arbogast.

They would never know who had done away with Arbogast. They wouldn't even take the trouble to attempt finding out. They had Arbogast listed as a cheap crook and it would be a convenience to cross him off the list. All very quick and automatic, easy to picture. Someone would come across the body and police would identify the body and bury it and say good riddance. But the picture was upside down.

The whole thing was upside down. And the world was spinning in the wrong direction. They had it completely diagnosed. There wasn't a segment of doubt in their minds. This man had killed his wife. And then he had gone ahead and killed his best friend. And then while he was at it he had sought out the woman who had testified against him and he had pushed her through a window.

His lips were building a dim smile. The taxi driver was coming into his mind, along with Coley. He wondered if they were still speaking to each other. Probably, because they couldn't discuss their awful mistake with anyone else. The taxi driver would say it didn't pay to be nice to people. Coley would say there was nothing they could do about it and they might just as well forget about it. And they would never forget about it. They would always feel certain they had helped a killer to kill two more people. He felt sorry for them. He wished there was a way he could straighten them out on that.

Someone said, "Do these buses ever run on schedule?"

A skinny woman with two children on her lap said, "What do they care? You think they're worried about us?"

"That's the way it goes." The someone was a tall man wearing a straw hat. He had a thin mouth that flapped down at the corners. His tie was knotted a good two inches below the collar. "Yes," he said, working his mouth as if there was something sour inside, "it's just one big battle royal all the way through. Nobody gives a hang about the other fellow."

"It's so hot in here," the woman said. The smaller child started to slip away from her lap and she pulled him back and said, "Sit still."

The man sighed. He took off the straw hat, scratched the top of a bald head. "Yes," he said, gazing at the wall, "that's the way it goes."

"Sometimes," the woman said, "I get tired. I just get sick and tired of everything. Nothing to look forward to."

The man gestured toward the children. "You got them kids," he said. "That's something. Look at me. I got nobody."

"These are my sister's kids," the woman said. "She's been sick and I been caring for them. Now she's all better and I'm taking them back."

"Where?"

"Tucson. Then I'll be coming back here and I'll be alone again. I tell you it aint bearable when a person has nothing to look forward to."

"You mean these aint your kids?"

"I wish they were. Look at them. They're fine little boys."

The man was looking at the woman. The man handled his tie and brought the knot up to the collar. The knot glowed like a lamp far down a dark road.

Parry left the bench and walked out of the bus depot. He was walking fast. He went into a drugstore on the corner and picked up a telephone book. He found the number he wanted and went into the booth and put a nickel in the slot. He dialed and waited while the other phone rang once and then twice and then she said hello.

He said, "It's Allan."

"Where are you? Are you all right?"

"Yes. What are you doing?"

"Just sitting here."

"All right. Listen. It was Madge. But I can't use it. I went up there for a showdown and she did away with herself. Went through the window. You'll read all about it in the afternoon edition. You'll read I pushed her out. I just want you to know I didn't push her out."

"That's not why you called. There's something else you want me to know."

He grinned while tears arrived. He said, "It's nice when you have something to look forward to. Get yourself a map of South America. In Peru there's a little town on the coast. Patavilca. Say it. Tell me where it is."

"Patavilca. In Peru."

"Good. Now listen. I won't write. There can't be any connection whatsoever. And we've got to wait. We've got to give it plenty of time. Maybe they'll get a lead on you and they'll keep an eye on you for a while. Meanwhile if I manage to make it down there I'll be waiting there for you. And if you see your way clear—listen to all these ifs."

"We'll skip the ifs," she said. "I get the idea and that's all I require. The general idea. Now hang up on me. Just like that—hang up."

He hung up. He hurried back to the depot and saw the bus gliding into the parking space alongside the waiting room. The passengers formed a jagged line and going into the bus they moved hungrily toward empty seats. Parry found a seat in the rear of the bus and gazing frontward he saw the man in the straw hat sitting next to the skinny woman and the two children sat together across the aisle. The driver came hopping into the bus and closed the door. A few people on the outside were waving good-by. The driver started the motor and then he faced the passengers and he said, "All set?"

NIGHTFALL

Chapter One

I T WAS one of those hot, sticky nights that makes Manhattan show its age. There was something dreary and stagnant in the way all this syrupy heat refused to budge. It was anything but a night for labor, and Vanning stood up and walked away from the tilted drawing board. He brushed past a large metal box of water colors, heard the crash as the box hit the floor. That seemed to do it. That ended any inclination he might have had for finishing the job tonight.

Heat came into the room and settled itself on Vanning. He lit a cigarette. He told himself it was time for another drink. Walking to the window, he told himself to get away from the idea of liquor. The heat was stronger than liquor.

He stood there at the window, looking out upon Greenwich Village, seeing the lights, hearing noises in the streets. He had a desire to be part of the noise. He wanted to get some of those lights, wanted to get in on that activity out there, whatever it was. He wanted to talk to somebody. He wanted to go out.

He was afraid to go out.

And he realized that. The realization brought on more fright. He rubbed his hands into his eyes and wondered what was making this night such a difficult thing. And suddenly he was telling himself that something was going to happen tonight.

It was more than a premonition. There was considerable reason for making the forecast. It had nothing to do with the night itself. It was a process of going back, and with his eyes closed he could see a progression of scenes that made him shiver without moving, swallow hard without swallowing anything.

There was a pale blue automobile, a convertible. That was a logical color, that pale blue, logical for the start of it, because it had started out in a pale, quiet way, the pale blue convertible cruising along peacefully, the Colorado mountainside so calm and pretty, the sky so contented, all of this scene pale blue in a nice even sort of style. And then red came into it, glaring red, the hood and fenders of the smashed station wagon, the hard gray of the boulder against which the wrecked car was resting, the hard gray turning into black, the black of the revolver, the black remaining as more colors moved in. The green of the hotel room, the orange carpet, or maybe it wasn't orange—it could have been purple, a lot of those colors could have been other colors—but the one color about which there was no mistake was black. Because black was the color of a gun, a dull black, a complete black, and through a whirl of all the colors coming together in a pool gone wild, the black gun came into his hand and he held it there for a time impossible to measure, and then he pointed the black gun and he pulled the trigger and he killed a man.

He took his clenched fists away from his eyes, opened his eyes and brought himself back to this room. Turning, he saw the drawing board, and it threw an invisible rope toward him, the rope pulling him in, urging him to get away from yesterday and stay with now. Because now had him listed as James Van-ning, a commercial artist specializing in the more intricate kind of work that art departments of advertising agencies hand out to proven experts. Tonight he was mixed up with one of the usual rush jobs and the deadline was four tomorrow afternoon. But if he went to sleep now he could get up early tomorrow and finish the assignment in time to satisfy the art director.

If he went to sleep now. That was downright comical. Sleep. As if sleep was something that came automatically. As if all he had to do was put his head against the pillows and close his eyes and go to sleep. He laughed without sound. He laughed at the picture of himself trying to sleep. Every night he had a debate with sleep and it was one rebuttal after another and it kept on like that until it knocked him out just about the time when the sun got started. That was his sleep.

He walked into the bathroom and saw himself in the mirror. Average height but on the husky side. Curly blond hair and quite a lot of it, so that was no worry. The worry came in where suggestions of silver showed here and there through the blondness. Very little silver, hardly noticeable against gold, but even the little that was there was too much silver for a man only thirty-three. And the lines under his eyes and around his lips, those lines weren't age. Those lines were ordeal. And even his complexion. It still retained considerable South Pacific, specifically Saipan and Okinawa, but the darkness of it was more shadow than sun. It seemed that there was shadow all over him, all around him.

More shadow moved in, and he decided to fight it. He took a shower and a shave, he put on a freshly cleaned and pressed palm beach suit. And he was getting his arm through a sleeve when he heard the noise from down the hall.

"A cop," the voice said. "Get a cop."

Another voice from out there. "What's the matter with you?"

"Get a cop."

Vanning's teeth came together, biting at nothing. He couldn't breathe. He stood there, waiting.

"What are you all excited about? What's wrong?"

"Who's excited? All I want is a drink. Bring me a cop of water."

"Why don't you learn to speak English?"

"Shut opp and bring me a drink."

From there on it became a typical husband-and-wife discussion, the wife yelling for a drink of water and continuing the yelling after she got it. Vanning used up a minute or so trying to decide whether they were Spanish or Italian or Viennese. He wondered when they had moved in. He wondered about all his neighbors. It was a point he made, keeping away from them. Keeping away from everybody.

He told himself to get a move on. He didn't know where he was going, but wherever it was, he was in a big hurry to get there.

Chapter Two

THE HEAT came in waves, big rollers of heat wallowing in from all parts of Manhattan and down from a sky of melted asphalt. The heat flowed into Washington Square Park and stayed there despite a sporadic breeze. Vanning remained in the park only a few minutes. As he left the park, he aimed toward the corner of Christopher Street and Sheridan Square. There were a lot of lights in that direction, and he figured on a drink or two and maybe a chat with some unimportant person who would talk about unimportant things.

He was crossing a street and turning a corner when a man came up to him and asked for a light. There were no street lamps in this particular area and Vanning couldn't get a good look at the man. He could see, however, a small figure and a mustache and neatly combed black hair. He lit a match and applied it to the man's cigarette. And in the glow he obtained a fairly comprehensive view of the face. But it lasted only a moment. There was no special reason for analyzing the face.

"Hot night," the man said.

"Terrific."

"I saw some kids diving off the docks," the man said. "They got the right idea."

"If we did it," Vanning said, "people would call us crazy."

"The trouble with people is they don't understand people."

The man had a pleasant voice and a free-and-easy air, and Vanning told himself there was nothing unusual about the matter. The man merely wanted a light and a minute or so of chewing the rag, and if he was going to start worrying about all these little things he might as well put himself in a sanitarium.

The man leaned against a building wall. Vanning lit a cigarette for himself. They stood there like a couple of calm animals in a calm forest. The night was all around them and the streets were quiet and the heat was dominant.

"I wonder how they stand it in the tropics," the man said.

"They're born into it."

"I don't think I could stand it," the man said. "Ever been near the Equator?"

"A few times."

"What's it like?"

"Great," Vanning said. "You go nuts but you don't mind it, because everybody goes nuts."

"I've never traveled much."

"Don't go near the Equator," Vanning said. "This is twenty per cent of what it's like."

"When were you there?"

"During the war."

"I didn't get in," the man said. "A wife and kids."

"They put me in the Navy," Vanning said, and listened to himself saying it, and told himself to put a lock on his big mouth. He figured it was about time to start moving.

But the man said, "You see much action?"

"Enough."

"Where?"

"Around Borneo." He told himself it was all right. It would last maybe another minute and then he would tell the man he had to meet someone at Jimmy Kelly's or someplace and he would go away and the incident would fade into one of those vague little incidents that never make the front pages or the history books.

"I envy you," the man said.

"Why?"

"Farthest I've ever been away from New York is Maine. I used to go there summers, before things got tough."

"Hard going?"

"Lately," the man said.

"What's your line?"

"Research."

"Business?"

"More or less."

"I'm in advertising," Vanning said.

"Agency?"

"Free-lance artist."

"How do you fellows make out?"

"It runs in cycles. We don't know what we depend on. Maybe the sun spots."

"I think we're in for another depression," the man said.

"It's hard to say."

The man let his cigarette fall to the sidewalk. He stepped on it. "Well," he said, "I think I'll be going. She always waits up for me."

Vanning was about to let the whole thing pass, but he found himself saying, "Been married long?"

"Eleven years."

"I wish I was married."

"You say that as though you mean it."

"I do."

"It has its points," the man said. "In the beginning we were all set to break up. Times I'd be eating breakfast and there she'd be across the table and I'd wonder if it was possible to get rid of her. Then I'd ask myself why and I couldn't think of a good reason."

"Maybe the freedom angle."

"You're free."

"It gets monotonous. I think if you're normal you've got to have someone. You've got to have something special and it's got to be around all the time."

"Can't that get monotonous?"

"How do you feel about it?"

"Monotony's a relative thing."

"That isn't a pun, is it?"

"No," the man said. "I'm saying it in a positive way. You go out and look for a thrill and when you get it there's no thrill. The only thrill is looking for it. When you have someone you can look for a thrill together."

"Isn't that going a little deep?"

"I met her at a dance," the man said. "I had a devil of a time really getting to know her. She hadn't been around much, and you know how it is in New York. I bet you'll find more virgins in New York than any other town in the country. I mean in ratio. Even the little towns in the sticks. This is one burg where they build a defense mechanism at an early age. You can wear yourself out breaking it down. But don't get the wrong idea. That isn't why I married her."

"Why did you marry her?"

"I got to like her," the man said. "We had a lot of fun to-gether. I don't know who you are and I'll never see you again in a hundred years, so it's all right to talk this way. I think it's a good idea to get things off your chest with strangers now and then."

"There's something to that."

"I developed a feeling for her," the man said. "I wanted to put my hands on her and at the same time I didn't want to do that and I got to thinking about it. It reached the point where I was buying things for her and I got a kick out of watching her face light up when she opened the packages. That had never happened before. We went around together for a little more than a year and then I went out and bought a ring."

"It always works that way."

"Not always," the man said. "I think I really fell in love with her about two years after the marriage. She was in the hospital then. We were having our first kid. I remember standing there at the bed, and there she was, and there was a baby, and I got all choked up. That was it, I guess. That was the real beginning."

"How many you got now?"

"Three."

"Three is just right."

"They're great kids," the man said. He raised a wrist toward his eyes and peered at the dial of a compact little watch. "Well," he said, "I've got to be running. Keep in trim."

"I will," Vanning said as the man started away. "Good luck."

"Thanks," the man said, and he was crossing the street. He turned a corner and walked up another block and crossed another street. A taxi came down the street in a listless way, the driver indifferent at the wheel, a cigarette miraculously hanging onto the driver's lips. The man raised his arm, waved it, and the taxi pulled toward the curb.

The man got in and gave the driver an address on the east side, slightly north of Forty-second Street, in the section known as Tudor City. The driver threw his cab into second gear and they were on their way.

In a little more than five minutes the man was home. He had an apartment on the seventh floor of a place once in the high-rent category but now toned down a bit. In the elevator he lit a cigarette, glanced again at his wrist watch as he left the elevator, and saw the hands indicating a quarter to twelve. Walking down the hall, he took a key ring from his trousers pocket, and as he came to the door marked 714 he glanced once more at his wrist watch. Then he inserted the key, opened the door and entered the apartment.

It was a pleasant little place, definitely little for a family of five, but furnished to give an impression of more space. The main element was a large window that showed the East River. And there was a grand piano that had put him in the red for several months. There was a presentable secretary desk with some intelligent-looking books behind glass. The top row was given over to a set of The Book of Knowledge, but underneath that it was all strictly adult stuff. A good deal of Freud and Jung and Horney and Menninger, and some lesser-known works by other psychiatrists and neurologists. The kids were always standing on chairs to get at The Book of Knowledge, and once in a while they'd mess around with the other books and sometimes use crayon on the pages, but the top row was the only place for The Book of Knowledge because the other rows weren't high enough. There'd been a bit of discussion about that, especially when the six-year-old daughter had torn out all the pictures in one of the more involved and pathological works on Man's Nervous System, but there just wasn't enough room for another bookcase and it was rather useless to make a big issue over the matter.

He came into the living room and his wife put down a book and stood up and walked toward him.

"Hello, Mr. Fraser."

"Hello, Mrs. Fraser."

He kissed her on the cheek. She wanted to be kissed on the mouth. He kissed her on the mouth. She was an inch or so taller than he was, and she was on the skinny side and had the kind of face they use in fashion magazine ads where they don't want to concentrate too much on the face. It was an interesting face even though there was nothing sensational about it. It was interesting because it showed contentment but no smugness.

She put her hands on the sides of his head. She rubbed his temples. "Tired?"

"Just a little."

"How about a drink?"

"I could eat something."

"Sandwich?"

"No meat. Something light. God, but it's hot."

"I couldn't get the kids to sleep. They must be swimming in there."

"You look cool."

"I was in the bathtub an hour," she said. "Come on in the kitchen. I'll fix you something."

In the kitchen he sat down at a small white table and she began preparing a salad. It looked good to her and she added things to it and made enough for two. There was a pitcher of lemonade and she put more ice and sugar and water in it and sat down at the table with him.

She watched him as he tackled the salad. He looked up and smiled at her. She smiled back.

She poured some lemonade for him and as he lifted a forkful of lettuce and hard-boiled egg toward his mouth she said, "Didn't you have dinner?"

"Who can eat in this weather?"

"I thought we'd get a breeze from the river."

"Should have sent you and the kids to the country."

"We went through that."

"It isn't too late," he said.

"Forget about it," she said. "The hot spell's almost over."

"I could kick myself."

"We'll go next year."

"We said that last summer."

"Is it my fault?"

"No," he said, "it's mine. I'm sorry, honey, really I am."

"You know something?" she said quietly. "You're a very nice guy."

"I'm not nice at all. I was thinking of the money."

"They want too much these days," she said. "The prices they ask, they're out of their minds. Out on Long Island you should see what they're asking."

"I'm thinking of the country."

"You're worried about the kids."

"You and the kids."

"Oh, stop it," she said. "You're making enough."

"I'm making a fortune. Next week I'm buying a yacht."

She added some mayonnaise to her salad, mixed it in, ate for a while, and while concentrating on the food she said, "Anything new?"

"Still checking." He sipped some lemonade. "It's a tough one."

"Is he still there?"

"Still there. Tonight I talked to him."

She stopped eating. She looked up. "What happened?"

"I just talked to him. Nothing phenomenal. He came out about eleven. Walked to the park. I followed him. He left the park and I walked up and asked for a match. That's about all."

"Didn't he say anything?"

"Nothing I could use. He's a difficult proposition. If there's anything criminal in that direction, I can't see it."

"Now, now——"

"I mean it, honey. He's got me buffaloed. For two cents I'd walk in and tell Headquarters they're on the wrong track."

"Suppose I gave you two cents?"

"I'd back out," he said.

She poured more lemonade into his glass. "I took your brown suit to the cleaner's. And you could use another pair of shoes."

"I'll wait till fall."

She studied his eyes. She said, "You never buy yourself anything."

"I do all right."

"You do fine," she said. She got up and walked toward him. Her fingers moved through his hair. "Someday you'll be important."

He smiled up at her. "I'll never be important," he said. "But I'll always be happy." He took her hand and kissed it and looked up at her again. "Won't we?"

"Of course."

"Sit on my lap."

"I'm gaining weight."

"You're a feather."

She sat on his lap. He drank some more lemonade and gave her some. She fed him a little more salad and took some herself. They looked at each other and laughed quietly.

"Like my hair?"

He nodded. He put his hand against her head, played with her hair. "You women have it tough in summer. All that hair."

"In winter it comes in handy."

"I wish it was winter already. I wish this case was over with."

"You'll get it over with."

"It's a problem."

She gave him a sideway smile. "And you eat it up."

"Not this one," he said. "This one's different. Something about this one gives me the blues. The way he talked. That tone. I don't know——"

She stood up. "I want to see if the kids are asleep."

Fraser lit a cigarette, leaned back a little to watch her as she crossed the living room. When the wall cut her off, he leaned forward and dragged deeply at the cigarette and stared at the empty glass in front of him. A frown moved onto his forehead and became more of a frown. The empty glass looked very empty.

Chapter Three

I N THIS particular Village place there wasn't much doing.
Four men at the far end of the bar were having a quiet discussion concerning horses. A young man and a young woman
were taking their time with long, cool drinks and smiling at each
other. A short, fat man was sullenly gazing at a glass of beer.

Vanning turned back to his gin rickey. A peculiar sense of
loneliness came upon him, and he knew it was just that and
nothing more. He wanted to talk to someone. About anything.
And again he saw himself in a mirror, this time the mirror behind the bar, and he saw in his own eyes the expression of a
man without a friend. He felt just a bit sorry for himself. At
thirty-three a man ought to have a wife and two or three children. A man ought to have a home. A man shouldn't be standing here alone in a place without meaning, without purpose.
There ought to be some really good reason for waking up in
the morning. There ought to be some impetus, there ought to
be something.

Again one of those sighs got past his lips, and he recognized
it and didn't like it. He was sighing that way too much these
days. He finished the drink, downing the last few gulps too fast
to get any real taste out of it, and then he ordered another
drink and while waiting for it he saw the short, stocky beer
drinker looking at him in a hesitant sort of way. It was evident
that the fat fellow wanted to strike up a conversation, the fat
fellow was lonely, too. Just then the drink arrived.

Vanning offered the fat fellow a kindly smile, and the smile
was appreciated and returned. Vanning moved his drink down
along the bar, holding onto the smile, and said, "Well, this is
one way of beating the heat."

The fat fellow nodded. "One thing I like about beer," he said.
"It stays cold once it gets in you. Whiskey don't work that way."

"I guess whiskey's a winter drink," Vanning said, and suddenly he realized this was going to be an extremely dull conversation, and if he didn't push the topic onto another track they
would be talking about liquor for the rest of the evening. He
wondered what they ought to talk about and he considered

baseball for a moment but had to discard it because he certainly wasn't up on his baseball. He didn't even know the league standings. It had been a long time since he had last opened a newspaper to the sports page.

And now, since there was nothing to say and nothing better to do, Vanning went to work on his drink.

The fat fellow said, "She's giving you the eye."

Vanning gulped and got it down. He looked at the fat fellow. He said, "What?"

"A number just walked in."

Vanning leaned far over the bar and studied the glass and its contents. Without fully knowing why, he said nastily, "Numbers are always walking in."

"This isn't bad."

"None of them are bad," Vanning said. "They're all wonderful."

"I just thought I'd mention it."

"Thanks," Vanning said. "Thanks for mentioning it."

The fat fellow shrugged and put some beer down his throat. He was quiet for a little while and then he said, "Too bad you're not interested."

"Why?"

"She is."

"That's nice," Vanning said. "It always builds the ego."

"I wish she was looking at me."

"Maybe I'm in the way."

"Oh, that's all right," the fat fellow said.

"No, really." And Vanning gave a brief, quiet laugh. "I'll move on down the bar. Or I'll take a walk outside. Anything you like."

"Don't do that. It wouldn't help me. I'm not her speed."

The nastiness cruised away. Vanning turned to the fat fellow and said sympathetically, "Now why carry on like that?"

"Oh, cut it out," the fat fellow said morosely. "I'm just a fat slob and I don't have enough brains to make people overlook it."

"Glands?"

"No, not glands. Appetite. I've had six meals already today and the night is still young. I'd have as much chance with that item as Eskimos in the Sahara."

"Go on," Vanning said, a little amused. "It isn't that hopeless. Give it a try. Nothing ventured——"

"Yes, I know all about that, and if I thought there was one chance in a thousand of getting a hello, I'd start an operation. But if I ever saw a hopeless state of affairs, this is it. I'm not in that league. Take a look at her and you'll see what I mean."

"Don't let them scare you," Vanning said, again lifting the glass. "They're not poison."

"Maybe you could sell me on that, but the way you say it, you don't mean it. You've been hurt, brother, you can't kid me. You've been hurt plenty."

Vanning's hand tightened around the glass. He put it down. He tapped ten fingers on the surface of the bar and took a deep breath and gazed straight ahead. "All right," he said. "What about it?"

"Nothing," the beer drinker said. "I've been hurt too."

"That's a shame. Should we start crying on each other's shoulder or do you think maybe it's a good idea to skip the whole thing? Have another beer?"

"She sure is looking at you."

"All right, then," Vanning said, "don't have another beer. And do me a favor. Don't give me a play-by-play of what's taking place at the end of the bar."

"I bet I know what's the matter." And the fat fellow wore a gleeful, shrewd little smile. "You're one of those bashful guys. I bet you're afraid."

"Afraid?"

"That's what I said."

"Afraid," Vanning murmured. He gripped the rounded edge of the bar. "Afraid. I'm afraid."

The beer drinker waited awhile, and then he said, "I beg your pardon, friend, but would you mind telling me what the hell is wrong with you?"

"I'm afraid," Vanning said.

"I'm going out for a sandwich," the fat fellow said. "Food settles all my problems, and yet my biggest problem is food itself. That's the way it goes, my friend, and I tell you it's a vicious circle, it certainly is."

"I guess so," Vanning said.

The fat fellow was paying his check, turning away from the bar, walking toward the door. Vanning watched him, and then Vanning's eyes hopped away and to the side and toward that part of the bar where she was standing alone in a yellow dress. Her figure was on the buxom side. Voluptuous, but in a quiet, wholesome way.

She was about twenty-six, Vanning estimated while he looked at her and while she looked directly back at him. And then the first coherent thought that entered his head was the idea that she didn't belong in this place, she ought to be home reading a good book, and tomorrow morning she ought to be in the park wheeling a baby carriage. And all that was in his eyes as he stood there looking at her, and agreement with all that was in her eyes as she looked back at him.

Even at this distance he could see there was no paint on her face except for some lipstick. But all the same there was color in her face, quite a bit of it aside from a beach tan, and it was deep rose all over her cheeks. He didn't think he was causing that. The deep rose was probably a permanent condition in her face. It was definitely a face, and it went along with the rest of her, and he knew why the fat fellow had retreated from the situation. The shining blond hair, loose and wispy and lovely around her shoulders, was something else that must have given the fat fellow a bad time.

She kept on looking at Vanning, and he kept on looking at her, and finally he told himself it was curiosity and nothing else that was making him pick up his drink, walk toward her.

Going toward her, it was more as though she were coming toward him, and the effect of her was something tremendous. He couldn't understand that, because along with it there was something uncanny, made all the more uncanny by the fact that she looked to be anything but uncanny or hard to figure out. He asked himself to stop trying to understand it.

He said, "Think you know me?"

"No."

"Then why are you looking at me?"

"Can't I look?"

He frowned and glanced at her with his head inclined a little. She stood there and looked at him. He had a feeling that she was a few strides ahead of him and he didn't like that.

"I guess you can look if you want to," he said. "I don't know what you expect to see."

"I'm not sure either."

"If you have pencil and paper," Vanning said, "I'll be glad to write a short autobiography."

"That won't be necessary. But you can tell me what you do."

He laughed. It was a way to pass some time, anyway. That was what he told himself. He wasn't able to tell himself the truth. But the truth was there, inside him, and the truth was that a female, in a few startling, swift moments, had gotten a hold on him and he had no inclination to free himself.

He said, "I paint."

"Houses?"

"Houses, horses, fountain pens, anything they want."

"Oh," she said, "then you're an artist."

"With apologies to Rembrandt."

"I didn't expect you'd be an artist. I thought——"

"Truck driver, longshoreman, heavyweight wrestler."

"Something along those lines."

"Disappointed?"

"Oh, no. Aren't artists glamorous?"

"I'm a commercial artist," Vanning said. "That means I'm a salesman, I'm part of a big selling job, and I actually get paid for painting pretty pictures."

"It sounds like a nice way to earn a living."

"It has its advantages," Vanning said. "But I do it all day long and at night I like to get away from it."

"I'm sorry."

"Don't be sorry. Talk to me. That's why I came in here."

"To see if you could meet a girl?"

"To see if I could find someone interesting to talk to."

"That's very strange," she said.

"How come?"

"I had the same idea."

"I don't think so," Vanning said. He got his eyes away from her and he watched his fingers rolling back and forth along the smooth roundness of the highball glass. "I think you came in here because you're an unhappy person, desperately unhappy and very disappointed with men, and probably disillusioned but not disillusioned to the extent that you're ready to throw all men aside. Do I hear the sound of a click?"

"Go on. Talk."

"Well"—Vanning went on playing with the glass—"I think

you came in here a little on the frantic side, as if you're giving yourself a few last chances to meet someone worthwhile. Or maybe this was the final try. And you saw me standing there and you told yourself it was a bull's-eye if you could only attract my attention."

"Do all artists know this much about human nature?"

"I couldn't say. I don't hang around with other artists. Suppose we take one thing at a time. Suppose we talk about me after we get through with you. Is that all right?"

"If it isn't all right we'll do it anyway," she said. "Because you have your heart set on it. You're getting pleasure out of it."

"Not exactly what you'd call pleasure. But I think it would do us both some good if we skip the jockeying around. I mean come right out at the beginning and put it all on the table. That saves a lot of time. Sometimes it saves a lot of grief later on."

"What makes you think there will be a later on?"

"I didn't say there would be. What I'm really trying to do is catch up with you. I'm sure you're mature enough not to take offense at that."

She smiled. "My name is Martha."

"Jim."

"Hello, Jim."

"Hello. Have another drink?"

"I've had enough, thanks. Too much, I guess, on an empty stomach."

"We can fix that," Vanning said. "Come to think of it, all I had tonight was a sandwich and a malted."

He paid for the drinks and they walked out of the bar. Now it seemed that the heat was letting up a bit and the Hudson was sending over a breeze. Going toward midnight, the streets were quieting down and it was the bars and night clubs that were getting all the play.

Vanning looked at her. He said, "Got any special place in mind?"

"There's a little restaurant off Fourth Street. I don't know if it's still open."

"We'll try it."

The place was well off Fourth Street, and the weak yellow light from its window was the only light on the narrow street. Vanning took her in there and they sat at a small table near the

window. They were alone in the place. It was very small. Their
waiter was the proprietor, and he was a man who looked as if
one of his own meals would do him a lot of good. He was
trying to be friendly, but weariness prevented him from getting
it across. He took their order and went away.

"All right," Vanning said, and he leaned toward her. "Now
tell me."

"Yes, I've been married. Divorced. No children. I'm a buyer
in a department store. Glassware. I live alone in a two-and-a-
half here in the Village."

"I'll want that address. And the telephone number."

"Now?"

"Here's why. There's a slight possibility I might have to leave
you in a hurry. Don't ask me to explain, but just on the chance
that things work out that way, I'll want to see you again."

She opened a handbag, took out a pencil and a small pad.
She did some writing and handed him the slip of paper. Without looking at it, he folded it and put it in his wallet.

"Now," she said, "what about you?"

"Never been married. I come from Detroit and I took engineering at Minnesota. If you like the rah-rah, I was an All-
Western Conference guard. Then I was in Central America and
we were showing them some new stunts with electricity and
water power and so forth. While I was down there I began
painting. For relaxation. Someone told me I could paint and I
took him up on it. I did a lot of painting down there. Wind-up
was engineering played second fiddle and I came back to the
States and enrolled at an art school in Chicago. If there'd been
a lot of money I would have gone in for the fine arts. But there
was very little money and I had to go commercial. Things were
breaking very nicely and the luck stayed with me all through
those years and all through the war. I wasn't even scratched."

"Doing what?"

"Navy. I was a damage-control officer on a battleship."

A dull tone had crept into his voice and he wanted to get rid
of it, he wanted to be amusing, diverting. He wanted to show
her a nice time. He told himself this was a good thing, this
thing happening to him now. She was something clean and
refreshing; he felt sure this was the something he had sensed
was going to happen tonight. He was glad, and yet there was a

certain uneasy feeling along with that gladness, and he couldn't figure it out.

The food came and they ate silently. Every now and then he lifted his eyes and watched her for a moment or so. He liked the way she ate. A quiet sort of gusto. She took her time and yet she didn't waste any time. Her table etiquette was an easy, relaxed thing that made it a pleasure to sit here with her.

After the food, Vanning ordered peach cordials. They sipped the cordials and smiled at each other.

"I should be ashamed of myself," she said. "I mean, you picking me up like this. Or rather, me picking you up. But you called it right, Jim. I was very lonely, or let's even say desperate. I'll be looking forward to seeing you again."

"When?"

"Whenever you feel like seeing me."

"You don't know how good that sounds."

They finished their cordials and Vanning paid the check and they moved toward the door. They had to go down a few steps, because the door was below street level, with other steps leading up to the pavement, and now Vanning was opening the door, now they were going up the steps, now he knew something was wrong, he saw the shadows cutting in on light issuing from the restaurant, he saw the forms following the shadows and he told himself to twist away and race back into the restaurant and try a rear exit. But already it was too late for that, and the lateness was within him. He was angry, and the anger got the better of discretion, and he was going up the steps, taking her with him but not knowing she was there with him. And suddenly, as the three men came out of darkness and confronted him, he knew he had been expecting it. This was really it. This was the something he had expected would happen tonight.

The three of them stood up there at the top of the steps.

And one of them, his face half black, the other side of his face orange-yellow where the light hit it, smiled and took a cigarette from his lips, lowered his eyes toward Vanning and said, "Okay, bud. It's all over."

Her hand gripped his wrist, and he realized she was there, and along with that realization there was another, and it was a thunder burst; it made him blink, it made him stagger without budging. He took hold of her clutching hand, twisted her hand with violence, threw her away from him. She gasped.

There was a laugh from one of the men up there.

Vanning walked up the steps toward him. They stepped back to give him room, and yet they surrounded him, the three men and the girl beside him.

And then one of the men looked at Martha and said, "Thanks, honey, that was a beautiful piece of work."

"Yes," Vanning said. "It was terrific."

"You," said the man who had just spoken, and he smiled easily at Vanning, "you don't talk now. You do your talking later." Then he looked past Vanning, looked at the girl and said, "You can go home now, honey." He laughed with pure enjoyment. "We'll call you when we need you."

"All right," she said. "Do that."

Then she came walking up the steps and, coming abreast of Vanning, she looked at him with nothing in her eyes, and it lasted for an exploding second, and then she turned and walked away.

The three men closed in on Vanning. Two of them had their hands in the pockets of dark tropical worsted suits, but hands alone couldn't make the pockets bulge that much, and Vanning told himself to stop thinking in terms of a break.

One of the men said, "Let's take a little walk across the street."

The four of them crossed the street, walked down the block to where a large, bright green sedan was the only interference with thick midnight blackness.

The man who was doing most of the talking said, "Now we'll take a little ride." He climbed into the front seat. In the back, Vanning sat with a man on either side of him. His brain was empty. His mouth was dry and a coldness was getting itself settled within him, and now the car was in gear, going down the street, making a turn and picking up speed. They made a turn. They were going downtown, then they were swinging away from a wide street and going toward Brooklyn Bridge.

"If you tell us now," said the man behind the wheel, "we'll let you out and you can go home."

"I can picture that," Vanning said.

"Why don't you tell us now?" the man said. "You're going to tell us sooner or later."

"No," Vanning said. "I can't do that."

"You can't do that now, you mean. Because you're tough. But it won't last long. When we get you to the point where you're not tough any more, you'll say what we want you to say."

"It isn't that," Vanning said. "I don't feel like getting myself hurt. If I knew, I'd tell you."

"Come off that," the man said. "That's in the heartache department. That's crying the blues. You know where you'll get with that? Nowhere."

"That's too bad," Vanning said. "Because then we'll both be nowhere."

"He's too tough," the driver said. "He's much too tough, I think. What do you say?"

"I say he's too tough," said the man who sat on Vanning's left. He was a big man and he wore glasses, and now he took them off very slowly, put them in a case and put the case in his pocket.

"What do you say, Sam?"

"Yes, he's too tough," said the man on Vanning's right, a short, wiry man with very little hair on his head. His arms were folded but slowly unfolding.

"I'm not tough at all," Vanning said. "I'm scared stiff."

"Now he's being funny," the driver said. They were on Brooklyn Bridge. The lights were whizzing in and passing the car, dropping other lights on sides of other cars, and all the light was bouncing around like captured lightning in a black vault.

"How about it?" Sam said.

"Hold it a second," the driver said. "Wait till we get off the bridge."

"I think the bridge is the best place," said the man who had been wearing glasses.

"We'll hold it awhile," the driver said. "Just for a little while, Pete, and then you can have your fun."

"Fun?" Vanning said.

"Sure," Pete said, and he laughed. "The bigger they are, the more fun they are."

"You mean with their hands and feet tied, don't you?"

"I can see you're going to be a lot of fun," Pete said.

The green sedan tore away from Brooklyn Bridge and went slashing into Brooklyn. It went through the city and away from the city and into a section of vacant lots and shallow hills.

"I think now ought to be all right," Pete said. "What do you say, John?"

"Hold it awhile," the driver said.

"We're almost there," Sam said. "How about it, John? Just to get him accustomed to it."

"Maybe you're right," John said. "And then get him down on the floor and keep him there. I don't want him to see the layout until after we got him inside. So now, if you want to, you can go to work on him."

Pete twisted and threw a punch that hit Vanning on the side of the head, and an instant later Sam smashed him on the jaw, using brass knuckles. He lowered his head, testing the pain and the dizziness, feeling another blow and still another and yet another, and then he was going to the floor and they were kicking him. He wondered how long it would be until he lost consciousness. He looked up and saw the brass knuckles coming toward his face, and he threw himself to the side and the brass knuckles went past his head. Then the edge of a shoe caught him in the mouth and he realized there was only one way to stop this sort of thing. They weren't quite ready to kill him, and if he was going to get the slightest satisfaction out of this entire deal, now was the time to get it.

He came up from the floor, feinted at Pete, then swerved and let go with both hands, sending his fists into Sam's face. There was an opportunity for a follow-up, but instead of using it, Vanning swerved again, turned his attention to Pete. He leaned away from Pete's outstretched arm, then got under the arm, got his elbow under Pete's chin and heaved with the elbow, sending Pete's head quite a distance back, and then he hit Pete in the mouth, pistoned the same hand into Pete's mouth, then used both hands on Pete's face. That was about all he could do with Pete, because now Sam was showing a revolver and Sam was cursing and a lot of blood was flowing from Sam's nose.

"Bullets already?" Vanning said.

"Put the gun away," John said.

"I feel like blasting him." Sam was holding the gun a few inches away from Vanning's head.

"I told you to put the gun away," John said. "You're too fidgety with a gun, Sam. That's no good. I've told you that a lot of times. Give the gun to Pete."

"Sure," Pete said, the sound staggering through blood. "Let me have that gun."

"Be careful with it," John said. "We have a long night ahead of us. Just keep him covered and keep him on the floor."

Pete's foot thudded into Vanning's chest, forcing him against the floor and the front seat. "Stay there," Pete said. "Just stay there and regret the whole thing."

"I thought it was fun," Vanning said. "Didn't you?"

"The real fun hasn't started yet," Pete said.

The car made an acute turn, its wheels squealing. Vanning closed his eyes and told himself it was time to accept the thing for what it was. And it was very clear. It was very simple. Tonight he was going to lose his life. It was inevitable that someday this thing should catch up with him, and although he had sensed that all along, he had tried to stretch it as far as possible. That was a wholly natural way to take it and he couldn't condemn himself for acting in a natural way. All in all, it was one of those extremely unfortunate circumstances, and it had started on a day when it simply hadn't been his turn to draw good cards. He could have died on that day or on the day following or the week following. He could have died on any of those several hundred days in the months between then and now, so what it actually amounted to was the fact that all this time he had been living on a rain check and it was only a question of how long it would take until payday arrived.

The car was making turns, going long stretches without turns, making more turns, then sweeping around somewhere in a wide circle, slowing down.

"Put something around his eyes," John said.

"Why bother?" Sam said. "This is the last stop."

"Don't talk like that," Vanning said. "You make me feel blue."

"Bring your hand over here," Pete said. He was handling a large breast-pocket handkerchief, folding it over, folding it again, then winding it around Vanning's head, drawing it tightly, knotting it.

"That's too tight," Vanning said.

"That's too bad," Pete said.

The car had stopped. They were getting out. They were taking Vanning across some sort of field. He could feel high grass brushing up against his ankles. Then the high grass gave way to hard-packed soil and it went on that way for a few minutes, and then they were walking up steps that had to be wood because there was considerable creaking. After that the sound of a key in a lock, the sound of a door opening, the feeling of entering a large room, going through the room with big hands pushing him, holding him back, pushing him again. Now a stairway, a long climb, and now a corridor, and then another door opening, and the sound of a wall switch and light getting through the fabric that covered his eyes. He was working his lips toward a smile. He managed to build the smile. There was some fatalism in it, and a trace of defiance. And underneath the smile he was terribly frightened.

Chapter Four

LAVENDER LIGHT came down on a purplish river. There was a huge ferry boat crammed with people. The ferry had shut off its power and was floating toward the wharf when suddenly a monster wave came from noplace and hit the ferry on starboard and knocked it over on its back. And there were no people to be seen. Only the ferry, floating on its back. And the river, calm again. And Fraser twisted his face against the pillow and let out a groan. He opened his eyes. He closed them again, opened them again, and saw his wife sitting up beside him, looking at him.

"You're all worked up," she said.

"What was I doing?"

"Making noise."

"Did I say anything?"

"I couldn't make it out. Can I get you something?"

"No," Fraser said. "Just put on the light."

She switched on a lamp at the bedside. Fraser blinked and rubbed his eyes. He reached toward a table near his side of the bed, fumbled with a pack of cigarettes and a book of matches. She didn't want a cigarette. She wanted him to go back to sleep. Lighting his cigarette, he got out of bed, walked to the window and looked out. The East River was glimmering black pitch and the lights were points of spears lancing a smoldering night.

He took several short puffs at the cigarette. "I can't get it out of my mind."

"You should be on time and a half for overtime," she said. "You work twenty-four hours a day."

"Not always."

"Want a drink of water?"

"I can get it."

"Let me get it."

She climbed out of bed, and Fraser was alone in the room and he wanted to get dressed and leave the apartment. He was putting on his socks when she came back with the water. She let him finish the water and then she picked up his shoes and took them back to the closet.

"Take off your socks," she said, "and stop the nonsense."

"I feel like doing something."

"On what basis?"

"I don't know," Fraser said.

"I wish you'd get yourself a job in Wall Street. Keep this up and you'll be gray in no time."

She sat down beside him on the edge of the bed. She put a hand on his shoulder. For a while they sat there quietly, then Fraser got up and walked to his dresser. He opened the top drawer of the dresser and took out a brown paper portfolio and began extracting paraphernalia. He stood there at the dresser, studying various papers.

This went on for several minutes, and then she came toward him. He looked at her, and she had her arms folded and she was saying, "Now stop it."

"Go back to sleep."

"I can't sleep with the light on."

"Put on your eyeshade."

"You're being inconsiderate."

"I'm sorry," Fraser said. "I can't help this."

"What is it?" she said. "What's all the fuss?"

"So many angles I can't figure."

"Tomorrow. Please, dear. Tomorrow."

"You go back to sleep. I'll go in the other room."

She went back to the bed. Fraser walked out of the room. In the living room he switched on the light and sat down with the paraphernalia. A few minutes later she came into the living room.

"I can't sleep," she said, "when you aren't sleeping."

He picked up the papers and began putting them back in the portfolio. "All right," he said, "I'm done now."

She stopped him. "No, you're not. You won't close your eyes all night. Sit here. Talk to me. Tell me."

Fraser smiled at her. "You've got a very nice nose."

"It's too thin."

"I think it's very nice." He ran his finger along the bridge of her nose. Then he looked away from her and began punching a fist into a palm, punching lightly, steadily. "They're letting me do it my own way," he said. "If I ruin it, it's my own fault, mine alone. I'm sure I know where I'm going, but I'm not in-fallible. No man is."

"Don't make excuses to me. I'm a college graduate. I understand things."

Fraser let out a sigh. "It's a very difficult setup. It's like one of those cryptograms where the more steps you solve, the harder the rest becomes."

"You'll work it out."

"I wonder."

"You mean that, really?"

He looked at her. He nodded slowly. "It's a bad one, honey. It's definitely a bad one. With what I've got now, I can turn him in tomorrow. With what they have on him already, they can put him on trial and it's a hundred to one he'd get a death sentence. That's why I find it a little hard to sleep."

"But if that's what he deserves——"

"If."

"Is that your worry?"

"Not under ordinary conditions. But this is a very unusual state of affairs. The record says the man's a bank robber. A murderer. It adds and it checks and it figures. They've got witnesses, they've got fingerprints, they've got a ton of logical deduction that puts him in dead center. And what I've got is a mental block."

"What is this, the old humane element?"

"Just a theory."

"You've got a theory and they've got the facts."

"I know," Fraser said. "I know, I know." He rubbed the back of his head. "If I could only talk to him. I mean really talk. If I wasn't in such a delicate spot. It's one hell of a jam, and every time I walk into Headquarters they look at me with pity."

"You need help on this one."

"I need a miracle on this one."

"You're doing all you can."

"That's what bothers me," Fraser said. "The best shadow job I've ever done. Know every move he makes. Got it down to a point where I can leave him at night and pick him up when he walks out in the morning. I know what he eats for lunch, what kind of shaving cream he uses, how much money he makes with the art work. I know everything, everything except what I need to know."

"He's just clever."

"He's not clever," Fraser said. "That's another thing. I'll be dogmatic about that. He's intelligent, but he's not clever. Talk about a paradox, this one takes the cake."

"You're not a mind reader. You're not an adding machine. You've only got one brain and one set of eyes. Stop trying to knock yourself out."

Fraser stood up. He walked across the living room and came back to the sofa and looked at the wall. "It's a shame," he said. "It's a damn shame."

"What is?"

"They had to go and lose track of those others. That's what they get for putting two-bit operators on a big case. When I think of how they fumbled——"

"That's their fault, not yours."

"It's my fault if Vanning gets the chair."

"What makes you so sure he's innocent?"

"I'm not sure."

"Then what are you worried about?"

"For a college graduate that's a foolish question."

"Are you quarreling with me?"

"I'm quarreling with myself."

She pulled him down to the sofa. She put her hands against the sides of his head and made him look at her. "Let me fix you some tea."

"Black coffee."

"I said tea."

"All right, tea."

She walked into the kitchen. Fraser sat there on the sofa for a while and then he went into the kitchen. She was standing at the stove.

He stood behind her and said, "Can I bore you awhile?"

"Please do."

He took a very deep breath. "Here's one for Aesop," he said. "Three men rob a bank in Seattle. They run away with three hundred thousand dollars. They get as far as Denver. In Denver they register at a hotel under assumed names. They have a contact man in Denver, a smooth manipulator named Harrison. This man Harrison has the job of taking the money, getting it in a safe place or putting it in various channels or something. You follow me?"

"I've heard this a thousand times."

"Hear it again. The Harrison party comes to the hotel. He walks out with one of the men, a personality registered under the name of Dilks. Now get this, because this part was witnessed. Dilks was carrying a small black satchel. The money. All right, all that's under the heading of fact. Now we go into theory."

"Yours?"

"No, Headquarters'. Harrison and Dilks take a little stroll. And somewhere along the line this Dilks gets a bright idea. He decides three hundred thousand is a neat little sum and why give it to Harrison? Why not keep it for himself? He waits until he and Harrison are on a dark, quiet street and then he pulls a gun and kills Harrison. He runs away and hides the money. Now we leave theory and come back to fact."

"Here's your tea."

"Put it on the table. Listen. Dilks gets out of Denver. But he leaves fingerprints on the gun found near Harrison's body. He leaves a blue convertible with a California license. Police go to work and start checking. And they find out this man Dilks is not Dilks at all, he's a former Navy officer named James Vanning. They start looking for him."

"Lemon?"

"Just a drop. On a night like this I need hot tea."

"It's good for you. They say it's the best thing in hot weather."

"Do you want me to go on?" Fraser said. And she nodded soberly and he said, "They rack their brains trying to figure this Vanning. No former record, nothing except a few minor traffic violations, and that from way back. Before the war he was a commercial artist in Chicago. Made a fairly nice living at it. Why does this man rob a bank? Why does he commit a murder?"

"A lot of men came back from the war and had the wrong outlook and got themselves in trouble."

Fraser nodded. "That's what Seattle says. That's what Denver says. That's what Headquarters says. Maybe they're right."

"And so?"

"Maybe they're wrong. Now look, do you want to hear the rest of this?"

"I'm not interrupting." She gave him an indignant look. "I'm just discussing it with you."

Fraser stirred the sugar in his teacup. He blew on the tea and took an experimental sip. "Too hot," he said. "I'll let it cool for a while." He took another deep breath and leaned forward. "They look for Vanning. They can't find him. They look for the other two men. No trace. A time interval, and then we see these two other men here in Manhattan. We follow them. We're about to pick them up and then we get very brilliant and we lose them.

"And then we get a call from someone who spots a man answering Vanning's description. We check. It's Vanning. And Headquarters wants to move in, but Seattle doesn't feel like losing three hundred thousand and there's the factor of making sure. Headquarters disagrees with Seattle, but Seattle claims it would be a very nice thing if the money was picked up along with Vanning. Of course Denver puts up a kick because Denver wants to wrap up a murder case. There's something of a delay and then they give me the assignment and I'm supposed to settle this little discussion between three cities.

"So I focus on Vanning. I wait. I wait some more. I follow him like I've never followed anyone. And I wait. I wait for some indication of a lot of money being spent or hidden or invested. No indication. Nothing. Just Vanning from day to day, and if I don't hurry up and come in with something, they'll give me orders to grab him."

"And they'll be right."

"No, they won't be right. They'll be making a terrible mistake. Why did those other men come to New York? Because Vanning's here. They trailed him. They know he's somewhere in town and they're looking for him. They want that money. If we take Vanning, we lose the chance of an established contact between him and those other men. Headquarters says forget about those other men, but I've got the feeling we'll never wind up this case if we don't grab all three."

"But isn't Vanning the killer?"

"Yes."

"That's definite?"

"Yes."

"In your own mind?"

"Yes."

"Well, then?"

Fraser lowered his head. He hit his fists against the table. "I don't know, I can't get rid of the notion. He's a killer and yet he's not a killer."

She leaned her head sideways and gave her husband a careful look. "Is this man your cousin or something?"

He picked up the teacup and took a few gulps. "I wish you'd try to follow me. If I thought this was a hunch or a brain storm I'd laugh at myself. But it's so much deeper than that." He leaned across the table. "I know Vanning. For months now I've been walking behind him, watching every move he makes. I've been in his room when he wasn't there, when I knew it would take him a half-hour to finish a restaurant meal. I've been with Vanning hour after hour, day after day. I've been living his life. Can't you see? I know him, I know him. I"—and the rest of it came out in a low tone, rapid and strained— "I understand him."

She got up from the table and gathered the teacups and took them toward the sink. She turned the faucet handle and the water came out in too much of a rush. She turned it down a little. Quickly, efficiently, the cups were washed and dried and she put them back in the kitchen cabinet. As she closed the door of the cabinet she heard him getting up from the table and she turned to see him walking out of the kitchen. She started to follow him, but just then her eye caught the top of the smooth white table and there was something on the table that caused her to frown. She moved toward the table.

She had seen this sign of extreme agitation once before on a night when their youngest child, stricken with pneumonia, had been approaching the crisis.

She stood there at the table and looked at the scraps of fingernail.

Chapter Five

"ALL RIGHT," John said. "Let him see where he is."

The blindfold was removed. Vanning blinked a few times and then he looked at John. It was the same John. The same hunched shoulders, rather wide, the same creased leathery face and large, flat nose and thick lips that didn't have very much blood in them. The same stringy necktie. Everything the same, even the way John wore his hair, a salt-and-pepper brush that covered his head like a mat of steel wool.

John put a cigarette in his mouth and lit it. He seated himself on the edge of a studio couch. Sam and Pete were up against the wall, standing there like statues. That left Vanning in the center of the room, with light from the ceiling doing a slow fall onto the top of his head. There was some pain in his face from the brass knuckles, and there was a quantity of dizziness, but not so much that he couldn't stand there balancing himself on two feet. He turned his back on the two men who stood against the wall. He looked at John.

"Well?" John said.

"Your move," Vanning said.

They were gazing at each other as if they were alone in the room. John leaned back on an elbow, crossed one leg over the other and took a long, contemplative haul at the cigarette. He blew out the smoke in a single quick exhalation and said, "All I want is the cash."

"I don't know where it is."

"Now say that again," John said. "Just say it to yourself and hear how foolish it sounds."

"I know it sounds foolish, but that's the way it is and I can't help it."

John looked at the black-and-white shoes, the suit and shirt and blue-and-black tie and he said, "Nice clothes you have on."

"I like them."

"They cost money."

"They're not bad clothes," Vanning admitted. "But they're not the real high quality. Not the kind of quality I'd be wearing if I had that cash you're talking about."

"It's a point," John said. "But not much of a point. What are you doing these days?"

Vanning liked that question. It was more of an answer than a question. It told him something he was hungry to know, and it offered a foundation for some strategy.

He said, "Nothing much." He tossed a few ideas around in his head, selected one of them and added, "I have a photo studio uptown, West Side. I manage to make a living, and there's a studio couch and a bathroom, and that way I save on rent."

John looked at the floor and blew some smoke toward a faded violet rug. Vanning studied John's face and told himself it had been a clever play. At least he understood now they didn't know where he was living. He put it together rapidly. They had spotted him in the Village. Followed him. Made a fast contact with the girl and told her to work on him, to get him out of the bar and out of that street and into the restaurant on the dark and empty street. It was reasonable. It checked. It was a typical John manipulation. Because John had just so much brains and no more. John wasn't exactly a fool, but he was harder than he was clever, and probably he knew that about himself, because he had a habit of laboring to be clever.

"Look," John said. "You've got a fair amount of intelligence. You're on one side and I'm on the other. That's clear enough. So we'll take it from there. It's got to be managed along those lines. In order for you to stay alive and have a long, happy life ahead of you, what you have to do is tell me where you put that cash, then we keep you here until I have the cash, and then we let you go. Does that make sense?"

"It would make wonderful sense," Vanning said, "except that I don't know where that cash is located and that's why I can't tell you. Now does that make sense?"

"No, it doesn't. I can see a man misplacing a ten-dollar bill. Maybe even a hundred-dollar bill. But it doesn't figure that a man will let three hundred thousand dollars slip out of his fingers just like that. And that brings us to another angle. If you really lost the money, you lost it in Colorado. And that means you wouldn't be here if you didn't have the money. You'd still be in Colorado, looking for it."

"Colorado is a big place."

"Three hundred thousand dollars is a lot of money. Most people I know would use a magnifying glass and search every inch of the state."

"Maybe you and I don't know the same kind of people."

John threw the cigarette onto the floor, waited until it burned the rug, then stepped on it. He looked at the mashed stub. He said, "We're not getting anywhere." Then he looked up at Vanning without raising his head. "Are we?"

Vanning sighed. "We can't get any further than this. I don't know where it is. I tell you I don't know where it is."

"Don't get excited," John said. "We have plenty of time."

"I don't look at it that way. If I did, I'd try to stall. I'd try to bargain. I'd ask for some assurance that you'd leave me alone after you had the money, and I'd give you assurance that I'd leave you alone."

"You wouldn't have to do that," John said. "We know you'd leave us alone. We know you wouldn't go to the law. How could you go to the law when the law is looking for you?"

Vanning frowned. "What do you mean, looking for me?"

"You're wanted for murder," John said. "Didn't you know that?"

"You're way ahead of me," Vanning said. "I don't remember murdering anybody."

John smiled with understanding and patience and allowed it to coast for a while. Then he beckoned with his fingers and said, "Come on, come on."

Vanning, without moving his head, could see part of the window at his side, and he wondered if he could make it in one leap. He wondered how far it was to the ground. With a big effort he got his mind away from the window and he said, "How much do you know?"

"We know you killed him," John said. "We know the law has you tagged. People saw you with him that night. So the law found out what you looked like. And the car license. That was another thing. Your description tallied with the description of the car owner. And still another thing, the big thing. You bought the car in Los Angeles and you got a license there. That gave them a record of your fingerprints, and the prints checked with prints on the gun."

"How do you know all this?"

"It's the kind of news that gets around," John said. "Newspapers and people talking and so forth. We hung around in Denver for a while, and then we picked up on you from a tip that came from New Orleans. Later we got another tip from Memphis. And then a third tip from New York. We figured you'd stay in New York for quite a time. It's a nice place to hide. What happened was you were spotted in a Village bar. The man who made the contact had to go and lose you in a traffic jam, but we figured we'd tag you again, sooner or later. And that's the way it adds, so now maybe we can come to terms."

"I wish we could," Vanning said. "I wish I had something to offer."

"Put yourself in my place," John said. "I'm very hungry for that cash. I'm so hungry that I'm willing to give you a slice. Say fifty thousand. How does it sound?"

"It sounds great. That's what makes this picture so miserable. I just don't know where that money is."

John stood up. He said, "Final?"

"Final," Vanning said.

"No," John said. "I don't think so." He looked at the two men who stood motionless against the wall.

"Well?" Pete said.

"All right." John was walking toward the door. "You can have him now."

Beyond the pain, beyond the spinning and all the gleaming red, and beyond the falling rocks that crashed and clanged, and beyond the black flood shot with more red, with some livid purple in there, beyond all that, there was a stillness and it was the stillness of memory, and he groped his way toward it. And he came out in the bright gold of a springtime afternoon in Colorado, and in the pale blue convertible coupé he had bought in Los Angeles after receiving his discharge, he was driving toward Denver with the idea that he would stay in Denver for a while and then take his time going up to Chicago.

The convertible purred its way along the mountain road, and the radio purred along with it, Noro Morales handing out a suave rhumba. The top was down and the sky was very clear and it was good to know that the war was over and that agency in Chicago was the kind that kept its promises, a big firm with stability and energy, and they had liked his work and in reply to his letter they had told him to come on back and go to work. They asked him if seventy-five hundred a year was all right. He was thinking, before the war they had paid him five thousand a year. That was the kind of outfit it was. He felt good about going back. He felt good about everything. Chicago was an all-right place, and someday in the not too far distant future he ought to be meeting a nice girl and getting married and starting a home. It was a fine thing to be thirty-two and alive and healthy. It was a marvelous thing to be starting fresh.

He whistled along with Noro Morales and the convertible floated along the road.

Suddenly, away up there ahead of him, where the road went curving its way up along the mountain, there was a violent noise, and it sounded as if an automobile had crashed into something. Vanning pressed hard on the accelerator and the convertible leaped, and it took a few turns, made a whizzing straightaway run as the road sliced into a tunnel, came out to make another turn, then he saw a branching road, very narrow, almost at right angles to this road, and saw a wreckage.

It was a station wagon, and it was turned over on its side against a rock. Two men were stretched out on a patch of bright green near the rock, and a third man in his shirt sleeves was leaning against the rock.

Vanning turned the convertible onto the narrow road and raced it toward the scene of accident. As he brought the convertible to a stop, the man who was still upright came walking toward him. The man had a leathery face and hair that looked like a mat of steel wool. There was a leather contrivance under the man's left shoulder and it was held there by straps, and now the man reached toward it, took something out of it, came up to Vanning and pointed the revolver in Vanning's face.

"Get out of the car," the man said. "Give me a hand."

"Why the gun?"

"I said get out of the car."

Vanning climbed out of the convertible and the man walked along with him. The two men on the ground were moving about and groaning. One of them, a big man with glasses hanging from one of his ears, was slowly forcing himself to a sitting position, adjusting the glasses and staring around stupidly. The other man, small and wiry and getting bald, was out cold.

The man with the gun was saying, "How is it, Pete?"

"I think I'm all right," the big man said. "Had the wind knocked out of me." He looked at Vanning. "Where did you pick this up?"

"He just came along."

The big man inclined his head to get a look at Vanning's automobile.

"It's a lucky break," the big man said.

"Yeah, we're overloaded with luck today," said the man with the gun. He looked at the smashed station wagon. "Overloaded. Take the gun and keep it on this guy. I'll have a look at Sam."

"Maybe we ought to hurry," Pete said.

"That's why we smashed up. We were in too much of a hurry. Press the gun on him. He looks nervous."

"Why should I be nervous?" Vanning said.

"You shut up," Pete said. He prodded the gun against Vanning's spine, held it there. A few moments later he said, "How does it look, John?"

"I think he's done for," said the man with steel-wool hair. "I think he busted his head. But he's still breathing."

"You think he'll last long?"

"I can't say."

"I always told you Sam was a lousy driver. I told you he was no good in a squeeze."

"Close your head. I'm trying to think what we should do."

"Should we leave him here?"

"That's why I asked you to close your head. Because every time you open your mouth you prove you were born without brains. How can we leave him here? Look at him. He's still alive."

"I know that, John, but you just claimed he won't last long. What's the use of letting him suffer? We'll be doing him a favor if we put a bullet in him. All I got to do is——"

"Keep that gun where it is," John said. "And keep your head closed while I figure this out."

Just then the man on the ground let out a loud groan and opened his eyes.

"I don't know, John. We ain't got much time," Pete said.

John looked down at the man on the ground. He said, "Sam, you drive like a monkey."

Sam let out another groan and closed his eyes.

"You," John said, and he pointed at Vanning, "you come over here and lend a hand."

"Wait a minute," Pete said. "What do you figure on doing?"

"What does it look like?"

"We can't take Sam with us," Pete said. "He'll slow us down."

"Sure, that's right," John said. "And if we leave him here and they find him and he's still alive, the first thing he'll think of is that we left him. I don't think he'll appreciate that. You never know. He might even open his mouth."

"But if he's dead he won't be able to open his mouth."

"What's the matter, Pete? Don't you like Sam?"

"I get along with Sam. You know that. But why take chances?"

"We won't shoot him," John said. "And we won't talk about it any more. We're taking him with us and if we can find a doctor somewhere we'll see if he has a chance." He glanced up at Vanning. "All right, you. Let's go to work."

Vanning and John carried the injured man to the convertible, placed him in the back seat. Then John ran back to the wrecked station wagon, got inside and came out, carrying a black satchel. He brought it back to the convertible, threw it on the floor near the front seat and said to Vanning, "Get in there and put the top down."

"What do you want with me?" Vanning said. "Why don't you take the car? Leave me here."

"And have you describe the car to the law?" John smiled in appreciation of his own strategy. He shook his head. "Nothing doing. You come with us. And you drive. Pete, you stay in the back seat and look after Sam."

"I still think," Pete said, "it would be better if I put a bullet in Sam."

"I think," John said, "you ought to cut out that line of thought."

"It ain't that I have anything against him. It's just that I——"

"Come on," John said. "Let's be on our way."

They were in the car now, the top was down, the car was

rolling. It made a turn onto the other road, it ran down the other road, and the road ran up and out and once more skirted the side of the mountain. Vanning watched the rear-view mirror.

"You keep your eyes on the road," John said.

"I'm getting a little nervous," Vanning said.

"So am I," John said, and he brought up the revolver so that Vanning could see it was still around. "Suppose we both calm down and then maybe nothing will happen."

"Should I put on the radio?"

"No," John said. "I'll entertain you. I'll tell you a little story. Once upon a time there were three bad men. They were very bad. They robbed banks. In Seattle they robbed a bank and got away with three hundred thousand dollars in thousand-dollar notes. Then they stole a station wagon and scooted out of Salt Lake City. Then they were chased and they had to go fast. They went so fast that their station wagon smashed up. But a kind man came along and helped them out. He had a blue automobile and he was very good-natured about the whole thing."

From the back seat Pete's voice came whining in, "I don't see why you have to tell him about the three hundred grand."

"I'll tell him what I feel like telling him," John said. "I got the funny feeling he's going to be with us for a while." He turned to Vanning. "How about it? Would you like that?"

"I'd love it," Vanning said.

"Turn off at the next crossing," John said. "There's a road brings us into Leadville. There's a doctor in Leadville—anyway, I think it was Leadville—it was a long time ago, but this doctor, if I remember correctly, he was willing to talk business. Anyway, we'll try Leadville."

A quarter of an hour later the blue convertible arrived in Leadville and cruised around for a while, and John was trying to remember where the doctor was located.

Finally they pulled up in front of a hotel and John went in and came out a few minutes later and they went on down the street, made a turn, stopped in front of a wooden structure that had given up the fight a long time ago. John got out of the car, looked up and down, waited for two middle-aged women to cross the street and go on to another street, and then

he gestured to Pete. While Pete carried Sam out of the car, John
entered the dead house, his gun nudging Vanning, who walked
along just a bit ahead of him as they came into the hallway.

The doctor wanted five hundred dollars now and another
five hundred to be paid in three weeks, at which point Sam
would be ready to travel again. John paid the doctor and then
he and Vanning and Pete left the house and got back into the
car.

"Now we'll go to Denver," John said.

They arrived in Denver just as the sun was starting to drop.
They went into a small hotel in a shabby part of town and they
were given a fairly large room on the third floor. John sent a
boy out for liquor. The boy came back with liquor and ice and
bottles of ginger ale and several packs of cigarettes. John gave
the boy a dollar bill and Vanning looked at the boy, but the
boy was looking at the dollar bill and then the boy was walking
out of the room, the door was closing, the door was closed,
the room was quiet.

John opened a bottle and went to work with ice and ginger
ale. Pete was stretched out on the bed, and every few moments
Pete would complain about Sam and whine that he didn't like
the Sam angle. Finally John told Pete that if he didn't keep
quiet he would be hit over the head with a liquor bottle.

"I can't help worrying," Pete said.

"Go out and get some air," John said. "Do your worrying
outside. No. Wait a minute. I have another idea. Stay here. Hold
the gun on him a minute. I want to look in the bathroom."

"What's in the bathroom?" Pete said.

"Usually a skylight, when it's on the top floor."

Pete looked at Vanning, pointing the gun at Vanning. "We
ain't on the top floor."

"I'll make sure," John said. "Hold the gun on him."

John went into the bathroom, came out and said, "It's all
right. No skylight, no windows." He smiled at Vanning. "Get in
there."

Vanning walked into the bathroom. They closed the door
on him. He could hear them talking in the next room. All at
once their voices dropped, and although he had his ear pressed
against the door crack, he couldn't make it out. The low-toned
conversation went on for quite a while. And then it faded and

there was nothing and the nothing went on for a very long time and Vanning couldn't understand that.

He stood at the door and said, "How long do you figure on keeping me here?"

There was no answer.

He said, "It's getting stuffy in here."

No answer.

"At least," he said, "you might let me have a cigarette."

Nothing.

"Anyway," he said, "a drink."

And there was no answer.

And he said aloud, "Maybe you're not even there. Maybe you went out for a walk."

No answer.

"All right," he said. "I'll find out."

He opened the door and stood there looking at the empty room.

The room was terribly empty. The door was closed. And the room was empty. It was good. And that was why it was bad. It was too good. What made it ridiculously good was the revolver that calmly gazed back at him as he stared at it where it rested, emphatically black against the white bedspread. He walked to the bed, picked up the revolver and put it in his coat pocket. For no good reason at all he walked to the window and looked out. He saw an alley, a dark sky, and nothing else. He moved across the room and picked up a half-empty bottle of whiskey and looked at it and put it down. He picked up a ravaged pack of cigarettes and put one of them in his mouth. He didn't quite know what to do. He told himself that a little calm reasoning ought to get him at the source of this. And he sat on the bed, looked at the floor and tried to reason calmly.

What they should have done, if they were smart, was to get him alone somewhere, out in the woods or on a dark street, and then kill him in a hurry and take themselves out of Denver. That was the way to do it without complication. This business of walking out on him, leaving him here alone, leaving the revolver on the bed, it added up to an odd maneuver, and the only way to find the answer was to put himself in their place and think along the same lines as they would think. He told himself he ought to be intelligent enough to box with them, as long as they were in the mood for boxing. He told himself, despite the fact that he and John were in two widely separated fields of endeavor, he ought to be able to outwit John, anyway draw up even with John.

Knowing that liquor wouldn't help, he decided to have a drink, regardless. He stood up, walked toward the dresser where the bottles and ice were assembled, and then he stopped dead, at first frowning, then widening his eyes until they hurt, and then frowning again. And he was staring at the top of the dresser, not staring at the bottles, but staring at the satchel.

There it was, right there in front of him. The black satchel that John had taken out of the station wagon. A new satchel of finely grained leather. Whatever was in it was filling it, making it strain with bulging. He knew what was in it. He told himself he didn't know what was in it. He told himself to leave the satchel alone, put the gun back on the bed, get out of here and get out of Denver. And do it fast and get it started now. Hurry on to Chicago, go to work at the drawing board, meet a nice girl and start a home. Leave the satchel alone. Leave it alone.

"Use your head," he said aloud. "Leave it alone."

He rubbed his hands into his eyes. His teeth clicked and clacked. His head was lowered and then he was shaking his head.

"Come on," he said. "Come out of it."

And then he raised his head and looked at the satchel. It was there, fat and black and shiny and bulging. There was something luscious about it. It looked very smug, sitting there on top of the dresser.

Vanning moved toward the dresser, his hands stretching toward the satchel, then suddenly veering away, clutching at the nearest bottle. He worked whiskey into a highball glass, studying the amount of whiskey he had poured, telling himself he had never taken that much whiskey in a single drink. He took the glass toward the bathroom door, leaned against the door, looked at the satchel, kept his eyes on it as his head went back, as he raised the glass toward his mouth. Then his eyes were closed and the whiskey was flowing down his throat, exploding in his belly. And the empty glass fell out of his limp hand and hit the floor and made considerable noise as it cracked apart.

The noise echoed within Vanning's brain. He told himself to

go to the window and lean out and call for help. Then he laughed at himself. He laughed out loud. The sound of it was attractive in an eerie way and he laughed harder. Maybe if he laughed loud enough, someone would come in and see him here and talk to him. He wanted that badly right now. If he only had someone in here with him, someone with whom he could discuss this. He stared at the satchel.

He rubbed his hands together, telling himself he looked like a safety man waiting for a punt. Then he walked toward the dresser. He rubbed his hands again. He took hold of the satchel, lifted it, brought it over to the bed and opened it and saw United States currency.

Thousand-dollar bills. In small packets, ten bills in each packet, and he counted thirty packets. That made three hundred thousand dollars, he told himself. He placed the packets in the satchel, closed it and stared at it.

Then he came bounding up from the bed, and he picked up the satchel and walked out of the room. He walked down the hall toward the stairway. Just before he reached the stairway someone moved in behind him, something pressed against his side. And the party said, "Keep walking. Be good."

Vanning turned his head and he was looking at a man he had never seen before. The man wore a white panama and a pale green suit, a dark green shirt and yellow tie and a yellow handkerchief flowing largely, gracefully, from the breast pocket. The man was tall and heavy, and he had a square face and his skin was sun-darkened.

"Just keep walking," the man said. "Downstairs and to the right and we'll go out through a side door."

"You can have the money," Vanning said.

"I don't want the money."

"Are you a policeman?"

The man let out a laugh that suddenly got itself sliced clean. "Just keep walking," he said.

They arrived on the second-floor landing. The gun nudged Vanning's side, then pressed hard, and Vanning winced, and then he was going downstairs with the man that way beside him, the gun that way against him, and they were in the lobby and a few people were standing around doing nothing the way only people in hotel lobbies can do nothing.

"So help me," the man said, "if you let out a whimper I'll let you have it. Now go toward that side door as if you're going out with me for a stroll."

They went toward the side door, the man opened the door, they walked out and down a dark street, and nothing was said until the man told Vanning to make a turn. A minute later he told Vanning to make another turn. They were on a narrow street, weakly illuminated by yellow light coming from second-story windows.

"Now," the man said, placing himself in front of Vanning, "let's have that bag."

Vanning handed over the satchel. He looked at the man. The man was smiling. Vanning sighed. He saw the revolver coming up and pointing at his chest. He sighed.

He said, "I knew it."

"Tough," the man said, "but that's the way it's got to be."

"Can I have a minute?"

"That's too long."

"Half a minute."

"All right."

"How about a break?"

"Don't waste time asking for a break. If you want to talk about the weather, we'll talk about the weather, but if you keep asking for a break I'll only get annoyed."

"Working for John?"

"That's right."

"Why does John use you?"

"He always uses me for this sort of thing. He doesn't like to do it himself."

"Then why didn't he use Pete?"

"Because Pete don't have a head on his shoulders. Pete has a habit of making mistakes."

"I see."

"I'm glad you see. I'm glad everything is clear."

"Except for one thing."

"Ask me, and if I can answer you I'll give you an answer."

"Why did they give me this?" Vanning said, sincere as he said it, completely naïve as he took the revolver out of his pocket and showed it to the man. And the man looked at the revolver and then Vanning looked down at it and realized that it was actually a revolver and that he had it in his hand. And he looked up at the man's face and saw the dismay. And just as the dismay gave way to rage, Vanning pulled the trigger, pulled it again, then again, the shots bouncing back and forth, up and down, as the man was lowered on an invisible elevator. Vanning stepped back. Now the man was on the ground, squirming, his arms stretched out, his revolver resting near a wrist, his fingers twitching. Then his whole body twitched, gave a convulsive movement that took him over on his back, he twitched once more, his eyes opened wide, his mouth came halfway open, and he was dead.

Vanning ran. He ran as fast as he could go. There was a hill. He ran up the hill. There was a field. He ran across the field. There was a narrow stream. He went into the stream, and the water came up to his knees, then his waist, then his chest, and he lifted one arm high, wondered why he was doing that, looked at the arm, the thing that dangled from his hand, and it was the satchel. He tried to remember picking up the satchel. He couldn't remember. But he must have picked it up. It hadn't walked into his hand. It wasn't alive. Or maybe it was. The water came up to his chin. He told himself to drop the satchel, let it sink in the stream. He told himself the bullets had hit the man, the man had fallen and dropped the satchel. And he had stood there looking at the dead man. And then he had picked up the satchel and started to run away with it.

That part of it was too much for him. He didn't have the gun. He had the satchel. He had left the gun there and had picked up the satchel. He wondered what he wanted with the satchel. He wondered why he had taken it in the first place. For that one he had an answer. He had intended to give the satchel to the police. So that was all right. But he couldn't figure out why he had taken the satchel from the dead man. Perhaps the answer was identical with the first answer. Perhaps he had still intended to visit the police. And yet that was sort of weak, because now he couldn't remember holding that idea in his mind. The only thing he now completely realized was that he had killed a man and now in his possession he had a satchel containing three hundred thousand dollars and he was running away. And he was very much afraid of the satchel.

Gradually, as his physical endurance lessened, the mental

side became clearer, and he was putting pieces together and drawing conclusions. The thing that made it very bad was the way John had held the gun so close to him that people couldn't notice the gun. Even the doctor in Leadville had not seen the gun. And the hotel clerk in Denver. And the people in the lobby. Nobody had seen the gun. All they had seen was John and Pete and himself, together in the blue convertible, together in the hotel, and that made the whole thing miserable. But it had to split somewhere along the line. It couldn't keep up this way. Maybe in another ten or twenty minutes or so he would have a hold on himself and he would be ready to visit the police and tell them all about it.

The thought was in there, solid and compact, very pure and logical. But it lasted for only a few moments. After that it began to float away from him because he was telling the story to himself as he would tell it to the police, and it seemed like a foolish story. It seemed a little fantastic and more than a little ridiculous. The bathroom, for instance. They had put him in the bathroom but they had not locked the door. That was the start, and from there on it became downright comical. They had gone out of the room, leaving him in the bathroom with the door closed but unlocked. He had come out of the bathroom. And there on the bed, all ready for him, was a revolver. And there on the dresser, shining and plump, was the little black satchel with all that money in it. He could see the faces of policemen, he could see them looking at each other, he could see them leaning toward him with disbelief jumping out of their eyes. And yet, with all that, one big weapon remained on his side. He still had the satchel.

He told himself that. He still had it and he could go to them and hand it over and he still had the satchel. He begged himself to believe that he still had it as he raised his hands and looked at his hands, saw two white hands against the background of black woods. And no satchel.

There was a moment of nothing. No thought, no motion, nothing. Then an attempt to reason it out. Then the realization that he couldn't reason it out, it was too far away from him. It was away back there an hour ago, or two hours ago, miles away back there. Maybe during the minutes when he was crossing the stream. Maybe ten minutes later in these vast woods. Maybe an hour later. But there was no way of putting it on a definite basis, no way of remembering when he had let the satchel fall from his hand, or where he had let it fall.

Again Vanning saw the faces of policemen. Big pink faces that formed a circle around him, came moving in on him. And one of them was bigger than all the rest and the mouth was moving. He could hear the voice. The voice hit him, bounced back. He stumbled toward the voice and the voice hit him again.

The voice said, "You say you came out of that room and you were carrying the satchel. Is that right?"

"Yes," Vanning said.

"What were you going to do with the satchel?"

"Hand it over to you."

"All right. Then what?"

"He came in from behind me and put a gun in my back. We went out of the hotel. Then when we were on that narrow street he took the satchel away and told me it was too bad, but he was forced to do away with me."

"Then what?"

"I took the gun out of my pocket and shot him."

"Just like that?"

"Yes," Vanning said.

"What about his gun?"

"He didn't use it."

"Why not?"

"I guess he was too surprised. I guess that was the last thing he expected, my having a gun."

"Your own gun?"

"No," Vanning said, "I told you how I got it."

"Yes, you did tell us that, but I'm wondering if you expect us to believe it. Doesn't matter. We'll skip that section. We'll put you on that street with him. He's dead. You're standing there, looking down at him. And now what do you do?"

"I start running."

"Why?"

"I'm afraid."

"What's there to be afraid of? You haven't done anything wrong. You've killed a man, but you've done it in self-defense. You're in the clear. What bothers you?"

"The satchel. I saw that I had it in my hand. I couldn't remember picking it up. But there it was, in my hand."

"Well," the policeman said, "that was all right too. You still had the satchel. Why didn't you come into Denver and hand it over?"

"I was afraid. I didn't think you'd believe my story. You know the way it sounds. It's one of those stories that doesn't check."

"I'm glad you understand that," the policeman said. "It makes things easier for both of us. So now we have you in those woods and you're running and still have the satchel. And what happens?"

"I don't have the satchel any more."

"It takes a jump away from you and runs away, is that it?"

"I just don't have that satchel any more," Vanning said. "I can't remember where I dropped it. I must have been in the woods for two or three hours and I couldn't have been traveling in a straight line. And the woods were thick, there was so much brush, there was a swampy section, there were a million places where I could have dropped the satchel. Can't you understand my condition? How confused I was? Try to understand. Give me any sort of a test. Please believe me."

"Sure," the policeman said. "I believe you. We all believe you. It's as simple and clear as a glass of water. You took the satchel. You ran away with it. That's what you say and that's what we believe. And that brings us to the other thing. In order to get that satchel you had to kill a man. So we've circled around now and we've come back to it and honest to goodness, mister, you're so far behind the eight ball that it looks like the head of a pin. It's too bad you had to go and get yourself mixed up with the wrong people. We're holding you on grand larceny and murder in the first degree."

"But I gave myself up. I came to you. I didn't have to do that."

"You didn't bring the satchel."

"I don't know where it is."

"Oh, now, why don't you cut that out?"

"I tell you I don't know where it is. I dropped it someplace. I lost it. Look, I didn't have to come here and tell you all this. I could have kept on running. But I came here."

"It's a point in your favor," the policeman said. "As a matter of fact, you have quite a few points on your side. No past record. The fact that the other man was holding a gun when you killed him. The fact that you had a legitimate occupation waiting for you in Chicago. So all that may get you some sort of a break. We may be able to work something out. Tell you what. You tell us where you've got that satchel hidden."

"I can't tell you that. I don't know where it is."

The policeman looked at the other faces and sighed. Then he looked at Vanning. His face loomed in front of Vanning as he said, "All right, you can still help yourself out a little, even if you want to be stubborn about that three hundred thousand. What you can do is plead guilty to grand larceny and murder in the second degree. That's giving you a break, bringing it down to second-degree murder, and that ought to send you up for about ten years. If you behave yourself you ought to get out in five, maybe even two or three if you're lucky."

"I won't do that," Vanning said. "I won't ruin myself. I'm an innocent man. I'm a young man and I'm not going to mess up my life."

The policeman shrugged. All the policemen shrugged. The woods shrugged and the sky shrugged. None of them especially cared. It meant nothing to them. It meant nothing to the universe with the exception of this one tiny, moving, breathing thing called Vanning, and what it meant to him was fear and fleeing. And hiding. And fleeing again. And more hiding.

He stayed in the woods for another day and another night, went on through the woods until he found a clearance, and then railroad tracks. A freight came along and he hopped it. Later he hopped another freight and still another and finally arrived in New Orleans. He called himself Wilson and got a job on the water front. The pay was good, and with time and a half for overtime he soon had enough for more travel.

In Memphis he called himself Donahue and worked as a truck driver. Then up from Memphis, a short stay in Washington, and winding up in New York with three hundred dollars in his pocket. He called himself Rayburn and took the room in the Village. He went out and bought artist's materials and for two weeks he went at it furiously, building up a portfolio.

Then he went around with the portfolio and after a week of that he received his first assignment. At the beginning he had a thick mustache and wore dark glasses and combed his hair with a part in the middle. Later he discarded the glasses, and after that the mustache, and eventually he went back to the old way of combing his hair. He knew he was taking a big gamble, but it was something he had to do. He had to get rid of the hollow feeling, the grotesque knowledge that he was a hunted man.

He worked, he ate, he slept. He managed to keep going. But it was very difficult. It was almost unbearable at times, especially nights when he could see the moon from his window. He had a weakness for the moon. It gave him pain, but he wanted to see it up there. And beyond that want, so far beyond it, so futile, was the want for someone to be at his side, looking at the moon as he looked at it, sharing the moon with him. He was so lonely. And sometimes in this loneliness he became exceedingly conscious of his age, and he told himself he was missing out on the one thing he wanted above all else, a woman to love, a woman with whom he could make a home. A home. And children. He almost wept whenever he thought about it and realized how far away it was. He was crazy about kids. It was worth everything, all the struggle and heartache and worry, if only someday he could marry someone real and good, and have kids. Four kids, five kids, six kids, and grow up with them, show them how to handle a football, romp with them on the beach with their mother watching, smiling, so proudly, happily, and sitting at the table with her face across from him, and the faces of the kids, and waking up in the morning and going to work, knowing there was something to work for, and all that was as far away as the moon, and at times it seemed as though the moon was shaking its big pearly head and telling him it was no go, he might as well forget about it and stop eating his heart out.

The moon expanded after a while, and it became a brightly lit room that had two faces planted on the ceiling. One of the faces was big and wore glasses. The other face was gray and bony and topped by a balding skull. The faces flowed down from the ceiling and became stabilized, attached to torsos that stood on legs. And Vanning groaned.

Then he blinked a few times and put a hand to his mouth.

The hand came away bloody. He looked at the blood. He tasted blood in his mouth.

A door opened. Vanning turned and saw John entering the room. He grinned at John.

John had his hands in trousers pockets and was biting his lip and gazing at nothing special. Vanning stood up, stumbled and hit the bed and fell on it.

Pete moved toward Vanning and John said, "No."

"Let me work on him alone," Pete said. "Sam gets in my way."

"You hit him too hard," Sam said. "You knocked him out too fast. That ain't the way."

"I don't need Sam, I can operate better alone," Pete said. He was removing brass knuckles from his right hand. He rubbed his hands together and took a step toward the bed.

"Leave him alone," John said. "Get away from him."

"I'd like a drink of water," Vanning said.

"Sure," John said. "Sam, go get him a drink of water."

Sam walked out of the room. Pete stood there, near the bed, rubbing his hands and smiling at Vanning. Quiet streamed through the room and became thick in the middle of the room. Finally John looked at Vanning.

"Hurt much?" John said.

"Inside of my mouth. Cut up."

"Lose any teeth?"

"I don't know. I don't care."

"Let me work on him alone," Pete said.

John looked at Pete and said, "Get the hell out of here."

Pete shrugged and walked out of the room and John took a revolver from his shoulder holster and played with it for a while. He sighed a few times, frowned a few times, twisted his face as if he was trying to get a fly off it, and then he stood up and went to the wall and leaned there, looking at Vanning.

The quiet came back and settled in the center of the room. Vanning collected some blood in his mouth, spat it onto the floor. He took out a handkerchief and dabbed it against his mouth and looked at the blood, bright against white linen. He looked at John, and John was there against the wall, looking back at him, and it went on that way for several minutes, and then the door opened and Sam came in with a glass of water.

Vanning took the glass, and without looking at it he lifted it to his mouth, sent the water into his mouth, choked on the water, pegged the glass at Sam's face. The glass hit Sam on the side of his face, broke there, and some glass got through Sam's flesh. Sam threw a hand inside his lapel.

"No," John said.

"Yes. Let me." Sam's eyes were blank.

"What did you put in the water?" John said.

"Nothing," Sam said.

"Salt," Vanning said. "Try tasting salt water when your mouth is all cut up."

John walked over to Sam, gestured with the revolver, and Sam walked out of the room. John turned and faced Vanning and said, "You see the way it is? They like this. They get a kick out of it. That's what you're up against. Every few minutes they'll get a new idea and they'll want to try it on you."

"I feel sorry for myself," Vanning said, "but I can't do anything about it."

"I'll let you in on something," John said. "If you think I'm enjoying this, you're crazy."

"Then why don't you stop it?"

"The cash."

"Suppose you were in my place," Vanning said. "Suppose you knew you were going to go out the hard way if you didn't talk. Would you talk?"

"Sure," John said. "I'm no fool. I'd save myself a lot of grief. Money means a lot to me, but it doesn't mean that much."

"Do you think it means that much to me?"

"I think you're sore, that's all. You're so burned up that it's got the best of you. Either that or you're one of these morons who thinks it's the trend to be brave."

"You're way off," Vanning said. "I'm too mature for the Rover Boy act. I'm too scared to be angry. And I have enough common sense to realize that eventually I'll be dead if I don't tell you where that money is. That's why it's such a rough situation. I don't know where it is and there's no way I can convince you of the fact."

John sighed again. He said, "I've been in this game a long time. I was sent up once for seven years. When they let me out

I made up my mind to play level. It lasted for a while. I worked for a brewing outfit in Seattle. I met a girl. I don't remember, maybe I was happy. Anyway, my health was good, I had an appetite, I hardly ever took a drink. Then I began to see things. The way so many people let themselves wide open for a smart play. Even the big people. So you can figure out what happened to me. I went back to the old game. Just jockeying around at first. A few gasoline stations, a store now and then. Then a small bank in Spokane. And then a bigger bank in Portland. Finally the important job in Seattle. And that was going to be the last transaction."

"Even this won't do you any good," Vanning said. "How can you sell me something when I'm in no position to buy?"

As if Vanning had not interrupted, John went on, "It was going to be the last. After the split and expenses, I figured on a little more than two hundred grand for myself. And then I'd wait awhile until things blew over and I'd go back to Seattle and get in touch with that girl. Look, I'll show you something."

Holding the revolver at his side, John used his other hand to extract a wallet from a hip pocket. He opened the wallet, handed it to Vanning. Under celluloid there was a picture of the girl. She was very young. Maybe she wasn't even twenty. Her hair came down in long, loose waves that played with her shoulders. She was smiling. The way her face was arranged it was easy to see that she was a little girl, and skinny, and probably not too brilliant.

Vanning handed back the wallet. He bit his lower lip in a thoughtful way and he said, "She's pretty."

"Good kid." John replaced the wallet in his pocket.

"Does she know?"

"She knows everything."

"And where does that leave her?"

"Up a tree, for the time being," John said. "But she doesn't care. She's willing to wait. And then we're going away together. You know what I always wanted? A boat."

"Fishing?"

"Just going. In a boat. I know about boats. I worked on freighters tripping back and forth between the West Coast and

South America. Once I worked on a rich man's yacht. I've always wanted my own boat. That Pacific is a big hunk of water. All those islands."

"I've seen some of them."

"You have?" John leaned forward. He was smiling with interest.

"Quite a few of them. But I didn't have time to concentrate on the scenery. There was too much activity taking place. And smoke got in the way."

John nodded. "I get it. But just think of working out from the West Coast with all that water to move around in. All those islands out there ahead. A forty-footer with a Diesel engine. And go from one island to another. And look at them all. No real estate agent to bother me with the build-up. Just look them over and let them give me their own build-up. And let me make my own choice."

"You wouldn't stay long."

"You don't know me."

"You don't know yourself. You'd start thinking about another bank and another three hundred thousand. You're built that way, John. It's not your fault."

"Whose fault is it?"

"Who knows? Something must have happened when you were a kid. Not enough playgrounds in your town."

John grinned. "You talk like a defense attorney. It's a funny thing. I like you. You're game. You don't make a lot of noise. You can handle yourself. Maybe I'll take you along on my boat."

"I'll be looking forward to it."

John twisted his face and stared past Vanning. "I'll bet we could actually strike up a friendship. What do I call you?"

"Jim."

"Cigarette, Jimmy?"

"Okay."

And then after the cigarettes were lit, John said, "That's what I have in mind. That boat. And you're wrong about my coming back. I'd never come back. Just that little island and the girl and me. We'd have everything two people need. Figure it out."

"That's what I'm doing," Vanning said. "And there's a piece in there that doesn't fit. The money. Why would you need all that money?"

"The boat. Supplies. General expenses. It adds up."

"It doesn't hit a couple hundred thousand. Nowhere near that. If we made an itemized list you'd see how little you needed."

"We'll do that later," John said. "After I have the money."

Vanning hauled at the cigarette. He liked what was happening. It was giving him time, and he wanted that more than anything else. With time he could think, and with enough thinking there would be some sort of plan. Up till now the atmosphere had exhibited a completely hopeless quality. And now he had reason to think there might be a way to go on living.

"When I have that boat," John said, "I won't wait. I'll get on the boat with her and we'll shove off. Did you ever stop to think how cities crowd you? They move in on you, like stone walls moving in. You get the feeling you'll be crushed. It happens slow, but you imagine it happens fast. You feel like yelling. You want to run. You don't know where to run. You think if you start running something will stop you."

"I don't mind cities," Vanning said.

"Cities hurt my eyes. I don't like the country, either. I like that water. I know once I get on that water, going across it, going away, I'll be all right. I won't be nervous any more."

"You don't seem nervous."

"My nerves are in bad shape," John said. "I have a devil of a time falling asleep. How do you sleep?"

"The past eight months haven't been so good."

"You'll sleep fine after we get this deal cleared up."

"I guess so."

"How about it, Jimmy?"

Vanning squeezed the cigarette, watched the burning end detach itself from unlit tobacco, watched shreds of tobacco dripping from the paper shell. Emotion became an unknown thing, replaced now by curiosity. He wanted John to go on talking. He wanted an explanation of that sequence in Denver, the peculiar combination of revolver and satchel and empty room. But he couldn't ask about that. If he did ask, and if John gave him an answer, he would be strangely obligated to John, and he couldn't afford to be placed in that position. He had nothing to offer in return.

"I'm thinking about it," he said.

"That's fine," John said, and there was a faint touch of desperation in his voice. "You go on thinking about it. Don't worry about it. Just give it some thought. We'll figure out something."

They traded smiles, and John went on talking about the boat. He got to talking about boats in general. He seemed to know his boats. They stayed with the boats for a while and then they gradually came back to the business at hand.

"Funny," John said, "how we spotted you tonight."

"It was funny and it was clever."

"Why clever?"

"The girl," Vanning said.

"What girl?"

"Come on," Vanning said, and his heart climbed to the top of a diving platform and waited there.

"Oh," John said. "That girl. That girl in the restaurant. I didn't get a good look at her. What about her?"

"That's the point," Vanning said. "What about her?"

"You ought to know."

"All I know is, she couldn't have worked it better. I'm not the smartest man around by a long shot, but I don't get fooled like that very often."

John laughed. "You're nowhere near it," he said. "She wasn't working with us. We never saw her before."

"I don't see why you're trying to save her face."

"Maybe you'll want to see her again. Maybe you like her."

"Crazy about her," Vanning said. "Why shouldn't I be? Look at all she's done for me. I ought to buy her a box of orchids."

"You make it sound as if it's important."

"It's important because it's one of those things that makes a man want to kick himself. Bad enough that I talked to her in the first place. What hurts the most is that I let her take me down a street with only one small light on it."

"Maybe it's all for the best," John said. "Now we'll get this whole thing straightened out and everything will be fine."

"And dandy. Don't forget the dandy."

"Fine and dandy," John said, and he grinned, and then he stopped grinning.

Because Vanning was in there, too close to him, and Vanning was moving, Vanning's hand sliding out, going toward the revolver, veering away from the revolver as it came up, closing over John's wrist. And Vanning twisted John's wrist, twisted hard, and the revolver flew out of John's hand as Vanning twisted again. Then Vanning chopped a short right that caught John on the side of the head. As John tried to straighten, Vanning clipped him again, and a third time, and John was going down, hitting the edge of the bed, trying to get up.

Vanning allowed him to get halfway up, allowed him to start opening his mouth. Then Vanning reached back, hardened his right hand, sent it in on a straight line, direct and clean and exploding. John's eyes closed and John sagged, reached the floor, rolled over and stayed there.

Vanning stepped to the window and looked down. There was a ledge a few feet below. He climbed out of the window and placed himself on the ledge, looked down, saw another ledge, descended to that as he noticed the way the porch roof was placed. He was going down. Hanging from finger tips, he worked his way to a spot reasonably close to the porch roof, then let go. He didn't make much noise as he hit the porch roof, but it seemed like thunder. He waited there, and the echo of the thunder passed away and there was no more noise. He jumped from the porch roof, and he was wondering if they had left the keys in the green sedan.

Chapter Six

THERE WAS another ferryboat, much larger than the first one. And the big wave was moving in again. Fraser opened his eyes, twisted his head and saw a gleam of gray-lavender slicing through the venetian blinds. He rolled over and got out of bed, and immediately his wife was awake and sitting up.

"I'm getting dressed," Fraser said.

"So early?"

"I shouldn't have left him last night."

"Get back in bed."

"No," he said. "I've got to make sure." He moved toward the dresser. He opened a drawer and took out a tan leather case with a long strap attached to it. He dressed quickly, slung the strap over his shoulder, and he looked as though he was headed for the races at Jamaica.

"Breakfast?" she said.

"No, I don't have time."

"A glass of orange juice?"

"No," he said. "Thanks, honey, but this is on the double."

"Call me," she said. "I want to know."

He nodded and hurried out of the room. He was impatient in the elevator and more impatient on the street that was quite empty and especially empty in regard to taxis. He had to walk a block before he spotted one.

The taxi took him down to Greenwich Village, stopped a half block away from where he wanted to go. He walked quickly the rest of the way, entered a house across the street from Vanning's place, ran up to the room he had rented for the purpose of watching Vanning's room. He opened the leather case and took out a pair of binoculars.

At the window he held the binoculars to his eyes and focused on Vanning's room. He saw the empty room and a bed that had not been slept in. He stood there at the window with the binoculars against his eyes and the empty room looked back.

He put the binoculars back in the case. They were wonderful binoculars. They had cost plenty and if they weren't so valuable he would have kept them in this room, but the house was a shabby place and some of these tenants had a habit of visiting other rooms by means of a skeleton key. Now, however, he didn't particularly care if someone took the binoculars. He left the case on a table and walked out of the room.

There was a need for talking to someone, and Fraser decided to call Headquarters. Downstairs there was a pay phone, and he inserted a nickel, moved his hand toward the dial, discovered that he was not calling Headquarters, but his wife. She must have been sitting near the phone and waiting for the call, because she answered at once.

"He's gone," Fraser said.

"Are you sure?"

"I tell you he's gone."

"Please don't get excited."

"I've ruined it."

"Please——"

"I was too sure of myself. When I left him last night I could have sworn he'd head for his room and go to sleep. He'd been working at his board. He had an appointment today with an art director. I had it all checked, I was so sure, I'm gifted that way, I always know what I'm doing, I'm terrific——"

"Now cut it out, will you?"

"I think I'll resign——"

"Stop it. Come on home——"

"No," Fraser said. "I feel like taking a walk. I know where there's a grammar school around here. I think I'll enroll in kindergarten."

"Stay there. Maybe he'll come back."

"No, he's gone."

"I said stay there."

"Do you still like me?"

"Yes."

"Do you?" he asked. "Really?"

"Yes, dear."

"I don't think there's much to like. I shouldn't be giving you my troubles."

"If you didn't I wouldn't like you. But do you want me to like you a great deal?"

"Yes," Fraser said. "I want you to like me very much."

"Then stay there."

"He won't come back."

"Maybe he will. Please stay there."

"What for?"

"There's a chance——"

"I don't think so. I think they got him."

"Who?"

"Those other men. It's the first time he hasn't come home. What other kind of work do you think I'm fitted for?"

"I'm getting very angry at you."

"Maybe I'll go down to Headquarters."

"I don't want you to do that."

"I've got to go down there. I've got to tell them. Tell them now. Get it over with. Get the whole goddamn thing over with. I'm going down——"

"No——"

"See you later——"

"I said no. Stay on the phone. Don't you hang up——"

"Why?"

"I want to talk to you."

"What about?"

"Us."

"You and me?"

"And the kids," she said.

"All right, talk. I'll listen."

"I have faith in you," she said. "You're the finest man I've ever known. Sometimes I feel like walking up to strangers and telling them all about my husband. And the kids are so proud of you. And I'm so proud——"

"You ought to see me now."

"Does it mean anything when I say I have faith in you?"

"It makes me feel worse," he said. His voice was very low. He had lived a fairly quiet life, considering the field he was in, and aside from the technical excitement and ups and downs he had suffered no more disappointments and setbacks than the average man. He had been able to take all that without too much grief or self-dislike, but now he was extremely despondent and he was rather close to hating himself. Not for what he had done to himself, but the connection between the ruin of his career and the future of his wife and children. He had a feeling that right at this point his family was very insecure. And not because Headquarters would kick him out. They wouldn't kick him out. He had been with them too long. His record was excellent.

That was it. His record was much too excellent.

They'd pat him on the back and tell him to forget all about this one. They'd tell him to take a week off and get a rest and come back refreshed. But he wouldn't come back that way. He would come back with the rigid, icy knowledge that he was going downhill. And already he was descending. The moment he walked into Headquarters to report this matter, he would be going downward at a terrific rate, with no support or elevation in sight. And that was what he had to do. He had to tell Headquarters about this, and immediately.

"I've got to hang up now," he said. "I'm going to Headquarters."

"Will you do something for me?" There was a desperation in her voice and it was as though she had seen inside his mind. "Will you wait there another hour? Just give it another hour."

"That's against regulations. We've got to report these things right away."

"I'm asking you to gamble."

"High stakes," he said. And he meant it. Despite his record, despite his many years on the job, he couldn't defy routine procedure without taking the risk of being fired. Even though they liked him very much, they had a habit of taking this sort of thing quite seriously. Maybe they would throw him out, after all, just to set an example.

"I know it's taking a big chance," she said. "But do it anyway. For me."

He bit at the inside of his mouth. "An hour?"

"Just an hour."

There was an odd certainty in her voice. He had to smile. It was a strained, weary smile. "You're selling me something," he said. "You want me to think you're clairvoyant."

"Promise me you'll stay there an hour."

He waited for several moments, and then he said, "All right."

"You promise? Really?"
"Yes."

And he put the receiver back on the hook. He walked up the dusty stairway, went into the room. He picked up the binoculars and moved toward the window.

Chapter Seven

THERE WAS morning gray in the sky as the sedan crossed Brooklyn Bridge. There was some pale blue in the sky as Vanning parked the car in an alleyway off Canal Street. He used the subway to get back to the Village, and upon entering his room the first direct move he made was to start packing his things. After some minutes of that he changed his mind, sat on a chair near the window and smoked cigarettes while he toyed with various angles. He was certain they didn't know his address. He told himself not to be too certain of anything. The logical step at this point was something simple, something easy. And the easiest thing he could think of was sleep.

He slept until late afternoon, showered and shaved, concluded after a mirror inspection that he looked just a little too banged up for an appearance at the advertising agency where his illustrations were due. After breakfast, he used the restaurant phone booth, told the agency art director that he was sick with an upset stomach. The art director told him tomorrow would be all right, joked with him about the effects of alcohol on a man's stomach, told him milk was the best medicine for a raw stomach. Vanning thanked the agency man and hung up. He took a subway uptown. He didn't know where he was going. He wanted to get away from the Village. He wanted to think.

It kept jabbing away at him, the desire to get out of this city, to travel and keep on traveling. But it wasn't traveling. It was running. And the desire was curtained by the knowledge that running was a move without sensible foundation. Retreat was only another form of waiting. And he was sick of waiting. There had to be some sort of accomplishment, and the only way he could accomplish anything was to move forward on an offensive basis.

He was part of a crowd on Madison Avenue in the Seventies, and he was swimming through schemes, discarding one after another. The schemes moved off indifferently as he pushed them away. He walked into a drugstore and ordered a dish of orange ice. Sitting there, with the orange ice in front of him, he picked up a spoon, tapped it against his palm, told himself to take it from the beginning and pick up the blocks one by one and see if he could build something.

There weren't many blocks. There was John. There was Pete and there was Sam. There was the green sedan. There was the house on the outskirts of Brooklyn. None of those was any good. There was the man who had died in Denver. And that was no good. There was Denver itself. There were the police in Denver. The police.

A voice said, "You want to eat that orange ice or drink it?"

Vanning looked up and saw the expressionless face of a soda clerk.

"It's melting," the soda clerk said.

"Melting," Vanning said.

"Sure. Can't you see?"

"Tell me something," Vanning said.

"Anything. I'm a whiz."

"I'll bet you are. I'll bet you know everything there is to know about orange ice."

"People, too."

"Let's stay with the orange ice."

"Whatever you say. It's no longer a sellers' market. Nowadays we've got to please the customers."

"It doesn't take much to please me," Vanning said. "I'm just curious about this orange ice."

"No mosquitoes in it. We spray the stuff every day."

"I mean the way it melts."

"It don't melt in winter, mister. But this is summer. It's hot in summer. That's why the ice melts. Okay?"

"Okay for a start. But let's go on from there."

"Sure. Just as soon as I fix a black-and-white for Miss America down there."

Vanning waited. He dipped the spoon into the melting pale orange dome and left it there. The soda clerk came back and said, "Now where were we?"

"The orange ice. Look, it's nearly all melted."

"That's the way things go. It's a tough world."

"But suppose we use our heads about this. Suppose we freeze it again. What I'm driving at is, a thing may look ruined, but if you give it a certain treatment you can bring it back to normal. You can still use it."

"That's what I claim," the soda clerk said. "Never say die. Someday I'll own Manhattan. Just watch my speed."

"Good for you," Vanning said. He picked up the check, put a fifty-cent piece on the counter and walked toward the telephone booths. There was a buzzing in his mind and it was a healthy buzzing. He liked the feel of it, the soundless sound of it. He entered a booth, closed the door, took some change out of his pocket.

He put a nickel in the slot.

"Number, please?"

"I want to call Denver."

"What is that, sir?"

"Denver, Colorado."

"What number, sir?"

"Police headquarters."

"Station to station?"

"That's right, and don't cut in on me. I'll signal when I'm finished."

"Just a moment, sir."

He waited several moments. Then the operator waited while Vanning left the booth and got the necessary change. She was arranging the connection for him, he was putting quarters and dimes into the slots, he was waiting.

And then he heard her saying, "New York calling. Just a moment, please."

A voice said, "Yes? Hello?"

Vanning leaned toward the mouthpiece. "Is this police headquarters in Denver?"

"That's right. Who is this?"

Vanning gave the name of a New York newspaper. He said, "Features department. This is Mr. Rayburn, associate editor. I'm wondering if you could help me out."

"Just a minute."

The voice handed him over to another voice. And then a third voice. And a fourth.

The fourth voice said, "All right, what can we do for you?"

"May I know whom I'm speaking to?"

"Hansen. Homicide. What's on your mind?"

Vanning repeated the self-introduction he had given to the

first voice. He said, "We'd like to do a feature story on a murder that took place in Denver some time ago."

"That's not telling me much."

"Eight months ago."

"Solved?"

"That's what we don't know. We got the shreds of it from
hearsay."

"Any names?"

"No," Vanning said. "That's why I'm calling. We don't have
any record of it in our files. But from what we've picked up, it's
one of those sensational things."

"Is that all you can tell me?"

Vanning stared at the wall beyond the telephone and told
himself to hang up. This was a crazy move. It was packed
chock-full of risk. If he stayed on the phone too long, if he
made one slip, they would trace the call. Maybe they were tracing it already. He couldn't understand why he was staying on
the phone. For a moment he wanted them to trace the call, he
wanted them to nab him, once and for all, get the entire affair
over with, one way or another. In the following moment he
told himself to hang up and walk out of the drugstore and
leave the neighborhood. But something kept him attached to
the phone. He didn't know what it was. His mind was filled
with an assortment of jugglers and they were dropping Indian
pins all over the place.

He said, "We know the victim was a man. The killer was
identified, but he got away."

"Wait a minute. I'll have a look at the files."

Vanning lit a cigarette. The quiet phone was like an ocean
without waves. He blew smoke into the mouthpiece and
watched it radiate. The minute went by. Another minute went
by. And a third. And a fourth. The operator was in there for a
few seconds, and Vanning told her to come in at the end of the
call and tell him what he owed the phone company. Then the
phone was quiet again. And another minute went by.

And then the voice from Denver was on again, saying,
"Maybe this is it. You there?"

"I'm listening."

"Eight months ago. A man named Harrison. Shot and killed

a few blocks away from the Harlan Hotel. Suspect a man named James Vanning. Still at large."

"That's it."

"What about it?"

"Can you give me anything?"

"Nothing you could build into a story. But then again I'm not in the newspaper business."

"Anything at all."

"Listen, if it's this important, why don't you send a man down?"

"We will, if I think the thing can be shaped into something."

"I doubt it, but you're paying good money for the call. You want to take it down?"

"I'm ready. Shoot."

"Harrison, Fred. Record of six arrests. Served time for robbery. Arrested on a murder charge in 1936 but case thrown out of court for lack of evidence. On probation at time he was murdered. From there on we're in the dark. No motive. No trace of the suspect."

"You sure about your suspect?"

"No doubt about it. Fingerprints on the gun. Vanning's car parked near the Harlan Hotel. Vanning registered at the Harlan Hotel under the name of Dilks, along with two other men."

"Their names?"

"Smith and Jones. You can see what we have to work with."

"Anything more on Vanning?"

"He was spotted with Harrison in the lobby of the hotel. About ten minutes before the murder. Someone piped them leaving the hotel together. That was the last time he was seen."

"Try to stay with him," Vanning said. "I don't want to promise anything definite, but we may be able to dig up a few facts you can use. Try to give me more on the man."

"There isn't much to give. On the face of it, we'd say that the job was handled by a hired killer. But this Vanning keeps us guessing. No record of past arrests. Worked as a commercial artist in Chicago. Served as a lieutenant, senior grade, in the Navy. Damage-control officer on a battleship. Silver Star. Excellent record. No past connection with victim. It's an upside-down case. We know he did it, but that's all. You said you could hand us a few facts."

"We may have something for you. Say in a few days. We're not sure yet, but there's an interesting connection that has possibilities."

"Why not let me have it now?"

"I don't want to make a fool of myself. It may not mean anything. I don't want to lose my job. Remember, I'm only an associate editor. There's a boss over me."

"Let me speak to the boss. I'll hold the phone."

"Wait," Vanning said. "Let's see what I can do with this." He turned his face away from the mouthpiece, said to empty air, "Johnny, is the boss around?" Then he waited. Then he came back to the mouthpiece and said, "Wait there a minute."

"I'm waiting."

Vanning lit another cigarette, took small, rapid puffs at it, closed his eyes, his forehead deeply creased in groping thought. All at once he snapped his fingers. The idea was glaring and he didn't see any holes in it. He whipped out his breast-pocket handkerchief, put it across the mouthpiece, put his voice on a high-pitched, nasal plane as he said, "Callahan speaking. Features editor."

"This is Hansen. Denver police. Homicide department."

"What did Rayburn tell you?"

"Nothing. He only asked questions. But he said he might be able to tell me something. He said it was a little over his head, so I asked if I could speak with you."

"If Rayburn was a good newspaperman, he wouldn't be dragging me in here. I don't know why they're always putting these things on my shoulders."

"Look, Callahan, that's between you and Rayburn. I'm a policeman and we're trying to catch a murderer. You're trying to get a story. If we can help each other out, that's fine. But you can't expect me to throw information your way and have you sit there in New York and hold back on me. If you have something you think we can use, let's have it. Otherwise, stop wasting your time and mine."

"I guess you make sense."

"I guess I do."

"Okay," Vanning said. "I'll give it to you but I want you to understand it's not a definite lead. It's just something we picked up more or less by accident. Some character called us up and told us a story about a bank robbery in Seattle. About eight or nine months ago, he said it was. A big job, three hundred thousand dollars. He said it was connected with a murder in Denver. We called Seattle and they told us the bank robbers were traced as far as Colorado."

"That's interesting."

"Is it new to you?"

"Brand-new. Tell me something. How many men were in on that Seattle thing?"

"Three," Vanning said, and he tried to bite it back before it hit the mouthpiece, but it was already in the mouthpiece, it was already in Denver.

"Three men. That adds up to Dilks and Smith and Jones. That brings Vanning in on the bank job. I'm going to check with Seattle. I think you've handed us something we can use. Will you hold the phone a minute?"

"Don't be too long," Vanning said.

He took a deep breath, blew it out toward the handkerchief spread and tightened across the telephone mouthpiece. He wondered how long he had been in the phone booth. It seemed as if he had been here for a full day. And it seemed as if he was making one mistake after another. There were too many things to remember, and already he had forgotten one of the most important, that angle concerning Sam, the fact that Sam had been absent from the Denver affair. Sam had been in Leadville, under the care of that doctor. Three men in the Seattle robbery. Three men in the Denver deal. He felt like rapping himself in the mouth. Now he had gone and done it. Now he was glued to Seattle as well as Denver. Now he had taken Sam's place in the line-up. He was only a substitute, and yet at the same time he was the headline performer. He was the star, the stellar attraction, he was the goat, the ignoramus who deserved every rotten break he got. This phone call was just another major error in a long parade of major errors. He was kidding himself now and he had been kidding himself all along. He wasn't a criminal, he wasn't even an amateur criminal. He was a commercial artist, a grown man, an ordinary citizen who believed in law and order, a man who looked upon too much excitement as an unnatural, neurotic thing. He didn't belong in this muddle, this circle that went round and round much too fast.

The voice from Denver was there again. "Hello. Callahan?"

"Still here."

"We're checking with Seattle. Can you hold on?"

"I'll wait."

"Good. We won't be long."

Vanning put another cigarette in his mouth, had no desire to light it. He put his hand in front of his eyes, wondered why his fingers weren't shaking. Perhaps he had gone beyond that. Perhaps it was actually a bad sign, his steady fingers. He sat there, his head lowered, feeling sorry for himself, feeling sorry for every poor devil who had ever stumbled into a spot like this. And then, gradually lifting his head, he gradually smiled. It was such a miserable state of affairs that it was almost comical. If people could see him now their reactions would be mixed. Some of them would have pity for him. Others would smile as he was smiling at this moment. Maybe some of them would laugh at him, as they would laugh at Charlie Chaplin in hot water somewhere up in the Klondike.

He sighed. He thought of other men, thousands of them, hundreds of thousands, working in factories, in offices, and going back tonight to a home-cooked meal, sitting in parlors with their wives and kids, listening to Bob Hope, going to sleep at a decent hour, and really sleeping, with nothing to anticipate except another day of work and another evening at home with the family. That was all they looked forward to, and Vanning told himself he would give his right arm if that was all he could look forward to.

"Callahan?"

"Yes?"

"Just stay there. Be with you in a jiffy. We're still talking to Seattle on another phone."

"Make it snappy, will you?"

"Be right with you."

Vanning struck a match and applied it to the cigarette that waited in his mouth. He took in some smoke, blew it out, turned his head and saw a girl waiting outside the phone booth. She seemed to be fed up with waiting, and her pose was typical, the hand on the hip, the head tilted to one side, the lips tightened sarcastically and saying, Go on, take all day, it's so silly to consider other people. He smiled sheepishly, and her expression changed, she glared at him. She looked very attractive, glaring. Pretty girl with an upsweep, pretty and slim and extremely Madison Avenue. It was getting on toward the cocktail hour and evidently she wanted to check on her date at Theodore's or the Drake and it was a shame he had to keep her waiting like this. It was really unfair. All she wanted to do was keep that date, and all he wanted to do was keep himself alive. Now her expression had changed again and she seemed really worried about getting to the phone. He was just a little annoyed at himself, because he was getting an eerie sort of satisfaction watching her frown of worriment. At least he wasn't the only worried individual in this world.

The girl shifted her position, breathed in and out in an exasperated way.

Vanning opened the booth door, leaned out and said, "I'm calling Denver."

"How lovely."

"I'm awfully sorry it's taking this long."

"We're both sorry."

"Maybe one of the other booths——"

"No, darling. Everybody's calling Denver."

"I'll try to rush it."

"Please do. I want to break the date before he gets there."

"I thought you wanted to keep the date," Vanning said.

"I want to break it. I hope you don't mind."

"It depends. Maybe he's a nice guy."

"He's very unexciting," the girl said. "He wants to get married. What are you doing with that handkerchief over the mouthpiece?"

"I have a cold. I don't want anyone else to get it. I——"

Denver was in again. Vanning closed the door, came back to the mouthpiece.

The voice was saying, "I think you've started something, Callahan. We have Seattle all worked up. They tell us three men did that bank job. Got away in a phaeton. Two men in the bank and one waiting in the car. One of the men was big. Hefty around chest and shoulders. Wore a felt hat and a loafer jacket with a wide collar turned up. That was probably Vanning, alias Dilks. Now we're going to check with the Navy to see when he got out. The way we have it lined up, Harrison was waiting in Denver, acting as contact man. There must have been an argument over the split, and Vanning pulled a gun and that's about as close as we can come to it right now. That character you were telling us about, if he calls up again see if you can meet him somewhere. See if you can hold him down. And listen, if anything new turns up, get in touch with us, will you?"

"By all means."

"And thanks for the tip."

"I'm thanking you," Vanning said. "I think we'll have a swell story."

"You bet. 'Bye now." And the other party hung up.

The operator asked for more money and Vanning paid it. He put the handkerchief back in his pocket, and as he left the phone booth the girl went whizzing in to take his place. He walked through the drugstore, arranged his lips to whistle a tune, couldn't get the tune past his lips.

On Madison Avenue again, he waved to a cab, climbed in and fell back against leather-looking upholstery, and the cab started south on Madison.

"Where to?"

"Fifth Avenue and Eighth Street."

"You in a hurry?"

"No," Vanning said. "Why?"

"Just wondered."

Vanning closed his eyes, slumped in the seat, stayed that way for several seconds and then slowly opened his eyes and gazed at the driver's head. There was considerable traffic in front of the taxi's windshield, but Vanning didn't see it. He was studying the driver's head. The driver wore a cloth cap. The driver had recently treated himself to a haircut. The barber was either a newcomer to the trade or not too much interested in the work. It was a very bad haircut.

The taxi made a turn, made another turn and came onto Fifth Avenue.

The haircut was bad because it took too much hair from the

driver's skull, and instead of shading gradually from hair to shaven neck, it broke up acutely, so that there was a distinct cleavage between black hair and white flesh. That was one thing that made the driver seem a little wrong. And another thing was the way the driver sat at the wheel. The driver leaned to one side, and didn't seem to be watching the traffic in front. Instead, the driver seemed to aim attention at the rear-view mirror.

"Where did you get that haircut?" Vanning said.

"What's the matter with it?"

"Everything."

"Makes no difference," the driver said. "Who sees me?"

"Don't you care how you look?"

"All I care about is getting rid of hair in the summer. If men had any sense, they'd shave their entire heads. Nothing like it if you want to keep cool."

The taxi made another turn. It was going toward Sixth Avenue.

"Why not stay on Fifth?"

"Too much traffic."

"I'm a New Yorker," Vanning said. "Just as much traffic on Sixth. Just as many lights."

"Should we try Eighth?"

"That's taking me out of my way."

"You said you weren't in a hurry."

Vanning leaned forward. "That's what I said. That's why I'm wondering why we didn't stay on Fifth."

"You want me to cut off the meter? I don't need the money. I make out."

The taxi passed Sixth Avenue, passed Broadway, moved on toward Eighth.

"Sure," the driver said. "I break even. I don't have to stretch a ride. I never go in for that sort of thing. And I don't like to be accused of it, either. I been driving a cab for fifteen years and I never stretched a ride. I like when people start telling me how to operate a cab."

"What do you want me to do, sit here and argue with you?"

"I like when these people think they're doing me a favor when they get in the cab. I got more money in the bank than most of the people who ride with me. And you don't have to tip me if you don't want to. I'm not asking for a tip. I don't want anybody to think they're doing me favors."

"Now we're passing Eighth," Vanning said. "If this is a sight-seeing tour, why not start with Grant's Tomb?"

"You want me to stop the cab?" the driver said. "You can get out here if you want to."

"It sounds like an idea."

"We'll stop right here," the driver said.

The taxi was slowing down, going toward the curb. The driver turned around and stared at Vanning as Vanning looked at the meter. The driver stared past Vanning. And Vanning was taking money from his pocket and then he was looking at the driver, whose eyes remained focused on the rear window.

"All right," Vanning said. "Let's forget the beef. Let's keep going."

"Maybe you better get out here."

"Keep going," Vanning said.

"It's got to be level. I can't do it if it ain't level. You know how it is."

"I said keep going."

The taxi moved away from the curb, stopped for a red light. The light changed. Traffic was thinning out. Vanning folded his arms, sat stiffly on the edge of the seat.

"Down Ninth Avenue?" the driver asked.

"Try Tenth."

"A lot of trucks on Tenth."

"All right. Ninth. Give her some speed."

"Now look, mister——"

"You heard me."

The taxi commenced racing down Ninth Avenue. A red light showed and the taxi ignored it, raced toward the next red light.

"Make a turn," Vanning said. "Turn left."

"Can't do that. One-way street. We'll be bucking traffic."

"Make the turn," Vanning said.

The taxi started a turn, veered away to remain on Ninth Avenue, cut past the next red light, then turned down a side street, and there was the sound of a policeman's whistle, and the taxi raced on.

"Back to Fifth," Vanning said. "Go past Fifth. Go toward the river. Don't stop for anything."

"It ain't no good," the driver said. "We're in the center of Manhattan. We don't have no room to move. First thing you know, we'll have a smash-up. It's bound to happen."

"Don't look back at me. Keep your eyes on the windshield. Keep us moving."

"If I stop in heavy traffic you can hop out and——"

"Don't tell me how to plan my day," Vanning said. "Just drive your taxicab and let's see if we can do something smart."

"I sure did something smart when I picked you up."

"Drive, Admiral. Just drive."

They were going past Sixth. Past Fifth. There was another red light. They went past it. They went rushing toward the rear of a huge truck, and the truck came to a stop, and the truck became an expanse of dull green wall in front of them.

"On the sidewalk," Vanning said.

Two wheels of the cab climbed up on the sidewalk, stayed on the sidewalk as the cab fought to get free. A man appeared in front of the cab, and the man's eyes bulged, the man leaped toward the wall of a building. The cab returned to the street, went tearing its way past the red light that showed on Madison.

"I needed this," the driver complained.

"Don't worry," Vanning said. "Everything's going to be all right. We're doing great."

"I'm glad you think so. That makes me feel a lot better."

Another truck blocked them off on Lexington Avenue. The driver twisted the wheel, they cut between two other cars, and the two other cars came together and there was the sound of a crash. Vanning's cab continued on its way, and in the distance there was the sound of a policeman's whistle. And another whistle.

"You hear that?" the driver said.

"I heard it."

"But that's the law."

"That's why it sounds so good."

"You don't get me, mister. I said the law. I'm doing the best I can, but we're working in a crowded city and there's too much law and not enough space. They're going to catch this cab."

"And the car in back of us."

"You know who's in back of us?"

"Sure," Vanning said. "A green sedan. Right?"

"Wrong," the driver said. "Take a look. See for yourself."

Vanning stared at the driver's third-rate haircut. Then very slowly he turned and looked through the rear window and he saw another cab. It was quite a distance behind, and some cars were in front of it, but it was pushing its way past the cars. It was coming on.

"The cab?" Vanning said.

"Of course it's the cab. I thought you knew from the beginning."

"When was the beginning?"

"When you climbed in. When we started out on Madison. I saw him making a beeline for that other cab. That's why we took the long ride. I was trying to help you out."

Vanning smashed a fist into his other hand. "It's John," he said. "It's got to be John. It's got to end here. They've got to catch me and they've got to catch John. This is the wind-up. The only way it could end." He knew he was getting onto the hysterical side, but there was nothing he could do about it. His voice sounded odd as he said, "You hear me?"

"I hear you, mister, but I don't know what you're talking about."

"I'm talking about a bank robber named John."

"In that other cab?"

"Right."

"Wrong," the driver said. "The guy in that other cab is no bank robber. I know what he is."

"What?"

"Detective."

At first it didn't click. It was too far away. Too high up or too far underground, and Vanning had to close his eyes and rub his palms into his eyes, and then he had to take himself back to the phone booth in the drugstore, and he had to remember how long he had stayed on the phone, talking to Denver, and he had to estimate how long it would take Denver to trace the call, how long it would take Denver to call Manhattan police, how long it would take Headquarters in Manhattan to send a man to the drugstore. Vanning figured that out in terms of minutes, and then he shook his head in a convulsive way, he tried to forget that he was in a racing taxi. And just then the whole thing clicked, and it made a tremendous noise in his head. And it was too much for him.

"Take me to the river," he said. "I may as well jump in."

"Don't go nuts on me," the driver said. "Past Second Avenue I'll drive up an alley and you can hop out. We got a nice lead."

"How do you know he's a detective?"

"I've seen him around."

"You sure?"

"I'm telling you he's a plain-clothes man. I've seen him operate. What I ought to do is mind my own business. But you looked all right. You look like a guy who needed a break."

"Where's that alley?"

"Not far," the driver said. "From now on," he promised, "I'll get my excitement in the movies."

"Drive," Vanning said. "I'm an innocent man. Believe me——"

Slashing past Second Avenue, the cab almost made contact with another truck, curved away, then out in front of the truck, then past a jalopy, then made a turn into a wide alleyway. On one side there was a gate that ran the length of the alley, and beyond the gate a grim line of wall with no windows showing. On the other side there was a warehouse, and Vanning saw windows and he saw doorways, and a few of the doors were open.

His wallet was out, he was flipping a twenty-dollar bill toward the front seat, the cab was coming to a stop.

"Keep moving," he said. "Drive up the alley. After that I don't care what you do."

He jerked the door handle, leaped out of the cab, sprinted across the alley and threw himself at the nearest open doorway. As he went in, he could hear the noise made by an approaching siren.

The warehouse was a huge place. It was quite dark in the area across which Vanning moved. He had to move slowly because it was so dark. Men's voices came from somewhere on the floor above. Vanning walked into a column of boxes, grabbed them as they started to topple over.

"Charlie Chaplin again," he murmured. "Come on, you. Cut out the comedy."

But he was having trouble getting the boxes back in place, and they were large boxes and they almost knocked him over. He knew he was grinning. And as he kept on grinning he became a little afraid of it. To grin at a time like this was all wrong, unreasonable. And the wrongness of it harmonized with all the other wrong stunts he had pulled.

The absurd phone call to Denver. He couldn't get his finger on the exact reason why he had called Denver. Maybe because he wanted to find out how much they knew. Maybe because he wanted to throw some bait their way in the hope of making a bargain. Just what kind of bargain he had figured on making he couldn't remember. There had to be a trickle of logic in it somewhere, but now, at this special juncture, he saw the phone call as an extremely foolish thing.

And those other foolish things. Assuming that the car behind the cab had been a green sedan with John and Pete and Sam in it. So very sure that it had been a green sedan, failing to remember that he had taken the green sedan on a ride from the outskirts of Brooklyn. Now he remembered the ride but he couldn't remember the geography of the ride, he couldn't remember the location of the house where they had negotiated with him. Not even the approximate location of the house. And he couldn't remember where he had parked the green sedan. Somewhere near the subway station on Canal Street, but that was no good. There were too many streets, too many alleys near the Canal Street subway. And all this harmony of error was harmonizing with that first tremendous error, that satchel business, and it didn't get him anywhere to tell himself he was absent-minded. Lapse of memory might be good for a laugh in a courtroom, but bad otherwise.

All this was saddening, it was downhill. Vanning begged himself to get away from the negative side. Too much of it would lead to complete fear, and if he ever reached that point he might just as well take gas. Defeat was a whirlpool, and the only thing to do was swim away from it, keep swimming, no matter how strong the downward drag. He still had his life, he still had his health, his brain had stalled several times but it was still a brain, it still functioned.

And now it told him there was no such thing as a super-human being, and even Babe Ruth had suffered a batting slump every now and then, and even Hannibal had undergone military set-backs, even Einstein had flunked in mathematics on one amazing occasion. And then there was another way to look at it.

Gravity was a powerful thing, but someone had invented the parachute. Oceans had tremendous depths, and yet someone had invented a vessel that would go down and down and then come up again and reach the surface. Vanning told himself to invent an idea that would get him clear of the downhill path and bring him up. It was time for that. He had gone down far enough, too far. It was time to start climbing. It was time to stop the foolish grin and the relaxed submission to all the leering goblins.

He walked through the warehouse. There was a door leading out to air and sunlight. There were some men standing near the door. A few were in their shirt sleeves. Others wore overalls. A husky man wearing a cap and smoking a cigar was loudly enthusiastic over a new welterweight from Minneapolis. Vanning walked toward the group. They blocked his path to the door. They turned and looked at him. He stared at them as he approached. He stared past them, indicating that he intended leaving the warehouse. They continued to block the door. They all looked at him.

"Going out," Vanning said.

The big man with the cigar was lowering the cigar from tobacco-stained lips. "You connected here?"

"City inspector," Vanning said.

"Inspecting what?"

"Plumbing."

"How we doing?"

"Water's still running," Vanning said. "That's good enough."

The big man stepped out of Vanning's way. And Vanning walked through the doorway. Adding distance between himself and the warehouse, he moved on toward First Avenue. He walked fast on First Avenue, watching the street, looking for a cab. There was slightly less than five minutes of this, and then a cab, and then a slow ride downtown, a few cigarettes, and then a short stroll across part of Washington Square, and finally his apartment.

He took off his coat, seated himself near the window. He sat there doing nothing for quite a while. Heat came up from the Village pavements and threw itself against him. He picked himself up from the chair, walked to the kitchenette, opened the refrigerator. Busy with bottles and ice, he anticipated his drink and enjoyed the idea that he was doing something constructive. He mixed a third of scotch with two thirds of soda, used a good deal of ice, took the glass back to the window, sat down and took his time with the drink.

Three drinks later he was in a fairly comfortable frame of mind. He looked out and saw the sky taking on a blend of orange and purple, lighting up in the fierce, frantic glow that tries and fails to conquer dusk. When dusk arrived, Vanning told himself to go out and get something to eat.

There was a lot of satisfaction in that, knowing he could still go out. That part of the situation was the best part, the fact that they didn't know where he lived. Or to put it another way, they didn't know where he was hiding out. It was sensible to look a thing like this in the face, because there was a great deal of difference between a home and a hiding place.

Chapter Eight

IN THE Fraser apartment the phone rang. She raced to it. And the first thing he said was a big thank you, thanks for everything.

"You feel better?" she said.

"I'm with him again."

"I knew that," she said. "I knew it the moment I heard your voice."

"I wanted to call earlier——"

"Of course——"

"But I couldn't get away. I've been with him ever since he came home this morning."

"You sound so excited."

"I ought to be," he said. "Something's happened. It's big. He's home now and I have a chance to breathe. I just checked with Headquarters. They told me he called Denver. The call was traced and they put two and two together. I knew he was making a long call but I couldn't do the tracing myself. Too many booths in the drugstore. A big place on Madison Avenue. He called Denver and pretended to be a newspaperman. He told them what they already knew. Denver can't figure that one out. Neither can Headquarters. But I think I can."

"You mean he's working toward giving himself up?"

"Not yet. I figure he wanted to find out how much they knew."

"Wouldn't a smart criminal do that?"

"No," Fraser said. "A smart criminal would know for sure they'd trace the call. Everything he's done today backs up my ideas about this case. When he left the drugstore he got in a cab. I followed him. Somehow he knew he was being followed and he managed to lose me."

"How did you find him again?"

"He went back to his apartment. He's there now, across the street. I'm watching the front door."

"He got away from you and then he went home?"

"Right."

"He must be stupid."

"Not stupid," Fraser said. "It's just that he isn't operating like a guilty party. That phone call to Denver. And then knowing he was being followed. And coming back to his apartment instead of leaving town. A guilty man wouldn't do things like that."

She sighed into the phone. "I guess I'm thick. I just don't get it. You say he's a killer and yet he isn't guilty."

"I know. It sounds all mixed up."

"Why do you think he's staying in town?"

"I've got an idea he wants us to find those other men."

"Why?"

"I don't know," Fraser said. "I'm trying to hit an answer."

"What did Headquarters say?"

"They wanted me to bring him in. I begged for more time."

"How much more?"

"Not long," Fraser said. "Forty-eight hours."

"Do you have a plan?"

"Vaguely."

"Anything to work on?"

"Just Vanning. I better hang up now. I'm beginning to worry again. Vanning isn't enough. I need something else. It's like waiting for rain in the desert."

"Maybe you can talk to him again."

"If I could find a good excuse."

"But there's only forty-eight hours——"

"Don't remind me," he said. "Every time I look at my watch I get sick."

"Does it make you feel better, talking to me?"

"A lot."

"Stay there and talk to me."

"All right, dear."

"Tell me things."

"Things you don't know already?"

"Anything you want to tell me."

"Even if it's unimportant?"

"Even if it's silly," she said.

"Headquarters told me something funny," he said. "I shouldn't even mention it. I haven't any right to think about it. Not at this point, anyway. It all depends whether you're in a mercenary mood."

"I'm in any mood you're in."

"I don't know what mood I'm in, dear. I only know right now money's a side issue. Now I wish I hadn't said anything."

She laughed. "You've already opened your big mouth."

"How much do we have in the bank?"

"Seventeen hundred."

"Headquarters got a wire from Seattle," he said, and felt rather cheap saying it. But he was thinking of his wife and his children and the things he wanted to give them, and underneath that he was impelled by the desire to talk, to talk about anything except the big worry at hand, and he might as well talk about this; at least it was something practical, it was a basis for talk. And he said, "If I can get Vanning to tell where the money is, I'll get a reward of fifteen thousand."

"Fifteen thousand?"

"That's a lot of cabbage."

"Fifteen thousand."

"Let's both forget about it."

"We might as well. Even if you bring him in, he'll never own up."

"I'm sorry I mentioned it."

"Don't be sorry," she said.

"We'll forget about it."

"Sure."

"How are the kids?"

"Fine."

"And how are you?"

"Oh, I'm——"

"I've got to hang up," Fraser said. "He's out there, coming out of the house. Talk to you later——"

The receiver clicked. She lowered the phone. She started to light a cigarette, but suddenly there was a commotion in the next room and it sounded as though the children were beating each other over the head. She put down the cigarette and tightened her lips as she went in to break it up. As she entered the room the riot came to an immediate halt, and the three of them looked at her with innocent faces. She tried to appear severe, but she wasn't much good at this, and all at once she laughed lightly and the children started to laugh and she ran at them, gathered them to her, hugged them and kissed them and said, "You little Indians——"

Chapter Nine

THE RESTAURANT was a popular sea-food establishment, noted especially for its lobster. Vanning ordered a cup of clam broth and a large lobster. He ate slowly, getting pleasure from the rich pink-white meat dripping butter. It was luxury, this lobster. It was one of the things that made life worth living. There were considerable things that made life worth living. Luxurious things, rich, colorful things, tasty things, and then the quietly pleasant things, abstract things, certain contentments that couldn't be analyzed in terms of statistics. He thought of those things for a while, but only a little while. The lobster brought him back to the other things, and he found himself thinking in terms of the luxurious, the joys in a materialistic category. Somewhere along that path a few colors entered. There was deep rose against a background of rich tan. There was shining gold. There was blue, a good, definite blue, not bright, not at all watery, but deeply blue. And then the tan again. Healthy tan. And all that added up, and it became Martha.

The thought became action, and Vanning's hand shot back and away from the table, went sliding into his coat pocket. For a moment it wasn't there, and he told himself if it wasn't there it was no place. Then it came against his fingers, and he took it out of his pocket, the folded paper secure and actual and living against the flesh of his fingers. He unfolded it. He looked at the name. Just Martha. And then the address.

It was a fake address, of course. It had to be fake. If she was clever enough to fool him as she had done, she would certainly be clever enough to give him a fake address. He congratulated himself on the deduction. And yet that was all it amounted to right now. Nothing more than a deduction. In order to make it a fact, he had to check on that address.

All right. Granted that the deduction was faulty and she actually lived there. He wouldn't be able to do anything about it. Certainly he had nothing to gain from it. Or maybe he did have something to gain. Maybe if he played fox sufficiently well, he could have his cake and eat it too. The folded paper with her address on it would give him a potential contact with John, without giving John a contact with John's quarry.

It was an important consideration. Potential contact with John. It was important on the surface, much more important beneath the surface, but he didn't feel like going into that now. There was something vital and glowing in the possibility that the address was on the level. It was an exceedingly vague possibility, but there it was, and Vanning told himself there would be a change of mood tonight. The hunted intended to do a little hunting.

He wasn't in too much of a hurry. He treated himself to a dessert of cherry cream pie. Then black coffee. Then a brandy and another brandy and a cigarette. Walking out of the restaurant, he felt well nourished and the taste in his mouth was a good taste, and even though it was starting out as another hot, sticky night, he felt cool inside. And calm. And strangely self-assured.

The address was on Barrow Street. To get there he had to cross Christopher and Sheridan Square, and that took him past the bar where he had met her. As he passed the bar, a feeling of boldness came over him, there was the desire to gamble. He turned around. He smiled.

He entered the bar, and almost instantly he recognized the fat beer drinker of the preceding night. The fat fellow was right there at the bar, and again he was drinking beer.

Vanning walked up, gestured to the bartender. As the man in white apron approached to take the order, the fat fellow turned and looked at Vanning.

"Well, now, what do you know?"

"Hello," Vanning said. He smiled at the bartender. "A brandy and water chaser for me. A beer for my friend."

The bartender nodded and went away.

"Another hot night," Vanning said.

"What brings you in here?"

"What brings anyone in here?"

"We're speaking about you. In particular."

"I'm looking for her," Vanning said.

"I knew it." This was said with tight-lipped emphasis. "I was willing to bet on it. One of those things that have to happen."

"As sure as that?"

"Like that," the fat fellow said, and he snapped his fingers.

"You make it seem like arithmetic."

"And that's what it is. Two and two makes four and you can't get away from it. Or maybe I should say one and one makes two. Now wait——" And the fat fellow frowned and ran a fat finger through a puddle of beer on the bar. "We have a problem here. Sometimes one and one doesn't make two at all. One and one makes one. You see what I'm getting at?"

"Nup."

"You'll see. Just follow me. I promise you, I won't go into a long production. I'll make it simple. Like this. You and that girl, you're a natural team."

"You do this often?"

"Do what?"

"Play Cupid."

"It's the first time. I usually look out for myself. But that deal last night, it was different, it was one of those sensational things. A setup if I ever saw one. I said to myself when I walked out of here, I said, I'll give ten to one he looks at her. Small odds, at that. And I said, I'll give five to one he gets to talking with her. Then the odds went up again. Twenty to one he likes her. Fifty to one she likes him. A hundred to one they walk out of here together."

"Keep it up. You're making money."

The fat fellow misinterpreted Vanning's mild sarcasm. The fat fellow said, "All right, even if it didn't happen last night, it's bound to happen. You and that girl are a combination. In every way. Mark my word, it's going to happen. Just as sure as I'm alive, I know it. And it makes me feel good. I don't know if I'm getting this idea across, but I feel terrific, just thinking about you and that girl. You in a full-dress suit, and the girl in white satin. I get a picture of her in satin. Gorgeous, there's no other word for it. And I go past that, I get a picture of the two of you, I see you on a train together, I see you on a boat, on the boardwalk in Atlantic City or someplace. I keep on going. I get such a kick out of it. I get a picture of what your kids will look like. Chubby kids, all of them blond, all of them healthy, rosy faces just like her face, and blue eyes, and——"

"All right, that's all."

"What's wrong? What did I say?"

"Nothing. That's the point." Vanning sighed and shook his head slowly. "Don't get me wrong. I'm not sore. You're a nice guy. But I don't want to listen to you any more. I don't want to see you any more."

"Don't leave. I hardly ever get to talk to anybody. Let me buy you a drink. I promise to keep my big mouth shut."

"Sorry," Vanning said. "Thanks a lot, but you're such a good pal that you give me the blues."

He walked out. And it was all gone, that good feeling from the lobster and the brandy and the technical line of thought. It was replaced by a certain amount of confusion and some despair mixed in, and some loneliness and some bitterness, and topped off with a dash of desperation.

The house on Barrow Street was a four-story white brick affair, externally in good shape. On a panel at right angles to the front door there was a list of the tenants, with a button adjoining each name. Vanning struck a match and looked for a Martha. He went down past a Mr. and Mrs. Kostowski, a Mr. Olivet, a Mrs. Hammersmith, a Miss Silverman, and then there was only one more name and it wouldn't be the name he wanted. It was absurd to think she had been fool enough to have given him a level address.

He looked at the name. He brought the match closer to the panel. And there it was, Martha Gardner.

A forefinger went thudding into the little black button. Then there was waiting. The finger hit the button again. More waiting. Then a buzzer, and Vanning opened the door and came into a small, neatly laid out foyer. Whoever took care of this place really believed in taking care of it. Vanning walked up a stairway carpeted in dark green broadloom. The walls were white, really white, blending with the quiet that flowed evenly through each straight and stolid hallway. There wasn't much light, just enough of it. She lived in a place where people obviously lived quiet lives.

As he came to the third floor, a door opened for him. Light from the hall hit the doorway, merged with bright light coming from the room, and flowed down and framed her face.

She was wearing a bathrobe, quilted blue satin. He expected her to step back into the room and close the door. And if she didn't do that, he expected her to stare, or gasp, or register some other form of surprise. She didn't do any of that. She even disregarded his damaged face. There was no particular response other than the ordinary process of standing there and looking at him.

"Remember?" he said. "You gave me your address."

"What do you want?"

"I would like to straighten things out."

"I don't think that's necessary."

"There's an explanation forthcoming."

"Really, I'm not interested in hearing your explanation."

Vanning frowned, taking that in and tossing it around for a few hollow moments. Then he offered her a dim smile and said, "You've got it backwards. What I meant was, there's an explanation due from you."

This time she did the frowning. She looked at him and yet she wasn't looking at him. She was looking at last night. He tried to gaze into her mind and gave it up after several crazy seconds.

Then she was saying, "All right, come in."

It was a small apartment, but it was clean, it was attractive, it went right along with the rest of the house. A living room with a studio couch, a bathroom and kitchenette. Something about the colors and furnishings gave Vanning the idea that she had done her own decorating. The general scheme was blue and burnt orange, the blue demonstrating itself in various shades that climbed from the very pale to an almost black. A few passable water colors on the wall and one extremely interesting gouache.

He was looking at the gouache. He could hear her closing the door behind him. He told himself it was idiotic to have come here. There was a closet door not very far away, and he wasn't being at all absurd in juggling the possibility that John might be hiding in the closet. And yet he wasn't sorry he had come here. John or no John, he was here and he was satisfied to be here.

The gouache was simple and quiet and relaxed, showing a fishing boat in a lagoon, with sunset throwing dead blue and live orange onto the deck of the boat, the orange rising from the deck and flowing across green-gray water.

"Who did this painting?" Vanning asked.

"Pull yourself together. The name is on the bottom."

"Let's start over again. Where did you get the painting?"

"A little art shop on Third Street."

"It's an interesting job."

"I'm so glad you like it."

"Cut that out," he said, still looking at the gouache. "It doesn't go with the rest of you."

"Does that matter?"

"Yes," he said. He turned around and faced her. She had her arms folded, as if she were sitting in a jury box. "Yes, it matters more than you think. I want to know how you got tied up with those men. I want to know how a girl like you goes and lets herself wide open for a wrong play. You didn't belong in that picture last night and you know it as well as I do."

"Are you telling me I didn't belong?"

"I'm telling you."

"That's very funny," she said. "All day I've been telling myself I didn't belong in that picture."

"Why did you do it? Money? Sure. What else could it be? It had to be money."

"Do you always talk to yourself? Do you always answer your own questions?"

He didn't like what she was saying, and he didn't at all care for the way this was going, but he had to admire the way she was handling herself, the way her voice remained calm and level, the way she stood there, very straight, balanced nicely on her two feet without making too much of an effort at it.

"Why did you do it?" he said. "Why did you go to work for them?"

"I wasn't working for them. But suppose I was? Would it make any difference? You did something wrong and you were running away and you were bound to be caught. That's all I know. I don't feel like knowing any more."

"Say, what are you doing? Are you fencing with me?"

"I wouldn't attempt that. I'm not smart enough, Jim."

"What?"

"Jim."

"Thanks. It was nice of you to remember."

"I couldn't help remembering. Tell me, Jim. What did you do? How did you get yourself involved with the police?"

He stared at her. He studied her eyes as though they were rough diamonds and he was about to operate. And then he said, "You thought those men last night were police?"

"Weren't they?"

Vanning let out a laugh, drew it in a tight knot of sound that kept on tightening until it became a grinding gasp. "I think I get it now," he said. "You really thought they were police. That's why you took off so fast. And they knew you had them figured as police. They put you in the role of stool pigeon, and that made you go away faster. As long as you thought they were police, as long as you had me down as some criminal being taken in, your only move would be to clear out of it and stay out. It was clever on their part. It was stupid on my part not to see through the whole thing. And yet I'm glad it worked out like that."

"But all this doesn't tell me anything. It goes around in a circle."

"Nobody knows that better than I."

"Jim." She was coming toward him, came close enough to touch him and then stopped. "Who are they? What's going on?"

"Why should I tell you?"

"I can't answer that. You'll have to answer it for yourself."

He moved away from her, sat down on the studio couch. She came over and sat down beside him.

She said, "Can I fix you a drink?"

"No."

"Smoke?"

"No."

"Can I do anything?"

"You can sit there and listen."

She sat there and listened. He talked for almost a half-hour. When it was all over, when there was nothing more to say, they looked at each other, breathed in and out in unison. He started a smile, worked at it, got it going, and she helped him out with it. Then she stood up.

"Sit there," she said. "Let's see if we can cool off with some lemonade."

He watched her as she walked away, moving toward the kitchenette, a little alcove all by itself. From where he was sitting, he couldn't see her in the kitchenette. Now he began to get all sorts of thoughts, and the thoughts jabbed at one another, and he told himself it didn't make any difference now. No matter what the thoughts were made of, no matter what their sum, he couldn't do anything with it. That was all right. He was even a little glad. All he wanted to do was sit here and wait for Martha to come back.

She came back with a tray. A pitcher of lemonade, a bowl of ice. And glasses. Lemonade filled a glass, and she offered it to him.

"Drink this," she said.

"You make it sound as if I'm sick and you're taking care of me."

"Drink it."

For a while all they did was sip lemonade. Then Vanning put down an empty glass and he looked at her and said, "Do you believe what I've told you?"

"Yes, Jim. Do you believe me when I say yes?"

He nodded.

She put her hand against the back of his head, patted him as if he were her little son. "Go home now. Go to your drawing board and finish that work you were telling me about. Get it all finished. Then go to sleep. And please treat me to dinner tomorrow night?"

"Seven."

"Where?"

"I'll meet you here. Good night, Martha."

He walked out without looking back at her. Going back to his room, he walked rapidly. He was in a hurry to get at the drawing board.

Chapter Ten

FRASER TOLD himself it was a matter of selection. He stood outside the white dwelling and watched Vanning going away. He had placed a little more than twenty yards between himself and Vanning during the walk from the bar to here, and he had remained across the street as Vanning entered the place, and he'd been hoping a light would show in one of the front windows. When it failed to show, he wondered on the feasibility of going up and visiting the back rooms. Somehow it hadn't seemed like a good idea. He'd had the feeling it wouldn't give him anything solid.

And now he stood here and watched Vanning going away. He had the choice of following Vanning now or going up and trying the back rooms. He had his own system of questioning people so that they gave answers they didn't think were usable but which Fraser was able to use. He would probably get something from one of those back rooms and yet he still had the feeling it wouldn't be enough.

He decided to stay with Vanning. He lit a cigarette and followed his man to the place where his man lived. He saw his man entering the place, and then he crossed the street, went up to the room he had rented, seated himself behind the dark window, and waited.

And he saw the light arriving in Vanning's room. He saw Vanning moving around in a preparatory sort of way. The binoculars picked up the bright spots and the shadows, and Vanning's eyes were distinct, they were the eyes of a man in confusion, a confusion that had some strange happiness mixed in. Tonight there was something different in Vanning. The binoculars took it all in and clarified it, but it was clear only on the visual side, and not in the analysis. For some reason Vanning was hopeful and perhaps just a bit cheery, and Fraser began to use his imagination and kept it up until he disciplined himself, told himself imagination was no part of science. It was all right in art, but this wasn't an art. This was on the order of mathematics.

The binoculars saw Vanning seating himself at the drawing

286

board. There were manipulations with a soft pencil. Vanning would never be a Matisse. He was much too precise. He went at it more like an engineer. He used a T-square and a slide rule. He leaned close to the work and studied it carefully after each small movement of the pencil.

It was interesting to watch him at his work. He had a cigarette going and the smoke of it shot a straight, rigid column of blue past his head, the column quite permanent because once the cigarette was lit he left it in the ash tray and paid no attention to it. When it was burned out he lit another and treated it the same way.

The pencil work completed, Vanning commenced mixing gouache pigments. This took a long time. Fraser sat there with eyes burning into the binoculars, telling himself three hundred thousand dollars was a fortune. A man with three hundred thousand dollars didn't have to sit up all night with T-squares and gouache and shoulders bent over a board. It was something he had told himself many times, and this time it was in the nature of a conclusion.

And yet there was another consideration, and it was evolved from the way Vanning addressed himself to his work. The thorough, accurate method, the painstaking manner in which he mixed the paint, the slow, careful application of paint to rough paper. Again Fraser said it to himself. An engineer, he said, a patient calculator. Perhaps a fanatic for doing things in a precise way. Doing this sort of thing, anyway. And the possibility of his doing other things in the same way could not be completely disregarded.

Fraser sat there and watched. And the longer he sat there, the longer he watched, the more subjective he became. The more subjective he became, the more he began to doubt himself. There was so much he didn't know. About zoology, even though he had read many books. About crystallography, even though at one time he had taken a course at the museum. About judo, despite having been taught by one of the true experts. About Vanning, even though he'd been telling himself he knew Vanning.

And about psychology, and neurology, and man's way of thinking, doing things, reacting. The books were all good books and represented a great deal of study and experimentation and summaries based on years of formularizing. But the field was still in its infancy. There was so much as yet unlearned, even by the top people. And the top people were Fraser's tutors, and Fraser told himself he was a novice. If he'd been someone else examining Fraser, he would have called Fraser a naturally humble man. But he was Fraser. And he was calling Fraser a fool for having considered Fraser a walking textbook on Vanning.

There was so much he didn't know about Vanning. There was so much a man didn't know about other men. Conversation was an overestimated thing. Such a large part of conversation was merely a curtain for what went on in the mind. So many madmen were walking around and fooling people. It wouldn't be ridiculous to ponder the possibility that Vanning was a victim of dementia praecox, extremely shrewd about hiding it, underneath the disease a good man, but dominated by the disease, a murderer and a terror. Ponder that, Fraser told himself.

And ponder the other roads. Because there were many roads. The road he had selected could be the wrong road. And it was as though he was in a car and he was going up that road, and the farther he traveled, the more he worried about its being the wrong road. But like any man behind a steering wheel, he tried to tell himself he was steering straight. Rationalizing, he knew he was rationalizing. But he couldn't do anything about that. All he could do was sit there and worry about it.

In the binoculars, Vanning labored with a paintbrush. The interior of the binoculars gradually became a magnetic little world. Fraser became a magnetized object being drawn into the little world. And as he arrived there, he talked to Vanning.

He said, "Tell me about yourself."

Vanning's lips did not move. He was concentrating on the drawing board. But somehow he said, "I'm a man in a lot of trouble."

"I know that," Fraser said. "Tell me about it."

"Why should I? Would you help me?"

"If I believed you deserved help."

"How can I make you believe?"

"Just tell me the truth," Fraser said.

"Sometimes truth is a very odd thing. Sometimes it's amazing and you refuse to believe it."

"The front of this thing is amazing. I'll understand if the background's the same way."

"I don't think you would," Vanning said. "I don't think any man would."

"Try me out."

"No," Vanning said. "I'm sorry but I can't take the chance."

"Don't you want to get out of this mess?"

"Getting out of it is very important to me. Staying alive is more important."

"Don't you trust me?"

"I'm in a position where I can't trust anyone."

"Is that all?" Fraser said.

"I'm afraid so. I'm sorry."

Fraser was about to ask another question, but just then the little world was blanketed with darkness. It became a black, meaningless thing until he took the binoculars away from his eyes and realized he'd been watching Vanning in the process of leaving the drawing board, getting into bed, switching off the light.

The room across the street was dark, a room of sleep, and Fraser liked the idea of getting some sleep himself. He liked the idea very much. He smiled wistfully at the idea, brought his chair closer to the window, leaned an elbow on the sill and sat there with his eyes half opened, waiting.

Chapter Eleven

THERE WAS a feeling that sleep would come easily tonight. When it finally reached Vanning it was like a vapor closing in on him. He rolled around in it, he floated down through it, down and down, going through the endless tides of thick slumber. And somewhere down there the tide twisted, started up in an arc, brought him toward the surface. He attempted to fight the tide, but it kept pulling him up in that circle. When it had him on the surface, when his eyes were wide open and he was staring at the black ceiling, he tried to continue the circle, go down again. But he couldn't close his eyes.

Worry was doing this. It couldn't be anything except worry. He was in her apartment again and he could hear himself talking to her, he could hear the replies she was making. And dancing around somewhere in there was an unsatisfactory element, and he wondered what it was.

All at once he jumped out of bed and switched on the light. On a Governor Winthrop desk the alarm clock announced three-fifteen. He remembered leaving her apartment at nine-thirty or thereabouts. He measured it with his fingers. An intervening time of approximately six hours.

That was a long time. It was too long. It was time wasted, and he had to stop making these errors. Especially the kind of errors that concerned a woman. He had started out tonight on a mechanical basis and that was good, and he had allowed himself to fade from the mechanical to the emotional and that was very bad. She had given him nothing, anyway nothing that he could use. And he had given her plenty. He had given her everything. If she felt like using it, there was no limit to what she could do with it. And she could do a great deal in six hours.

He didn't bother to tie his shoelaces. He tripped once going down the stairway, saved himself from a complete fall by grabbing the rail. On the street he started out with a fast walk, ended up with what amounted to almost a sprint. And then he was panting as he stood outside the white brick house on Barrow Street.

The button was beside her name on the panel, and it was a

shiny button and it was tempting. But he found himself thinking in terms of an alley. He walked around the side street at right angles to Barrow, and there was a narrow alley and the first thing he saw against the blackness of the alley was a light showing from a rear window on the third floor of a house facing Barrow.

Without counting the houses he knew it was that house.

Moving down the alley, he was figuring at first on a rear entrance, and wondering how he would get past the lock. And then he noticed a garden court, one of several garden courts at the other side of the alley, and the trees came into focus, and a few of them were quite high. One in particular was getting considerable play from the light that flowed out through the window. The light dipped and hopped through the upper branches of the tree, made puddles of silver on black leaves.

He walked up to the gate that separated the alley from the garden court. For a few moments he stood there, looking up at the shining leaves, rubbing his hands together, and then lightly, quickly, he climbed over the gate, he approached the tree. Again he looked up. Again he rubbed his hands together. Then he took off his coat.

It wasn't an easy climb. This was a very big tree, big in every way, particularly in the thickness of the trunk. In several places the trunk was much too smooth, and he felt himself slipping, felt the strain on his legs, told himself to stop being in such a hurry. He rested awhile, then went on climbing, took hold of a branch, pulled himself up, and now he was going up through the branches, the leaves swishing against his face.

A few thin branches gave him trouble, and he had to come in toward the center of the tree, where there was more thickness. Then up a couple more feet, and a couple more, and just a couple more. He turned slowly, to face the lighted window.

He saw her in there. She no longer wore the blue quilted satin bathrobe. Now she was wearing a yellow dress trimmed with green. There was a cigarette in her mouth and she had a highball glass in her hand. She moved toward the window and turned so that her back was to the window. Then she moved again to the side, and he couldn't see her. There was only the lighted window and the motionless room beyond the window. And Vanning waited.

A shadow fell across the light. Vanning leaned forward. He saw her again. She was back at the window, and he saw her in profile. She was smiling. Her lips were moving. She took a drink from the highball glass. She took a puff at the cigarette. Vanning's fingers twisted, pressed into the branch that supported him. He saw her gesturing with the cigarette. Then once again she walked away from the window.

There was another wait. It lasted a few years. Then the shadow again, falling across the light. And Martha again, leaning against the window sill. And then another shadow, falling across Martha, remaining there.

And then a hand, holding a highball glass. A man's hand, a man's coat sleeve. Cigarette smoke between Martha and that hand. And no motion now, nothing, only another wait. But suddenly a quick movement on the part of Martha. She was going away from the window. The other things remained there, the man's hand, the highball glass, the coat sleeve. And gradually the coat sleeve moved out across the lighted space, and there was a coat, and a shoulder, and a man's head, turning slowly and getting into profile. And there he was.

John.

Chapter Twelve

IT WAS ENOUGH. It was hollow and yet there was a shattering in it. Vanning began his descent. He sighed a few times, he shook his head a few times, and as he came onto the ground he hit his fists together lightly, shook his head again, and then he grinned. He wasn't angry at John. He wasn't angry at anybody, not even himself.

He had to pass out a little credit. Some of it to John for engineering the thing from the beginning, but more of it to her, because her performance had been sheer perfection. Every move, every word, the smallest gesture, she had carried it out in major-league style. If this was the work she had cut out for herself, she was certainly doing it on a blue-ribbon basis.

As he walked down the alley, getting his arms through the sleeves of the coat, he knew he was rationalizing, but it didn't bother him. He was too tired to be bothered by anything right now. He was at the point where the open-field runner had already run past him and he had tried for the tackle and missed, and now all he could do was rest back on his elbows and listen to the crowd cheering the other team's touchdown.

He was going up the side street, turning, coming onto Barrow, and he was making his way along Barrow, listening to his own footsteps breaking through the quiet black. There seemed to be an echo to his footsteps. There seemed to be noise beyond the echo. Then the echo and the noise came together and moved up toward him, and he stopped dead and waited, and the sound now was purely that of footsteps behind him, and coming closer. And he waited there.

"That's right," a voice said. "Just wait there."

Vanning turned. He saw the man. It was quite dark around here, and yet he began to get the feeling he had seen this man before. And then he saw the gun.

"Will I need this?" the man said, and he pointed to the gun in his hand.

"You'd better keep it ready."

"I'll put it in my pocket," the man said. "Lift your arms a little. I want to see what's on you."

293

The man had the gun in his pocket as he came toward Vanning, and he hit Vanning lightly, swiftly, in the frisking process. Then he stepped back and waited for Vanning to do something.

"What do you want?" Vanning said.

"I'm not sure yet."

"Make up your mind. It's past my bedtime."

"Let's walk," the man said.

They walked down Barrow, crossed Sheridan Square. The man seemed to be walking at Vanning's side, but actually he was just a little to the rear.

"Let's walk to the park," the man said. "I want to have a talk with you."

"Why the gun?"

"Guess."

"Police?"

"You guessed it." And the man displayed a badge.

"I'm glad," Vanning said. "You don't know how glad I am. Now it's off my hands. Now it's your worry."

"My name is Fraser."

"Who cares what your name is? Who wants to know your story? You're the police and you're taking me in. Why don't we leave it at that?"

"Because there's more to it than that."

"All right, take me in and we'll find out."

"We're going over to the park and have a talk."

"You're the doctor."

"Now that's funny, your saying that. I always wanted to be a doctor. Maybe I am, in a way. I like to think it's possible for me to help people, rather than make their lives miserable. Lately I've been studying psychology."

"Good for you."

"I'd appreciate it if you helped me out."

"With your homework?"

"Call it that."

"Take me in, will you? Just take me in."

"We're going to the park."

"I'm tired," Vanning said. "You don't have any idea how tired I am. I'm glad you finally grabbed me and I wish you'd take me in."

"Why did you do it?"

"Oh, come on," Vanning said. "Don't start that now. I'll get enough of that later."

"You must have had a reason. We never do things like that without a reason."

"Read tomorrow's late edition and you'll find out all about it."

After that the detective was quiet. They crossed another street, went down another block. They were entering Washington Square Park. They went across grass, came onto pavement, and the detective gestured toward a bench.

They sat down. The detective took out a pack of cigarettes. "Have one?"

"Anything to make you happy," Vanning said. Then he smiled wearily. "No, I don't mean that. You're only doing your job. I'll have a cigarette, thanks."

The detective lit a match. Smoke sifted between the detective and Vanning.

They took in more smoke and blew it out and watched it rise. Then the detective said, "I've had my eye on you for quite a time."

"You don't need to tell me."

"You felt it?"

"No. You fooled me. But I'm not surprised. I should have known."

"Of course," the detective said. "The way you were running down that street. I could even see your shoelaces were untied."

Vanning frowned at the smoke. It made a weird pattern in front of his eyes. Some of it boomeranged and got into his eyes and he blinked. But he kept on frowning.

"All right," the detective said. "What's your name?"

"Van——"

"What?"

"Van."

"Van what?"

"Van Johnson."

"Be reasonable."

"Van Rayburn."

"That's an unusual first name. Van."

"Johnson does all right with it."

The detective made himself as comfortable as the park bench would allow. He took a long pull at the cigarette. "Now let's see," he said. "I'm walking down the street at three-thirty in the morning and I gander a man going someplace in a big hurry. Really flying. So I figure I'll stay behind and see what happens. So I follow this man as he tears down Barrow Street. I watch him go up the side street and the alley. I watch him climbing the tree. At first I figure too many Tarzan pictures, but then I notice he's got himself across from a lighted window. So then I figure a Tom. I've still got to figure a Tom. That is, unless you can talk your way out of it."

Vanning looked at the detective.

"And that's all?"

"Why? Is there something else?"

"No," Vanning said.

"Tell me, Van. What's troubling you? Don't you have a girl friend?"

"I did," Vanning said. "At least I thought I did. Until a little while ago."

"That's the idea," the detective said. "Now tell me all about it."

"I was with her earlier tonight," Vanning said. "I accused her of playing around with another party. She said it wasn't true. So I took her word for it and went home. I couldn't sleep. I had to find out for myself. Without her knowing. That's why I climbed the tree."

"He was in there with her, wasn't he?"

"What do you think?"

"I don't think. I know. All I had to do was get a good look at your face. Tell me, Van, what do you do for a living?"

"Commercial artist."

"Okay," the detective said. He stood up. "That's all, Van. Go on home. Forget about her. If she lied to you once, she'll lie again. If you allow yourself to see her any more, you deserve every kick in the pants you get."

Vanning came up from the bench and faced the detective. "You're letting me go?"

"Why not? All you did was climb a tree."

Vanning turned and walked away. After a while he felt choked up and the pain in his lungs was a suffocating pain. He wondered why that was happening, then gradually realized it was because he was holding his breath. The stale air came out in a violent rush. He breathed in pure air. He breathed it in with desperation, as if he were in a tube where there was very little air remaining.

The streets paraded toward him like collections of black shapes, living but not moving. They instilled a definite discomfort, and he was in a hurry to arrive at his room. When he got there, he opened the door with a rapid, jerky motion, closed it the same way. Then he leaned back against the door and looked at the room.

"Well," he said, "we're still here."

He went into the bathroom, splashed cold water on his face. Doing it with his hands didn't give him as much cold wetness as he felt he needed. He put a stopper in the drain opening, filled the bowl with cold water, ducked his head in it, kept that up for several moments. When he lifted his head he saw himself in the mirror. He grinned at himself.

"All you did was climb a tree," he said.

The face in the mirror grinned back at him for a few seconds. Then, when it stopped grinning, it became expressionless.

"Buck up," Vanning said without sound. "It's not that bad. Give me the grin again."

The face stared back at him.

"What's the kick?" Vanning said. "Tonight you got a real break. You ought to be happy. You're a lucky boy tonight."

And without sound the face said, "Tonight was tonight. But then comes tomorrow."

"Get off the gloom wagon, will you? They say tomorrow never comes."

"They're all wet."

"You're all wet," Vanning said. "Dripping wet. You give me the blues, brother. Sometimes you make me sick. Why don't you go to sleep?"

"I'll try."

"Don't worry. You'll sleep."

"I hope so."

"Sure, you'll sleep. All you've got to do is close your eyes and think about nothing."

"It sounds easy, but sometimes the thoughts keep coming in

like sticky air through an open window. You can't keep it out. The more you try, the faster it comes in. You have a date with her tomorrow night at seven o'clock. See how it is? There's your tomorrow. You'll think about that. You'll think about John. You'll think about Denver. What's that name again? Harrison, wasn't it? You killed Harrison. See if you can get away from that. You killed him, that's all there is to it, and they know you killed him, and now you're started, so you might just as well think about Seattle, and there's where the three hundred thousand comes in, so that brings you to the satchel. You're really moving now. You're wondering again, wondering as you've wondered a thousand times already, wondering why John left you in that room in the hotel, left you alone in there with the gun and the satchel, and somewhere in that there's an ounce of maybe, a fraction of an ounce. Maybe if you could figure that one out you'd have a door that you could open, you'd have something to give a lawyer, you'd have some actual ammunition on your side. Try to figure it out. Try to figure out the whole business. There must be an answer somewhere. You see the way it is? How can you keep these things out of your mind? Where did you drop that satchel? How can you fall asleep?"

"If I only had someone to talk to."

"Me."

"You? Don't make me laugh. You help me out like iodine helps sunburn."

Later, when his head came against the pillow, the pillow felt like granite. He tried to tolerate it, but after a while it was unbearable, and he sat up, switched on the bed lamp. He lit a cigarette.

In an ash tray near the bed, the stubs became a family that grew through the night.

Chapter Thirteen

FOR A MAN leading a normal life it would have been a pleasant day. The weather was pleasant, there was a bright sun, but an ocean breeze came up the Hudson and gave Manhattan a break. There was a good breakfast, and a smooth bus ride uptown. Fifth Avenue seemed lively and contented, perhaps just a bit smug, but then Fifth Avenue could afford that.

In the advertising agency, the art director was pleased with the work and handed out another assignment. That was nice. The deadline was generous, and that was even nicer. Lunch was nice too. And Fifty-seventh Street was showing some extremely interesting work by some new people, and so the remainder of the afternoon went riding along gently and at just the right speed.

In one of the larger galleries on Fifty-seventh Street he became engaged in a conversation with one of the more successful surrealist painters, and the two of them moved along from oil to oil, discussing the importance of shadow in surrealism, the effect of color on shadow, the effect of shadow on color, the effect of color and shadow on line, and it became one of those conversations that could very easily go on for years. The surrealist was more than a little interested in Vanning's point of view, and the whole thing led to a dinner invitation. Politely refusing, Vanning said he already had a dinner date for tonight.

"Oh, I'm sorry."

"So am I."

"Maybe you can break it."

"I could do that. But I don't think I will."

"Business?"

"In a way. Maybe some other time. All right?"

"By all means," the painter said. "I'll be here every day through the end of August, when the exhibition closes. You do like my work?"

"Very much. It has depth. It has technique. Very fine technique. You'll go places, I'm sure of it."

"It makes me so happy to hear that. I'm going to tell my

wife about you. There's so much in what you say about painting. You don't talk like the ordinary experts. Your judgment is
so fair, so objective, so calm. I don't usually tell my wife these
opinions expressed toward my work. As a matter of fact, I only
tell my wife the things that affect me deeply. You see, I have a
very deep feeling toward my wife. We've been married for sixteen years."

Vanning stared at an open space of wall above the highest
painting. "Why do you people pick on me?"

"I beg your pardon?"

Vanning kept staring at the wall. "Why do you rub it in?"

"I'm sorry. I fail to understand."

"Skip it. I didn't say anything. I do that every now and then.
Don't mind me. Here, let's shake hands. I hope you and your
wife will always be happy together. There's nothing like having
a wife and being madly in love with her. Is there?"

On the painter's face a perplexed look gave way to a shining
smile, and as he shook hands with Vanning he said, "My wife
means everything to me. More than my art. That's why I'll
never be a truly great painter. But it doesn't matter. Success in
love is success in life. Are you married?"

Vanning nodded. He said, "It isn't a good marriage. I don't
trust her. I ought to let her go. I know she's bad for me. That's
the practical side. The other side of it is way over my head."

"Give her a chance. She's only a human being. And she's
probably young. She can be molded. You listen to me. I'm
much older than you. In the beginning, in Paris, my wife gave
me a lot of trouble. She was a little imp. You know what I did
once? I went on a hunger strike. After two days of that she got
down on her knees, she cried like a little child. I told her I
would eat if she prepared the kind of dinner I liked. She prepared a feast. We feasted together. We got drunk. We laughed
ourselves unconscious. That's living, my friend. That's loving."

"You have something there."

"Fight with her. Make some noise. Give her excitement. Give
her color. Give her children. My wife and I, we have three girls
and a little boy. Every night I come home to a festival, a beauty
pageant, a delightful comic opera right there in the little house
where I live. There's so much yelling. It's wonderful."

"I'll bet it is," Vanning said. He smiled. He patted the

painter's shoulder and walked out of the gallery. On the street, walking south on Lexington, he kept on smiling, and very slowly a frown arrived and he was smiling and frowning at the same time, and it showed he was a man in deep thought, somewhat amused at what he was thinking, somewhat puzzled. And when the smile faded and the frown stayed there, it showed he was a man who had made up his mind about something.

There was an hour to kill. He walked, he looked in some windows, he did more walking, he went into a haberdasher's and bought several shirts, a few ties, a few pairs of socks. He splurged on a brocaded robe. Splurging like that on himself gave him an idea, and a little later he was buying a five-pound box of candy and a large bottle of expensive perfume. Then he went home and showered and shaved, got himself into one of the new shirts, stood in front of a mirror, experimenting with the new tie.

At a few minutes to seven he walked down Barrow Street.

Again the door was open when he reached the third-floor landing. She was all ready. She was smiling.

She took a step toward him. "My, but you look nice."

"Here's a little something I picked up." He was extending the fancy packages.

"For me?" She took the packages and stared.

"I was going to try fur, but I didn't know what kind you liked."

She didn't get that. He decided to let it pass. They were going into the room. She opened the packages. The big box of candy brought a murmur of delight. The ornate bottle of perfume caused her to step back, her eyes wide. He was watching her as if she were under a microscope.

Gesturing toward the perfume, she said, "You shouldn't have done that."

"Why not?"

"That's very expensive."

"Don't you think I can afford it?"

Her eyes were on the perfume. "That's an awful lot of money."

He didn't say anything. He was lighting a cigarette. It was starting out the way he wanted it to start. The gifts leading to a mention of money, the money a potential path to the satchel. It was up to her to guide the way along the path. He waited, telling himself to step along with extreme caution. The type he was dealing with was the most dangerous and clever of them all. On the surface a soft-voiced innocence, an unembroidered sincerity. Beneath the surface a chess player who could do amazing things without board and chessmen.

"Really," she said, "you shouldn't have spent all that money."

"It wasn't so much, considering."

"Considering what?"

He studied the way she was looking at him. "Considering," he said, "what I have."

"I didn't think you had a lot."

"It all depends on what you mean by a lot."

She laughed. "Maybe you haven't told me everything about yourself."

"For instance?"

"Maybe you're heir to a fortune."

"That's possible."

"Should I guess again?"

"Sure," Vanning said. "Give it a try."

They stood facing each other, and it was as if lengths of foils separated them. He was trying to get rid of his own thoughts, his own strategy, trying to bring her thoughts into his mind so he could take a close look and figure how far she was ahead of him. Because even in this short time she had taken the lead, she was out there in front, her pace steady and yet relaxed, her confidence a thing of menace, her relaxed superiority almost like a panther's playing with a zebra.

"Maybe," she said, "you've been fooling me all the time and it's some sort of a gag. Actually you're a young wizard of Wall Street."

"Try again."

"You made a fortune playing cards."

"Do I seem as if I'd be clever at poker?"

"That's why you'd be clever. Because you don't seem to be clever. Or perhaps shrewd would be a better word. The shrewdest people give you the impression that they're exactly opposite."

"That's a keen observation," Vanning said. "I'm going to make a note of it and keep it on file."

"Do that. You'll find out it comes in very handy now and then."

"You still have another guess coming."

"Feed me first," Martha said. "I can think better on a full stomach."

They went out and found a restaurant. It was one of those places where people concentrated on food, and yet each booth was a little rendezvous in itself. There was an emphasis on privacy and yet it was a casual sort of privacy. While they waited for their order, their conversation was affected by the atmosphere of the place and it became pleasant, meaningless chatter with a laugh here and there. She had a fine sense of humor, deviating in a marvelous way between the dry and the robust. For detached moments Vanning was enjoying her presence, and the worry and peril were completely out of it. She began telling him of amusing incidents at the glassware counter, and her imitations of various customers were definitely blue-ribbon. At one point his laughter came out in a burst, at another point he smiled and nodded appreciatively as she pantomimed to perfection the undecided buyer of glass.

When the steaks arrived, they stopped fooling around. It was phenomenal food and they gave it their undivided attention.

Later, while they sipped brandy, they looked at each other.

And Vanning said, "You still have that one more guess."

"Oh, yes. I forgot about that."

"I didn't."

"Are you trying to find out how smart I am?"

"I already know how smart you are," Vanning said. "Now I want to see how good you are at guessing."

"Suppose it isn't a guess?"

"If it isn't a guess it's deduction. If it isn't deduction it's mind reading and I'll put you in business on Broadway. Now let's have it. This is the big one."

He grinned at her. She didn't return the grin. A strange quiet became a bubble growing larger in the center of the table, and he could see her through the bubble. He could see her face, and that was as far as he could see. It frightened him, and he didn't know why. There was no reason for fright. The situation held no immediate danger. But he was very frightened, and gradually, as he sat there watching Martha, he realized that it was not Martha he feared. And it was not John. And it was not the police. It was himself.

And then all at once there was a bursting in his brain, and this place, and Martha, the table, the brandy, everything, it all assumed the substance and dimensions of a horrible reality. Horrible only because it was real, so very real that it refused to be reined in. He was in love with her.

It was not logical, it was impossible. And yet there it was. The attraction, the feeling were beyond measurement, beyond the limits of self-analysis. The thing itself was clear and definite, and yet the reasons were vague and far away and he had no desire to itemize those reasons. There was an eerie resemblance between this matter and something else that had happened to him, but right now he couldn't remember what that something else was. His mind was too busy accepting the fact, the ghastly truth that he had fallen in love with this woman. Shackles of some fierce, unbreakable metal were already locked, holding him secure. And that, too, was an awful paradox, because he had not the slightest wish to free himself. No matter what she was, no matter what she had done or was doing now, no matter what trouble and heartache the hidden Martha represented for him, he was in love with the Martha that showed herself to him now.

It was a phenomenon of huge proportions. It was bigger than life. And yet, as big as it was, there was something even bigger. And he knew what that was, too, only with this new realization there was no explosion, the knowledge reached him in a calm sort of way. He was certain she had fallen in love with him.

"I'm ready," he said.

"I'm thinking."

"Make it good."

"If it's too good," she said, "it won't be any good at all. It will wreck everything."

"I'm willing to gamble."

"Maybe that's because you don't have too much to lose."

"And you?"

"I'll be losing a lot. You have no idea how much I'll be losing. Do you mind if I back out?"

"Yes," he said. "I do mind. I want you to make that guess."

"It's not a guess any more. I'm sure I know. If I'm correct, the whole thing blows up in my face. If I'm wrong, you'll walk out on me and nobody can blame you. I don't want to lose you, Jim. Maybe you know that already."

"I've been playing with the idea."

"No matter what you are," she said, "I don't want to lose you."

He stared at her. She had repeated what he had told himself. And it was no act. Because she meant it, actually meant it, her eyes and her words were far more dreadful than an act, and he could think of only one explanation. There were two sides to Martha Gardner, and what he had thought was the hidden side was not hidden at all, it was actual, it was living, breathing, performing. And doubtless she feared and hated that side of herself just as he did.

"You're halfway across the tightrope," he said. "You can't turn back."

"You're really asking for it, aren't you?"

"Put it another way. Say I'm demanding it."

A tinge of indignation came into her eyes. "You sound as if I'm obligated."

"We're both obligated. It's just about time to take off our masks."

"I don't know what you mean."

"I mean take off the masks. Walk off the stage. Remove the greasepaint. Any way you want to put it."

"I'm sorry, Jim." A confused little smile crept back and forth across her parted lips. "You have me in the dark."

"Do I really?" He leaned toward her, his eyes a set of lances.

She touched finger tips to her chin. "It's so strange, the way you're looking at me."

"I'm looking at the life ahead of me. With you."

She gave him a sideways glance. "I'm not bothering you, am I?"

"You don't catch the drift," he said. He bit at a thumbnail. "Let's get out of here."

He paid the check. They left the restaurant. The Village was under twilight, and nothing much was happening on the street. They went down the street and came onto Fifth Avenue, and then they turned toward the arch that officially welcomed people to Washington Square. He was waiting for her to say something, knew she was waiting for him. Eventually he realized it was up to him.

"I'll let you in on something," he said. "I've been playing a game with you."

"You didn't have to tell me that." There was an ache in her voice.

"I thought it might do the trick. Crazy notion, wasn't it? Like trying to hook a marlin with trout bait. I never underestimated your brains. It was just that I overestimated my own. Now I don't feel like fighting any more. Whatever it is you're trying to win, you've won it."

She stopped. She looked at him. And then all at once it came out and there was fury in it, pain in it as she said, "Don't throw puzzles at me. Don't try to twist me around and have fun with me. You told me a story and I believed you. Because I wanted to believe you. That's all it was. It was very simple. But you weren't satisfied with that. You had to make it complicated, with question marks in it, with me on one side of the fence and you on the other. I wanted to come over on your side, but you wouldn't have it that way. And I suppose I can't very well blame you. Who am I? Why should you share all that money with me?"

"Is that the guess I've been waiting for?"

"It's no longer a guess. I know. How could you expect me to know otherwise? Why would you keep digging away, trying to find out if I had suspicions?"

"You make it sound as though I'm a guilty party."

"Aren't you?"

"All right, let's assume I am. Let's assume I never lost that satchel, and now I have the three hundred thousand hidden away in a nice safe place. What are you going to do about it?"

"Nothing."

"Oh, come, come. I'm a crook. I'm a killer. You don't intend going to the police?"

"I intend going home," she said. "I want you to leave me

alone. From now on, I mean. Please—I don't want to see you any more."

"What you really mean is, this Martha doesn't want to see me any more. What about the other Martha? The other Martha, the bad one, the one who's tied up with John."

She gasped. Her eyes bulged and she stepped back, kept going back, suddenly pivoted and started to run. And it was as if goblins were chasing her. Vanning stood there, watching her as she ran away. When she was out of sight, he turned and went onto Fifth Avenue and got into a bus. He had no idea of where he wanted to go. The bus made its run, made a turn and got started with another run. At the end of the run Vanning got off and walked into a bar and stayed there for an hour, and then he walked across the Village and arrived at the place where he lived. He didn't feel like going to sleep. He wasn't at all tired. And it was still an early hour. He leaned against the iron rail of the front steps and put a cigarette in his mouth, looked across the street, took out a book of matches and started to light the cigarette, then dropped the lighted match and stared across the street. And the cigarette fell out of his mouth.

And the man came walking toward him.

Chapter Fourteen

"REMEMBER ME?"

"What do you want?" Vanning said.

"I'll bet you don't even remember my name. I did give you my name, you know."

"I don't remember."

"Fraser."

"Oh, yes," Vanning said mechanically. "That's right."

"And you're Van."

"Van Rayburn."

"No," Fraser said. "That was last night when you climbed a tree and I had a father-and-son talk with you. Tonight you're Vanning. You're James Vanning."

"You have a nice change of pace."

"No, it's the same old routine day after day. I get pretty tired of it now and then, but I know what it's all about."

"I wouldn't bet against that," Vanning said. He took a deep breath. "I'm ready to go along with you now."

"I'm not ready yet," Fraser said.

"What do you want from me?"

"Why can't we stand here and talk?"

"That was last night," Vanning said. "Remember? The psychology attraction was last night. You've done your jockeying already. Now you're in there for the kill. You've made it. You've done a wonderful job and now it's all over and what are we hanging around for?"

"If you don't mind, I'll handle it the way I think best. It's my case."

"I thought Denver had it."

"Denver gave it to New York, and New York gave it to me. I mean entirely. If anything goes wrong, it's all my fault. I'll get it from all sides. From New York and from Denver. And Seattle."

"I don't get Seattle."

"I told you they gave me the entire case. By that I mean the entire case. What I'm supposed to do now is take you in, then I look for the other two men."

"The other three men."

"See what I mean?" Fraser said. "You've already given me something."

"That's fine. What can you give me?"

"Every possible break. I don't think you're a killer."

"But I am."

"Why?"

"Self-defense."

Fraser put his hands in his coat pockets, thumbs overlapping the pockets. "Suppose we go up to your room and talk it over?"

He didn't wait for Vanning's reply. He walked past Vanning. He led the way up the stairs. It would have been easy for Vanning to take him from behind.

They both knew it. They didn't need to talk about it. Going up to the room, they remained quiet, as though they had something definite and logical ahead of them, as though they were members of a closely knit organization.

At the door, Fraser stepped aside. Vanning moved in, put his key in the lock, opened the door. Just before he walked in, he looked at Fraser's thin, sharp face. The sharp, black eyes. The black mustache. Fraser smiled at him. He responded with a wide grin, standing relaxed but very straight nevertheless, and he was breathing easily. It was as if a tremendous weight had been lifted from his shoulders.

Fraser walked over to the drawing board, stood there looking at it.

"Here's something else," he said. "You gave me some truth last night. You told me you were a commercial artist."

"I didn't tell you everything last night, but what I told you was true."

"You have anything to drink?"

"I'll make something."

"Plenty of ice. It's a scorching night."

Vanning prepared drinks, brought them in. There was some serious concentrating on the drinks, and then Fraser lowered his glass and said, "All right, I'm ready to listen. I want everything. Every move, every detail. I want the whole business, from the very beginning."

It lasted the better part of an hour. Fraser made only a few interruptions, and did that only when it was necessary to straighten out a sequence here and there. Vanning was speaking in a low voice, but without a stumble, without a repetition of facts. He was finding it easy to speak. Despite the low pitch, his voice was clear. Toward the end there was more than a little of confidence in it.

When it was finished, Fraser walked toward the drawing board, tapped his fingers against it, turned and faced the chair where Vanning had one leg crossed over the other.

"Only one thing," Fraser said. "Only one thing bothers me. Let's go back to it. Let's put you back again in that hotel room in Denver. I'll see if I can repeat it the way you told me. You're in that room with John and Pete. They put you in the bathroom. They don't lock the bathroom door. They have a conversation in whispers. That's reasonable. Okay, you're waiting in the bathroom. Suddenly you realize there's complete quiet in that other room. You can't make that out. So finally you decide to take a chance. You open the door. And the other room is empty. But there on the bed you see a gun. And there on the dresser you see the satchel. And that, my boy, is a very strange state of affairs."

"If I could explain it, I would."

"That's understood," Fraser said. "At least I understand. But other people wouldn't buy it. In a courtroom they'd laugh at you. You see the spot we're in. That setup with the gun and the satchel. It doesn't add. It's fantastic."

"Then I guess I'm finished."

"Don't talk like that," Fraser said. "I'm an optimistic sort of person, but if you lose your grip you'll only make it hard for me."

"I'll hold on."

"You've got to. We're going to work this out together. I'm convinced you're an innocent man, and I'll do everything in my power to bring you out of this. What we've got to do now is find the answer to that crazy picture in the hotel room. I don't think we'll find the answer here. What do you think?"

And he was looking at Vanning. It wasn't necessary to say anything. The look was a request, and Vanning took it in and examined it and knew what it meant. He thought of Martha. He thought of Martha's eyes. And her lips. And the way she walked. The sound of her. The presence of her. He told himself to put her out of his mind.

Fraser folded his arms, bent his head to the side, kept on throwing the look. Seconds built themselves into a full minute. And then Fraser said, "Well, what about it? Can you put us on the starting line?"

"I think so."

"Good. Far from here?"

"Barrow Street."

"I thought so. I had the house spotted, but there's more than one in that house."

They went out of the room. Walking down the street, they weren't going fast, they weren't going slowly. They walked side by side, two men going somewhere.

As they came onto Barrow Street, a shiver ran through Vanning, and after that he let out a sigh. Fraser was looking at him.

"What's wrong?" Fraser said.

"The girl."

"What about her?"

Vanning closed his eyes, pressed finger tips into his forehead. "I thought I had common sense," he said. "I thought I knew something about life."

They were standing still. Fraser was lighting a cigarette. "We all think we know something about life. We think we know ourselves. If we did know, we'd be adding machines instead of human beings. You're in love with that girl and you don't want to destroy her. You're very much in love, because Vanning doesn't matter now, does he?"

"I can't get a practical thought in my head."

"Take a drag at this cigarette."

"That won't help. Maybe if you clipped me in the teeth——"

"That won't help, either. Let's see if we can take it from a long-range point of view. You think she was in on that Seattle affair?"

"I don't know."

"What about Denver?"

"I don't know."

"We'll make it dark. We'll make it as miserable as we can. Let's assume they had her working for them from the very beginning. Remember, we're stretching the point. All right, she helped out with the Seattle robbery. Probably a few jobs before that. And probably she has a prison record. Let's say she gets ten years. How old are you?"

"Thirty-three."

"You're forty-three when she gets out. Are you willing to wait?"

Vanning turned away from Fraser and stared down the street, his eyes soldered to the white brick front of the house where she lived. "I can't let it happen," he said. "I don't know what got her into this kind of life. I know she isn't made for it. She's such a healthy girl, she's full of living. She needs a guy. She needs a home. And kids. If they put her in prison, she'll decay. I want to see her laughing. I want to see her bending over a stove. Wheeling a baby carriage down the street. I can't see her behind bars. I can't see that."

Looking at his wrist watch, Fraser said, "If we get a move on, maybe we can put a head on this thing before morning."

"Ten years."

"Remember, I said it was the dark side."

"Promise me you'll do something for her."

"I'll be level with you. I can't promise anything. Once I bring her in, it's out of my hands."

"She wasn't in that station wagon. Maybe she had nothing to do with Seattle."

"Maybe."

"Everything is maybe. Everything."

"It's maybe as long as we stand here," Fraser said. "Why don't we go ahead and find out?"

"Do you need me there?"

"You'll have to face her sooner or later."

Vanning began to walk ahead. Fraser came up at his side. They were going down Barrow Street.

"Look what I'm doing," Vanning said. "Look what I'm doing to her."

"Think of what you're doing for yourself."

"I had to travel to Chicago by way of Colorado. I couldn't take another road. No, I had to go and use that road."

"And then you would have never met her in the first place."

"That's what I mean."

"So all right then," Fraser said. "It adds up to the same thing."

"No, it doesn't. I can't look at it that way. I guess I would have met her somewhere. I don't know. I was bound to meet her."

"Brother, you need a shot in the arm. You need a cold shower. You're in a bad way, do you know that? And if you go on like this, you won't be of much help to me. That means I won't be able to help you."

"Can't you help her? Can't you do something?"

"Not if she's a criminal. If she's a criminal, we've got to put her in prison. That's why society hires us. You'd be amazed how some of us hate our jobs. But somebody has to do this kind of work. Otherwise you'd see broken store windows and dead people all over the street. Now try to think along these lines." He turned and got a glimpse of Vanning's face. "No," he said, "don't even try. Don't think of anything. Just take me to that address."

They walked on. The houses marched past them in funereal parade. The house of white brick came nearer. The white stood out against the black street like something dead surrounded by mourners.

"That one," Vanning said. And he pointed.

"Come on."

They came to the door and Fraser looked at the panel bearing the tenants' names. "Which one is it?"

"Gardner."

Fraser pressed the button.

"Maybe she isn't there," Vanning said. "We'll find out."

"Maybe she packed up and left."

"It's very possible."

"I guess that's what she did. She packed up and left."

"Sure," Vanning said. "That's what she did. If she was there, we'd get a buzz."

"I'll try again."

"There's no use trying. She's gone."

Fraser showed a pair of tightened lips. "And if she's gone," he said, "your goose is cooked. Do you realize that? You can't take me to that house outside of Brooklyn. You told me you have no idea where it's located. If the girl is gone, we've lost our only contact. Think that over."

"I've thought it over already. I don't even care."

Again Fraser pressed the button; he held his finger against it as he watched Vanning.

And then there was a buzz, and Fraser said, "She's home."

"I didn't hear anything."

"I said she's home. We're going up." Fraser's hand moved down and touched a bulge in his coat pocket. "Come on, Vanning. This is the wind-up."

Fraser opened the door. He flattened himself against the door.

"You first," he said.

"Don't you trust me?"

"Not in the condition you are now. Do me a favor, will you? Don't make me use the gun. Please."

Vanning moved past Fraser, started up the steps, heard Fraser's footsteps behind him. The stairs and the walls seemed to have a high polish, seemed to glow in a way that made them unreal. The glow increased. Vanning told himself it was really that, it was unreal. When he came to the second-floor landing, he stopped.

Behind him, Fraser murmured, "Where is it?"

"Third floor."

"Up we go."

"This is hell."

"Climb."

They went up to the third floor, and her door was open and she was standing there and again she was wearing the quilted blue satin robe. When she saw Vanning, her eyes lit up. When she saw Fraser, her eyes widened and she stepped back into the room, leaving the door open, going back and back into the room, looking at Vanning, at Fraser, at Vanning again.

Fraser closed the door. He walked across the room as if he had lived in it for years. He pulled down the shade and turned his back to the window. He leaned against the window sill and folded his arms as he looked at Martha.

He said, "Sit down. I want to talk to you."

She moved toward a chair, her eyes on Vanning. She sat down and her eyes kept watching Vanning.

Fraser said, "Are you Martha Gardner?"

"That's my name."

Gesturing toward Vanning, the detective said, "Do you know that man?"

"Yes."

"Who is he?"

"James Vanning." Now, for the first time since the door had been closed, she took her eyes away from Vanning and faced the detective.

"We're going to step on the gas," Fraser said. "We're going to use a good, sharp knife and cut away everything that doesn't matter. Now, Miss Gardner, what do you do for a living? Fast. I want it fast."

"I sell glassware in a department store."

"How long have you worked there? No, we'll change that. How long have you been in New York?"

"Three years."

"And this address?"

"Five months."

"When you took that trip to Seattle, you went by train, didn't you?"

"I've never been to Seattle."

"All right then, in what town did you meet John?"

"John who?"

"Just John. Come on, Miss Gardner, come on."

She looked at Vanning. Suddenly she smiled at him. She said, "What's the matter, Jimmy boy? Why do you look so sad?"

Vanning's gaze dropped to the floor. He was standing on his own two feet, and yet his whole body seemed to be dropping to the floor, going through the floor.

"We're talking about John," the detective said. "The man who was here last night. In what town did you meet him? When did you meet him?"

"Last night," she said. "In this room. For the first time."

"Really?"

"Really," she said. "I'll tell you about it, if you want."

"By all means. And you'd better make it good, Miss Gardner, because you're in a terrible jam."

"I don't think so," she said. "I'm not worried about it at all. I know everything is going to be all right." She turned and

smiled at Vanning. "Isn't it, Jimmy?" And then she came back
to Fraser and the smile went away and she said, "The man you
call John, the man who was here last night, he told me his
name was Sidney. He said he was an old friend of James Vanning. I'm quoting him now. Just as he said it. He said he had
forgotten Vanning's address. He asked me if I knew. I told him
I didn't know."

"How did he pick up your address?"

"I asked him that. He said Vanning had told him about me,
and one day when they were walking down Barrow Street,
Vanning pointed out the house where I lived."

"Did you believe him?"

"No."

"All right then, how did he find out your address?"

"I haven't the slightest idea."

"Then you're not connected with him?"

"No."

"Have you ever been in prison?"

"No."

"Now this John, or Sidney, or whatever his name is, what
else did he tell you last night?"

"That was all. He just wanted Vanning's address. But he
stayed for quite a while, trying to get it. He went at it in a
roundabout way. I let him talk. I made him feel at home. I
even gave him a few drinks. I didn't want him to catch on."

"What do you mean, catch on?"

"I know who he is."

"You don't have to keep your face so straight, Miss Gardner.
You're not playing poker. You say you know who he is. How
do you know?"

"Jimmy told me. Jimmy told me everything."

Fraser made a chin gesture toward Vanning. "Why do you
call him Jimmy?"

"Because he's Jimmy."

Fraser took a pack of cigarettes from his coat pocket. He
tossed the pack from one hand to the other. He said, "I think
we're going around in a circle. We still don't have anything."
His head went down, snapped up, his eyes jabbed at Martha
and he said, "Are you really in love with that guy standing
there?"

"Madly."

"You realize what a spot he's in?"

"Yes."

"And what a spot you're in?"

"Yes."

"Tell me, Miss Gardner, is love an important issue with you?"

"It's everything."

"Then why the devil don't you come clean?"

"I've told you all I know. I'll do anything you want me to do."

Fraser stood up. He walked across the room, reached the door, took a swing at it and pulled the punch. Then he started to turn, and then he stopped and his arms fell and hung loosely at his sides. And he just stood there.

That went on for several foolish seconds, but when the foolishness faded it faded quickly, energetically, and Fraser whirled, faced the door, went through rapid motions that got the door open and got the revolver out of his pocket, his finger against the trigger. And he stepped back into the room, beckoned with his other hand.

"Come on in," he said. "Open house tonight."

Chapter Fifteen

JOHN CAME walking into the room. John was very surprised. He had a gun in his hand, but it wasn't pointing at anything in particular.

"Put the gun on the floor," Fraser said. "Don't start anything because then we'd both get hurt. Close the door, Vanning."

Vanning moved in behind John and closed the door. He stayed there, behind John, waiting.

Fraser took a step toward John and said, "I told you to put your gun on the floor."

"That's asking a lot," John said.

"I'm in a position to ask a lot."

Now John had lifted his gun and the two guns were pointed and ready, and John said, "I'm in a position to refuse."

"We can stay this way all night."

"I guess we can."

"Or else we can start shooting and get it over with."

"You play it your way and I'll play it mine."

Fraser bit his lower lip. He studied his own gun for a few moments and then, when his eyes lifted, his gaze rested on Vanning for a very small part of a second, and after that he was grinning at John and he was saying, "I'm not very good at this. My nerves can't take it."

He shrugged and tossed the gun away and watched it land on the studio couch. Just as the gun made contact with the upholstery, Vanning moved in and took hold of John's arm and did some twisting. John let out a moan and went to his knees. John's arm was far up behind his back and his limp fingers allowed the revolver to break loose. Vanning caught it before it could hit the floor. He walked away from John and gave the gun to Fraser. And Fraser put the gun in his pocket, stepped over to the studio couch and regained his own gun. He smiled at Vanning. He said, "That wasn't bad."

John was sitting on the floor and rubbing his arm. When he started to get up, Fraser motioned him down with the gun.

"Just stay there," Fraser said. "We don't need to be formal about this."

"I'm a fool," John said. "And I guess guns don't like me. I've never had much luck with guns."

Fraser looked at Martha. And then he looked at John. His gaze went back to Martha, but he was addressing John as he said, "What about her?"

"She's not in it," John said.

"That's not enough. You'll have to tell me why. And it's got to be very good."

"Vanning can tell you why," John said. "We had him unconscious the other night, and while he was out I looked through his pockets. I wanted to see if I could find out where he lived. It was no go, he wasn't carrying any personal papers, not even a card in his wallet. Only a note with the girl's name and address on it. I copied the information and put the note back in his pocket."

Fraser looked at Vanning. "All right?"

Vanning wore a tired smile. He nodded slowly. He said, "It figures."

"Now then," Fraser said, putting himself in a chair, his eyes arrows, with John the motionless target, "you're in a position to make life miserable for Vanning. You understand that?"

"I can see it."

Fraser's eyes were almost closed, and it was as if his eyes were the fine lenses of a fine camera. He said, "It goes along this way, John. You're not exactly a young man any more, and if I'm guessing right, this manipulation is going to send you up for a long, long time. You won't be very happy in prison, but if you have any good in you, I think you'll sleep better at night knowing that you went to bat for our friend here."

John went through a brief facial contortion. He said, "I'm not comfortable here on the floor."

"Make yourself comfortable."

John stood up and walked to the nearest chair. He sat on the edge, his hands folded between his legs. There was a quiet, and it churned, and John stared at the wall across from him, and then there was a strange little interval during which John's eyes skipped from Fraser to Vanning to Martha and back to Fraser again.

It all came to a head. It broke, and John said, "Can we make an exchange?"

"We can trade facts," Fraser said. "Nothing else."

"That's what I want. The facts. I want to see where I stand. Let's hear what you have on your side."

"The main thing on my side is Seattle. I know you headlined the bank job. Three hundred thousand dollars. It points at you for so many reasons that we won't even bother to count them. Do you want me to keep talking?"

"I guess you've told me enough," John said. "It's a fair exchange. I only wanted to be sure about Seattle. That puts me in the soup, and there's no good reason why Vanning should be in there with me. He's clear."

"You'll stick with that?"

"He's clear," John said. "He had nothing to do with Seattle. He's an innocent man, but if you want that three hundred grand, only Vanning can tell you where it is."

"We'll come to that," Fraser said, and he looked at Vanning.

There was a moment of shock, followed by a moment of complete realization, and after that the first thing Vanning felt was a greatly multiplied admiration for Fraser's thinking power. That lasted for a few hazy moments, and it contained the knowledge that Fraser had taken him for a beautiful ride. But he couldn't hate the detective. He couldn't blame the detective. He couldn't blame anyone for doubting that story of the lost satchel. He was close to doubting it himself. In a frantic effort to erase the doubt, he hurled his mind back to Colorado, and he tried to see Denver, and a dark street in Denver became part of the swishing, droning circle that went round and round and round with no indication of a halt.

Fraser was lighting a cigarette. He went about it slowly, methodically. When he lifted his head, his eyes rested on John. "Let's have a look at Denver," he said. "If you really want to set things right for Vanning, you'll explain that business in the hotel. You'll explain why you left Vanning alone with the gun and the satchel."

"You ought to be able to figure that out. You're a detective."

"I'm not psychic."

John placed folded hands against the back of his head. "The whole thing was set up by Harrison. It was all his idea. I've never gone in for killing. I don't believe in it. I was trying to figure out a way to get rid of Vanning without killing him. I couldn't get any ideas, and finally Harrison convinced me that there was only one thing to do and the sooner we did it the better. Harrison said it was his job. He was a specialist at that sort of thing. He did it in terms of arithmetic. He always used to tell me there was no sense in risking a charge of first-degree murder when you could angle it toward second-degree or even manslaughter."

"You're taking me in deep," Fraser said. "Go a little deeper."

"Harrison was waiting there in Denver. So here's the way things stood. The bathroom door was unlocked. Vanning was in there and I was in the bedroom with another man."

"His name?"

"When you catch him," John said, "he'll tell you his name." He waited for that to sink in. Fraser nodded to signify that it had sunk in. And then John said, "Harrison knew the hotel we would use. He took a look at the register after giving us a high sign in the lobby. Then he came up to the room and the three of us talked it over. Harrison told us to go out and he would handle the rest of it. He said he wasn't taking any chances on a charge of first-degree murder. He said he was going to give Vanning a chance to put fingerprints on that gun. And if Vanning wanted to, Vanning could pocket the gun. Figuring on a percentage basis, Vanning would do that. He would pick up the gun and then he would put it in his pocket. Later on, if things developed the wrong way, Harrison could claim that Vanning made a try for him with the gun. No sense doing it in the hotel. Harrison wanted a dark street. A fast powder."

"Wasn't that doing it the hard way?" Fraser said.

"Harrison was very sure of himself. He was too sure of himself. That was a bad habit he had."

"Didn't you have any say?"

"I told him he was taking a big chance," John said. "But it was his play and I let him go ahead. He was sure it would work out. So what he did was to leave the gun on the bed and the satchel on the dresser, then go out and wait in the hall. And then out comes Vanning with the satchel and the gun, and what happens after that I've never been able to figure. What I mean is, the way Vanning came out on top, because Harrison was a very talented agent when it came to guns."

"I had the gun in my pocket." Vanning said it as if he was

talking to himself. As if he was in the woods again, running through the dark, trying to get away from the narrow street where Harrison's body grew cold.

"Sure you had it in your pocket," John said. "And that's why it's so mixed up. Harrison had a gun in his hand, didn't he?"

"Yes. He had the gun pointed at me." And Vanning's voice was a drone, as if it was coming out automatically while his mind was somewhere else. And in his mind he saw the black of the night all over Denver. And the woods. And then the hill. He climbed the hill. There was a field. He crossed the field. There was a stream. He stepped into the stream and the water came up to his knees and went on rising and came up to his waist.

"So he's standing there," John said. "He's pointing the gun at you——"

"I took the gun out of my pocket and showed it to him. It's hard to explain. At the time, at that exact second, I wasn't thinking of using the gun. I don't know what I was thinking. I knew he had his mind made up to kill me and I guess the whole thing was a little insane, the way I took out the gun and showed it to him. All he did was stand there and stare at the gun as if it was some new kind of gadget. I don't even remember telling myself to pull the trigger."

"When you produced that gun," Fraser said, "you must have given him the shock of his life. The way you took it out. The way you showed it to him. If you had actually drawn the gun with the intention of using it, you would have had as much chance as a fly arguing with a spider. What you did was throw him completely off balance, but even so it was a crazy thing for you to do."

"I've been doing a lot of crazy things," Vanning said, and for an instant his eyes hit Martha.

Fraser hauled deeply at his cigarette. "I think we're finally tying it up," he said, and then he looked at Vanning. "There's only one more thing, and if you can give me that, we'll have this entire business boxed and wrapped and ready to ship."

"I can't," Vanning said.

"Try."

"I've been trying. I've tried a million times. I just can't do it. I can't tell you where it is because I don't know where it is."

"Go back," Fraser said. "Take it step by step. Try to remember every detail."

And then John let out a laugh and said to Fraser, "What a panic this is. He's kidding you and you're kidding him and the two of you aren't kidding anybody. Sure, he knows where it is, but if he tells you he's a fool."

"And if he doesn't tell me," Fraser said, "he's part of that bank robbery and he goes to prison. And nothing that I say or you say or that the girl says will make any difference. Just picture it in court."

"I've done that," Vanning said. "I've done that so many times I can't stand thinking about it."

"I'll think about it for you. I'll picture it for you." There was hardness in Fraser's voice. "You're in court. They're telling you what you did. Now, here it comes. You take out the gun. You point it at Harrison——"

"I explained that."

"Explain it in court and see what happens. It's a knocked-out story, there's not an ounce of logic in it, because there's nothing to back it up. Seattle doesn't want to know from your personal troubles. Seattle wants that three hundred thousand. Listen to the way it goes. Listen——" And Fraser's voice took on a machine-gun quality, the words coming out with fire in them, coming out fast and faster, saying, "You take out the gun and you kill Harrison and you grab that satchel. You run away with it, it's three hundred thousand dollars, it's all the money in the world, it's yours, it's yours, you're not a crook and actually you didn't steal this dough, but now it's yours and you'll be damned if you're going to let it slip out of your fingers. So you take it in the woods and you dig a hole and you hide it, telling yourself when you're good and ready you'll come back and pick it up——"

"But that's not true," Martha blurted.

Quiet came in like a blade as they all stared at her.

Then Fraser slowed down a little. "I don't care if it's true or not," he said. "That's what they'll say. Go argue with them. Go try and make them believe otherwise. You, John. You're on the sidelines now. Do you believe him?"

"Do I look like a moron?" John wanted to know. He grinned at Vanning. "No offense, bud. You're playing it the smart way.

Stay with it. You'll be out in a few years and then it's all yours. It's a lot of jack and it'll buy you a lot of pretty things."

Vanning was staring at the floor, his head going from side to side, his hands pressing hard at his temples. "I don't know where it is. I don't, I don't know where it is."

"Think," Fraser snapped. "Think."

"Why don't you leave him alone?" John said. "You're carrying on like a third-rate detective."

Fraser blinked a few times. Then he smiled at John and he said, "All right, I'll leave him alone. I'm going to do better than that. I'm going to walk out, and he can have the gun."

John was a statue with big glass eyes as Fraser handed the gun to Vanning, and then the glass eyes moved slowly, following Fraser as he headed toward the door, and John said, "You must be crazy."

"Maybe I am," Fraser said. "But I trust this man. I can't help it."

"You're still not telling me anything," John said. "What's all this good-bye?"

"No good-bye." Fraser held onto the smile. "I'm only going outside to have a chat with your friends."

The glass eyes became foggy. "How do you know they're outside?"

Fraser swerved away from the door and moved across the room toward the studio couch. He let go of the smile as his eyes took in the other gun. And he said, "Even a third-rate detective would know they're outside."

Chapter Sixteen

IT WAS strange, the way Fraser picked up the other gun. It was strange, the expression on his face as he walked out of the room. And the quiet that followed was very strange. There was a lot of ending in it. And it seemed that most of the ending was concentrated where John's gaze rested on nothing. It seemed that the ending and nothing were coming together and creating a blend. And the quiet went on. And Vanning had the gun aimed at John's face, the gun heavy in his hand, the gun seeming to gain weight with every passing second of that dismal quiet.

The quiet went on.

Finally John said, "I don't figure this. I've been trying but I can't figure it nohow."

"I could use a drink of water," Vanning said.

"I have some lemonade in the icebox," Martha said. She moved toward the kitchenette. She became busy with pitcher and glasses. For a few moments Vanning forgot entirely about John, and although his eyes drew a straight path between himself and John, he was seeing Martha in the kitchenette, he was seeing her walking down the street. He was seeing her in a small restaurant, and on the subway, and walking through the park. And she was alone, all the time alone. In this little place she called home, she was alone. Night after dreary night she was alone. He saw her sitting in a chair in this room, alone, and then he saw himself making his way across the stream in the black woods outside Denver, and he saw himself going through the woods, and he heard his own soundless speech as he told himself he was afraid of the satchel.

Somehow he had a glass of lemonade in his hand. He sipped at it and there was no taste. A big tree, blacker than the black of the woods, far blacker than the sky, loomed up in front of him. He was going fast, and in order to get away from the tree he had to throw his body quickly to the side. He could see part of the moon coming into view as he veered away from the tree. He couldn't see the remainder of the moon because a blotch of cloud was dangling up there. There was a flicker of white,

then black, then white again, and the cloud and segment of
moon came together and took on a fleshy color and the mixture molded itself into John's face. John was gulping at a glass
of lemonade.

Martha was saying, "I have some scotch around here, if
anyone feels like it."

"None for me," John said. "I'd better get used to the idea of
no liquor."

Martha walked back and forth for no reason at all. She stood
in front of the closed door that separated her little home from
the rest of the house. Lightly and slowly she patted her palms
against the white door, cleaned to a very white, and she said,
"He's been out there a long time."

"He shouldn't have gone out alone," Vanning said.

John was shaking his head. "He shouldn't have gone out,
period."

"A wife and three kids," Vanning said, the moment bursting
as he remembered his first meeting with Fraser.

John frowned. "How do you know?"

Vanning didn't answer, since in a single, jumbled second he
had forgotten what the question was, and besides, he was too
busy dodging another tree. This was an awfully big fellow with
branches going out wide, clutching frantically at the vacant sky
like a punctured octopus, and there was a miniature ravine a
few steps farther on, and Vanning stumbled into it, came up
and out of it, got past the big rock with the sound of leather
against rock a distinct recollection in his pounding brain. The
leather was the satchel, so that particular tree and that particular rock didn't matter, because he still carried the satchel at that
time.

Again Martha was walking back and forth. "I have a telephone here," she said. "Maybe if we made a call——"

"Better not," Vanning said. "Fraser would have made the
call if he thought it was best. I guess he didn't want to take the
chance of losing them. At the first sign of police they'd get
scared and start running. We don't want to horn in on this.
Fraser knows what he's doing."

"What's he so hungry about?" John said. "Sam and Pete
don't figure now."

"Everything figures now," Vanning said. "It's Fraser's case and he wants to get all the answers tonight."

"All the answers?" John said.

"All of them."

"Except one," John said. "There's one answer he won't get, unless you lose all your brains all of a sudden. I tell you, if you hold out you'll get away with it. And suppose you do spill it, what will you get? A merit badge? Put it together and see for yourself. A cop is a cop and Fraser isn't doing anybody any favors. And if you think he doesn't have his own eye on that dough——"

"Cut it out," Vanning said. "You're way off."

"Am I?" John said. "You're new at this sort of thing. Maybe you ought to listen to an old hand. I don't claim Fraser will pull monkey business. I do claim he's given more than a single thought to the reward money, and believe me, there's bound to be some important reward money. Maybe he's not a bad guy and maybe he likes to give people a break now and then, but you can bet your sweet life Fraser comes first."

"That's why he walked out," Vanning said with weary sarcasm. "That's why he put a gun in my hand."

"Can't you see through that?"

"I see the gun in my hand. I see Fraser trying to give me a fair deal."

"And I see Fraser playing you for a sap," John said. "Sure, he puts a gun in your hand. Sure, he walks out, and you're in charge, you're the good boy of the class, old faithful in person, mister true blue, loyal to the end. And when Fraser comes back, if he does come back, you're still the good boy and you hand over the gun like a good boy. And then Fraser takes you in, and you go to prison. Like a good boy."

"What's the matter, John? Are you trying to give me ideas?"

"I'm trying to get a few angles across," John said. "If you get the point, swell. But you won't get the point. Because you like the idea of stooging for Fraser. It's easier that way. But when you see those bars in front of your face you'll remember what I told you. And you're going to hate yourself for losing out on a cute little chance that was handed to you on a silver platter."

"Save it," Vanning said. "I'm not buying anything today."

John looked at Martha and said, "Maybe you can sell it to him."

"He can do his own thinking," Martha said.

John came back to Vanning. And John's face was solemn, a rather sad note in his voice as he said, "I can see it as if it happened already. You went and got cold feet and you told them where they could find the money. So they talked to Denver and Denver laid hands on the cash and gave it back to Seattle. That made everything nice and pretty for everybody, and everybody was tickled pink. But there was one piece of business that had to be taken care of. You see, they still had to put you up on trial. And it was certainly a crying shame, but even though you owned up, they still had to put you in jail because, after all, you got yourself in on the tail end of that bank job, you got your mitts on that dough and you stashed it away. It was too bad, but even though that money, every last cent of it, was back in the vault where it belonged, they still had to give you a few years. And when I say a few years I'm giving you the benefit of a great big doubt."

"It sounds very good," Vanning said. "But it doesn't mean a thing, because I don't know where that money is."

John let out a huge sigh. He turned to Martha and said, "Honest to goodness, I'm beginning to believe him." Then his head made a snapping, mechanical turn and his eyes slashed at Vanning as he said, "If you don't know where that dough is, if you really and truly don't know, then do me a little favor. Tell me one thing. You've got that gun in your hand. You've got that door in front of you. Tell me, what are you hanging around for?"

Vanning mixed a shrug with a smile as he said, "I'm trying to be a good boy."

John made a reply, but it didn't reach Vanning, because Vanning was moving through thick brush that took him downhill where there were no trees, where the moonlight made a spray of pearls on the jet velvet of moss-covered rocks, and one of the rocks became transparent, with a scene beneath its glassy substance, the scene showing Fraser going down a stairway. Everything turned inside out and Fraser's skull became transparent, and inside Fraser's mind there was the plan to make a rear exit and take the alley and work it roundabout to Barrow Street, the anticipation of two men on the other side of the street, waiting behind a tree or behind an automobile or in an automobile or in some doorway. The realization of that was a flash containing all sorts of color, and it flashed again, and again, and then it rose and took its place on an observation post, with Fraser far below, Fraser walking alone down the dark street.

"I hate the thought of it," Vanning said. "Fraser out there alone."

John smiled like an old fox. "I knew it. Here it comes."

Vanning beckoned to Martha and said, "You take the gun." She didn't move. She said, "I'm afraid I don't understand."

"I'm going out there," Vanning said.

"And he'll keep on going," John said. "He'll get away while the getting is good. He's not such a fool, after all." Then, as he addressed Vanning, his voice dropped a little. "While you're at it, you might as well give me a break too. I won't bother you any more. All I want to do is get myself lost."

"No go," Vanning said. "You stay here." And again he beckoned to Martha, his eyes soldered to John.

Martha stayed where she was.

Vanning's voice was almost down to a whisper. "I want you to take the gun, Martha. I want you to keep it on John. I'm going out there. You can decide for yourself. You can believe anything you want to. If you take John's word for it, I'm walking out on the whole thing and you'll never see me again."

She was breathing deeply. "And if I take your word for it?"

"I'm going out to see what I can do for Fraser."

John lifted his eyes to the ceiling as he crossed his legs and threw his hands around a knee. "That one gets four stars," he said. "That's the best I've ever heard."

Vanning bit into his lip. "I'm sorry, Martha. I hate like the devil to put you on the spot, and it's a thousand to one that John is calling it right. I mean the way it looks on the surface. I know it's giving you a lot of worry——"

"That's not what I'm worried about." There was feminine indignation in Martha's tone. "I don't like your going out there without a gun. All you have is your two hands. What are you trying to do, show me you're a big brave man?"

"Sure," Vanning said. "And I can do somersaults, too. Here, take the gun."

Martha was moving in toward the gun, and John banged a fist into a palm and said, "I'm closing up shop. I'm way behind the times. He's actually sold her a bill of goods."

The gun in Martha's hand pointed at John's chest, and Vanning took in that picture a couple of seconds and then he stepped toward the door.

"Just keep it on him," he said. "He won't do anything. You won't do anything, will you, John? Look how nervous she is. If you let out a sneeze she'll pull the trigger."

"Is that all I have to do?" Martha said. "Pull the trigger?"

"That's all you have to do," Vanning said. He had his hand on the doorknob. "Good-bye now."

John looked at Vanning and nodded slowly, emphatically. "Good-bye is right."

The door opened, banged shut as Vanning raced down the hall, down the stairs. Now the moonlight in the black woods showed another large rock against which Vanning leaned for a few moments to catch his breath, but his hand did not touch the rock because the satchel was in there between his hand and the rock. And so that particular rock didn't matter, either. Beyond the rock, flowing in toward Vanning, there was a parade of small trees, so straight they looked as if someone had tried to start an orchard in the woods. Their amazingly well-ordered progression stood out against the rest of the woods like good soldiers in a riotous crowd. The moonlight seemed to pick them out and honor them. They passed in smart review as Vanning moved on. And then, just as Vanning reached the second-floor landing, he heard the sound of a shot.

Chapter Seventeen

IT CAME from the street, entered the house and ripped through like an insane intruder. There was another shot. Vanning winced. He told himself to keep moving. There were more shots. The stairway rushed up at him, went past him, and he was thinking that in all probability Fraser had a little house up in Kew Gardens or someplace like that and there was a bit of grass around the place and every night when Fraser came home, Fraser's wife was there, waiting. And the children were in their beds, and Fraser would come up and kiss the children, kiss them softly, tenderly, so as not to wake them. And in the morning Fraser and the wife and the three kids would be sitting there at the breakfast table with sunlight getting through a tree out on that little lawn out there, the sunlight coming through and glowing on the toaster on the breakfast table, the chromium bright, the faces glowing, the little Fraser family.

The sunlight glowing, but then it was no longer sunlight, it was a street lamp throwing glow into the front doorway as Vanning ran out. Against the black street the glow was intense, there was some red in it, some bright red streaming, curving away from a motionless form in the center of the street, the nucleus of the red a distinct blotch on the side of Sam's balding head.

That was the first thing. The second thing was the big rubber band of quiet that stretched and stretched before the next shot. When he heard the next shot, he traced the sound of it to a doorway across the street, he saw a big man moving out of the doorway, saw the big man making bold progress down the stone steps. Then he saw something moving slowly, going down at the side of a telegraph pole, knees giving way. His eyes switched back to the big man who advanced across the street, the big man pointing a gun toward the weak and sagging thing that was trying to wrap itself around the telegraph pole, trying to push the pole between itself and the gun.

All of this was coming nearer, getting larger, especially the big man, who was now very big. And on the border of all this, as another shot sounded, there was sideline activity, windows opening, the sound of people, but it was part of the vague black, it was absurdly unimportant. The only thing that mattered was the big man, so terribly big now, the bigness suddenly blending with a swift turning, the motion clumsy yet definite, and all that blending with the new direction of the pointed gun, and then the blast, quickly followed by another blast from the gun now pointed at the sky because Vanning had a hold on Pete's wrist, and with his other hand he was bashing away at Pete's face.

Pete wouldn't let go of the gun. He aimed a knee at Vanning's stomach, missed and tried again, and this time his knee made contact and Vanning fell back, doubled up, lost his balance and fell heavily on his side. And he stared at the gun, the huge, twisted face behind the gun. On the gun there was a gleaming and in the black woods outside Denver there was moonlight gleaming and then from somewhere behind the moonlight there was the sound of another gun, and Pete stood very straight just before he arched his back and dropped the revolver and followed the revolver to the street. He did some groaning, a little gurgling, and then he was all finished.

Vanning pulled himself up, made a dash to the telegraph pole. He took hold of Fraser and saw the pain on Fraser's face.

"How did I do?" Fraser said.

"Very nice. Where has it got you?"

"A knee job. Hurts like hell." And all at once Fraser's eyes were very wide but not with pain. "What are you doing here?"

"It's all right," Vanning said. "She's watching him. She has the other gun."

"She sure has," Fraser said, grinning through the pain, his eyes going past Vanning, so that Vanning had to turn and see what it was all about. For an instant all he saw was people running out of doorways. The instant crumbled and the people faded and he saw John approaching, followed by the gun and then Martha. He felt like laughing out loud. It was a wonderful little picture. Martha looked so serious about it all, and John looked so weary.

A hand touched his shoulder, and he came back to Fraser, and Fraser was saying, "You sure put yourself out for me. It's going to be tough on me, taking you in."

"That's all right," Vanning said. "Don't let it bother you."

He was ripping the fabric of a trouser leg, using the freed fabric to fashion a tourniquet. As he tightened the tourniquet, he heard Fraser's groan, but he went on with the tightening, then the knotting, and just as he finished the knotting he saw Martha and John standing there, and all the gaping people behind him. He saw that and yet he didn't see it, because he was staring at the black of the woods where it was all very thick and jumbled compared to the twenty yards or so of muddy clearing that separated this thick vegetation from the mathematically arranged trees.

Someone was talking, but Vanning didn't know who it was and he didn't know what was being said. Now, in this heavy foliage, he didn't have the satchel, but moments ago while going past the final tree in that strangely straight row, he had held the satchel in his hand. And his brain took a skip and a jump. The satchel was somewhere in that small clearing. Between the tree and the foliage, and closer to the foliage, and it was there, it had to be there.

Fraser was watching him. Martha was watching him. And John. He didn't know that. He was back there in the woods, going toward the satchel.

And all at once a voice said, "Where?"

It was Martha's voice. He looked at her, and he could see the pleading in her eyes, the hope and the fear. And then he couldn't see her eyes but he could see the satchel. His eyes were shut tightly and he could see the satchel glimmering as it dropped away from him and went into a little muddy crevice about three yards away from the foliage.

And there it was, and it was still there, a little thing of black leather glowing in the moonlight, a little lost thing waiting for someone to come along and pick it up.

No doubt. No fear. Only the knowledge. The bursting, wonderful discovery. And the wonderful realization that the woods were extremely dense and there were no paths in that vicinity and the satchel would still be there and the landmarks were convenient and specific and he could lead them to the satchel.

His eyes lit up and he grinned at Fraser.

The detective grinned back. "You finally hit it?"

Vanning nodded. "On the button."

"It isn't buried, is it?"

"No," Vanning said. "It's in the open."

"You dropped it?"

Vanning nodded.

"You dropped it and kept moving," Fraser said. "That's what I was hoping you'd tell me. I'll go along on that trip to Denver. I'll back you up, even though it isn't really necessary. Any good psychiatrist could figure this without any trouble."

"Do you have it figured?"

"A hundred per cent," Fraser said. "It's what they call regressive amnesia. You identified the satchel with your killing a man. Subconsciously you forced yourself to forget the location. Something important had to happen to get you past that barrier. Now if the important something will hand over the gun——"

Martha placed the revolver in Fraser's extended hand. That made two guns on Fraser's side. The guns aimed casually in the direction of John, but John wasn't looking at the guns. He seemed far away from the whole business. He didn't even blink when he heard the sirens, although he knew they were coming toward him and toward no one else.

THE BURGLAR

Chapter I

A T THREE in the morning it was dead around here and the
windows of the mansion were black, the mansion dark
purple and solemn against the moonlit velvet green of gently
sloping lawn. The dark purple was a target and the missile was
Nathaniel Harbin who sat behind the wheel of a car parked on
a wide clean street going north from the mansion. He had an
unlit cigarette in his mouth and in his lap there was a sheet of
paper containing a diagram of burglary. The plan gave the
route aiming at the mansion, moving inside and across the
wide library to the wall-safe where there were emeralds.

In the parked car Harbin sat with his three companions.
Two of them were men and the third was a blonde skinny girl
in her early twenties. They sat there and looked at the mansion. They had nothing to express and very little to think about,
because the mansion had been thoroughly cased, the plan had
been worked and re-worked with every move scheduled on a
split-second basis, the thing discussed and debated and rehearsed until it was a fine, precise plan that looked to be foolproof. Harbin told himself it was foolproof, allowed that to
simmer for a while, then bit hard on the cigarette and told
himself nothing was foolproof. The haul was going to be risky
and as a matter of fact it might prove to be more risky than any
they had ever attempted. It was certainly the biggest haul they
had ever attempted and it was these big hauls that offered the
most danger. Harbin's thinking went that far and no further.
He was inclined to pull the brakes on thinking when his mind
began looking at risk.

Harbin was thirty-four and for the past eighteen years he had
been a burglar. He had never been caught and despite the
constant jeopardy he had never been forced into a really tight
corner. The way he operated was quiet and slow, very slow,
always unarmed, always artistic without knowing or interested
in knowing that it was artistic, always accurate with it and always extremely unhappy with it.

The lack of happiness showed in his eyes. He had grey eyes
that were almost never bright, subdued eyes that made him

look as though he was quietly suffering. He was a rather good-looking man of medium height and medium weight and he had hair the color of ripe wheat, parted far on one side and brushed flat across his head. His mode of attire was neat and quiet and he had a soft quiet voice, subdued like the eyes. He very seldom raised his voice, even when he laughed, and he rarely laughed. He rarely smiled.

In that respect he was on the order of Baylock, who sat next to him on the front seat of the car. Baylock was a short, very thin man in his middle forties, getting bald, getting old fast with pessimism and worry, getting sick with liver trouble and a tendency to skip meals and sleep. Baylock had bad eyes that blinked a lot and small, bony hands constantly rubbing together with the worry and the memory of several years ago when there was prison. Baylock had been in prison for what he considered a very long time and on certain occasions he would talk about prison and say what an awful thing it was and claim that he would rather be dead and buried than be in prison. Most of the time Baylock was a bore and sometimes he could really get on one's nerves and at certain times he was truly intolerable.

Harbin could remember specific occasions when he had been fed up with Baylock, finally weary of Baylock's continual whining and nagging, the sound of complaining and pessimism that was like a dripping faucet, going into the nerves and going in again and again until the only thing to do was walk away from Baylock and keep on walking to keep away from him until he got tired of hearing himself talk. Baylock always took a long time to get tired of that, and yet Baylock was completely dependable during a haul, valuable after a haul because of his ability to appraise loot, and valuable mainly because all his motives and all his moves were always displayed out in the open.

Harbin recognized and appreciated that rare trait in Baylock, and so did the others, the two in the back seat, the girl and Dohmer. Although Dohmer at times showed active hostility toward Baylock, it was a temporary hostility that always bubbled and climbed and blew up and died. Dohmer was a tall, heavy Dutchman, touching forty, with a wide, thick nose and a thick neck and a thick brain. The brain never tried to accomplish what it knew it couldn't accomplish and for that reason

Dohmer was just as valuable to Harbin as Baylock was. Dohmer was quite clumsy on his feet and he was never allowed to work the inside of houses, but from the outside he functioned well in the capacity of lookout and during emergencies he was more or less automatic, reacting like a network of gears and wires.

Harbin took the cigarette from his mouth, looked at it and put it back in again. He turned his head to look at Baylock, then went on turning his head to look at Dohmer and the girl. The girl, Gladden, looked back at Harbin and as their eyes met and held there was a moment of strain and difficult waiting, as though this was as far as it could go, this thing of just looking at each other and knowing it couldn't go any farther than just this. Glow from a streetlamp far back came through the rear window, came floating in to settle on Gladden's yellow hair and part of her face. The glow showed the skinny lines of her face, the yellow of her eyes, the thin line of her throat. She sat there and looked at Harbin and he saw her skinniness, this tangible proof of her lack of weight, and in his mind he told himself she weighed tons and tons and it all hung as from a rope around his neck. He looked at this burden that was Gladden, tried to smile at her but couldn't smile because he saw her in that moment as a burden and nothing more than a burden, then drew himself up and away from that moment and saw her only as Gladden.

Only as Gladden she was quiet and kind and it was pleasant to have her around. When it came to the hauls she was completely mechanical and went through her maneuvers as though she was knitting. On all the hauls she did all the casing and she did it in a relaxed, somewhat detached manner that made it look almost easy although it was really very difficult, sometimes more difficult than the haul itself. On this haul, aiming at something around a hundred thousand dollars worth of emeralds in a wall safe, Gladden had worked for six weeks to get in good with certain servants who worked in the house, to get into the house on the pretext of visiting with the servants when the family was away for a weekend, to line up the information and take it back to Harbin and Baylock and Dohmer. She did all that with each move carried out according to plan, getting her directions from Harbin, asking no questions and going through with the directions exactly as specified, coming back with all the facts she was told to obtain, and just standing there quietly when Baylock began to whine and nag and complain. Baylock said she should have come back with more, there were undoubtedly more burglar alarms than the ones she had listed. Baylock said it was an unsatisfactory job of casing. But then Baylock was always getting his digs in at Gladden.

There was nothing personal in the digs. Baylock was really fond of Gladden and when they weren't working on a haul he was amiable toward her and he showed her a kindness now and then. But the hauls were the big things in Baylock's life and he saw Gladden as a drag, her femininity a negative force working against the success of the hauls, and even if the hauls were successful, Gladden was a woman and sooner or later a woman causes grief and Baylock was constantly taking Harbin aside and drilling away at this issue. Gladden was Baylock's major complaint though he never made the complaint bluntly in her presence. He would wait until she wasn't around, and then he would start on it, this favorite complaint of his, telling Harbin that they didn't need Gladden, they ought to give her some money and send her away, and she would be better off and most certainly they would be better off.

Harbin always did his best to change the subject, because this subject was something he not only didn't want to talk about, it was something he didn't want to think about. He knew he couldn't convey to Baylock the reasons why they had to retain Gladden. The reasons were deep and there were times when he tried to study them and could not figure them out himself, could only see these reasons as vague elements floating in sinister depth, his contact and relationship with Gladden a really weird state of affairs, something about it that was unnatural, and it was like a puzzle that threw itself in front of one's eyes and stayed there, wouldn't go away, persisted there and grew there. He had gone through countless nights when there was no sleep, only the black ceiling of a room above his eyes, the thought of Gladden a hammer that dangled from the ceiling and clanged against his brain. It was as though he could see the hammer, its metal shining against the darkness of the room, the force of it swinging toward him, coming hard, coming into him. And it was as though he was tied there hand and foot and there was no getting away. The thing was planted. It was set. There was no getting away from Gladden.

Looking at her now, seeing her face there in the rear of the car, he made another attempt to smile at her. He couldn't smile at her. But she was smiling at him. There was sweetness in her smile, soft and gentle and yet it was a blade going through him and he had to turn his head away. He bit into the cigarette and wished he could light it, but they had their own rules about lighting matches during a haul. He shifted the cigarette across his mouth and glanced at his wristwatch.

Then he turned to Baylock and said, "I guess we're ready."

"Check your tools?"

"I'll check them now," Harbin said, and from his coat pocket he took a small metal sliver that could have been a fountain pen, and pressed the edge of it and tested the light it stabbed to the floorboards. From another pocket he took a flannel case tied with a shoelace, undid the shoelace, took out the little tools one by one and held them close to one eye, the other eye closed, studying the fine tips and edges of the tools, touching the smooth metal with a forefinger, closing both eyes to concentrate on the feel of the cold, accurate metal against his flesh. It was wise to always check each tool just before the beginning of a haul. Harbin had learned long ago that metal is an unpredictable element and sometimes it chooses embarrassing moments to give way.

The tools seemed to be all right and he had them back in the case and put the case in his pocket. He glanced again at his wristwatch and said, "All right, get your eyes wide open."

"You going now?" Dohmer said.

Harbin nodded and opened the door and stepped out of the car. He crossed the wide smooth black street, came onto the curving pavement bordering the flowers of the lawn of the mansion. Coming onto the lawn he moved toward the window that had been selected. Again the flannel case came out of his pocket and from the case he took an instrument designed to cut glass. The glass-cutter did its work quietly as Harbin turned the little lever putting the little blade in motion. Finally the glass-cutter sliced a small rectangle permitting Harbin to get his fingers inside to open the window lock. He had the window going up slowly and quietly. He told himself that just about now Gladden ought to arrive. There was a sound near him, and he turned and looked at Gladden. She smiled at him, then a quick gesture with her right hand, something like brushing a fly away from her nose, signified that Dohmer and Baylock were now in their specified placements. Dohmer was at the rear of the house, watching the rear upstairs windows, to see if and when a light would go on. Baylock was on the lawn up toward the front, where he could watch the front and side windows, and where he could get a good view of the street and their parked car. It was very important to keep an eye on their parked car. The police along Philadelphia's Main Line knew most of the cars in this section of mansions, and would be inclined to check any cars that looked like strangers.

Harbin lifted a finger toward the window, and Gladden climbed in. Light from Harbin's small flashlight streaked under her arm as he followed her in. She took the flashlight from him and he followed her across the room toward the wall-safe. No attempt had been made to camouflage the safe and the flashlight displayed it as a square of hammered brass, centered with an ornamented combination dial. Harbin nodded slowly and Gladden went back to the window to stand there where she could watch for flashlight signals from Dohmer and Baylock.

At the safe, Harbin took another look at his wristwatch. He gazed at the safe, ignoring the combination dial and concentrating on the edges of the brass square. He glanced again at his wristwatch and gave himself five minutes at the outside. He began chewing on the unlit cigarette as he removed the important tool from the flannel case.

The important tool was a tiny circular saw revolved by a pumping process, on the order of a hypodermic syringe. The teeth of the saw bit through oak that panelled the brass square. Harbin had his face close to the oak, but every now and then he took it away to see if there was any green light on the wall near him. The green light would be from Gladden's flashlight, in case she needed to use it. The chances were he would see the signal anyway, if it came, but he had to be sure, because here her flashlight threw a wire of green glow, and if it wasn't aimed just right, he would miss it. But if the green light did come, it would mean that Gladden had received an alarm from either

Dohmer or Baylock, or both of them. It would mean that Dohmer would come running to the window, to climb in and intercept anyone coming down from upstairs, to use the special brand of Dohmer technique to silently yet firmly quiet the intercepting party. Or possibly it could mean interception coming from the outside and Dohmer and Baylock would be forced into a decoy set-up. It could mean a great many things and Harbin had all the potentials carefully listed in his brain.

The saw finished one side of the square. The rhythm of the saw made a sound something like that of a man groaning deep in his throat. It was a night sound and it could be an insect out there in the springtime air. Or it could be the distant sound of an automobile. It was a sound that Harbin had tested many times at the Spot, and Gladden had used the saw downstairs while Harbin, his head against the pillow, strained his hearing, and threw aside all rationalization, and finally decided the sound was passable. At the Spot they were always going through this sort of testing, and they practiced constantly. They all hated the practicing, especially Harbin, but it was Harbin who quickly stifled all arguments against the practicing.

Three sides of the square were sawed and he was on the final side when grass-on-fire came into his eyes. He turned and saw the bright green flame from Gladden's flashlight. It went on and off, on again, stayed on, then three bursts from it and he knew there was disturbance on the outside and Baylock had given the signal and it was police and they were at the parked car. He opened his mouth just a little, the chewed cigarette fell out from between his teeth, bounced off his elbow and hit the floor. He leaned over and picked it up, his eyes seeking Gladden at the window, waiting for more from her flashlight. He saw her standing there at the window, giving him her profile in what was almost silhouette. For such a skinny girl, he told himself, she had reasonable height, somewhere around five feet three. She really ought to put on some weight, he told himself. She had an appetite like a wren. The police, he imagined, were now walking around the parked car. He imagined their bandit chaser was parked beside the car and now they were walking around it and looking at it and not saying anything. Now they were inside it. They would see the interior of the automobile. They were tremendous, these police, because the next thing they would do was to look at each other. Then they would look around at the night air. They would just stand there. The police, he told himself, were marvelous when it came to just standing there. Sometimes they elaborated on it a little and pushed their caps back and forth on their heads. Nobody could push a cap back and forth on his head like a policeman. He went on looking at Gladden and waiting for more from her flashlight. Her flashlight stayed dark. Harbin looked at his wristwatch. The next time he looked at his wristwatch it was eight minutes later and he knew he must do something about the policemen, because the lack of further news from Gladden meant the police were still out there.

He moved across the room, came toward Gladden.

He stood beside her profiled face and said close to her ear, "I'll go out."

Her only movement was breathing. She kept her eyes on a garden wall where lights from the other flashlights would show. She said, "Tell them what?"

"Car broke down," he said. "I went to look for a mechanic."

For some moments she had no reply. He waited to hear something. It was a real emergency, yet whatever she said wouldn't mean anything to him in a practical sense, because he was going out anyway. But he liked to know his ideas were solid, and he wanted her to say this was solid. He handed her the tools and his flashlight. He waited.

She said, "You always underestimate the cops."

It wasn't the first time she had said that. It didn't annoy him. Perhaps it was true. Perhaps it was actually a serious weakness in his campaigning, and some night it would truly backfire. But it remained a perhaps and he was never affected strongly by the possible or even probable. The only merchandise he ever bought was the definite.

He said, "Watch your diet," just to say something before he climbed out. Then he was through the window and out on the lawn, working close to the house, getting toward the rear. Shrubbery came up in front of his face and he circled it and saw Dohmer crouching near the stone steps leading to the kitchen door. He made a little sound through the corner of his mouth. Dohmer turned and looked at him. He gave Dohmer a small smile, then moved on, passing Dohmer, working his way around to the other side of the house, cutting across the lawn and seeing Baylock pressed hard against a wall of the garage on the far side of the lawn. He came up behind the garage, edged his way in toward Baylock, making just enough noise so Baylock could hear him coming. Baylock moved a little, stared at him. He nodded and Baylock returned the nod. He faced around, retraced his steps to bring himself on the other side of the garage. Then there was more shrubbery. He went through it. Another line of shrubbery brought him down near the end of the driveway, toward a curving street lowering its way around the north side of the mansion. He came out and onto the street, took off his coat, opened his shirt collar, put a cigarette in his mouth and struck a match.

Puffing at the cigarette, he walked up the street, holding his coat over one arm, then made the turn at the summit of the climbing street. It brought him in view of the parked black car and the parked red car and the two policemen.

They stood there and waited for him. He sighed and shook his head slowly as he walked up to them. One of them was large and past forty and the other was a young handsome man with pale blue eyes, like aquamarine.

The large cop said, "This your car?"

"I wish it wasn't." Harbin looked at the car and shook his head.

"What you doing around here?" the young cop said.

Harbin frowned at the car. "Know where there's an all night mechanic?"

The large cop rubbed his chin. "You kidding?"

The young cop looked at the black car. It was a 1946 Chevrolet sedan. "What's wrong with it?"

Harbin shrugged.

"Let's see your cards," the large cop said.

Harbin handed his wallet to the large cop and watched the young cop walking around the Chevrolet and examining it as though it was something new in the zoo. Harbin leaned against a fender and went on smoking his cigarette as he watched the large cop looking through the cards and checking them with the license plates. He saw the young cop opening the front door on the other side and sliding in behind the wheel.

The large cop handed back the wallet and Harbin said, "I

must have walked a couple of miles. Nothing. Not even a gas station."

"You realize what time it is?"

Harbin looked at his wristwatch. "Jesus Christ."

From inside the car, the young handsome cop said, "Where's your keys?"

"What do you mean?" Harbin said.

"I mean where's your keys? I want to try it."

Harbin opened the front door next to the steering wheel, reached in toward the ignition lock and found only the lock. He frowned up at the long nose of the young cop. He withdrew himself from the car, threw a hand toward his rear trousers pocket, then went through an act of searching for the keys, telling himself he didn't like the eyes of the young cop.

The young cop came out of the car and folded thick arms and watched him as he searched for the keys.

"God damn it," Harbin said. Now he was going through his coat pockets.

The young cop said, "How come you lose keys?"

"They're not lost," Harbin said. "They got to be around somewhere."

"Been drinking?" The young cop moved in a little.

"Not a drop," Harbin said.

"All right then," the young cop said, "where's the keys for your car?"

Instead of answering, Harbin leaned his head inside the car, under the steering wheel and began to search on the floor for the keys. He heard the young cop saying, "You look at his cards?"

"They're in order," the large cop said.

A hand touched Harbin's shoulder, and he heard the young cop saying, "Hey."

He came out from underneath the steering wheel. He faced the young cop. He said, "Some nights a man just shouldn't go out."

Again the young cop had his arms folded. His aquamarine eyes were lenses. "What do you do?"

"Installment business," Harbin said.

"Door to door?"

Harbin nodded.

The young cop glanced at the large cop and then he turned his handsome face toward Harbin and said, "How do you make out?"

"I break even," Harbin pushed a weak grin onto his lips. "You know how it is. It's a struggle."

"What ain't?" the large cop said.

Harbin rubbed the back of his head. "I must have had the keys in my hand when I got out of the car. Must have dropped them while I was walking." He waited for the policemen to say something, and when they didn't he said, "I might as well crawl in the back and go to sleep."

"No," the young cop said, "you can't do that."

"Can you run me into town?"

The young cop pointed to the red bandit chaser. "Does that look like a taxi?"

Harbin put his hands in trousers pockets and gazed dismally at the street. "Might as well go to sleep in the car."

There was a long wait. Harbin kept his eyes away from their faces. He had a feeling the young cop was watching him closely. He knew it was now at the point where it would go one way or another, and all he could do was wait.

Finally, the large cop said, "Go on, get in your car. The night's half shot anyway."

Harbin crossed in front of the aquamarine eyes of the young cop. He opened the rear door of the car, climbed in, curled up on the upholstery and closed his eyes. Around a minute later he heard the engine of the red car starting up. He heard the red car going away.

The long hand on his wristwatch traveled for seven minutes before he raised his head to peer through the car window. Turning the handle that brought the window down, he listened for engine noise, but the night air was empty of sound. He inhaled the quiet, enjoying it. Then, climbing out of the Chevrolet, he put another cigarette in his mouth and moved toward the mansion.

Gladden was at the window as he climbed in. He gave her a grin while she handed him the tools. He turned on his flashlight, aimed it at the wall safe, followed the path of white light across the room to the square of hammered brass, and beyond the brass, the emeralds.

Chapter II

THEY WERE looking at the haul. The four of them were on the second floor of a small dingy house in the Kensington section of Philadelphia. The house was in Dohmer's name and it was very small, part of a narrow street of row houses hemmed in by factories. The house was their dwelling place, their head-quarters, and they called it the Spot. Dust and dirty air from the mills was always coming in even when the windows were closed. Gladden had a habit of throwing a cleaning-rag at the windows and saying it was no use trying to fight this dust. After awhile she would sigh and pick up the rag and go on with the cleaning.

The table in Baylock's room on the second floor was in the center of the room and they stood around and watched Baylock as he examined the emeralds. Baylock's fingers were pincers of thin metal as he picked up the gems one by one and held them against the glass fitted into his left eye. Dohmer had beer going down his throat from a quart bottle, and Gladden's hands were clasped behind her back, her shoulder resting slightly against Harbin's chest, the smoke from his cigarette spraying through the yellow hair of Gladden and floating toward the center of the table where the stones flamed green.

After awhile Baylock took the glass from his eye and picked up a piece of paper on which he had been making an itemized list with the estimated value of each jewel. "Come in around a hundred and ten thousand. Cut the stones down, melt the platinum, shape it up again and it ought to bring around forty."

"Forty thousand," Dohmer said.

Baylock frowned. "Less the expenses."

"What expenses?" Dohmer said.

"Overhead," Baylock said, biting at the corner of his mouth.

Harbin looked at the emeralds. He told himself it was a nice haul and he ought to feel good about it. He wondered why he didn't feel good about it.

Baylock said, "We better move this rapid." He got up from the table, walked up and down, came back to the table. "I figure we go tomorrow. Pack up in the morning and start out. Take it down to Mexico."

Harbin was shaking his head.

"Why not?" Baylock asked.

Harbin didn't answer. He had his wallet out and he was tearing the operator's license and registration card in little pieces. He turned to Dohmer. "Get new cards printed and take care of the Chevvie. Get it done fast. Get new upholstery, now, new paint job, melt the license plates. Everything."

Dohmer nodded, and then he said, "What color you want it?"

Gladden said, "I like orange."

Harbin looked at her. He was waiting for Baylock to commence an argument about Mexico. He knew Baylock would have something to say about Mexico.

"Make it a dull orange," Gladden said. "I don't like bright colors. They're cheap. They're common. When I buy dresses, I buy them in the soft colors. With good taste. With class. Make the car a smoky orange or a grey orange or a burnt orange."

Dohmer took the beer bottle from his mouth. "I don't know what you're talking about."

"I wish," Gladden said, "sometime I could get to talk with women. If once a month I could talk lady talk with ladies I'd be happy."

Baylock rubbed fingers across his balding head. He frowned down at the emeralds. "I figure we go tomorrow and head for Mexico City."

"I said no," Harbin let it come cool.

As though Harbin had not spoken, Baylock said, "Tomorrow's the best time to go. Soon as we get the car changed over. Go down to Mexico City and get the stuff to a fence. Get it done rapid."

"Not tomorrow," Harbin said. "Not next week. Not next month."

Baylock looked up. "How long you want to wait?"

"Between six months and a year."

"That's too long," Baylock said. "Too many things can happen." And then for some unknown reason he looked directly at Gladden and his eyes became almost closed. "Like stupid moves. Like painting the car bright orange."

"I didn't say bright orange," Gladden said. "I told you I didn't like bright orange."

"Like getting up in society," Baylock went on. "Like getting in with the servants on the Main Line."

"You leave me alone," Gladden said. She turned to Harbin. "Tell him to leave me alone."

"Like getting high ideas," Baylock went on. "With good taste. With class. First thing we know she'll be in circulation."

"Now you shut up, Joe," Gladden cried. "You got no right to talk like that. I got in with the servants 'cause that's the only way I could case the place." Again she turned to Harbin. "Why does he pick on me all the time?"

"God, first thing we know," Baylock said, "she'll be up in the world with Main Line society. We'll have rich people coming up here to play bridge and have tea and look at our emeralds."

Harbin turned to Gladden, "Go out in the hall."

"No," Gladden said.

"Go on," Harbin said, "go out and wait in the hall."

"I'll stay right here." Gladden was quivering.

Baylock frowned at Gladden and said, "Why don't you do like he tells you?"

Gladden turned fully upon Baylock. "You shut your God damn lousy face."

Harbin felt something twisting around in his insides, something getting started in there. He knew what it was. It had happened before. He didn't want it to happen again. He tried to work it down and stifle it, but it kept moving around in there and now it began to climb.

Baylock said, "I claim we start tomorrow. I claim—"

"Drop it," Harbin's voice sliced the room. "Drop it, drop it—"

Gladden said, "Hey, Nat—"

"You, too," Harbin was up from the chair, he had the chair in his hand, up in the air, high up, then heaving the chair against the wall, moving toward the dresser and picking up a half-empty bottle of beer, bashing it to the floor. He took his fist and slammed it into the air. His breathing sounded like broken machinery. He was pleading with himself to stop it, but he couldn't stop it. They stood there and looked at him as they had looked at him many times when it had happened before. They didn't move. They stood there and waited for the thing to die down.

"Get out," he shouted. "All of you, get out of here." He threw himself on Baylock's cot, his fingernails cutting through the sheet, then the sheet underneath, his fingers tearing at both sheets as he arched his back to destroy the fabric in his hands. "Get out," he screamed, "get out and leave me alone."

They worked their way out of the room. He was on his knees, on the cot, tearing the sheets, ripping them until they were scraggly ribbons. He fell on his side, rolled off the cot, hit the table so that it went off balance and the gems splattered on the floor. He was on the floor among the emeralds, his flesh touching them without feeling them. He closed his eyes and heard voices in the hall. Dohmer's voice was loud, getting louder against the loudness of Baylock's voice. Gladden yelled something he couldn't make out, but he knew what was happening. He wanted to remain there on the floor and let it grow and let it finally happen. He picked himself up from the floor, and as he heard the shriek from Gladden, he staggered across the room toward the door.

He was in the hall, throwing himself between Dohmer and Baylock, getting in low to put his arms around Dohmer's knees, his shoulder against Dohmer's thigh, his feet bracing hard, then the push and the heave as his arms went even lower so that he took Dohmer with him to the floor.

Dohmer's eyes didn't see him. Dohmer was gazing past him, up at Baylock. There was a good deal of grief on Baylock's face. Baylock's left eye was swollen and purple and the eyebrow was cut.

Rising slowly, Harbin said, "All right, it's over."

"It isn't over." Baylock was weeping without tears.

"If you feel that way," Harbin said, "don't stand there thinking about it. Here's Dohmer right in front of you. If you want to hit him, go ahead and hit him."

Baylock had no reply. Dohmer had risen and now stood rubbing his brow as though he had a severe headache. A few times he opened his mouth, wanting to say something, but he was unable to choose words.

Gladden lit a cigarette. She gave Harbin a scolding look. "This is all your fault."

"I know it is," Harbin said. Without looking at Baylock, he murmured, "Maybe if certain people would stop needling me, it wouldn't happen."

"I don't needle you," Baylock wept. "All I do is say what I think."

"It isn't thinking," Harbin said. "It's crying the blues. You're always crying the blues." He gestured toward the bathroom. "Fix him up," he said to Gladden, and she took Baylock into the bathroom. Harbin turned and moved into the bedroom and began putting things back in order.

In the doorway, Dohmer rubbed palms across his knuckles. "I don't know what got into me."

Harbin set the table on its legs. He put the chair back in place. He gathered the scattered gems and when they were all collected and in their cloth on the table, he turned to Dohmer and said, "You make me sick."

"Baylock makes you sick."

"Baylock makes me sore. You make me sick."

"I didn't mean to do it," Dohmer said. "I swear I didn't really mean to hit him."

"That's why you make me sick. As long as you do what you mean to do, you're a utility. But when you lose your head you're worse than nothing."

"You're the one went out of control."

"When I go out of control," Harbin said, "I punch air, I don't punch a face." He pointed to the torn sheets. "I damage that. I don't damage the people I work with. Look at the size of your fists. You could have killed him."

Dohmer moved into the room and sat on the edge of the cot. He went on rubbing his knuckles. "Why do these things have to start?"

"Nerves."

"We've got to get rid of that."

"We can't," Harbin said. "Nerves are little wires inside. They stay there. When they're pulled too tight, they snap."

"That ain't good."

"Nothing you can do about it," Harbin said, "except try to

steer it when it happens. That's what I try to do. I try to steer it. Instead of aiming that hand at Baylock, you should have aimed it at the wall."

"I'm too big," Dohmer stood there very dismally. He looked with pleading at Harbin. "You've got to believe me, Nat, I got nothing against Baylock. I like Baylock. He's been good to me. He's done me more favors than I can remember. So look what I go and do. I walk in and slam my hand into his eye. This hand here," and he displayed his right hand, holding it out as though offering it to be cut off.

Harbin saw Dohmer's head go down, the immense shoulders slumped, the big head descending into cupped hands. Something midway between a moan and a sob came from Dohmer's throat. It was evident that Dohmer wished to be alone with his remorse, and Harbin walked out of the room and closed the door.

He entered the bathroom to see Baylock with head tilted far back under the light above the washbowl. Gladden pressed gently with a styptic pencil, then she held the white pencil under cold running water, then applied it again. Baylock made a thin sound of pain.

"It's awful," Baylock said. "It's like fire."

"Let me see." Harbin stepped in close to examine the eye. "Not too deep. You won't need stitches, anyway."

Baylock gazed morosely at the floor. "Why did he have to hit me?"

"He feels worse about it than you do."

"Does he have this eye?"

"He wishes he did," Harbin said. "He feels lousy about it."

"That helps the eye a lot," Baylock whined.

Harbin lit a cigarette, taking his time. Then, after a few puffs, he looked at Gladden. "Go downstairs and fix us something to eat. Later on I'll take you out for a drink."

"Should I dress up?" Gladden asked. "I'd love to dress up."

Harbin smiled at her.

She said, "I get a real kick when I'm all dressed up. What I like best is that number with the silver sequins. You like that one, Nat? That yellow dress with the sequins?"

"It's very pretty."

"I'm dying to wear it tonight," Gladden said. "I got a real itch to take that dress out and put it on and wear it. Then I'll be out with you and I'll be wearing that dress."

"Nice," Harbin nodded. "Real nice."

"It's always real nice when I'm all dressed up in a dress I'm crazy about, and I'm sure crazy about that sequin thing. I'll put it on and I'll be wearing it when we go out, and I'll have it on and I'll feel fine. I feel real good just thinking about it."

She was walking out. They heard her as she reached the head of the stairs, saying aloud to herself, "Just thinking about it." They heard her going down the stairs.

"That there," Baylock said, "is something I can't make out." He was forgetting his bad eye and looking directly and thoughtfully and probingly at Harbin, and saying, "It ain't me that gets on your nerves. It's the girl. The girl always gets on your nerves. The girl is a dumbbell and you know she's a dumbbell. I think it's time you did something about it."

"All right," Harbin waved wearily. "Cut that."

"She's dumb," Baylock said. "She's plain dumb."

"Why don't you drop it?"

"Look at it, Nat. Take a look at it. You know I got nothing personal against Gladden. She's straight and she means well but that ain't the point. The point is, she's dumb and you know it just like I know it. The difference is, I come out with it and you hold it back inside. You choke yourself up with it and that's why you broke loose tonight and went haywire. I can't take it any deeper than that, but I know it goes way deeper."

"Can't we just leave it like this?"

"Sure we can," Baylock said. "Another thing we can do is close up shop."

"You're walking a wire, Joe. I don't like what you're saying."

"I'm saying what I know to be a fact. You got things you want to do and I want to be with you when you do them. Dohmer too. But with the girl it's another play. Everything she does, she does because you tell her to. Using her own brains, she couldn't move an inch, anyway not in the direction we take. There's trouble there, and sooner or later it blows right up in your face. Don't tell me you don't see it coming."

Harbin opened his mouth wide, shut it tight, then opened it again. "You trying to give me the creeps?"

"You already got them."

Then Harbin's voice was down to almost a whisper, "You be careful."

Baylock's manner went into an abrupt change. "What the hell's wrong?" he whined. "Can't I even disagree? If you make a point and I don't see it your way, I have the right to come out with it, don't I?"

"It's always something," Harbin said. "No matter what I say, with you it's no. Everything is no."

"I can't agree when I don't agree."

"All right, Joe."

"I can't help it," Baylock said. "That's the way it is."

"All right."

"I don't want to keep harping away, but I keep worrying about that girl. She has a real wrong effect on you and it's got to the point where I always know when it's up to your neck." He moved in close to Harbin, "Let her go." He moved in closer, his voice low. "Why don't you let her go?"

Harbin turned away. He took in some stale air and swallowed it with an effort and a certain pain. "We're an organization. One thing I won't allow is a split in the organization."

"It wouldn't be a split. If you told her to go, she'd go."

"Where would she go?" Harbin's voice was loud again. "What would she run into?"

"She'd be all right," Baylock said. "And I can tell you one thing. She'd be a lot better off than she is now."

Harbin turned away again. He closed his eyes tightly for a moment, wished he was sound asleep and away from everything.

Baylock was close again. "You know the way it is with you? As though you've been in some courtroom and got yourself a life sentence to take care of her."

"God damn it," Harbin said, "leave me alone." He walked out of the bathroom. He came into the room where Dohmer was still sitting on the cot with his big head covered by big hands. Baylock came in a few moments later. The two of them stood there, watching Dohmer.

Dohmer slowly lifted his head. He looked at them, he sighed heavily and began shaking his head. "I'm so sorry, I'm so sorry, Joe."

"It's all right," Baylock let a hand rest for a moment on Dohmer's shoulder. And then his eyes moved and came to a stop on Harbin, and he added, "I wish everything was all right."

Harbin bit hard at his lip. He felt his head jerking to one side. He couldn't look at either of them.

Chapter III

IN AN after-hour club that gave out membership cards for five dollars a year, the light from pale green bulbs tossed a watery glow on Gladden's hair. The glow was on the top of her head, floating there. Her head was bent toward the tall glass with the rum and ice in it, and Harbin watched her as she sipped the drink, smiled at her as she lifted her head and looked at him. They sat at a very small table away from the center of activity, an absurdly small dance floor faced on the other side by three Negro musicians who constantly played with all their might. The place was on the second floor of a Kensington Avenue restaurant, and it kept its lights low, its customers happy, its blue-uniformed visitors paid off promptly each week. It was a pretty good place.

"They give us a nice drink," Gladden said.

"Like the music?"

"Too jumpy."

"What kind of music do you like?"

"Guy Lombardo."

"I used to play the violin," Harbin said.

"No."

"But I did," Harbin said. "I took lessons for five years. There was a conservatory in our neighborhood. They'd take in twenty kids at a time. We'd all be in a little room with the old guy up front, and he'd scream at the top of his lungs as if we were all a mile away and he was trying to make himself heard. He was a maniac, the old guy. I wonder if he's still there."

"Tell me," Gladden said. "Tell me about the neighborhood."

"I've told you a thousand times."

"Tell me again."

He picked up the short glass and swallowed some whiskey. He beckoned to a colored girl who was walking in and out through the tables with a big tray above her head. "Why?"

"I get dreamy."

The colored girl was at the table and Harbin ordered a few jiggers of whiskey for himself and another rum collins for Gladden. He leaned back in his chair, his head to one side a little as he studied the pale green glow on the top of Gladden's head. "Always," he said, "after we do a job you get dreamy like this. The haul doesn't seem to interest you."

Gladden said nothing. She smiled at something far away.

"The haul," he said, "becomes a secondary thing with you. What comes first?"

"The dreamy feeling," Gladden slumped languidly. "Like going back. Like resting back on a soft pillow that you can't see. Way back there."

"Where?"

"Where we were when we were young."

"We're young now," he said.

"Are we?" Her tall glass was lifted, her chin magnified through the rum and soda and glass. "We're half in the grave."

"You're bored," Harbin said.

"I've been bored since I was born."

"You looking for kicks?"

"Who needs kicks?" She gestured toward the dancers crowding the tiny floor. "They're all crazy." She shrugged again. "Who am I to talk? I'm crazy, too. So are you."

Harbin saw the pale green glow coming down a little and making a wide pale green ribbon across her forehead. Now her yellow hair was a zig-zag of yellow and black, her eyes under the ribbon a distinct and bright yellow, her face dark but getting lighter as the ribbon lowered, and Harbin saw the whiteness of her teeth as she smiled again. He returned the smile, not knowing why. And then, not knowing why, he said, "You want to dance?"

She pointed to the slow chaos on the dance floor. "Is that dancing?"

He looked at it and it wasn't dancing. He listened to the music and it gave him nothing. He threw a drink into his stomach and there was no tingle. He looked at Gladden and she was watching him and he knew she was studying him and he said, "Let's leave."

She didn't move. "You tired?"

"No."

"Then where will we go?"

"I don't know, but let's get out of here." He started to rise.

"Wait," she said. "Sit down, Nat."

He sat. He had no idea of what she intended to say. He waited for it with a nervousness that bothered him greatly because there really was no reason for it. Finally he said, "You're terrific when it comes to times like this."

"Nat." She leaned her elbows on the table. "Tell me. Why do you go out with me? Why do you take me places?"

"I like company."

"Why not Dohmer? Why not Baylock?"

"You're better to look at than they are."

"You go for scenery?"

"You're not bad."

"Don't be sweet to me, Nat. Don't give me compliments."

"It isn't a compliment. It's a statement." He didn't care for the direction this talk was taking. He shifted a bit in his chair. "I'll tell you what I would like. I'd like to see you enjoy yourself once in a while. Times I look at you and you look like hell." He leaned toward her, his arms flat on the table. "What I want you to do is go away for a while."

"Go where?"

"Anywhere. Baltimore. Pittsburgh. Atlantic City."

"Atlantic City," she mused. "That would be all right."

"Sure it would. You really need a rest. You'll get out on the boardwalk and sit there in the sun and breathe some salt air. Do you a world of good. Get to bed early and put some decent food in your stomach. Put some color in your face."

Her face was coming closer to him. "You want to see some color in my face?"

"You'll take in some shows," he said, "and go for rolling chair rides on the boardwalk. You can lie down on the beach and get that sun—"

"Nat," she said.

"And you can go for boat rides. They have boat rides out on the ocean and at night you can walk on the boardwalk and they have some smart shops where you can buy those dignified dresses you're always talking about."

"Nat," she said. "Nat, listen—"

"They have these smart shops on the boardwalk and you'll have yourself a fine time."

"Nat," she said. "Go with me."

"No."

"Please go with me."

"Stop being stupid, will you?"

She waited awhile, and then she said, "All right, Nat, I'll stop being stupid. I'll do what you want me to do. What you expect of me. I'll turn it off, just like that," and she imitated the turning off of a faucet. "I'm good at that. I've practiced and practiced and now I know how." Once more she turned the invisible faucet.

"Tomorrow," he said, "you'll grab a train."

"Fine."

"Atlantic City."

"Marvelous."

He put a cigarette in his mouth and began to chew on it. He took it out and bent it and broke it and let it fall in the tray. "Look, Gladden," he started, and didn't know how to continue. The line of his thinking refused to stay on one path, and split up like a wire coming apart and branched off wildly in countless directions. He saw the colored girl passing the table and he touched her arm and said he wanted the check.

Chapter IV

THERE WAS no phone at the Spot, and the next afternoon, at three, while they waited at the station for the Atlantic City train, they decided that she should make calls to a certain drugstore booth at stipulated intervals. Then the train arrived, and he stood back as she entered the train. Suddenly she put down her bags and faced him and said his name.

He grinned. "Don't fill up on salt water taffy."

"We haven't said goodbye."

"When you go to China we'll say goodbye."

She gave him a look he couldn't classify. Then other passengers were crowding him in, and there was no more time. He turned, walked down along the platform. Descending the steps leading to the waiting room, he heard the train going away. It occurred to him that this was the first time he had seen Gladden going away, and for some odd reason it was disturbing. He told himself Atlantic City was only sixty miles away. It was the place where Philadelphians went to get the sun and the salt air. It wasn't China. It was practically right next door, and he would be in constant touch with Gladden. There was no cause for him to be disturbed.

He stood outside the terminal and wondered where he should go. It was always a problem, where to go and what to do. Sometimes he came close to envying the people whose lives were based on compulsory directives, who lived by definite need and command, so that every morning they had to get up at six or seven, and be at a specific place by eight-thirty or nine, and stay there and do specific things until five or six. They never wondered what to do next. They knew what they had to do. He had nothing to do and no place to go. He had plenty of money to spend, around seven thousand dollars remaining from his share of the two previous hauls, but he couldn't think of a way to start spending it. There was nothing special that he wanted. He tried to think of something that he wanted, but a wall came up in his mind and blocked off everything tangible.

So he went back to the Spot because there was no other

place to go. The Spot was reassurance. The Spot was security. In its own strange way, the Spot was home.

Entering, he heard Baylock's voice from the kitchen. He walked into the kitchen. Baylock and Dohmer were at the table, playing their original variation of two-handed poker. Dohmer showed a hole card, an ace that matched another and gave him the hand. Dohmer collected a dollar and seventy cents, and then they put aside the cards and looked at Harbin.

Baylock said, "She go?"

"Took the three-forty." Harbin looked out the window.

They were quiet for a few moments. Dohmer let out a big yawn. Then he pointed to the window and said, "Look at that sun. Look at that sun out there."

"Let's go romp in the park," Baylock said. He scowled at the cards. He picked them up and shuffled them, riffled them, stacked them and shuffled them again and put them down.

Harbin stood at the kitchen window and looked at the sunlit sky above the alley and the grey dwellings. He was thinking of Atlantic City, picturing the boardwalk and the beach and the beach-front hotels.

Dohmer said, "I think I'll have something to eat."

"You ate an hour ago," Baylock said.

"So now I'll eat again."

Dohmer and Baylock went on arguing, and Harbin stood at the window, gazing out at nothing. He thought about Gladden and her father, and about himself. He thought of when he was a little boy in a little town in Iowa, an only child, his father a merchant of dry goods, his mother a timid, soft-voiced, sweet-souled woman who tried hard to like everybody. When her husband died she took over the business and did what she could with it and finally lost it. There came a day when she had to borrow money, a day when she had to borrow more, a day when the son heard her weeping in a dark room, and a day when a chest cold became pneumonia and she didn't have the strength to fight it. She lasted only a few days. He was in high school at the time. He didn't know what to do. The world was an avalanche, taking him down, and he found himself on a road going away from the little town. He was sixteen years old and during that year he wandered and groped and resented and feared. It was the year when a good many people were hungry, and it was known generally to be very bad times. He almost starved to death that year. He would have starved to death if it hadn't been for a man named Gerald Gladden.

The thing took place in Nebraska and Gerald Gladden was driving south from Omaha, accompanied by his six-year-old daughter. Gerald was approaching middle age and he was a paroled convict who now felt sure he had learned enough to continue the science of burglary without getting caught. It was late in the day when he saw the boy with lifted thumb begging for a ride. His car whizzed past the boy and then in the rear-view mirror he saw the boy sagging to the ground. He put the car in reverse and picked up the boy.

That was the way it started. The way it exploded was raw and unexpected. Harbin had just passed his nineteenth birthday and he and Gerald were on a second-story job in the suburbs of Detroit. A shrewdly concealed burglar alarm went off and some ten minutes later police bullets hit Gerald in the spine and then a slug smashed through his brain and that was the end of him. Harbin had better luck. Harbin worked his way back to the rooming house where the little girl was asleep and for the first time in his three-year association with Gerald he took a good look at Gerald's daughter. This was a tiny, sad little girl whose mother had died while giving birth to her. This was Gerald Gladden's daughter. It occurred to Harbin he had an obligation. When he edged his way out of Detroit a few weeks later, he took the little girl with him. A month after, in Cleveland, he had a birth certificate and some other papers drawn up by an individual who specialized in this sort of thing, and the little girl was officially designated as his kid sister. He couldn't think of a good first name for her, so he decided on Gladden. The last name was unimportant. It was the name he was using then, and unimportant because he was changing his name every time he entered a new town. He enrolled Gladden in an inexpensive private school and went out and found a job selling kitchen utensils on a door-to-door basis. For five years he stayed away from burglary. He sold the kitchenware, door-to-door, and averaged about thirty-five dollars a week, and it was just about enough for Gladden and himself. Then one day he met Baylock, and Baylock introduced him to Dohmer, and a few nights later they were out on a job.

The amazing thing was the war. They had ways and means to get out of all sorts of situations, but they couldn't evade the war. It was fast and blunt, the way the Army snapped them up. Only Baylock could sidestep the Army, because Baylock had a record and also a bad set of kidneys. Baylock offered to take care of Gladden while Harbin was away. Baylock had a sister in Kansas City, and Gladden went to live with the sister and Harbin went away to war.

Then five years passed and the war was ended and Harbin came back. Dohmer was already back and doing jobs with Baylock. That was something Harbin expected. What he hadn't expected was to see Gladden being used on the jobs. They were using Gladden for jobs that required inside work. Gladden was now nineteen, and she was still tiny and still sad and she seemed unhappy with what she was doing, and Harbin had no idea of what to say. He had a feeling she was waiting for him to say something, and after awhile he knew what it was she wanted. She wanted him to say this was no good, they must get out of it now, he would go back to selling kitchenware door-to-door, and she would get herself a job washing dishes or something. But he couldn't say it.

They made rather large hauls but they couldn't accumulate much money. They began having trouble with the fences. Baylock couldn't get along with the fences. Then Baylock got into the habit of involving other individuals in the projects and this developed until there were a great many people who for various reasons had to be paid off. Finally Baylock managed to complicate things to the point where they were in actual jeopardy, not from the law, but from these other people, and it was Harbin who took over then and smoothed things out. That made Harbin the leader. Baylock began screaming his head off, and he made so much noise that Harbin finally told him he could have the leadership back again. But Dohmer and Gladden refused to accept this, and Baylock eventually admitted that Harbin was best fitted to run the projects. But now Baylock was beginning to complain about Gladden. And another thing, Baylock said, Harbin's operations were too slow.

Harbin was really very slow. It took him weeks to plan a job and then more weeks before the job was activated. Then it took months before the fence was contacted. Then it took more months until the deal with the fence was consummated. But this was the way Gerald had taught him to operate, and most of what he knew he had learned from Gerald. With Gerald it was a science and a business and Gerald had learned it from a wizard who had finally gone to Central America with close to a million dollars in ice-cold money and had died there an old man. Gerald had always dreamed of accomplishing the same feat, had always claimed it could be done and it would be done provided one could learn the science of taking one's time and knowing all the grooves and potentials before making a move. With Gerald that was the big thing, the patience, the waiting, and yet even Gerald had succumbed to the poison of impulsiveness. That night in Detroit the death of Gerald could have been avoided if Gerald had only waited another fifteen or twenty minutes, if he had taken the time to look for additional wires that meant auxiliary burglar alarms. Gerald had thirty-odd dollars in his pocket when he died, but as he hit the ground with his bullet-slashed skull he was pointing his body toward Central America, his hands reached out, clutching for the million dollars in ice-cold money.

Chapter V

ALL THE rest of the day Harbin stayed at the Spot. It suddenly became evident that with Gladden absent there was no housekeeper, and Harbin put himself to work straightening things out, dusting around in a more or less spiritless way. Dohmer sprawled in a dingy sofa and supervised Harbin's work between gulps of beer. Baylock stood in a doorway and suggested Harbin should put on an apron. Harbin suggested it might be a damn good idea if they shook their legs and helped out. For a couple of hours the three of them swept and dusted. Gradually the momentum of the work became an attraction in itself, they began to scour and scrub, and the Spot was considerably cleaner except for the places where Dohmer worked. Dohmer succeeded in upsetting a bucket of soapy water. Harbin told him to clean up the mess and he opened a window and said the sun would dry it out. He then flopped on the sofa and claimed he was completely exhausted.

Toward seven o'clock, Harbin left for the phone booth to receive the scheduled call from Gladden. The drugstore was on Allegheny Avenue, going away north from Kensington. They had chosen the second booth from the left in a row of four. He entered the booth at two minutes to seven, sat there smoking a cigarette and deliberately calling a wrong number. At seven o'clock the phone rang in the booth.

Gladden's voice from Atlantic City was low and he told her to talk louder. She said her hotel room was very nice, looking out on the ocean, and she was going to buy herself a good dinner and then take in a movie and get to bed early.

Then she said, "What are you doing?"

"Nothing in particular. I'm sort of tired." He wasn't the least bit tired. He couldn't understand why he had said it.

She said, "Tired from what?"

"We cleaned up the Spot today. Now it's almost fit to live in."

She said, "Tell Dohmer not to start with cooking. Once he begins in that kitchen we'll have a regiment of cockroaches. You know what I'm seeing tonight? A Betty Grable picture."

"She's good."

"It's with Dick Haymes."

"Yeah?"

"It's all in color. With a lot of music."

"Well," he said, "enjoy the picture."

"Nat?"

He waited.

She said, "Nat, I want to ask you something. Look, Nat. I want to ask you this. I want to know if it's all right if I go out."

"What do you mean, if you go out? Sure you can go out. Aren't you going out tonight?"

"Tonight I'm going out alone. And tomorrow night I guess I'll be going out alone. But maybe one of these nights I'll go out with somebody."

"So?"

"So is it all right?"

"Fine," he said. "If you're asked out, you'll go out. What's wrong with that?"

"I just wanted to make sure."

"Don't be sappy. You don't have to ask me these things. Just use your own judgment. Now look," he added quickly, "you won't have enough change to pay this phone bill. Hang up and call me same time tomorrow night."

He put the receiver on the hook. Walking from the drug-store he picked up an *Evening Bulletin* and his eyes were on the headline as he dropped a nickel in the slotted cigar box. The headline said it was a hundred-thousand-dollar burglary and there was a picture of the mansion. He tucked the paper under his arm. A few minutes later, in a small restaurant, he began reading the story while telling a waitress to bring him a steak and some french fries and a cup of coffee. The story said it was one of the slickest jobs ever pulled on the Main Line and there were absolutely no clues. They didn't mention the two policemen and the parked car near the mansion, and this of course was understandable because mentioning it would make the police look like idiots.

He finished the paper and worked on his steak, and watched the other customers. His eyes worked their way toward two middle-aged pudding-eaters, and across the room to a lonely young man, then toward the woman who sat at a nearby table, then toward three girls who were sitting together, then quickly back to the woman, because the woman was looking at him.

He couldn't be sure whether she was smiling. Her lips were relaxed and so were her eyes. He sensed there was something intentional in the way she sat there, looking at him. It wasn't bold, it wasn't what he would call cheap. But it was a direct look, coming right at him. For a moment he figured perhaps the woman was deep in her own thought and had no idea of what she was looking at. He turned his head away, tried that for a few seconds, then brought his eyes back to hers. She was still looking at him. He noticed now she was something out of the ordinary.

It began with the color of her hair. Her hair was a pale tan, not blonde, and he would swear it wasn't dyed. It was glistening tan hair. She wore it tight and flat on her head, parted far on one side, then brushed back to her neck where he saw the edge of a little brown ribbon. The eyes were the same color as the hair, the special tan, and the skin was perhaps a shade lighter. He told himself either she was an expert with a sunlamp or her beautician was a wizard. The nose was thin yet not stingy, taking up just about the right amount of room on her face, a graceful oval of a face unlike any face he had ever seen. He could see her body was slender, and there was something sleek about it even though her attire made no effort at sleekness. The longer he looked at her, the more certain he was that he ought to stop looking at her.

He knew if he kept on looking at her he would start getting fascinated, and it was almost a religion with him, his refusal to allow himself to be fascinated by any of them. He pulled his eyes away from her and just to do something he began toying with the strap of his wristwatch.

Across the room, someone put a nickel in the music machine and a weak, whispery baritone begged the world to show pity because a girl in an organdie dress had gone away and would never come back. Harbin finished the steak and lit a cigarette while he creamed his coffee. He found himself becoming quite restless. He decided to go downtown and shoot some pool at one of the large, respectable places. Then he changed his mind, sensing there might be something better to do. Maybe he ought to visit the public library. For several weeks now he hadn't been to the library. He liked it in the library, the big one on the Parkway, where it was an endless flow of quiet and calm and he could sit there reading the thick volumes dealing with precious stones. It was a very interesting subject. Many times he had imitated the people he saw there in the library with their notebooks, doing research. He had brought a small notebook to the library and made notes from the books on precious stones. Tonight, he told himself, would be a good night to go to the library. He started to get up from the table, keeping his eyes on the door but knowing he would turn his head just for one more look. He turned his head. He looked at her and her eyes were on him.

She was only a few feet away, but her voice seemed to be coming from a distant area. "Enjoy your meal?"

He nodded very slowly.

"I don't think so. You didn't seem to be enjoying it."

Without moving from where he stood, he said, "You do this all the time? Visit restaurants to see if people enjoy their food?"

The woman said, "Maybe I've been rude."

"You're not rude," Harbin said. "You're just interested." He moved toward her. "What makes you interested?"

"You're a type."

"Special?"

"Special for me."

"That's too bad." Harbin smiled. He smiled as kindly as he could.

He had a feeling she had been married at least twice, and he was ready to bet she had a man now and at least three more on the string. He asked himself, what did he need this for? He had always avoided this and why was he allowing it to grab at him now? The answer came, rapid and keen. Never before had he seen anything that even approached this.

"If you're looking for company," he said, "you can come along with me."

"Where?"

"All right," he said. "Forget it."

He turned his back on her, moved to the cashier's stand. He paid his check, left the restaurant and stood on the corner waiting for a cab. The night air had a thick softness and the smell of stale smoke from factories that had been busy in the day, and the smell of cheap whiskey and dead cigarettes and Philadelphia springtime. Then something else came into it and he breathed it in, and he knew the color of this perfume was tan.

She stood behind him. "Usually I don't gamble like this."

He faced her. "Where would you like to go?"

"Maybe someplace for a drink."

"I don't feel like a drink."

"Tell me," she said. "Are you hard to get along with?"

"No."

"You think we can get along?"

"No." A cab rolled through the middle of the street, and he beckoned to it. Entering the cab, Harbin told himself he had handled it the way it should have been handled, and any other way would have been a mistake, and as it was, he had made enough of a mistake in even beginning to talk with her. He started to close the door, but she was already climbing into the cab, and he found himself sliding across the seat to make room for her.

The driver leaned back. "Where we going?"

"The Free Library," Harbin said. "On the Parkway." He studied her and for a few moments she gazed frontward, then slowly turned her head and looked at him. She smiled and her mouth opened just a little. He could see her teeth.

She said, "My name is Della."

"Nathaniel."

"Nat," she said. "That's an all right name for you. It's soft but it has a snap to it. A soft snap. It's a patent leather name." She pulled in some smoke and let it out. "What do you do for a living?"

"Do you really want to know, or are you just trying to make talk?"

"I really want to know. When I'm interested in a man, I want to know all about him."

He nodded a bit dubiously, "That's either a good policy or a very bad one. You let yourself in for a flock of disappointments. Suppose I told you I was a shoe salesman and I made forty a week?"

"You'd be lying."

"Certainly," he said. "I'm much too smart to sell shoes for a living. I have that snap quality, that soft snap. Tell me all about it. Tell me the story of my life so far and what I should do with the rest of it." He frowned at her with nothing in the frown but honest curiosity. "What is it you want? What are you out for?"

"Basically?" She was no longer smiling. She held the cigarette close to her mouth but she had forgotten it. Her eyes were slightly wide, as though she was surprised at the reply she was about to give. "Basically," she said, "I'm out to find myself a lover."

The impact of it was like the initial touch of an oncoming steamroller. He told himself to get back on balance. The presence of women in his life had never represented much of a problem, although the potential was always there, and he could always see the potential. He had always found it not at all difficult to sidestep and maneuver himself away from annoying involvement. The thing was purely a matter of timing. To know just when to walk out. And he knew as sure as he was sitting here, this was the time to walk out. Right now. To tell the driver to stop the cab. To open the door and slide out, and walk away, and keep walking.

She held him there. He didn't know how she was doing it, but she held him there as though she had him tied hand and foot. She had him trapped there in the cab, and he looked at her with hate.

"Why?" she said. "Why the look?"

He couldn't answer.

She said, "You frightened?" Without moving, she seemed to lean toward him. "Do I frighten you, Nat?"

"You antagonize me."

"Listen, Nat—"

"Shut up," he said. "Let me think about this."

She nodded slowly, exaggerating the nod. He saw her profile, the quiet line of her brow and nose and chin, the semi-delicate line of her jaw, the cigarette an inch or two away from her lips, and the smoke of the cigarette. Then he took his eyes and pulled them away from Della, and then without looking at Della, he was seeing her. The ride to the library took up a little more than twenty minutes, and they weren't saying a word to each other, yet it was as though they talked to each other constantly through the ride. The cab pulled up in front of the library and neither of them moved. The driver said they were at the library, and neither of them moved. The driver shrugged and let the motor idle and sat there, waiting.

After a while, the driver said, "Well, what's it gonna be?"

"The way it's got to be," she said. As she floated her body toward Harbin, she gave the driver an address.

Chapter VI

IT WAS up in the north of the city, in a section known as Germantown. To get there, the cab had to follow the Schuylkill River, following the night sheen of the river up along the smooth river-drive and curving away and following Wissahickon Creek and then past the rows of little houses of working people who lived on the outskirts of Germantown. The cab went deep into Germantown and finally pulled up in front of a small house in the middle of a badly lighted block.

The inside of the house was a combination of creamy green and dark grey, the green predominating, the furniture green, the wallpaper the same green, the rugs dark grey. It was an old house that had been done over. Above the fireplace, within a wide tan frame, there was a line drawing of Della's face, and it was done in tan tempera on very pale tan boardpaper. The artist's name was on the Spanish side.

Harbin said, "You have a lot of money, don't you?"

"A fair amount."

He turned away from the line drawing. "Where'd you get it?"

"My husband died a year ago. Left me an income. Fifteen thousand a year."

She had seated herself in a deep sofa that looked like it was fashioned from pistachio ice cream and would melt away any minute. He started toward the sofa, then moved to one side, kept moving in that direction, stopped when he reached a wall. "How do you spend your time?"

"Miserably," she said. "I sleep too much. I'm sick and tired of sleeping all the time. One of these days I'll open a shop or something. Come over here."

"Later."

"Now."

"Later." He remained there facing the wall. "Got many friends?"

"None. No real friends. Just a few people I know. I go out with them and the evening starts to drag and it gets to a point where I feel like lighting firecrackers. I can't stand people who aren't exciting."

"You find me exciting?"

"Come over here and we'll find out."

He gave her a little smile and then he looked at the rug. "Aside from that," he said, "what do you figure we can offer each other?"

"Each other."

"Entirely?"

"Everything," she said. "I wouldn't have it any other way. This you've got to know about me. The first time I was married I was fifteen. The boy was a couple years older and we lived on neighboring farms in South Dakota. We were married a few months and then he got run over by a tractor. I went out to look for another man. It wasn't the idea of marriage, exactly, it was just that I needed a man. So I found me a man. And then another. And another. One after another. And each had something to offer, but it wasn't what I wanted. I've always known what I wanted. Six years ago when I was twenty-two, I got married for the second time. That was in Dallas and I was selling cigarettes in a night club. The man was married and he was down there with his wife for their first real vacation in ten years. He was forty and worth a fortune. Copper mines in Colorado. He started running around with me and finally his wife went back to Colorado and got a divorce. The man married me. After four years of it he began getting on my nerves. He started with the jealousy. That's all right, the jealousy, when it's carried out with finesse. You know, the soft snap. It's attractive that way. But with him it was all red hot temper. He threatened to tear my head off. One night he hit me in the face. With his fist. That was just a little more than a year ago. I told him to pack up and go to the other side of the world. He went out and a few days later he threw himself off a fishing boat. I started looking for another man. All my life I've been looking for a certain man. You think I should keep on looking?"

He didn't say anything.

"I want it now. I want an answer."

"It takes time."

"Don't bore me," she said. "Don't stand there thinking it over." A certain rigidity came into her voice. She behaved as though they were in the midst of a crisis. "I've waited for to-night. I've waited a long time. I sat there tonight and watched you at that table. I watched you eating your dinner. And I knew. Not the trace of a doubt."

He glanced at his wristwatch. "We've known each other exactly two hours and sixteen minutes."

She was up and away from the sofa and coming toward him. "You letting that wristwatch make your decisions? I've never been guided by time. I won't let myself be guided by it. Jesus Christ in Heaven, I know, I know, I'm standing here and telling you I know. And you know, too. And if you deny that, if you doubt it, if you can't make up your mind right now, I swear I'll throw you out of here—"

Closing in on her, he smothered her mouth.

The liquid of her lips poured into his veins. There was a bursting in his brain as everything went out of his brain and Della came in, filling his brain so that his brain was crammed with Della. For a single vicious moment he tried to break away from her and come back to himself, and in that moment they were helping him, Dohmer and Baylock. They were helping him as he tried to pull away. But Gladden wasn't helping. Gladden was nowhere around. Gladden ought to be here, helping. Gladden was letting him down. If Gladden hadn't gone away, this wouldn't be happening. It was all Gladden's fault. He took it that far and he couldn't take it any farther, because from there on it was all Della. It was very distant from the earth and there was nothing but Della.

A little past six in the morning he stood under a shower and let the water run as cold as it cared to. He heard her voice beyond the bathroom door, asking him what he wanted for breakfast. He told her to go back to sleep, he would get something outside. She said he would eat breakfast here. When he came downstairs, the orange juice was already fixed and she was busy in the kitchen with eggs and bacon.

They sipped orange juice. She said, "Soon we'll do this in the country."

"You like the country?"

"Far out," she said. "I already have a place. Midway between here and Harrisburg. It's a farm, but we won't farm. We'll just live there. It's a marvelous place. My car's being fixed but maybe it'll be ready by noon. We'll drive out today and I'll show it to you."

"I can't."

"Why not?"

"I have a couple of people to see."

"You mean you have to work?"

"In a way."

"How long will you be away?"

"I don't know. Talk to me. Tell me more about this place in the country."

"It's about thirty miles the other side of Lancaster. The famous rolling hills of Pennsylvania. This is a very high hill. We're not at the top, but on the side of the hill where it has a gradual slant, then levels off for awhile before it goes down again. What you see from here is all the other hills going out, the greenest hills you ever saw in your life. Then away, far away, but somehow so close that it seems right next door, we have mountains. Lavender mountains. You see the river but before that you see the brook. It runs coming up toward you in a lot of soft easy jumps, curving up to the pond that's where you can reach in and get your hand wet if you lean out the bedroom window. It's deep enough, this pond, so in the morning if you feel in the mood, you can roll yourself out the window and go into the water."

"What do we do there?"

"We just stay there. Up there together in that place on that hill. Not a soul anywhere near. We'll be together there."

He nodded. Inside himself he repeated the nod.

They finished breakfast, had an extra coffee and a few cigarettes and then she walked him to the door. He put his hands on her face.

"You stay here," he said. "Wait for my call. I'll come back a little past noon and we'll drive out to see our estate."

Her eyes were closed. "I know this is permanent. I know it—"

As he left the house, it seemed to him that he had no weight at all.

The cab let him out at Kensington and Allegheny and he decided to walk the seven blocks back to the Spot. He didn't feel like returning to the Spot. He had no desire to see the Spot, wishing there was some other place he could go. What he really wanted to do was hail another cab and drive back to Della.

He moved toward the Spot with a drag in his legs, a frown that became deeper as he came closer to the emeralds and Dohmer and Baylock.

He walked into the Spot to hear Dohmer cursing the kitchen. "Mice," Dohmer was shouting. "These damn mice." Then Dohmer appeared from the kitchen and stared at him. "Where you been all night?"

"With a woman. Baylock sleeping?"

"Dead," Dohmer said. "We played cards until four-thirty. I took him for near a hundred. We got a flock of mice in the kitchen."

"Go upstairs and wake him up."

"What's wrong?"

"Do I look wrong?"

"You bet your life you do," Dohmer said. "You look from the clouds. Someone stick a needle in you?"

Harbin didn't answer. He watched Dohmer climbing the stairs, and put a cigarette in his mouth and began to chew on it, then pulled it from between his teeth and shredded the tobacco onto the floor. From upstairs, Baylock protested whiningly that all he wanted from life was to be let alone, to be allowed to sleep and die.

They came down and Baylock took one look at him and said, quickly, anxiously, with a bit of a hiss, "What happened? I bet something happened."

"Stop it," Harbin started to light the cigarette but it was a mess. He took another one. "I'm out."

Dohmer looked at Baylock and Baylock gazed at a wall. Baylock's head turned like the head of a puppet. His eyes came back to Harbin and he said, "I knew right away." His head went on turning, aiming toward Dohmer. "I knew something happened."

"Nothing except that I'm walking out," Harbin said. "Listen to it and take it or don't take it. But I found myself a woman last night. I'm going away with her. Today."

"He's away," Dohmer gasped. "He's all away."

Harbin nodded slowly. "That's the only way, the only way to put it."

Baylock scratched the side of his face. He looked at Harbin, looked away. "I don't see how you can do it."

"Easy," Harbin said. "With the legs. Right foot, left foot and you're walking out."

"No," Baylock shook his head quickly. "No, you can't do it."

"You can't do it," Dohmer told Harbin. "For God's sake."

"The woman," Baylock asked. "Who's this woman?"

"Just a woman," Harbin said. "That's all you get."

"You hear this?" Baylock posed Dohmer. "You hear it? He says that's all we get. No rundown, no listing, no nothing. Just a woman, and he's going away. Like that," and Baylock snapped his fingers. And then turned to Harbin, "How well do you think you know me? How well do you think you know him?" and he pointed toward Dohmer. "You really believe we'll stand here and watch you walk out?" Then he started to laugh, sliced it hard, peered at Harbin as though his eyes looked through slits in a wall. "You're so wrong, Nat. You're so wrong it's almost comical. We can't let you walk out."

Harbin felt the floor under his feet. It began to sag just a little. He waited for it to get firm again. He said, "Keep the thing technical."

Baylock held his arms wide. "It's a hundred per cent technical. If you walk out, there's a crack in the dam. The dam gets wider. The water starts coming in. Your own words, Nat. We're an organization. We're hot as a furnace in seven big cities and you know how many small towns. If they get Dohmer, it's ten to twenty. Same with Gladden. If I get caught, goodbye everybody. Makes me a three-time loser and that's twenty to forty at a minimum. Listen, Nat," and Baylock crouched, his eyes almost closed. "When I die, I want to die in the sunshine."

Harbin waited a moment. Then he shook his head slowly. "You haven't made your point."

"My point is," Baylock's voice held a slight tremor, "the minute you walk out of here, you're on the debit side."

"You think," Harbin said, "I'd play it filthy? You think I'd ever open my mouth?"

"I don't think so," Dohmer spoke huskily. "I'd bet a million to one against it. But all the same it remains a bet." He resumed shaking his head. "I don't want to make this kind of a bet."

"Another thing," Baylock said. "What about your split of the haul?"

"I'll want that." Harbin was taking his mind ahead of them.

He felt no interest in his split of the haul but now the thing was becoming stud poker and he saw the need for maneuvering himself out of the wedge they had created around him.

Baylock moved in. "He wants his split of the haul. That's real nice."

"What's not nice about it?" Harbin made his voice a little louder. "When you say my split, you mean my split. Don't I get it?"

"No," Baylock was testing him, weighing him. It wasn't good testing. It wasn't sufficiently hidden. Baylock's face showed the testing and gave Harbin the formula for the next move.

Harbin walked across the room and sat down on a chair that looked sick. He gazed thoughtfully at the floor. "You're a dog, Joe. You know that? You realize what a dog you are?"

"Look at me," Baylock shouted. "You see me trying to walk out?" Baylock worked his way toward Harbin, seeming to be pulled along on tracks. "I'm willing to talk it over but you won't talk." Baylock waited for talk and Harbin offered nothing, and eventually Baylock said, "All we want is the reason. Something we can believe." Then Baylock was away from the poker table. "Give it to us, will you? If you give it to us, maybe we'll understand. We can't believe this thing with the woman, we want to know what it really is."

Harbin had it now, seeing the closed card Baylock had displayed, and knowing fully that he sat alone at the table with all the winnings, because actually they weren't in a class with him, they couldn't begin to compete with him when it came to manipulating a situation. It was definite. Yet, underneath his expressionless face he was angry with them. They were forcing him into an area of deceit, actually urging him to lie. And he hated to lie. Even in the line of business with outsiders he felt unsanitary when he was lying. And now they had so arranged it that he had to give them a lie.

He said, "If you really want it, I'll give it to you. I'd hoped you wouldn't make me say it, but the way it is, I guess I'll just have to tell you." He figured it was time for a sigh, and then, while they stared and didn't breathe, "There's big jobs I want to do, and you just don't fit in. You don't have what I need. You don't have it, that's all."

The quiet that came then was a quiet with their shock in it, their dismay, their agony. Dohmer had a hand to the side of his face, and he was shaking his head and making odd little noises deep in his throat. Baylock began walking aimlessly around the room, trying to say something and unable to pull a sound from his mouth.

"I didn't want to say it," Harbin said. "You made me say it."

Baylock leaned against a wall and gazed at empty air. "We don't have what you need? We ain't first-rate?"

"That's the thing. It's the nerves, mostly. I saw it coming and I didn't want to believe it. You've been getting shaky, the two of you. And Gladden doesn't have the health. I saw it the other night. I was bothered by it. Bothered too much."

Baylock turned to Dohmer, "He means we ain't in his league."

"I want to hit very big jobs," Harbin told them. "Triple the risk. Jobs where every move is high-class dancing, where even your toenails have to be in place. I need the best people I can get."

"You got them already?" Baylock asked.

Harbin shook his head. "I'm going out to look for them."

The quiet came again, and finally Dohmer stood up and sounded an immense sigh with a grunt in it. "If it's got to be this way, it's got to be this way."

"One thing." Harbin was moving toward the door. "Be good to Gladden. Be real good to her."

Now he had his back to them. The door came closer. He heard Dohmer's heavy breathing. He thought he heard Dohmer gasping, "Nat, for God's sake—" and a final pleading whimper from Baylock, and then another voice, and a shudder went through him as he sensed it was Gladden's voice. All their voices were with him as he opened the door, then floated away behind him as he walked out.

Chapter VII

DELLA'S CAR was a pale green Pontiac, a new convertible, and they had the top down as they ran past Lancaster, going west on Route 30, holding it at fifty miles an hour with the sun over their heads and honeysuckle coming into their faces. The road dipped evenly, the hills rising smoothly, softly on both sides of the road. Then the road followed the lines of the hills and they were climbing.

"I notice," Della said, "you didn't bring your things." She indicated his attire. "Those all the clothes you have?"

"They're all I need."

"I don't like the suit."

"You'll get me another one."

"I'll get you everything." She smiled. "What do you want?"

"Nothing."

The Pontiac curved and climbed and reached the top of a hill from where they looked out ahead, saw more hills, higher than this one, green hills a quiet glimmer under the heavy sun. A snake made of silver curled its way around one of the hills and as it came closer he knew it was the hill she had talked of, and the house was on that hill. He could see it now, a house of white stone and a yellow gabled roof, set on the slight plateau that interrupted the rise of the hill, and the silver snake was the brook, and now the pond, another thing of silver, and the river down and away to the north, and the lavender mountains.

She drove the car down, went up and down a few more hills, turned it onto a narrow unpaved road and again the car began to climb. They were going up the hill. Alongside, maybe fifty yards away, the brook going down from the pond to the river seemed to be climbing with them. He had a feeling they were going away from all the people of the world. There was another road, narrower than this one, and tall grass and trees came up and crowded them for awhile, and then the house was there. She parked the car beside the house, and they got out of the car and stood there looking at the house.

"I bought it four months ago," she told him. "I've been coming up here week-ends, staying here alone, wanting someone to be here with me. In this place. Here, completely here, and never to go away."

They entered the house. She had done it in mostly tan, the color of her hair, with yellow here and there, and a tan broad-loom rug that stopped only when it reached the yellow kitchen. From the kitchen they could see the barn, the same oyster-white as the house. Then the rest of the small plateau that was a green table-top beyond the barn.

She seated herself at the piano and played something from Schumann. He stood near the piano. For awhile he heard the music, but gradually it became nothing. He felt the frown cutting into his brow. Then he heard the abrupt quiet that meant her fingers were off the keys.

"Now," she said. "Now start telling me."

He put a cigarette in his mouth, took a bite at it, took it out of his mouth and placed it carefully in a large glass ashtray. "I'm a crook."

After awhile she said, "What kind?"

"Burglar."

"Work alone?"

"I had three people with me."

"What about them?"

"This morning I said goodbye."

"They argue?"

"A little. I had to make it fancy. I said I had big plans and they didn't rate high enough to be included."

She crossed the room and settled herself in a tan chair. "What's your specialty?"

"We went in for stones. Now they got themselves a haul in emeralds and they'll have to wait a long time before making it into money. But all that's away from where I am now. It's strictly yesterday."

"But it still bothers you."

"One part of it."

"I want to know about that. We've got to clear up anything that bothers you. We're starting now, and I don't want a single thing to bother you."

"One of us," he said, "was a girl." Then he told her about Gladden, and Gladden's father, and all the years of it. "She always wanted to get out, but drilled it into herself she would never get out unless I did. Now I'm out. And where is she?"

"That's a question."

"Help me with this," he was walking up and down. "Driving out here, I kept thinking about her. I felt rotten about it and I still feel rotten. I wish I knew what to do."

Della smiled dimly. "You have a feeling for this girl—"

"It isn't that. She depends on me. I've been her father. I've been her older brother. There were times I went away but she knew I'd come back. Now she's in Atlantic City, and tonight at seven she'll call a phone number and there won't be any answer. That eats away at me. I don't think she'll be able to take it. I think she'll go to pieces. It's getting worse inside me and I feel real bad about it, I wish I knew what to do."

She put the palms of her hands together, took them away, put them together again. "We'll have something to eat and then we'll start driving back to Philadelphia. You'll take that call at seven. Then I'll come back here. And I'll come alone."

"No."

"Mean it when you say it. Say it again."

"No." He made the decision out loud. "The hell with her, let her call, let the phone ring a thousand times. I'm clear of all that, I'm away from it. I'm here with you, and that's all."

Yet deep in the night he came halfway out of sleep and on the black of the ceiling he saw Gladden. He saw her walking alone on the boardwalk in Atlantic City, the black of the beach and ocean and sky all a black curtain, her yellow hair a vague yellow, her skinny body vague and seeming to float.

Blindly, to get away from Gladden, he reached for Della. His body twisted, almost lunging as his arms swept across the wide bed. But there was nothing under the blanket. Della wasn't there.

He sat up in the bed. She wasn't there. He was coming awake very quickly now, and his brain went into gear and told him to be quiet and accurate.

Enough moonlight came into the room to let him know where he was going. Invisible ropes pulled him across the room to the door. A new and unreasonable feeling came into his spine and his stomach and his brain. He had no idea what it was, only that it pumped away at him and caused him to stand motionless for a moment, facing the dark door, visualizing the hall beyond in terms of something bleak and grim.

He decided to use a method he had used many times in the past when there was an abundance of jeopardy. The method was simple. It was a matter of swerving his mind from night to day, forcing himself to see sunlight rather than darkness. He imagined it was broad daylight, and he was going out in the hall to call Della.

Opening the door, he stepped out in the hall. The bathroom door was wide open and the bathroom was dark. She wasn't upstairs. He wondered what she was doing downstairs. He knew now what the pumping was, this thing he was feeling for the first time in his life. It was the beginning of regret.

He returned to the bedroom, and groped for his clothes. He didn't realize the pumping was beginning to fade. It didn't occur to him he was riding away from himself, that the thing was becoming a project and now his moves were all arithmetic as they were when he was on a job. The moves were slow, precise, each move, even the tying of his shoelaces, a separate step in a series of steps carefully arranged.

He was in the hall again, moving down the hall toward the stairway. Downstairs it was dark. Midway down the stairs he waited, listened for a sound, any sound at all. There was no sound. There was no light down there. Instead of thinking now, he was calculating. The sum of it came easily. She was not in the house. He headed for the kitchen.

In the kitchen, his hand worked the doorknob as though it were an instrument that had to be worked with pure silence or not at all. There was no sound as he opened the door, and no sound as he stepped outside. The smell of the night was a smell of field and hill and tree, thick with springtime and flowers in the night. He moved across grass, toward the white shape of the barn, then out away from the barn, coming back toward the house but staying wide of it to see what else there was to see. He saw the Pontiac parked beside the house. Then he saw something else, two things that moved. They moved just a little, near the trees that bordered the far side of the pond. He made them out as human figures, and one of them was feminine, and he knew it was Della.

Instead of focusing on Della, he centered his attention on the other figure, the man. The man was in silhouette and stood close to Della and it grew evident that they were in deep and urgent discussion. Then, as Harbin watched, the man and Della became a single silhouette, and they were in each other's arms.

They retained the embrace for several moments. When they broke it, the conversation was resumed. Harbin decided on the trees. He saw that he could circle around behind the barn to bring himself in on the far side of the trees on that side of the pond. Once in among the trees, he could wriggle in toward them and get close enough to hear what they were saying.

He did it that way, and began getting words, then phrases, then all of it.

"—in a couple of days."

"It ought to be sooner than that," the man said.

"Let's not be in too much of a hurry."

The man said, "Why don't we do this my way?"

"Because your way is wrong; now look, let's cut it out."

"I don't want to cut it out. I want to talk about it. God damn it, a thing like this we should talk about. It's a big thing. You know what a big thing it is. I want to be sure it's handled right."

Della said, "It will be."

"When should we make it?"

"Saturday," Della said. "At three in the afternoon."

The man's voice became a bit louder. "By Saturday night we ought to have it all wrapped up. Even then maybe it'll be too late. I still claim we're doing it too slow. If we did it my way, we'd be done by now."

"You want to do it your way? You do it alone. I think that's a good idea. You better do it alone."

"Did anyone ever tell you you're a nasty proposition?"

"I'm not at all nasty. I'm just certain. I'm certain of everything I do. If you haven't learned that by now, you better hurry and get wise to it."

There was a long wait, and it ended with the man saying something so quietly that Harbin couldn't hear. Della answered in the same low tone. Harbin edged his face out from behind the tree and saw them embracing again. There was only one thing on his mind, and it was estimating. He estimated that they would keep on embracing long enough to allow him to get back into the house and undress and climb into the bed.

It took less than a minute. When he entered the bedroom he already had his coat and shirt off. He waited until he was in bed before sliding into his pajamas. He worked his head into the pillow and closed his eyes. He felt the full feeling of having been lured, completely deceived.

It was like the in and out movement of a bellows that had been inserted in his flesh. He waited there in the bed with the pumping banging away at his insides, his brain trying to sit still but pulled around and around by the pumping. A few moments later the door opened and he heard her entering the room.

He listened as she moved around the room, felt her weight coming into the wide bed. But the weight didn't hit the bed fully. He sensed she was sitting there in the bed, looking at him. Then, at the very instant when he wished he had the impetus to reach up and put his hands around her throat and choke the life out of her body, he felt her lips on his forehead. Not wanting to open his eyes, he opened his eyes. He murmured sleepily, and saw the shine of her lips and her eyes. Then her lips crashed into his mouth, and something lifted him high and hurled him out into space, his body speeding toward an unreal world.

Chapter VIII

I N THE morning, while she prepared breakfast, Harbin came back to himself, and began to figure his moves. The big thing he had to do was find out who the man was. But that would have to wait until Saturday. On Saturday, at three, she would meet the man and it would be in the afternoon, he would see the man in daylight and know what the man looked like. That would gradually reduce the element of question and bring it toward an answer.

Until Saturday, he realized, there was nothing for him to do but wait. In terms of clock time, it wasn't very long, but he knew this waiting would be an extremely difficult thing for him. He could already feel it, the impatience, the anxiety. Glancing at Della during breakfast, he saw her watching him. He told his face not to give him away. He knew it was these little things that could give him away. Like a sudden change of facial expression. Or a word in the wrong place.

In the afternoon they decided to take a long walk. She said it would be marvelous, walking through the hills. Maybe, she said, they would see some flowers they could collect. She was crazy about flowers, she told him, especially wild flowers. She put on a sporty skirt and blouse and low-heeled shoes. They started on their walk. They moved past the barn, followed a path that took them toward the top of the hill.

They went for a walk the next day, too, and Harbin kept on waiting for Saturday.

Saturday morning they slept late, didn't get to eat until around eleven. Della prepared a combination of breakfast and lunch. Afterwards, Harbin walked outside and strolled around, wondering what sort of pretext Della would use to get rid of him in the afternoon, and where and how she'd keep her appointment with the man.

A half hour later he found out. "I have to run down to Lancaster," she said. "I want to do some shopping."

Harbin knew that the next thing he said had to be said just right. "When will you be back?" he asked.

"Past five, anyway. Tons of things I've got to buy."

He shook his head emphatically, showing a dim smile.

"I can't wait that long."

It did what he wanted it to do. There was no way for her to answer. All she could do was copy his smile.

Then she said, "You want to go with me?"

"Anywhere you go, I want to go with you."

"Then you'll go with me. Except during the shopping. That's something a woman's got to do alone. I'll put you in a barber shop. You can stand a haircut."

He said, "You put me in a barber shop, you'll never get me out. Once I get in, I get the whole works. I stay there for hours."

"Good," she said. "Because I've a lot of marketing to do."

"I'll bet you do," he said, without saying it aloud.

Later they climbed into the Pontiac and started toward Lancaster. Approaching the town, he said he could use a little money and she gave him close to a hundred dollars. She gave it to him without comment. He took it without comment. For the first time since leaving the Spot, he remembered that he had seven thousand dollars in small bills stashed away at the Spot. It didn't bother him. A few days ago, seven thousand dollars had been very important because it was all the money he had in actual cash. Now it was a minor detail.

They arrived in Lancaster at twenty after two. He said he could stand a few sport shirts, and waited for her to suggest that he choose his own store and pick them out himself. He waited for a trace of uneasiness in her voice, because she had less than forty minutes until her appointment with the man. Yet when she said she'd go with him to get the shirts, he wasn't at all surprised. It was already at the point where nothing she did surprised him.

It took a good half hour to buy the shirts. She did the selecting and the buying. When the package was wrapped and they were headed toward the door, she had less than ten minutes before her appointment with the man. She behaved as though she had all day. They passed a counter of neckties and Della stopped and looked at the ties.

She said, "Like regimental stripes?"

"I go for polka dots."

The salesman closed in and began to discuss the new styles. Della looked at the salesman as though he was peddling shoe-laces. She said, "I can't pick out these ties while you're talking."

"Beg your pardon, Madam." The salesman acted as though he had been given a good clout on the side of the head.

Harbin looked down at his wristwatch. Six minutes. He looked at Della. She was completely immersed in the subject of neckties.

"I'm not enthused about any of these," she said. "What else do you have?"

The salesman excused himself and went into a side room.

Della spent a good ten minutes selecting three neckties. Harbin could see the man at the meeting-place, maybe smoking one cigarette after another, or cracking the knuckles or biting the lips, waiting there for Della while Della was here, buying neckties.

Harbin said, "I better get to the barber shop."

"What's the hurry?"

The calm, easy way she said it threw a flag of warning against his eyes. He had displayed a touch of impatience, and with this woman, with this manipulator, he couldn't afford to display anything along that line.

He said, "Saturday afternoon. They get busy around three. I hate to sit around waiting."

"Thank me for the neckties."

"Thank you for the neckties."

They were out of the store and she looked up and down the street, told him if they tried the next block they'd probably see a barber shop. They tried the next block and there was a barber shop near the far corner, but when they arrived there, Della said she didn't like the looks of it. Harbin studied his wrist-watch. It was now twenty-two minutes past three.

"What's wrong with this place?" he asked. "It looks clean."

"The barbers look stupid."

"Let's spend the day hunting for intelligent-looking barbers."

It was another five minutes before they found the barber shop on Orange Street. Harbin smiled at Della and then he threw another look at his wristwatch. This time he let her know he was looking at it. He said, "Where do we want to meet? What time?"

She peered through the big window of the barber shop, a big clean shop with many chairs. "There's four ahead of you. You're good for an hour and a half, at least. Wait here for me."

He entered the shop, turning in time to see her headed in the direction from which they had come. It would take her twenty seconds at the minimum to reach the corner at the end of the block. He had to get outside to see whether she would turn the corner. He counted up to eight and then moved out of the shop and saw her turning the corner, going right. He crossed the street, walked fast to the corner, arrived there in time to see her turning another corner.

There was a crowd farther ahead, and still another coming out of a department store across the wide street that Della had just crossed. Della was entering the department store. Harbin bumped into a trio of old women and almost knocked them down. They wanted to discuss it with him but he was already in the middle of the street, traveling against the light, racing the people who were aiming at the revolving doors of the big store. He beat them to the door, but going through it he could see the maze of people in the store and he knew he had lost her. He started to chew on the cigarette. An aisle said lingerie and another aisle said luggage and a third said toiletries. He selected luggage and halfway down the aisle he saw her among a flock of women waiting at the elevators.

Wondering how many floors this place had, telling himself he should have thought of that before, he stopped and turned his back on the elevators, and kept on chewing at the cigarette as he realized it was now necessary to gamble on what floor she would call.

It was difficult to let the seconds go by. He let fifteen of them pass before turning to face the elevators. She had already gone up. He took his time walking to the elevators. One of them arrived and opened for him, and he went in with a crowd of women and children. The colored girl took the elevator to the second floor and called out furniture, rugs, radios, household essentials. At the third floor the colored girl called sporting goods and men's wear, and Harbin got out. He told himself it was a fairly good bet, a basic thing. A reasonable place for the man to wait would be in the men's wear department.

It was rather crowded, and they were mostly boys and young

men in this section that had the baseball bats and gloves, the tennis racquets and swimming trunks. He moved slowly, and a salesman walked toward him and he smiled easily, shook his head, murmured something about just looking around. He was in there with the suits and slacks now, his head turning slowly this way, that way, and going toward windows as he maneuvered to always stay behind a row of hanging suits but sufficiently away from the suits so he could get a reasonable view of that part of the room near the windows.

He went up and down past two long rows of suits. Then he saw Della. He saw the man. They stood a little away from one of the windows. The salesmen were leaving them alone. The man had his back to Harbin, but not all the way. The man was about five-ten and had a heavy build, and was young and had thick blond hair, blonder than Harbin's, a wealth of blond hair combed straight but sort of loose.

Harbin lifted a sport jacket from its hanger and held it up in front of his face, going through the motions of taking it toward a window where he could see it in the light. He maneuvered the jacket to keep it in front of his face as he went sliding in toward Della and the blond man. He was coming toward them from an angle.

He pulled the jacket slowly away from his face, as though the jacket was a curtain. A fuzzy sleeve went past his eyes. A sizzling fuse began eating itself away as Harbin told himself he had seen the face before, had seen it very recently, had seen that nose and mouth. And the eyes. The eyes were an unusual color. Very pale blue with a bit of green. Aquamarine eyes. A couple of nights ago, two cops had questioned him about the car parked near the mansion. This was the young cop.

Chapter IX

As Harbin entered the barber shop, a man got up from one of the wire-backed chairs in response to the barber's beckoning finger. Harbin lowered himself into the wire-backed chair. He leaned back, closed his eyes, saw the mansion in the night and the car parked on the wide clean street north of the mansion, the police car, the aquamarine eyes of the young cop.

Now he had to take it from there. He began to take it, very slowly, considering each item before buying it. He had to check his own moves in ratio with the moves of the young cop, the things they were doing at the same time, the things in the mind behind the aquamarine eyes. That mind had decided to come back alone and have another look at the parked car. Maybe the aquamarine eyes had seen the flashlight signals going across the lawn minutes before Harbin had appeared. Maybe it was something else. Whatever it was, the young cop had decided the older cop was a hindrance, and it was best to come back alone.

And so the blond man, no longer to be considered a policeman, had come back alone and had placed the police car so he could not be seen. He had watched the parked Chevrolet. He had seen them coming from the mansion with their haul. He had watched the Chevrolet as it went into first gear. Maybe he had followed them without using his headlights. That maybe didn't last long. In Harbin's brain it became an emphatic yes. He remembered having examined the rear-view mirror and not seeing any headlights.

Without headlights, this blond man had followed the Chevrolet to the Spot. He had watched them entering the Spot with their haul. That was for certain and another thing for certain was the fact that he had gone back to the police station and reported nothing.

Harbin realized it was necessary to check on that, check with himself, his own conception of how certain people react to certain situations. The aquamarine eyes had seen the luxurious mansion, the token of great wealth, had decided it would be a big haul, had waited calmly for the report to come in. When the report came in, when the house sergeant put it down in the book, and the fact that it amounted to around a hundred thousand dollars in emeralds, the man aimed his eyes and his body and his brain at the hundred thousand dollars.

And now it was all quite clear to Harbin and he could see the rest of it as though he sat at a table and looked at tangible things set neatly before him. He saw the man walking around and thinking it over, deciding to play it carefully and with accuracy. A policeman would have gone after the burglars, but this man was a policeman only when he wore a uniform and moved in the company of other policemen. This man was a rather special sort of operator, loyal only to himself and what he wanted. And what he wanted was the emeralds. This man realized the emeralds were in the shabby Kensington house and the only way to get them out and into his own hands was by using another brain. The other brain was a woman named Della.

The man had made contact with Della. They must have taken turns, keeping their eyes on the Spot, the legs that walked out of the Spot and then returned and walked out again. They must have decided on a time, the initial forward move. And Della had seen him entering the restaurant that night, and that was it, that was the arrangement she needed. If that hadn't worked, she would have tried something else. But that had worked. It had worked beautifully. It had kept on working until now, but now it was all over.

Harbin saw a thick finger pointing at him. The barber was smiling, inviting him to the chair. He climbed into the chair and the barber gave him a shave and then a haircut and after that a shampoo and scalp massage and then went back to the face and put pink cream on the face and worked it in with the thick fingers and followed with a sunlamp treatment. A folded towel kept the light out of Harbin's eyes. In the black under the folded towel he could see the Spot, he could see their faces, the three in the organization when it ought to be four in the organization. He was in a great hurry to get back to the Spot.

The barber took the folded towel from Harbin's eyes and

pushed a button that then lifted the chair electrically to sitting position. Harbin got off the chair and saw Della standing near the door.

They left the barber shop and walked back to the car. They drove out of Lancaster and pulled onto the road going back to the hill. Della worked the radio and got some light-opera music. She pushed the car at medium speed, sat there behind the wheel with a relaxed smile on her face as she listened to the music. Without looking at Harbin she was communicating with him and once she reached out and let her fingers go into the hair at the back of his head. She gave his hair a little pull.

He poked around in his brain and wondered if it was possible to figure her out. He thought of her kisses. In his lifetime he had been kissed by enough women and had experienced a sufficient variety of kisses to know when there was real meaning in a kiss. Her kisses had the real meaning, and not only the fire, but the genuine material beyond the fire. If it hadn't been genuine he would have sensed it when it happened. This woman had immense feeling for him and he knew clearly it was far above ordinary craving and it was something that couldn't be put on like a mask is put on. It was pure in itself and it was entirely devoid of pretense or embroidery.

It was the true feeling that made the entire business a quaking paradox, because the one side of Della was drawn to him, melted into him, and the other side of Della was out to louse him up. Even now, knowing of her purpose, knowing she was out to get the emeralds, fully aware of her scheme, seeing the situation as a sort of arena with her on one side and himself on the other, he felt the magnetic pull, he realized his desire for Della, the depth of the desire and the knowledge it was permanent desire. He knew he wanted Della more than he had ever wanted anything. This was a solid problem, this woman, a thing he had to deal with, a trouble he had to blast apart. Because it was a threat, and since it aimed at the emeralds, it had to aim at the Spot. And the Spot was the organization. The Spot was Dohmer and Baylock and Gladden. And there, right there, the quiver went through him, the edge of the knife sliced everything else away. This thing was aiming at Gladden.

Not knowing it, he had his eyes dulled and heavy with guilt.

There was hammering in the guilt and it sent the heaviness through his veins. Every thread in his body became a wire drawn tight. Gladden needed him and he had deserted Gladden. Here he was, sitting at the very side of this thing that aimed a threat at Gladden. For days he had been with this thing, away from Gladden. Gladden needed him and if he wasn't there it would be the end of her. This woman sitting beside him was an element that he must quickly erase.

He glanced around at the hills, the woods beyond the hills. There were some narrow hills going to left and right of the concrete highway, and he said, "Let's try some new scenery."

She gave him a look. "Where?"

"One of these little roads." He said it with his eyes going into her, the words nothing more than ripples on the surface.

It worked. She nodded slowly. "All right, we'll find a quiet place. Where we'll have a lot of trees around us. Like a curtain."

They took one of the little roads, followed it up along a hillside, went up and around and down to the other side of the hill, followed the road into the woods where it became a set of tire tracks. They were going far into the woods and the path became dim. Harbin glanced over the side of the car and watched the thick high green grass sliding along, some purple sliding with the green.

He felt the car slowing down and he said, "No, keep going."

"It's wonderful here."

"Keep going."

"Put your hands on me."

"Wait," he said.

"I can't."

"Please wait."

The woods around them was thick and up ahead it seemed to be thicker, very dark because the leaves were mobs of solid green high in the trees and holding the sun away. He knew she would say nothing now until he said something and he remained quiet while they went on through the woods. They went deeper and deeper into the woods and through an hour and through another hour, the car going very slowly because it was bumpy ground and there was considerable climbing and turning. He felt the immense yet gentle pressure of the woods and he felt the nearness of Della and for moments that choked him he was pulled away from his idea, his purpose, the thing he meant to carry out in these woods. He took hold of the moment and twisted it away from himself.

He said, "All right. Just about here."

She stopped the car. She turned off the radio.

He said, "Get rid of the lights."

She switched off the headlights and he opened the door on his side and stepped out of the car. Moonlight came down through the woods. Della was getting out of the car, circling it to come toward him. Her body came toward him through the moonlight. As she reached him he took her hand, he walked her away from the car, off the path, heard the sound of her breathing as he took her into the trees.

He took her on toward the rippling sound of water. Eventually they could see the water, the glimmer of a brook far down below from where they stood on a high mound of wild flowers.

He took her down to the brook and they stood there looking at the moon-glazed water, the points of rocks showing like bits of crystal against the dark. He lowered himself to the ground, felt the smooth flatness of it here on the bank, felt Della as she came against him. He sensed the approach of her lips. He drew his face away from her lips.

"No," he said. He said it tenderly, almost like a caress, and yet he knew it had the force of a spear going into her.

He waited. He wanted to look at her, he wanted to see the effect, but this was only the start of what he was going to do to her, only an ounce of the full measure aiming at this thing that aimed the threatening aim in a long line going up from the emeralds to the Spot to the organization, and to Gladden. Inside himself he spoke softly to Gladden and told her he was about to make up for what he had done.

Della was quiet for many moments. Finally she said, "What bothers you?"

"Nothing."

"You don't seem to be with me."

"I'm not." He was smiling at the brook. He knew she could see the smile and he knew what it was doing to her.

There was another long wait and then she said, "I know what this is."

He went on smiling at the brook.

"You're drifting," she said. "I can see you drifting."

He shrugged. "I imagine so."

She stood up, had her back to him but he knew what was happening on her face. He could almost see inside her, see the tumult, the piercing shock, the agony she didn't want him to see. She was trying to hold back but couldn't hold back because finally it broke away and came out, bursting, hissing, her body twisting to show him her face as she said, "God damn you, you dirty son of a bitch."

He looked at her only for an instant, then swerved his eyes to the brook and went on smiling at it.

"Why?" She shot it at him. "Why? Why?"

He shrugged.

"You tell me why," she gasped, her voice almost cracking. "You better tell me why."

The smile on his face became dim but inside himself he was smiling widely because this was the way he had planned it and it was working just right. He thought of certain people who had it in for other people and went ahead and did their killing. But there was never any real benefit to be derived from killing, and the results, sooner or later, were always bad. So it was always stupid and crazy to kill, and this was so much more effective than killing. This was the worst possible thing he could do to her. It was the worst thing any man could do to any woman. It was the meanest form of torture, because he was rejecting her without qualifying the rejection, throwing her into a gully of dismay, watching her flounder and choke, her brain seething, trying to reach the reason while he held the reason just a trifle out of her reach.

He stood up. "Guess that's about it."

"You can't," she said. "How can you? How can you do this? It isn't human. It's what a devil would do. At least give a person a reason, let me know why—"

"Why?" He made a little gesture with his arms. "Go ask the trees. They know as much about it as I do."

"I don't believe that."

"I'm sorry."

"You're not sorry. If you were, you'd tell me. You'd tell me what goes on in that mind of yours. What thoughts are you having? What are you feeling?"

"I don't know." He said it as though she had asked him what time it was. Then, as he began to turn away from her, "I don't know anything about it except I just don't want to be around you anymore. I want to get away."

And as he moved away, as he went up the steep rise going away from the brook and into the woods, he could hear no sound behind him other than the sound of the water against rocks. Moving steadily through the woods, seeing the car, he crossed the moonlit path far in front of the car and followed a stretch of climbing terrain to get up high enough so he could obtain a view of the main highway, and started down in that direction.

On the highway, about an hour later, a truck picked him up and took him into Lancaster. He climbed into a taxi and went to the railroad station and bought a ticket to Philadelphia.

Chapter X

OPENING THE door, he saw only darkness. He called Baylock's name, then he called Dohmer. A weak light came down from upstairs, and he heard their voices. He switched on a lamp, took out a handkerchief and wiped some rain from his face. He waited for them to come down the stairs.

They came down rather slowly, looking at him as though they had never seen him before. They were both dressed, but their trousers were rumpled and he knew they had been sleeping in their clothes. They moved down into the living-room and stood close together, looking at him.

He opened his mouth. Instead of words coming out, a lot of air and worry rushed in. He didn't know how to begin.

They waited for him to say something.

Finally he said, "Where's Gladden?"

They let him wait. He asked it again and then Dohmer answered, "Atlantic City."

He put a cigarette in his mouth. "I guess I figured she'd come back here."

"She did come back," Dohmer said. "We told her about you, so she went back to Atlantic City."

Harbin took off his wet jacket and hung it on a chair. "You talk as though she's gone for good."

"You hit it," Baylock said.

"Don't lie," Harbin moved quickly toward them, caught himself and told himself to handle it another way. His voice was calm. "What happened with Gladden?"

"We tell you she's pulled out," Baylock said. "She packed her things and pulled out. You want to make sure? Go to Atlantic City." Baylock dipped a hand in his trousers pocket, took out a folded slip of paper and handed it to Harbin. "Here's the address she gave us." Baylock took a deep breath that had grinding in it. "Anything else you want?"

"I want you to listen while I talk."

He studied their faces for a sign of trust. There was no sign. There was nothing.

He said, "I want to come in again."

"You won't come in," Baylock told him. "You're out. You'll stay out."

"I'll come in," Harbin said. "I've got to come in because if I don't, you stand a good chance of losing the haul and getting yourselves grabbed. Now either show some sense and listen to me or you'll wind up in a mud puddle."

Baylock looked at Dohmer. "I like how he walks back in and right away he takes over."

"I'm not taking over," Harbin said. "All I can do is tell you the way things are shaped. We've got ourselves a package of grief." He let that come against them, waiting until it went into them, and then giving it to them. "We're being looked at."

They moved in no special direction. They stared at each other and then they stared at Harbin. For a moment he was with them, he felt what they felt. He wanted to come out and put the whole thing in front of them, the thing as it had happened and the way it was. But he realized they wouldn't accept the truth. They hadn't accepted it the last time and they wouldn't accept it now. He would have to slice most of it away and give them nothing more than a mouthful to chew on.

He said, "A party's been trailing me. It took me four days to find out. Another day to shake him. But I've added it up and I can see that shaking him won't do any good. At least not for the time being. Anyway, not until we get out of here."

Baylock took another deep breath. "Be careful, Nat. We got a lot more brains now than the day you walked out. We been educating ourselves." He grinned at Dohmer. "Ain't we?"

"Yeah," Dohmer said. "We took it serious, what you said, Nat. We made up our minds to get smarter. Now we're smarter and we're not nervous like we were."

"Try to follow it." Harbin was begging himself to stay away from anger, to hold on, to keep it cool. "At the mansion we had the police. When they went away I thought for sure that was the end of them. But one of them came back. He followed us here. And now, in plain clothes, he's been following me."

Baylock held onto the grin and shook his head. "No fit. When they want you, they don't follow you. They move in and grab you."

"The point is," Harbin said, "he doesn't want me." Harbin let some quiet come in, let it settle. "All right, if you can't figure it out, I'll tell you. The man stays with me but he doesn't want me. He wants the emeralds."

Baylock turned and stopped, turned again, came back to where he had been standing. Dohmer lifted a hand and rubbed a long, heavy jaw. Then Baylock and Dohmer frowned at each other and that was all they could do.

Baylock said, breathing very heavily, "Who is he? Who is this bastard?"

"I don't know. All I know is, the man is hungry for emeralds. He's got his police uniform to fall back on and when it lines up like that, the only way to deal with them is stay away from them."

"But maybe," Dohmer blurted, "all he wants is a cut."

Harbin shrugged. "They all want just a little cut. To begin with. Then they come back and say they want another little cut. Then later they're back again." He lit a cigarette, took several small puffs at it, blew out the smoke in one big cloud. "What we've got to do and do fast is get the hell out of here."

"Where to?" Dohmer said.

Harbin looked at him as though it was a silly question. "You know where. Atlantic City."

"For God's sake," Dohmer groaned.

Baylock said, "If she's pulled out, she's pulled out."

"No," Harbin said. "We go there and pick her up."

"Answer me this," Baylock shouted. "What do we need her for?"

"We don't need her," Harbin admitted. "But she needs us."

"Why?" Baylock wanted to know.

"We're an organization." Harbin knew he shouldn't have said that, but it was said and all he could do was wait for Baylock's blast.

"Are we?" Baylock shouted. "Jesus Christ, give us credit for half a brain anyway. You walk out of here and say you're through and now almost a week later you show up again and once more we're an organization, just like that. I don't like it handled that way and I won't see it handled that way. Either it's black or it's white. One or the other."

"I won't argue," Harbin said. "If you want to break it up we can break it up here and now. On the other hand we can hold it. And if we hold it, I stick. We all stick. That includes Gladden."

Dohmer hit his hands against his thighs. "I'm with that."

"You're with everything." Baylock looked Dohmer up and down. He turned his face to Harbin. He started to say something and then his mouth tightened up and he walked to the window and looked out at the rain.

The rain was coming down very hard, pouring off the rooftops in solid sheets of silver water against the black. Baylock stood there looking at the rain and hearing the thud of it and saying, "It sure is a fine night to ride down to Atlantic City."

Harbin made no reply. He started up the stairs, then stopped and looked at Dohmer, "I'll do the driving. I hope you got the cards printed."

Dohmer took out his wallet and extracted a few cards, including an operator's license, a registration card, and a social security card and handed these to Harbin. He examined them, saw that the alias was neither far-fetched nor too common, then he beckoned to Dohmer and Baylock. The three of them went upstairs and packed their bags. They loaded the emeralds into a ragged suitcase, picked up their baggage and moved slowly out of the Spot and walked through the rain.

The Chevrolet was parked in a nearby one-car garage they had rented from an old couple who didn't have a car and were out of touch with the world. Dohmer had made the necessary changes so that now the Chevrolet was a darkish orange and had different license plates, a different engine number and looked altogether like a different car.

Harbin drove and Baylock sat beside him. Dohmer was in the back and sound asleep before they hit the Delaware Bridge. There were very few cars on the Bridge. When they had driven halfway across the Bridge, Baylock began to worry.

"Why did we have to paint it orange?" Baylock wanted to know. "Of all the colors we could have used, we had to use orange. Some color for a car. Who paints a car orange?"

"You're worrying about the law," Harbin said, "and our worry right now is not the law."

"Another thing," Baylock said. "Why in Christ's name did we have to take the car anyway? Why didn't we grab a train?"

"And put the emeralds on a train. And being there on a train going eighty miles an hour and not being able to get off if something goes wrong. If you want to make talk, let's make talk with sense."

The car reached the New Jersey side of the river and Harbin paid New Jersey twenty cents for the use of the Bridge. In Camden the rain died down a little. Coming onto the Black Horse Pike the rain started again. It grew to become a wide rain with a great deal of Atlantic Ocean wind in it.

Harbin worked the car up to fifty-five and held it there on the wet black road. The rain was seemingly coming straight at the car and he had to bend over a little, getting his eyes closer to the windshield to see where he was going.

Baylock said, "Gladden looked good."

"What do you mean, she looked good."

"Her face. She looked good in the face. She had some color."

"The salt air," Harbin said. "It's good for everybody. The salt air and the sun."

"It wasn't sunburn," Baylock sounded emphatic. "And where does salt air affect the eyes? I took one look at her and right away I noticed the eyes."

"What's wrong with her eyes?"

"Nothing. Her eyes look great. I never saw her eyes like that before. I guess that's what happens to the eyes in Atlantic City. They get that real Atlantic City look. She sure was anxious to get back. As if there was something there that she was lonesome for. Like the salt air. And the sunshine."

"All right," Harbin said.

"And so," Baylock said, "the thing I keep asking myself is why we're going to all this trouble, going down there to Atlantic City to take her away from what she wants."

Harbin couldn't form a reply. He had his mind completely on the road and the fight he had to make against this attack of northeaster wind and rain.

"All this trouble," Baylock suddenly whined. "And all this risk."

"Quit harping on the risk." Harbin was annoyed. "There's no risk. Why don't you rest your head back and take a nap?"

"Who can sleep in this weather? Look at this God damn weather."

"It'll let down." Harbin knew the storm wouldn't let down. It was getting worse, there was more rain, heavier wind, and now he had to keep the car down to forty, and even at that speed he had difficulty hanging on to it.

"I'll make book," Baylock said, "we're the only car tonight on the Black Horse Pike."

"That's a safe bet."

"Even the cats," Baylock whined, "stay home on a night like this."

Harbin was about to say something, but just then the car hit a chughole in the road and there was a nasty sound as the rear springs strained to keep themselves alive. The car went down and up and down again, and Harbin waited for it to fall apart. It went on riding through the northeaster. The headlights found a road sign that said Atlantic City was forty-five miles away. Then the road sign was past them and in front of them was the black and the booming storm. Harbin had an odd feeling they were a thousand miles away from Atlantic City and a thousand miles away from anywhere. He tried to convince himself the Black Horse Pike was a real thing and in daylight it was just another concrete road. But ahead of him now it looked unreal, like a path arranged for unreal travel, its glimmer unreal, black of it unreal with the wet wild thickness all around it.

Baylock's voice came to him, the whine of it cutting through all the clashing noise of the storm. "I know for sure now," Baylock said, "we made a big mistake. We were crazy to start this. I can't tell you how sorry I am we started it. And while we still got the chance we got, we better junk off this road."

"We'll get there." Harbin knew it was a stupid thing to say. It signified he was trying to reassure himself, as well as Baylock.

And Baylock said, "You're always the brains and we're always the goats. But now I'm wondering after all how much brains you really got. This party who trailed you, maybe he's the big brains. So let's see how his brains would work. Enough brains to find the Spot. Enough to keep checking on us. Here's a maybe for you. Maybe he trailed Dohmer, too. Maybe he trailed Dohmer to the garage and watched Dohmer painting the car."

"You sound like you're from nowhere. Drop it."

"It just can't be dropped. You grab hold of high voltage, you can't let go. This party, like you claim, is after the emeralds, not us. That fits. But here's another thing. If he loses us, he loses the emeralds. So now we've got to think of it the way he would think of it. Even though he ain't with the law, he can still give the law enough inside dope to make sure we don't break away."

"You tell me how he could manage that."

"Why should I have to tell you? You ought to know yourself. You're an expert on everything. And even a dumbbell can figure what the man does. He puts in a call to the station house, and he's anonymous, and he makes a few statements about an orange Chevrolet. Says it's a dark orange and has a lot of fancy chrome. Says nothing about the emeralds or the haul, just says it's a stolen car."

"Come out of the trees."

"You're in the trees. You're trying to dodge away from it but you know, just like I do." Baylock's voice had climbed so that it was no longer a whine, but somewhere near a screech. "You and your brain. You and your obligations. This skinny girl who needs Atlantic City. Who likes the color orange. You and your girl Gladden."

Harbin took the car up to forty. Then past forty. And then he took it up to fifty, and then to sixty. He felt the tremor of the car as he pushed it to seventy miles an hour through the bedlam of northeaster force and water. He heard every loud noise in the world blending to become one big banging noise, and through it he heard the wail of Baylock, thought Baylock was begging him to slow down, then listened hard, knew the wail meant something else.

"I told you," Baylock shrieked and wailed. "You see? I told you."

Baylock's fingers tapped the rear-view mirror, Baylock's hand shaking, his fingers on the mirror showing Harbin the two little spheres of bright yellow in the black mirror.

"It's nothing." Harbin lessened his pressure on the accelerator. The two glowing spheres became just a bit larger, and he gave the car more gas. Again there was a wail, but almost instantly he knew it wasn't Baylock's wail. It was mechanical. He listened to it, studied it, and knew it was a police siren and it came from back there where the headlights sent their gleam into his rear-view mirror.

"Wake Dohmer," he shouted. He looked at the speedometer. The car was holding seventy. He heard Dohmer grumbling, coming out of sleep, and then the clash between Dohmer's voice and Baylock's voice. From the corner of his eye he saw Baylock opening the glove compartment, reaching in deep to open another compartment that had been built by Dohmer for the concealment of revolvers. He saw the flash of the gun barrels as Baylock took them out. Dohmer in the back seat was bumping around like a big animal, twisting to look through the rear window.

"Put the guns back," Harbin said.

Baylock was checking the guns, making sure they held slugs. "Quit kidding yourself." Baylock hefted the guns.

"Put them back," Harbin said. "We've never used them before and we won't need to use them now."

"You better be damn certain about that."

"I am. Put them back."

"For God's sake," Dohmer shouted. "Go faster, will you? For God's sake, what in God's name is happening here? Why don't you go faster? What are you slowing down for?"

The car was down to sixty. It kept slowing down and the two dots of light in the rear-view mirror became larger. Harbin turned his face a little toward Baylock.

"I want you to put the guns back," Harbin said.

The siren wail of the police car came biting through the northeaster, getting the fire of its drastic sound into Harbin's head, burning there in his head as he kept telling Baylock to put the guns back and close the contrived compartment.

Baylock said, "I know we need guns."

"You start with guns and you're dead."

"We're using the guns."

Harbin had the car down to forty miles an hour. "I won't tell you again," he said, "put them back."

"You sure you want me to do that?"

"I couldn't be more sure," Harbin said.

He saw the flash again as the guns went back into the glove compartment, Baylock's arm deep in there getting the guns into the space on the side, and he heard the click as the side panel closed. Now he could no longer hear the police siren. From back there they could see he had slowed down and would be waiting for them to come up. The Chevrolet faded from thirty down to twenty, down to fifteen, and then it stopped altogether at the side of the road.

Harbin wondered whether it would be a good thing at this point to light a cigarette. In front of him the rain washed down across the wearily sliding windshield wipers, more rain washed down and through the black beyond that, and more rain beyond that. He put a cigarette in his mouth and leaned his head back as he lit the cigarette. Now he could hear the engine of the police car coming up, and there was the floating wide swath of its headlights making bright white designs on the ceiling of the Chevrolet. There was something else he heard, and when he saw it happening it was already too late, he couldn't stop Baylock now, he couldn't close the glove compartment to catch Baylock's hand. Baylock already had the gun and was holding it close to his side as the police car pulled up alongside the Chevrolet, and Harbin twisted his head to stare at Dohmer. He saw Dohmer nodding slowly and knew that Baylock had maneuvered it quickly and nicely and Dohmer had the other gun.

"Don't use them," Harbin said. "I'm begging you not to use them."

He didn't have time to say anything else. A big man wearing a hooded raincoat had stepped out of the police car, the spotlight of the police car shooting past Harbin's face and giving enough light to brighten up the entire area and display the other two police faces in the official car.

Harbin lowered the window and let some smoke come out of his mouth. He saw the big shiny face of the big policeman, very shiny and weird in the mixture of light and rain.

"What's the big hurry?" the policeman said. "You know what you were hitting?"

"Seventy."

"That's twenty too much," the policeman said. "License and owner's card."

Harbin took the cards from his wallet and gave them to the policeman. The policeman was studying the cards but made no move to pull out his book.

"We people in Jersey want to stay alive," the policeman said. "You drivers from Pennsylvania come over here and try to kill us."

"You see what kind of a night it is," Harbin argued. "We only wanted to get out of this weather."

"Call that an excuse? That's all the more reason to stay inside the speed limit. And you were doing something else, too. Crossing over that white line. You were way over on the wrong side of the road."

"The wind kept pushing me over."

"The wind had nothing to do with it," the policeman said. "If you're a careful driver and obey the law you don't have to worry about the wind." He turned to the other policemen. "I told you he'd blame it on the storm."

"Well," Harbin sighed, "I know I've seen better weather than this."

"You going down the shore?"

Harbin nodded.

The policeman said, "You want nice weather, you won't find it in Atlantic City. Not for the next day or so, anyway. And I tell you I wouldn't want to be down there tonight. When that ocean gets it from the northeast, there's no worse place to be."

He handed the cards back to Harbin and Harbin put them in the wallet. The book had not appeared and Harbin told himself it was all right, it was over, and what remained wouldn't be important.

"Now you be careful," the policeman warned. "Unless you're inclined to be a lunatic you won't do more than forty miles an hour. Go into a skid on this road and you'll wind up in a grave."

"I'll remember that, officer."

The policeman turned to get back into the official car, and just then one of the other cops steered the spotlight so it would swish its wide glow into the Chevrolet, and the big policeman kept turning his eyes automatically to follow the path of the spotlight. The glow went riding past Harbin's head into the rear of the Chevrolet. Harbin pivoted his head, saw the glow catching Dohmer in the back seat, the revolver in Dohmer's hand in the middle of the glow. Then, as the big policeman let out a grunt and went for his own revolver, Dohmer raised the gun and pointed it at the big shiny face.

"No, don't, don't, don't," Harbin pleaded, but he heard the explosion of Dohmer's gun as the policeman went for his own gun. On the other side of the car Baylock already had the door open and was leaping out. Harbin tried to move and couldn't understand why it was impossible to move. He stared at the big policeman.

The face of the big policeman was completely destroyed, split wide open by the bullet and now sinking under the path of the spotlight. Harbin saw convulsive movement in the police car, sensed his own body moving, the backward rush as he threw himself toward the door that Baylock had opened. Falling out of the car, going backwards, he saw Dohmer leaping away toward a vague mass that was bush fringing the muddy ditch that fringed the road. He heard the crash of more bullets, heard the yelling of the policemen as they circled their car and came running toward the bush. They were running toward Dohmer and shooting at him as he sought to get inside the bush. Dohmer was more clumsy now than he had ever been before. He had managed to get past the ditch, but now he tripped with the bush coming up in front of him, got up and tripped again and fell into the bush and became entangled there. Then Dohmer knew he was due to be hit and he let out a scream, and right after that he was hit. He squirmed, his hands mixed with the bush. His body was an arc as he threw his shoulders far back. The policemen ran in close to him and shot him again as he twisted to give them his face and his stomach. They shot their bullets into his stomach. He screamed at the policemen. He screamed at the rain and the raining sky. He began to fall, but he was too clumsy to merely fall. He stumbled as he fell, and while stumbling he lifted his revolver and fired one and two and three shots at the policemen. One of the policemen died instantly, his heart pierced. The other policeman began to sob and let out a choking, gurgling noise as he clutched at his chest. Dohmer's body collided with him and they both went to the ground. The policeman pulled himself up and away from the corpse of Dohmer and crawled on his hands and knees toward the ditch, then rolled into the ditch.

Harbin, crouching at the side of the Chevrolet, waited for the policeman to climb out of the ditch. But all Harbin could see was the quiet legs of the policeman, coming from the top of the ditch. Then there was sound from another section of the bush, and Harbin turned to see Baylock emerging from the bush, Baylock following the line of bush toward the legs of the policeman. Harbin called to Baylock, and Baylock stopped, turned quickly, looked at him, then moved on toward the policeman. Now the legs were moving, the policeman was trying to pull himself from the muddy water. Baylock, his arm extended with the revolver at the end of the arm, walked up to the policeman, stared at him, aimed the revolver at him.

The revolver was only inches away from the policeman's head as Harbin came lunging toward Baylock, calling to him, pleading with him to forget the policeman and pull out of there. Again Baylock turned and looked at Harbin, motioned Harbin to stay away, then put two bullets in the policeman's skull.

Rain came showering into Harbin's eyes. He wiped the rain from his eyes and stood still and looked at Baylock. He had no thoughts about Baylock. He had no thoughts about anything or anyone in particular. He saw Baylock examining the bodies of Dohmer and the policemen. He followed Baylock toward the road and watched Baylock examining the body of the policeman who had been hit in the face.

"Get in the car," Harbin said.

Baylock straightened himself, walked away from the Chevrolet and blindly opened the door of the police car and began to climb in.

"Not that car," Harbin said.

Baylock turned. "Where's our car? The car we got?"

"Right in front of you. You're looking at it."

"I can't see it," Baylock let out a cough, then a series of coughs. "Let's go back to the Spot. Let's be at the Spot."

Harbin walked over to Baylock and took him toward the Chevrolet and helped him get in. Then Harbin was behind the wheel of the Chevrolet, putting it in gear, taking it out onto the road, getting it in second gear, working it up fast, the transmission grinding hard as the car went into high gear. The tires made a big splash through water that filled a hollow in the road. Then the water became higher further on up the road and they began running into a succession of lakes in the road.

It seemed to Harbin that the interior of the car was a part of the lakes. The steering wheel felt like water. His body felt like it was all water.

"What are we doing?" Baylock asked.

"We're in the Chevrolet. We're going to Atlantic City."

"I don't want to go there."

"That's where we're going."

"I want to go back to the Spot. That's the only place I want to go."

"Where's your revolver?" Harbin wanted to know.

"Look at all the rain. Look how it's raining."

"What did you do with your revolver?" Harbin asked. "Did you drop it?"

"I guess that's what I did," Baylock said. "I must have dropped it. We better go back there and get it."

"What we better do," Harbin was saying aloud to himself, "is get off this road."

"Let's get off this road and go back to the Spot."

The road was level again and there were no more little lakes. Lights showed up ahead and Harbin could see it was one of the small towns that blotted the Black Horse Pike on its way to Atlantic City. He looked at his wristwatch and the hands read past two in the morning. It was too late to catch a bus or even a train. Their only way to get to Atlantic City was to stay in the car and take it onto a side road and keep it on the side roads away from the policemen who would soon be cluttering the Pike and stopping every car. He saw a road branching off to the right and knew it represented a chance. It might be a negative chance but he couldn't stop to think about that. The Chevrolet went onto the side road and followed it for a few miles, then cut onto another road that paralleled the Pike.

Baylock said, "We're going the wrong way."

"Why do you say that?"

"Because I know. We been making wrong turns."

"You're crazy," Harbin said.

Baylock said, "We ought to have a gun."

"We ought to have a lot of things. We ought to have a special apparatus that pulls back on your hand when you go for a gun."

"I tell you," Baylock insisted, "what we need is a gun. If I hadn't dropped my gun back there I'd have it now. I can't begin to tell you how much I miss that gun."

"If you don't shut up," Harbin said, "you'll go even crazier than you are now. And you're plenty crazy now. Why don't you shut up? Why don't you try to get some rest?"

"That's what I ought to do," Baylock admitted. "I ought to fall asleep. I'd feel a lot better if only I could sleep."

"Give it a try."

"Wake me up if anything happens."

"If anything happens," Harbin said, "I won't have to wake you."

He sent the Chevrolet onto a narrow road that aimed east. For the better part of an hour he followed the road, then had to turn where the road turned, going north. Instead of taking him toward Atlantic City, the road was pulling him away, but he had to follow the road and wait for it to start east again. He heard the heavy breathing of Baylock and every now and then Baylock mumbled something that had no meaning. A new atmosphere came into the car and it was the atmosphere of complete solitude, as though Baylock did not exist. Outside the car, the storm came sweeping in from the ocean. Now the road was sliced by another road that went east. Harbin made the turn. He listened to the rain and the bang and smash of the storm.

Chapter XI

T HEN, FAR out in the ocean, something unnatural took place with the northeaster and threw it acutely off its course. The waves that had been big and fast, dashing in on Atlantic City, now began to calm down, and the rain became a light rain that lessened to a drizzle, and toward four in the morning the storm was ended. It ended completely only a few minutes before the Chevrolet arrived in Atlantic City, the full thick black that meant soon it would start getting light, and Harbin took the car down a small street leading to the Bay. He parked the car at the end of the street, walked to the dock and saw a few cabin cruisers were bouncing lightly on the water. It seemed that here the water was deep enough for the purpose Harbin had in mind. He knew he had to do it before the sky lighted up. He walked quickly to the car, got in, put the car in reverse and took it back up the street for thirty yards or so, then pulled the emergency brake and gave the sleeping Baylock an elbow in the side.

"You got the legs, Baby," Baylock moaned. "You got the wonderful kind of legs. Keep your dresses short so I can see your legs."

"Come on, wake up," Harbin said.

"Now see here, Baby, you—" Baylock blinked several times, opened his mouth, held it open and closed it hard, tasting his mouth and making a face at the taste of it. He sat up straight and rubbed his eyes. He looked at Harbin.

"We're here," Harbin said. "I'm throwing the car in the Bay. Help me get the bags out."

"What bay?"

"You'll see it. Let's do this fast."

They took the bags from the car, all the bags except Dohmer's big brown suitcase. Then Harbin climbed into the car and put it in gear, driving it toward the Bay. He had the door open and he opened it wider as the car approached the water. The edge of the dock came up and he leaped out of the car and started running back toward the bags and Baylock. He heard the splash and hoped the water would be deep enough to cover

413

the car, maybe even deep enough to hide it, but he didn't have time to go back and make sure. Approaching Baylock, he waved Baylock on. Baylock picked up the two smaller bags and began running, leaving Harbin one more small bag and the suitcase containing the emeralds.

They covered two long city blocks and were on the third when a cab cruised up the street. Baylock yelled to the cab and it stopped for them. They piled in with their bags. Harbin said he wanted a cheap hotel. The driver took a second look at Harbin's attire. Harbin, amiable, asked him what he was look-ing at, and he said he wasn't looking at anything special.

The cab pulled up in front of a miserable-looking place on a small street off Tennessee Avenue. Harbin paid the fare, tipped the driver a quarter and said he wished he could give more. The driver smiled good-naturedly, threw the cab in gear and drove it away.

They entered the hotel and the clerk took them up to a room on the second floor. It was a two-dollar double. It looked ter-rible. The window opened out on the wall of another building and Baylock said they would suffocate in here. Harbin said they wouldn't be here long enough to suffocate.

Baylock asked, "How long we staying?"

"Until I get Gladden."

"When you getting her?"

"Now." Only he didn't feel like going now. He wanted the bed. He was very anxious to hit the bed. His muscles were tired, his arms, after all the arduous driving, were extremely tired. But worst of all were the eyes. His eyes wanted to close and he had to work hard to keep them from closing.

Harbin lit a cigarette, and walked out of the room. Down-stairs in what they used for a lobby he saw a pay phone on the wall and mechanically he took from his coat pocket the folded paper on which was written the address of her hotel and the phone number. He wanted to call her, to tell her he was in town and would see her tomorrow. It would be more convenient to call. It would allow him to walk upstairs and fall into bed. He couldn't remember a time when he had been so tired. The pay phone invited him to start dialing, but he knew that phoning wouldn't be enough. He was deeply aware of the importance of going to her, being with her.

On Tennessee Avenue he walked toward the boardwalk. The sky was still black when he reached the boardwalk, but far out past the beach and the broken line of white breakers he saw the beginnings of thin dawn above the ocean. The boardwalk, still wet, looked as though a corps of polishing experts had been at work on it for weeks. Every fourth lamp along the railing was dimly lit and that was the only light except for the faint push of dawn coming in from the ocean. With that, there was the heat, the unnatural heat that couldn't be coming from the ocean. It had to be coming from the meadows and swamps of New Jersey to the north of the seashore. Along the boardwalk the faces of the beachfront hotels were quiet and listless, waiting passively for the throngs who would come when summer arrived, merely tolerating the sprinkle of guests who now had the best rooms at off-season prices.

He looked back at what had happened on the Pike. It was an actual display of the law of averages. It had been bound to happen sooner or later. Something on the same order had happened once before, a long time ago in Detroit, the night when Gerald Gladden had made the pavement wet with the red coming out of his skull. That night had formed itself to a pattern, and it was being repeated tonight. Because that night, as he ran from the police, he had moved in a direction that took the little girl who was Gerald Gladden's daughter. And tonight the same thing was happening. He was moving toward Gerald Gladden's daughter, to lift her up and carry her away before anything bad could happen to her.

The pattern. And all these years, in modified ways, his every move had followed within the pattern. It was always necessary to get back to Gladden, to be with Gladden, to go with Gladden. It was more than habit and it was deeper than inclination. It was something on the order of a religion, or sublimating himself to a special drug. The root of everything was this throbbing need to take care of Gladden.

A contradiction came into it. He saw the contradiction coming in, beginning that night in the after-hour club when he had suggested to Gladden that she go to Atlantic City and get herself a bit of rest. The contradiction lengthened as he remembered Gladden's asking him to come with her and his saying no. It meant the pattern was beginning to fall apart, making him susceptible to the formation of another pattern and another drug and another religion or whatever in God's name had happened to him as he sat there in the restaurant and found himself being dragged across space by the woman's eyes.

Yet now he was back within the vague yet stern boundaries of the Gladden pattern. As he concentrated on it the vagueness gradually took on emphasis, like a wispy scene gradually brought into clear focus by the turning of a lens. He was digging through the reasons, digging through the layers of reasons for all the moves he had made since the afternoon when Gerald Gladden had found him sick and starving on a western road. He had been an infant, sixteen years old but all the same an infant, an orphan infant, sixteen years old, with nothing in his mind but a drastic need for food, and the piteous bewilderment of an infant begging for aid from a world that wouldn't listen. Only Gerald had listened. Only Gerald had picked him up and given him food. It was stolen food because Gerald had paid for it with money gained from the sale of stolen goods. It was illegal food but it was food, and if he hadn't eaten it he would have died. Later, after their first job together, Gerald had explained this to him. Gerald liked to explain, not only about the tactics and science of burglary, but the philosophy behind it, anyway Gerald's philosophy. Gerald was always contending that burglary is no special field of endeavor, and every animal, including the human being, is a criminal, and every move in life is a part of the vast process of crime. What law, Gerald would ask, could control the need to take food and put it in the stomach? No law, Gerald would say, could erase the practice of taking. According to Gerald, the basic and primary moves in life amounted to nothing more than this business of taking, to take it and get away with it. A fish stole the eggs of another fish. A bird robbed another bird's nest. Among the gorillas, the clever thief became the king of the tribe. Among men, Gerald would say, the princes and kings and tycoons were the successful thieves, either big strong thieves or suave soft-spoken thieves who moved in from the rear. But thieves, Gerald would claim, all thieves, and more power to them if they could get away with it.

He had listened to Gerald because there was no one else to whom he could listen. There was no one else around. He had listened and he had believed. Gerald was the only external. Gerald's teachings were the only teachings. Gerald's arguments were not only forceful in delivery, they were backed with fact and qualified with history. Gerald's mother had been part Indian, her mother all Indian, all Navajo. For Christ's sake, Gerald would yell, take a look at how they robbed the Indians, and how they arranged a set of laws to justify the robbery. Always, when Gerald got himself started on the Navajo theme, he would go on for hours.

Gerald would say that aside from all this, aside from all the filthy dealing involved, the stink of deceit and lies and the lousy taste of conniving and corruption, it was possible for a human being to live in this world and be honorable within himself. To be honorable within oneself, Gerald would say, was the only thing could give living a true importance, an actual nobility. If a man decided to be a burglar and he became a burglar and made his hauls with smoothness and finesse, with accuracy and artistic finish, and got away with the haul, then he was, according to Gerald, an honorable man. But the haul had to be made correctly, and the risks had to be faced with calm and icy nerve, and if associates were involved, the associates had to be treated fairly, the negotiations with the fence had to be straight negotiations. There were categories of burglars just as there were categories of bankers and meat-packers and shoemakers and physicians. There was no such thing as just a burglar, Gerald said, and always when he said this he would bang a fist onto a table or into his palm. There were scientific burglars and daredevil burglars and burglars who moved like turtles and burglars who darted in like spears. There were gentle burglars and semi-gentle burglars and of course there were the lowdown sons of bitches who were never content unless they followed it up with a blackjack or switchblade or bullet. But the big thing to remember, Gerald would say, was this necessity of being a fine burglar, a clean and accurate operator, and honorable inside, damn it, an honorable burglar.

This big thing, Gerald would say, this thing of being honorable, was the only thing, and actually, if a human being didn't have it, there wasn't much point in going on living. As matters stood, life offered very little aside from an occasional plunge into luxurious sensation, which never lasted for long and even while it happened it was accompanied by the dismal knowledge that it would soon be over. In the winter Gerald had a mania for oyster stew, and always while he ate the stew he would complain the plate would soon be empty and his stomach would be too full for him to enjoy another plate. All these things like oyster stew and clean underwear and fresh cigarettes were temporary things, little passing touches of pleasure, limited things, unimportant things. What mattered, what mattered high up there by itself all alone, Gerald would say, was whether things are honorable.

Gerald would always come out strongly and challengingly with the contention that he himself was honorable and had always been honorable. Every promise he had ever made he had kept, even when it made him sick to do so, even when it placed him in actual jeopardy. There was a night when he had promised a girl he would marry her, and knew a moment later it would be a big mistake to marry her, to marry anyone. But he had promised. He couldn't break the promise. He married the girl and he stayed married to her until she died. Telling of it, he would yell and curse himself but he would always end up by describing her as a marvelous woman and it was a damn shame she had to go and die. And besides, Gerald would say, maybe the marriage had not been such a bad mistake, after all. In order for a man to be honorable within himself, it was necessary to carry some sort of a responsibility, a devotion. It was natural and correct that this devotion be aimed at a woman.

Looking back at the times long ago when Gerald had said all these things, Harbin heard them distinctly as though Gerald were talking aloud to him now. The sum of it was the center of it, the core of it, this big thing, this being honorable. Gerald had taught him how to open the lock of a door, the lock of a vault, and how to analyze the combination of a safe, and how to get past certain types of burglar alarms, but the important thing Gerald had taught him was this thing of being honorable.

That was why, when he saw Gerald dead on the pavement, he had raced mechanically to get Gerald's daughter and why, all these years, he had looked after Gladden. That was the only thing for him to do, because it was the honorable thing.

Ahead of him, and rather near, the black bulk of the Million Dollar Pier took itself out upon the ocean. Just a little this side of the pier he saw the unlit electric sign of the hotel where Gladden was staying. It was a small hotel, hemmed in between boardwalk shops and apartments above the shops, but it had a certain independence about it, almost seemed to flaunt itself as one of the beachfront hotels, more dignified and elegant than the hotels off the boardwalk.

Walking in, he couldn't see anyone in the lobby. He hit the bell on the clerk's desk, hit it again and kept on hitting at it in intervals for more than a minute. Then the clerk came in from a side room and showed him a tired, yawning, aged face, some white hair far back on the head, a pair of tired, drooping shoulders.

Automatically the old man said, "We got no rooms." Then he began to wake up as he moved in behind the desk. "Maybe," he said, "we got one empty."

"I don't want a room." Harbin was lost for a moment and then it came to him, the name she said she would use. "I'm looking for Miss Green."

"Nobody here by that name." The old man started to move out from behind the desk, yawning again.

"Why don't you call Miss Green and then you can go back to sleep."

"Buster," the old man said, "I'm going back to sleep right now and I ain't calling Miss Green because we ain't got no Miss Green."

The old man was on his way to the side room when Harbin stepped into his path and showed him a couple of one-dollar bills.

"It's awfully important that I see Miss Green."

The old man looked at the money. "What was that name again?"

Harbin repeated it for him and spelled it for him.

"I think," the old man said, "maybe we got a Miss Irma Green." Now he had the bills and was stuffing them into a vest pocket. "But I'm ready to swear she checked out a couple days ago."

"Let's make sure about that."

The old man started back toward the desk and then stopped and circled his throat with his thin hand. "She's a small, skinny girl? Blonde hair?"

Harbin nodded.

The old man made a face that was meant to be a smile, but it looked as though he was in pain. "Miss Irma Green," he said. "Yes, a very nice little lady. Very nice indeed."

"Call her for me, will you?"

The old man yawned again. He twisted his head and stared up at the wall-clock above the desk. "You know," he said, "this ain't the best hour to go visiting people."

"Call her." Harbin indicated the phone. "Just pick up the phone and call her room."

"We got certain house rules."

"I know you have. You got rules providing a guest with the right to know when she has a visitor."

"Say look, Buster," the old man said. "You standing there and arguing with me?"

Sliding a hand into his trousers pocket, Harbin took out more money, selected a five-dollar bill and showed it to the old man.

"All I want you to do," he said, "is put me on the phone as though it's an outside call."

The old man thought it over for a moment. "I guess there ain't no harm in that."

Harbin gave him the money, frowned slightly while waiting for the switchboard to make contact. The old man nodded toward the phone, and Harbin took it and heard Gladden's voice.

He said, "I'm calling from a few blocks away. I'll be there in five minutes. What's your room number?"

"Three one two. What's wrong? What's happened?"

"We'll talk about it when I see you." He hung up and turned to the old man. "I only want to see the man who's with her. You have my word there won't be any trouble. I won't even talk to him. I just want to see who he is." He watched carefully to get the effect of his words on the old man. The effect was all right and it allowed him to add, "He won't even get a look at me. I'll be in that side room and keep the door open. He won't even know I'm around."

The old man was somewhat mixed up and worried. "Well,

all right," he said, "but we can't afford to have violence. A jealous husband comes to these places looking for his wife and he finds her with a boyfriend and right away we got a battle on our hands. Maybe you'll see him and you'll lose your temper."

Harbin smiled. "I'm not the jealous husband. I'm only a friend looking out for her welfare."

He walked into the side room. It was black in there and he opened the door just wide enough to get a reasonable view of the lobby. He was halfway behind the door and from there he could see the old man fidgeting nervously near the desk. A minute passed, then another minute and Harbin put a cigarette in his mouth and began to chew on it. He watched the movement of the big hand on the wall-clock above the desk. The sound of a descending elevator came against his hearing and he saw the face of the old man turned toward him, the aged eyes very worried, the brow severely wrinkled. He heard the sound of the elevator as it came to a stop, and then the footsteps, and then he saw the double-breasted gabardine suit, the healthy crop of blond hair, the handsome features and aquamarine eyes of the young cop moving past his range of vision beyond the partly opened door.

Chapter XII

H E WAITED there in the side room, unable to handle it. After the initial moments of amazement he knew it wouldn't do any good to think about it. It was something that went beyond thinking. He was scarcely conscious of the old man coming toward him, talking to him, telling him that he could come out now, the man left the hotel and it was all right to come out now.

As he emerged from the side room into the lobby he heard the old man saying, "Was it someone you know?"

Harbin shook his head.

"Then I guess everything's all right," the old man said.

"Sure." Harbin smiled, and stepped toward the elevator.

"Now hold on there." The old man moved quickly between Harbin and the elevator.

"I promised there wouldn't be any trouble," Harbin said. "Besides, she's expecting me."

The old man searched for some kind of a rebuttal, couldn't find any, made a gesture of surrender with his two hands and turned away from the elevator. Harbin entered the elevator, put a lit match to the cigarette in his mouth. He closed the elevator door and pushed the button.

As he entered Gladden's room, as he saw her stepping back and away from the door, the first thing he noticed was the white of her face. It was paper white and her yellow eyes were dull with some weird kind of fatigue. He wasn't smiling at her. He knew he ought to start this with a smile, but getting a smile started now would be like trying to walk on water.

"Start packing," he said. "Snappy."

She didn't move. "Tell me."

"We're hot." He knew there was no way of getting around it. Without looking at her, he said, "Dohmer's dead." He told her of what had happened on the road. He told her to hurry and start packing.

But she didn't move. She stood there gazing past him, at the door. He began taking her clothes from the narrow closet and throwing them on the bed. Then he had dresser drawers open and he was rapidly filling her suitcase.

He heard her saying, "I can't go with you."

That took him away from the suitcase. "What's the rub?"

"I've met someone."

"Oh." He came back to the suitcase but didn't continue to fill it. She had her back to him and he was curious to see the condition of her eyes. He took a step toward her, then decided to stay where he was, to let her build it in her own way.

A long string of silent moments ended as she said, "I want to get out, Nat. From now on I want to be out of it. I always wanted to be out of it but you kept me in."

"How do you figure that?" he asked. "I never told you to stay in against your will."

"My will was to stay," she said. "Because of you." Now she turned and faced him. "I wanted to be near you. I wanted you and I wanted you to want me. But you didn't want me, you never wanted me, you never will. I've had a lousy time, I've gone through nights when I've torn pillows apart with my teeth, so hungry for you I wanted to smash down the wall and break into your room. You knew it, Nat. Don't tell me you didn't know it."

He put his hands behind his back and cracked his knuckles.

Gladden said, "All right, so I've never been much with brains. But it didn't need a lot of thinking. The point was, I went through something we all go through. I grew up. You didn't see it taking place but it was taking place all the time. I was growing up, from a little girl into a woman, and I wanted to be your woman. But what the hell could I do? I couldn't bang you over the head."

"Maybe you should have tried that." He sat down on the edge of the bed. "This comes at a wonderful time."

She moved toward him, reached out to touch him, then pulled her hand back. "You've always been so good to me, you've taken care of me, you've been everything to me but what I was hoping you'd be. That isn't your fault. It isn't mine, either. It's just a miserable state of affairs."

He smiled dimly. "Miserable is one way of putting it."

She detected the odd currents underneath his tone. She said, "I hope you won't hold this against me."

He looked up at her. "What's his name?"

"Finley. Charles Finley."

"What does he do? Tell me about him."

"He sells automobiles. Salesman on a used car lot in Philly. I met him the second day I was here. On the boardwalk. We just got to talking and it happened sort of fast. I guess I was ripe for it, ready for it, he got me at just the right time, that night I went back to Philly and they told me you walked out and I came back here and called him up."

"You really go for him?"

"He has a lot of charm."

"I didn't ask you that."

"All right," she said, "I think I go for him."

Harbin stood up. "When did you last see him?"

"He was here tonight. He was here when I got your call. When you said you were coming I told him to leave and I'd see him for lunch." She took a deep breath. "Don't ask me to break the date. I really want to see him, I want to keep on seeing him. I don't want to let him go." She took hold of Harbin's arms. "I won't let him go and you can't make me let him go."

"Don't get wild," he spoke gently.

"He's overboard for me," she said, "and if I told you I wasn't glad about that I'd be a no-good liar. I want to have some kind of a life for myself and you've got no right to keep me from having it."

"Quit ripping my sleeves." He frowned at her.

She was breathing very hard. Her fingernails cut through the fabric of his jacket. He twisted, got a grip on her wrists, forced her away. Going away, she staggered, bumped against a wall, stayed flattened against the wall, staring at him and taking deep, gasping breaths.

Harbin shook his head slowly. He gazed at the floor. "It's a pity. It's a damned pity."

"Not for me."

He looked at her. "Especially for you." Then he waved her to quiet as she opened her mouth, and he said, "Listen, Gladden, just listen to me and try to take it relaxed. You've been sucked in. This man is manipulating."

"Don't."

"This man, I tell you, is working on a job."

"Don't. Please don't."

"This man Finley is a cop—"

"Nat, Nat," she cut in pleadingly. "I told you I'm not a little girl anymore. I've grown up, I know the alphabet. Quit selling me short, will you?"

He was suddenly hit by too much weariness and he threw himself on his back on the bed, his arms flopping down, spread wide against the bedcover. "If you'll try to listen," he said, his eyes half-closed, "I'll try to tell you. This Finley is one of the cops I talked to on the night we made the haul. A few minutes ago I was in a side room off the lobby as he came from the elevator and walked out. I recognized him."

"Why are you doing this?" she cried. "What are you trying to arrange?"

"I'm not doing the arranging. Finley's taking care of that." Something like a sigh came from his lips. "The cop angle doesn't mean anything. He holds on to that only for convenience. And from his position, you don't mean anything, either. He doesn't want you. He wants the emeralds."

He saw her looking at him in a way she had never before looked at him. He heard her saying, "Why do you lie to me?"

"Have I ever lied to you?"

"No," she said. "So why do you lie to me now?"

"I'm not lying. If you want all of it, I'll give you all of it."

She nodded slowly, and he started to tell her. It was easy to start, but when he came to the Della proposition, he had trouble handling it, making it clear, moving ahead with it. She stood there and watched him as he struggled with it, as he managed to take himself back to the house on the hill and then the maneuvering in Lancaster and the transit from the black woods to the road to the train to Philadelphia to the Black Horse Pike and to here and now.

He said, "I can see Finley planning the thing, making sure there's no hitch. The day I took you to the train, he followed us. I can see him following us. He already had checked the Spot, and Della was watching the Spot. So there at the station when you got on the train, he got on, too. When you arrived here in Atlantic City, he was right behind you, watching you as you checked in at this hotel, then beginning to work on you here in Atlantic City while Della was working on me back there."

She moved toward the bed, sat down on the edge of it. Her breathing had quieted somewhat. She said, "Some people do things in a roundabout way."

"Finley's way is not roundabout. It's quality from the word go. He has his eye on a hundred thousand dollars worth of emeralds. That's all. But that's plenty. He built this thing so it would work slowly, going upstairs a step at a time, first establishing the contact, bringing your guard down while Della brought mine down, figuring on a week or two weeks or three or maybe a couple of months. And even if it took six months and maybe even more than that, it was still a matter of a hundred thousand dollars and it would be worth all the trouble and all the waiting."

She stared at the bedboard behind Harbin's head. "Emeralds," she said. "Chunks of green glass."

Harbin sat up just a little. "Forget the emeralds," he said. "The major item is three dead policemen. That's something new with us." He sat up completely, swung his legs over the side of the bed. "It's why you've got to go with me. Stay with me. You're implicated, Gladden. I wish you weren't but you are. You and Baylock and myself. The three of us, we're in a situation where we've got to run. We've got to keep on running."

"Are we that hot?"

"I don't know exactly how hot we are. I do know we can't stay around just in order to find out. If we move now, we'll be able to keep on moving."

Gladden was quiet for a little while. Then she said, "I thought I was out of it. The feeling I had was wonderful, like getting rid of a terrible throbbing headache that I'd had all my life. Now I'm back in it again. I have the headache again." She stood up, walked around the bed to the door, faced the door as though it was an iron wall. She turned again, coming toward him. "You've pulled me back into it."

"Circumstances."

"Not circumstances." There was a lack of reasoning in her eyes and in her voice. "No, not circumstances. You. You, Nat. Keeping me in this time just like you've always kept me in. I tell you I don't want to be in." Her entire body quivered. "I don't want it, I don't want it, I never wanted it, I want to be out of it." She came close to him. "Out of it, out of it."

"If you'll think it over," he said, "you'll see the point."

Gladden said, "There's only one reason you keep me around your neck. It's safer that way."

He couldn't speak. The thing that crushed down on him was the sum weight of all the years, and her voice was a lance cutting through it, breaking it all up and showing him it added up to nothing but a horrible joke he had played on himself.

But he knew something more was coming, and he waited for it like a man tied to railroad tracks waiting for the impact. He looked at her and saw the whiteness of her face, the strange blaze in the yellow of her eyes.

And then it came. "You bastard," she said. "You made me think you were looking out for me. You were looking out for yourself. You dirty tricky bastard, I hate your guts—"

He moved his head, but her arm was quicker, her extended fingers jabbing at his face, her fingernails ripping and he felt the slash, the icy burn. He saw her stepping back and away, her face twisted, her teeth showing.

"Here's your chance," she said. "Why don't you make it a real guarantee? Do what you've wanted to do all along. Get rid of me once and for all. Make sure I'll never talk and you'll always be safe." She pointed at her throat. "Look how skinny, how easy it would be. Take you no time at all."

The door seemed to be moving toward him. As he opened it, with Gladden behind him, he waited and didn't know what he was waiting for. The room became quiet like a chamber with nobody in it. He opened the door wider, walked out, closed the door slowly as though Gladden was asleep in there and he didn't want to wake her up. He walked down the hall toward the elevator.

Chapter XIII

BAYLOCK SEEMED dead except for his breathing, a sick troubled grinding breathing, the chest going up and down in a spasmodic way. Very little air was coming into the room and Harbin saw that he could open the window wider if he wanted to but he didn't have the inclination or the strength. He lowered himself onto the sagging bed beside Baylock and just before closing his eyes he told himself at least he ought to take off his shoes. But already he was going into sleep and his last conscious thought was that he had forgotten to put out the light and the light would have to stay on.

Almost eleven hours later Baylock woke him up. He asked Baylock what time it was and Baylock said three-fifteen. He rubbed his eyes and saw a thin slice of sunlight coming through the window after edging itself around the wall of the neighboring building.

"I knew she wouldn't be there," Baylock said.

"She was there."

"Why didn't you bring her here?"

"She didn't want to come."

"What's that again?"

Harbin was off the bed, moving toward a chipped washbowl. He put some cold water in his mouth, swished it around in there, put more in and swallowed it, put some on his face and turned and looked at Baylock.

"You'll like this," he said. "This is what you've been wanting."

"Maybe you better wake up more," Baylock was taking his turn at the washbowl. "You're still from fog."

"I'm wide awake," Harbin studied Baylock at the washbowl. "You wanted her out of it. All right, now she's out of it."

Baylock frowned. "How come?"

"That's the way she wants it."

"You told her what happened?"

"I told her everything."

"You told her everything," Baylock said, "and she wants to be out of it. Now that's good. That's really pretty good. She finds out we got ourselves in a serious mess and we're wanted and she comes out with this interesting statement that she ain't with us any more."

Harbin lit a cigarette. "I can use some coffee."

"Just like that," Baylock said, "she's out of it."

"Let's get some coffee."

Baylock didn't move. "I'm too worked up to drink coffee. I'm too worried."

"You don't know what worry is," Harbin forced a smile. "Here's real worry for you. Our friend made contact with her."

"Our friend?" Baylock was far away from it.

"The cop."

Baylock remained far away, unable to get himself to move any nearer.

Harbin said, "His name is Finley. Charley Finley. He traced her down here and it seems he's that sun and salt air you were talking about."

Reacting like an animal, Baylock made a move toward the door, changed his mind, started toward the suitcases, changed his mind about that, began to move here and there, darting little motions that got him back to where he had started. He whined, "I told you, I told you, don't tell me I didn't tell you."

"All right," Harbin said. "You told me. You were correct and I was wrong. Does that clear it up or do you want me to start chopping off my fingers?"

"We're hemmed in. Now we can't budge."

"Why not? Finley doesn't know where we are."

"You sure of that?" Baylock said. "Look at the way he moves around. This is a trace artist. It's a very special gift. One in a million has it. Like a mind reader, a dealer in some kind of magic, and don't laugh, I tell you don't laugh." He saw that Harbin was not laughing and he went on, "For all we know he may have us spotted right now."

"I wouldn't say that's impossible."

"What do we do about it?" Baylock asked.

Harbin shrugged. He looked at the door. Then he looked at the window. Baylock followed his eyes. And then they looked at each other.

"The only way to know," Harbin said, "is to find out." He frowned just a little, thinking it over. "Finley could have followed me from her hotel last night. Followed me here. I doubt it and if I didn't know what he's done already I'd bet a grand against a nickel it couldn't be possible." He rubbed fingers across his chin. "All I know for sure is I need some coffee. While I'm out I'll look around. You wait here."

"How long?"

"Half hour."

"Suppose it's longer."

"It won't be."

"But suppose it is?"

"In that case," Harbin said, "you'd better skip and skip fast."

"With the emeralds?"

"Listen," Harbin said. "If it was you going out and me waiting here, and you said you'd be back in thirty minutes and you didn't come back in thirty minutes, I'd go for that window, and I wouldn't take the emeralds. And when I'd hit the street I'd start moving in a hurry."

Baylock shook his head very slowly. "I wouldn't leave the emeralds here. You know I wouldn't leave them here."

Harbin shrugged.

Baylock said, "If you're not back in thirty minutes, I'll start aiming toward my sister's place in Kansas City. You know the address and you know if I say I'm going there, I'm going there. And if you can manage to get there, you'll find me there with the emeralds." He tightened his lips. "Unless I'm grabbed before I can get there. Or dead."

Harbin said, "Should I bring you some coffee? Something to eat?"

"Just bring yourself back."

Harbin started toward the door. Baylock moved quickly, with a kind of frenzy, went sliding in to place himself against the door, to face Harbin and show him a pair of disturbed eyes.

Baylock said, "I want to get it straight about Gladden. What do we do with her?"

"Nothing."

"What if she rats?"

"Why would she do that?" Harbin asked.

"She's out of it, that's why. When they're out of it they're in a position to rat. I'm worried, I tell you, and I think we ought to do something about Gladden."

"Do this for me," Harbin said. "Don't mention her name." He opened his mouth wide and something like a sob came out, and he turned his head quickly to hide his face from Baylock, and he took his fist and slammed it hard into his opened palm. He threw one swift glance at Baylock and saw Baylock looking at him with pity. It went into him like the orange end of a poker. He pulled the door toward him, went through and heard the door crash shut. He started fast down the narrow hall, came to the stairs and told himself to stop the rush. There was no need to rush. He was going out to take a look around and drink some coffee.

Downstairs, he could feel midday heat pouring in on him. It was like syrup. He felt his face get sticky and just a bit itchy. On the street moving slowly down Tennessee Avenue he saw the striped pole of a barber shop and decided on a shave.

The shave did something for him and he felt more alive as he came off Tennessee and hit Atlantic Avenue. But the sticky heat was really serious in Atlantic and the tingling effects of the shave were fading away while he looked around for a restaurant. Very few people were on the street. He saw some natives of the city walking across Atlantic in the direction of the beach. They seemed sullen, annoyed with their town for allowing itself to be messed up with this wet heat and angry at their ocean for not doing something about it. They wore beach robes and sandals and there was a sacrificial air about them as they headed toward the beach, as though this was something unfit for natives of Atlantic City at this time of year. It was all right for the vacationers because anything was all right for the vacationers, but natives of this town didn't deserve this weather, and it was an outrage.

He glanced at his wristwatch. Eight minutes. He had been out for eight minutes, and twenty-two minutes remained. A restaurant sign displayed itself on the other side of the street. He crossed and entered, sat down at a sloppy counter and told the waitress he wanted coffee. The waitress made a comment about how hot it was today for coffee, and maybe he would like it iced. He said he didn't want it iced. The waitress said it was good when it was iced. Harbin said he had never tried it iced and would appreciate their terminating the discussion; the waitress said the reason the world was like it was could be attributed to the fact that too many people were hard to get along with. She gave him a cup of black coffee and stood there watching him as he started on it. She was a short girl who looked Italian and restless, and below the short sleeves her fat arms were shiny with sweat. Harbin raised his eyes from the coffee and saw that she was watching him. He smiled at her. She took her eyes away from him and gazed through the opened doorway at the yellow, steaming street. She let out a long sigh and folded her arms and leaned back against the selling side of the counter.

Harbin glanced at his wristwatch and ordered another cup of coffee. She gave it to him and he lit a cigarette and began sipping the coffee, watching her as she stood there looking out toward the street. The sun came in and sent a yellow glaze all over her, so that it seemed as though she stood in the center of a bowl filled with bright yellow syrup. She put out her tongue and licked some wetness away from under her lip. Then a dark ribbon slanted across the yellow, so that she was in shadow and the shadow was caused by someone entering the restaurant. The Italian girl moved to greet the customer, and Harbin lowered his head toward the cup, started the coffee toward his mouth, felt the cup shake in his hands as the perfume hit him and he knew it was the perfume of Della.

Chapter XIV

DELLA SAT down at the counter beside him. She wore an ivory-colored blouse and skirt but even before he took note of her appearance he knew she would appear cool. Her tan hair gleamed in a quiet way, her face was quiet and cool, her voice cool as she told the waitress to fix her an orangeade.

Turning to look outside, Harbin saw the green Pontiac parked on the other side of Atlantic. His fingers made a little drumbeat on the counter. "You get around."

"Only when it's necessary."

He looked at her. "What's necessary?"

"Being here," she said. "With you."

"Unless I'm very much mistaken, I thought that was a dead issue."

"You know it isn't dead."

He worked on a little sigh and got it going. "Tell me all about that."

Della sat there looking at the orangeade. She said, "I want you to do something for me. I want you to listen very carefully and try to believe what I'm saying. There's a chance you know already, but if you don't know, you'll hear it now. If you refuse to believe it, I can't do anything about that. It happens there are quite a few things I can't do anything about. Like turning night into day. Like stopping the rain when it's raining." She turned fully to him.

She said, "The night I met you there in that restaurant it was no accident. It was planned. A solid plan to have me work on you and get the emeralds. Of course you remember what happened the night you made the haul. You remember having a chat with two policemen outside the mansion? You remember that clearly?"

He nodded. He took a toothpick from a glass container, broke it in two and began to play with the pieces.

"One of them," Della said, "you saw was a rather young man. Early thirties. I want to tell you about that party. His name when he functions as a policeman is Charley Hacket. When he functions for the sake of Charley his last name is Finley." She lifted the glass of orangeade, looked at it as though the color pleased her, then put it down. "This man Charley is out to get the emeralds. Most of the time he's a shakedown artist and he's usually satisfied with a cut. I know that because I know the way he operates. I've been working with him for a little more than a year. But this time he sees big loot and he wants all of it."

Harbin took his eyes away from the toothpick production and he looked at her. He saw Della and nothing more than Della. Not the menace. Not the enemy in the woods. Only Della.

"This Charley Hacket," she said, "is very much from brains and when I first met him I could see that right away. And then of course I could see the looks he had and the charm and there was something else I thought he had and even when I found out he didn't have it I went on trying to believe it was there. When he asked me to work these jobs with him I did it only because it meant being with him. I certainly didn't need the money. And for sure I'm not the kind of mental case that does it for excitement. I did it because it meant being with him, and I had drilled it into myself that I needed to be with him. The night I changed my mind about that was the night I came across you."

Harbin took another toothpick from the container and broke it in half. He put one piece at right angles to the other and then he switched them around. Then he pushed the bits of wood aside. "Why did you wait until now? Why didn't you tell me all this before?"

"I was afraid," she said. "I wanted it to be just you and me, no emeralds, no Charley, no deals and transactions, just you and me. I was trying to work it out in my mind, find a method to slide away from Charley, get that ended so it would be just you and me. In order to do that I needed time. I wanted to tell you, I was dying to tell you. But I was terribly afraid of losing you."

"Not afraid of Hacket?"

"No." Then she gave a little shrug. "I know the way it is with Hacket. I know I mean more to him than the emeralds. I know I'm his major weakness and he wants me more than he wants life. So what? So if he discovered the way I feel about you he would probably kill me. Or both of us. But I've never really been afraid of that. I've only been afraid of losing you. Last night in the woods when you walked away I had the notion of killing myself; the idea actually seemed attractive."

She picked up the glass of orangeade and took some. She savored it, took some more. "I did a lot of thinking about it, knowing definitely that life is worthwhile only when you have a chance of getting what you want. I told myself if I couldn't have you it wouldn't pay to continue. All night long I thought about it and early this morning I was still thinking about it, ripping myself apart thinking about it when the phone rang and it was Hacket calling long distance from here, telling me you were here, wanting to know what went wrong. I told him I didn't know, I said you had just walked out on me without giving a reason. Hacket told me not to worry about that. He said it would work out much better this way—" She frowned just a little. "I don't see any reaction. I thought you'd react when I said that Hacket was here in town."

He smiled at her. "Most of what you're telling me, I already know. I know he came here to work on Gladden."

She sat there and stared at him. "How did you find out? What put you on the track?"

"You did. I'll tell you all about it when we're old and grey. Maybe sooner." He played with the toothpicks again. "What did Hacket say on the phone?"

"He kept patting himself on the back, telling me how clever he was, the way he handled it when you came to her room at the hotel, how he waited in a doorway or someplace until you walked out on the boardwalk, how he followed you to that little dump off Tennessee Avenue."

Harbin looked at Della, then at the toothpicks, then at Della again.

Della said, "I told him I was coming to Atlantic City. He said no, he could handle it alone. I told him he shouldn't get too hasty and I was coming here and we wouldn't discuss it further. He said he'd be sitting in his car, parked on Tennessee Avenue, keeping an eye on your hotel. I met him there and said I'd take over. I said he looked beat and it would be a good idea if he went back to his room and got some sleep. We fought about that for a while but finally he gave in. I backed my car up on Tennessee Avenue, waited there, and then I saw you coming out from the side street. Then and there I would have called to you but I saw you going into a barber shop and I knew we couldn't talk in a barber shop. So I waited. And when you came out, I followed you. And here I am now, I'm here with you, and I want to stay with you, go with you—"

"Where?"

"Our place."

His head went down, then it came up very slowly, then down again. And he was nodding. And then he trembled suddenly, as though trying to pull himself out of a trance. He tasted metal in his mouth, trembled again, went very deep into himself and said, "It's got to be figured out."

"Let's figure it."

"There's Hacket."

"We'll get rid of him."

Harbin leaned his elbows on the counter. "I guess there's no other way of getting around it."

"No other way," she said. "It will have to be done." She took more orangeade. "Anything else?"

He looked at her. He didn't say anything.

She said, "You're thinking of Gladden."

He took his eyes away from her. He didn't say anything.

She said, "Do something for me. Stop thinking of Gladden."

It was difficult, but he managed to do that for her. He worked at it, pushed with his mind as though he was heaving against a wall with his shoulder. He felt the resistance, and then strangely and suddenly it melted away but there was something else and he said, "There's something else."

"All right, we'll face it. What is it?"

"It's a situation. Maybe you saw the papers today. Maybe you didn't." He gave way to a sigh. "Last night there was some heavy trouble on the Black Horse Pike."

He told her of the three policemen who had died from bullets on the Pike, and of how Dohmer had died, and of what was now happening to Baylock, the fear and the worry, the lack of control, Baylock jittery, Baylock more or less immobilized. And he said, "I can't walk out on Baylock without first telling him about it."

"What good will that do?"

"He needs assurance. He needs instructions. I can't leave him with the feeling he's being let down. I've got to go back to the room and have a talk with him."

"He'll argue with you."

"I'll meet all his arguments."

"He'll get excited. Maybe you'll have trouble."

"There won't be any trouble."

"He'll think you're trying to put something over."

"He won't have any reason to think that," Harbin said. "I'm letting him have all the emeralds. Then I'm saying goodbye to him. Then I'm coming back here. To you. We'll get in your car and we'll start driving. We'll go to the place on the hill and we'll stay there together. I know for sure now that's the only way it can be. Nothing can break this up between you and me. Nothing. It was bound to be this way. We have something here that neither of us can get away from. When I left you there in the woods last night, you were someone else and I was someone else. But last night was a long time ago."

He put some silver on the table and stood up. He smiled at her and he saw her smiling back at him and he didn't want to leave, even though it was firm in his mind that he would be returning within minutes. Then Della nodded toward the door, her eyes telling him to go and come back quickly. He left the restaurant and crossed Atlantic Avenue and walked fast toward Tennessee. He came onto Tennessee and walked faster as he approached the narrow side street. Entering the hotel, he felt light, his head was clear.

In the upstairs hall the heat was dark and thick and carried the decay of the people who lived in these rooms. Harbin came to the door and opened it and the first thing he saw was two suitcases wide open, their contents flung around. The third suitcase, the one containing the emeralds, was closed. The next thing he noticed was Baylock. On the floor, knees bent, Baylock had one arm across his eyes and the other arm rigid behind him. Baylock's eyes were very wide and the pupils were trying to climb into his forehead. Blood from his hammered head was bright and flowing and spilling down from the split skull in a wide stream that stayed wide as it reached the shoulder, then became a glistening red ribbon headed toward the elbow. Baylock was almost dead and while Harbin stood there and looked at him he tried to open his mouth to say something. This was as much as Baylock could do, and in the midst of trying to open his mouth, he pulled back his head and died.

Chapter XV

HARBIN ALLOWED his head to turn slowly and he looked at the unopened suitcase. It told him what he needed to know, but it was a matter of reaching a conclusion and not being able to do anything about it. He wouldn't have time to make the door, and the window was foolish. The closet door, partly open, now opened wider, and Charley Hacket came out of the closet with a revolver. The butt that had smashed Baylock's head was red with Baylock's blood.

"For Christ's sake," Harbin said, "don't use that thing, keep your head. Whatever you do, keep your head."

"Shut up." Hacket's voice was smooth pebbles on velvet. "Get on the bed, face down."

Harbin put himself on the bed and let his face go into the pillow. He saw himself receiving it as Baylock had received it. His lips moved against the pillow. "This won't gain you anything."

"Quit bargaining," Hacket said, "unless you have something to sell."

Harbin had his brain focused on the unopened suitcase, the suitcase Hacket had been about to open when footsteps coming down the hall had told Hacket to slide into the closet. He wondered what Hacket was doing now. He wondered whether Hacket was looking at the suitcase.

"Where are the emeralds?"

There was a sudden hysteria in Hacket's tone and Harbin grabbed at it as though it were a rope dangling toward him with quicksand the only other thing around.

Harbin said, "It's got to be business."

"You're in no position to talk business."

"You want the emeralds?"

"Now."

"That's an order I can't fill," Harbin said. "I can't manufacture emeralds for you. All I can do is take you to where you'll find the haul."

There was a quiet. Then Hacket told him to turn around.

Harbin turned, started to sit up and Hacket said, "What I don't like about you is you're too scared."

"Sure." Harbin inclined his head toward the gun. "What have I got to be scared about?" He indicated the gun. "Just be sensible, Charley. That's all I ask. Be sensible."

"All right, I'll be sensible. I'll ask you a sensible question. Where are the emeralds?"

"If I tell you," Harbin said, "you'll kill me anyway. And even then you have no guarantee I was telling the truth."

"We can't get around that."

"Be smart, Charley. I don't have to give you ideas. You know how to frame ideas."

"What are you pitching?"

"No pitch, Charley. Just trying to stack things up and get a total. There's you, there's me, there's the emeralds. And—"

"And that's all."

"That isn't all." Harbin said it slowly and with great emphasis. He waited.

He saw the hysteria in Charley Hacket's eyes and in the little jerky movement of the underlip. He knew he had to depend on the hysteria but he couldn't depend on it too long, because it was the hysteria that had caused Hacket to go in for killing. It was hysterical impatience that had brought Hacket up to this room, pure compulsive ignition working Hacket's arm to bring the gun butt crashing into Baylock's skull. Harbin told himself he was dealing with a certain kind of twisted personality and at any moment the gun might go off.

He heard Hacket saying, "What else is there?"

"The girl."

"The girl," Hacket said, "is nowhere. Is nothing. You can't tell me anything about the girl." Then the lips worked up a little at the corners, the teeth showed and it was almost a smile. "You've known her for years and I've only known her for days. But I think I know her better than you."

"You don't even know her right name." Harbin sat up straighter. "Her name isn't Irma Green. Her name is Gladden. Now if you want it, I'll let you have it." Without waiting, he went on, "You were sucked in, Charley. She lured you in. You started the game but after that it was strictly her play. You were handed a fast hustle and don't be too surprised now when I tell you she has you down pat, you're in the palm of her hand, she can do whatever she wants with you."

The corners of Hacket's lips came down. "She knows from zero."

"From plenty."

"Like what?"

"Your identity."

"My face?" Hacket chuckled for a moment. "What's a face?"

"I don't mean your face, Charley. I mean your name. Not the name you gave her, not Charley Finley. I mean the other name, the real name, the name you didn't want her to know. But she found out."

Hacket stared. "You're a liar."

"Sometimes," Harbin admitted. "But not at this point. I tell you Gladden found out. Don't ask me how. I've never been able to figure the way she operates. All I know is, she thinks a hundred moves ahead of anyone she's dealing with. That goes for me as well as you."

Hacket threw a hand toward the back of his head and rubbed his hair up and down. "What did she tell you my name was?"

"Hacket."

Hacket said quickly and loudly, "How did she find out? Tell me how she found out."

"I asked her that and she told me to go get her a drink of water. So I went and got her a drink of water. You see, Charley, I work for her. You see how it is? She's the head figure. She gives the orders. She's in charge of everything. You see what I'm getting at?"

"Say it, God damn you. Go on and say it."

"Gladden has the emeralds."

Behind the gun the face became hard wax, becoming white and whiter as the lips stiffened. The aquamarine eyes looked down at the gun and then looked at Harbin. The eyes frightened Harbin and he wondered how much longer he would be alive in this room. He knew the chances were that in less than a minute from now he wouldn't be alive. He realized he had made a good try and he had pushed it across as well as it could be gotten across. But the one thing he couldn't handle was the fact that Hacket was very hysterical and in the mood to kill. He wondered if there was anything he could say.

He said, "Neither of us want to die."

"I'm holding the gun."

"The gun," Harbin said, "is a minor item. I'm not talking about the gun. I'm talking about the rap." He indicated Baylock on the floor. "There's something." He said it as though it was comparatively unimportant, and then he put the big worry out in front where they could both look at it. "Maybe you saw the papers this morning."

"No."

"Last night. On the Black Horse Pike. All they did was stop us for speeding. Three of them in a patrol car. One of them saw one of us with a gun. That started it. The business ended with all of them dead and one of us dead." Again he indicated the body on the floor. "Now we have that. And don't you think that's enough grief for this party?"

"I want the emeralds."

"As hot as they are?"

"I want them."

"As far as I'm concerned, you can have them."

"I don't believe you," Hacket moved in a little to aim the revolver at Harbin's stomach. "You still want them, don't you? Don't you?" The teeth showed. "Don't you?"

"No," Harbin said, wanting to say it again, wanting to plead, knowing it wouldn't do any good to plead. Just then he heard the sound in the hall outside near the door. He saw Hacket's head turning and knew Hacket was hearing it.

The sound was directly outside the door and the next thing was knuckles against the door. Then they both heard her voice. Hacket opened the door, keeping the gun on Harbin.

As Della walked in, her eyes were pulled to the red on the floor and Baylock's dead face resting against the shiny red. She turned away quickly from that. She waited until Hacket had closed the door and then she stared at him. Her voice was low and quivered just a little. "What are you, a lunatic?"

Hacket stood looking at the door. "I couldn't help it."

"That means you're a lunatic." Della glanced briefly at Harbin. Her head turned slowly, her eyes came back to Hacket. "I told you to wait in your room."

Hacket blinked a few times. "I've had too much waiting. I got fed up with waiting."

"I'm getting fed up with you." Della pointed to the dead body on the floor. "Look at that. Just look at it."

"Quit giving me hell." Hacket blinked a few more times. "I'm having enough hell." Suddenly he frowned at her. "What made you come here?"

"I called your room." The quivering had gone out of her voice. "There was no answer." Her eyes were drawn back to Baylock on the floor. She moved strangely toward the body and all at once she whirled and came toward Hacket and cried, "What in God's name is the matter with you?"

"I want to get this thing ended."

"This is a fine way to get it ended."

"You worried?"

"Sure I'm worried."

"Quit worrying." Hacket suddenly smiled widely. He seemed extremely pleased about something. "I'm glad you're here. It's a good thing you came. You couldn't have come at a better time. That's one of the nicest things about you, Della. You always know just when to arrive. As he finished it, he sent the smile toward Harbin. "Thank the lady," he told Harbin. "If she hadn't walked in, you'd be dead now."

"I know that." Harbin nodded seriously. He looked at Della, his face expressionless. "Thanks, lady."

Hacket continued to smile. He gestured with the gun. "Say it again."

"Thanks, lady. Thanks very much."

"Now say it once more—" Hacket began to laugh. He let his head go far back and his body vibrated with the laughing. It was sick laughing and it was getting louder. Della waited until the laughing filled the room and then she stepped in close to Hacket and sent the back of her hand across his face. He went on laughing and Della hit him again. While she hit him he had his eyes wide open and aiming along with the gun at Harbin.

Della hit Hacket hard across the face and gradually the laughing stopped. Hacket blinked a great many times. He began to shake his head slowly as though trying to figure himself out and couldn't do so. After some moments he gazed pleadingly at Della and stood there and waited for her to say something. When she didn't respond to this, Hacket pulled himself away from the depth of himself, came up to the surface of himself, showed it in the way he pushed his chest out, lifted his chin, set his feet solidly against the floor. A brightness came into the aquamarine eyes and it was surface brightness. Harbin realized Hacket was trying to re-establish himself with himself and with Della. It seemed that Hacket believed fully in his ability to do this.

Hacket's tone was in harmony with the way he stood there. "The girl's name is Gladden. Now I pay her a visit and when I walk in I call her Irma, Irma Green. And when I walk out I have the emeralds." He glanced at Della. "When I come back here I have the emeralds and you'll be waiting here for me." He looked at Harbin. "You'll be here, too, and once I have the emeralds I'll be in a happy frame of mind, maybe I'll let you walk out of here alive. Remember, I say maybe, I don't guarantee anything."

Harbin was thinking of Gladden. He tried hard not to believe that Hacket was going out to kill Gladden. He heard Hacket talking to Della but the words didn't mean anything, the words were vague symbols blanketed by the realization that he was saving his own life at the expense of Gladden's life. In order to keep from dying, he had decided to use something, and he had used Gladden. He saw Gladden dying. He saw Gladden dead. He closed his eyes and saw it and felt it. Then he opened his eyes and looked at Della. He told himself it would be all right. Soon he would be here alone in the room with Della and together they would know how to work it out, they would scheme a way to get to Gladden before Hacket got to her. They would work it out. He told himself he was sure it would all be all right.

His head came up and he saw Della. She looked deeply thoughtful. Then a different look came onto her face as Hacket offered her the gun. Hacket was moving toward the door. Della stood still with the gun in her hand, showing it to Harbin, showing him the look on her face that was a puzzling kind of look, the kind of look he had never seen on her face before. Now Hacket was at the door. The strange look stayed on Della's face. It began to bother Harbin. He heard Hacket opening the door.

He heard Hacket saying, "This won't take long. Just hold him here and entertain him until I get back."

The door opened and Hacket walked out.

Chapter XVI

Harbin looked at the closed door and heard the footsteps going away down the hall, then going down the stairs and fading. He felt his head turning toward the gun in Della's hand.

It was time for her to lay the gun aside. The gun remained in her hand. The strange look remained on her face. His eyes asked her why she was pointing the gun at him and her eyes gave him no answer.

He said, "We didn't arrange it this way. Why did you come here?"

"You heard what I told Charley. That's it. I had a feeling. I phoned his room and he wasn't there. I just had a feeling."

"That isn't enough." For a moment he forgot about the gun. His eyes went into her. "How did you know it was this room?"

"Charley had given me the number."

Harbin took his eyes away from her and stared at the wall behind her head. "I'm wondering how Charley knew the room number."

"He got it when he followed you here last night. When he follows people he really follows them. He had his eyes on you from the time you left Gladden until the time you walked up here."

"Charley's brilliant."

"You're brilliant too." Her face did not change. "What took place here? What did you sell him?"

"He came to get the emeralds and after he killed Baylock he opened two suitcases. He was about to open the third when I arrived. I had to talk him out of shooting me. He was very anxious to shoot me."

Della looked at the unopened suitcase. "They in there?"

Harbin nodded. He made a gesture to indicate that she should put the gun aside. The gun stayed on him.

His lips pressed hard against his teeth. "What are you doing?"

"Keeping you here."

"Like Charley ordered?"

"Charley has nothing to do with it."

"Then why?" he asked. "What do you want?"

"It's not what I want. It's what I don't want. I don't want you to go away."

"I'm not going away. I only want to get to Gladden before Charley gets to her. He's out to kill her. You understand that, don't you? You know as well as I, we're up against a time element."

Della spoke slowly. "I'm giving Charley all the time he needs."

"Della—"

"I want him to kill her."

Harbin was up and away from the bed. He was moving toward the gun.

Della pushed the gun at him. "Stand back. You try to take it from me and I'll pull the trigger. Then I'll pull it on myself."

Harbin felt very weak. He leaned against the edge of the bed. "You really want me that much?"

"There's nothing else I want."

"Thanks." He smiled weakly. "Thanks for loving me so much. But I can't let Gladden die."

"I can't let her live."

"You're crazy jealous. If you saw me looking at the clouds, you'd be jealous of the clouds."

Della said, "I can't get rid of the clouds. I can certainly get rid of Gladden." Her voice climbed a little. "I won't let you hold onto Gladden."

"Believe me, will you?" He could feel a fever in his brain. "I swear to you, there's nothing there."

"There's everything." And all at once she was smiling sadly and her voice was very sad. "You don't realize it, my sweet, but that's the way it is. Your entire life is Gladden. Last night in the woods you walked away from me, but you really didn't want to walk away. It was Gladden, pulling you, dragging you away."

He lifted his hands, bent his fingers, pushed them hard into his shut eyes. "I can't remember. I don't know what it was."

"I tell you it was Gladden. I want to release you from that. I want to cure you of this sickness you have. This sickness from all the way back. Her father."

He stared at Della and she nodded and said, "Gerald, Gerald," and he felt as though he was being strangled.

Della said, "All you could do was tell me the story. You couldn't figure it. I had to do the figuring for myself."

He reached out and gripped the wood post of the bed and tried to crush the wood.

He heard Della saying, "You're controlled by a dead man."

"No."

"Gerald."

"No."

"Gerald," she said. "This man who picked you up and kept you alive when no one else gave a good God damn. You were a kid there, standing in the road. You were dizzy and starving, you were sick, and the cars went past, one after another. They didn't even look at you. But Gerald looked. Gerald picked you up. And that was it, that was your wonderful luck. It had to be Gerald who picked you up, Gerald who cared for you, fed you, put clothes on you, schooled you. Everything was Gerald. His ideas became your ideas. His life became your life. Now listen carefully while I tell you that when Gerald died his daughter became your daughter."

The room closed in on Harbin. The walls slanted and moved down on him. He could feel the nearness of the moving walls.

He heard her saying, "All these years you've been ruled by it. Every move you make, guided by Gerald. Always, every minute, asleep or awake, Gerald telling you what to do, how to do it—"

"Please, will you?" He shouted it. "Shut up."

"I want you to break loose. Be free of it once and for all."

Harbin heard something that sounded like, "Really, I can't do that. It wouldn't be honorable." He wondered where the voice was coming from. He wondered whether it was coming from his own lips or whether it was some other voice that he could hear inside himself. He was looking at the door. He moved toward the door and the gun followed him. He knew it followed him and he knew it was a gun and what it could do. He went toward the door.

"I'll shoot you," Della said. "I'll shoot you dead."

He was past the edge of the bed and he heard Gerald telling him to take the haul. He walked past Della and picked up the unopened suitcase and went on toward the door. He heard Gerald telling him to hurry. The door was in front of him as he sensed the pointed gun behind him. He heard a sob coming from behind him. The door was opening. He continued to move, feeling the heaviness of the suitcase. Then from behind him he heard the sob again, and then a sound like a thud, and he knew it was the gun hitting the floor. Now the door was closed behind him. He was in the hall. For another moment he could hear the sobbing in the room behind him but something caused him to stop hearing it and the only thing behind him was Gerald, urging him down the hall, urging him toward Gladden.

Chapter XVII

On the boardwalk, he approached the hotel, he saw the sun hitting the silvery rail that separated the raised boards from the beach. There were a lot of people on the beach and most of them wore bathing suits. The beach was white-yellow under the sun. He looked at the ocean and it was flat and passive, with the heavy heat coming down on it, giving it the look of hot green metal. The waves were small and seemed to lack enthusiasm as they came up against the beach. In the water the bathers moved slowly, without much enjoyment, getting wet but not cool. He knew the water was warm and sticky and probably very dirty from the storm of Saturday night. Even so, he told himself, he would like to be in there in the ocean with the bathers, and maybe he and Gladden would have themselves a swim before leaving Atlantic City. The thought was an extreme sort of optimism but he repeated the thought and kept repeating it as he moved toward the entrance of the hotel.

The old man was there behind the desk and Harbin came up to him and smiled and said, "When do you sleep?"

"Snatches." The old man was doing something to his thumbnail with the point of a pen.

Harbin put down the suitcase. "I'd like to see Miss Green."

The old man pushed the pen-point against the cuticle. "It's a scorcher. It's a real scorcher today." He looked at Harbin. "For this time of year it's what I call flukey weather. I never seen such rotten heat. This town ain't had a day like this in twenty years."

"Miss Irma Green."

"You look melted down," the old man said. "We got a bathhouse here. Want to get into a suit?"

"I want to see Miss Green. Call her, will you please?"

"She's out."

"Checked out?"

"No, just went out."

"Alone?"

The old man showed a perfect set of teeth that spent part of each night in a glass of water. "You make me out to be an information desk." He worked the pen-point against the side of his thumbnail, looked up sufficiently to see the bill in Harbin's fingers. He took the bill from Harbin, crumbled it in his fist, then let it slide into the breast pocket of his grimy shirt. "She went out alone."

"When?"

Turning his head slowly, his chin raised, the old man studied the wall-clock. It said four-forty. "Must have been a couple hours ago."

"Has the man been here since then?"

"What man?"

"You know who I mean."

"I don't know anything unless I'm told about it." The old man glanced calmly toward the little bulge in the breast pocket of his shirt, then his eyes traveled to the wall across the lobby and stayed there.

"I mean the man who was here last night," Harbin said. "The good-looking man with the blond hair. The man I watched from the little room while he walked out."

"Oh," the old man said. "That man." He waited a few moments, then he was too old and too weary to be ambitious for more money. "Yes, that man was here. Came in about twenty minutes ago. I told him she wasn't in and he hung around long enough to light a smoke. You smoke?"

Harbin gave the old man a cigarette, lit it for him. "Mind if I wait here?"

"Make yourself comfortable."

There was a sofa and a few chairs. He let the suitcase remain where it was and sat in the sofa and after some minutes he checked the suitcase with the old man and strolled out of the lobby, walked across the boardwalk to the rail and stood there looking at the entrance of the hotel. He went through a few cigarettes, discovered that he was ready to eat something. The hotel was flanked by souvenir stores and sandwich stands that opened on the boardwalk. He bit into a ham-and-cheese sandwich, downing it with coffee while his eyes focused on the entrance of the hotel. He had another sandwich, some more coffee and then he bought a couple of newspapers and walked into the hotel and took the sofa again.

Later, much later, it seemed to him that he had covered

every word in both newspapers. He glanced at his wristwatch and it put the time at close to seven. The sun was still going strong outside and he was relieved to see the sunlight. Bringing his eyes back to the lobby he saw the old man behind the desk, working on another fingernail.

He went back to the newspapers. It became seven-thirty. It became eight. Then eight-fifteen and eight-thirty. He was out of cigarettes and as he put the papers aside he sensed night coming in from the boardwalk. He looked toward the door and saw it was black out there.

Near the door there was a cigarette machine and he was taking the pack from the slot when someone came into the lobby and pulled his eyes up and he saw it was Gladden. He said her name and she turned and stared at him.

He moved toward her. She wore a hat that looked very new. It was a small hat, a pale and powdery orange, nothing on it but a long pin with a bright orange plastic head, like a big round glistening drop of juice.

Getting in close, Harbin kept his voice low. "We skip. We got to do it now."

He wasn't looking at her but he knew her eyes were on him. He heard her saying, "I told you I was out of it."

"Not yet."

She bit hard into each word. "I'm out of it."

"Your friend Charley doesn't know that." He took her arm.

She pushed him away. "Go, will you? Just go. Get away from me."

"Let's walk the boards." He turned his head a little and saw curiosity on the face of the old man.

Gladden said, "I want you to leave me alone. For the rest of my life I want to be left alone."

"The rest of your life is a matter of minutes if you don't let me help you."

Now he was looking at her and he saw it coming onto her face. It began with the eyes and after the eyes widened the lips parted and she could just about get the words out. "I won't be bothered by Charley. So he is what he is. So what? There's no reason why Charley should bother me. I'm not scared of Charley."

"You're plenty scared," he said. "You're paralyzed. You're so stiff you haven't been able to budge. So much in a fog you didn't have the brains to pack up and leave town. All you could do was float along the boardwalk and buy yourself a hat." He turned, moved across the lobby, handed the old man some change and came back with the suitcase. Gladden looked at the suitcase. Harbin smiled and nodded and then he was talking her out of the lobby, onto the boardwalk. It was still very hot out, but now the beginning of a breeze came in from the ocean. The boardwalk lights made a curving parade of yellow spheres against the black, curving out to meet the majestic brilliance of the big pier, the entertainment bazaar, the white blaze of it far up ahead, Steel Pier.

"My arm," she said.

He realized he was pressing it too hard. He let go. In front of him, a mile away, the lights of Steel Pier dazzled his eyes, and he blinked. He felt his walking motion on the boards, and Gladden walking beside him. He saw the other people on the boardwalk and it was a satisfying thing to see them there, all out there on the boardwalk to get the breeze.

Gladden moved a step out in front of him to gaze up at his face. "Why did you come back?"

He was lighting a cigarette. He got it lit, took in the taste of it, a harsh taste now after all the previous cigarettes. But still it tasted good, and the wood of the boardwalk felt good under his feet. He puffed at the cigarette, and then, his voice coming easily, he told her why he had come back. He made it as technical as he could, getting in all the details without elaborating on them. When he was finished they had covered half the distance to Steel Pier. He smiled dimly, contentedly at all the lights and all the people between his eyes and the Pier, and he waited for Gladden's voice.

She wasn't saying anything. Her head was down and she was looking at the shiny wood of the boardwalk as it went flowing past her moving feet.

"Thanks," she said. "Thanks for coming back."

Her voice was grey and dismal, the heaviness of it came against him. He frowned. "What's wrong with you?"

"I have a feeling. Maybe it would have been better the other way." Before he could reply, she murmured, "Nat, I'm tired."

There was a pavilion close by, and he took her to it. The

pavilion was a little more than half filled, mostly middle-aged people who sat there with nothing on their faces. There were some children moving restlessly among the benches, and a man wearing a white marine cap was selling bricks of ice cream.

The bench Harbin selected was toward the middle of the pavilion where it went away from the boardwalk to hover over the beach. As he came against the bench he felt the secure comfort of it and he looked at Gladden and saw that she was leaning her head far back, her eyes closed, her mouth set in a tight line.

He said, "That's a nice hat you bought."

She didn't respond. Her face stayed the way it was.

"Really an elegant hat," he said. "You got good taste."

Gladden opened her eyes and looked at him. "I wish you hadn't come back."

"Quit talking foolish." His lips curved upward in a scolding smile. "This isn't the time to talk foolish. What we do now is plan. We have the opening and what we do is use it."

"For what good reason?"

"To stay alive."

"I'm not too sure that I want to stay alive."

Harbin sent his eyes toward the boardwalk in front of him, where the parade of people was a stream of mixed pastels. He shook his head slowly and sighed heavily.

"I can't help it," Gladden said. "That's the way I feel." She put a hand to her eyes. "I'm tired. I'm so tired of keeping it in, holding it back, the way I feel." She began to breathe like a marathon runner finally giving up. "I can't go on with it anymore. There's nothing to gain."

"That's right." He looked at her. "Make it complicated. Make it miserable."

"I've always made it miserable for you." She made a move to take his arm, then pulled her hand away. "All I've ever done was hold you back."

"Let's do a smart thing. Let's let it ride."

"Ride where?" she asked, then answered it. "Nowhere." Now she took his arm, but only to make him pay close attention. "The way it lines up, it's no good. Last night," and now there was a choking in her voice, "I threw you out of my room. I called you names because I couldn't tell you what I really felt.

I've never been able to tell you what I feel. Until now. Because now it's like when they say the time has come. Like in a story I read once where there's a walrus and he says the time has come."

Her hold on his arm was very tight and he wondered for a moment if that was where the pain was. And then he knew it wasn't in his arm.

"So now," she said, "the time has come. I love you, Nat. I love you so much I want to die. I really want to die, and whether it comes from Charley or no matter how it comes, I don't care, I just want to die. You see," and she turned her head away from him, not wanting him to see, "it's no good when you're sad all the time."

He tried to get rid of the big heavy thing in his throat. "Don't say that." He knew it only made things worse and wanted so much to make things better and didn't know how. "I've given you one hell of a rotten trip."

"Not your fault. Not the least bit your fault." She took her hand away from his arm. "I get the blame. I knew I wasn't needed, so what did I do? I hung around. Like a leech." Her eyes, condemning herself, were dreary yellow. "That's all I've ever been. A leech." And then, the lips barely moving, "The only time a leech comes in handy is when it dies."

For an instant he wasn't able to move, to breathe, to think. It was the complete stillness that comes just before a cannonade. And as the thing hit the sky and split the black apart, he told himself it was love. He drilled it, with a hard and wild frantic drilling, telling himself it was love, drilling it into himself as his arms shot out to take Gladden, to pull her against himself and hold her there. With him.

"You won't get away," he said. "I'll never let you get away."

Staggered, dazed, her eyes reaching toward Harbin's eyes, the softness of her voice covered the screaming inside. "You do care?" And then, her voice still soft, "You do care. You do, you do, I know you do."

"I do." Just then the knowledge came and he understood what it all was, and who had sent the cannonade, and who had done the drilling, who had moved his arms for him and kept his arms where they were now. He knew it with complete knowing. He knew it was Gerald and it was Gerald causing him to say it as he said, "I love you, Gladden."

Chapter XVIII

THE BREEZE coming in from the ocean was swifter now, and the news of the breeze must have reached the streets, because more people were coming onto the boardwalk and arriving there with pleasure on their faces. Lit brightly with the faces and the lights, the white lights of the boardwalk lampposts and the colored lights of the boardwalk shops and cafes and hotels, the boardwalk was a ribbon of movement and high glow, many colors and many sounds, sparkling there, its brightness slicing the black of sky and beach and ocean.

From the boards there was a steady flow of people coming into the pavilion and it became filled. The man selling ice cream was doing good business, and a competitor saw what was happening and moved mechanically toward the pavilion. The people sat there and bought ice cream and took in the breeze, feeling the cool of it, breathing in the salt of it, content to sit there and take it. There was very little talking in the pavilion. They were there to get the breeze.

Harbin wanted more talking, more sound. It was time, he knew, to shape a plan and he couldn't very well talk plans with Gladden against this quiet. He turned his head and looked toward the rear of the pavilion where it hung over the beach. There was one empty bench and it was on the last row, set close to the rail and somewhat isolated. The edge of it was near the stairs going down to the beach. He stood up with the suitcase and Gladden followed him to the rear of the pavilion and they took the bench. Ahead of them there was a slight scurry as some people raced toward the bench they had vacated. There was some pushing and shoving up there and the beginning of an argument. The voices climbed, an elderly woman called another woman a name and was called a name in return and that more or less settled it and the pavilion was quiet again.

"Let's figure it." He lit a cigarette. Gladden leaned against his shoulder and the pale gold under his eyes was her hair flowing across his chest, gliding in the breeze.

"Money," Gladden said. "All my cash is in the room. We'll have to go back."

"No." His thoughts were moving out across a mixture of checkerboard and blueprint. "I'm carrying enough. Almost seven grand."

"Big bills?"

"Mostly."

"That's a problem."

"Not for awhile. There's enough tens and fives to keep us moving." He took a long pull at the cigarette. "What bothers me is transportation."

He looked up at the jet sky. It was sprinkled heavily with stars and there was a full moon. Between the stars and the moon he traced a pattern of travel, sending a map up there and seeing Gladden and himself moving across the map, going somewhere. He wondered where. He wondered how long it would take to get there, and whether they would ever get there. The map in the sky became a dismal map and he told himself to quit looking at it. The map wasn't giving him any ideas. He needed ideas and they weren't coming. He tried to force them but that was no good, he knew it was no good and he decided to let them flow in toward him of their own accord.

"The buses," Gladden said. "I don't think they'll be watching the buses."

"When they watch, they watch everything."

"Don't mind me," Gladden said. "I'm new at this."

"So am I." He looked at the suitcase at the side of the bench. "You scared?"

"Sure I'm scared."

"We'll get out of it."

"But meanwhile, I'm scared. I don't want to kid you. I'm really very scared."

"I know what it is," Gladden said.

He nodded slowly. "From last night on the Pike. From today, with Baylock." He stiffened just a little. "One thing for certain. We didn't do it. I wanted those three cops to live. I wanted Dohmer to live. I wanted Baylock to live. For Christ's sake," he said, and he saw her gesture, telling him to talk lower, "I never wanted anyone to die." He stared ahead, at the people seated in the pavilion, the people on the boardwalk, and indicating them, he said, "I swear I have nothing against them. Not a thing. Look at them. All of them. I like them. I really like them, even though they hate my guts." His voice went very low. "Yours too."

"They don't know we're alive."

"They'll know it if we're caught. That's when it starts. When we get grabbed. When we're locked up. That's when they know. It tells them how good they are and how bad we are."

"We're not bad."

"The hell we're not bad."

"Not real bad." She looked closely at his eyes.

"We're bad enough," he said. "Plenty bad."

"But not as bad as they'll make us out to be. We're not that bad."

"Try to sell them that."

"We don't have to sell them anything." She patted his wrist. "All we have to do is keep ourselves from getting caught. Because if we don't get caught, they'll never know."

"But we know."

"Listen, Nat. We know we didn't do away with anybody. Not today, not last night, not ever. If they say we did, we know they're wrong. That's one thing we know."

"We can't prove it. But then, suppose we could—?"

"What if we could?" She was looking at him with puzzlement, with something that grew in her eyes and made her eyes wide.

"If we could," he said, "it might be worth a try."

"Nat, don't give me riddles. Tell me what you're talking about."

"Giving ourselves up."

"You really thinking about that?"

He nodded.

She said, "Why are you thinking about it?"

"I don't know."

"Then stop."

"I can't," he said. "It's there, that's all. I'm thinking about it."

"You won't go through with it."

"I don't know about that, either."

"Please stop," she said. "Please, you're worrying me."

"I can't help it. I don't want to worry you, but I just can't help it. I'm thinking maybe we ought to do it."

"No."

He took her hands and pressed them between his palms. "Listen to me. I want to tell you something and I want you to listen very carefully." He pressed tightly on her hands, not knowing how much pressure he was using. With a gesture of his chin he indicated the faces that passed in a thick stream going back and forth along the boardwalk. "Look at them. Look at the faces. You'd think they have trouble. Trouble? They don't know what real trouble is. Look at them walking. When they take a walk, they take a walk, and that's all. But you and I, when we take a walk it's like crawling through a pitch-black tunnel, not knowing what's in front, what's in back. I want to get out of it, I want it to end, there's no attraction and I want it to end."

She had her eyes closed and she began to shake her head in long, slow swings, her eyes tightly closed. That was all she could do.

"Listen," he said. "Like you listen when we talk plans. Listen that way. It's really the same as a plan, except it's more clear, it's open, it's got more to it than plans. So try to listen to me. We'll go in. We'll give ourselves up. We'll give it to them, put it there in front of them. They'll go for that. They won't know what to make of it at first but I'm sure they'll go for it. We'll make it plain we could have skipped but instead of skipping and making them come after us we saved them the trouble, we came in. Nobody brought us in. We came in ourselves. We brought ourselves in. That's like doing the work for them, saving them the headaches, solving it for them, clearing up the business on the Pike, and Baylock in the room. But especially with the Pike. That's important, the Pike, because it's always a rough deal when cops die, and other cops always itch to find out who and how and why. So here we'll be giving it to them and they'll know, and they'll understand they'd never know if it wasn't for us, coming in to tell them how it happened and who did it. And here's the important thing, the emeralds. We'll be giving back the emeralds. I know that'll do some good. Maybe they'll really go easy on us."

"Maybe," she said. "And maybe. And another maybe."

"They will," he insisted. "I know they'll go easy on us."

"Easy like a sledgehammer."

"If we—"

"Now it's if," she cut in. "Before it was maybe and now it's if."

"There's no guarantee. There's never a guarantee. But coming in cold, bringing ourselves in, giving back the emeralds, that sort of thing goes over big. We'll be out in no time."

Gladden pulled away from him and regarded him quietly, as though looking down on him from a platform. "You say it, but you don't believe it. You know how long we'll be in." And then, when he was unable to make a reply, she went on, "You say we but you really mean only yourself. I know what you'll do. Because I know you. You'll take the weight of the rap."

He gave a little shrug. "I'll get that anyway."

"No you won't. You'll try to get it. You'll make it as rough on yourself as you possibly can." She leaned toward him. "To make it easier for me." And then slowly, evenly, "That's only one reason. But there's another."

He looked at her as though she was something frightening coming toward him, something that was not frightening when he had it covered up deep inside but which was very frightening when it came toward him from the outside.

"You want it," she said. "You're aching for it. You'll be glad when they put you in. The longer they keep you in, the better you'll like it."

He turned his head away from her. "Quit talking like an idiot."

"Nat, look at me."

"Make sense and I'll look at you."

"You know it's true. You know you want it."

He tried to say something. The words formed a tight string and the string was broken in his throat.

"You want it," she said. "You feel it's coming to you. And you want it."

Then it was like being in a game of tag and he knew she had tagged and there was no use trying to veer and dodge. He still didn't know what to say. He turned to face her again and saw her wincing and knew it was the look in his eyes that caused her to wince. He tried to pull the look away but it stayed there. All his torture was in the look and it caused her to wince again.

"Please," she said, "don't go all to pieces. Try to think clearly."

There was a moving of gears in his brain. "I'm thinking very clearly." And then it came out, the flood of it, the burst of it, the seething. "I want it because I'm due for it. Overdue. I'm nothing but a no-good God damn thieving son of a bitch and I have it coming to me and I want it."

"All right." Her voice was soft, gentle. "If you want it that much, I want it too. I want whatever you want. We'll get it together."

He looked at her, waited and wondered what he was waiting for, and gradually realized he was waiting for her to crack. But there was no sign of cracking. All she did was sigh. It was almost like a sigh of relief.

"Now," he said. "We won't wait. We'll do it now." He took her wrists, to help her up from the bench, but he saw she wasn't looking at him. She was looking at something else, something behind the bench. He turned his head to see what she was looking at.

He saw the gun. And above the gun, the lips faintly smiling, the aquamarine eyes quietly satisfied, the face of Charley.

Chapter XIX

HARBIN TOLD himself it was just like sudden bad weather and the bad pattern of it followed the pattern of all the other things that had happened. He knew the aquamarine eyes had watched them as they came out of the hotel, had followed them along the boardwalk, had followed them here, had waited, and Charley had selected the moment. And this was the moment.

The gun showed only long enough to let them know it was there, then Charley put it underneath his jacket, the jacket bulging just a little where the muzzle pressed against the fabric. Charley was standing with his back to the rail of the pavilion and now he began to slide himself toward the stairs going down to the beach.

"Come along," Charley said. "And don't forget the suitcase."

Harbin studied the tone of it, caught the trace of hysteria in the tone and knew there was nothing to do but take the suitcase and go along with Charley to the beach. Gladden looked up at him, to see what he wanted her to do. He smiled for her, then he shrugged, and carrying the suitcase he followed her toward the stairs, then down the stairs with Charley's face in front of them as Charley backed his way down to the beach.

The three of them were on the beach. Charley moved around to get the gun pointed at their spines. Charley said, "Let's take a walk. Let's go look at the ocean."

They were walking across the beach toward the ocean. The full moon splashed a blue-white glow against the black water. The glow seemed to melt and widen as it came into the beach. It floated onto the beach, a floating of a pale blue gauze that took shadow and weaved in and out in front of them as they walked toward the water.

The sand was soft and thick and moved in little hills under their feet. The sound of the ocean, a big sullen sound, blended with the hum and drone coming from the boardwalk. They moved toward the hard wet sand near the water. The boardwalk sound began to fade and as they came onto the damp sand it was all very far away from the boardwalk and away from everything.

"Turn around," Charley said.

They faced Charley. They saw the shine on the barrel of the gun pointing at them.

Charley made a gesture with the gun. "Slide the suitcase over here."

Harbin shoved the suitcase across the sand. Charley picked up the suitcase, felt the weight of it, nodded very slowly and shoved it back toward Harbin.

"Open it," Charley said.

The gun moved closer to Harbin. He unstrapped the suitcase and opened the lid. He displayed the green flame of the stones and sensed the flame of Charley's eyes looking at the stones. He heard Gladden's breathing. He raised his head and saw the gun and then Charley's face. There was something very unusual in Charley's face. The features seemed completely out of balance.

"Now I got them," Charley said. "Now you're giving them to me."

"All right, take them."

"Not yet. That wouldn't be proper. Just to make it fair all around I think I'll give you something."

"You use the gun," Harbin told him, "and they'll hear it on the boardwalk. You'll have a thousand people on the beach and you'll be hemmed in."

Charley moved in closer and the moonlight was full on his twisted features. "The last time you gave me information, I took it. You pulled my mind away from the suitcase and you had me turning my back on it and walking out of the room. That was a pretty move, and you're a classy engineer. So it means this, it means I can't afford to let you louse me up again."

"Look, you've got the haul. Why don't you just take it and go away?"

Charley inclined his head so that it rested on his shoulder. His voice was mild. "You really want me to do that?"

"It's the only thing you can do."

"And what will you do?"

Harbin shrugged. "Nothing."

"You sure?" Charley was smiling. "You really sure?"

Harbin shrugged again. "Examine it for yourself. We can't afford to move against you. We're too hot ourselves."

Charley let out a mild laugh. "You're real classy, you are. I get a kick from the way you evade an issue. I like the way—" The laugh became sort of wild. "You know what you want to do." With the gun he indicated Gladden, his eyes staying on Harbin, his voice jagged. "You want to get rid of this girl and go back to Della. That's what you want. And I got half a mind to let you do it. I'd like to be with you when you get back there to that room. I want to be there, watching you when you stand there. When you look at Della. I want to watch your face very close. I want to hear what you have to say. You'll do all the talking because I'll just be standing there, I won't be saying a word. And I know Della won't be talking."

Harbin felt something slicing into him, felt part of himself being sliced away.

He heard Charley saying, "Maybe the thing Della liked about you was your class. Maybe that was it. She used to tell me I ought to have more class. She never liked when I talked loud and got excited. You don't talk loud and you don't get excited, so maybe that was what she went for. Whatever it was, she sure went for it. I mean all the way, completely, way up to the point where there I am coming back to the room and I find her sitting on the bed and you're not there. So naturally I want to know what happened, and Della started giving me a story and I know she's giving me a story from the way it's coming out. I see she's in very bad shape and then she started crying and she couldn't talk anymore. So then I knew. I put it together and when I had it together it was too much, and something happened, and I put my hands around her throat. I choked her. I choked Della until she was dead."

Charley was breathing hard, his face shining above the gun, and suddenly he kicked viciously at the suitcase, sent it over on its side so that the emeralds went flying out and made a green flash and glittered green on the sand.

"I don't want them," Charley said. He started to weep, loud wracking weeping. "I don't care about them, you hear? Only one thing I ever really cared for. I cared for Della. I want her back, you hear?" The weeping was very loud. The heavy tears went running down Charley's face. "Will I ever find another

Della? No. Never. There was only one Della. Now she's dead and I got nothing in my life. But I know this—" Charley lowered his head, his eyes trying to smash Harbin apart. "I know if it wasn't for you—"

"No, don't," Harbin pleaded quietly.

"You—"

"Don't."

"Please don't," Gladden said. "Please, Charley, please—"

Charley laughed through the weeping and came moving in with the gun and Harbin saw the split taking place in Charley's brain, saw the brain coming apart as the gun came up in a slanting path that ended when Charley shoved the gun very close. Charley's eyes were opened wide, the white shining like white platters surrounding aquamarine. Then Charley had the gun pressing against Harbin's chest, the finger getting hard on the trigger. Harbin saw it coming, felt it coming, but then it wasn't coming because Gladden moved and brought her arm down on Charley's arm, her weight against Charley, her other arm swinging hard against Charley's face. Harbin was underneath the gun, slamming his shoulder into Charley's groin, getting his shoulder in there solid, pushing and then heaving to knock Charley off his feet and go with Charley to the sand. He was on top of Charley and he reached out and grabbed Charley's wrist and used his own arm as a lever to bend Charley's wrist, bend it back and far back. He saw the gun in Charley's hand, saw the fingers coming loose and away from the gun, saw the gun falling away from the hand, bright blue and in the air, curving and going away and onto the sand. He reached for the gun. Charley hit him in the mouth. He made another try for the gun. Charley hit him again, sent a fist against the side of his head. He went on reaching for the gun. Charley put two hands around his throat and began to choke him.

He tried to pull his throat away from Charley's hands. He could feel the thumb banging into his jugular vein. The pain was deep, and it went riding up into his eyes. He knew his eyes were starting to bulge. It was difficult to see anything. His mouth fell wide open and his tongue was hanging out. He tried to work his arms but there was no feeling in his arms. All the feeling was in his head now and it was the feeling of going up and back and around and down toward nothing. He could see the sky and the stars, the lights in the dark blue, the big dark blue that went sliding slowly, falling toward him but sliding away. And then he heard Gladden.

"Let go," Gladden said. "Let go of him."

He heard the grunt as Charley went on choking him. He felt his head going far to one side and it seemed that his head was being taken away from his body. Then he saw Gladden, and in the same moment he saw the face of Charley hovering over his own face. He saw the gun in Gladden's hand, and all this was very close to his eyes and it blotted out the sky. He heard the shot, saw the flash, felt the choking, heard another shot, saw nothing, felt the choking, and then another shot and then another and Charley's hands came away from his throat. He saw Charley's face and saw Gladden standing there with the smoking gun. That was for just a moment, and after that the sand came up and pounded into his skull.

Chapter XX

GLADDEN HAD her hands under his arms. She spoke to him but he couldn't make out what she was saying. The pain grew very bad and he didn't think he would be able to get up. Gladden tried to get him up off the sand. His legs were liquid. He had his eyes closed and he was fighting to get up, trying to hear what Gladden was saying.

Then he could hear it as it went in past the pain. She was telling him that he had to get up. Even if he couldn't get up, he had to get up.

"They heard the shots," she said. "They're coming."

He worked with her, came forward to his knees, facing the boardwalk. He saw a rapid movement on the boardwalk, people coming toward the rail and crowding the rail. All along the boardwalk within the range of his vision they were pushing toward the rail, trying to see what had caused the explosive sounds in the darkness of the beach. He had his arm around Gladden's shoulder as she brought him to standing. He looked down and saw Charley.

The moonlight was on Charley and it was rather bright where it came against the head and shoulders. There it seemed to be moving moonlight because the blood was still flowing. Only a small part of Charley's face remained. The rest of it caused Harbin to turn his head fast. He looked at the boardwalk. He saw the moving mob and under the boardwalk lights they were small enamel figures heading toward the various stairways going down to the beach. His head clouded for a moment and he had to close his eyes. When he opened his eyes he saw the gun on the sand near Charley. He turned his head and saw Gladden. She was looking at the boardwalk. Then she looked at the dead man on the sand. Then again at the boardwalk.

"We can't run," she said. "There's no use running."

"We better run. Let's move."

"Where?" she said. "Look." And she pointed up and down along the boardwalk. All along the boardwalk they were coming down the stairways, the stairway directly ahead, the stair-

466

ways on both sides, then more stairways, and more stairways. Harbin looked at it. He heard the drone of it, the rising sound of droning, and suddenly a sound that split the droning. A sound of whistles. He knew it was police whistles and something caused him to take another look at the dead man. He told himself the dead man was a policeman and would be eventually identified as a policeman. He knew it meant a very quick decision from any jury, so they had to run, he told himself, but they couldn't run because if they ran they would run into the people and the police coming toward them from the front and from both sides. He looked at Gladden. She had her face turned to the ocean. He took hold of her wrist. His heart began to beat very fast.

"That's it," he said. "That's the only way."

"We'll have to go far out."

"Very far out." They were running now, running toward the water, he could see the plan of it, and as the design took shape, he took himself above the pain and the weakness and held himself there as he ran with Gladden toward the water.

"Nat," she panted. "Can you swim?"

"You've seen me swim."

"But now. Can you swim now?"

"Don't worry, I'll swim." They were on the wet shining sand and she was going ahead of him and then losing stride to wait for him and he said, "Keep going. Just keep going."

They ran into the water. They ran through the shallow water where it came in little waves snapping at the beach. The foam of the big waves was thick and very white out there against the black, and they were going toward the big waves, the water up to their knees, the waves breaking just ahead of them. He saw that Gladden still had the hat on, the new hat she had bought in the boardwalk shop. The hat was distinct and bright orange against the black water. He was directly behind Gladden as she threw herself under a wave, and he followed her under the wave, came up alongside her and saw that she still had the hat on.

"Take off the hat," he said. "They might see it from the beach."

"I better take off more than the hat." She was removing the hat-pin from her hair. "My shoes feel heavy."

"Wait until we're further out." But he knew they couldn't

wait very long. His clothes and his shoes were pulling him down. It made him feel as though he were dragging a wagon behind him through the water. He swam ahead of Gladden while she went under water to take off the orange hat and crumble it and let it sink. He remembered times when Gladden was a kid and he had watched her swim at municipal pools. She had been a smooth little swimmer and swimming was a practice that never went away once it was acquired. It helped some, to know Gladden was a good swimmer. He sent himself under another wave, going under deep, then looked around and saw Gladden swimming toward him. He could see her face clearly against the dark water and she was grinning. He forgot what they were doing out here in the ocean in the night and he figured he was out here with Gladden for some fun and swimming in the Atlantic. Then he felt the drag of his clothes and his shoes pulling him down in the water and he realized what he and Gladden were doing out here, what they were trying to do, and he felt the panic.

He felt the big panic because everything was big. The sky was big and the ocean was big. The waves were very big. The tops of the waves were high above his head, the foam coming like the foaming mouths of big beasts leaping at him. He went under, came up, went under again to slide himself underneath the heavy current of the waves. Gladden came up alongside him and they went under a wave together. Harbin failed to go under deep enough and the rush of the wave caught him full and knocked him off balance. He hit the bottom of the ocean. The panic was there very big and he had a feeling he was several hundred feet down at the bottom of the ocean underneath the night. But coming up he was standing and the water reached only to his chest. He was facing the boardwalk, seeing the lights and the movement of color against the glow and some vague action on the beach, but that was all. He didn't want to take the time to study it further. He turned and went under another big wave as it came lunging at him. He saw Gladden was some yards ahead and she was swimming nicely. He saw her hair flowing, glowing gold along the black water.

They swam through the waves, went out past the breakers, swimming out and came to the deep water and went on going. They went swimming out, staying close together, concentrating on the swimming. The water was calm out here. Harbin decided it was time to really start swimming and in order to do that they would have to get rid of the clothes and the shoes.

"Hold it," he said. "Tread water."

"You all right?"

"I'm fine. Take off your things."

They treaded water while they took off their clothes. Harbin had trouble with the shoelaces and he went down a few times and felt the drag of the effort while he struggled with the shoes. Finally he had the shoes off and he liked the free movement of his legs in the water. He took off his clothes and pulled his wallet from the trousers, took the bills from the wallet and pushed them deeply into his socks, so that he could feel the security of the paper money against his ankles and the soles of his feet. He had all his clothes off except his shorts and the socks, with the money in the socks. He thought of the money and it was a good thought, because he knew to what extent they would need the money when they came out of the water.

He wondered when they would come out of the water. He wondered if they would ever come out of the water. That brought the panic again and he began to call himself names for allowing these things to occur to him. He told himself it was going to be all right. That was the only way to look at it, because it was going to be all right. He looked at Gladden. She was grinning. It was the same grin she had given him when they were back there going through the breakers. All at once, staring at the grin, he knew there was something wrong with the grin. It wasn't really a grin. It seemed to be more on the order of a grimace.

"Gladden."

"Yes?"

"What's wrong?"

"Nothing's wrong."

"Tell me, Gladden."

"I tell you nothing's wrong."

"You tired?"

"Not a bit." Her face bobbed up and down in the water. She grinned.

"Gladden," he said. "Listen, Gladden." He treaded water toward her. "We'll work our way out of this."

"Sure we will."

"We'll swim out far. We've got to swim out very far."

"Way out," she said.

"Very far out. They may look at the water. Maybe they'll look far out."

"I know."

"And then," he said, "when we're out far enough, we'll turn and follow the line of the beach. We'll do that for a while and then we'll start turning in toward the beach."

She nodded. "I get it."

"We'll come in," he said, "where it looks safe."

"Sure," she nodded. "That's the way we'll do it."

"I've kept the money with me," he said. "I've got it right here with me. In my socks. As long as we have the money, we'll manage. There's plenty of money and I know we'll manage."

"After we come back to the beach."

"It won't be too long."

"How long?" She lost the grin, then quickly picked it up again.

"Not very long," he said. "What we've got to do is not get tired. We'll take our time and we won't get tired."

"I'm not the least bit tired." The grin became wider. "I bet it's a very crowded beach right now."

"Mobbed." He wanted to look toward the beach but something told him he shouldn't look at it. He knew it would be very far away and he didn't want Gladden to see him looking at the distant beach. He said, "I guess they're just standing around. Just a mob of them standing around and figuring he probably did away with himself."

"That's good," she said. "That means we're clear."

"I'm glad you're not tired," he said. "Now, look, Gladden—"

"Yes? Yes?"

"If you get tired, I want you to tell me. You hear?"

"All right," she said. "I'll tell you."

"I mean it." He came in close to her and took a close look at her. "If you get tired it's important that you tell me right away. We have a lot of swimming to do."

"All right," she said. "Let's start doing it."

They resumed the swimming. Without the clothes and the shoes it was easy swimming now and they cut their way through the calm water, going out, the black a thick black ahead of them, nothing ahead of them but the black of water and sky, except where the moonlight came against the ocean. The moonlight was far to one side, and it went running slowly along with them as they swam out.

Chapter XXI

A ND AS he swam, staying just a little behind Gladden so he
could keep his eyes on her and see how she was doing,
Harbin began to think about Della. He didn't realize he was
thinking about Della. It was just that Della floated into his
mind and began to take control of his mood. More of Della
floated in and he saw her somewhere. It was beyond the ordinary.

That was one of the things about Della, her manner of going
beyond the ordinary. And yet the basic things she had wanted
were really very ordinary. All she had wanted was to be with
him in the place on the hill, just be there with him. It couldn't
be more ordinary than that. Certainly she hadn't asked a lot,
wanting that.

The golden hair in the water ahead of him came into his
eyes and into his mind, pushing softly at Della and sending
Della away. He could feel it happening and for a moment he
didn't want it to happen. He fought it. But it was happening.
Della was going out and away from his mind. He had his
thoughts entirely on Gladden.

He called her name. She stopped swimming and he came up
close to her. They treaded water.

"What is it?" she grinned at him.

"Want to rest my arms." But that wasn't it. His arms felt all
right. All of him felt all right and he managed to keep himself
high above the pain in his throat. He said, "I want to promise
you something. I promise I'll never get ideas like the ideas I
had up there on the boardwalk. I mean about giving ourselves
up. The way it was, there was a point to it, but now there's no
point, no point at all. They'd throw the entire rap at us and
we'd have no comeback."

"That's for certain. I took it for granted." Instead of the
grin, she was looking at him in an odd way. "Why do you tell
it to me?"

"Just to let you know."

She nodded. "I'm glad you're telling me." Then suddenly

472

the grin was there again. "Really, Nat, you don't have to tell me."

"Listen," he said. "Is anything the matter?"

"Why?"

"What are you grinning about?"

"Grinning?" She worked on the grin and made it fade. "I'm not grinning."

"What bothers you?"

"Nothing bothers me," she said. "We're out here swimming and after a while we'll go back to the beach." And again she showed him the grin that was not actually a grin.

Then suddenly she was going through the water toward him, her arms were around his neck. "Hold me," she said. "Please hold me."

He held her. He felt the weight of her and he knew she was forgetting to tread water. He held her up in the water and had the thick wet of her hair against his face.

She said, "I ruined it. You see what I do? I always ruin it for you. I've always wanted everything to be good for you and I've always made everything bad."

"That isn't true. I don't want you to say that."

"Pulling you down. Like I'm pulling you down now. I've always pulled you down."

"Quit it," he said. "Quit it. Quit it."

"I can't."

"I want you to quit it. Come away from it."

"The gun," she said. "I can still feel the gun."

"The gun was a situation. You couldn't help the situation."

"It feels heavy. I can't let go of it."

"Now check this," he told her. "You had to use the gun. If you hadn't shot the gun, I would have died."

"That's right."

"Sure," he said. "That's the only way to see it."

"It was the only thing I could do. I had to use the gun."

"Of course you had to use the gun."

"To kill him," she said.

"To keep him from killing me."

"But look," she said, "I killed him. I killed him."

"For my sake."

"No." And she released herself from Harbin, stepped back through the water, held herself up with a certain lack of effort so it looked as though she was balanced on a platform in the ocean. "Not for your sake. I wasn't thinking of you. I was thinking of myself. Only of myself. So I shouldn't lose you. You see? I didn't want to lose you and that's why I killed him. Not to keep you alive for your own sake, but for my sake. That makes it selfish. Makes it murder. You see what I mean? I murdered him."

"Don't. Don't, please—" and he went to her and held her again.

"No, let go."

"Gladden—"

"Let go." She writhed in his arms. Her head went under the water. She pulled her head up from the water and there was a spray. "Let me go." It became a shriek. "Damn you, let go." She had her hands in his hair, pushing his head back to get him away from her. "I don't want you to hold me. You hold me as if I'm a child and you're my father."

Water came into his eyes. He felt dizzy and somehow lost track of what was happening. Then he saw Gladden swimming away. She was swimming very fast. There was a frenzy in the way she swam, going out and away from him. He called to her and told her to stop the crazy swimming. He watched the pace of her swimming and knew she couldn't keep up the pace very long. A little wave hit his face and sent more water into his eyes. Then a lot more water came cutting into his eyes and it was because he had his arms flailing the water, going after Gladden.

But she was going very fast and soon he lost sight of her. He shouted and there was no answer. He shouted again and tried to see her but all there was to see was the black of the water and the sky, and suddenly there was no feeling of direction and he sensed he was getting nowhere. Just then he saw the lights, the thin glowing line of the lamps on the boardwalk. The lights were very far away. He couldn't believe it was that far. The vast distance between himself and the shore lights threw a terrible scare into him and he turned quickly from the sight of the lights. He shouted to Gladden.

There was no answer. He shouted again. His voice went out on a lonely ride across the water and came back to him like a sound in an abyss. He shouted as loud as he could and now he was swimming hard, knowing he had to reach Gladden, knowing deeply and fully true that he had to swim faster because Gladden was far out there and getting exhausted.

His eyes burned into the blackness ahead, trying to see Gladden. All he could see was the blackness. He went on shouting her name as he went on thrashing through the water. The water came into his mouth and choked him. Then, from what seemed like very far away he heard a cry. It was Gladden. She was calling his name. Her voice was faint, and he knew she was in serious trouble. He begged himself to swim faster, hearing Gladden calling to him, knowing Gladden had not been able to think with reason when she swam away from him, knowing her senses had returned in this moment when the trouble came. She was calling to him, asking him to hurry, she needed help, she was drowning.

And then, far ahead of him, there was something golden in the ocean. It was there for a moment and then it wasn't there. He smashed his arms through the water, kicked his way through, saw her golden hair appearing again, saw something white and thin going up on both sides of the golden hair. It was Gladden stretching her thin little arms toward the sky, clutching at the sky, and he knew Gladden was really drowning.

He knew he was swimming much faster than he could really swim. He told himself he would get to Gladden and get to her before she went down, and kept telling it to himself, racing himself toward where he could see the golden hair now flat and smooth on the surface of the ocean, the arms still showing but motionless, and less and less of the arms because the rest of the body was being taken down.

And now all he could see was Gladden's hands above the water. The hands stayed there for just a moment, then went under and there was only the black ahead of his eyes.

Nothingness glided in. He was in the center of the nothingness, taken into it, churned by it, going down in it, knowing the feeling of descending. What he saw next was the liquid green, a dark green with circles of light wheeling their way up past his vision. He realized he was swimming down through the water, going down after Gladden. He knew he was going down deep and he told himself to keep going down, get down there to find Gladden. A streak of pain went shooting from his eyes to the back of his head. He wanted to close his eyes. He held his eyes wide open, straining to see Gladden.

He saw her. Off to one side, and floating down easily, very gently going down, Gladden had her head lowered on her chest, her arms away from her body, her gold hair weaving in the green water. He swam down and saw Gladden's arms moving out toward him. It was as though the arms were reaching toward him. He told himself it was too late, he couldn't do anything for her now. They were down very very deep in the water and he realized there was no more air in his lungs. He told himself to hurry and kick his way to the surface. But he saw Gladden's arms reaching toward him, and it was Gladden, it was Gerald's child, and there was only one thing to do, the honorable thing to do. He went down toward Gladden and got to her and held her and tried hard to lift her and himself up through the water and couldn't do it and they went down together.

THE MOON IN THE GUTTER

1

AT THE edge of the alleyway facing Vernon Street, a gray cat waited for a large rat to emerge from its hiding place. The rat had scurried through a gap in the wall of the wooden shack, and the cat was inspecting all the narrow gaps and wondering how the rat had managed to squeeze itself in. In the sticky darkness of a July midnight the cat waited there for more than a half hour. As it walked away, it left its paw prints in the dried blood of a girl who had died here in the alley some seven months ago.

Some moments passed and it was quiet in the alley. Then there was a sound of a man's footsteps coming slowly along Vernon Street. And presently the man entered the alley and stood motionless in the moonlight. He was looking down at the dried bloodstains.

The man's name was William Kerrigan and he was the brother of the girl who had died here in the alley. He never liked to visit this place and it was more on the order of a habit he wished he could break. Lately he'd been coming here night after night. He wondered what made him do it. At times he had the feeling it was vaguely connected with guilt, as though in some indirect way he'd failed to prevent her death. But in more rational moments he knew that his sister had died simply because she wanted to die. The bloodstains were caused by a rusty blade that she'd used on her own throat.

At the time it had happened, he'd been flat on his back in a hospital ward. He was a stevedore, and on the docks a large crate had slipped off its mooring and hit him hard, breaking both his legs. During his third week in the hospital he was told of his sister's suicide.

It was definitely a case of suicide but the circumstances were rather unusual and the authorities decided on a post-mortem examination. They discovered she'd been raped, and the assault had deprived her of virginity. They concluded that she couldn't bear the shock, the shame, and in a fit of despair decided to take her own life.

There were no clues to indicate who had assaulted her. It was the kind of neighborhood where the number of suspects would be limitless. A few were hauled in, questioned, and released. And that was as far as it went.

Seven months ago, Kerrigan was thinking. He stood there looking down at the bloodstains. Attempts had been made to wash them away, and summer rains had thinned them a lot, but the dried red blotches were now a part of the alley paving, stains that couldn't be erased. The moonlight poured on them and made them glisten.

Kerrigan lowered his head. He shut his eyes tightly. His mood was a mixture of sorrow and futile anger. He wondered if the anger would ever find its target. His eyes opened again and he saw the red stains and it was like seeing a permanent question mark.

He sighed heavily. He was a large man, with the accent more on width than on height. He had it mostly in the shoulders, and it amounted to a powerful build composed of hard muscle, two hundred pounds of it, standing five feet ten. His hair was black and thick and combed straight, and he had blue eyes and a nose that had been broken twice but was still in line with the rest of his face. On the left side of his forehead, slanting down toward his cheek, there was a deep jagged scar from an encounter on the docks when someone had used brass knuckles. On the other side, near the corner of his mouth, there was another ridge of healed flesh, from someone's knife. The scars were not at all unique, just a couple of badges that signified he lived on Vernon Street and worked on the docks. Just a stevedore, thirty-five years old, standing here in the dark alley and thinking of a dead girl named Catherine.

He was saying to himself, She had the real quality, straight as they come, and it adds up to a goddamn pity, but you gotta give her credit for what she was, she was born and raised on this street of bums and gin hounds, winos and hopheads, and yet with all that filth around her, she managed to stay clean, through all the twenty-three years of her life.

He sighed and shook his head slowly and started out of the alley. Just then someone called his name and he turned and saw the torn and colorless polo shirt, the slacks that couldn't be patched any more. He saw the sunken-cheeked cadaver, the living waste of time and effort that added up to the face and body of his younger brother.

He said, "Hello, Frank."

"I been lookin' for you."

"For what?" But he already knew. One look at Frank's face and he could tell. He could always tell.

Frank shrugged. "Cash."

He was anxious to get rid of Frank. He said, "How much you need?"

"Fifty dollars."

Kerrigan smiled wryly. "Make it fifty cents."

Frank shrugged again. "All right. That oughta do it." He accepted the silver coin, hefted it in his palm, then slipped it into his trouser pocket. He was twenty-nine. Most of his hair was white. His daily diet consisted largely of five-cent chocolate bars and slot-machine peanuts and as much alcohol as he could pour down his throat. He was fairly gifted at cards and dice and cue sticks, although he'd failed miserably as a purse-snatcher. They hadn't sent him up for it, they'd merely hauled him into a back room at the station house and beat the daylights out of him, and after that he'd stayed away from petty theft. But he was nevertheless proud of his criminal record and he liked to talk about the big operations he'd handle someday, the important deals and transactions he'd manipulate and the territories he'd cover. A long time ago Kerrigan had given up hope that Frank would ever be anything but a booze hound and a corner bum.

"Got a spare weed?" Frank asked.

Kerrigan took out a pack of cigarettes. He gave one to Frank, put one in his own mouth, and struck a match.

He noticed that Frank was gazing past him, the watery eyes aiming down through the darkness of the alley. Frank's expression was thoughtful, then probing, and finally Frank murmured, "You come here often?"

"Now and then."

Frank's eyes narrowed. "Why?"

Kerrigan shrugged. "I'm not sure. I wish I knew."

Frank was quiet for some moments, then he said, "She was a good kid."

Kerrigan nodded.

"One hell of a good kid," Frank said. He took a long drag at the cigarette. He let the smoke come out, and then he added, "Too good for this world."

Kerrigan's smile was gentle. "You know it too?"

They were looking at each other. Frank's face was expressionless. Then his lips twitched and he blinked several times. It seemed he was about to say something. He clamped his mouth tightly to hold it back. The cords of his throat moved spasmodically as he swallowed the unspoken words.

Kerrigan frowned slightly. "What's on your mind?"

"Nothing."

"You look nervous."

"I'm always nervous," Frank said.

"Loosen up," Kerrigan suggested. "Nobody's chasing you."

Frank jerked the cigarette up to his mouth and took a quick draw and bit off some shreds of tobacco and spat them out. He looked off to one side. "Why should anybody chase me?"

"No reason at all," Kerrigan said easily. But inside he felt himself stiffening a little. "That is, unless you've done something."

Frank took a deep breath. He seemed to be staring at nothing. His lips scarcely moved as he said, "Like what?"

"Don't ask me. I don't keep tabs on you."

"You sure you don't?"

"Why should I? You're old enough to look out for yourself."

"I'm glad you know that," Frank said. He straightened his shoulders, trying to look cold and hard. But his lips were twitching, and he went on blinking. He took another conclusive drag at the cigarette and said, "See you later."

Kerrigan watched him as he walked away, crossing the cobbled surface of Vernon Street and heading toward the taproom on the corner of Third and Vernon. The name of the place was Dugan's Den and it was the only dive in the neighborhood that sold legitimate liquor. All the other joints were in the back rooms of wooden shacks or in the cellars of tenements. Most of the alcohol sold along Vernon Street was homemade and the authorities had long ago given up trying to catch all the bootleggers. Every once in a while there'd be a raid, but it didn't mean anything. They never kept them locked up for long. Just long enough to let them know that payoffs had to be made on time. So a few days later they'd be back in business at the same old stand.

He stood there at the edge of the alleyway and watched the scarecrow figure of his brother moving toward the murky windows of Dugan's Den. When the fifty cents was used up, Frank would hang around Dugan's and beg for drinks, or maybe he'd steal some loose change off the bar and make tracks for the nearest establishment where twenty cents would bring him a water glass filled with rotgut. But there was no point in worrying about Frank.

There was no point in even thinking about Frank. It was a damn shame about Frank, but then, it was a damn shame about a lot of people.

Approaching voices interrupted his thoughts. He looked up and saw the two men. He recognized Mooney, the sign painter. The other man was a construction laborer named Nick Andros. They came up smiling and saying hello, and he nodded amiably. They were men of his own age and he'd known them all his life.

"What's doing?" Nick greeted him.

"Nothing special."

"Looking for action?" Nick asked. He was short and very fat and had a beak of a nose. Totally bald, his polished skull shone in the glow from the street lamps and moonlight.

Kerrigan shook his head. "Just came out to get some air."

"What air?" Mooney grumbled. "Thermometer says ninety-four. We might as well be in a blast furnace."

"There's a breeze coming from the river," Kerrigan said.

"I'm glad you feel it," Mooney said. "For supper I had a plate of ice. Just plain ice."

"That only makes it worse," Kerrigan said. "Try a lukewarm bath."

"I'll hafta try something," Mooney said. "I can't stand this goddamn weather." He was a tall, solidly built man with sloping shoulders and a thick neck. His hair was carrot-colored and he had a lot of it and always kept it combed neatly, parted in the middle and slicked down. His skin was very pale, almost like the skin of an infant. Although he was thirty-six, there were no lines on his face, and his gray-green eyes were clear and bright, so that the only sign of his years was in his voice. He looked more or less like an overgrown boy. Actually he was a widely-traveled man who'd studied painting in Italy on a fellowship and had been hailed as an important discovery in the art circles of Europe. He'd come back to America to find that his water colors were acclaimed by the critics but ignored by the patrons. So he'd changed his style in an effort to make sales, and the critics roasted him and then forgot about him. Then everybody forgot about him. He returned to Vernon Street and started painting signs in order to eat. Sometimes when he was drunk he'd talk about his art career, and if he was terribly drunk he'd shout that he was planning another exhibition in the near future. But no matter how drunk he was, he never said nasty things about the critics and the collectors. He never said anything about them one way or another. His primary grudge was against the weather. He was always complaining about the weather.

Nick was laughing. "You shoulda seen him eating the ice. He has a big block of ice on a plate and he's biting it like it's meat or something. He musta et up about ten pounds of ice."

"That's bad for you," Kerrigan told Mooney. "You'll ruin your stomach, doing that."

"My stomach can take anything," Mooney said. "Anything at all. If I can chew it, I can eat it. Last week in Dugan's I won three dollars on a bet."

"Doing what?" Kerrigan asked.

"Eating wood."

Nick nodded. "He actually did it. I was there and I saw him bite the edge off a table and chew it up. Then he swallowed it, the whole mouthful, and he collected three dollars off the slummer."

"Slummer?"

"The playboy," Nick said.

"What playboy?"

"The playboy from uptown," Nick said. "Haven't you seen him?"

Kerrigan shook his head.

"Sure," Nick said. "You musta seen him. He always comes to Dugan's."

Kerrigan shrugged. "I hardly ever go in there, so I wouldn't know."

"Well, anyway, he's one of them playboys who likes to go slumming. One night about a year ago he walked into Dugan's and now he's one of the regulars. Comes in two, three times a week and drinks himself into a coma. But some nights he only has a few and then he goes out looking for kicks." Nick shook his head solemnly. "A queer proposition if I ever saw one. I've watched him, the way he looks at a woman. Like he ain't satisfied, no matter how much he gets."

"Maybe he ain't getting anything," Mooney commented.

"Maybe," Nick conceded. "But on the other hand, I think he knows how to operate. I got that impression when I offered to get him fixed up. It was something he said when he turned me down."

Kerrigan looked at Nick. "What did he say?"

"He claimed it does nothing for him when he has to pay for it. Paying for it takes away the excitement."

"Maybe he has something there," Mooney said.

"He makes a lot of sense, the way he explains himself," Nick went on. "I asked him if he was married and he said no, he'd tried it a couple times and it always bored him. I guess it's a kind of ulcer in the head that gives him loony ideas."

"You think he's really sick that way?" Kerrigan murmured.

"Well, I'm not an expert in that line."

"The hell you're not," Mooney said.

Nick looked at Mooney. Then he turned again to Kerrigan and said, "I guess most of us are sick with it, one way or another. There ain't a man alive who don't have a problem now and then."

"Not me," Mooney said. "I don't have any problem."

"You got a big problem," Nick told Mooney.

"How come? I got no worries. There's nothing on my mind at all."

"That's your problem," Nick said.

Kerrigan was gazing past them. He said, "I wonder why he comes to Vernon Street."

"Hard to figure," Nick said. "Lotta ways of looking at it. Maybe in his own league he don't rate very high, so he rides down here where he don't hafta look up to anybody."

"Or maybe he just don't like himself," Mooney remarked.

"That's an angle," Nick agreed. Then he frowned thoughtfully. "What it amounts to, I guess, he's probably safer down here."

"Safer?" Kerrigan said.

"What I mean is, he knows he can pull certain stunts on Vernon that he couldn't get away with uptown."

"What kind of stunts?" Kerrigan asked quietly.

"Whatever he has in mind." Nick shrugged. "Who knows what he's gonna dream up? It's a cinch there's something wrong with him, otherwise he wouldn't need this Vernon Street routine."

Kerrigan turned his head slightly and looked into the darkness of the alley behind him.

Then he looked past the heads of Nick and Mooney and focused on Dugan's Den.

He said, "I could use a cold drink."

"I'm dry myself," Nick said.

"Me, I'm dying from thirst," Mooney moaned.

Kerrigan smiled dimly. "I got some loose change. It oughta buy us a few beers."

The three of them started walking toward Dugan's Den. As they crossed the street, Kerrigan turned his head again for a backward glance at the dark alley.

2

DUGAN'S DEN was twice as old as its proprietor, who was past sixty. The place had never been renovated and it retained its original floor and chairs and tables and bar. All the paint and varnish had vanished long ago, but the ancient wood glimmered with a high polish from the rubbing of countless elbows. Yet, aside from the shiny surfaces of the tables and the bar, Dugan's Den was drab and shabby. It was the kind of room where every timepiece seemed to run slower.

But few of the customers owned watches, and as for the clock on the wall, it wasn't even running at all. At Dugan's there was very little interest in time. They came here to forget about time. Most of them were very old men who had nothing to do and no place to go. And some were white-haired women with no teeth in their mouths and nothing in their heads except the fumes of cheap whisky. The specialty of the house was a double shot of fierce-smelling rye for twenty cents.

There was no jukebox and no television set, and the only entertainment came from Dugan himself. He was a skinny little man with only a few strands of hair on his head and he was always whistling or humming or singing off key. It was a habit he'd developed long ago to keep the place from becoming too quiet. Most of the drinkers were not talkers, and when they did talk it was generally a meaningless jumble of incoherencies that made Dugan wish he were in another line of business. Occasionally there was a loud argument, but it seldom grew to anything really interesting. And on the few occasions when they'd throw fists or bottles, Dugan never made a move to stop them. He led a very monotonous life and he could stand to see a little action now and then.

There were only a few patrons at the bar when Kerrigan came in with Nick and Mooney. Behind the bar, Dugan was dozing standing up, with his arms folded and his chin on his chest. Nick banged his fist on the bar and Dugan opened his eyes and Kerrigan ordered three bottles of beer.

"No bottles," Dugan said. "Ran out of stock late this afternoon. This is a thirsty neighborhood today."

"I'm a thirsty man tonight," Mooney stated. "Let's have it from the tap."

Dugan filled three big glasses and Kerrigan put money on the bar. Behind the bar there was a dirty mirror and he looked in it and saw a man sitting at one of the tables against the wall on the other side of the room. The man had his head lowered to his folded arms on the table and he seemed to be sleeping. Kerrigan noticed that the man was neatly dressed.

"This beer is warm," Mooney was saying.

"There's a shortage of ice," Dugan said.

"You're always short of ice," Mooney complained. "What good is beer if it ain't cold?"

Dugan looked at Mooney. "Did you come in here to raise an issue?"

"I came in to cool off," Mooney said loudly.

"Then cool off," Dugan said. "Just relax and cool off."

"Might as well be drinking hot soup," Mooney grumbled. "It's a damn shame when a man can't get relief from the heat."

Through the mirror Kerrigan was studying the huddled figure on the other side of the room. He saw that the man had yellow hair cut short, with some silver showing through the yellow. He told himself to stop looking at the man, and he went on looking at him.

"I'm suffocating," Mooney was saying. "It's a goddamn furnace in here. And this beer makes it worse. I feel like I'm melting away to nothing."

A white-haired gin-drinker raised his head from the glass and looked at Mooney. "Why don't you walk down to Wharf Street and jump in the river?"

Nick laughed. But Mooney looked thoughtful, and after a moment he said solemnly, "That ain't a bad idea. Not a bad idea at all."

Mooney turned away from the bar and started out of the taproom. Nick went after him and pulled at his arm.

"Let go," Mooney said. "I reed relief from this heat and I'm gonna get it if I have to stay in the river all night."

"It's a cinch you'll stay longer than that," Nick said. "You know you can't swim."

"Well, I'll float." Mooney released his arm from Nick's grasp. He continued toward the door. At the door he turned and looked at Nick and Kerrigan. "You coming with me?"

Nick sighed. "I better be there when you jump in. You'll need someone to pull you out." He went back to the bar and gulped the rest of his beer. Then he looked at Kerrigan. "You coming?"

Kerrigan wasn't listening, and Nick repeated it, and then Nick saw that Kerrigan had his mind on something else. He saw what Kerrigan was looking at in the mirror. Nick's face was expressionless as he watched Kerrigan staring at the mirror that showed the man at the table on the other side of the room. Mooney had already made an exit, and after some moments Nick went to the door and opened it and walked out.

Dugan was dozing again, his head down and his arms folded on his chest as he stood behind the bar and hummed a squeaky tune. The white-haired gin-drinker was gazing tenderly at the few drops remaining in the glass. The other drinkers were bent over the bar and looking at nothing in particular. Then the door of the men's room opened and Frank came out and saw Kerrigan and walked toward him, saying, "What are you doing here?"

Kerrigan took his gaze away from the mirror. He looked at Frank.

"You never come to this place," Frank said. The corner of his mouth went up and came down and went up again. "Why'd you come here tonight? You don't hafta put any tracers on me. I know how to take care of myself. What's your point, anyway? Were you worried how I'd spend your fifty cents?"

"I came here to drink a glass of beer," Kerrigan said.

"Then why don't you drink it?"

Kerrigan lifted the glass to his lips and took a long drink. He put the glass down and Frank was still standing there, breathing hard, the mouth still moving in up-and-down spasms. Frank's eyes were shiny and he was having difficulty standing still.

"What's the matter, Frank?"

"You see anything the matter?"

"Something's on your mind."

"Quit digging." Frank spoke jerkily, as though he'd been

running and was out of breath. "You been watching me lately as if you're waiting for some kind of flash news. Every time I look at you, I see you watching me. I'm warning you to lay off."

Kerrigan stood motionless. Frank was moving past him and out of the taproom. He heard a sound that was something like a rumbling roar and it became louder and then he realized it was the dense quiet and stillness that made all the noise. But gradually he was aware of another sound and he concentrated on it, the squeaky little tune that came humming from Dugan's lips. He tried to stay with the music, tried to think of the words that went with the melody, but while his brain moved in that direction his eyes moved to the mirror that showed the man at the table on the other side of the room.

He turned away from the bar and walked slowly toward the table.

He sat down facing the yellow-haired man, who was still slumped over, head buried in folded arms. For almost a full minute he sat there looking at the man. Then he touched the man's wrist and said, "Hey, Johnny, wake up."

"Go away." The man didn't look up. He scarcely moved, except to draw back his wrist from Kerrigan's hand.

"Come on, Johnny. Get with it."

"Leave me alone," the man said.

"Don't you know your old friend Bill?"

The man lifted his head just a little, but his arms still covered his face. He spoke slowly, more distinctly now, measuring his words. "I'm not acquainted with anyone named Bill. And I don't have any old friends."

"But this is Bill Kerrigan. You remember Bill Kerrigan."

"I don't remember anybody," the man said. "I don't like to remember people. All the people I've known I'd rather forget."

"Is it that bad?" Kerrigan wondered if he could really make contact with this man.

"It isn't bad at all," the man said. "It's delightful. It's positively delightful."

"What's delightful, Johnny?"

"The calendar," the man said. "The calendar with the picture of the girl on it. She wore an ermine wrap and it was unbuttoned and she didn't have anything on underneath. That's what

I was dreaming about when someone wakes me up and starts calling me Johnny. It so happens my name isn't Johnny."

"What was the name of the girl?"

"What girl?"

"The girl in the dream."

"She didn't have a name," the man said. "None of them have names. They're just a lot of telephone numbers. This one didn't even have a telephone. I like them better when they don't have telephones. And the ones I like best are the dead ones. The dead ones never come around to bother me, not even in dreams."

"But you said it was delightful."

"That's why it bothers me," the man said. "It gets too delightful. It gets so damned delightful that it becomes anguish. Maybe I owe you something for breaking up the dream. You want me to buy you a drink?"

"Sure."

The man raised his head. He had a sallow complexion, and his features were fragile and sensitive. The shadows under his eyes were like a dark reflection of what he had in mind most of the time. He was of average height and weight and he looked to be in his early thirties.

He offered Kerrigan a weary smile. "What are you drinking?"

"I'll have a beer, Johnny."

The smile became dim and sort of sad. "You still think it's Johnny?" He didn't wait for a reply. He got up and went to the bar. Kerrigan watched him as he stood there talking quietly to Dugan. Then he was back at the table with the beer, and a water glass half filled with whisky for himself.

Kerrigan raised his glass. "Good luck, Johnny."

"There's no such thing," the man said. "It's all bad." He grinned at the whisky. Then he took a big gulp of it. He had trouble getting it down and he tried to curse while he was coughing and began to choke. He put a stop to that with another gulp. While it went down he had his eyes shut tightly. Then he was grinning again and he said, "You're lonesome too, aren't you?"

"Sometimes," Kerrigan said.

"I'm lonesome all the time." The man stopped grinning and gazed at the whisky in the glass. "I've been everywhere, I've done everything, and I've known everybody. And what it amounts to, I'm lonesome."

"Maybe you need a woman," Kerrigan ventured.

The man didn't even seem to hear it.

Then it was quiet for some moments and finally the man grinned again and said, "Who are you?"

Kerrigan decided to play it straight. He said, "I'm sorry, mister. I knew I'd never seen you before. It's just that I wanted company. I'm Bill Kerrigan."

"And I'm Newton Channing. Ever hear of Newton Channing? Does the name mean anything?"

Kerrigan shook his head.

Channing said, "You know, it means nothing to me, either."

There was a long silence. Kerrigan took a sip of beer, and then he said, "Where do you live?"

"Uptown," Channing answered absently. And as he went on talking, it was obvious that his thoughts had nothing to do with what he was saying. "Nice clean neighborhood. Too goddamn clean. Strictly middle-class. House and garage and a lawn in front. I live there with my sister. Just the two of us. She's a nice girl and we get along fairly well. One night last week she knocked me cold."

Kerrigan didn't say anything.

"She's really a very nice girl," Channing said. He lifted the glass to his mouth and finished the whisky. Then he got up from the table and went to the bar and came back with another beer and a pint bottle of whisky. Pouring the whisky, he went on in the detached tone, "I was trying to set fire to the house and she used the heel of her shoe on my head. I was out for at least ten minutes."

"Well, there's nothing like a happy home."

Channing filled the water glass to the brim. He lifted the glass very carefully and drank the whisky as though he were drinking water. He consumed more than a third of the glass before he said, "You know, I admire my sister. I really do. Only thing I object to, she has some notion I can't take care of myself. It makes her maternal. Lately she's been coming here to pick me up and drive me home."

"Can't you make it alone?"

Channing shrugged. "Usually I'm too drunk to handle a

car. When that happens, Dugan calls for a taxi. I don't like to see my sister coming down here. I'd much rather go home in a taxi."

"It's a lot safer," Kerrigan said. "I mean, it's safer for your sister. After all, this is a rough neighborhood."

"She doesn't care about that."

"The point is," Kerrigan said, "it's a very rough neighborhood and it's especially bad for a woman."

Channing inclined his head and gave Kerrigan a side glance. "Maybe you're just sitting here and pulling my leg."

Kerrigan didn't reply.

"Something bothers you," Channing said. "You're not chatting with me just to pass the time." He leaned forward, and his gaze was intent. "What's really on your mind?"

"Nothing special," Kerrigan said.

Channing drank more whisky. He kept the glass in his hand and stared at it. "Maybe you're a mugger. Maybe you're building up to some clever dodge. Like getting me alone somewhere and knocking my brains out and taking my wallet."

"Could be," Kerrigan agreed. "In a neighborhood like this, you never know who you're dealing with. It's always smart to be careful."

Channing laughed softly. "My friend, let me tell you something. I don't give a damn what happens to me."

Kerrigan watched him as he finished the whisky in the glass and lifted the bottle to pour some more. The glass was filled again and Channing had it almost half empty when there was the sound of a door opening and Kerrigan looked up and saw the woman coming into Dugan's Den.

She was walking toward the table. She moved slowly, casually, with a certain poise that blended with her face and body. She had a very beautiful face and her figure was slender and elegant. She had long wavy hair and greenish eyes. Her height was around five-four and she appeared to be in her middle twenties.

But he wasn't thinking about her age. He wasn't exactly sure what he was thinking. He could feel the tingling fascination of her physical presence and at the same time he was irritated with himself for staring at her.

He didn't realize that she was returning his stare. Whatever her reaction was, she did a nice job of hiding it. It lasted that way for a few minutes or so, then she was looking at her brother and saying, "All right, Newton. Finish your drink and let's go home."

Channing smiled at the whisky glass. "I ought to pay you a salary. What are nursemaids getting these days?"

"It isn't that kind of job." Her tone was quiet and amiable. "It isn't a job at all. I don't mind it in the least."

Channing shrugged. "You might as well sit down and have a drink. I'm not ready to go yet. I still have some drinking to do."

"How much have you had?"

"Very little, really."

"That means you've had almost a quart."

"It hasn't hit me yet," Channing said. "I've got to stay here until it hits me."

"One of these nights it'll really hit you and you'll be carried out on a stretcher." She was looking down at her brother as though examining a curious exhibit. "I'm absolutely certain you'll wind up in a hospital. Is that what you want?"

"I want you to leave me alone." He looked up at her, smiling faintly. "I hope it's not asking too much, but I'd really be grateful if you'd leave me alone."

"I can't do that," she said. "I'm much too fond of you."

"That's awfully sweet," Channing said. He looked at Kerrigan. "Don't you think that's sweet? Wouldn't you say I'm fortunate to have such a nice sister?"

Kerrigan was silent.

He heard her saying, "You're not polite, Newton. You ought to introduce your friend."

"By all means," Channing said. Then, to no one in particular, "Please forgive my bad manners." He half stood, and waited for Kerrigan to stand. But Kerrigan sat there. Channing shrugged, lowered himself to the seat, and poured more whisky into the glass. Then he went to work on the whisky.

"I'm still waiting," she said. "I'm waiting for the introduction."

"Oh, the hell with it." Channing took a big gulp of whisky. "As a matter of fact, the hell with everything."

She looked at Kerrigan. She said, "I'm sorry. He doesn't really mean that. It's just that he's drunk."

"It's all right."

She studied Kerrigan's face. "Please don't be offended."

He spoke a trifle louder. "I said it's all right."

"Sure it's all right," Channing said. "Why shouldn't it be all right?"

She looked at Channing. "You be quiet," she said. "Just sit there and drink your whisky and don't say anything. You're in no condition to say anything."

Channing sat up stiffly. He stared off to the side, his eyes focused on nothing. "What do you know about my condition?"

She didn't bother to answer. She turned to Kerrigan. "May I introduce myself? I'm Loretta Channing."

"That means a lot to him," Channing said. "It's very important that he should know your name. Why don't you give him your address? Tell him he's welcome any time. Invite him to dinner."

She went on looking at Kerrigan.

And Channing said, "He doesn't think you mean it. You've got to make it more sincere. Don't stand there looking down at him. Sit beside him."

"I told you to be quiet."

"Go on, sit beside him. Take hold of his hand."

"Will you shut your mouth?"

Channing was laughing. "Prove it to him, let him know you're on the level. Maybe you'll convince him if you drink from his glass."

"Maybe I'll slap your face," she told Channing. "You're not too drunk to get your face slapped."

Channing went on laughing. It was almost soundless laughter and gradually it subsided and became a series of little gasps, more like sobs. He made a grab for the glass and tossed more whisky down his throat. Then he turned so that he faced the wall. He sat there drinking and staring at the wall as though he were in a room alone with himself.

She was looking at Kerrigan, waiting for him to tell her his name.

He swallowed hard. "My name is Kerrigan." He said it through his teeth. "William Kerrigan. I live right here on Vernon Street. The address is Five-twenty-seven."

Then he got up from the table, and he was facing her and

standing close to her. There was a heaviness on his chest and it caused him to breathe hard.

He said, "Got it straight? It's five-twenty-seven Vernon." He was trying to say it calmly and softly, with velvety sarcasm, but his voice trembled. "You're welcome to visit there any time. Come over some night for dinner."

She winced and took a backward step. He moved past her and headed for the door and walked out.

As he hit the street he felt better, remembering the way she'd winced. It wasn't much, but it was something. It offered a little satisfaction. But all at once she faded from his mind and everything faded except the things in front of his eyes, the rutted street and the gutter and the sagging doorsteps of decaying houses.

It struck him full force, the unavoidable knowledge that he was riding through life on a fourth-class ticket.

He stared at the splintered front doors and unwashed windows and the endless obscene phrases inscribed with chalk on the tenement walls. For a moment he stopped and looked at the ageless two-word phrase, printed in yellow chalk by some nameless expert who'd put it there in precise Gothic lettering. It was Vernon Street's favorite message to the world. And now, in Gothic print, its harsh and ugly meaning was tempered with a strange solemnity. He stood there and read it aloud.

The sound was somehow soothing. He managed to smile at himself. Then he shrugged, and turned away from the chalked wall, and went on walking down Vernon Street.

3

H<small>E WALKED</small> slowly, not with weariness, but only because he didn't feel quite ready to go home and he wanted the walk to last as long as possible. From a small pocket in his work pants he took out a nickel-plated watch and the dial showed twenty past one. He wondered why he wasn't sleepy. On the docks today he'd put in three hours' overtime and he'd been up since five in the morning. He knew he should have been in bed long ago. He couldn't understand why he wasn't tired.

He moved past the vacant lots on Fourth Street and walked parallel to a row of wooden shacks where the colored people lived. One of the shacks contained a still that manufactured corn whisky. The bootlegger's neighbors were elderly church-going people who continually reported the bootlegger to the authorities, and were unable to understand why the bootleg-ger was never arrested. The bootlegger could have told them that he always handed his payoffs to the law when his neighbors were in church. It simplified matters all round.

Bordering the wooden shacks there was an alley, then an-other vacant lot, then a couple of two-storied brick tenements filled with Armenians, Ukrainians, Norwegians, Portuguese, and various mixed breeds. They all got along fairly well except on week ends, when there was a lot of drinking, and then the only thing that could stop the commotion was the arrival of the Riot Squad.

Passing the tenements, he crossed another alley and arrived at the three-storied wooden house that was almost two hun-dred years old. It was owned by his father and it had been handed down through four generations of Kerrigans.

He stood there on the pavement and looked at the house and saw the loose slats and the broken shutters and the caved-in doorsteps. There was only a little paint clinging to the wooden walls and it was chipped and had long ago lost its color, so that the house was a drab, unadorned gray, a splin-tered and unsightly piece of run-down real estate, just like any other dump on Vernon Street.

The Kerrigans occupied only the first floor; the two upper floors were rented out to other families, who were always bringing in more relatives. There was really no way to determine how many tenants were upstairs. From the noise they usually made, it sometimes seemed to Kerrigan that he was living underneath a zoo crammed to the limit with wild animals. But he knew he had no right to complain. The first floor did all right for itself when it came to making noise.

He opened the front door and walked into a dimly lit parlor that featured a torn carpet, several sagging chairs, and an ancient sofa with most of the stuffing falling out of the upholstery. His father, Tom, was sound asleep on the sofa, but he awakened and sat up when Kerrigan was halfway across the room.

Tom Kerrigan was fifty-three, an extremely good-looking man with a carefully combed pure-white pompadour, a tall and heavy and muscular body, and absolutely no ambition. At various times in his life he had shown considerable promise as an Irish tenor, a heavyweight wrestler, a politician and a salesman and a real-estate agent. He might have attained the heights in any of these fields, but he was definitely a loafer, and the more he loafed, the happier he appeared to be. As he sometimes put it, "It's a short life and there ain't no sense in knocking yourself out."

Sitting on the edge of the sofa, Tom let out a tremendous yawn, and then he smiled amiably at his son. "Just coming in?"

Kerrigan nodded. "Sorry I woke you up."

Tom shrugged. "I didn't feel like sleeping anyway. This goddamn sofa was breaking my back."

"What's wrong with your bedroom?"

"Lola threw me out."

"Again?"

Tom frowned and rubbed the back of his neck. "I don't know what the hell's wrong with that woman. She's always been an evil-tempered hellcat, but lately she's been carrying on something fierce. I swear, she tried to murder me tonight. Threw a table at me. If I hadn't ducked, it would've knocked my brains out."

Kerrigan sat down in a chair near the sofa. He sensed that his father was in a talkative mood, and he was perfectly willing to sit here and listen. Somehow he always felt relaxed and content when he was alone with Tom. He liked Tom.

"Let me tell you one thing," Tom said. "It ain't no cinch living with a woman like that. It's like playing around with a stick of dynamite. The thing that beats the hell out of me is why I stay here and take it." Tom shook his head slowly and sighed.

Kerrigan shifted his position in the chair. He settled back halfway against the wooden arm and flung both legs over the other arm.

Tom said, "It's always something. Last week she claims I'm monkeying around with some woman lives upstairs. Now for God's sake, I ask you man to man, would I do a thing like that?"

"Of course not," Kerrigan murmured, and checked it off as a lily-white lie. Tom had quite a reputation in the neighborhood.

"You're damn right I wouldn't," Tom declared. "When I marry a woman, I stay faithful to her. If I say so myself, I think I'm one hell of a good husband. I was good to your mother and after she died I was loyal to her memory for three entire years. For three years, mind you, I wouldn't let myself look at a skirt. Now that's the truth."

Kerrigan nodded solemnly.

"Come to think of it," Tom said, "your mother wasn't so easy to live with, either. But let her rest in peace. She was an awful nag, but she wasn't so bad compared to these other wives I've had. Like that second one, that Hannah. I swear, that woman was completely out of her mind. And the next one I married, that Spanish woman. What was her name?"

"Conchita."

"Yes," Tom said. "Conchita. She was one hot tomato, but I didn't like that knife she carried. It bothers me when they carry a knife. That's one thing I can say for Lola. She never reaches for a knife."

"Why'd she heave the table at you?"

Tom sighed heavily. "We had a discussion about the rent. She claims the tenants upstairs are four months behind."

"She's right about that," Kerrigan murmured. "It adds up to more than a hundred dollars."

"I know," Tom admitted. "And we sure can use the cash. But I just don't have the heart to put the pressure on them.

Can't squeeze money out of people when they don't have it. Old Patrizzi ain't worked for a year. And Cherenski's wife is still in the hospital."

"What about the others?"

"They're all up the same creek. Last time I went upstairs to make collections, I heard so much grief it gave me the blues and I stayed drunk for three days."

From one of the other rooms there was the sound of a door opening, then heavy footsteps approached through the hall. Kerrigan looked up to see Lola entering the parlor. She was a huge woman in her middle forties, with jet-black hair parted in the middle and pulled back tightly behind her ears. Weighing close to two hundred pounds, she had it distributed with emphasis high up front and in the rear, with an amazingly narrow waist and long legs that made her five feet nine seem much taller. She moved with a kind of challenge, as though flaunting her hips to the masculine gender and letting them know she was the kind of woman they had to fight for. The few who had dared had wound up with badly lacerated faces, for Lola was an accomplished mauler and she'd been employed as a bouncer in some of the roughest joints along the docks.

Her complexion was dark, and some Cherokee red showed distinctly when she was riled. Actually the Cherokee was mixed with French and Irish, with accent on the more explosive traits of each.

Lola moved toward the sofa, her hands on her hips, directing her full attention to Tom. Her booming lower-octave voice was like the thud of a heavy cudgel as she said, "You gonna go upstairs and collect that rent?"

"Now look, sweetheart. I told you—"

"I know what you told me. It's for the birds, what you told me. You're gonna get that money and you're gonna get it tonight."

"But they don't have it. They swore to me—"

"They're nothing but a bunch of goddamn liars," Lola shouted. "I'd go up there myself and make them pay off or get the hell out, but that ain't my department. You're the owner of this house and it's your job to deal with the tenants."

"Well, after all, I've been busy."

"Doing what?" Lola demanded. "Sitting on your rear all day

and drinking beer? That's another thing I'm fed up with. Morning, noon, and night it's beer, beer, beer. We got enough empty bottles in the back yard to start a glass factory."

"The doctor says it's good for my stomach."

"What doctor? What are you giving me? When you been to see a doctor?"

"Well, I didn't want to worry you."

Lola moved closer to the sofa and pointed a thick finger in Tom's face. "You're so goddamn healthy it's a downright disgrace. Why shouldn't you be healthy? All you do is eat and sleep and drink beer. If it wasn't for your son here bringing in the pay check, we'd all be living on relief."

Tom assumed a hurt look. "Is it my fault if times are hard?"

"It ain't the times, and you know it. If anyone came and offered you a job, you'd drop dead, you'd be so scared." As though addressing a roomful of spectators, she indicated Tom with an extended palm and said, "I tell him to go upstairs and get the rent money and he claims it wouldn't be charitable." She whirled on Tom and yelled, "Where do you come off with that charity routine? You're just too goddamn lazy to climb a couple flights of stairs."

"Now look, sweetheart—"

Lola cut in with another burst of condemnation, spicing it with oaths and four-letter words. The walls of the parlor seemed to vibrate with the force of her loud harangue. Kerrigan knew from past experience that it would go on like this for the better part of the night. He walked out of the parlor and moved slowly down the narrow hallway leading to the small bedroom he shared with Frank. But all at once he stopped. He was looking at the door of another room. It was an empty room and no one lived in it now and he wondered what caused him to stare at the door.

He tried to drag his eyes away from the door, but even while making the effort he was putting his hand on the knob. He opened the door very slowly and went in and flicked the wall switch that lit the single bulb in the ceiling. He closed the door behind him and stood looking at the walls and the floor, the bed and the chair, the small dresser and tiny table. He was thinking of the girl who had lived here, the girl who'd been dead for seven months.

Without sound he spoke her name. Catherine, he said. And then he was frowning, annoyed with himself. It didn't make sense to sustain the sorrow. All right, she'd been his sister, his own flesh and blood, she'd been a fine sweet tenderhearted creature, but now she was gone and there was no way to bring her back. He tried to shrug it off and walk out of the room. But something held him there. It was almost as though he were waiting to hear a voice.

Then suddenly he heard it, but it wasn't a voice. It was the door. He turned slowly and saw Frank coming into the room.

They looked at each other. Frank's mouth was twitching. The eyes were very shiny, the arms hanging stiffly and the hands slanted out at an odd angle with the fingers stretched rigid. Then Frank was staring at the wall behind Kerrigan's head and saying quietly, "What goes on here?"

Kerrigan didn't reply.

"I'm asking you something," Frank said. "Whatcha doing in this room?"

"Nothing."

"You're a liar," Frank said.

"All right, I'm a liar." He made a move toward the door. Frank wouldn't get out of the way.

"I want to know what you're up to," Frank said. He blinked a few times. "We might as well get it straight here and now."

"Get what straight?" Kerrigan's eyes were drilling the face in front of him and trying to see what was going on in Frank's mind.

Frank began to breathe very fast. Again he was staring at the wall. He said, "You're not fooling me. You got a long way to go before you can fool me."

Kerrigan made a weary gesture. "For God's sake," he said. "Why don't you knock it off? Quit looking for trouble."

Frank blinked again, and then for a moment his eyes were tightly shut as though he were trying to erase something from his mind. Whatever it was, it wouldn't go away, and the weight of it seemed to push down on him, causing his skinny shoulders to sag. His head was bent low, and light from the ceiling bulb put a soft glow on his white hair. There was something gloomy in the way the light fell on him. It was like an eye looking down at him, feeling sorry for him.

It occurred to Kerrigan that he ought to show kindness toward Frank. He sensed that Frank was headed toward a breakdown, the total result of too many bad habits, especially alcohol. He thought, Poor devil looks all washed out, just about ready to drop.

He smiled softly and reached out and put his hand on Frank's shoulder. Frank hopped backward as though he'd been jabbed with a hot needle. And then he went on moving backward, crouching and breathing fast with his mouth opened so that his teeth showed. His trembling lips released the choked whisper, "Keep your hands off me."

"I'm only trying—"

"You're trying to ruin me," Frank gasped. "You won't be satisfied until I'm all smashed up, done for, finished. But I won't let you do it. I won't let you." His voice went up to a thin wail that twisted and snapped and then he was staring at floor and walls and ceiling, like a trapped creature frantically seeking escape.

"Want a cigarette?" Kerrigan said.

Frank didn't seem to hear. His lips were moving without sound and it appeared he was talking to himself.

Kerrigan lit a cigarette for himself and stood there watching as Frank sat down on the edge of the bed and lowered his head into his arms. Kerrigan thought, It ain't that he's afraid of me, it's got nothing to do with me, he's afraid of the world, he's finally got to the point where he can't face the world.

He heard Frank saying dully, "I want you to leave me alone."

"I'm not bothering you, Frank. Seems to me it's the other way around."

"Just lay off. That's all I ask."

"Sure, Frank." His voice was as soft and gentle as he could make it. "That's what I've been doing all along. I've never stood in your way. Whatever you do is your own affair."

Frank stood up. He was calmer now, he seemed to have control of himself. But as he moved toward the door, he wasn't looking at Kerrigan. It was as though Kerrigan weren't there.

When Frank had gone, Kerrigan took a long drag from the cigarette. He went on dragging at it until it was down to a stub that scorched his fingers. He hurled the stub to the floor and stepped on it.

Suddenly he felt smothered in here. And somehow it had nothing to do with the tobacco smoke that filled the room. He made a lunge for the doorknob, telling himself that he needed air.

He hurried through the hall and across the parlor. He opened the front door, came out on the doorstep, and saw the other female member of the household. Her name was Bella and she was Lola's daughter. She was sitting on the top step, and as she sensed his presence, her head turned very slowly, and her eyes drilled him with a mixture of icy scorn and fiery need.

4

"HELLO," KERRIGAN SAID.

"You go to hell."

"Still mad at me?"

"Do me a favor. Drink some poison."

Bella was in her middle twenties. She'd been married three times, once by a judge and twice by common law. Somewhat tall and on the plump side, she was a slightly smaller edition of her mother. Her hair was the same jet black, her eyes dark and flashing, her complexion a Cherokee russet. She had the same generously rounded build as Lola, and emphasized it with tightly fitting blouses and skirts.

She had a loud and very bushy mouth, an evil temper, and she wasn't afraid of a living soul with the exception of her mother. Some weeks ago, during an argument in the parlor, she'd kicked Kerrigan and really hurt him, and Lola grabbed her and tore her up so badly with an ironing cord that she couldn't leave the house for two days.

Kerrigan smiled at her. "What's the gripe this time?"

"Take a walk," Bella snapped. "I told you a week ago you're off my list."

He sat down beside her on the doorstep. "I still don't know what you're sore about."

Bella stared straight ahead. "You got a short memory, mister."

Somehow tonight he found her presence invigorating and her nearness gave him a feeling of comfort and pleasure.

He said, "I think it was something about a blonde."

She scowled. "Can't you remember which one? Maybe you got so many on the string, you forget their names."

"Was it Vera?"

"No, it wasn't Vera. And while we're at it, who the hell is Vera?"

Kerrigan shrugged. "She's a waitress. When I'm in a diner I gotta talk to the waitress. I gotta tell her what I wanta eat."

Bella didn't reply. Kerrigan offered her a cigarette and she grudgingly accepted. He pulled a book of matches from his trousers pocket and lit it. For a while they sat there just smoking.

Finally Bella said, "It wasn't no waitress I saw you with. To me she looked like a two-dollar type. You took her for a walk up Second and then you went in a house with her."

"What house? What are you talking about?" He frowned with genuine bewilderment and rubbed the back of his head. Then, as the incident came back, "For God's sake, that was no house, it was a store. She's married and has five children. Her husband sells secondhand furniture. I told her we needed another lamp for the parlor. If you don't believe me, go inside and take a look. You'll see the lamp I bought."

Bella was convinced, but not mollified. She said, "Why didn't you tell me that when I asked you the first time?"

"I didn't like the way you asked me, that's why. Didn't even give me a chance to explain. Just came leaping at me like a wildcat."

"Did you have to punch me in the face?"

"If I hadn't, you'd have torn my eyes out."

"One of these days I will."

He showed her an easy grin. "Don't do it when your mother's around."

"She won't stop me the next time. Nothing will."

Kerrigan let the grin fade. He didn't like the look on Bella's face. There was a grimness in her eyes that made him know she meant every word she said.

"What's the big beef?" he said. "What's eating you?"

For a moment she was quiet. Then she said, "I'm tired of waiting."

"Waiting? For what?"

Her eyes drilled him. "You know."

He looked away from her. "Hell," he muttered. "Are we gonna start that again?"

"I want it settled once and for all," Bella said. "We getting married or ain't we?"

He took a final pull at the cigarette and flipped it into the street. "I don't know yet."

"What do you mean, you don't know? What's holding you back?"

He groped for an answer, and couldn't find any. His shoulders were hunched, his folded arms pressing on his knees as he scowled at the pavement.

"Why shouldn't we get married?" Bella demanded. "We go for each other, don't we?"

"It needs more than that."

"Like what?"

Again he couldn't provide an answer.

"Where's the complication?" Bella wanted to know. "We're living in the same house, we eat at the same table. It ain't as if you gotta make some major changes. All we do is kick Frank out of your room and put him in mine. Then I bring my clothes across the hall and we're all set."

His scowl deepened. He tried to say something but his lips wouldn't move.

She inclined her head slightly, studying him with open suspicion. "Maybe you got some other plans that don't include me."

He didn't reply. He had the vague notion she'd spoken an important truth that he couldn't admit to himself.

Bella said, "Whatever you do, don't play me cheap. I ain't in the market for any raw deals."

He frowned at her. "You're too jealous."

She didn't say anything for some moments. Then, very quietly, "I got every right to be jealous."

His eyes flared, his voice climbed. "Whatcha want me to do, lock myself up in a closet?"

"I wish you would." She wasn't looking at him. She stared at the cobbled street as though its lifeless stillness were the only audience for her deeper thoughts. "What is it with me?" she murmured. Then, moving her head slightly to indicate Kerrigan, "I got this guy in my blood like a disease. It's reached the point where I can't think about anything else."

Kerrigan gaped at her. For the first time he was fully aware of Bella's great need for him, the extent of her want, which went far beyond the physical drive. He had long known that she was genuinely attracted to him, and her behavior on the mattress was always sufficient proof that he gave her something special. But he'd never anticipated that her hunger for him would become the major factor in her life. He realized now that he'd been taking Bella for granted, that although he always looked forward to being with her, he'd never had the deeper feeling, the feeling she was now expressing toward him.

Suddenly he sensed that he'd been giving Bella a bad time. His eyes clouded with guilt. He wanted very much to say something affectionate and reassuring, but he couldn't find the phrases.

She was looking at him. She was saying, "Some nights in bed I sit up wide awake, trying to figure out what it is with me and you. For some crazy reason I keep having a dream where I see you standing on top of a mountain. I'm somewheres around, just where I don't know. And there's a hundred thousand other women reaching up to get you. For months now I've been having that same dream."

Kerrigan smiled gently. "Don't let it bother you. You got no competition."

"If only I could believe that."

"I'm saying it, ain't I?"

"Saying it ain't enough." There was worry in her eyes, and her voice was dull and heavy with doubt. "I just can't get rid of this jealous feeling. Why should it hit me so hard?"

He shrugged. "Beats the hell out of me. All I know is, I haven't messed with any other skirt since you and me got started."

It was evident that she believed him. And yet the worry stayed in her eyes. "It's not that I'm imagining things. And it ain't the way you look at women, either. It's the way they look at you. Even when they're on the other side of the street and you come walking past, I see them turning their heads. I know just what's in their minds."

He shrugged again. "These Vernon dames'll look twice at anything wearing pants."

"No, they won't," she said. "I'm one of them, I ought to know. It's just that there's something about you that women go for."

There was nothing complimentary in the way she said it. Her tone was sullen and resentful. "I'll be damned if I know what makes them so weak for you. After all, what are you? Just a big chunk of beef, an ordinary dock-walloper who never even finished high school. And you sure as hell ain't pretty. I've seen punch-drunk pugs who could give you cards and spades and come out in front. So I know it ain't looks. And it ain't brains. I wish to God I could figure out what it is."

Kerrigan was vaguely uncomfortable and somewhat annoyed with this probing of his physical and mental make-up. "Don't knock yourself out trying to figure me. Just relax and take me as I am."

For a long moment she just sat there and looked at him. Then gradually her lips shaped a smile, the sparks came into her eyes, and the red of her cheeks grew redder.

She stood up and said, "Come on, let's go in."

He started to move. But something kept him seated there on the doorstep. He frowned slightly and said, "I want to sit here for a while."

"How long?"

"Just a few minutes."

"All right," she said. "But don't make it longer. I don't feel like waiting."

He heard the door opening and closing behind him, and told himself that he was alone now. It was as though a weight had been lifted from his shoulders. But at the same time he wondered why he was thinking in terms of a burden instead of enjoyment.

As he sat there gazing moodily at the pavement, there was the purring sound of an automobile approaching at low speed. He looked up and saw an open-top sport car gliding toward the curb.

He winced, then stiffened, staring at the golden hair of Loretta Channing.

5

THE SPORT car came to a stop directly in front of the Kerrigan house. Loretta climbed out and walked toward him. He winced again, trying to ignore a strange stir of excitement. Gradually he managed to get a sullen look in his eyes. And he could feel his resentment growing when he saw how relaxed she was. As she came up to him, he muttered, "You sure you got the right address?"

She nodded. She wasn't smiling. "I'm accepting your invitation."

"It's a little late for dinner."

"I didn't come for dinner."

He sat there on the doorstep and scowled at her.

She said offhandedly, "It's just a visit. Just felt like seeing you."

"That's nice." He gazed past her. "You make a habit of calling on people at two-thirty in the morning?"

She shrugged lightly. "I was hoping you wouldn't be asleep."

"If I was, you'd probably wake me up. Maybe you'd force the door open and break into my room."

"Not really," she said. "I never take it that far."

He gave her a side glance. "I'm not so sure about that."

It was quiet for a few moments. Then she said, "Like to go for a ride?"

It caught him off guard. He frowned at her, his eyes asking questions that were aimed mostly at himself.

She said, "It's a perfect night for a ride." She pointed backward to the car. "The top is down and we'll get a breeze. Nice way to cool off."

Before he realized what he was doing, he stood up and followed her to the car. It was a pale gray MG with yellow leather upholstery.

She climbed in behind the wheel. He stood there hesitantly. Then he saw her looking at him. She was smiling. It was a dim smile, like a dare. He had the feeling he was bracing himself for a test. His teeth were clenched as he walked around to the other side of the car.

He opened the door. He started to climb in and then he stopped and said, "This is very nice upholstery. You sure I won't get it dirty? I'm wearing my working clothes."

"Please get in."

She was starting the engine. He got in and settled back in the seat. The car moved away from the curb. They took a corner and then another corner and the MG came back onto Vernon. She wasn't pushing it, just letting it glide. He settled back and told himself to enjoy the cruise. The hell with her. It was a nice hunk of automobile and it was giving him a smooth ride and that was all. But then he wondered if his grimy trousers were dirtying the upholstery. He bit at the side of his mouth.

Then he noticed they were headed in the direction of Wharf Street and he said, "We're going toward the docks."

"Yes, I know."

"You been here before?"

"Many times," she said. "But I've never seen the river at night. Do you mind if we have a look at it?"

He shrugged. "You're the driver."

The MG came onto Wharf Street and turned left and moved parallel to the docks. They were going very slowly now, cruising past the hulking shadowy shapes of piers and warehouses. In the black water along the wharves the big freighters were settled like motionless oxen waiting for morning. Within another hour the river activity would begin, the trucks would arrive to receive cargo from incoming ships, and workers would be straining under the weight of bales and crates and heavy cardboard boxes. But now, in the moonlight, the piers were deserted, and the only sound was the engine of the MG.

The car made a sudden and unexpected turn. He saw she was taking it onto the planks of a wide pier. On one side of the pier there was a big Dutch tanker, and the other side showed the suspension bridge that spanned the river like a huge curved blade of silver in the black sky. In front, the edge of the pier gave way to a couple of miles of deep water, its blackness streaked and dotted with the reflection of city lights. It was like millions of varicolored sequins on black satin.

They were parked at the edge of the pier and she was gazing out at the river. "It's breath-taking."

He didn't know what she meant. He looked at her.

She moved her hand to indicate the river and the sky and the ships and the bridge. "It's really magnificent."

He grunted. "Well, that's one way of looking at it." Then, with a shrug, "I guess it's a nice view for the sight-seers."

"Why do you say that? Don't you think it's a nice view?"

"Maybe I'd think so if I didn't work here." He gazed down at the calloused palms of his hands. It was quiet for a long moment, yet he could sense the question she was putting to him. And finally he said, "I'm a dock laborer, a stevedore. It's rough work, and I guess it gives me a different outlook."

"Not necessarily," she murmured. She pointed to the moon-lit river. "We're both seeing the same thing."

"Take a closer look," he said. He gestured toward the splintered pilings of the pier, where scum and garbage were floating. "See that green stuff? That's bilge from the holds of the ships. There's nothing dirtier. If it gets on your skin it crawls right through you. You never get it off you, no matter how hard you scrub. The smell—"

She shuddered. He saw her mouth twisting in a grimace of disgust. She swallowed, pulling in her lower lip.

"Feel sick?" He was grinning at her.

"I'm quite all right," she said.

His eyes were wide and innocent while he told himself to rub it in deep, really let her have it. "I'm only trying to give you the full picture. You come down to see the dirt, I'm showing you the dirt."

"Why do you call it the dirt?"

"That's as good a name as any." He saw the way she was watching him, her eyes intent, and he said, "Don't get too curious, Miss Channing. You're messing around with rough company."

"You're not rough," she said lightly. Then, more seriously, "You remembered my name."

He looked away from her. He didn't say anything.

"You're attracted to me," she said.

He was staring past the windshield, at the dark water of the river. He told himself the best move was to get out of the car and take a walk.

"You're really interested," she said. "Why don't you admit that you're interested?"

There was a strange thick feeling in his throat. He wanted to look at her and he was afraid to look at her.

"Of course," she murmured, "I could be wrong about this. Maybe you just don't go for my type."

"Let it ride."

"I can't."

"That's tough," he said.

"For both of us."

"Not for me."

"You're lying," she said. "You know you're lying."

His fingers gripped the door handle. He begged himself to open the door and get out and walk away.

He heard her saying, "You excite me."

"All right, cut it out."

"But you do," she murmured. "You know you do."

Without looking at her, he knew that she was leaning toward him. He tried to open the door but somehow the handle would not move.

"Look at me," she said.

He looked at her. She was entrancing and he could feel the warmth coming from her body and flowing into him. He told himself he mustn't touch her. His brain pulled frantically at the reins, but she was close and coming closer, sort of floating. Or maybe he was moving toward her, he wasn't sure. The only thing he was sure of was that he was getting dizzy with the nearness of her. And then the reins snapped and there was nothing he could do about it. He had his arms around her and his eyes were closed and he was kissing her.

It was something he'd never felt before, something he'd never known or even imagined. It put him on a cloud going up and away from Vernon Street and the docks and the city, and far away from all the world. It was a feeling of immeasurable delight and it had a flavor that made him terribly thirsty for more and more. But all at once he was able to think. And his brain said, She's just fooling around; all she's doing is getting her kicks in a new way for her.

He pushed her away. He did it roughly and she winced. Then she sat there staring at him and shaking her head slowly. She said, "What happened? What's wrong?"

He couldn't talk.

"Please," she said. "Please tell me what's the matter."

He opened the door and got out of the car. But he couldn't take it past that. He was standing away from the car and wondering why he couldn't move.

"You look frightened," she said. Then, her eyes widening, "You are frightened."

He looked at her. He said very quietly, "Get going."

For a long moment her eyes remained wide. Aside from that, she was quite calm. Finally, with a slight shrug, she started the engine. The MG backed off the pier and drove away.

6

It was several minutes later and he was on Vernon Street, headed toward home. But as he came closer to the Kerrigan house, he thought of Bella and the battle that would undoubtedly flare up when he got there. She was probably sitting in the parlor waiting for him, and chances were she had some heavy object in her hand, all set to heave it at him the instant he opened the door. Momentarily there was something downright appetizing in the prospect of a clash with Bella. He wanted to hear some noise, and make some himself, and maybe hand her a clout or two. He sure was in the mood for hitting something.

He came to an abrupt stop under a street lamp. No, he told himself, he didn't feel like fighting with Bella. The only thing he felt like hitting right now was his own face. He pulled a pack of cigarettes from his work pants and jabbed one between his tightened lips and struck a match. He leaned against the post of the street lamp, gazing out at the street and taking deep drags of smoke.

A voice called, "Hey, man."

He turned and looked at the window of the wooden shack and saw the long, glimmering earrings, the lacquered black hair, the coffee-and-cream face of Rita Montanez. In the Vernon Street market, which rarely ran as high as three dollars, she alone had the nerve to charge five. She got away with it because she was constructed along the lines that caused men to swallow hard when she passed them on the street. Rita was a mixture of African and Portuguese and she featured the finer physical characteristics of her internationally-minded ancestors. Her onyx eyes were long-lashed and she had a finely shaped nose and medium-thick lips. She was in her early thirties and didn't look a day over twenty.

Kerrigan smiled at Rita and walked toward the window. Although he was not a customer, he had a definite affection for her, going back to the days when they were kids playing in the streets.

"Got another smoke?" Rita asked.

He gave her a cigarette and lit it for her.

She winked at him, beckoned with her head, and said, "Wanna come inside?"

He laughed lightly. She laughed with him. They were always going through this routine and taking it just this far and no farther.

"What's new?" she asked. "How's my friend Thomas?"

Kerrigan shrugged. He wasn't affected one way or another by the fact that his father was one of Rita's steady customers. Long ago he'd become accustomed to Tom's dealings with the Vernon professionals.

Rita took an open-mouthed drag at the cigarette. She let the smoke come out slowly, and watched it climbing past her eyes. She said, "I like Thomas. He is much man."

Kerrigan's thoughts were only half focused on what she was saying. He said absently, "You better watch out for Lola."

Rita narrowed her eyes. It was purely technical, an expression of business strategy. "You think Lola knows something?"

He shrugged. "I don't know what she knows. But sooner or later she's gonna pay you a visit. You better be ready to run."

"From her? She's nothing but a lot of fat and a lot of noise." Rita blew smoke away from her face. "Lola don't worry me. No woman worries me." She made a motion toward the back of her head, and her fingers came away holding the tiny black-beetle knob of a five-inch hatpin. "This here's the equalizer," she said. "One jab with this and they know who's boss."

He grinned. "You're a hellcat, Rita."

"Gotta be. This street is no place for softies."

The grin faded. He stared at the splintered wall of the shack. He said, "You got something there."

She studied his eyes. Suddenly she knew what he was thinking. She reached out and touched his arm. "Don't let it get you."

He didn't say anything.

Rita kept her hand on his arm. "I was good friends with your sister."

He blinked. He looked at the painted face of the five-dollar woman.

Rita nodded. "Real good friends," she said. "And I don't

make friends easy. Especially women. But it was different with Catherine. She was strictly Grade A."

He stared at Rita. He said, "I didn't know she was friends with you."

"She was friends with everybody." Rita gazed past Kerrigan's head. "I used to see her giving candy to the kids in the street. Giving pennies to the bums and the cripples. Always giving."

His voice was thick. "She sure got paid back nice."

"Don't think about that."

For some moments he didn't speak. And then, very low in his throat, "It was my fault."

She looked at him. She frowned.

He said, "I knew she didn't belong here. I should have taken her away."

"Where?"

"Anywhere," he said. "Just to get her away from this mess. This goddamn street."

"You don't like the street?"

"Look at it." He pointed to the rutted paving, the choked gutter, the littered doorsteps. "What's there to like?"

"She liked it," Rita said.

"She had no choice. She lived here all her life and she never knew anything better."

"But she liked it. She was happy here. That's what you gotta remember."

"I can only remember one thing: I could have taken her out of this fouled-up rut and I didn't do it."

"Quit blaming yourself," Rita said.

"There's no one else to blame."

"Yes, there is. But there's no way to point at him, you don't know his name. Maybe you'll never know. After all, it happened almost a year ago. Best thing for you to do is forget about it."

He wanted to say something, to disagree with Rita's viewpoint, but as he searched for a way it was like groping in a dark closet that had no walls. He shook his head slowly, futilely, and finally he murmured, "Good night, Rita," and walked away.

At the corner of Fourth and Vernon he took out his pocket watch. The hands pointed to twenty past three. He had to be up very early and it hardly paid to go home and get in bed. And now the prospect of a battle with Bella was not at all appetizing. He winced at the thought that she'd still be sitting up, preparing to greet him with a flood of curses. Suddenly he was thinking of the railway ticket office, the bus depot, the freighters docked at the piers. But that had nothing to do with Bella. He just felt like taking off, that was all. He just wanted a long trip that would carry him far away from Vernon Street.

Skip it, he told himself. Think about it later.

He shrugged. But it was more than a casual effort. His shoulders felt strangely heavy. And then, trying to shake off the weighted feeling, he began to walk fast. But suddenly he came to an abrupt halt. He turned his head slowly and looked at the dark alley, where moonlight fell on a broken bottle, a crushed tin can, and the dried bloodstains of his sister.

He moved toward the alley. Then he was in the alley, looking down at the bloodstains. He wondered why his eyes felt cold. Quit it, he told himself. Get out of here. Go home. But he stood there looking down at the crimson stains on the rutted paving. A minute passed, another minute, and then all at once he had the feeling that someone was watching him.

He turned very slowly. He saw the carrot-colored hair and thick neck and sloping shoulders of Mooney. The sign painter had his head slanted and his arms folded and seemed to be appraising Kerrigan as though lining him up for a charcoal sketch.

Kerrigan smiled uncertainly. "I didn't know you were there."

"Just happened to see you," Mooney said. He shifted his position, leaning against the wall of the shack at the edge of the alley. His hair was damp and shiny.

"Enjoy your swim? Cool you off any?" Kerrigan asked.

Mooney had a look of grumbling displeasure. "That goddamn river. Cooled me off, hell. Only thing it did, it almost drowned me."

Kerrigan grinned. "Was Nick there to see it?"

Mooney nodded. He said offhandedly, "Reached me just in time. I went down twice before he dived in."

Kerrigan was still grinning. "Where's Nick now?"

"Went home. That's what I oughta do." He shrugged again. Then he looked at Kerrigan and said quietly, "Making progress?"

"What?" Kerrigan said. "What are you talking about?"

"This situation here," Mooney murmured. He was looking down at the bloodstains. "I've seen you in this alley more times than I can count. Of course, it ain't none of my business—"

"All right, let's drop it."

"You won't drop it."

"I'm dropping it now. It's a dead issue."

"The hell it is. You'll come here again. You'll keep coming here."

"If I do, I'm a damn fool," Kerrigan said.

"I wouldn't say that." Mooney spoke very quietly, almost in a whisper. "I've never had you checked off as a damn fool."

For a long moment they stood there looking at each other. Then Mooney said, "You come here to investigate."

"There's nothing to investigate," Kerrigan said. But while he said it, he was making a careful study of Mooney's face, especially the eyes. He went on, trying to speak casually. "She did away with herself. There's no question about that. She picked up a rusty blade and cut her throat and then she laid down to die. So the point is, she did it with her own hands. I'm not trying to take it past that."

"It goes a long way past that," Mooney said. "She did it because she was ruined and she couldn't stand the pain or the grief or whatever it was. There's never been any secret about that. You weren't here when it happened, but there was a big commotion and the entire neighborhood was looking for the man who did it. You see, everybody liked her. I liked her very much."

"You did?"

"Yes," Mooney said. "Very much."

"I didn't know you were acquainted with her."

"Don't look at me like that," Mooney said.

"What's the matter?" Kerrigan said gently.

"I don't like the way you're looking at me." Mooney's face was expressionless. "Don't jockey with me. I'm talking straight."

"I hope so," Kerrigan said. "How well were you acquainted? I never saw you talking to her."

"We talked many times," Mooney said. "Someone told her I used to paint pictures. She liked to talk about painting. She wanted to learn about it. One time I showed her some of my water colors."

"Where? In your room?"

"Sure."

Kerrigan looked at Mooney's thick neck. He said, "She wouldn't go into a man's room."

"She would if she trusted the man."

"How do you know she trusted you?"

"She told me," Mooney said.

"Can you prove it?"

"Prove what?"

"That you're on the level."

Mooney frowned slightly. "I'm sorry I started this," he said to himself. Then, gazing directly at Kerrigan, "You're suspicious of everybody, aren't you?"

"Not exactly," Kerrigan said. "I'm just doing a lot of thinking, that's all."

"Yes, I can see that." Mooney was nodding slowly. "You're doing a hell of a lot of thinking."

Kerrigan took a slow deep breath. Then he said very quietly, "I'd like you and me to take a little walk."

"Where?"

"To your room."

"What for?" Mooney asked. "What's in my room?"

"The water-color paintings," Kerrigan said. He smiled dimly and added, "Or maybe there's no paintings at all. Maybe there's just a bed. I'd like to have a look and make sure."

Mooney's face was blank. "You're checking on me?"

"Sure," Kerrigan said, and he widened the smile.

For some moments Mooney didn't move. Finally he shrugged and backed out of the alley and Kerrigan moved up beside him. They walked down Vernon Street toward Third. Near the corner of Third and Vernon they turned down another alley. It was very narrow and there were no lights in the windows of the wooden shacks. Mooney was walking slowly and Kerrigan followed him and watched him very carefully. Mooney's shoulders were sort of hunched, his arms bent just a little and held away from his sides, and he seemed to be bracing himself for something.

"You there?" Mooney asked.

"Right behind you."

Mooney slowed to a stop. He started to turn his head.

"Keep moving," Kerrigan said.

"Listen, Bill—"

"No," Kerrigan cut in. "You can't stall now. You're taking me to your room."

"I only want to say—"

"You'll say it later. Keep moving."

Mooney walked on. Kerrigan followed him and they went halfway down the alley and arrived at a two-story shack that had no doorstep and no glass in the front windows. Mooney went up to the door and then he stopped again and started to move his head to get a look at Kerrigan.

"Inside," Kerrigan said.

"Bill, you've known me all your life."

"I wonder," Kerrigan murmured. Then, through his teeth, "Go on, get inside. Get the hell inside."

Mooney opened the door. They came into a room where a lot of people were sleeping. There weren't enough beds and the floor was a jumble of sleeping grownups and children. Kerrigan stayed close behind Mooney, treading carefully to avoid stepping on the sleepers on the floor. They made their way across the room and went into another room where there were more sleepers. For an instant Kerrigan forgot about Mooney and he was wondering how many families lived in this dump. Goddamn them, he thought, they don't hafta live like this. At least they can keep the place clean. But then his mind aimed again at Mooney as he saw the sign painter turning toward the stairway. And he thought, Be careful now, it might happen when we're halfway up the stairs.

But nothing happened. Mooney didn't even look back. They came up on the second floor and went down a very narrow hall. The ceiling was low and there wasn't much air. It seemed there was hardly any air at all.

He followed Mooney into a room. It was a tiny room and there was no furniture. The only thing he saw was a mattress on the floor. But then Mooney switched on the light, and other objects came into view.

There was a large vase, almost four feet high. It was some kind of glazed stone and was cracked in many places and looked very old. Kerrigan looked to see what was in it and he saw it was filled with cigarette stubs and ashes. Next to the vase there was a stack of large rough-surfaced paper used for water-color paintings. And then he saw the jars of paint, the little tubes, and the brushes. Paint brushes of various sizes were scattered all over the room. He figured there must be at least a hundred brushes in here. He came closer to the stack of papers and lifted the edges and saw that some of the sheets hadn't been used. But the others were all water-color landscapes and still lifes and a few portraits. And that was what he had come here to see. It was the tangible proof that Mooney hadn't been lying.

"Well," he said quietly, "you got the paintings here, all right."

He waited for a reply. There was no reply. He turned slowly to look at Mooney, who stood facing the wall on the other side of the room. Then there was no sound in the room, not even the sound of breathing.

They were both looking at the wall and what was on the wall.

It was a rather large water color on thick board paper. It was the only painting on any of the walls. The dominant color was the yellow-gray background for the greenish-gray of her face and the cocoa-gray-yellow of her hair. It was just the head and neck and shoulders against the background. The head was slightly lowered and there wasn't much expression on the face and it was merely the portrait of a very thin girl with long hair, not much to look at, really. But she was alive there on the wall. She seemed to be living and breathing and fully conscious of what she was and who she was. She was Catherine Kerrigan.

"I didn't want you to see it," Mooney said. "I tried to tell you."

Kerrigan was moving backward. He kept moving backward until he bumped into the large vase. He reached back and gripped the edge of the vase. His fingers merged with the glazed stone and then his arms felt like stone and he wondered if his entire body were turning to stone. He was looking at his sister and telling himself she couldn't be dead.

He heard Mooney saying, "Damn it, I tried to tell you. I didn't want you to come here."

"It's all right," he said. But the words meant nothing.

He looked at her up there on the wall and without sound said, Catherine, Catherine.

And then, without seeing Mooney's face, he was hit by something coming out of Mooney's eyes. He looked at Mooney and knew the way it was, the way it must have been for a long time, and the way it would always be. The knowledge of it came to him very slowly, going into him very deep and pushing aside all the shock and astonishment, causing him to understand fully that Mooney had worshiped her and would go on worshiping her.

For some moments he stood looking at Mooney and they were having a silent conversation. They were talking about her, telling each other what a special item she'd been, and all the kindness and sweetness of her nature, the gentle manner and the sincerity. In the quiet of the room she gazed down at them and it seemed she joined them in their soundless discussion, saying, Don't give me such a build-up, I didn't really amount to much, just another Vernon girl with very little brains and no looks at all.

Mooney spoke aloud. "She was quality. The real quality."

Suddenly Kerrigan felt very tired. He looked around for a place to sit. Finally he sat down on the mattress on the floor. He folded his hands around his bent knees and lowered his head and his eyes were half closed.

He heard Mooney saying, "She never knew how I felt about her. I'm not sure if I can tell it to you now."

"I think I know already."

"No, you don't," Mooney said. "She was your sister, and it's an entirely different feeling. You never had to fight against something inside, something that said you were male and she was female. I wanted her so much that I used to steal from drugstores to poison myself so I'd get an upset stomach and have the cramps to think about."

Kerrigan looked at him.

"Why didn't you let her know?"

"I couldn't. She'd have felt sorry for me. She might have done something that she didn't want to do. Just to make things easier for me. It would have been an act of charity. You see, if I thought she went for me, I'd have asked her to marry me."

"You should have told her."

Mooney sighed slowly. He looked at the floor. He said, "She was clean. And I'm a dirty man. It's the kind of dirt that don't wash off. It's in too deep. Too many memories of dirty places and dirty women."

"You're not so dirty. And I think you should have told her."

"Well maybe I wasn't man enough." Mooney turned and looked up at the picture on the wall.

Kerrigan looked at Mooney and felt very sorry for him and couldn't say anything.

"Not man enough," Mooney said. "Just a specialist in the art of wasting time and lousing things up. There was a time the critics had me ranked with the important names in water color. They said I'd soon be pushing Marin for the number-one spot on the list. Today I'm pushing the sale of window signs for butcher stores and tailor shops. My weekly income, according to latest reports, is anywhere from twelve to fifteen dollars. If the Treasury Department is interested, the current bankroll is a dollar and sixty-seven cents."

Mooney was telling it to the dead girl, speaking in a conversational tone, as though he thought she could actually hear what he was saying.

"Comes a time," he told the painted face on the wall, "when the battery runs down, the stamina gives out, and a man just don't care any more. That happened long ago with this fine citizen. Not a damn thing I could have done for you, except lean on your shoulder and weigh you down. I'm a great leaner, one of the finest. I have a remarkable talent for making people tired."

Kerrigan figured it was time for him to say something. "You have a pretty fair talent for painting pictures." He gazed at the portrait on the wall.

"Thank you," Mooney said quietly and formally, as though he were addressing an art critic. Then his tone became technical. "There was no live model. This work was painted from memory. There were more than thirty preliminary sketches. The portrait took three months to complete, and this is the first time it's been exhibited."

Kerrigan nodded, although he was scarcely listening. He went on looking at the painted face that was framed there on the wall and gradually it became a living face as the gears of time shifted into reverse, taking him backward five years to a summer night when he stood with Catherine on the corner of Second and Vernon. He'd been walking up Second Street and he'd seen her leaning against the lamppost on the corner. Coming closer, he'd noticed that she was breathing heavily, as though she'd been running. He said, "What's wrong?" and for some moments she didn't answer, and then she smiled and shrugged and said, "It's really nothing." But he knew the smile was forced, and the shrug was an effort to hide something.

He put his hands on Catherine's shoulders. He said quietly, "Come on, tell me."

She tried to hold the smile, tried to shrug again. But somehow she couldn't manage it. Her lips quivered. Her pale face became paler. All at once she gripped his arms, as though to keep herself from falling, and she said, "I'm so glad you're here."

"Catherine." His voice was gentle. "Tell me what happened."

She hesitated. Then, whatever the issue was, she made an attempt to evade it. She said, "You look so tired and worn out. Work hard today?"

"Overtime," he replied. "They were short of men." In the glow of the street lamp he saw the delicate line of her features, the fragility of her body. She always wore low-heeled shoes and loose-waisted schoolgirl dresses and looked much younger than eighteen. The dress was cotton, plain drab gray, and it needed sewing here and there. But it was clean. She wouldn't wear anything that wasn't clean.

She was smiling again and saying, "You really look knocked out. Let's go somewhere and sit down."

She was always saying, "Let's go somewhere," as if there were anywhere to go except the candy store, which had a small fountain and a few battered stools.

"Come on," she said. "I'll treat you to a soda."

She took his hand. He sensed she was anxious to get off the corner. They walked two blocks to the little candy store and went in and sat down at the fountain. She asked him what he wanted and he said, "Orange," and she put a dime on the counter and ordered two bottles of orange pop.

He took a few long gulps and his bottle was empty. She sipped hers from a straw. He watched her as she sat there taking tiny sips and enjoying the flavor of the soda. There was a look of pleasure on her face and he thought, It takes so little to please her.

Suddenly he got off the stool and went to the magazine rack. She liked movie magazines and he stood there checking them to see if there was one that she hadn't read yet. He was reaching for a magazine when the door opened and three young men came into the candy store. They sort of barged in, and he turned and looked at them. They were wearing torn shirts and ragged trousers and battered shoes. It was hard to tell which one of them was the ugliest, which face was most misshapen.

The three of them were winking at each other as they moved toward Catherine. She was still sipping the soda and hadn't yet seen them. Kerrigan was waiting to see what they'd do. He saw the shortest one, who looked like a middleweight, slide onto the seat next to Catherine. The middleweight grinned at her and said, "Well, whaddya know? We meet again."

Catherine was trembling slightly. Kerrigan had a fairly adequate notion as to why she'd been out of breath when he'd met her on the corner.

The middleweight went on grinning at her. The other two were snickering. One of them was scar-faced and the other featured a yellowish complexion and crooked buck teeth that prevented him from closing his mouth. Scarface sat down so that Catherine was hemmed in between him and the middleweight. Then Scarface said something in low tones that Kerrigan couldn't hear, and Catherine winced. She turned her head to see Kerrigan standing there at the magazine rack. He gave her a reassuring nod, as though to say, Don't worry, I'm still here, I just want to see how far they'll take it.

The middleweight widened the grin. It became a grimace as he said to Catherine, "Why'd you run away?"

Catherine didn't answer. The aged candy-store proprietor was standing behind the counter and scowling at the three young men and saying, "Well? Well?"

"Well what?" Scarface said.

"This is a store. Whatcha wanna buy?"

"We ain't in no hurry," the middleweight said. He turned to

Catherine. "I like to take my time. It makes things more interesting." He edged closer to her.

"Please go away," Catherine said.

The proprietor was pointing to a sign on the wall behind the counter. "You read English?" he demanded of the three young men. "It says, 'No Loafing.'"

"We're not loafing," the middleweight said mildly. "We're here to keep a date, that's all."

Catherine started to get up from the stool. But she was crowded from all sides and they wouldn't give her room. Kerrigan didn't move. He told himself he would wait until one of them put a hand on her.

The proprietor took another deep breath. "This is a store," he repeated. "If you're not here to buy something, get out."

"All right, Pop." The middleweight reached into his pocket and took out a dollar bill. "Three root-beer floats." He made a casual reach for the bottle in Catherine's trembling hand. He took the bottle away from her and said to the proprietor, "Make it four."

Catherine looked at the middleweight. She wasn't trembling now. There was just the slightest trace of a smile on her lips. It was a kind smile, something pitying in it. She said very softly, "I'm sorry I ran away from you and your friends. But you were talking sort of rough, and then when you came toward me—"

"I wasn't gonna hurt ya," the middleweight said. He was frowning just a little; he seemed uncertain of what to say next. He aimed the frown at Scarface and Bucktooth, as though blaming them for something. Catherine went on smiling at the middleweight. Gradually his frown faded. "Damn, I shoulda known how it was from the way you walked. You didn't swing it like them teasers do."

Catherine grinned. She looked down at her skinny body. She gave a little shrug and said, "I got nothing to swing."

The middleweight laughed, and the other two joined in. Kerrigan told himself to relax. It was all right now. He saw Bucktooth sitting down beside Scarface and the proprietor placing four root-beer floats on the counter and he heard the middleweight saying, "Hey, look, my name is Mickey. And that's Pete. And that's Wally."

"I'm Catherine," she said. She turned and beckoned to Kerrigan, and he came forward. "This is Bill," she said. "My brother."

"Hi," the middleweight said. He told the proprietor to mix another root-beer float.

Kerrigan wasn't thirsty now, but he decided to drink the float anyway. He thanked the middleweight and saw the pleased smile on Catherine's face. She was happy because everyone was friendly.

He sipped the root-beer float and listened to the soft voice of Catherine as she chatted with the three young hoodlums. Her voice was like a soothing touch. He looked at the face of his sister and saw the gentle radiance in her eyes.

Then time shifted gears again and it was now, it was Mooney's room again. He was sitting there on the mattress on the floor and staring up at the portrait on the wall.

"You look knocked out," Mooney said. "Why don't you roll over and go to sleep?"

He gazed dully at Mooney. "Gotta be up early. There's no alarm clock."

"That's all right. I'll wake you. Got a watch?"

Kerrigan was already prone on the mattress and his eyes were closed as he took out the pocket watch and handed it to Mooney. "Get me up at six-thirty," he whispered, and while sleep closed in on his brain he wondered what Mooney would be doing awake at that time. But before he could put the question into words, he was asleep.

7

AT TEN in the morning the sun was like a big muzzle shooting liquid fire onto the river. Near the docks the big ships glimmered in the sticky heat. On the piers the stevedores were stripped bare to the waist, and some of them had rags tied around their foreheads to keep the perspiration from running into their eyes.

Alongside Pier 17 there was a freighter that had just come in from the West Indies with a cargo of pineapples, and the dock foremen were feverishly bawling orders, spurring the stevedores to work faster. There were some wholesale fruit merchants scurrying around, screaming that pineapples were rotting on the deck, melting away in the heat, while these goddamn loafers took their time and carried the crates as though they had lead in their pants.

Kerrigan and two other workers were struggling with a six-hundred-pound crate when a little man wearing a straw hat came up and shrieked, "Lift it! For God's sake, lift it!"

They were trying to lift the crate onto a wheeled platform. But on this side of the pier there was a traffic problem. They were surrounded by a jam-up of crates and bales and huge boxes and they had insufficient space to get leverage.

Stooped over, with the crate leaning against their backs, the two stevedores were panting and grimacing while Kerrigan knelt on the planks, his hands under the edge of the crate, trying to coax it onto the platform.

"You morons!" the little man screeched. "That ain't the way to do it."

The edge of the crate came onto the platform. The wheels of the platform moved just a little and the crate slipped off. Kerrigan's hands were under the crate and he pulled them away just in time.

"I told you," the little man yelled. "You see?"

One of the stevedores looked at the little man. Then he looked at Kerrigan and said, "All right, Bill. Let's try it again."

The other stevedore was arching his back and rubbing his spine and saying, "We need more room here."

The little man shouted, "You need more brains, that's what you need."

Kerrigan wiped sweat from his face. He took his position at the side of the crate, pushed a smaller box against the platform to keep it from rolling, and said to the stevedores, "Ready now?"

"All set."

"Heave," Kerrigan grunted, and the men braced their backs under the weight of the crate, while Kerrigan strained to work it onto the platform. Again he managed to lift it over the edge, but just then a sliver of rusty metal went stabbing into his fingernail and he lost his hold on the crate. "Goddamnit," he muttered as the crate fell off the platform and slammed onto the planks of the pier. He stood up and put the injured finger in his mouth and sucked at the blood.

"Go in deep?" one of the stevedores said.

"It's all right." Kerrigan winced and took his finger out of his mouth and looked at the torn cuticle. He said, "I guess it's all right."

"It don't look good, Bill. You better have it bandaged."

"The hell with it," Kerrigan said.

The little man was hopping up and down and shouting, "What are you standing around for? What about the pineapples? Look at the pineapples. They're rotting away in the sun." He beckoned to a dock foreman on the other side of the pier. "Hey, Ruttman. Come here, I want you to see this."

The dock foreman made his way through a gap in the pile-up of pineapple crates. He was a very big man in his late thirties. His head was partially bald and he had a flattened nose and thick scarred lips and a lot of chin and jaw. His arms were tattooed from wrist to shoulder and the hair on his chest was like a screen of foliage in front of the large tattoo, the purple-brown-black head of an African water buffalo.

As Ruttman approached, the little man continued to hop up and down, yelling, "What kind of men you got working here? Take a look at this situation."

"Easy, Johnny, easy." Ruttman had a deep, furry voice. He came up to the crate, glanced at the wheeled platform, and then looked at the three stevedores. He said, "What goes on here?"

"We just can't handle it," one of them said. "We ain't got enough space to work in."

"You're a liar," the little man shrieked. "There's plenty of space. You're just goofing, that's all, you're trying to kill time."

Ruttman told the little man to go away. The little man started to yelp, claiming that he had a lot of money invested in these pineapples and he'd be damned if he was going to let them get spoiled. Ruttman said the pineapples wouldn't get spoiled and it would help matters if the little man went away. The little man folded his arms and shouted he was going to stay right here. Ruttman sighed wearily and took a slow step toward the little man. The little man scampered away.

The three stevedores moved toward the crate and Ruttman shook his head, waving them back and saying, "This ain't no good. We gotta do it another way." He looked at Kerrigan. "Bring me a chain and a crowbar."

Kerrigan turned and walked down along the length of the pier, wiping sweat from his face. In the tool shed he found a roll of adhesive tape, and he cut off a strip and slipped it around his torn finger. He came out of the shed carrying the heavy chain and the crowbar. He took a few steps and stopped short and the crowbar fell out of his hand, the chain slipped away from his fingers. He stood motionless, staring at Loretta Channing.

She was sitting at the wheel of the MG. The car was parked on the pier. A few men wearing Panama hats and tropical-weave suits were leaning against the car and it was evident she'd got special permission to come onto the pier.

As Kerrigan stood there, unable to breathe, Loretta waved to him. He could feel the heavy awkwardness of the moment as the men in Panama hats turned to look at him, their faces showing vaguely puzzled smiles.

He told himself to pick up the chain and crowbar and get out of here. But as he reached down, he stiffened again. He was staring at an object in Loretta's hands. It was a small camera. She had it focused on him.

He straightened, breathing air that seemed to burn. His arms were away from his sides, his hands were clenched, and he didn't realize he was showing his teeth.

The camera made a clicking sound. It was a very small noise, but in his brain it was amplified. It cracked like a lash hitting him in the face.

He moved toward the MG. He walked very slowly. His head jutted like an aimed weapon. A fruit clerk wearing an apron came into his path and he pushed the man aside, not hearing the whine of protest. The men in Panama hats were moving uneasily as they detected the menace in his approach. Instinctively they got out of his way. But Loretta didn't move. Loretta sat there at the wheel, smiling at him, waiting for him, the camera held loosely in her hand.

He came up to the door of the MG and pointed to the camera and said, "Give it to me."

Loretta widened her eyes in mock surprise. "You want it for a gift?"

"All I want is the film."

The mockery remained on her face. "What will you do with it?"

"I'd like to shove it down your throat."

The men in Panama hats were swallowing hard and looking at each other. One of them braced himself and tapped Kerrigan on the shoulder and murmured, "No need to take offense, fellow. All the lady did was take your picture."

"You keep out of it," Kerrigan said.

The man said, "Now look here, I'm one of the owners of this pier."

Ignoring the man, Kerrigan reached out toward the camera. But Loretta was faster. She opened the panel of the glove compartment, slid the camera in, and closed the panel.

Kerrigan gripped the door, leaned across the steering wheel, and moved his hand toward the glove compartment. The pier owner grabbed his arm and said, "Just a moment here. Just a moment."

In the next instant the Panama hat was falling off the pier owner's head. He was shoved backward, with Kerrigan's flat hand covering his face. He tripped over a loose plank and sat down very hard and stared up at Kerrigan with his mouth opened wide.

Loretta hadn't moved. She was smiling at Kerrigan and saying, "I can't understand why you're so upset. All I did was take your picture."

His voice was low and even but it whipped at her. "You want it for a souvenir. You'll show it to your uptown friends. Picture of a man, stripped almost naked, like something on exhibit in a cage."

Again he reached for the glove compartment. Loretta sat there quietly, making no move to stop him as his finger found the chromium button. He pressed the button, the panel swung open, and he groped for the camera. His hand closed on it and he pulled it out and at that moment he felt the iron pressure coming down on his arm, gripping him above the elbow and causing him to blink.

He turned his head and saw the face of Ruttman.

"Easy, bud," the dock foreman murmured. "Easy now."

"Let go." He tried to jerk his arm away, but Ruttman held him there.

The pier owner, still hatless, had come forward and was saying to Ruttman, "Throw this man off the dock. Give him his pay and get him out of here."

"Yes, sir," Ruttman said. He took a deep breath that was like a sigh. "All right, bud. Let's go."

Kerrigan didn't move. He was looking at the faces of the men with the Panama hats. They were smiling at him; they felt safe now. They saw him taken in charge by a larger man, a stronger man, a man who was obviously capable of handling him.

"I said let's go." Ruttman's tone was louder.

But he didn't hear it. He was staring at the other faces, the faces of the stevedores who'd left the crates and were moving in to see what would happen. Ruttman was the undisputed boss of Pier 17 and there were scores of dock-wallopers who'd tried their best to disprove it, only to get their teeth knocked out, their noses caved in, their jaws broken. All along the docks of Wharf Street the opinion was unanimous: It never paid to trifle with Ruttman.

Kerrigan looked at the face of Ruttman and saw the strength, the quiet confidence, saw the warning that was almost friendly. Ruttman's eyes seemed to be saying, Don't force me into it, I really don't want to hurt you.

And then, as caution was mixed with the reasonable knowledge that he had no complaint against Ruttman, he turned his head, a gesture of submittal. In that instant he saw Loretta smiling at him, a mocking smile.

He let the camera fall way from his fingers, and the back of his hand cracked across her mouth.

It was a hard blow and it sent her head twisting all the way to the side. But he didn't have time to see what damage he had done, because Ruttman was already hitting him.

Ruttman was smashing him with a straight right that caught him under the eye. He fell back with his arms wide, his feet off the ground. He collided with a crate, bounced away, started to fall, made up his mind he wouldn't fall, and lunged at Ruttman with his fists flailing.

He found Ruttman's head with his right hand, staggered Ruttman with another blow to the temple, then came in close and ripped both hands to the body. He heard Ruttman grunting and again he punched to the body, and Ruttman started to double up, falling forward, trying to clinch.

Kerrigan stepped back and hooked a short left to Ruttman's jaw, followed it with another left to the side of the head, stepping back again and chopping with the right and missing, and then taking a terrible, thundering blow from Ruttman's right hand. It was a roundhouse smash, a punch that started wide, came in short, exploded on his jaw, and knocked him down.

"That winds it up," someone said.

Kerrigan's eyes were closed and he was flat on his back. There was no pain, only the feeling of wanting to stay here and keep sinking into the darkness.

But then he heard a voice saying, "Finished?"

He opened his eyes and looked up and saw Ruttman. He grinned and said, "Not yet."

Ruttman sighed reluctantly and stepped back, giving him a chance to get up. He got up slowly, now feeling the pain, the grogginess, and it was as though his jaw were bolted to his skull and a wrench were tightening the bolt.

He saw Ruttman walking in to measure him, the right hand taking aim. In Ruttman's eyes there was no satisfaction. Ruttman came in close, feinted with the left, and threw the right.

Kerrigan moved his head, got away from the big fist, blocked a left that tried to find his ribs, blocked the right coming again toward his jaw, then side-stepped going away from another right. Ruttman grunted, lunged, missed with both hands, lunged again, and missed again as Kerrigan crouched going backward, weaving and dodging, ducking and coming up and then moving away from where Ruttman wanted him to be.

Ruttman's expression had changed. Now his eyes showed impatience. He took a deep breath and charged at Kerrigan, putting everything he had in an overhand right that whizzed toward Kerrigan's head. The fist hit empty air and nothing else. Ruttman lost his balance and stumbled and fell to one knee.

Someone laughed.

Ruttman came up fast. He rushed again, his left arm swinging hard. Kerrigan went inside the hook, shot a short right to Ruttman's belly, used the right again, ripping it to the ribs. Ruttman lowered his hands to protect his midsection, and Kerrigan took a backward step, took aim, and hauled off and smashed a straight right hand to the chin.

He saw Ruttman staggering sideways, the thick arms flailing. The dock foreman struggled to keep his balance, managed to hold on and stay on his feet, moving unsteadily, eyes dull, then bracing himself and coming in again.

Kerrigan was ready. He jabbed with his left, jabbed again and again, finding Ruttman's nose and mouth. Then another vicious jab that had all his strength behind it, his fist twisting as it landed against Ruttman's brow. He saw the flaring red streak above Ruttman's eye, and he sent another left to the same place, that widened the cut.

The dock workers were silent, staring in disbelief as they saw Ruttman taking it and falling backward and still taking it. They were watching the downfall of a man they believed to be invincible. And they didn't like it.

Kerrigan put another left against Ruttman's bad eye. Ruttman let out a groan of pain, tried to cover up, and Kerrigan, working very fast now, hooked a left to the head, hooked again to the body, chopped with the right and brought more blood and a couple of teeth from Ruttman's mouth.

Someone yelled, "Come on, Ruttman! Don't take it. Go after him."

"Get him, Ruttman!"

"Knock his brains out!"

As the stevedores shouted encouragement to Ruttman, it

was like a heavy weight falling on Kerrigan's chest. Suddenly he realized he was fighting a man he had no right to fight. He was defeating the man and he hated the idea.

Because the adversary was not Ruttman. The true enemy was sitting there at the wheel of the parked car, her golden hair glimmering, her eyes taunting him.

It was as though she were saying, You're afraid of me.

He could hear the grinding of his teeth as he realized it was true. He had the feeling of facing a high fence, much too high for him to climb. The fists of Ruttman were coming toward him but it wasn't important, he didn't care. He scarcely felt the knuckles that bashed his face. It wasn't a fight any longer, it was just a mess, a loused-up comedy without any laughs.

Something crashed against his mouth. He tasted blood, but he wasn't conscious of the taste, or the grinding pain.

He was thinking, You can't handle her, you know you can't.

A big fist hit him on the side of the head, sent him falling back. He saw Ruttman moving in for the follow-up, saw Ruttman's arms coming in like pistons. But it didn't matter. He didn't even bother to lift his hands.

His head jerked to the side as Ruttman's right hand caught him on the jaw. Ruttman hit him in the midsection with a short ripping left that caused him to double up, then straightened him with a long left, then another right to the jaw, setting him up now, gauging him, sort of propping him there, and then winding it up and sending it in, a package of thunder that became a flashing, blinding streak of light going up from his chin to his brain. He sailed back and went down like a falling plank and rolled over on his face.

The onlookers stood motionless for several moments. Then a few stevedores moved forward to join Ruttman, who was bending over Kerrigan and muttering, "He's out. He's out cold."

"Is he breathing?"

"He's all right," Ruttman said.

They turned Kerrigan over so that he rested on his back. For a few seconds they were silent, just staring at his face.

His eyes were closed, but the men weren't looking at his eyes. They were watching his mouth.

"He's smiling," one of them said. "Look at this crazy bastard. What's he got to smile about?"

Kerrigan was deep in the soothing darkness and far away from everything, yet his blacked-out brain was speaking to him, smiling and saying derisively, You damn fool.

8

THEY LIFTED Kerrigan and carried him into the pier office and put him on a battered leather sofa in the dusty back room that was used for infirmary purposes. They splashed water in his face and worked some whisky down his throat, and within a few minutes he was sitting up and accepting a cigarette from Ruttman. He took a long drag and smiled amiably at the dock foreman.

Ruttman smiled back. "Hurt much?" Kerrigan shrugged.

The other stevedores were slowly leaving the office. Ruttman waited until all of them were gone and then he said, "You gave me a damn nice tussle. For a while there you had me going. But all of a sudden you quit cold. Why?"

Kerrigan shrugged again. "Ran out of gas."

"No, you didn't. You were doing fine." Ruttman's eyes narrowed. "Come on, tell me why you quit."

"I just lost interest. I got bored."

Ruttman sighed. "Guess I'll have to let it ride." And then, deciding on a final try, "If you'll open up, maybe I can help you."

"Who needs help?"

"You do," Ruttman said. "For one thing, you're out of a job."

Kerrigan tried to take it casually, but he felt the bite of genuine panic as he thought of the family's financial condition. His weekly pay check was the only money coming into the house these days. Of course, there were Bella's three nights a week as a hat-check girl, but she had the gambling habit, mostly horses, and she was always in the red. So here he was with five mouths to feed and no job and the picture was definitely unfunny.

He made an effort to cheer himself up. "This ain't the only pier on the river. I'll go see Ferraco on Nineteen. He's always got a shortage."

"No," Ruttman said. "He won't hire you. None of them'll hire you."

"Why not?" he asked, but he already knew the answer.

"You're blackballed," Ruttman said. "It's going down the line already."

Kerrigan stared down at the uncarpeted floor. He took another drag at the cigarette and it tasted sour.

He heard Ruttman saying, "I'd like to go to bat, but you won't give me anything to work on."

He went on staring at the floor. "The hell with it."

Ruttman let out a huge sigh. "I guess it ain't no use," he said aloud to himself. Then, looking at Kerrigan, "Better stay here and rest a while. When you come out, I'll have your pay check ready."

The dock foreman walked out of the room. Kerrigan sat there on the edge of the sofa, feeling the dizziness coming again, starting to feel the full hurt of the big fists that had rammed his ribs and his belly and his face. Very slowly he pulled his legs onto the sofa and lay back. He closed his eyes and told himself to fade away for an hour or so.

Just then he heard a footstep, the rustle of a dress. He opened his eyes and saw Loretta Channing looking down at him.

She stood there at the side of the sofa, her hands holding the camera. She wasn't aiming it, and he saw that her fingers were manipulating a lever and getting the camera open and taking out a small roll of film.

Her face was expressionless as she extended her hand to offer him the film.

He grinned wryly and shook his head.

"Take it," she said.

"What'll I do with it?"

"Whatever you wish. You said you'd like to shove it down my throat."

He went on grinning. "Did I really say that?"

She nodded. Then she stepped back a little, studying him. Her eyebrows were lifted slightly, as though she was seeing something she hadn't expected to see. He knew she'd anticipated another bitter outburst from him, another display of uncontrollable rage.

He lowered his legs over the side of the sofa, then leaned back, comfortably relaxed. He watched her as she walked across the room and dropped the roll of film into a waste basket. Then she turned and looked at him and she was waiting for him to say something.

He saw the bruise on her lip, and he winced.

"I'm sorry I hit you," he said. Then, with the feeling that he had to say more, he added, "I didn't mean to do it. Just lost my head for a second." He stood up and moved toward the window that looked out upon the sun-drenched river. His voice was very low, not much more than a husky whisper. "I'm really very sorry."

It was quiet for a few moments. Then he heard her say, "Please don't apologize. I'm glad you did it."

He turned and looked at her.

"Yes," she said. "I know I deserved it. I shouldn't have come out there on the pier, and I certainly had no right to snap your picture."

"Why did you do it?"

She opened her mouth to answer. Then she changed her mind and her lips shut tightly. He saw her face go red. She blinked a few times, then looked past him and said, "Whatever my reasons were, it was inexcusable, and I'm very much ashamed of myself." With an effort she gazed directly at his face. "I hope you'll forgive me."

For some strange reason he wasn't able to meet her eyes. He looked at the floor and swallowed hard. "It's all right," he said gruffly. "Let's forget it."

"I can't. I want you to know how badly I feel about this. I've caused you a lot of trouble. You took a bad beating out there on the dock. And now they tell me you've been fired."

He rubbed the back of his neck. "Well, that's the way it goes. I was looking for grief, so they gave it to me."

"But it's all my fault," she said. And then, in a lower tone, "Won't you let me make it up to you?"

He looked at her. "How?"

"I know one of the pier owners. I'll tell him it wasn't your fault. Maybe he'll let you keep your job."

His eyes hardened, and he could feel the cold anger coming. But as he stood there and looked at her, his gaze gradually narrowed and his thoughts became more reasonable. He was thinking, For God's sake, take it easy. Don't blow your top again.

She was saying, "All you need to do is say the word. I'll arrange for an appointment right away."

He was able to say easily, "You really think it'll work?"

"I'm sure it will."

"Well," he said, "whichever way it goes, it's damn nice of you to try."

"Not at all." Her tone was level. "I'm only doing what I think is fair. All this was my fault and there's no reason why you should suffer for it."

He didn't say anything. He had a relaxed feeling, an awareness that it was happening the way it should happen. Somehow it was as though they were meeting for the first time.

His smile was pleasant. "If I get my job back, it'll take a load of worry off my chest. You'll be doing me a big favor."

She had moved toward a table near the window. She put the camera on the table, then turned slightly and gazed out the window and for a few moments she didn't reply. Then, very quietly, "Maybe you'll get a chance to repay it."

He caught no special meaning from her statement, and he said lightly, "I hope so. It'll be a pleasure."

"Well," she said, moving toward the door, "we probably won't be seeing each other again."

"I guess not."

For a long moment she stood in the doorway, looking at him. Her eyes were intense, and it seemed she was trying to tell him something that she couldn't put into words.

Then very slowly she turned and walked out of the room.

Kerrigan moved toward the leather sofa. He felt the weight of heavy fatigue and it had no connection with the battering he'd taken from Ruttman. Nor was it due to the fact that he'd had less than three hours' sleep the night before. As he lowered himself to the sofa, he realized what an effort it had taken to control his anger and discuss matters calmly. It seemed to him that he'd never worked so hard in all his life. . . .

For hour after hour he slept heavily, oblivious of the loud voices of the stevedores on the pier, the clanging of chains, the thudding of crates against the planks. At a few minutes past five he was awakened by a hand shaking his shoulder, and he looked up and saw the grinning face of Ruttman.

"The front office just called," Ruttman said. "They're putting you back on the job."

Kerrigan sat up slowly, rubbing his eyes and dragging himself away from sleep.

Through a veil he heard Ruttman saying, "I'll be damned if I can figure it out. That call came from the big boss himself."

Kerrigan didn't say anything.

Ruttman was looking at him and waiting for an explanation and not getting any. The dock foreman turned away, started toward the door, then pivoted and stared at the table near the window.

Kerrigan stiffened as he saw what Ruttman was looking at. It was the camera.

"Well, whaddya know?" Ruttman breathed. "She give it to you for a gift?"

Kerrigan shook his head slowly, dazedly. "I didn't know she left it here."

Then it was quiet in the room while Ruttman walked slowly to the table and picked up the camera. He looked at it and murmured, "This ain't no ordinary gadget. If it's worth a dime, it's worth fifty bucks. Not the kind of a thing you leave around on tables."

Kerrigan's lips tightened. "What are you getting at?"

Ruttman hefted the camera in his hand. He brought it to the sofa and let it drop into Kerrigan's lap. "It's like a game of checkers," he said. "Now it's your move. You find out where she lives and you take it back to her. That's why she left it here."

The anger was coming again and he tried to hold it back but it flamed in his eyes. "The hell with her," he muttered. "I ain't running no lost-and-found department."

"You gotta take it back to her. Think it over and you'll see what I mean. If it wasn't for her, you'd be out of a job. Now you're obligated."

Ruttman turned and crossed the floor and went out of the room. Kerrigan sat there on the edge of the sofa, his hands gripping the camera. It felt like a chunk of white-hot metal, scorching the skin of his palms.

9

HE WALKED slowly along Wharf, came onto Vernon Street, then walked west on Vernon toward home. The slimy water in the gutter was lit with pink fire from the evening sun, and he looked up and saw it big and very red up there, the flares shooting out from the blazing sphere, merging with the orange clouds, so that the sky was like a huge opal, the glowing colors floating and blending, and it was really something to look at. He thought, It's tremendous. And he wondered if anyone else was looking up at it right now and thinking the same thing.

But as his gaze returned to the street he saw the dirty-faced kids playing in the gutter, he saw a drunk sprawled on a doorstep, and three middle-aged colored men sitting on the curb and drinking wine from a bottle wrapped in an old newspaper.

Under the vermilion glory of the evening sun, the vast magnificence of an opal sky, the Vernon Street citizens had no idea of what was up there, they scarcely bothered to glance up and see. All they knew was that the sun was still high, and it would be one hell of a hot night. Already the older folks were coming out of shacks and tenements to sit on doorsteps with paper fans and pitchers of water. The families who were lucky enough to have ice in the house were holding chunks of it in their mouths and trying to beat the heat that way. And a few of them, just a very few, were giving nickels to their children, to purchase flavored ice on sticks. The kids shrieked with glee, but their happy sound was drowned in the greater noise, the humming noise that was one big groan and sigh, the noise that came from Vernon throats, yet seemed to come from the street itself. It was as though the street had lungs and the only sounds it could make were the groan and the sigh, the weary acceptance of its fourth-class place in the world. High above it there was a wondrous sky, the fabulous colors in the orbit of the sun, but it just didn't make sense to look up there and develop pretty thoughts and hopes and dreams.

The realization came to Kerrigan like the sudden blow of a

hammer, putting him down on solid ground where a spade was never anything but a spade. He looked at the torn leather of his workshoes, the calloused flesh of his hands. He thought, You better wise up to yourself and stay out of the clouds.

His mouth hardened. His hand moved toward the pants pocket where he had the camera. He asked himself what he was going to do with it.

All right, he thought, it ain't no problem. All you gotta do is find out where she lives and mail it to her.

But he could visualize her face as she opened the package and saw the camera. He could see her lips curved in contempt, and almost hear her saying to herself, He's afraid to come here and ring the doorbell.

He wondered what would happen if he went up there to the uptown street where she lived, and actually rang the doorbell. Hell, he thought, what's there to be scared about? Nobody's gonna bite you. But damn it, you'd be out of place up there.

Maybe it would be all right if he looked decent, if he was bathed and shaved and properly dressed. He needed a bath anyway, and it wasn't as though he'd be using soap just to pass some sort of test. It wouldn't hurt him to put on his Sunday clothes. There wasn't any law that said he had to wear them only on Sunday.

Maybe it would really be all right, and these uptown characters wouldn't give him any trouble. Maybe they wouldn't notice that he was different, that he didn't belong.

But no. In no time at all they'd have him sized up, they'd see him for what he was. Perhaps they'd try to be polite and not say anything, but he'd know what they were thinking. It would show in their eyes, no matter how they tried to hide it.

The thing to do, he told himself, was take this goddamn camera and throw it down a sewer or someplace. Just get rid of it.

And there it was again, the stabbing thought that he didn't have the guts to face the situation squarely. He was frightened, that was all.

He walked on down Vernon Street, wondering what to do with the camera.

Arriving at the Kerrigan house, he opened the front door and walked into the parlor. He glanced at the sofa, where Tom was snoring loudly, holding a half-empty beer bottle, the picture of utter contentment.

The only sound in the parlor was the noise coming from the kitchen, the clatter of dishes, the loud voices of Lola and Bella. At first he paid no attention to what they were saying, and his thoughts played idly with the idea that he ought to go in there and get some supper. He wondered if there was anything warm on the stove.

He started across the parlor, headed toward the kitchen, and then he heard Bella yelling, "Just wait till I see that two-timing sneak. Wait till I get my hands on him."

"You'll leave him alone," Lola shouted at her daughter. "If you know what's good for you, you won't start anything."

"It's already started," Bella raged. "What do I look like, an idiot or something? You think I'll let him push me around and make a fool of me? I warned him what would happen if he messed around. I'm gonna show that louse I mean what I say."

"Not in this house you won't," Lola shouted.

"The hell I won't," Bella blazed. "And you won't stop me, neither."

There was the smacking sound of a hand against a face. He heard Bella screaming. Then another smack. And Bella screamed again.

He heard Lola say, "Talk back again and I'll slap you so hard you'll go through the wall."

Then it was quiet in the kitchen. Kerrigan decided to wait just a little while longer before having supper, and perhaps Bella would be cooled off entirely by the time he was ready to eat.

He walked down the hall and into his room and took off his clothes. Then he went into the bathroom, filled the tub, and climbed in and soaped his body. In his room again, he put on a clean shirt and shorts and socks, opened the closet door and took a gray worsted suit off the hanger. It was his Sunday suit, the only suit he owned, and it needed pressing, some sewing here and there, and one of the buttons was missing. As he stood before the mirror, pulling at the lapels and trying to stretch the fabric to get rid of the wrinkles, he wished he had a better suit to wear. And while the thought ran through his mind, he was slowly lowering the camera into the jacket pocket.

He slipped a tie under his collar, knotted it three times before he was satisfied, then leaned close to the mirror and gave his wet combed hair a few final pats with his palms. Stepping back from the mirror, he studied himself from various angles, frowned appraisingly, then shrugged and decided that it would have to do.

Coming into the kitchen, he saw Lola arranging the dishes on a shelf. Bella was at the sink with a towel in her hands. The moment she saw him, her face darkened and reddened and fire came into her eyes. She took a deep breath and opened her mouth to say something. But from the other side of the room she saw her mother watching her. She took another deep breath and shut her mouth tightly and closed her eyes, grimly trying to control her temper.

Lola was smiling at Kerrigan and saying, "Want something to eat?"

He nodded and sat down at the splintered table, which had several match books under one leg to keep it balanced. Bella had turned back to the sink as if she had no idea he was in the room. But he could hear her breathing heavily and he knew she was having a hard time holding back the rage that strained to break loose.

Lola picked up a large spoon and moved majestically toward the stove. She was an excellent cook, extremely proud of it, and always anxious to prove it. She bent over the stove, studied the contents of a huge pot and a couple of smaller ones, and murmured, "It'll take just a minute to warm up."

"No hurry," Kerrigan said. He lit a cigarette and leaned back.

Lola was stirring the spoon in the pots, lifting the spoon to her mouth, testing the flavor of the beef stew and the rice and the summer squash.

"Needs pepper," Lola murmured. She looked at Bella and said, "Get me the pepper."

"Let him get it." Bella spaced the words distinctly.

"I told you to get it," Lola said.

Bella sucked air in between her teeth. She moved away from the sink, opened the kitchen cabinet, and grabbed at the pepper shaker. She brought it to the table and slammed it down in front of Kerrigan.

"Not there," Lola said. "I told you to bring it here. To me. And bring your face here so I can smack it again."

Bella swallowed hard. She was afraid to move. Kerrigan reached for the pepper shaker and handed it to Lola, who took it without looking at it. Lola aimed a dim but dangerous smile at her daughter.

"You're gonna get it," Lola said. "I can see you're itching for it, and before the night's over you're gonna get it like you never got it before. I'm telling you, girl, you got a rotten evil temper and I'm gonna knock it out of you if I have to break every bone in your body."

Bella's lips were trembling. She started toward the doorway leading out of the kitchen. Lola caught her arm, pulled her away from the doorway, then shoved her back to the sink.

"You ain't finished here yet," Lola said. "You gotta do them knives and forks. And when he's through eating, you'll have his plates to do."

Bella seemed to be choking. "Me do his plates? I gotta clean up after him?"

"You heard me," Lola said.

Kerrigan squirmed in his chair. "I can wash my own dishes."

"I said she's gonna wash them," Lola said loudly and firmly.

Kerrigan shrugged. He knew there was no use arguing with Lola.

She heaped his plate with the beef stew and the rice and the squash. She put six slices of bread on the plate, poured coffee into a thick cup, then backed away from the table and watched him tackle the meal.

Kerrigan ate slowly, chewing thoroughy, savoring each mouthful. As he sat there enjoying the meal, the kitchen was quiet except for the busy noise of his knife and fork on the plate. He completely forgot the presence of Bella, whose eyes alternated between raging glares at him and wary glances at her mother.

His plate was empty now, and Lola said, "Ready for more?"

He nodded, pushing bread into his mouth.

Lola looked at Bella and said, "Don't stand there. Pick up his plate."

Bella swallowed hard. Her voice cracked slightly as she stared pleadingly at her mother and said, "It ain't bad enough I gotta wash his dishes. Now you want me to bring him his meal. Like a servant."

Lola's eyes softened just a little. She shook her head slowly. "No," she murmured. "Not like a servant. After all, you're his woman, ain't you?"

Kerrigan winced. He looked up and studied Lola's face and all at once he knew what was in her mind. In her own blunt way she was saying to her daughter, If you want him for a husband, I'll show you how to get him.

He shifted uncomfortably in the chair. He had a strange feeling that the walls were closing in on him and he itched to get out of the house. Until now it hadn't occurred to him that Lola wanted him for a son-in-law. But as he noticed how Lola was nodding approvingly, he realized there was a plan in action, and for a fearful moment he could see himself married to Bella.

But then, as the steaming food was placed before him and he saw the smooth richness of Bella's skin, he said to himself, Why not?

He watched her as she turned away from the table, and saw how her hips moved. The construction was there, the face was there, and all he had to do was buy her a ring and he'd have all that for keeps.

Another thing. He'd soon be thirty-five and it was high time he got married. What the hell was he waiting for?

He pictured himself putting the ring on Bella's finger. He had the feeling it would settle a lot of questions that clouded his brain and circled around in there, a vague merry-go-round of issues that he just couldn't figure out. Since last night he'd been walking back and forth in a fog, doing things he didn't want to do, operating way off the beam and wondering what in God's name it was all about. Things had happened much too fast, making him dizzy, taking his feet off the ground. But there was a fast way to fix all that.

There'd be no problem in finding the right person to perform a quick ceremony. On Third Street, off Vernon, a little old Greek was capable of legally tying the knot in a matter of seconds. The Greek's son worked in City Hall, in the Marriage Bureau, and was faced with no trouble at all when it came to stealing licenses. The father and son were extremely popular in the neighborhood, for when Vernon men decided to make it legal, they didn't like to wait.

A blunt voice cut in on his thoughts. He heard Bella saying, "More coffee?"

He looked up. She was standing at the stove. He glanced around the kitchen, but Lola wasn't there and he wondered when she'd walked out of the room. Then he gazed down at his plate and saw that it was empty and he couldn't remember having finished the second helping.

"Come out of it," Bella said, and he knew she'd been watching him for some time. "I asked you if you want more coffee."

He nodded. But it wasn't for the coffee. It was just to make a reply.

Bella brought the percolator to the table and poured coffee into his cup. She poured a cup for herself and sat down across from him. Then she put cigarettes on the table and asked him if he wanted one. He nodded again, looking at her intently and trying to establish contact with her. As he leaned forward to get the light from the match she offered, he wondered what the hell was wrong here. He had the downright uncanny feeling that he wasn't here in the kitchen with Bella, he was someplace else.

"What is it?" Bella said. "What's the matter with you?"

"Nothing." He shrugged. "I had a rough day."

"You look it," she murmured. "Who slugged you?"

"It happened on the pier. It didn't last long."

"They carry him away?"

"No," he said. "They carried me."

She gave him a side glance. "How come? Lose your punch?"

He didn't say anything. He sipped at the coffee and took long drags at the cigarette and tried not to look at her. But he was focusing on her face, and seeing a parade of questions coming out of her eyes. He compared her present mood with the explosive anger of minutes ago, and realized that she'd calmed down considerably, almost to the point of passivity. He'd never seen her like this, and it made him uneasy. His throat felt tight and he worked his head from side to side, trying to loosen his collar.

"Unbutton it," she said.

"It's all right."

"Don't you feel hot? Why don't you take your jacket off?"

"I want it on." He spoke just a little louder. "You don't mind, do you?"

He was hoping she'd curse him, or say anything that would get the shouting started, their normal means of communication.

But all she said was, "Of course I don't mind. I just want you to be comfortable."

"All right, I'm comfortable. You satisfied?"

She didn't reply. For some moments she just sat there looking at him. Then, in a strangely quiet tone, "I want to know why you're all dressed up."

He opened his mouth to give her an answer. His mouth stayed open but no sound came out.

Bella leaned forward, her elbows on the table. "Come on, let's have it. You might as well tell me who she is. I've seen her already."

He blinked a few times.

"Last night," Bella said. "I was in bed, waiting for you. When you didn't come in, I got up to see what you were doing. I went into the parlor and took a look through the front window. I saw you talking to her. And then the two of you got into the car and drove away."

He managed to look away from her. "It wasn't what you think."

Her face was expressionless. "I haven't told you what I think. I'm waiting to hear what your plans are."

"What plans?"

Bella's eyes were drills going into him. "You and her."

"For God's sake!" He shouted it, and jumped up from the table. "What are you building here? That broad don't mean a thing to me. I hardly even know her!"

He jammed his hands into his trousers pockets and started to walk up and down alongside the table.

"Another thing," Bella said. "You didn't come home last night. I stayed up, waiting for you. Where'd you go? Where'd you sleep?"

The floor seemed to be moving under his feet and he wished it would keep on moving and take him away from all these questions he couldn't handle. But the floor kept him there near the table, holding him on the track, setting him there like a slowly moving target while the sharpshooter took aim.

Then Bella shot it at him. "Whoever she is, she's doing something to you. She's got you wrapped around her finger."

It was like a crowbar hitting him in the eyes. He backed away from the table, staring at Bella. "What gives you that crazy idea?"

"I can tell. It's plastered all over your face."

He took several deep breaths. But that didn't help. He turned his back to the table, folded his arms, and glowered at the floor.

And he heard Bella saying, "You see what I mean? It shows. You can't even look me in the eye."

For a moment he wished he were one of the smooth talkers, the con artists who could handle this sort of thing and slide out of it without any trouble. But then, as he pivoted hard and faced her, he was glaring and his voice was blunt. "Now listen," he said. "I'll tell you once and then it's ended, you hear? There ain't a goddamn thing happening with me and that chippy. She's one of them phonys from uptown. She came down here to play around and get some kicks. All I did was tell her off and send her on her way."

Bella's features were impassive. Then gradually a smile worked its way onto her lips, a perceptive smile that narrowed her eyes as she murmured, "She's got you so mixed up, you're dizzy. You really go for her."

"Sure," he snarled. "Like a fish goes for dry land. You don't know what the hell you're talking about."

"Don't I?" Bella slowly arose from the table. She looked him up and down. She smiled and said, "This tickles me. It's really very funny."

He stiffened. "What's funny?"

Her smile was pure disdain. "You," she said. "You're the comedian. And what takes the cake is that getup you're wearing. Making a social call uptown?" She started to laugh at him.

"Stop it," he said.

She went on laughing.

He stood rigid and his fists were clenched and he spoke through his teeth. "Goddamn you," he said. "Stop it."

He stood rigid and his fists were clenched and he spoke through his teeth. "Goddamn you," he said. "Stop it."

"I can't." She was holding her sides, as though her ribs were cracking. Her laughter climbed to a screaming pitch.

Kerrigan moved toward her, his eyes burning, his teeth grinding. But suddenly he stopped short, staring past Bella, seeing something that caused him to stiffen. His eyes were aiming at a small mirror on the wall and he saw his carefully combed hair and the Sunday suit.

The mocking laughter jabbed at him like hot needles inserted in his brain. But he heard it, the jeering sound wasn't coming from Bella. He told himself it came from the mirror.

He turned away and hurried out of the kitchen. The laughter followed him down the hall, through the parlor, and went on jabbing at him as he opened the front door and walked out of the house.

10

H E WALKED aimlessly on Vernon, crossing the street several times for no good reason at all. On Wharf Street he turned around and went back on Vernon all the way to Eleventh, then walked eleven blocks back to Wharf, and turned around again. It didn't occur to him how much ground he was covering, how many hours it was taking. The only definite feeling he had was the weight of the camera in his jacket pocket.

The sky was dark now. He continued to walk back and forth along Vernon Street and finally he stood outside a store window, staring at the face of a clock that read eleven-forty. He scowled at the clock and asked himself what in hell he was going to do with the camera.

He turned away from the store window and resumed walking along Vernon. The heat-weary citizens were grouped on doorsteps, the perspiration gleaming on their faces. As Kerrigan walked past, they stared at him in wonder, seeing the buttoned collar and the necktie and the heavy worsted jacket and trousers. They shook their heads.

But although he wasn't thinking about it, the sticky heat seeped into his body and he moved with increasing difficulty. His mouth and throat were aching for a cold drink. He saw the light in the window of Dugan's Den, and it occurred to him that he could use a few beers.

Entering the taproom, he heard the squeaky tune that Dugan hummed off key. There were three customers at the bar, a couple of hags with a lot of rouge on their faces and an ageless humpbacked derelict bent low over a glass of wine. The hags were glaring at Dugan, who had his arms folded and his eyes half closed and was concentrating on the music that came from his lips.

One of the hags leaned toward Dugan and yelled, "Shut up with that noise. I can't stand that goddamn noise."

Dugan went on humming.

"You gonna shut up?" the hag screeched.

"He won't shut up," the other hag said. "Only way to quiet him down is shoot him."

"One of these nights I'll do just that," the first hag said. "I'll come in here with a gun, and so help me, I'll put a slug in his throat."

Kerrigan was at the bar. He caught Dugan's attention and said he wanted a beer. Dugan filled a glass and brought it to him. He finished it quickly and ordered another. He looked up at the clock above the bar and the hands pointed to twelve-ten. In his jacket pocket the camera was very heavy.

The first hag was pointing to Kerrigan and saying loudly, "Look at that goddamn fool. Look at the way he's all dressed up."

"In a winter suit," the other hag said.

"Maybe he thinks it's wintertime," the first hag said. She was short and shapeless and her hair was dyed orange.

The other hag began to laugh. She made a sound like two pieces of rusty metal scraping against each other. Her throat was ribboned with several knife scars and on her face she had a hideous vertical scar that ran from the right eye down to the mouth. She was of average height and weighed around eighty pounds. Pointing a bony finger at Kerrigan, she jeered, "You tryin' to suffocate? Is that whatcha wanna do? You wanna suffocate?"

"He don't even hear ya," the shapeless hag said. "He's all dressed up to go somewhere and he don't even hear ya."

"Hey, stupid," the scarred woman hollered. "You goin' to a party? Take us with you."

"Yeah. We're all dressed up, too."

Kerrigan looked at them. He saw the rags they wore, the cracked leather and broken heels of their shoes. Then he looked at their faces and he recognized them. The shapeless woman with orange hair was named Frieda and she lived in a shack a few doors away from the Kerrigan house. The scarred woman was the widow of a ditchdigger and her name was Dora. Both women were in their early forties and he'd known them since his childhood.

"Hello, Frieda," he said. "Hello, Dora."

They stiffened and stared at him.

"Don't you know me?" he said.

Without moving from where they stood at the other end of the bar, they leaned forward to get a better look at him.

"I know what he is," Frieda said. "He's a federal."

Dora slanted her head and looked Kerrigan up and down and then she nodded slowly.

"A goddamn federal," Frieda said. "I can spot them a mile away."

"What's he want with us?" Dora's voice was wary.

"I'm wise to these federals," Frieda declared in a loud voice. "They can't put anything over on me. Hey, you," she shouted at Kerrigan. "Whatever you got in mind, forget it. We ain't bootleggers and we ain't peddling dope. We're honest, hardworking women and we go to church and we're all paid up on our income taxes."

"And another thing," Dora cut in. "We're not counterfeiters."

"We're decent citizens," Frieda stated. Her voice climbed to a shrill blast. "You leave us alone, you hear?"

Kerrigan sighed and went back to his beer. He knew there was no use trying to prove his identity. He knew that Frieda and Dora were mixing their fear of the law with a certain pleasure, a feeling of importance. They visualized the United States government sending an agent to deal with two clever queens of vice. But they'd show him. They'd trip him up on every move he made.

He called to Dugan and said he was buying drinks for the ladies. They ordered double shots of gin and didn't bother to thank him because they were in a hurry to get it down. And when it was down they forgot all about him; they gazed at the empty glasses and tried to drown themselves in the emptiness.

While Dugan hummed the squeaky tune, Kerrigan leaned low over the bar, not hearing it. He was gazing at the half-empty glass of beer and feeling the weight of the camera in his pocket.

Then the door opened and someone came into the taproom. The women looked around at the newcomer, who smiled a quietly amiable greeting and moved toward a table at the other side of the room. The hags made oaths without sound as they glowered at the delicately chiseled face of Newton Channing. He was wearing a clean white shirt and a light summer suit that was freshly pressed. As he seated himself at a table he lit a cigarette with a green enamel-cased lighter. It sent a pale green glow onto his thin, sensitive features and gave a greenish tint to his yellow hair.

The two hags went on looking at Newton Channing, their eyes reflecting a mixture of curiosity and absurdly futile envy.

Kerrigan had raised his head and he was staring at the mirror behind the bar. He watched the smoke climbing languidly from the cigarette in Channing's mouth. His hand moved slowly along the side of his jacket and he reached into the pocket containing the camera.

He waited until Dugan served Channing a water glass filled with whisky. Then he walked across the room to Channing's table. He took the camera out of his pocket and put it on the table.

"What's this?" Channing asked without interest.

"It belongs to your sister."

"Where'd you get it?"

"She left it with me."

Channing frowned slightly. He picked up the camera and turned it around in his hands, holding it close to his eyes and giving it a careful inspection. Then he put it down and his head turned slowly and he looked at Kerrigan.

He said, "Aren't you the man I met last night?"

Kerrigan nodded. "You bought me a beer. We talked for a while."

"Yes, I remember." Channing turned his attention back to the camera. "What's the story on this?"

Kerrigan laughed.

"What's funny?" Channing asked. His voice was very soft.

Kerrigan moved to the other side of the table and sat down. Channing had pushed the glass of whisky aside and was leaning forward and frowning puzzledly, his eyes still on the camera.

Kerrigan drummed his fingers on the tabletop. He said, "You better have a talk with your sister. Tell her she was very lucky this time. Maybe next time she won't be so lucky."

Channing looked at him. "I don't know what you mean."

"Can't you add it up?"

Channing shook his head. His eyes were blank.

"She made a play for me," Kerrigan said. He leaned back in the chair and waited for Channing's reaction.

But there was no reaction, except that the puzzlement faded just a little. And then Channing shrugged. He reached out for the water glass filled with whisky, lifted it to his mouth, and took a long drink. Then he put the cigarette to his lips and pulled at it easily. The smoke came out of his nose and mouth like the smoke from an incense burner, thin columns climbing lazily.

Kerrigan could feel himself stiffening. He tried to loosen up, but his eyes were getting hard and his voice sounded tight and strained. "Didn't you hear what I said? She made a play for me."

"So?"

"You don't seem to care."

"Why should I?"

Kerrigan spoke with bitter sarcasm. "She's got class. You don't want her mixing with bar flies and dock workers."

"I don't give a damn who she mixes with."

"She's your sister," Kerrigan said. "Don't she mean anything to you?"

"She means a great deal to me. I'm awfully fond of Loretta."

"Then why don't you look out for her?"

"She's old enough to look out for herself."

"Not after dark. Not in this neighborhood. No woman is safe in this neighborhood."

Channing lifted his gaze from the camera and studied Kerrigan's face. For some moments he didn't speak. Then he said quietly, "I'm not worried. Why should you be?"

It was a perfectly logical statement. Kerrigan swallowed hard and said, "Just trying to give you advice, that's all."

"Thank you," Channing said. He slanted his head a little. "I think you're the one who needs advice."

Kerrigan found himself staring toward the center of the table, at the camera.

He heard Channing saying, "Don't be afraid of her."

It seemed to him that the tabletop was coming up to hit him in the face. He pulled his head to one side. He wondered why he couldn't look at Channing.

"There's no reason to be afraid," Channing said. "After all, she's just a woman."

He tried to reply. He groped for phrases and couldn't find a single word.

"I'm saying this," Channing murmured, "because I know you want her."

"You're crazy."

"Possibly," Channing admitted with complete gravity. "But at times it's the lunatic who makes the most sense. Maybe you're not aware that you want her, but it shows in your eyes. You want her very much and you're terribly afraid of her."

Something tugged at Kerrigan's throat. He spoke in a whisper. "Sure I'm afraid. I'm afraid if she bothers me again I might clip her in the teeth."

Channing raised his eyebrows. For a long moment he was quietly thoughtful. Then he said, "Well, that's easily understandable. From your point of view she's just fooling around."

Kerrigan put his hands flat on the table. His palms pressed hard against the wood. He didn't say anything.

Channing said, "It's quite possible she's more serious than you think. Why don't you try to find out?"

"I'm not interested. Happens I got something else on my mind."

He paused, waiting for it to sink in.

Channing's face was impassive.

"It concerns you." And there was another pause, much longer. "I'd like to find out more about you."

"Me?" Channing frowned. "What for? Any special reason?"

"I think you know what the reason is. I'm not ready to say for sure. But I think you know."

Channing's eyebrows were up again. "That sounds rather sinister. Now you have me curious."

"Not worried?"

"No. Just curious."

"You ought to be worried."

Channing smiled. "I never worry. I suffer a lot, but I never worry." He reached for the glass of whisky. He took a very long drink, emptying the glass. Then he poured more whisky from the bottle and took another drink. He said, "I wish you'd tell me what this is all about."

"I'm not ready to tell you."

Channing went on smiling. It was a relaxed smile. "I hope it's something exciting," he murmured. "I like excitement."

"That's what I figured," Kerrigan said. "Anything for kicks."

"Sure." Channing lit another cigarette. "Why not?" He took an easy drag, let it go down deep, and then it came out in little clouds as he said, "A few weeks ago I thought it would be nice to see Alaska. I'd never been to Alaska and I had this sudden notion to make the trip. The idea hit me on a Wednesday afternoon. An hour later I was in a plane. Thursday night I was making love to a sixty-year-old Eskimo woman."

For some moments Kerrigan was silent. Then he said, "How was it in Alaska?"

"Very nice. Rather cold, but really very nice."

Kerrigan's hands were still flat on the table. He looked down at them. "You do these things often?"

"Now and then," Channing said. "Depends on what mood I'm in."

"I bet you have all kinds of moods."

"Hundreds of them," Channing admitted. He laughed without sound. "I ought to keep a filing cabinet. It's hard to remember such a wide variety."

Kerrigan closed his eyes and for a moment all he saw was black. And then something happened to the blackness and it became the dark alley and the dried bloodstains.

He could feel the trembling that began in his chest and went up to his brain and down to his chest again. His eyes were open now and he stared at his hands and saw that his knuckles were white. He said to himself, Cut it out, you're not sure yet, you don't have proof, you can't do anything if you don't have proof.

Just then something caused him to turn his head and he saw the two hags who stood at the bar. They were making hissing sounds and their eyes were focused on him and Channing. And then, somewhat hesitantly, they moved toward the table.

They approached the table with their faces sullen and belligerent and yet their twisted mouths seemed to be pleading for something. Frieda was trying to wriggle her shapeless hips and her hands made dainty adjustments to her orange hair. Dora swayed her bony shoulders and attempted to show the curves of a body that had no curves. As the two of them came closer, it was like a walking bag of flour and a walking broomstick.

"Get the hell away," Kerrigan muttered.

"We got a right to sit down," Dora said. And then she recognized him. "Well, whaddya know? It's Bill Kerrigan."

"Damn if it ain't," Frieda shouted.

"And he's all dressed up in his Sunday best," Dora declared. She let out a high-pitched, jarring laugh. "We thought you was a federal." She folded her arms and unfolded them and then folded them again. "Why the special outfit?"

"This here's a special table," Frieda said. She made a gesture to indicate Channing, who sat there relaxed and smiling dimly.

Dora had stopped laughing and her face was pleated with lines curving downward. "It may be special, but it ain't reserved. If they can sit here, so can we."

"You're goddamn right," Frieda said. She took the chair next to Channing. Then she shifted the chair so that the grimy fabrics covering her hip came up against the side of his clean jacket.

Dora sat down beside Kerrigan. She put her arm around his shoulder. He cursed without sound, took hold of her wrist, and pushed her arm away. But then her arm was there again. He said, "What the hell," and let it stay there.

"Gonna buy us a drink?" Frieda asked Channing.

"Why, certainly," Channing said. "What would you like?"

"Gin," Dora said. "We don't drink nothing but gin."

Channing called to Dugan and said he wanted a bottle of gin and two glasses. At the bar the humpbacked wino had turned and was looking at the table. The face of the wino was expressionless.

"Would you like something?" Channing asked the wino.

"Go to hell," the wino said. He said it with an effort. There was no more wine in his glass and he had seven cents in his pocket and wine was fifteen. He took a deep dragging breath and said, "You can go to hell."

"Same to you," Frieda yelled at the wino. "We want no part of you, you humpbacked freak."

"Don't say that," Channing said mildly. "That isn't nice."

Frieda twisted in her chair and glowered at him. "Don't you tell me how to talk. I'm a lady and I know how to talk."

"All right," Channing said.

"We're both ladies, me and my friend Dora. That's Dora there. My name's Frieda."

"Pleased to meet you," he said. "I'm Newton Channing."

Frieda spoke loudly. "We don't give a damn who you are. You ain't no better than us." She sat up very straight, and her eyes were hard. "What makes you think you're better than us?"

"Is that what I think?"

"Sure," Dora said. "You ain't kidding nobody."

Channing shrugged. Dugan arrived at the table with the bottle of gin and two glasses. Channing looked at Kerrigan. "What's yours?"

"I don't want anything," Kerrigan mumbled. "I'm getting out of here." He tried to twist away from the pressure of Dora's skinny arm. She put her other arm around him and held him there.

He didn't hear the sound of the door and he didn't hear the approaching footsteps in his struggle to pull away from Dora. Then something caused him to look up and he saw her standing at the side of the table, he saw the lovely face and golden hair of Loretta Channing.

She was looking at him. Her gaze was intent and she was ignoring the others at the table.

Frieda said, "Who's this tramp?"

"This tramp," Channing said, "is my sister."

"She ain't bad-lookin'," Dora commented.

"What's she doin' here?" Frieda asked. "She lookin' for a pickup?"

"There's one over there," Dora said, and pointed to the humpback at the bar. "Go on over and talk to him," she told Loretta. She didn't like the way Loretta was looking at Kerrigan. Her arm pressed tighter around Kerrigan's shoulder and she spoke louder. "Can't ya see we're teamed up here? Ya can't sit here unless you're with a man."

Loretta went on looking at Kerrigan.

Dora began to breathe hard. "All right, you," she hissed at Loretta. "You quit puttin' your eye on him. He's with me. Ya wanna see him, ya gotta see me first."

"That's right, tell her," Frieda said.

Channing was chuckling. "Be careful, Dora. My sister packs a punch."

"She don't worry me," Dora said. "She starts with me, she'll need nurses day and night."

She saw that Loretta was ignoring her and continuing to look at Kerrigan. She stood up and put her face close to Loretta's face and shouted, "Now listen, you, I told you to stop lookin' at him."

"Don't shout in my face," Loretta said quietly.

"You keep it up and I'll spit in your face."

Loretta smiled. Her eyes stayed on Kerrigan as she murmured, "No, don't do that."

"You dare me?" Dora screeched.

"Sure she dares you," Channing said. "Can't you see she's looking for trouble?"

"Well, sure as hell she's gonna get it," Dora stated. "When I'm with a man I don't want no floozie buttin' in."

Loretta looked at the skinny hag. "You're right," she said. "You're absolutely right. I'm very sorry." She backed away from Dora and then turned and walked toward the bar.

But Dora wasn't satisfied. Dora yelled, "You don't get off that easy, you tramp." She lowered her head and went lunging across the room. At the last moment Loretta stepped to one side and Dora collided with the bar and bounced back and landed flat on the floor. She rolled over on her side, tried to get up, and tripped over her own legs and went down again. She made another attempt to rise, managed to get on her feet, and saw Loretta standing with hands on hips, waiting for her. There was something in Loretta's eyes that told Dora to think in terms of personal safety.

As Dora backed away from Loretta, the humpbacked wino let out a quiet laugh of disdain. Dora whirled on the wino and began to blast him with a stream of curses. Loretta turned away from them and told Dugan she wanted whisky. At the table, Frieda was telling Channing that he ought to get himself a wife and settle down. She began to speak in low tones, discussing the various benefits to matrimony. Channing had turned in his chair to face her and give her his undivided attention. Frieda declared that every man needed a woman to live with, that in order to preserve one's health it was necessary to lead a wholesome domestic life. Channing agreed with her. He said he was definitely in favor of a wholesome domestic life. He asked Frieda what her age was, and she said forty-three. Channing nodded thoughtfully and then he asked her what she weighed and she said one-seventy. He told her that one-seventy was all right and then he asked her if she knew how to cook. She said no. Channing's eyes were steady and level on the shapeless hag with orange hair. His voice was serious as he told her that she might as well start learning how to cook.

Kerrigan sat there and listened to it and he was staring at the camera. He heard Frieda saying, "You mean it?" and Channing said, "Yes, Frieda," and then Frieda said, "Well, I'll be god-damned." Kerrigan was trying to drag his eyes away from the camera. He told himself to get up and get out of here. He heard the gin-rusty voice of Frieda as she said, "You mean I'll actually be your wife and you'll be my husband?" Without the slightest hesitation, Channing answered, "Absolutely, if that's what you'd like." Kerrigan took hold of the table edge and tried to lift himself from the chair, but the lens of the camera had hold of his eyes and he couldn't move. Frieda was saying, "When do we do it?" and Channing said, "You set the date."

The legs of Kerrigan's chair scraped the floor, and then he was up from the table. He looked down at the shapeless hag and said, "Why do you let him tease you?"

Frieda gazed up at him. Her mouth sagged. "Is that what he's doing?" She turned her head to study Channing's face. She said, "You just sittin' here and havin' fun with me?"

Channing was pouring more whisky into his glass. He took a long, slow drink, the equivalent of three shots. He said, "I told you to set the date."

Kerrigan scowled at Frieda and said, "You damn fool. Can't you see he's pulling your leg? He's making you pay for the gin. Only thing he wants is entertainment."

"Aw, dry up," Frieda said. "I ain't askin' for your opinion." She turned to Channing and smiled fondly at him. There was some sadness in the smile. "It's all right, I know it's just a gag. I know you can't really mean it."

"But I do mean it," Channing said. His voice was soft, his eyes were tender. He spoke to her as though Kerrigan weren't there. "Believe me," he said. "Try to believe me."

Kerrigan snorted. He pulled away from the table and turned toward the door. He took a step in that direction and then he saw Loretta at the bar on the other side of the room. He stood motionless, looking at her as she leaned over the bar. Gradually his eyes narrowed. He went back to the table and picked up the camera. He walked slowly across the room and came up beside her and put the camera on the bar.

He said matter-of-factly, "You left this in the pier office."

He was turning to leave. She put her hand on his arm. "Please don't go."

"I have a date."

She looked him up and down. "Is that why you're all dressed up?"

He didn't reply.

For a long moment she studied his eyes. Then she said, "Of course you have a date. With me."

"Since when?"

"Since you took a bath and shaved and put on your best clothes."

He frowned. "I didn't do it for you."

She slanted her head, regarding him from a side angle. "For who else would you do it?"

He opened his mouth to give her a fast vicious answer, but no words came out. He waited for her to let go of his arm so he could walk away from her. Then he realized she wasn't holding his arm, she'd released it several moments ago. He wondered why he had the feeling she was still holding onto his arm.

Behind the bar Dugan was waiting to be paid for a whisky and water. Loretta opened her purse and took out a dollar bill and gave it to him. He gave her the change, two quarters and two dimes. The transaction was made without haste and Kerrigan wished they'd speed it up. He couldn't understand his impatience. For some unaccountable reason he was in a hurry, and it was as though he couldn't move unless she moved along with him.

He stood there and waited while she put the seventy cents in her purse and slipped the purse into her skirt pocket. He shifted his weight from one foot to the other and watched her sipping the whisky and water. She sipped it slowly, and without sound he said, Come on, come on. She turned and looked at him. She placed the glass on the table, picked up the camera, and smiled at him as she murmured, "I'm ready now, if you are."

The floor seemed to slide under his feet, taking him away

from the bar. The ceiling moved backward and the walls moved and the door came closer. Behind him there was the sound of Dora's shrill voice as she went on yapping at the humpbacked wino. And the sound of lower voices, the continued conversation of Frieda and Channing. And also the sound of a squeaky tune that came humming from the lips of Dugan. But all the sounds were meaningless, a chorus adding up to nothing. What he heard was a roaring in his brain as he walked with Loretta toward the door, and past the door, and out of Dugan's Den.

11

HE STOOD with her on the corner outside the taproom. He saw the little sport car parked across the street. It was clean and shiny, and the moonlight seemed to give it a silvery gleam. It glimmered like a jewel against the shabby background of shacks and tenements. He thought, It don't belong here, it just don't fit in with the picture.

He looked at Loretta. She was waiting for him to say something. He swallowed hard and mumbled, "Wanna go for a walk?"

"Let's use the car."

They crossed the street and climbed into the MG. She started the engine. He leaned back in the seat and tried to make himself comfortable. He felt very uncomfortable and it had nothing to do with the seating arrangement. She saw him squirming and she said, "It's such a tiny car. There isn't much room."

"It's all right," he said. But it wasn't all right. He told himself he didn't belong in the car. He wanted to open the door and get out. He wondered why he couldn't get out.

The car was moving. He said, "Where we going?"

"Any place you'd like. Would you care to ride uptown?"

He shook his head abruptly.

"Why not?" she asked.

He didn't have an answer. He had his arms folded and he was staring straight ahead.

"I can show you where I live," she said.

"No." His voice was gruff.

"It isn't far away," she urged mildly. "Just a short ride. Not even twenty minutes."

"I don't want to go there."

"Any special reason?"

Again he couldn't answer.

She said, "It's very nice uptown."

"I bet it is." He spoke between his teeth. "A damn sight nicer than it is down here."

"That isn't what I meant."

"I know what you meant." His hands put a tight grip on the edge of the seat. "Do me a favor, will you? Quit trying to put things on an equal basis. You're from up there and I'm from down here. Let's leave it that way."

"But that doesn't make sense. That's stupid."

"All right, it's stupid. But that's the way it is. So just drive toward the river."

The car moved faster. It came onto Wharf Street and he told her to turn north. They went north for several blocks and presently he told her to park up ahead. He pointed to a wide gap between the piers. It was a grassy slope, slanting down to the water's edge.

It was mostly weeds and moss, not much more than a mud flat, and during the day it was nothing to see. But under the moon it was serene and pastoral, the tall weeds somehow stately and graceful, like ferns.

"Very pretty," she murmured. "It's nice here."

"Well, it's quiet, anyway. And there's a breeze."

For some moments they didn't say anything. He wondered why he'd directed her to this place. It occurred to him that he used to come here when he was a kid, coming here alone to feel the quiet and get the river breeze. Or maybe just to get away from the shacks and the tenements.

He heard her saying, "It's so different here. Like a little island, away from everything." Then he looked at her. The moonlight poured onto her golden hair and put lights in her eyes. Her face was entrancing. He could taste the nectar of her nearness.

He told himself he wanted her, he had to have her. The need was so intense that he wondered what kept him from taking her into his arms. Then all at once he knew what it was. It was something deeper than hunger of the flesh. He wanted to reach her heart, her spirit. And his brain seethed with bitterness as he thought, That ain't what she wants. All she's out for is a cheap thrill.

The bitterness showed in his eyes. He spoke thickly. "Start the car. Let's get away from here."

"Why?" She frowned slightly. "What's wrong?"

He couldn't look at her. "You're just fooling around. Having yourself a good time."

"That isn't true."

"The hell it isn't. I been around enough to know what the score is."

"You're adding it up backward."

"Am I?" He glowered at her. "Who do you think you're kidding?"

She didn't say anything, just shook her head slowly.

He pointed to the key dangling from the ignition lock. "Come on, start the car."

She didn't budge. Her hands were folded loosely in her lap. She looked down at them and said quietly, "You're not giving me much of a chance."

"Chance for what?" His voice was jagged. "To play me for a goddamn fool?"

She looked at him. "Why do you say these things?"

"I'm only saying what I think."

"You sure about that? You really know what you're thinking?"

"I know when I'm being taken. I know that I don't like to be jerked around."

"You don't trust me?"

"Sure I trust you. As far as I could throw a ten-ton truck."

She smiled again, but there was pain in her eyes. "Well, anyway, I tried."

He frowned. "Tried what?"

"Something I've never done before. It isn't a woman's nature to do the chasing. Not openly, anyway. But I knew it was the only way I could get to know you." She shrugged. "I'm sorry you're not interested."

His frown deepened. "This on the level?"

She didn't reply. She just looked at him.

"Damn it," he murmured, "you got me all mixed up. Now I don't know what to think."

She went on in a tone of self-reproach, "I tried to be subtle. Or clever. Or whatever it was. Like today on the docks, when I used the camera. But deep inside myself I knew the real reason I wanted your picture."

He looked away from her.

She said very quietly, "I wanted to keep you with me. I had to settle for a snapshot. But later, when I left the camera on the table, I was strictly a female playing a game. What I should have done was say it openly, bluntly."

"Say what?"

"I want you."

He could feel his brain spinning. He fought the dizziness and managed to say, "I'm not in the market for a one-night stand."

"I didn't mean it that way. You know I didn't mean it that way."

For some moments he couldn't speak. He was trying to adjust his thoughts. Finally he said, "This is happening too fast. We hardly know each other."

"What's there to know? Is it so important to find out all the details? The moment I met you, I felt something. It was a feeling I've never had before. That's all I want to know. That feeling."

"Yes," he said. "I know. I know just what you mean."

"You feel it too?"

"Yes."

They sat there in the bucket seats of the MG, and the space between the seats was a gap between them. Yet it seemed they were embracing each other. Without moving, without touching her, he caressed her eyes and her lips, and heard her saying, "This is all I want. Just this. Just being near you."

"Loretta—"

"Yes?"

"Don't go away."

"I won't."

"I mean, never go away. Never."

She sighed. Her eyes were closed. She murmured, "If you really mean it."

"Yes," he said. "I want this to last."

"It will," she said. "I know it will."

But it wasn't her words that he heard. It was like soft music drifting through the dream. And the dream was taking him away from everything he'd known, every tangible segment of the world he lived in. It took him away from the cracked plaster walls of the Kerrigan house, the noises of the tenants in the crowded rooms upstairs, the yelling and bawling and cursing. It took him away from the raucous voice of Lola, and the empty beer bottles cluttering the parlor, and his father snoozing on the sofa. And in the dream there was a voice that said good-by to Tom, good-by to the house, good-by to Vernon Street. It was a murmur of farewell to the tenements and the shacks, the thick dust on the pavements, the vacant lots littered with rubbish, the yowling of cats in dark alleys. But there was one dark alley that refused to accept the farewell. Like an exhibit on wheels it came rolling into the dream to show the rutted paving, the moonlight a relentless lamp glow focused on some dried bloodstains.

His eyes narrowed to focus on the kin of the number-one suspect.

His voice was toneless. "Tell me something."

But he didn't know how to take it from there. It was like a tug of war in his brain. One side ached to hold onto the dream. The other side was reality, somber and grim. His sister was asleep in a grave and she'd put herself there because a man had invaded her flesh and crushed her spirit. He told himself he had to find the man. Regardless of everything else, he had to find the man and exact full payment. His hands trembled, wanting to take hold of an unseen throat.

She was waiting for him to speak. She sat there smiling at him.

He stared past her. "You like your brother?"

"Very much. He's a drunkard and a loafer and very eccentric, but sometimes he can be very nice. Why do you ask?"

"I been puzzled about him." He looked at her. "I been wondering why he comes to Dugan's Den."

For some moments she didn't reply. Then, with a slight shrug, "It's just a place where he can hide."

"What's he hiding from?"

"From himself."

"I don't get that."

Suddenly her eyes were clouded. She looked away from him. "Let's not talk about it."

"Why not?"

"It isn't pleasant." But then, with a quick shake of her head, "No, I'm wrong. You have every right to know."

She told him about her family. It was a small family, just her parents and her brother and herself. An ordinary middle-class family in fairly comfortable circumstances. But her mother liked to drink and her father had his own bedroom. She said they were dead now, so it didn't matter if she talked about them. They had an intense dislike for each other. It was so intense that they never even bothered to quarrel, they hardly ever spoke to each other. One night, when her brother was seventeen and had just got his driver's license, he took their parents out for a ride. He came home alone with a bandage around his head. The father had died instantly and the mother died in the hospital. Within a few weeks Newton began to have fits of hysterical laughter, wondering aloud if he'd done it on purpose, actually doing them a favor and giving them an easy way out. A bachelor uncle came to take charge of the house but couldn't put up with Newton's ravings and strange behavior and finally moved out.

When Newton was nineteen he married the housekeeper, a woman in her middle forties. She was a short and very skinny woman and her face was dreadfully scarred from burns in a childhood accident. No man had ever looked twice at her and she did her best to please Newton but that wasn't what he wanted. He wanted her to be harsh and nasty and downright vicious. He was always trying to agitate her, trying to make her lose her temper. Whenever that happened he seemed delighted, especially when she'd claw him or throw dishes at him. After seven years she couldn't take it any more and she went to a lawyer and got a divorce. A few months later Newton married a Hungarian gypsy, a fortuneteller, a tall, bony, beak-nosed woman who already had several husbands in various parts of the nation. She was in her early fifties and used liquid shoe polish to keep her hair black. Sometimes she'd get very thirsty and drink the shoe polish. At other times she forced Newton to give her large sums of money so she could buy cases of expensive bourbon. He had an income of sixty dollars a week from his father's insurance money and some weeks the entire sixty dollars went for liquor. Loretta was working in a dental laboratory and making forty a week and couldn't keep much for herself because Newton and the gypsy woman were always asking for money.

When Loretta was twenty, she married a young dentist. For a while they lived in a small apartment. But she was always worried about Newton, she had a feeling there was a bombshell in him and sooner or later it would burst. Her husband kept telling her to forget about Newton but she couldn't do it, and eventually she insisted on moving back to the house. He refused. They argued. The arguments became worse. Finally he walked out on her. She blamed herself, and got in touch with him, told him she was sorry, and asked him to come back. But she didn't really want him back. By this time she was very confused and she wasn't sure what she wanted. She was really relieved when the dentist told her it was no use trying a reconciliation, he cared for her very much but he had enough sense to know when a thing was ended. He advised her to get a divorce. She got the divorce and went back to live in the house with Newton and the gypsy woman.

It wasn't easy, living there with them. They were drunk most of the time, the gypsy woman made no attempt to keep the house clean, and the sink was always stacked with dirty dishes. There were empty bottles all over the place. Sometimes the gypsy woman would hurl the bottles at Newton's head. At other times she'd try to crack his ribs with a broom handle. On one occasion she hit him very hard and broke two of his ribs. He sat on the floor, grinning at her, telling her that she was a fine woman and he adored her.

Loretta told herself she couldn't stay in this madhouse. But she had to stay. She had to look after Newton. He was getting worse, drinking more and more. One time he went out and purchased a skeleton costume. In the middle of the night the gypsy woman heard a noise in the room and woke up and saw the skeleton and began to scream at the top of her lungs. The skeleton moved toward her, laughing crazily, and she passed out cold. After that night, she walked around with a blank look in her eyes. Some weeks later she caught cold, neglected it, developed pneumonia, and died. At the funeral Newton had another of his laughing spells. Then, for some months, he was all right and he got a job in an agency selling foreign automobiles. He worked very hard, and kept away from liquor. He was extremely considerate of Loretta, and extravagantly generous. For Christmas he gave her the little British car, the MG. They had a very nice Christmas dinner, just the two of them. He was gracious and quietly gallant. She was so thankful, the way he was behaving these days. She was so proud of him. But less than a week later he had another laughing spell. And the next day he quit his job. And then he began to drink again.

"When was that?" Kerrigan asked.

"About a year ago."

"When'd he start coming to Dugan's?"

"Just about then."

He told himself to continue the questions. But something stopped him. It was the expression on her face. Her eyes were dry and yet it seemed she was weeping.

"Don't," he said. "Don't look so sad."

She tried to smile, but her lips trembled.

He said, "I know it ain't been easy for you."

Her head was lowered. She put her hand to her eyes.

Suddenly he felt the pain she was feeling. His brain pushed aside all thought of Newton Channing, all aspects of the grim issue he'd been trying to settle. The only thing he knew was the yearning to hold her and hold her and never let her go.

And again he was immersed in the dream that took him away from Vernon Street.

His voice was a husky whisper. "Look at me."

She took her hand away from her eyes.

He said, "I want to take care of you. From now on."

Her lips were parted. She held her breath.

"For keeps," he said.

She was staring at him. "You know what you're saying?"

He nodded slowly. But his thoughts were spinning and there was the flashing of a warning light. He didn't know what it meant. He told himself he didn't want to know.

"It's gotta be for keeps," he said. "It can't be any other way." And then blindly, in a frenzy of wanting her, needing her, he reached out and took hold of her wrists. His voice was a hoarse whisper. "We won't quit. We'll do it tonight."

"Tonight?"

His eyes were feverish. "I know where we can get a license."

"But—"

"Just say yes. Say it."

She went on staring at him. Then very slowly she turned her head and gazed out past the shoreline, looking at the moonlight on the river. For a long moment the only sound was the lapping of the water along the bank.

And then there was the sound of her voice saying, "Yes."

12

HE DIDN'T MOVE. It was a kind of paralysis, as though he'd been hit on the skull with a sledge hammer, just hard enough to put him in a daze. The air became a tunnel of mist.

"Well?" she said.

He flinched. Again he sensed the flashing of the signal light. But now it didn't give a warning. Instead it offered the blunt message: Too late now, you're in it up to your neck, there's no way out.

His lips moved mechanically. He told her to start the engine. And then, as the MG responded to the gas pedal, he watched the fading of the pastoral scene, the windshield framing a changing picture. He caught one final glimpse of moonlit water and serene meadowland. The car turned onto Wharf Street and he saw the rough cobblestones that smothered all the flowers. He saw the jagged splintered outlines of piers and warehouses. The car was approaching Vernon and now he could see the shacks and the tenements. He began to hear the night noises of Vernon Street, the yowling of alley cats, the barking of mongrels, the dismal drumming moaning sound that came from hundreds of overcrowded rooms.

"Slow down," he said.

She looked at him. "Should I stop the car?"

"I didn't say that. Just slow down."

The car slackened speed. He sat stiffly, staring straight ahead. She kept giving him side glances.

Finally she murmured, "What's the matter?"

"Nothing," he said.

In the distance there was the clattering screech of domestic discord. From some third-floor flat the cracked soprano of a fishwife's voice was a saw-toothed blade, while the rumbled oaths of the drunken husband were aimed past the woman, past the roof, going up to the sky.

And yet Kerrigan felt envious. The fishwife and her man would wind up in bed hugging each other. They'd stay together because they belonged together. They both came from the same roots, Vernon cradles.

He heard the calm voice of Loretta Channing, the voice of a stranger asking for directions. He scarcely heard his own reply. As he told her to make a turn on Vernon, a chorus of Vernon voices came to him with the sullen query, what's she doing down here if she don't know her way around.

On Vernon Street the car was moving very slowly. A stumbling drunk lurched into the path of the car, was missed by inches, and shouted some dirty words to the driver. The words were very dirty and she winced. Kerrigan looked back and recognized the man. It was his next-door neighbor.

She put more pressure on the gas pedal. The MG leaped away from the flood of obscenity.

She said, "I'm glad we got away from that."

He told himself to keep his mouth shut.

At Third and Vernon he told her to make a right turn and they went down Third going past the street lamps, and toward the middle of the block he told her to stop the car. She looked at him questioningly. He pointed to a two-storied wooden dwelling that had a cardboard placard in its front window. The glow from the nearest street lamp showed two words scrawled in crayon on the placard. One word was in Greek letters. Under it was the same word in English—"Marriages."

He motioned her out of the car. Then together they stood at the front door and he rapped his knuckles on the wood. There were no lights in the house and he had to rap for several minutes before the door opened. The old Greek stood there, wearing a tattered bathrobe, needing a shave, his eyes clouded with interrupted slumber.

"You got a license handy?" Kerrigan asked.

The Greek blinked once. Then he was fully awake. "Plenty of licenses," he said. "I always have licenses."

He was a small man in his middle seventies. His head was bald except for three little bushes of white hair, one above each ear and one in the center. He smiled and showed a toothless mouth. He said, "The ring. You have the ring?"

Kerrigan shook his head. He looked at Loretta. Her face was calm and she was gazing past the old Greek and breathing quietly and not saying anything.

The Greek said, "I'll find a ring somewhere."

He beckoned them into the house. In the small and shabby parlor he switched on a lamp, then went into another room. Loretta sat down on a flimsy chair. Kerrigan stood in the middle of the floor, not looking at her. His legs felt heavy, as though weighted with lead.

A few minutes passed, and then the Greek came into the parlor carrying a bottle of ink and a pen and a large sheet of white paper rolled up, fastened with a rubber band. He took off the rubber band and put the paper in Kerrigan's hand. Kerrigan stared at the scrolled border and the printed words that told him he was looking at a marriage license. He swallowed very hard, and then he walked to the chair in which Loretta was seated and he said, "You sign it first."

Loretta looked at the Greek. "Is this paper a legitimate document?"

The old man nodded emphatically. "It comes from City Hall. My son works in the Marriage Bureau. Tomorrow he takes it back and puts it in the file."

She said quietly, "I want to be sure this is legal."

Kerrigan frowned. "Sure it's legal," he said. "Look at the printing on it."

The Greek said, "Nothing to worry about. I make real marriages. For many years I do this work. Never any trouble."

"If it isn't legal," Loretta murmured, "it's worthless, it doesn't mean anything."

The Greek twitched his lips and looked up at the ceiling. Then he glared at Loretta and said loudly, "This is genuine marriage license. I tell you it goes into the files."

Loretta got up from the chair and walked to the small table where the Greek had placed the pen and the ink. She picked up the pen, dipped it in the ink bottle, and then for a long moment she stared at Kerrigan. His head was lowered and he was gazing at the carpet. Loretta took a deep breath and signed her name to the license and then she handed the pen to Kerrigan.

He moved slowly toward the table. The pen vibrated in his trembling hand. He knew she was watching him and he tried to keep his hand from trembling. The trembling became worse and he couldn't move the pen toward the paper.

He heard her saying, "What are you waiting for?"

There was no way to answer that.

"Just sign your name," she said. "That's all you have to do. Put your name on the dotted line."

He stood there gaping at the paper that had her name written on it, with the dotted line waiting for his name.

Then he heard the Greek saying, "Maybe this man cannot write. Many men they come here and they cannot write their name."

"I can write," Kerrigan mumbled. As he spoke, he could feel the perspiration dripping from his forehead.

"What is happening?" the Greek asked quietly and seriously. "Why you not sign the paper?"

"Don't hurry him," Loretta said. "Let him pull himself together."

"He looks nervous," the Greek said. "I think he is very nervous."

"Really?" Her tone was musing. "I'd say that's rather strange. After all, this was his idea."

"Maybe he changes his mind." The old man spoke solemnly. "After all, marriage is no joke. It is a big step. Many men, they get scared."

"Well," she said, "if he wants to back out, this is the time to do it."

Kerrigan turned slowly and looked at her. She was smiling at him. He pivoted hard, bent over the table, and signed his name to the marriage license.

Then he picked up the license, shoved it at the old man, and said, "All right, let's get this over with. Where's the ring?"

The Greek put his hand in a pocket of the bathrobe, groped in there for a moment, and then took out a nickel-plated ring. It was thick and had a hinge that allowed it to open and close. Kerrigan took a closer look and saw it was a ring from a looseleaf notebook.

"For God's sake," he said. "This ain't no wedding ring."

The old man shrugged. "It was all I could find." He looked at Loretta and said, "Later he gets you a better ring. This one here is only for the ceremony."

He handed the ring to Kerrigan. Then he opened a drawer of the table and took out a Bible. As he leafed through the pages, he said, "The price for the ceremony is two dollars and fifty-two cents. That is total price. Two dollars for performing marriage. Fifty cents for license. You will please pay in advance."

Kerrigan frowned. "What's the two cents for?"

"I charge two cents for ring," the old man said. He kept his eyes on the printed text while extending his palm for the money. Then the money was in his hand and he averted his eyes from the Bible just long enough to count the cash. He put the bills and silver in the pocket of his bathrobe, took a firmer grip on the Bible, and said, "Now the bride will stand next to the groom."

It was three hours later and Kerrigan had his head buried in a pillow. His eyes were shut tightly but he wasn't asleep. He was trying to grope his way through the fog of an alcoholic stupor. It was apparent to him that he'd consumed an excessive amount of whisky, and now his brain was crammed with a lot of little discs that wouldn't stop spinning. His skull felt as though it were swollen to many times its normal size. He told himself he was really in sad shape, and wondered how in hell he'd fallen into this condition.

He begged his mind to start working, to give him some information concerning tonight's events, but his thoughts stumbled along a tricky path leading nowhere.

Then gradually the fog cleared just a little, the discs slowed down, and he realized he was coming out of it. As his brain went into gear, he kept his eyes shut, telling himself not to think about now, not even to take a look and see where he was. What he had to do was straighten the track and follow it very slowly and carefully and bring it up to now.

On the wall of his closed eyelids a light showed and then widened and it became a series of pictures that told him what had happened. He saw himself placing the ring on her finger. Then sound came into it and he heard the old man saying, "I now pronounce you husband and wife." And then the old man was telling him to kiss her. She stood there smiling at him and waiting to be kissed. The old man said, "Go on, kiss her." He glared at the old man and growled, "Goddamnit, mind your own business." He heard her saying to the old man, "Please forgive my husband. I think he's upset about something."

The pictures continued. He saw himself walking out of the

old Greek's house, and heard her footsteps following. He turned and looked at her and said, "Where d'ya wanna go?" She shrugged and murmured, "It's up to you." He said loudly, "I guess we ought to celebrate." She shrugged again, smiling pleasantly and saying, "Anything you say, dear." And then the smile faded as she said, "You look as if you need a drink."

He closed his eyes and saw more pictures. They were in the car and she had it headed down Third Street, then coming up Fourth and arriving on Vernon. She said, "You really need a drink, I know you do." And then the MG was parked outside Dugan's Den and they were entering the taproom. The place was empty now and Dugan was getting ready to close up for the night. Loretta put some money in Dugan's hand and Dugan put a bottle on the bar. She poured the whisky into the jiggers. Then she lifted the glass and proposed a toast. "Here's to our wedding night," she said. He lifted his glass, gazed moodily at the amber liquor, then shot it down his throat. Again she tilted the bottle and filled the jiggers. She said, "Another toast. Here's to my husband." He looked at her and muttered, "Let's get out of here. I don't feel like drinking." But a moment later he had the glass to his lips and then he was waiting for it to be filled again.

Then the picture got hazy. They stood there at the bar, and the glasses were filled and emptied and filled again. It went on and on like that, and then they were walking out of Dugan's Den. Or rather, she was trying to keep him on his feet while he staggered toward the door. Then she helped him into the car and said, "Now you're really drunk." His head was down and he tried to lift it to look at her. But he couldn't. And he couldn't say anything.

The pictures were fading away but he managed to get a vague impression of the car coming to a stop, the weaving and stumbling as she helped him up some steps and through a doorway. He didn't know what house it was, he didn't know what room he was in now. For just the fraction of an instant he caught a flash of Loretta sitting on a sofa and watching him as he staggered across a room. Then everything was black and it stayed black. He buried his head deeper in the pillow and thought, The hell with it, in the morning you'll find out where you are. But just then he felt the hand on his thigh.

My God, he thought, she's in the bed with me.

He tried to pull way from the hand. An arm circled his middle and drew him closer to the warm softness of a woman.

"Come on," the woman said. Her voice was languid. "Come on," she said sleepily.

Again he tried to pull away. But now her grip was tighter.

"You hear me?" Her voice was louder. "I said come on."

"No," he mumbled. "Let go of me."

"What? What's that?"

"You hear me. Just keep away. Go back to sleep."

"You kidding?"

"I'm telling you to let go. Stay on your side of the bed."

"Are you talking to me?" Her tone was incredulous. "What's wrong with you? Why do you have your clothes on?"

He frowned. Either her voice had changed or his drunkenness caused him to think it was someone else's voice.

Or maybe it really was someone else's voice.

His head moved on the pillow, and very slowly he turned over so that he could look at her face. While he turned, his eyes were wide open, and he saw the dark wall, the moonlit ceiling, then the window that showed the moon far out there. The moon was like a big spotlight that seemed to be focused on himself and his companion.

He was staring at her.

It was his stepmother.

Their eyes were only inches apart and they were gaping at each other as though they couldn't believe what they saw. Lola had her mouth opened as wide as she could get it. Her lungs made a dragging sound as she gasped for air.

Kerrigan groaned without sound. He seriously pondered the problem of how to become invisible.

For a long moment neither of them could move. They just went on gaping at each other. Then all at once Lola gave him a violent push that hurled him off the edge of the bed. He landed on the floor with a heavy thud. For purely practical reasons he decided to stay there for the time being. He stayed there and listened to the sound of the bedsprings as Lola's ponderous weight came off the mattress, then rapid and frantic sounds as she moved around and tried to find something to cover her.

The sounds went on as he sat there on the floor and groaned and sighed and pressed his hands to his head. He heard the noise of the closet door, the rustling of fabrics as clothes were pulled from hangers. He was half sobered now, and he began to consider the feasibility of a fast exit from the room.

But before he could arrive at a decision, there was the click of a wall switch and the room was brightly lit. He blinked several times and then he looked up and saw the big woman who stood there wearing a nightgown. She had her hands on her hips, her eyes a pair of seething caldrons.

"What is this?" she demanded. "What the hell goes on here?"

He choked, gulped hard, choked again, then blurted, "It's nothing, I just made a mistake."

As he said it, he realized how stupid and crazy it sounded. He blinked again, gazing blankly at the face of his stepmother. But she was looking at the empty bed, focusing on the pillow that should have shown her husband's face but showed only a question mark.

"Where is he?" she asked loudly. "Where's your father?"

Kerrigan lifted himself from the floor. He sat down on the edge of the bed, his head in his hands. He made a vague guess as to where his father was. Chances were that Tom was in the house of Rita Montanez.

Lola said, "He claimed he hadda go to the bathroom." Her eyes narrowed. "I'm gonna have a look," she muttered grimly, "and he'd better be in there."

She went out of the room. Kerrigan groped through the haze of his drunkenness and told himself to make a rapid trip to Rita's house and drag Tom out of there. But as he lifted himself from the bed, the floor seemed to slant and he had trouble staying on his feet.

And as he moved toward the door, the whisky in his veins made it several doors instead of one. He was still trying to find the right door when Lola re-entered the room.

"He ain't in the bathroom," she announced through tightened lips. She glared at Kerrigan. She said accusingly, "What are you and him up to?"

He sat down very slowly and carefully on a chair that wasn't there. Again he was on the floor, wondering what had happened to the chair.

Lola studied him for a long moment. "How many quarts did you drink?"

He shrugged kind of sadly. "I didn't have much. Guess I can't hold it."

"The hell you can't. From the looks of you, you're holding a gallon."

She took hold of his wrists, pulled him up from the floor, and put him in the chair that he hadn't been able to find. "Now then," she said, "I want some information. Where is he?"

Kerrigan stared dumbly at Tom's wife and said, "Maybe he went for a walk."

"At this time of night? Where would he walk?"

The whisky fog came drifting in. Kerrigan blinked several times and said, "Maybe he got lost." He gazed longingly at the bed and thought how pleasant it would be to go back to sleep.

Lola studied him once more and saw he was in no condition to give sensible answers. She gestured disgustedly and turned her back to him.

Suddenly she snapped her fingers. Then her head turned from side to side as she made a hasty examination of the room.

"Sure enough," she said. "His clothes ain't here."

She started to take deep breaths. Lola was about to lose her temper on a grand scale.

Despite his drunkenness, he managed to say, "No use getting sore about it. After all, it's a helluva hot night. Maybe he went out for a bottle of beer. To cool himself off."

"I'll cool him off," Lola said. "I'll break his goddamn neck, that's what I'll do."

She started to move around the room, searching for a suitable weapon. Kerrigan winced as he saw her lifting a thick glass ash tray, hefting it in her hand to test the weight of it. Apparently it wasn't heavy enough. She slammed it to the floor, then darted to the open closet and reached in and pulled out a long-handled scrubbing brush. The business end of the brush was an inch of bristles and a two-inch thickness of wood.

Lola had a firm grip on the handle of the brush. She held it with both hands, aiming it at empty air and taking a few practice swipes. Then, wanting a better target, she looked around for something solid. Kerrigan heard footsteps in the hall and he thought, It's gonna be crowded in here.

The door opened and Tom walked in. An instant later there was a loud whacking noise and Tom yelled, "Ouch!" Then there was more whacking, more yelling, and considerable activity. Tom was trying to run in several directions at once. He collided with Kerrigan, bounced away, staggered sideways, and received a wallop from Lola that spun him around like a punching bag. He tried to crawl under the bed, but there wasn't enough space between the springs and the floor. He was much too bulky to squeeze through. The flat side of the brush landed on him and in a frenzied effort to get away from the blows he gave a mighty heave with his shoulders, so that the bed was raised on two legs. He heaved again and the bed fell over on its side. Lola kept swinging the brush and Tom was asking her to wait just a minute so they could talk it over. Lola's reply was another whack. The sound resembled a pistol shot. Tom looked at Kerrigan and shouted, "For God's sake, make her stop."

Kerrigan shrugged, as though to say there was no way to stop Lola once she got started. He grinned stupidly, drunkenly, and then he started toward the door. But again it was several doors, and it seemed as if the ceiling were coming down. He couldn't stay on his legs. The floor came up and he was flat on his face. The dazed grin remained on his lips as he heard the continued uproar. Somehow the noise of the violence was softened in his whisky-drenched brain. It was strangely soothing, almost like a lullaby. For a hazy instant he tried to understand it. But the feeling was so pleasant, so comforting, it told him to fall asleep, just fall asleep. And as the blackness enveloped him, he sensed there was nothing strange about it, after all. It was merely the sound of the house where he lived. It was as though he'd been away and he'd come back, and it was nice to be home again.

13

In the darkness of the alcoholic sleep, he drifted through a glass-lined canal that had the labels of whisky bottles on its walls. The labels were varicolored and there were too many colors floating past his eyes. He told himself to stop looking at the labels, he'd soon be getting a headache. But then the glass became wood and there was no canal at all, just a dark alley and some moonlight showing the sides of the wooden shacks. He followed the path of the moonlight as it flowed onto the rutted paving and he saw the dried bloodstains.

"Goddamn it," he said, waking up.

He could feel a pillow under his head, and he heard someone breathing beside him. Before he looked to see who it was, he sat up, groaning and holding his head and wishing he had an ice bag. He blinked hard several times, and suddenly his eyes were wide as he realized this was Bella's room.

His head turned slowly. He looked at Bella. She was sound asleep, resting on her side. It was very hot and sticky in the room and she wasn't wearing anything.

The window showed the dark gray-pink of early morning. On the dresser the hands of the alarm clock pointed to four-forty-five. He told himself to get out of bed and go into his own room. Looking down at himself, he saw that he was wearing only a pair of shorts. He glanced across the floor, searching for his clothes, and saw shirt and jacket and trousers draped carelessly over a chair, Bella's dress on top of the heap.

Moving carefully, trying not to make any noise, he climbed out of bed and headed toward the chair. It seemed as if a ton of rocks was pressing down on him and crushing his skull. As he reached for his clothes, he stumbled forward, hit the chair, knocked it over, and went down with it.

He cursed without sound, getting up very slowly. Then he had his shoes in one hand, his shirt in the other, the jacket and trousers dangling from his arm as he walked unsteadily toward the door.

He was only a step away from the door when he heard Bella's voice. "Just where d'ya think you're going?"

"I got my own bed."

"Yeah?"

"Yeah," he said. He groped for the door handle. His hand closed on it.

"Listen, louse," Bella said. She was off the bed and coming toward him. She gave him a shove that sent him away from the door. She pointed to the bed and said, "Get back in there."

"You talkin' to me?"

She put her weight on one leg and clapped a hand to her hip. Then, shifting slightly, so that she blocked his path to the door, she said, "You might as well make yourself comfortable. We're gonna have a discussion."

"Not now," he said.

"Right now." Her eyes dared him to make a move toward the door. "We're gonna have it out here and now."

"For God's sake." He pointed to the alarm clock. "Look what time it is. I gotta get some sleep. Gotta get rid of this hangover."

"That's what I want to talk about," she said. "How come you got drunk last night?"

He didn't reply. He dropped the shoes to the floor, flipped the clothes aside, and walked slowly to the bed. As he sat down on the edge of the mattress, his hands were pressed tightly to his temples, as though trying to squeeze the whisky fog from his brain.

Bella came around the side of the bed and stood facing him. "I know you're not a drinker," she said. "You musta had a reason for getting drunk. Come on, let's have it. What happened last night?"

"Nothing."

"I'll bet." She snorted. And then, her eyes narrowed, "I found you stretched out in the hall outside Lola's room. You were stiff as a board."

"So what?"

"So it made me curious. You wouldn't get loaded like that unless you had something on your mind. Something you couldn't handle."

He looked at her. "What gives you that idea?"

"I just know, that's all. I know you."

His eyes were dull, gazing past her. "You think you know me."

She stood there studying his face. She said, "I took the trouble to drag you in here and take your clothes off and put you in bed."

"Thanks," he said sourly. "Thanks a lot."

"I didn't do it for thanks. I did it so I'd be around when you come out of it. We got some things to talk about. I wanna know the score on this. I got a right to know."

He frowned at her. "You got one hell of a crust, that's what you got. I didn't ask you to put me in this room."

"It ain't the first time you been here. You been in this room a lotta times. More times than I can count. And I never dragged you in, either. You always come in on your own two feet."

He took a deep breath. He started to get up from the bed and she pushed him back. She did it roughly and he bounced on the mattress. He made another attempt to get up and she pushed him again, harder this time. His head went back against the pillow. It felt like iron banging his skull. He told himself to close his eyes and go to sleep. His benumbed brain said, Forget about her, forget about everything, just go to sleep.

But then she was leaning over him, shaking him. She said, "Come on, come out of it."

"Goddamnit, leave me alone."

He shut his eyes tightly and tried to roll over on his side but she pulled at his shoulder and wouldn't let him do it. He mumbled an oath and reached out blindly to shove her away, and as his hand made contact with Bella, a current passed through him from her to him, from him to her, and he was aching to hold on, hold her tighter, pull her to him and find her lips and taste her mouth. But just then he heard the soundless voice that said, No.

It was a blast of icy realization that sliced through the heat of his senses and the thick mist of the hangover. He moved spasmodically to the other side of the bed, then sat up stiffly, staring at her. Ice was in his eyes as he said, "Keep away from me."

She sat there on the other side of the bed. She didn't say anything. She just looked at him.

He said, "And put something on."

She smiled thinly. "Does it bother you?"

He clamped his lips tightly. He turned his head so he wouldn't see her.

Her voice was a light jab, flicking at him. "It excites you, don't it? You don't want it to excite you."

"Listen, Bella—"

"Yes?"

But he couldn't take it from there. He swallowed hard.

She said, "Well, go on. I'm listening."

He told himself he'd have to say it sooner or later. He might as well say it now and get it over with. For a moment his eyes were closed and he was trying to find the words. And then, gazing straight ahead and seeing the wall on the other side of the room, he said, "It's all finished. We gotta call it quits."

He waited for her to say something.

Long moments passed. There was no sound in the room.

He went on gazing at the opposite wall. Finally he said, "Last night I got married."

"You what?"

"Got married."

"You joking?"

"No."

There was another long pause. When she spoke again, her voice sounded queer, sort of strangled. "Where'd you pull this caper?"

"At the Greek's place," he said. He spoke tonelessly. "Bought a license. She signed her name to it. I signed my name. I put a ring on her finger."

"The girl I seen you with? That floozie from uptown?"

"Yeah." He sighed heavily. He wondered if there was anything else to say.

He heard Bella saying, "Tell me how it happened."

"It happened, that's all. It just happened."

"You know what you're saying?"

He nodded again.

Bella said, "Maybe I'm crazy. Maybe I'm hearing things." She stood up. She sat down. She stood up again. She began to walk back and forth along the length of the bed. Finally she stopped, and with both hands she gripped the bedpost, as though to steady herself. Then, biting her lip, her eyes shut tightly, she made a sound as though she were feeling intense physical pain.

He rubbed his knuckles across his brow. He wondered what caused him to stay in this room when there was every reason to walk out.

"Can't believe it," Bella said aloud to herself. "It just ain't possible." And then her tone changed, there was pleading in her voice. "Didja know what you were doing? You couldn't have known. After all, you were drunk."

"No," he said gruffly. "I got drunk later."

"With her?"

"Yeah," he said. "We were celebrating."

"Where?" Her hands tightened on the bedpost.

"What difference does it make?"

"I'm askin' you something. Where'd you do the celebrating? Was it in a hotel room?"

He shook his head. Again he gave a heavy sigh. He said, "We went to Dugan's Den."

"Then where'd you go?"

His jaw hardened. "All right," he muttered, "let's drop the questions."

"You'll sit there and answer them. You'll tell me where you went after you left Dugan's Den."

He turned and frowned at her. "What're you getting at?"

She wasn't looking at him. Her voice was a grinding whisper. "You know what I'm getting at. You've told me about the license and the ring. And the celebration. Now I want to hear the rest of it. I want to know all about the wedding night."

He aimed the frown at the floor. "We didn't do anything, if that's what you mean."

She let go of the bedpost. She breathed in and out and it was almost like a sigh of relief. The corners of her mouth moved up just a trifle, starting to build a smile.

Kerrigan went on frowning. He heard himself saying, "The way it happened, we walked out of Dugan's and she had her car parked outside and we climbed in. She drove me back here and she helped me into the house. Then she was sitting on the sofa and I was moving around, I didn't know where the hell I was going. Went down the hall and got the rooms mixed up and landed in the wrong bed."

"You weren't as mixed up as you thought you were," Bella said. She had the smile fully glowing in her eyes. "You were on your way to the right bed. You're in it now."

He stared at her. She was moving toward him, coming slowly across the room. He told himself to get up but somehow he couldn't lift his limbs. As he watched Bella approaching, it was like a wall closing in on him.

She was saying, "Don't you see the way it is? Last night was just a joke, it wasn't for real, and you know it. Whatever it was that made you do it, we'll check that off, it ain't important. Only one thing matters. You're here with me."

"No," he said. "No."

Her smile widened and brightened and she said, "You don't mean that. You mean yes."

"Now wait." And his hand was lifted, telling her to stay away.

She flung herself at him, wrapping her arms around his middle. He fell back with her weight pressing against him. Her eyes were wild and her lips found his mouth and he could feel the flame rising in his body, the red-black flame that curled and swept in wide arcs, and he held her tightly, his heart pounding. But just then he heard the soundless voice of his brain saying, You damn fool, you're falling into a trap, get out, get out.

He tried to push her away. She wouldn't let go of him. He seized her wrists and twisted hard, then gave her a violent shove that sent her to the floor. He stood up quickly, lunged across the room, and picked up his shoes and the shirt and the jacket and trousers. He started toward the door. Then abruptly he came to a stop. He glared at her. He said, "I oughta push your face in for trying a trick like that."

It seemed she was speaking to the bed. "Well, I tried."

"Damn right you did. And you saw what it got you. You're lucky it didn't get you a broken jaw."

She looked at him. "I'm still here, if you feel like slugging me."

"It ain't worth the effort," he said. Then he braced himself, expecting that she'd leap at him with clawing fingernails.

For some moments she didn't move. Then very slowly she got up from the floor. She walked across the room, picked up a robe, and put it on. He watched her as she reached into a pocket, took out a pack of cigarettes and a book of matches. Her voice was oddly matter-of-fact as she said, "Want one?"

He shook his head. Her eyes were blank, puzzled.

She was lighting a cigarette. "You sure you don't want one?"

He breathed hard. "Only thing I want from you is a definite understanding. From here on in you're gonna leave me alone. You'll hafta get it through your head I'm a married man."

"By the way," she murmured casually, "where is she?"

He blinked a few times.

She took a slow easy drag at the cigarette. "Well?" She watched the smoke drifting away from her lips. "Come on, tell me. Where's the bride?"

His mouth was opened loosely. He went on blinking.

"I'll tell you where she is," Bella said. "She's sound asleep in a nice clean bed. In a nice clean house. In a nice respectable neighborhood."

He swallowed hard. He couldn't say anything.

Bella said, "It stands to reason she wouldn't stay here. She'd be a damn fool to spend the night in this dump."

"All right," he muttered. "That's enough."

Bella looked at the cigarette held loosely in her fingers. She spoke to the cigarette. "Sure, the bride took a run-out. And who can blame her? The groom brings her to a house with the plaster chipping off the walls and the furniture coming apart and empty beer bottles all over the floor. It's a wonder she let herself sit on the sofa. This afternoon she'll be taking her dress to the cleaners, you can bet on that and your money's safe. Another thing she'll do, she'll go to the beauty parlor and have her hair washed, an extra soaping just to make sure. After all, in these Vernon rat traps you never know, you can pick up anything. What she really oughta do is spray herself with DDT."

"Shut up," he said. "You better shut up."

Bella shrugged. "Well, anyway, she's breathing easier now. That cleaner, fresher air uptown."

He stood motionless. The quiet in the room was unbearable, and he knew he had to say something. His mouth was tight as he said, "You don't get the point. All she did was walk out of the house. She didn't walk out on me."

"That ain't what I'm saying." Bella spoke very quietly. But now the cigarette trembled in her fingers. "Cantcha see what

I'm trying to tell ya? No matter how much she wants you, she can't get away from uptown. And sure as hell you can't get away from here."

"Can't I?" His eyes aimed past Bella, seeing past the walls, past Vernon rooftops and sky. "All it takes is streetcar fare. Just a matter of fifteen cents."

The cigarette split in half. The lighted end hit the floor and scorched the carpet. Bella stepped on the burning stub. She looked at the scattered ashes. She was sobbing without sound as she said, "Don't throw your money away. It's a dime and a nickel wasted. All you'll be doing is taking yourself for a ride."

"It's gonna be more than that," he said. "I'll be going somewhere." And then, as though Bella weren't in the room, he said softly to himself, "She's there, she's waiting for me."

"You fool," Bella whispered. "You poor fool."

He looked at her. There was a practical tone in his voice as he said, "I'm leaving tonight. As soon as I get home from work. Tell Lola not to cook for me. I'm gonna be in a hurry."

Bella nodded very slowly. She gazed vacantly at the door behind him. Her lips moved automatically. "All right, I'll tell her not to cook for you."

He turned away from her. He opened the door and walked out of the room.

Then in his own room he was putting on his work clothes. He was thinking, Tomorrow morning it'll be a different room, a different house, a different street. From now on everything's gonna be different, gonna be better. His brain could taste the pleasant flavor of saying good-by to all Vernon dwellings, all Vernon faces.

There was a sound from the bed where Frank was sleeping fitfully. Turning over on his side, Frank grunted and let out a dry cough. Frank's face was toward the window, and as the morning light hit him, he opened his eyes. He saw Kerrigan sitting in a chair near the window. Kerrigan had just finished tying a shoelace and he was sitting up straight.

Frank's eyes were shiny. His mouth began to twitch. He lifted his head from the pillow, bracing himself on his elbows. He said, "Quit watching me."

Kerrigan made a gesture of weary annoyance. "Go back to sleep."

"Why d'ya keep watching me?"

"For God's sake, come off that routine."

"I can't come off," Frank said. "You keep me on it. You won't leave me alone."

Kerrigan shrugged. It was no use going on with it.

"I'm warning you," Frank said. "You better stop watching me."

He told himself to go easy. He said softly, "All right, let's skip it. I got other things on my mind."

"Like what?"

He smiled amiably at his brother. "Well, I finally went and did it. I got hitched."

Frank blinked a few times. "For real?"

He nodded. "License and ring and the whole works. Last night at the Greek's."

Frank lowered his legs off the side of the bed. He leaned forward stiffly, his skinny torso slanted like something activated by a lever. His voice was dull and metallic as he said, "Who is she?"

"You don't know her."

"Maybe I do," Frank said. "What's her name?"

"Loretta."

"The blonde?"

Kerrigan flinched. He had an odd feeling, as though he were bolted to the chair.

"The blonde with green eyes?" Frank asked. "The tasty dish from uptown?"

He sat there and stared at Frank.

"Sure," Frank said. "I know her."

"What do you mean, you know her?"

Frank parted his lips, his mouth curled up at the corners, revealing his yellow teeth. He didn't say anything.

Kerrigan tried to get up from the chair. He couldn't move. He said very slowly, "Whatever's on your mind, don't hold it back. Let's have it."

The toothy grimace stayed on Frank's face. He was looking past Kerrigan and saying, "I've seen her in Dugan's Den. Seen her there a lotta times. One night she bought me a drink. We talked. We stood there at the bar and she bought me more drinks and we talked."

"What about?"

"I don't remember," Frank said. The grimace widened. "All I remember is looking at her and thinking she reminded me of someone."

"Who?" It was blurted, almost a shout.

But Frank didn't seem to hear. "It wasn't the face or the body. It wasn't the eyes, either. More like the feeling you get when you're in a room that looks different but somehow you know you've been there before. Can't put your finger on what it is, but you know it just the same. That's what I remember mostly, that feeling. It was sorta weird, it gimme the chills. But that don't matter. I like to get the chills. It feels nice when I start to shiver. So there we stood at the bar and I was shivering and it felt real nice. And then, when she walked out, I waited just long enough to say the alphabet from A to Q. Then I followed her."

"You did what?"

"Followed her," Frank said, speaking to the wall.

"Was she alone?"

Frank's head moved jerkily up and down. "She'd come to Dugan's to pick up her brother, the lush. But he wouldn't leave. He told her to go home alone. On the street I saw her walking toward that little car she drives. The little gray job with the wire wheels. It was parked on the other side of Vernon, halfway down the block. All the other spaces were taken up by trucks. So she hadda do some walking to get to the car. That gave me plenty of time to follow her. I was shivering real good then, nice and cold. She looked so slim and trim and neat, so clean and shining, like something you see in a dream. That's it. In a dream. And I'd been there before. The same moon. The same street. Everything the same except for one thing. Her name. It wasn't Loretta."

It seemed to Kerrigan that the walls were liquid, forming waves that rolled slowly toward him. He begged himself to get up from the chair and run out of the room. But he couldn't budge. He heard himself saying, "All right, you saw her walking to the car. Then what?"

"Nothing," Frank said. "She drove away in the car."

"You've pulled this stunt before? You've followed women down the street?"

Frank didn't answer.

"Tell me," Kerrigan said. He was up from the chair, moving toward the bed. He grabbed Frank's shoulders. "You're gonna tell me."

"Tell you what?" Frank uttered a soundless laugh. "Something you know already?"

He dropped his hands to his knees. He backed away from Frank, his eyes riveted to his brother's face. And yet his inner vision didn't show a face at all. It showed a dark alley, with the moonlight coming down and spraying brightly on dried bloodstains.

14

H E TURNED away from Frank, hurried out of the room, and walked out of the house. He was trying very hard not to think about Frank. He wished he could reach with his fingers into his mind and drag Frank out of there.

On Vernon Street, walking toward Wharf, he saw the row of wooden shacks off Vernon between Third and Fourth, and he thought, Maybe it was Mooney, after all, or maybe it was Nick Andros. He walked faster, seeing more wooden shacks and the shabby fronts of tenements and he muttered without sound, There's more than one creep lives in these dumps, more than one hophead and bay-rum drinker and all kinds of queers. It might have been any one of them and maybe you'll never know for sure who it was. He pleaded with himself to let it rest there, to bury it and forget about it. But his face was gray and his breathing was heavy and he was still thinking about Frank.

And hours later, hauling crates along Pier 17, he didn't feel the weight of heavy boxes tugging at his arms and pressing on his spine. The only pressure he felt was inside his head. He couldn't stop thinking about Frank.

At four in the afternoon the sky began to darken and the river took on a metallic sheen. Black clouds moved in and shadowed the piers and warehouses and the street that bordered the docks. At a few minutes past five, as some of the dock workers started to leave the piers and head for home, the air was split with thunder. Pier bosses and foremen shouted feverish commands. Then all at once it was coming down, and it hit with terrific force. It was like a lake falling from the sky.

The docks were deserted. And soon the streets were empty. There was no human activity at all. There were only the darkness and the rumble of thunder and the relentless cascade of rain. The river was choppy with white caps, and angry waves came smashing at the piers.

Cursing, drenched to the skin, Kerrigan huddled under the stingy roof of a loading platform. He tried the big door that led into the warehouse. But the door was locked, and all he could do was press his back against it and try to keep from getting wetter than he was already.

He looked out across a few yards of wooden pier, the planks giving way to a newer driveway of concrete. Through the wall of falling rain he saw the raging foam of the river, and he could feel the vibration of the pier as the waves crashed against its pilings. Muttering an oath, he told himself it was a northeaster, and that meant it was due to last for hours and hours, and maybe days. He decided to take his chances with a run for home, and he braced himself, preparing to leap off the platform and make a beeline toward Vernon.

Just then he heard a clicking sound behind him. Someone had unlocked the big door. He told himself he'd been seen through one of the windows and some kind-hearted character was inviting him to come in and get dry.

He worked the door handle and pushed against the door, and the heavy bulk of it swung slowly inward. As he entered the warehouse, he saw there were no bulbs lit, and he frowned puzzledly as he groped his way forward. He shouted, "Anybody around?"

There was no answer. The only sound was the dull roar of the storm outside.

His frown deepened. He took a few more steps, bumped into a barrel, circled around it, and kept on going. Scarcely any light came through the partially opened door to the loading platform, and now he moved in almost total darkness.

He decided the door had been unlocked by some gin hound who'd come out of it just long enough to do him a favor, and then had returned to an alcoholic slumber.

His hand came in contact with the edge of a large box. He sat down on the box and wished he had a book of matches and a pack of cigarettes. For a few moments he played with the idea of getting the hell out of here. But the air in the warehouse was warm and somehow comfortable, and a lot drier than the weather outside. He figured he might as well sit here for a while.

But then, he thought, the storm would probably get worse and last for hours, and he was pretty hungry, getting hungrier all the time. And the problem of love had remained.

"The hell with this," he muttered aloud, and turned his head, looking for the column of gray light that would reveal the exit.

All he saw was blackness, and the dim gray rectangles of the small windows. The windows were high off the floor, and that was one thing. Another thing was the fact that they were made of wired glass and he'd have one mess of a time smashing his way through.

And yet he wasn't thinking much about that. He was concentrating on the door, telling himself he'd left the door open and now it was closed.

His mouth was set in a thin line as he thought, Whoever let me in here is making sure I don't get out.

In that same moment, he heard footsteps.

The sounds came from behind him. He knew that if he turned his head, he would see who it was. His eyes had become accustomed to the darkness, and the windows afforded just enough light for recognizing a face. But in the instant that he told himself to turn and look, his instinct contradicted the impulse and commanded him to duck, to dodge, to evade an unseen weapon.

He threw himself sideways, falling off the box. There was a whirring sound that sliced the air, and then the crash of a thick club or something, landing on the top of the box where he'd been seated. He was on his knees, crouched at the side of the box, listening intently for a sound that would give him his assailant's position.

Again he heard footsteps, and the shuffling noises told him he was dealing with more than one attacker.

His sense of caution gave way to a grim curiosity. He raised his head above the edge of the box and saw the men. There were two of them. The dim gray light from the windows was barely sufficient for him to estimate their size and study their features. The initial glimpse told him he was facing serious trouble. This was a professional wrecking team, a couple of dock ruffians who charged a set fee for breaking a man's jaw, a higher fee for removing an ear or an eye. And if the customer was willing to meet their price, they'd go all the way and use the river to hide the traces of what had been done. Their business reputation was excellent. There were never any disappointed customers.

Kerrigan could see their wide shoulders, the thickness of their arms and wrists. They carried wooden clubs, and they wore brass knuckles.

Now there was no sound from the other side of the box. They were taking their time about it, and it was as though they were sending him a silent message, telling him they had him where they wanted him, and they'd be willing to wait until he made a move.

He bit his lip, wondering what he could do. He glanced around at the floor, but it offered nothing, there was no sign of ammunition or weapon. He cursed without sound. Whatever these men were planning to do, whatever damage they had in mind, they'd sure as hell arranged it carefully. He knew they'd followed him from Pier 17, and the thunderstorm had aided them in their scheme to corner him. But storm or no storm, they'd have cornered him anyway. They'd have waited for a convenient moment and a convenient place. As matters stood, they had trailed him to the warehouse, had peered through a window to make sure it was deserted, and then they'd found an entrance. They'd watched him getting soaked out there in the rain, so from there on it was easy. They'd simply unlocked the door to let him know it was dry in here and he was welcome. It was a friendly favor and he ought to thank them. He ought to tell them how much he appreciated their kindness.

There were five feet of wooden box separating him from the big men and the thick clubs and the brass knuckles.

One of the men was grinning at him.

The other man, somewhat shorter and wider than his partner, leaned forward just a little and said, "You ready for it? You ready to take it?"

"He looks ready," the taller man said.

They spoke quietly, yet their voices were distinct against the rumbling of the storm outside. In the shadows their eyes were little points of yellow and green light, and there was the bright gleam of the brass knuckles, the glow reflected on the thick clubs of rounded wood.

And then there was something else, another glow that caused Kerrigan to glance downward. He saw the glimmer on the metal handle attached under the lid of the box.

The short wide man was saying, "Let's find out if he's ready."

"All right," the other man said. "Let's take him."

Kerrigan grabbed the handle and got a tight two-handed hold on it and with all the power in his body he heaved upward and forward, doing it very fast so that the box was raised and pushed in almost the same moment. It was just as heavy as it was large, and he heard the loud thud as it collided with the men. There was another thud and he knew that one of the men had been knocked down. He was still pushing at the box and he went on pushing until the box toppled over onto the fallen man. There was the sound of something being crushed and the fallen man was screaming and trying to wriggle out from under the box and not being able to do it.

The short wide man had leaped backward and seemed to be debating whether to aid his partner or make a lunge at Kerrigan. Before he had a chance to arrive at a decision, Kerrigan rushed at him, coming in low, sending a shoulder against his knees and taking him to the floor.

As they hit the floor the short man used his club on Kerrigan's ribs. Kerrigan let out a cry of animal pain, and the man hit him again in the same place. It sent white-hot fire through his middle, then more fire as he took another blow from the club. He rolled himself away and managed to evade a blow aimed at his skull. The man leaped at him, kicked him in the spot where he'd been clubbed, then tried to turn him over, sort of prodding him with a heavy foot to get him over on his back. In the next moment he was on his back and he looked up and saw that the club was raised once more. The short man wore a businesslike expression and was taking careful aim with his eyes focused on Kerrigan's pelvis.

Then the club came down. Kerrigan raised both legs and took the blow on his thigh. In the same instant he snatched at the club, missed and snatched again and missed again, and the club slammed against his arm. But now he didn't feel the pain and he was getting to his feet and not thinking about the club or the brass knuckles. He walked toward the short wide man and feinted with his left hand. As the club flashed downward, he pulled away from it, going sideways, then moving in very close and chopping his right hand to the man's jaw. The man staggered backward and dropped the club. Kerrigan kept moving in, hooked a left to the side of the head, and then hauled off and threw a roundhouse right that lifted the man off the floor and sent him sailing to land flat on his back.

Kerrigan kept moving in. The man was scrambling to his feet. Kerrigan kicked him in the head and that sent him down again. The man was gasping as Kerrigan kicked him once more. Kerrigan reached down and pulled him to his knees and smashed him in the mouth.

The man screamed. He made a desperate attempt to flee. Headed for the door of the loading platform, he ran through the narrow path lined with crates and barrels. He found the door and opened it and leaped out upon the rain-swept platform.

But in the next instant the man was on his knees with Kerrigan on top of him. Kerrigan's eyes were calmer now. He was thinking in purely practical terms, knowing there was only one way to deal with these professional manglers. He thought, knock him out, then make him talk.

He had one arm circling the man's throat. His other arm was drawn back and then he let go with a kidney punch that caused the man to scream again. Then another kidney punch, and the force of it was enough to take the two of them off the loading platform and onto the planks of the pier. As they landed, the man made a frantic effort to break loose, pumping his elbow into Kerrigan's stomach. Kerrigan groaned and fell back and saw the man running past the planks and onto the concrete driveway that bordered the edge of the pier.

But there was too much rain, it was coming down too hard, and the man could scarcely see where he was going. The concrete driveway was a foggy, slippery path, made treacherous by the foam coming up from the big waves crashing against the pier. The man had taken only a few steps when he lost his footing. Kerrigan was up very fast, lunging at him and trying to grab him before he went over the edge. There wasn't enough time for that. The man went over and down and made a splash. The raging current caught him and carried him away and swallowed him.

Kerrigan walked back to the loading platform and went inside the warehouse. He moved very slowly, wearily, grimacing as he felt the hammering pain in his ribs and stomach. He went on leaden feet toward the spot where the other man was still trying to squirm out from under the heavy box.

"God in heaven," the man groaned. "Get this thing off me."

Kerrigan smiled dimly. "What's the hurry?"

"It's mashin' my chest. I can't hardly breathe."

"You're breathing all right. And you're talking. That's all we need for now."

The man had one arm free and he raised his hand to his eyes and let out a moan.

Kerrigan knelt at the side of the man. He took a close look at the man's face and saw there wasn't much color. The man's eyes were glazed and the lips were quivering with pain and supplication. He told himself that maybe the man's chest was crushed, that maybe the man would die. He decided he didn't give a damn.

He said, "Who hired you?"

The man's reply was another moan.

"If you won't talk," Kerrigan said, "you'll stay there under the box."

He stood up. He turned away from the moans of the crushed man. Facing the opened doorway of the loading platform, he listened to the sound of the rainstorm. It seemed to merge with the noise of a cyclone that whirled through his brain.

Just then he heard the man saying, "It was a woman."

And after that it seemed there was no sound at all. Just a frozen stillness. Again he turned very slowly, and he was looking down at the man.

"A woman," the man said. He moaned once more, and coughed a few times. He wheezed, "She lives on Vernon Street. I think they call her Bella."

"Bella." He said it aloud to himself. Then he reached down and lifted the heavy box off the chest of the man. He heard the man's sigh of relief, the dragging sound of air pulled into tortured lungs.

The man rolled over on his side. He tried to get to his feet. He made it to his knees, shook his head slowly, and muttered, "This ain't no good. I'm in bad shape. You might as well call the Heat. At least they'll take me to a hospital."

"You don't need a hospital," Kerrigan said. He put his hands under the man's armpits, then used his arms as a hook to raise him from the floor.

The man leaned heavily against him and said, "Where's my partner?"

"In the river," Kerrigan said.

The man forgot his own pain and weakness. He stepped away from Kerrigan, his eyes dulled with a kind of brute sorrow. Then he shook his head slowly and said, "It just don't pay to take these jobs. They're not worth the grief. I'm all banged up inside and he's food for the fishes. All for a lousy twenty bucks."

"Is that what she paid you?"

The man nodded.

Kerrigan's eyes narrowed. "She pay in advance?"

"Yeah." The man put his hand against his trousers pocket.

"Let's have it," Kerrigan said.

It was two fives and a ten. The man handed him the bills and he folded them carefully. He said, "You sure she didn't give you more?"

The man tried to smile. "If she wanted you rubbed out complete, it would have cost her a hundred. For this kind of job, to put a man outta action, we never charge more than twenty."

"Bargain rates," Kerrigan muttered.

It was quiet for some moments. And then the man was saying, "Look, mister, I got a record. I'm out on parole. Wanna gimme a break?"

Kerrigan smiled dryly. "O.K.," he said. He pointed to the doorway.

"Thanks," the man said. "Thanks a lot, mister."

Kerrigan watched him as he walked away, moving slowly and painfully, pausing in the doorway to offer a final gesture of gratitude, then limping out upon the loading platform and vanishing in the storm.

Kerrigan looked down at the money folded in his hand.

15

DESPITE HIS anxiety for a showdown with Bella, he purposely delayed going home. For one thing, he wanted to be very calm when he faced her. Also, and more important, he wanted the discussion to be strictly private. On Wharf Street he entered a diner, ordered a heavy meal, took a few bites and pushed the plate aside. He sat there ordering countless cups of coffee and filling the ash tray with cigarette stubs. Then later he walked along Wharf through the storm, found a thirty-cent movie house, and bought a ticket.

When he came out of the movie it was past midnight. The storm had slackened and now the rainfall was a steady, dull drone. He didn't mind walking in the rain and his stride was somewhat casual as he walked north on Wharf Street. But later, on Vernon, the anxiety hit him again and he hurried his pace.

Entering the house, he quickly checked all the rooms. Frank was nowhere around, Tom and Lola were asleep, and Bella's room was empty. He went into the unlit parlor, took a chair near the window, and sat there in the dark waiting for Bella to come home.

Some nights Bella came home very late. Maybe tonight she wouldn't be coming home at all. Maybe she was on a bus or a train, telling herself she'd evened the score and it was a wise move now to get out of town. But while the thought drifted through his mind, he saw Bella walking across Vernon Street and approaching the house. She moved somewhat unsteadily. She wasn't really drunk, but it was obvious she'd been drinking.

He stood away from the window. The door opened and Bella came in and plumped herself on the sofa. In the darkness of the parlor she didn't see him, but enough light came through the window so that he could watch what she was doing. Her handbag was open and she was taking out a pack of cigarettes. She put one in her mouth and then she searched for a match.

Kerrigan spoke very softly. "Hello, Bella."

She let out a startled cry.

"It's only me," he said. He flicked the wall switch, and the ceiling bulbs were lit.

Bella sat stiffly, holding her breath as she stared at him. It seemed that her eyes were coming out of her face.

Kerrigan moved toward her. He had a match book in his hand. He struck a match and applied the flame to her cigarette, but she didn't inhale. He kept the flame there and finally she took a spasmodic drag, her body shaking as the smoke came out of her mouth.

He blew out the match, dropped it into a tray. Then very slowly, as though he were performing a carefully rehearsed ceremony, he reached into his trousers pocket and took out the folded money, the two fives and the ten. He unfolded the bills and smoothed them between his fingers. Then he extended them slowly and held them in front of her bulging eyes.

She was trying to look at something else, trying to stare at the carpet, a chair, the wall, anything at all, just so she wouldn't be seeing the money. But although her head moved, her eyes were fastened on the money.

"Here," he said, offering her the money. "It's yours."

He waited for her to take the bills. She kept her hands down, her fingers gripping the edge of the sofa. Her throat contracted as though she were trying to swallow something very thick and heavy in her throat.

Then suddenly her shoulders sagged. She lowered her head. "Oh, my God," she moaned. "Oh, my God."

Kerrigan placed the bills in the opened handbag. He said, "Don't take it so hard. You haven't lost anything. After all, you got your money back."

She looked at him. "Why don't you do it?"

"Do what?"

"Knock my teeth out. Break my neck."

He shook his head. He said, "I think you're hurt enough already."

She dragged at the cigarette. Then she leaned back heavily against the sofa pillow, gazing past him and saying dully, "How'd you get the money?"

He shrugged. "I asked for it."

She went on gazing past him. "I should have known they'd louse things up." For a long moment she was quiet. And then, as though she were very tired, she closed her eyes. "All right, tell me what happened."

"Nothing much. But they made a nice try. They came damn near earning their pay."

She looked at his hands. His knuckles were skinned, and she nodded slowly and said, "It musta been a nice little party."

"Yeah," he said dryly, "it was a lot of fun."

"They get banged up much?"

"Enough to make it a sad ending," he said. "One of them is out of business for at least a month. The other one is out for keeps."

She took another drag at the cigarette. She didn't say anything.

He said, "Next time you hire a wrecking crew, don't pay them in advance."

The smoke drifted very slowly from her lips. Her eyes followed the uncurling tendrils as she said, "It wasn't me who paid them. And it wasn't my idea to hire them."

He seized her shoulders. "What was the setup?"

Her lips were locked tightly. She started to shake her head.

"Cut that out," he said. "You've started to tell me and you're gonna finish."

"I can't."

"But you will." His grip on her shoulders was like a set of metal clamps. "I had a feeling it wasn't your idea to begin with. It figures there was an agent in charge of this deal. It figures from every angle. There's someone in this neighborhood who knows I'm looking for him. He knows what's gonna happen when I find out who he is and get my hands on him. You check what I'm talkin' about?"

Bella blinked several times. Her mouth opened but no sound came through.

"I'm talkin' about my sister," he said. "She killed herself because she was jumped and ruined and driven crazy. Whoever he is, he knows I'll keep looking until I find him. So it stands to reason he don't want me around. You check it now?"

She stopped squirming. She stared at him.

He said, "The man is nervous. He's scared. What he'd like most is to see me in a wooden box. But he'd probably settle for less, like a twenty-dollar deal to cripple me. To put me out of action so he'd be safe for a while. And that's where you come in."

She shut her eyes tightly.

He kept the tight hold on her shoulders. "The way it lines up," he said, "you were used for sucker bait. The man knew you had it in for me. He appointed himself as a friendly adviser. Tells you there's a way to even the score, and before you know what you're doing, you give him the twenty dollars. Ain't that how it happened?"

She nodded dazedly.

Kerrigan went on, "He hands the money to the hooligans. He tells them you're the customer. That keeps his name out of it, just in case there's a slip-up. Anyway, that's what he thought. But you know his name and I'm waiting for you to open your mouth."

"No." She choked on it. "Don't make me tell."

"Come on," he gritted. His hands put more pressure on her shoulders.

She winced. His fingers burned into her flesh and there were pain and fear in her eyes. Yet it wasn't at all like physical pain. And it seemed the fear was more for him than for herself.

Then all at once there was nothing in her eyes. Her voice was toneless as she said, "It was Frank."

Then it was quiet in the parlor. But he had a feeling the room was moving. It was like a chamber on wheels going away from everything, falling off the edge of the world.

He took his hands away from her shoulders. He turned away from her, and heard himself saying, "As if I didn't know."

Bella had her head lowered. Her hands covered her face.

"Well," he said, "it adds up. The twenty dollars was the one thing he needed. He never has a nickel in his pockets."

She spoke in a broken whisper. "I should have guessed what was in his mind. But I couldn't think straight. I was half crazy. Or maybe crazy all the way. I just wanted to see you get hurt."

"He knew that," Kerrigan said. "He knew it wouldn't be no trouble to sell you a bill of goods."

She was quiet for some moments. And then, in a lower whisper, "I came near spending more than the twenty."

"Did he ask for more?"

"He wanted me to spend a hundred."

He turned and looked at her. "Why didn't you?"

Bella stared at the carpet. "I didn't have it."

"Did he tell you what a hundred would buy?"

"He said it would put you in a grave."

Kerrigan breathed in slowly. He thought, This is worse than a grave, worse than hell.

Then gradually his mouth hardened. His arms were stiff at his sides. "All right," he said. "Where is he?"

She raised her head. She looked at him and saw something in his eyes that made her go cold.

"You don't hafta tell me," he said. "I'll find him."

He moved toward the door. His hand was on the doorknob when Bella leaped from the sofa, ran to him, and grabbed his arms.

"No," she gasped. "No, don't."

"Let go."

"Please don't," she begged. "Stay here for a while. Think it over."

He tried to pull away from her. "I said let go."

She was using all her strength to drag him away from the door. "I won't letcha," she said. "You'll only do something you'll be sorry for."

Her grip was like iron. Now she had her arms wrapped around his middle and he could hardly breathe. "Goddamn you," he wheezed. "You gonna let go?"

"No," she said. "You gotta listen."

"I've listened enough. I've heard all I need to know."

"You know what'll happen if you go out that door?"

Instead of answering, he gave her a vicious jab with his elbow. It caught her in the side and she groaned. But she wouldn't release her hold on him. He jabbed her again as she went on dragging him backward. She grunted and held him more tightly. It was as though she wanted him to keep jabbing her, to take it out on her.

"If you don't let go," he hissed, "you're gonna get hurt."

"Go ahead and hurt me. You got both arms free."

"You're askin' for grief."

Her breath came in grinding sobs. "I'm askin' you to listen, that's all. Just listen to me. I want you to go in your room and pack your things. And then I'll walk you to the streetcar. You'll take that ride uptown. And you'll stay there. With her."

His arms fell limply at his sides.

Bella relaxed her hold just a little. "Will you do it?"

He was looking at the door. He didn't say anything.

"Please do it," Bella said. "Go to her and live with her and never come back here. Don't even use the phone. Or write. Just forget about all this. Forget you ever lived in this house."

"You make it sound easy."

"Sure it's easy. You said so yourself. Just a matter of spending the carfare." Her voice was torn with a sob. "Fifteen cents."

"That's cheap enough," he said. "Maybe it's too cheap. I think it costs more than that to break off all connections."

Then slowly, gently, he took hold of her wrists, he unfastened her arms from around his middle. She didn't look at him as she stepped away, giving him an unimpeded path to the door. But as she heard the sound of the doorknob turning, she made one last try to hold him back, calling on the only power that could stop him now, moaning, "Dear God, don't let him do it."

But the door was already open. Bella sank to her knees, weeping without sound. Through the window she saw him as he stepped down off the doorstep. His face was like something carved from rock, a profile of hardened whiteness, very white against the darkness of the street. Then he was crossing Vernon and she saw the route he was taking. He moved along a diagonal path aiming at a foggy yellow glow in the distance, the window of Dugan's Den.

16

As he entered the taproom he heard voices and saw faces but everything was a blur that didn't seem real and had no meaning. His eyes were lenses going past the faces and searching for Frank. But Frank wasn't there. He told himself to stand near the door and wait. And just then someone yelled, "Come join the party."

It was the voice of the skinny hag, Dora. She sat with several others at a couple of tables pushed together for what seemed like a celebration. Kerrigan focused on the drinkers. Dora was seated between Mooney and Nick Andros. The other chairs were occupied by the humpbacked wino and Newton Channing. Next to Channing there was an empty chair and the person who'd been sitting on it was prone on the floor, face down and out cold. He looked at the sleeper and saw the orange hair and shapeless figure of Dora's friend Frieda.

For some moments he stood there gazing down at Frieda. She had one arm outstretched and he saw something that glittered on her finger. It was a very large green stone and he didn't need to be told it was artificial.

Dora said, "It cost a goddamn fortune." She reached across the table to nudge Channing's arm. "Go on, tell him how much it cost."

"Three-ninety-five," Channing said.

"You hear?" Dora screeched at Kerrigan. Then again she nudged Channing. "Now tell him what it's for. Tell him why we're celebrating."

"Gladly," Channing said. He stood up ceremoniously. He was wearing a clean white shirt and a straw-colored linen suit. His face was solemn as he bowed to the sleeping woman on the floor. Then he bowed to Kerrigan and said, "Welcome to our little gathering. It's an engagement party."

"You're goddamn right it is," Dora hollered. She reached through a maze of bottles and glasses and found a water glass containing gin. Lifting the glass, she tried to rise for a toast and couldn't make it to her feet. She leaned heavily against

Mooney, spilling some gin on his shoulder as she pronounced a toast for all the world to hear:

> "The yellow moon may kiss the sky,
>   The bees may kiss the butterfly,
>   The morning dew may kiss the grass,
>   And you, my friends—"

"Knock it off," Nick Andros cut in. He pointed to the empty chair and shouted to Kerrigan, "Come on and sit down and have a drink."

Kerrigan didn't move. "I'm looking for my brother," he said. "Anyone here seen my brother?"

"The hell with your brother," Nick said.

"The hell with everybody," Dora yelled. "The yellow moon may kiss the sky—"

"Will you kindly shut up?" Nick requested. He kept beckoning Kerrigan to take the empty chair.

Kerrigan looked at Mooney. "You seen him?"

Mooney shook his head slowly. His eyes were half closed and he looked drunk. But he was studying Kerrigan's face and gradually his mouth opened, his eyes widened, and he sat up straight and stiffly. He tried not to take it further than that, but his hands were lifted and then came down hard on the table and a bottle fell off the edge and crashed to the floor. At the table all talk was stopped. The only sound in the room was the squeaky tune coming from behind the bar. Kerrigan looked in that direction and saw Dugan standing with his arms folded, his eyes closed, humming the melody that took him away from Vernon Street.

Moving toward the bar, Kerrigan said, "Hey, Dugan."

Dugan opened his eyes. The humming slowed down just a little.

"My brother been here?" Kerrigan asked.

Dugan shook his head. Then his eyes were closed again and he picked up the tempo of the tune.

A hand touched Kerrigan's arm. He turned and saw Mooney. The sign painter's face was expressionless.

"Is this what I think it is?" Mooney asked quietly.

Kerrigan pulled his arm away from Mooney's hand. "Go back to the table."

Mooney didn't move. He said, "Why don't you tell me?"

"It don't concern you." But then he remembered the water-color portrait in Mooney's room. He gazed past Mooney and said, "Well, I guess you got a right to know. I've been putting some facts together and finally got the answer."

Mooney just stood there and waited.

Kerrigan closed his eyes for a moment. He heard himself saying, "The creep who jumped my sister was her own brother."

"No," Mooney said. "Don't tell me that. You can't tell me that."

"But I am telling you."

"You know what you're saying?"

Kerrigan nodded.

"You sure?" Mooney's voice quivered just a little. "You absolutely sure?"

"I got it all summed up," Kerrigan said. "It checks."

"You have proof?"

"I know what I need to know. That's enough." He looked down at his hands. His fingers were distended, bent stiffly, like claws.

Mooney said, "We got some hundred proof on the table. I'll fix you a double shot."

"No," Kerrigan said. "I don't want that. All I want is to see him walking in here."

"Now look, Bill—"

But Kerrigan wasn't looking or listening. He wasn't feeling the urgent grip that Mooney put on his arms. He spoke in a choked whisper, saying, "Gonna wait here for him. He'll show. And when he does—"

"Bill, for God's sake!"

"Gonna put him where he put her. Gonna put him in a casket."

And then again everything was a blur. He heard a jumble of noises coming from the table where Nick Andros was telling Dora to shut up and Newton Channing laughed lightly at some comment from the humpbacked wino. From behind the bar the humming sound of Dugan's tune provided vague background music for the clinking of glasses and the drinkers' voices. It went on and on like that, with Mooney's voice begging him to come to the table and have the double shot, and his own voice telling Mooney to leave him alone. Then suddenly he heard a sound that wasn't glass on glass or glass on tabletop or anyone's spoken words. It was the sound of the door as someone came in from the street.

He turned his head and saw his brother.

He heard himself making a noise that was like air coming out from a collapsed balloon.

And after that there was no sound at all. Not even from Dugan.

The quiet stretched as a rubber band stretches and finally can't stretch any more and the fibers split apart. In that instant, as he moved, he sensed Mooney's hands trying to hold him back and his arm was a scythe making contact with the sign painter's ribs.

Mooney sailed halfway across the room, came up against a table, sailed over it, and took a chair with him as he went to the floor. Then Mooney tried to get up and he couldn't get up. He was resting on his side with all the breath knocked out of his body. He saw Kerrigan lunging at Frank, and Kerrigan's hands taking hold of Frank's throat.

"I can't let you live," Kerrigan said. "I can't."

Frank's eyes bulged. His face was getting blue.

"Your own sister," Kerrigan said. "You ruined your own sister." And then, to everyone in the room, to every unseen face beyond the room, "How can I let him live?"

He squeezed harder. There was a gurgling noise. But it wasn't coming from Frank. It came from his own throat, as though he were crushing his own flesh, stopping the flow of his own blood. He told himself to close his eyes, he didn't want to watch what he was doing. But his eyes wouldn't close and he was seeing the convulsive movement of Frank's gaping mouth. He realized that Frank was trying to tell him something.

His fingers reduced the pressure. He heard Frank gasping, "I didn't do it."

He released the hold. Frank was on his knees, trying to cough, trying to talk, making gagging sounds that gradually gave way to sighs.

"Talk," Kerrigan gritted. "Talk fast."

"I didn't do it," Frank repeated. "I swear I didn't."

For some moments there was no sound in the room. Yet in the stillness there was the feeling of something racing through the air, whirling around and around to turn everything upside down.

Frank was lifting himself from the floor. He staggered sideways and leaned heavily against the bar. His eyes were shut tightly and he had his knuckles pressed against his temples.

"You gonna talk?" Kerrigan demanded.

But Frank didn't hear. He seemed to be alone with himself. Then gradually his eyes opened and he was staring up at the ceiling. His hands were lowered, his arms loose at his sides. He spoke to whatever he saw there on the ceiling. "It's straight now," he whispered. "I finally got it straight."

Then it was quiet again. Kerrigan had his mouth open but he couldn't speak. He was trying to get hold of his thoughts, the hollow thoughts that wouldn't add and wouldn't fit and had him trapped somewhere between icy rage and the misty abyss of puzzlement.

And finally he heard Frank saying, "It comes back. All of it. Comes back on all four wheels."

"Spill it."

Frank's voice was level and calm. "The night it happened I was plastered. Couldn't remember where I went or what I did. And all these months it's been like that, getting worse and worse until it reached the point where I gave up trying. I told myself it was me who did it. I really believed it was me."

Kerrigan spoke slowly, the sound edging through his tightened lips. "You sure it wasn't you? You absolutely sure?"

"It couldn't be me," Frank said. And then, completely certain of what he was saying, not trying to force it, just saying it because it was true, "I spent that night in a joint on Second Street. Went in before dark and didn't come out till the next afternoon."

Kerrigan's eyes narrowed. He was studying Frank's face.

Frank said, "I been sick with this thing a long time. It's been like a spike jabbing into my head. I ain't been able to sleep, and couldn't eat, and there were times I could hardly breathe."

Kerrigan didn't say anything. He could feel the truth coming out of Frank's eyes.

He heard Frank saying, "A spike in my head, that's what it was. And every time you looked at me, that spike went in deeper. As if you were telling me what I was telling myself. It got so bad I couldn't take it any more."

"Is that why you hired the gorillas?"

Frank nodded. "I musta gone haywire, just crazy enough to want you out of the way. Musta figured the only way to get rid of that spike was to use it on you."

Kerrigan took a deep breath. It was more like a sigh, as though a tremendous weight had been eased off his chest.

Frank said, "You sure as hell choked it outta me." He grinned weakly and rubbed his throat. "You squeezed just hard enough to loosen that spike. So now it's out."

Kerrigan smiled. He put his hand on Frank's shoulder. Frank grinned at him with a mouth that didn't twitch and eyes that weren't glazed.

"I'm all right now," Frank said. "You see the way it is? I'm really all right now."

Kerrigan nodded. He gazed past Frank. The smile gradually faded from his lips as he thought of Catherine. And he was saying to himself, You still don't know who did it.

And then, very slowly, he felt the answer coming.

17

H E STOOD there and told himself he was getting the answer. He knew it had no connection with any man's face or any man's name. His eyes were focused through the window facing Vernon Street. He peered out past the murky glass and saw the moonlight reflected on the jutting cobblestones. It was a yellow-green glow drifting across Vernon and forming pools of light in the gutter. He saw it glimmering on the rutted sidewalk and going on and on toward all the dark alleys where countless creatures of the night played hide-and-seek.

And no matter where the weaker ones were hiding, they'd never get away from the Vernon moon. It had them trapped. It had them doomed. Sooner or later they'd be mauled and battered and crushed. They'd learn the hard way that Vernon Street was no place for delicate bodies or timid souls. They were prey, that was all, they were destined for the maw of the ever hungry eater, the Vernon gutter.

He stared out at the moonlit street. Without sound he said, You did it to Catherine. You.

It was as though the street could hear. He sensed that it was making a jeering reply. A raucous voice seemed to say, So what? So whatcha gonna do about it?

He groped for an answer.

And the street went on jeering, saying, Your sister couldn't take it, and the same goes for you. And it chose that moment to display its hole card. It opened the door of Dugan's Den and showed him the golden-haired dream girl from uptown. As he stared at Loretta, he could hear the street saying, Well, here she is. She's come to take your hand and lift you from the gutter.

Loretta was walking toward him. Something quivered in his brain and he thought, She reminds me of someone. And then it was there, the memory of the hopes he'd had for Catherine and himself, the hopes he'd lost in a dark alley and yearned to find again.

But taproom noises interfered. Two dimes clinked on the

table as Dugan poured a drink for Frank. At the table Nick
Andros poured gin for Dora. "Say when," Nick said. But Dora
said nothing, for gin had no connection with time. As the gin
splashed over the edge of the glass, Kerrigan looked toward
the table. He saw Frieda getting up from the floor. Mooney
was doing the same, and they almost bumped heads as they
came to their feet. Then Frieda staggered backward and
bumped the humpbacked wino off his chair. Channing caught
hold of Frieda and tried to steady her and she said, "Let go,
goddamnit, I can stand on my own two legs." There was a
shout of approval from Dora. It inspired Frieda to a further
statement of policy. She said to Channing, "Don't put yer
hands on me unless I tell you to."

Channing shrugged, preferring to let it go at that. But Nick
Andros frowned and expressed the male point of view, saying,
"You're wearing his engagement ring, he's your fiance." Frieda
blinked, looked down at the ring on her finger, and then with
some energetic twisting she pulled it off. For some moments
she seemed reluctant to part with the green stone. She held
the ring tightly, frowning at it. Then suddenly she placed the
ring on the table in front of Channing. Her voice was quiet as
she said, "Take it back to where you got it. This pussycat's a
self-supporting individual."

For a moment Channing just sat there with nothing in his
eyes as he thought it over. Then, with another shrug, he lowered the ring into his jacket pocket. So that took care of that,
and then he was smiling at Frieda and saying, "Have a drink?"

Frieda nodded emphatically. She sat down beside him and
watched him pour the gin. She lifted the glass and said loudly,
"This juice is all I need from any man. Even if he wears clean
shirts." But then, as though using her right hand to make up
for a left-handed swipe, she patted the side of Channing's head
and spoke in a softer tone. "Don't take it to heart, sweetie.
You're really cute. It's nice to sit here and drink with you. But
that's as far as we can take it. After all, it's every cat to his own
alley."

So true, Kerrigan thought. He looked at Loretta, who stood
there waiting for him to say something. His eyes aimed down
to what she had on her finger, the hinged ring from the Greek's
loose-leaf notebook. His brain said, No dice. She'll hafta take

it off. And his heart ached as he gazed at her face. Her face told him that she knew what he was thinking and her own heart was aching.

He said, "I'll have a talk with the Greek. He'll get rid of the license. All he has to do is light a match."

She didn't say anything. She looked at the ring on her finger. She started to take it off and it wanted to stay there, as though it were a part of her that pleaded not to be torn away.

He said, "It'll come off. Just loosen the hinge."

Her eyes were wet. "If we could only—"

"But we can't," he said. "Don't you see the way it is? We don't ride the same track. I can't live your kind of life and you can't live mine. It ain't anyone's fault. It's just the way the cards are stacked."

She nodded slowly. And just then the ring came off. It dropped from her limp hand and rolled across the floor and went under the bar to vanish in the darkness of all lost dreams. He heard the final tinkling sound it made, a plaintive little sound that accompanied her voice saying good-by. Then there was the sound of his own footsteps walking out of Dugan's Den.

As he came off the pavement to cross the Vernon cobblestones, his tread was heavy, coming down solidly on solid ground. He moved along with a deliberate stride that told each stone it was there to be stepped on, and he damn well knew how to walk this street, how to handle every bump and rut and hole in the gutter. He went past them all, and went up on the doorstep of the house where he lived. As he pushed open the door, it suddenly occurred to him that he was damned hungry.

In the parlor, Bella was lying face down on the sofa. He gave her a slap on her rump. "Get up," he said. "Make me some supper."

STREET OF NO RETURN

1

THERE WERE three of them sitting on the pavement with their backs against the wall of the flophouse. It was a biting cold night in November and they sat there close together trying to get warm. The wet wind from the river came knifing through the street to cut their faces and get inside their bones, but they didn't seem to mind. They were discussing a problem that had nothing to do with the weather. In their minds it was a serious problem, and as they talked their eyes were solemn and tactical. They were trying to find a method of obtaining some alcohol.

"We need a drink," one said. "We need a drink and that's all there is to it."

"Well, we won't get it sitting here."

"We won't get it standing up, either," the first one said. He was middle-aged and tall and very skinny and they called him Bones. He gazed dismally at the empty bottle between his legs and said, "It needs cash, and we got no cash. So it don't matter whether we sit or stand or move around. The fact remains we got no cash."

"You made that statement an hour ago," said the other man who had spoken. "I wish you'd quit making that statement."

"Well, it's true."

"I know it's true, but I wish you'd quit repeating it. What's the use of repeating it?"

"If we talk about it long enough," Bones said, "we might do something about it."

"We won't do anything," the other man said. "We'll just sit here and get more thirsty."

Bones frowned. Then he took a deep breath as though he were about to say something important. And then he said, "I wish we had another bottle."

"I wish to hell you'd shut up," the other man said. He was a short bulky bald man in his early forties and his name was Phillips. He had lived here on Skid Row for more than twenty years and had the red raw Tenderloin complexion that is unlike any other complexion and stamps the owner as strictly a flop-house resident.

"We gotta get a drink," Bones said. "We gotta find a way to get a drink."

"I'm trying to find a way to keep you quiet," Phillips said. "Maybe if I hit you on the head you'll be quiet."

"That's an idea," Bones said seriously. "At least if you knock me out I'll be better off. I won't know how much I need a drink." He leaned forward to offer his head as a target. "Go on, Phillips, knock me out."

Phillips turned away from Bones and looked at the third man who sat there along the wall. Phillips said, "You do it, Whitey. You hit him."

"Whitey wouldn't do it," Bones said. "Whitey never hits anybody."

"You sure about that?" Phillips murmured. He saw that Whitey was not listening to the talk and he spoke to Bones as though Whitey weren't there.

"I'll give odds on it," Bones said. "This man here wouldn't hurt a living thing. Not even a cat that scratched him."

"If a cat scratched me, I'd wring its neck," Phillips said.

"That's you," Bones said. "Whitey ain't made that way. Whitey's on the gentle side."

"Gentle?" Phillips had a thoughtful look in his eyes as he went on studying Whitey. Then he said, "Maybe gentle ain't the word. Maybe the word is timid."

Bones shrugged. "Whatever you want to call it. That's the way he is." He spoke to the third man who sat there, not saying anything. "Ain't that so, Whitey?"

Whitey nodded vaguely.

"He ain't even listening," Phillips said.

"What?" Whitey blinked a few times. He smiled mildly and said, "What are you talking about?"

"Nothing," Phillips said. "Let it drop."

Whitey shrugged. He aimed the mild smile at the empty bottle. The curved glass showed him a miniature of himself, a little man lost in the emptiness of a drained bottle. Aside from what he saw in the bottle, he was actually on the small side, five feet seven and weighing 145. His eyes were gray and he had the kind of face that doesn't attract much attention one way or another. The only unusual thing was his hair. He was thirty-three years old and his hair was snow white.

Another thing, not really unusual along Skid Row, was his voice. He always spoke in a semiwhisper, sort of strained and sometimes cracked, as though he had a case of chronic bronchitis. At times when he spoke there was a look of pain in his eyes and it seemed that the effort of producing sound was hurting his throat. But whenever they asked him about it, he said there was nothing wrong with his throat. They'd insist there was something wrong and then he'd smile and say that his throat was dry, his throat was very dry and he could use a drink. Some of them would check on that and treat him to a drink and maybe two or more shots. But no matter how many shots he had, he went on speaking in the strained painful whisper.

He'd arrived on Skid Row seven years ago, coming out of nowhere like all the other two-legged shadows. He made the weary, stumbling entrance to take his place in the soup lines outside the missions and the slow aimless parade up and down River Street. With nothing in his pockets and nothing in his eyes, he joined the unchartered society of the homeless and the hopeless, to flop on any old mattress and eat whatever food he could scrounge and wear what rags he could pick up here and there. But the primary thing was the drinking, and it was always a problem because there was always more thirst than cash to purchase drinks. In that regard he was identical with the others, and when they saw he was no different from themselves, they didn't bother to ask questions. He was accepted and included and completely ignored. There was an unspoken agreement that they'd leave him alone, they'd pay no attention when he got drunk and stumbled and fell and passed out. It applied to any condition he was in; they'd definitely leave him alone. That was all he wanted and that was why he liked it here on Skid Row.

The three of them sat there with Bones and Phillips discussing the alcohol issue and Whitey staring at the empty bottle. It was getting on toward midnight and the wind from the river was colder now, and much meaner. On both sides of River Street the taprooms and hash houses were crowded. In the hash houses there was a demand for hot soup. In the taprooms they hollered for double shots and gulped them down and hollered again. The bartenders hollered back and told them to be patient, a man had only two hands. The sounds of drinkers and bartenders were reaching the ears of Bones and Phillips and they were getting irritated and sad and then irritated again.

"Listen to it," Bones said.

"I'm listening," Phillips said. But as he said it the sounds he heard were not coming from the taprooms. These were new and abrupt noises from several blocks away. It was a clamor of shouts and screams, glass breaking and things crashing and footsteps running.

"They're at it again," Bones said.

"The hell with them." Phillips waved wearily in the direction of the violent noises.

"They buried two last week," Bones said.

The sounds were coming in waves, getting higher and higher, and at the top of it there was someone screeching. It was on the order of the noise an animal would make while getting crushed by a steam roller.

"It gets worse every day," Bones said.

Phillips made another weary gesture.

Bones said, "They've been at it for more than a month. You'd think they'd have it stopped by this time."

The screeching noise faded and then for some moments it was quiet down there three blocks away. But all at once there was a crash and more shouting and screaming and a raging flood of curses and then policemen's whistles and running feet.

Bones stood up to have a look. He was looking south along River Street but he couldn't see anything down there. Up here along Skid Row there were a lot of bright lights, varicolored and sprinkling the darkness with the all-night glow from eateries and cut-rate stores and pawnshops. But where Skid Row ended the bright lights ended, and down there south on River Street there were no lights at all, only the hulking shapes of four-story tenements and three-story warehouses, and here and there the masts and funnels of freighters docked in the river. Bones went on trying to see what was happening three blocks south and all he saw was the darkness. Finally he sat down again, and just as he did so there was a very loud scream from down there and then much more noise than before. Now some of it was automobile noise, the roar of engines picking up speed, the whine of tires making sharp turns, then the high-octave scream of brakes performing sudden stops. But the human screams were louder than the automobiles; the yelling and crashing and thudding seemed to stifle the noise of the police cars.

It went on like that and the noise of the police cars was like frustrated growling, confused and fumbling, unable to cope with the louder noise.

Phillips snorted. "Them clowns."

"Who?" Bones asked.

"The cops," Phillips said. "The city's finest. The sturdy enforcers of law and order."

"They sound like they need help."

"They need brains, that's what they need. That's what's wrong with them, they got no brains."

Bones frowned indignantly. He assumed the look of a solid citizen defending the abilities of the police force. He said stiffly, "Quit jabbing needles in them. It ain't easy to be a cop in this district."

Just then there was a very loud crashing sound, as though one of the cars had collided with a brick wall. Or maybe it had run into another police car.

Phillips laughed sourly and disdainfully. "Listen to them," he said. "Now they're running around in circles and getting in each other's way."

"That sounded like a bad accident," Bones said.

Phillips snorted again. "They're always having accidents. They're always making mistakes. They're really brilliant, them policemen."

Bones folded his arms and gave Phillips a glaring look. "It's easy to talk," he said. "Them cops are only doing the best they can."

"Yeah, I know." Phillips pointed toward the area of chaotic sound. "They're sure doing a wonderful job of it."

"I guess you could do better."

"Me?" Phillips looked thoughtful for a moment. "If I was a cop I'd stay the hell out of that neighborhood. They don't want cops down there. All they wanna do is raise hell and hammer away at each other. I'd let them do it to their hearts' content. I wouldn't give a damn if every last one of them wound up on a stretcher."

"It's no use talking to you," Bones said. "You just don't make good sense."

Phillips didn't bother to reply. He looked at Whitey to see if Whitey was interested in the conversation. Whitey's face showed no interest at all. He wasn't even listening to the hectic noises coming from three blocks south. Whitey sat there gazing at the empty bottle set between Bones's legs, and Phillips wondered seriously whether the small white-haired man was completely in touch with the world. He decided to find out, and he tapped Whitey's shoulder and said, "You hear the commotion? You know what's going on?"

Whitey nodded. But aside from that there was no reaction and he went on looking at the empty bottle.

"You know what it's all about?" Phillips persisted.

Whitey shrugged.

"They're fighting," Phillips said. "Can't you hear them fighting?"

Whitey shrugged again. "They're always having trouble down there."

"Not this kind of trouble," Phillips said. "This is different."

Bones nodded emphatically. "You can say that again," he said. "It used to be they'd settle for some black eyes and busted noses, and maybe some teeth knocked out. But now they're really at it. They're out for blood."

"They'll get tired of it," Whitey said. He sounded as though he weren't inclined to discuss the matter further. Again he set his gaze on the empty bottle.

Phillips shrugged inside himself and decided there was no use in trying to get an opinion from Whitey. And anyway, maybe Whitey had the right idea. Like that little country overseas that never got in a jam because it stuck to a policy of minding its own business. Except that Whitey took it a lot further than that. Whitey wouldn't even look, wouldn't even listen. Chances were that Whitey never gave a moment's thought to what was going on around him.

There was another burst of crashing and shouting and screaming from three blocks away and Bones said, "Listen to it. Good God, just listen to it."

Phillips didn't say anything.

"It's getting worse," Bones said. "The Lord only knows

what's happening down there. It sounds like a slaughter-house."

Phillips opened his mouth to utter a comment and then changed his mind and locked his lips tightly to prevent himself from voicing any further opinions. The effort was rather diffi-cult for him because he was a man who gave considerable thought to local issues and felt quite strongly about certain matters. But he realized he couldn't afford to feel too strongly; he suffered from a nervous stomach and at the clinic they'd told him it was important not to get excited. They said it was bad enough that he drank so much cheap wine and he shouldn't make things worse by getting excited.

But the noise from three blocks away was on the order of hammer blows banging at the skull of Phillips and he winced as though he could actually feel the impact. He had come to Skid Row to get away from the memory of hatred and violence in a little mining town where the miners went on strike and he'd scabbed. They had come to talk to him and he'd figured they wanted to do more than just talk, and before it was ended there were three of them shot dead and a smoking rifle in his hand as he made a beeline for the woods. They were still look-ing for him in that part of the country, but that angle wasn't what bothered him. What bothered him was the memory.

The memory hit him and went in very deeply every time he heard the violence down there three blocks away. It was like a voice telling him that Skid Row wasn't really the hiding place it was supposed to be. It was a locale that constantly got played for a sucker. The Tenderloin tried its best to keep away from contact with the world but somehow or other the world always managed to make contact. The world tossed the bait and tossed it again and again, kept tossing it to get a nibble, and sooner or later the hook was taken and the line reeled in.

Phillips closed his eyes for a moment and listened to the sounds of the fighting in the street three blocks south of Skid Row. With his eyes shut very tightly he wished that Skid Row were soundproof.

He wanted to run down there and beg them to stop it. It was a silly notion and he smiled bitterly, knowing how silly it was. They called that area the Hellhole, and for more than one good reason. Along Skid Row the uninformed were firmly advised, "Don't walk too far south on River Street. Stay away from the Hellhole." In the past month it was more than just a matter of avoiding getting mugged or slugged or dragged into an alley. It was the idea of keeping away from the cobblestone battlefield where the combat was on an all-out basis. They were fighting with the white-hot fury that men display when they forget that they are men. In the Hellhole, these nights, they were having race riots.

Phillips had no idea how it had started. He knew that no one was sure about that. He remembered that around a year ago some Puerto Ricans had moved into the tenements down there and then more had come. And some more. And then they were saying there were too many Puerto Ricans moving in. The talk went on for a while but it was just talk and gradually it died down. Then all at once, five weeks ago, there was a riot. A few nights later there was another riot. Some people were hurt but there was no serious damage and for a week things were quiet and it looked as though the trouble had ended. But then they rioted again and it was mean ugly fighting and three men died. In the fourth riot there were two dead and one blinded with lye and several taken to the hospital, badly cut up. Tonight was the seventh riot and Phillips wasn't sure how many had died altogether but he knew the number was considerable. He told himself it was very bad and getting worse and he wondered how it would end. Or whether it would ever end.

He told himself to stop thinking about it. After all, it was a matter of geography and this was Skid Row and the Hellhole was three blocks away. He was here on Skid Row and the Hellhole was a million miles away. And so was yesterday, and so were all the memories of the little mining town.

The thing to do was play it Whitey's way and not let it touch him, let nothing touch him. He turned his head and looked at Whitey, knowing that Whitey's eyes would be aimed at the empty bottle and the only thought in Whitey's brain would be the need for another drink.

But Whitey wasn't looking at the bottle. Whitey sat there sort of stiffly, his mouth halfway open. He was staring at something on the other side of the street.

2

PHILLIPS FROWNED slightly. He studied the look of rapt attention on Whitey's face. Then he looked across the street to see what Whitey was staring at. He didn't see anything unusual over there. It was just some Tenderloin scufflers coming out of a hash house and a man walking south on River Street and a woman walking north. The woman was nothing to look at. She was fat and shapeless and walked with the exaggerated wiggle of a very lonely female hoping for company.

Bones was saying, "We gotta find a way to get a drink. That's all it amounts to. We just gotta get a drink."

"That's right," Whitey said. But he didn't seem to realize he was saying it. The words came out mechanically. He sat there stiffly and went on staring at something on the other side of the street.

"What is it?" Phillips asked. "What're you looking at?"

Whitey didn't answer.

"The woman?" Phillips asked. "You looking at the woman?"

Whitey shook his head very slowly. Then, more slowly, he started to get up from the pavement. He was almost on his feet when he changed his mind and sat down again. He shrugged and turned his head and looked at the empty bottle. He grinned at the bottle as though it were telling him something funny. He spoke to the bottle, saying, "All right, I'll try it."

"Try what?" Phillips said.

"I'll try it and see what happens," Whitey said to the bottle. The grin on his face was vague and it went along with the dragging whisper coming from his lips.

"What is this?" Phillips said. He touched Whitey's shoulder. "What's wrong with you?"

Whitey didn't seem to hear. He went on grinning at the bottle and he said, "Sure, I might as well try it."

Then it was quiet and Phillips and Bones looked at each other. Bones shrugged as though to say there was no way to figure Whitey, and no use asking him what was on his mind.

Whitey stood up again. He put his hands in the pockets of

his ragged overcoat and hunched his shoulders against the wind coming from the river. He approached the curb and then stopped to pick up a cigarette stub. The cigarette was less than half smoked and he started to put it in his pocket, then tossed the stub to Bones.

Bones reached inside his coat and found a safety match and lit the cigarette. He took a long drag and handed the cigarette to Phillips. They sat there on the pavement sharing the cigarette and watching Whitey as he crossed the street. They were waiting to see what he would do when he was on the other side. He looked very small and shabby as he crossed River Street and it didn't seem to matter who he was or where he was going or what he intended to do. But they watched him as though it were very important that they pay careful attention. They had the unaccountable feeling that he was something special to watch.

They saw him arriving on the other side of the street. On the sidewalk he stopped for a moment to pull up the collar of his overcoat. Then again his hands were in his pockets and he was walking. He was walking slowly, his white hair wind-blown, his legs moving off stride as he went along River Street in a sort of lazy shuffle.

"South," Phillips murmured. "He's headed south."

"That's going toward the Hellhole."

"No," Phillips said. "He wouldn't go there."

"Well, where's he going?"

Phillips didn't reply. He squinted through the glare of the Skid Row lights, watching the small white-haired figure going south on River and coming to the end of the block and still going south.

"He's damn sure going toward the Hellhole," Bones said.

Phillips took the cigarette from Bones's mouth and put it in his own. He sipped the smoke through his teeth and it came out slowly through his nose. He didn't taste it going in or feel it coming out. He listened for the sounds of street fighting from the Hellhole but now there was no sound down there. Only the darkness.

Something was shining far down there in the darkness and it was the white hair of the small man walking south on River Street.

"We oughta go after him," Bones said.

Phillips nodded slowly.

"Let's go," Bones said.

But neither of them moved. They sat there on the cold pavement with their backs against the wall of the flophouse. They watched the thatch of white hair getting smaller and smaller and finally it vanished altogether. They looked at each other and for some moments they didn't say anything.

Then Bones stared glumly at the empty bottle and said, "We need a drink. How we gonna get a drink?"

Whitey was on the east side of River Street three blocks away from Skid Row. He was walking very slowly and every now and then he stepped into a doorway and stayed there a few moments. Once he crossed to the west side of River and stood beside an empty ash can, bent over it as though he were rummaging for something in the trash. But he wasn't looking inside the can. His head was turned slightly from the can and his eyes were focused on the man moving south on River.

It was the man he had seen walking past the hash house. The man was very short, around five-four, and extremely wide. The man's arms were unusually long, and came down past his knees. He moved somewhat like a chimpanzee, his head jutting forward and down, his arms swinging in unison as he went along in a bowlegged stride. He wore a bright-green cap and a black-and-purple plaid lumber jacket. He was walking without haste but with a certain deliberateness, his hard-heeled shoes making emphatic sounds on the sidewalk.

There was no other sound. There were no other people on the street. In the tenements the windows were dark. There were countless mongrels and alley cats and sewer rats in this area but none were visible now. It seemed that all living things were hiding from each other. The silence in the Hellhole was colder than the wind slicing in from the river.

On the pavement and in the gutter there were certain souvenirs of what had happened here tonight. There were broken bottles and the splintered handles of baseball bats and a lot of red stains, still wet. There was the cracked pane of a store window and the smashed front door of a tenement, the door leaning far out on its hinges. There were strips of torn clothing and someone's hat ripped across the crown and wet red smears on it.

Whitey saw all of that but it had no effect on him, it had no place in his thoughts. He wasn't conscious of the fact that he was down here in the Hellhole. His full attention was centered on the man in front of him.

He saw the man turning off River to go east on a narrow side street. He quickened his pace just a little, came onto the side street, and saw the man stopped near a dimly lit lamppost, looking toward an alleyway. The man made a move toward the alleyway, then stopped again. The man stood there as though trying to make up his mind whether to enter the alley. Some moments passed and then the man shrugged and continued on.

Whitey had ducked into a doorway and now he came out and resumed following the man. His pace was slackened again and he stayed close to the tenement walls, ready to use another doorway in case the man turned for a look. As he approached the lamppost he heard something that made him glance toward the alleyway. It was a quick glance and he couldn't see it distinctly and he kept on walking. He told himself to forget about the alleyway and what was happening there. Whatever it was, it had no connection with the man he was following. But then he heard it again and it seemed to reach inside him and beg him to stop.

He stopped. He listened to the sound coming from the alleyway. It was a gurgling, rattling noise. And then the faint voice saying, "Please. Please. Help me."

Whitey turned and walked quickly to the alleyway. He entered the alley and the glow from the lamppost showed him the brass buttons and the blue uniform. The policeman was sitting in the alley, his head down very low. His cap was off and his hair was mussed and the top of his head was all bloody.

The policeman looked up and saw Whitey and said, "Get an ambulance."

"I'll hafta phone."

"Use a call box. Call the station house. Ask for the Thirty-seventh District."

"Where's the nearest call box?"

The policeman opened his mouth to reply. The sound that came out was more gurgling and rattling. His head went down again and then he was falling over on his side. Whitey caught hold of him.

"The call box," Whitey said. "Tell me where it is."

The policeman gurgled very low in his throat.

"Tell me," Whitey said. "Try to tell me."

"It's on—" But the policeman couldn't take it further than that. His head was leaning against Whitey's chest and his hands clutched at Whitey's arms. Now he made no sound at all and his full weight was on Whitey. As Whitey knelt there holding him to keep him from falling, there was the sound of an auto and then the beam of a searchlight. Whitey turned his head and blinked in the glare of the light shooting into his face. He blinked again and saw the black-and-orange police car parked out there. The door opened and he saw the policemen getting out and running toward him.

They were young policemen and their faces were expressionless. One of them was grabbing for a revolver and having trouble pulling it from the holster. The other policeman grabbed Whitey's shoulder, couldn't get a good grip on the shoulder, and decided to hook his fingers around the back of Whitey's neck.

"Let go," Whitey said. "I'm not running."

"You telling me?" the policeman said. He tightened his hold on Whitey's neck.

"That hurts," Whitey said.

"Shut up." The policeman pulled Whitey to his feet. The other policeman had managed to get the revolver from the holster and was now trying to put it back in. Finally he got it in and then he knelt beside the injured policeman, who was now face down in the alley. He rolled the man over on his side and looked at the face. The eyes were half open and the mouth sagged at the corners. The color of the face was gray with streams of red running down the cheeks and dripping from the lips.

"It's Gannon."

"Bad?"

"Dead."

The policeman stood up. He looked down at the body and then he looked at Whitey.

3

THE STATION house of the Thirty-seventh District was on Clayton Street, six blocks west of the river and four blocks west of the Hellhole. It was a one-story brick structure that had been built some thirty years ago. At both sides of the front entrance there were frosted-glass lamps. In the glare of the lamplight Whitey stood between the two policemen. He was handcuffed but they weren't taking any chances with him. They were very young policemen and new to the force and this arrest was very important to them. One of them gripped Whitey's arm and the other had hold of his trousers. He looked very small standing there between the two tall policemen.

The entrance doors were wide open and Whitey could see it was very crowded in the station house. It was a noisy assemblage and some of them were shouting in Spanish. He saw a Puerto Rican woman pull away from the grip of a policeman and lunge at a yellow-haired man and her fingernails ripped the man's face. The man stepped back and hauled off and punched her in the breast. Three Puerto Rican men started toward the yellow-haired man and several policemen moved in and for some moments there was considerable activity. One of the Puerto Ricans was completely out of control and Whitey saw the worried looks on the faces of the policemen as they tried to handle him. They couldn't handle him and two of them were knocked down. Then a very large man wearing the uniform of a police captain came walking toward the Puerto Rican and grabbed his wrist and then very quickly and precisely lifted him in a wrestler's crotch hold, lifted him high in the air, held him there for a long moment, then hurled him to the floor. There was a very loud thud and the Puerto Rican stayed there on the floor, face down and not moving. Another Puerto Rican shouted something and the Captain walked over to him and shot a fist into his mouth. The American-born prisoners shouted encouragement to the Captain and one of them was grinning and aiming a kick at the Puerto Rican who'd been hit in the mouth. The Captain took hold of the American and put a short left hook in his midsection, chopped a right to his head, then hooked him again to send him flying against the wall, and when he bounced away from the wall the Captain hit him once more to put him on the floor on his knees.

"Next?" the Captain said very quietly, looking around at the Puerto Ricans and the Americans. "Who's next?"

"You can't do this," one of the Americans said.

"Can't I?" The Captain moved slowly toward the American, who had a black eye and a cut on his face.

"All right, hit me," the American said. He pointed to his damaged face. "As if I ain't hurt enough. Go ahead and hurt me some more."

"Sure," the Captain said. "Sure, I'll be glad to." He said it sort of sadly, somewhat like a doctor telling a patient it was necessary to operate. Then quickly and neatly he threw a combination of punches and the American went down and rolled over and began to moan.

The Captain looked at the other Americans and the Puerto Ricans. "You want riots?" the Captain said. "I'll give you riots. I'll give you all you want."

"We want to be left alone," a Puerto Rican said in accented English. He pointed to the Americans. "They won't leave us alone."

"You're a goddamn liar," an American said. "You bastards started it. You started it and we're gonna finish it."

"No," the Captain said. "I'll finish it."

"I wish you would," the American said. He had a swollen jaw and under his nose there was dried blood. His face was pale and he was breathing hard. As he spoke to the Captain he stared at the Puerto Ricans and his eyes glittered. "I wish you'd use a machine gun. Mow them down. Dump them in the river."

"Shut your mouth," the Captain said.

"Dirty no-good spics," the American said. He breathed harder. "They're no good, I tell you. They're lousy in their hearts, every last one of them."

"You gonna shut up?" the Captain said.

"They're filthy. Filthy."

"And you?" said the Puerto Rican who had spoken. "You're not filthy?"

"We're Americans," the American said, his voice cracking

with the strain of holding himself back from leaping at the Puerto Rican. "We were here before you."

"Yes," the Puerto Rican said. "And so were the sewer rats."

The Captain stood there between them. He looked from one to the other. His big hands were clenched and his big body bulged with power. But now he couldn't move. He couldn't open his mouth to say anything. He stood there in the middle and his eyes were dull and had the helpless look of someone caught in the jaws of a slowly closing trap.

The American went on shouting at the Puerto Rican and finally the Captain growled very low in his throat, reached out, and grabbed the American's hand by the fingers, twisting the fingers to bend them back from the knuckles.

"I told you to shut up," the Captain said. He went on twisting the man's fingers. The man's knees were bent and he was halfway to the floor, his eyes shut tightly. The Captain growled again and said, "You'll shut up if I hafta rip your tongue outta your mouth."

Then it was quiet in there and Whitey saw the Captain releasing the man's hand and walking back to the big high desk at the far side of the room. The Captain called out someone's name and a policeman took hold of a man's arm and brought him toward the desk. At that moment a man wearing a gray overcoat came out of a side room and crossed the floor to the front door, coming outside to face the two policemen who held Whitey.

"What are you standing here for?" the plain-clothes man said. "Why don't you take him inside?"

"We were waiting, Lieutenant."

"Waiting for what?"

"For things to quiet down in there."

The plain-clothes man smiled dimly. "That's good thinking, Bolton. That's the kind of thinking gets promotions."

"I don't know what you mean, Lieutenant."

"I mean your timing. You were timing it just right. Waiting until it was quiet and you'd have the Captain's undivided attention. Then make the grand entrance. Come in with the murderer."

The policemen didn't say anything. They knew he was having fun with them. This one had a habit of having fun with everyone. Usually they didn't mind and they kidded him back. But now it was an important arrest, it was a homicide and the victim was a policeman. Certainly it was no time for the Lieutenant to be having fun.

The Lieutenant stood there smiling at them. He hadn't yet looked at Whitey. He was waiting for the policemen to say something. Behind him, inside the station house, another commotion had started, but he didn't turn to see what was happening in there.

Finally one of the policemen said, "We weren't timing it, Lieutenant. Only timing we did was according to the book. Used the radio and made the report. Waited there for the wagon to come and get the body. The wagon came and got it and now we're taking this man in. I don't see why we're getting criticized."

"You're not getting criticized," the Lieutenant said. His tone was mild and friendly and only slightly sarcastic as he went on: "I think you've done very nicely, Bolton. You too, Woodling."

The two policemen glanced at each other. They could feel the sarcasm and they wondered how to handle it.

The Lieutenant put his hands in the pockets of his overcoat and leaned back just a little on his heels. He said, "I'm sure you'll get a commendation from the Captain. He's gonna be very pleased with this arrest. It'll come as a pleasant surprise."

"Surprise?" Patrolman Bolton said. "I don't get that. Ain't he been told about the murder?"

"Not yet," the Lieutenant said.

"Why not?" Bolton was frowning. "We sent in the report thirty minutes ago."

The Lieutenant glanced at his wrist watch. "Twenty minutes," he corrected. Then he flipped his thumb backward to indicate the noisy action inside the station house. "The Captain's been very busy these past twenty minutes. I figured it was best not to bother him."

"Bother him?" Bolton came near shouting it. "For Christ's sake, Lieutenant—"

And Woodling was chiming in, "Listen, Lieutenant, this is serious."

The Lieutenant nodded very slowly and seriously. "I know," he said. And then for the first time he looked at Whitey. He gave a little sigh and said to Whitey, "You sure picked a fine time to do it."

"I didn't do it," Whitey said.

"Of course not," the Lieutenant said conversationally. Then he shifted his attention to the two policemen. "We'll have to wait a while before we tell the Captain." Again he glanced at his wrist watch and at the same moment his head was slightly turned, he seemed to be measuring the noise from inside the station house. He said, "I think we'll have to wait at least fifteen minutes."

"But why?" Bolton demanded.

The Lieutenant spoke slowly and patiently. "I'll tell you why. When a man has diarrhea you don't give him a laxative. You give him a chance to quiet down."

"But this—" Woodling started.

"Is dynamite," the Lieutenant finished for him. And then, not looking at anything in particular, sort of murmuring aloud to himself, "If I had my way, I wouldn't tell the Captain at all. He'd never get to hear about it. I think when he hears about it he's gonna get sick. Real sick. I only hope he don't burst a blood vessel."

The two policemen looked at their prisoner. Then they looked at each other. They didn't say anything.

The Lieutenant went on talking aloud to himself. "As if things haven't been bad enough. Getting worse all the time. And now we got this."

"Well," Woodling said, tightening his hold on Whitey's arm, "at least we got the man who did it."

The Lieutenant gave Woodling an older-brother look of fondness and gentle schooling. "You don't get the point. You're thinking too much in terms of the arrest. Try to forget the arrest. Think about the Captain."

The two policemen stood there frowning and blinking.

"The Captain," the Lieutenant said. He leaned toward them. He took his hands from his pockets and put them behind his back. "You get the drift of what I'm talking about?"

They went on frowning puzzledly.

"Listen," the Lieutenant said. "Listen to me. And it's very important that you listen carefully." He took a deep breath, and then his lips tightened and the words came out sort of hissing, like sound pumped from a hose. "From here on in," he said, "you'll be playing with a firecracker. Whatever you say to the Captain, think twice before you say it. And whatever you do, make sure it's not a mistake. He's in no condition to see you making mistakes, not even tiny ones. I'm telling you this so you'll remember it, and I want you to pass the word around."

Bolton blinked again. "Are things that bad?"

"Worse than bad," the Lieutenant said. He was about to say more when Woodling made a warning gesture, indicating that they shouldn't discuss this topic in front of the prisoner. For a moment the Lieutenant hesitated. Then he looked at the ragged little Skid Row bum, the white-haired blank-eyed nothing who stood there wearing handcuffs. He decided there were just three men present and he could go on with what he was saying.

He said, "This situation in the Hellhole. These riots. It's got out of control. Two nights ago I'm with the Captain when he gets a phone call from the Hall. The Commissioner. Wanted to know if we needed help. Said he was ready to send reinforcements. Add twenty men to this district, give us seven more cars. You know what that was? That was a slap in the teeth. That was the Commissioner telling the Captain to clean up the floor or give up the mop. In a nice way, of course. Very polite and friendly and all that."

Bolton spoke in a low murmur. "What did the Captain say?"

"He told the Commissioner to leave him alone. He said he didn't need reinforcements, he could do this job without help from the Hall, and all he wanted was a promise that they wouldn't interfere. He said he'd been in charge of this district for nine years and he'd always been able to hold the wheel and if they'd only leave him alone he'd go on holding it.

"Now mind you," the Lieutenant went on, "that was only two nights ago. So what happens tonight? Another riot in the Hellhole, the worst yet. And something else. Something I knew was bound to happen sooner or later. We lose an officer."

It was quiet for some moments. Then both policemen turned their heads very slowly and they were looking down at the small white-haired man who stood between them. And Woodling said quietly to the prisoner, "You bastard, you. You miserable bastard."

Bolton jerked his head frontward as though he couldn't bear to look at the prisoner. He swallowed hard. "But—" he started, then blurted, "But my God, they can't blame the Captain for this."

"They will," the Lieutenant said.

"No." Bolton's voice was strained. "No. That ain't fair."

The Lieutenant shrugged. Then his face relaxed and the seriousness went out of his eyes. He was himself again and his voice went back to the easy, friendly, mildly sarcastic murmur. "Don't let it give you ulcers," he told the two youthful policemen. "You're too young to get ulcers."

"But this." Woodling spoke through his teeth, his thumb flicking to indicate the prisoner. "Who tells the Captain about this?"

"I'll tell him," the Lieutenant said. "I'll figure a way to break it to him." He bit his lip thoughtfully. "Tell you what. I'll take this man in through the side door. I wanna ask him some questions. Meantime, you go outside and wait."

The policemen released their holds on Whitey and entered the station house. The Lieutenant looked at Whitey and said, "All right, come with me."

They walked down the steps and around the side of the station house. The Lieutenant had his hands in his overcoat pockets and moved along with his head down, his lips slightly pursed to whistle a tune in a minor key. It was a song from many years ago and he couldn't remember past the first few bars. He tried it a few times and couldn't get it. Whitey picked it up and hummed the rest of it. The Lieutenant glanced at Whitey and said, "Yeah, that's it. Pretty number."

"Yeah," Whitey said.

"What?"

"I said yeah."

"Can't you talk louder?"

Whitey shook his head.

"Why not?" the Lieutenant asked. "What's wrong with your voice?"

Whitey didn't answer.

They were approaching the side entrance of the station house. The Lieutenant stopped and looked fully at Whitey and said, "You got bronchitis or something?"

"No," Whitey said. "I talk like this all the time."

"It sounds weird," the Lieutenant said. "As if you're whispering secrets."

Whitey shrugged. He didn't say anything.

The Lieutenant leaned in slightly to get a closer look at Whitey's face. A vague frown drifted across the Lieutenant's brow and he murmured, "I bet you're full of secrets."

Whitey shrugged again. "Who ain't?"

The Lieutenant mixed the frown with a smile. "You got a point there."

Then the Lieutenant was quiet and they went along the side of the station house. They came to the side door and the Lieutenant opened it and they went in. There was a narrow corridor and a door with a sign over it with the word "Captain" and then another door with the sign "House Sergeant" and finally a door with the sign "Detectives." The door was partially open and the Lieutenant shoved it with his foot to open it all the way.

It was a medium-sized room with a floor that needed wax and walls that needed paint. There were some chairs and a few small tables and a roll-top desk. A tall man with a very closely waved and nicely cut pompadour of light-brown hair sat working at the desk. He glanced up at them, gave Whitey a quick once-over, and went back to work.

"Have a seat," the Lieutenant said to Whitey. He pointed toward a table that had a chair on either side. Then he took off his overcoat and put it on a hanger. On the wall next to the hanger there was a small mirror and the Lieutenant moved in close to it as though looking to see if he needed a shave. He stood there for some moments inspecting his face and adjusting his tie. He tightened the knot, loosened it, tightened it again to get the crease under the knot exactly in the middle. When he'd finished with that, he moved his head from side to side to see if he could use a haircut. Whitey began to have a feeling that it was sort of a gag and the Lieutenant was making fun of the neatly groomed man who sat at the roll-top desk.

Finally the man at the desk looked at the Lieutenant and said, "All right, cut it out."

The Lieutenant leaned in very close to the mirror and pretended to squeeze a blackhead from his chin.

"Very funny," the other man muttered. He bent lower over his work at the desk, his shoulders very broad and expanded past the sides of the chair. He wore an Oxford-gray suit of conservative but expensively tailored lines and his shoes were black Scotch grain and had the semiglossy British look. The Lieutenant had moved away from the mirror and was standing near the roll-top desk, looking down at the Scotch-grain shoes.

"Where'd you get them?" the Lieutenant asked.

"Had them made," the other detective said.

"That's what I figured," the Lieutenant said.

The other detective sat up very straight and took a deep breath. "All right, Pertnoy. Lay off."

Lieutenant Pertnoy laughed lightly and patted the other detective's shoulder. "You're a fine man, Taggert. Really a fine man, and you always make a very nice appearance. We're all proud of you."

"Oh, drop it," the other said wearily. And then louder, almost hoarsely, "For Christ's sake, why don't you drop it? There's times you actually get on my nerves."

Lieutenant Pertnoy laughed again. "Don't get angry."

"I'm not," Lieutenant Taggert said. "But sometimes you go too far."

"I know," Pertnoy admitted. He said it with mock solemnity. "After all, there's a time and a place for everything."

Taggert swung around in the chair. He pointed to the mirror on the wall. "Let's understand something," he said very slowly and distinctly. "I put that mirror there. And I want it to stay there. And I don't want to be kidded about it. Is that absolutely clear?"

"Absolutely." It was an exaggerated imitation of the other's crisp official tone.

Taggert took another deep breath. He started to say something and then he noticed the ragged little white-haired man who sat at the table showing handcuffed wrists.

"What's that?" Taggert asked, gesturing toward Whitey.

"Nothing important," Pertnoy said.

"Why the cuffs? What's he done?"

Pertnoy smiled at Whitey. "Tell him what you did."

"I didn't do anything," Whitey said.

Pertnoy went on smiling. "You hear?" he said to Taggert. "The man says he didn't do anything. So it stands to reason he didn't do anything. It figures he don't need handcuffs." And then, to Whitey, "Want them off?"

Whitey nodded.

"All right," Pertnoy said. "You can talk better if you're comfortable. I'll take them off."

Pertnoy moved toward the table and took a key ring from his pocket. He selected a key and unlocked the handcuffs. Then the handcuffs were off and Pertnoy slid them toward the center of the table and said, "That better?"

"Yeah," Whitey said. "Thanks."

"Don't mention it," Pertnoy said. He walked across the room and stood near the roll-top desk. For some moments he stood there looking down at Taggert, who had resumed working with pencil and paper. Finally he tapped Taggert's shoulder and said, "Were you here when the report came in?"

Taggert didn't look up. "What report?"

"Nothing much," Pertnoy said. "I'll tell you later." Then, offhandedly, "Can you hold that work for a while? I want to talk to this man alone."

Taggert wrote a few more lines on the paper, folded the paper, and clipped it onto several other sheets. He put the papers in a large envelope and placed the envelope in one of the desk drawers. Then he stood up and walked out of the room.

Lieutenant Pertnoy glanced at his wrist watch. His lips moved only slightly as he said, "We got about five minutes." He looked at Whitey. "Let's see what we can do."

Whitey blinked a few times. He saw Lieutenant Pertnoy moving toward him. The Lieutenant moved very slowly and sort of lazily. For some moments he stood behind Whitey's chair, not saying anything. It was as though the Lieutenant had walked out of the room and Whitey was there alone. Then the Lieutenant moved again, circling the table and sitting down in the chair facing Whitey.

The Lieutenant sat almost directly under the ceiling light, and now for the first time Whitey saw him clearly and was able to study him. Lieutenant Pertnoy looked to be in his middle thirties and had a glossy cap of pale blond hair parted far on the side and brushed flat across his head. He had a gray, sort of poolroom complexion, not really unhealthy, just sun-starved. There was something odd about his eyes. His eyes were a very pale gray and had the look of specially ground lenses. They gave the impression that he could see beyond whatever he was looking at. Whitey had the feeling that this man was cute with a cue stick or a deck of cards. The cuteness went along with the Lieutenant's slim and well-balanced physique, around five-ten and 150 pounds. He wore a gray flannel suit that needed pressing but wouldn't look right on him if it were pressed. It seemed to blend with his easy relaxed manner and his soft lazy smile.

The smile seemed to drift across the table, almost like a floating leaf in a gentle breeze. The Lieutenant was saying, "Tell me why you did it."

"I didn't do it," Whitey said.

"All right." The Lieutenant shifted in his chair, facing the wall on the other side of the room. "Let's take it slower. We'll talk about the weapon. What'd you hit him with?"

"I didn't hit him," Whitey said. "I didn't touch him."

Pertnoy smiled at the wall. He waved his hand lazily toward Whitey and said, "Look at your clothes. Look at the blood on you."

"I got that trying to help him. He was sitting there and I was holding him to keep him from falling."

Pertnoy gave a slow nod of assent. "That ain't bad. It might even stand up in court."

"Will it reach court?"

Pertnoy looked at Whitey and said, "What do you think?"

"I think you oughta go look for the man who did it."

"You mean you didn't do it?"

"That's what I been saying."

"Maybe you'll get tired saying it."

"Maybe." Whitey shrugged. "I'm getting tired now."

"Wanna break down?"

"And do what?"

"Cry a little," Pertnoy said. "Make some noise. Confess."

"No," Whitey said. "I'm not that tired."

"Come on." The Lieutenant's voice was very soft and kindly, like a doctor's voice. "Come on," the Lieutenant said, opening the table drawer and taking out a pencil and a pad of paper. "Come on."

"Nothing doing," Whitey said.

The pencil was poised. "Come on. You can spill it in just a few words. He's chasing you down the alley and you pick up a brick or something. You don't really mean to finish him. All you wanna do is knock him down so you can get away."

Whitey smiled sadly. "You putting words in my mouth?"

"I wanna put some words on this paper," Pertnoy said. He flicked another glance at his wrist watch. "We only got a couple of minutes."

Whitey stopped smiling. "Until what?"

"Until I break it to the Captain."

"Then what?"

"God knows," Pertnoy said. And then his expression changed. His face became serious. It was the same seriousness he'd displayed outside the front entrance of the station house when he'd told the two policemen about the Captain.

Whitey sat there blinking and not saying anything.

"Look," Pertnoy said. "It's like this. You give me a confession and I'll put you in a cell. Then you'll be safe."

"Safe?" Whitey blinked hard. "From what?"

"Don't you see?" The Lieutenant leaned forward sort of pleadingly. "From the Captain."

Whitey gazed past the gray face of Lieutenant Pertnoy. But the wall of the room was also gray and it seemed to be moving toward him. "God," Whitey said to the wall. "Is that the way it is?"

"That's exactly the way it is," the Lieutenant said. He pointed his thumb over his shoulder to indicate something. It was the noise coming from the big room at the end of the corridor. It was the clashing mixture of shouts and curses in Spanish and English. There was a thud and another thud and then more shouting. "You hear that?" the Lieutenant said. "Listen to it. Just listen to it."

Whitey listened. He heard the cracking, squishy sound of someone getting hit very hard in the mouth. And then he heard the voice of the Captain saying, "Want more?" There was a hissing defiance in the voice replying, "Got any sisters?" Then a very cold quiet and then the Captain saying, "Sure. I got three." And there were three separate, precisely timed sounds, the sounds of knuckles smashing a face. After that it was just the vague noise of someone crumbling to the floor.

"You hear it?" Pertnoy said.

Whitey sat very low in the chair. He nodded slowly. He looked at Pertnoy's hand and saw the pencil poised above the pad of paper.

He heard Pertnoy saying, "You see what I mean?"

"Can't you stop him? Can't you do anything?"

"No," Pertnoy said. "We'd be crazy if we tried. There's no telling what he'd do. You heard what I told the blue boys. He's a sick man. He's getting sicker. I feel sorry for him, I swear I do. He's been trying his best to stop these riots, and the more he tries, the worse it gets. He's lost his grip on the neighborhood and he's losing his grip on himself. And now comes the pay-off. I gotta go in there and give him the news."

Whitey swallowed hard. He felt as if sawdust were going down his throat.

"I gotta give it to him," Pertnoy said. "I gotta tell him what the Hellhole did to him tonight. How it hit back at him. How it hit him where it hurts most. One of his own men."

Whitey swallowed again and there was more sawdust going down. His voice was scarcely audible as he said, "Do I hafta be there when you tell him?"

"It's up to you," Pertnoy said. The seriousness went away and he was smiling again. "Can we do business?"

Whitey opened his mouth to reply. But there was too much sawdust and it choked him and he couldn't say anything.

"Come on," Pertnoy said. He touched the pencil point to the pad of paper. "Gimme some dictation."

"Can't," Whitey said. "Can't tell you I did something I didn't do."

Pertnoy glanced at the wrist watch. "Not much time," he said.

Whitey shut his eyes and kept them shut for a long moment. Then he looked at the Lieutenant and inclined his head just a little. He frowned slightly and worked a very dim smile along the edge of it. "Lemme ask you something," he said. "You conning me?"

Pertnoy gestured toward the noise coming from the big room. "Does that sound like I'm conning you?"

Whitey listened. He heard it thumping and thudding and sort of galloping toward him. He sat there wishing the chair had wheels and a motor and a reverse gearshift.

Again the Lieutenant glanced at the wrist watch. "I'm looking at the second hand," he said. "Twenty seconds."

"That's close," Whitey said.

"Damn close," the Lieutenant said. He kept his eyes focused on the dial of the wrist watch. "Fifteen seconds."

Whitey grinned. He wondered why he was able to grin. He heard himself saying, "The hell of it is, I got no hospital insurance."

"Maybe you'll need a hearse," the Lieutenant said. His lips smiled as he said it but his eyes weren't smiling and there was no smile in his voice.

Whitey stopped grinning. "You think he'd go that far?"

"He might. Come on, buddy. It's ten seconds. Nine seconds."

Then it was very quiet in the room. There was only the tiny noise of the ticking of the watch.

"Five seconds," the Lieutenant said. He looked up. He kept the pencil on the paper, ready to write. The pencil was steady in his fingers, the point lightly touching the surface of the blank sheet.

"No?" the Lieutenant said.

"No." Whitey said it with a sigh.

"All right," the Lieutenant said. "No seconds. All gone." He stood up, motioning for Whitey to rise. "Come on, you're gonna meet the Captain."

4

THEY WERE in the corridor walking slowly and going toward the noisy action in the big room. The Lieutenant was lighting a cigarette and holding it between his thumb and little finger, his eyes intent on the cigarette as though it were an oboe reed that must be handled delicately. He didn't exhale the smoke, it simply drifted from his lips of its own accord. It drifted sideways and floated past Whitey's eyes to form a wispy curtain. Whitey gazed through the curtain and saw the big room coming closer and it was blurry and he had the feeling it was unreal.

The feeling grew in him and he told himself all this was strictly on the fantastic side. The chaotic sounds of the big room were sounds he'd never heard in any station house, or even in the alcoholic wards of municipal hospitals. At least in the alcoholic wards there were white-garbed people in control of the situation, and despite all the hollering in the beds, there was an atmosphere of order and system. He'd been in more than one alcoholic ward, and certainly he'd been in many station houses, and he'd never seen anything that compared with this.

As the Lieutenant led him into the big room and he got a full front view of what was going on, he winced in wonder and disbelief. He stared at four men who were unconscious on the floor, and a few sitting there on the floor with bloody faces, and several sprawled on the benches along the walls, their heads down and the gore dripping from their chins. One man, a Puerto Rican, had his hands pressed to his throat and was making strangled groans. Another man, with Slavic features, stood holding his groin and shaking his head as though refusing to believe how hard he'd been hit there. A policeman stood beside him, showing him the night stick and letting him know it was ready for another smash. The policeman was breathing very hard and his mouth was wide open and he seemed to be having more distress than the man he'd hit. It was the same way with all the other policemen. Their faces were paler than the faces of the prisoners, their eyes showed more agony, more fear. They were staring at the Captain, who was talking to one of the men sitting on the floor.

"Get up," the Captain said.

The man sat there grinning at the Captain.

"You gonna get up?"

"No," the man said.

The Captain leaned down and took hold of the man's ankle, lifting the leg and twisting the ankle. The man grimaced but managed to hold some of the grin and showed his teeth to the Captain.

"You're gonna need crutches," the Captain said. He tightened his hold on the man's ankle and twisted harder.

"That's right," the man said. "Break it off."

"You think I won't?" the Captain said. His features were expressionless. He had his coat off and his shirt was torn, one sleeve ripped from wrist to shoulder with the blue fabric dangling in shreds. His face was shiny with sweat and his hair was mussed. He had pitch-black hair with some narrow ribbons of white in it and the white was like foam on a storm-tossed black sea. The Captain had blue eyes and his complexion was the color of medium-rare beef. He was built along the lines of Jeffries, about five-eleven and well over two hundred. There was no paunch and hardly any fat and most of his weight was above his navel. He looked to be around forty-five and it was altogether evident that he took very good care of himself and was in excellent physical condition. Yet somehow he gave the impression of a helpless creature going to pieces and slowly dying.

He went on twisting the man's ankle. Now the man's leg was bent at a weird angle, and the man let out an animal cry. And then one of the younger policemen said loudly, "Captain. For God's sake."

The Captain didn't hear. He was concentrating on the man's ankle.

"Captain," the young policeman said very loudly. "Captain Kinnard—"

It reached the Captain and he looked up. He blinked several times and shook his head like someone emerging from water. He let go of the man's ankle and looked up at the ceiling and there was a straining yearning in his eyes, as though he wished fervently he could fly up there and go on through the roof and sail away.

Gradually the room became quiet. Whitey stood in the doorway with Lieutenant Pertnoy. He saw some of the policemen going to the aid of the men on the floor. He estimated there were some fifty people in the room. He counted eleven policemen and around twenty Puerto Ricans and the rest were Americans who looked to be of Slavic and Irish and Scandinavian descent. The policemen were moving in between the Puerto Ricans and the Americans, making sure there was plenty of space between the two groups of arrested rioters, then shoving them back toward the benches along the walls. Finally the floor was cleared and all the benches were taken. The Captain had walked to the big high desk and now he sat there with his head turning very slowly, looking at the Puerto Ricans on one side of the room, the Americans on the other side, and back to the Puerto Ricans, then back to the Americans.

"Now then," the Captain said, but that was all he could say. He went on looking from one side to the other. He opened his mouth again and no sound came out. His mouth stayed open and then very slowly he lowered his head and looked down at the surface of the desk.

It was very quiet in the room.

Lieutenant Pertnoy turned to Whitey and said quietly, "You wanna tell him?"

"Tell him what?"

"What you did. What you did to one of his men."

Whitey didn't get it. He looked blankly at Pertnoy. He said, "Ain't it your job to tell him?"

"That's the point," Pertnoy said. "I wish it wasn't."

Whitey shrugged. He knew there was nothing more for him to say, nothing to think about, nothing to do to stop what was coming. He knew it was coming, he told himself it was coming sure as hell, and again he could feel the sawdust in his throat as he gazed toward the desk and saw the wide shoulders and thick-muscled arms and heavy hands of Captain Kinnard.

He heard Pertnoy saying, "Wanna sit down?"

"I'd rather lay down."

"You'll lay down," Pertnoy said.

Whitey sighed softly. He tried to shrug again, but now his shoulders felt too heavy. He told himself it was going to be a very long night for Whitey. Then, thinking deeply and seriously, he took it further than that. He reasoned it was quite possible that he'd never get out of here alive. He'd heard stories about it, the way it had happened in certain station houses when they brought in a cop-killer and maybe an hour later they'd take the man out through the back door with a sheet over his face. With no mention of it in the newspapers. Or maybe they'd tell the reporters that the man tried to get away. Then again, they might simply state the facts and admit that they'd hit the man just a little too hard. Whichever way they handled it, they never got blamed too much. Not when it came to cop-killers. The papers and the public were never sorry for cop-killers.

He stood there waiting for Pertnoy to walk him toward the big high desk. Then he was conscious of voices at his side. He turned and looked and it was Pertnoy talking to the tall and well-built and impeccably attired Detective Lieutenant Taggert.

"Who told you?" Pertnoy was saying.

"I got it from the house sergeant," Taggert said. He gave Pertnoy a narrow look and his mouth tightened just a little. "Why didn't you tell me? What's all this cover-up?"

Pertnoy made an offhand gesture. "No cover-up. I just figured it could wait."

"Wait? I don't get that." Taggert's eyes were narrower. "It isn't a snatched purse, it isn't a drunk-and-disorderly. It's a homicide. And the victim's a policeman from this district." His head jerked sideways and for a moment he stared at Whitey. "Well," he said. "Well, now." Then he aimed the narrow look at Pertnoy and his voice was a needle jabbing gently. "You sure you know what you're doing?"

"I'm never sure," Pertnoy said. He smiled sort of wistfully. "I never give myself guarantees."

"Guess not," Taggert agreed. But his tone sent the needle in deeper. Then, still deeper, "The way you operate, there's no guarantee on anything. Or maybe you like it better that way. Sometimes I think you do it on purpose."

Pertnoy widened the smile. "Meaning what?"

"That it's more fun when it's thin ice. You're always out for fun, aren't you?"

Lieutenant Pertnoy shrugged and said, "It's a short life."

"Yeah," Taggert said. "Especially for cops. The cop who died tonight was forty-four years old."

Pertnoy didn't say anything.

"He was a twenty-year man with a perfect record," Lieutenant Taggert said, standing there tall and stalwart, solidly planted on his custom-made Scotch-grain shoes, his finely tailored Oxford gray correct in every detail, his fingernails immaculate, and his light-brown pompadour with every hair in place glimmering cleanly under the ceiling lights. He stood there exuding cleanliness and neatness and strength of mind and body. He said, "It's a serious loss. It's damn serious and it certainly doesn't call for fooling around."

"Fooling around?" Pertnoy smiled again. "Is that what I've been doing?"

Taggert's mouth was very tight. "All right, Pertnoy. I won't jockey with you. I want a direct answer and I think I'm entitled to it. Why'd you keep this thing quiet? Why haven't you told the Captain?"

Pertnoy looked across the room. Without words he was telling Taggert to look in the same direction. They both saw the Captain sitting at the big high desk on the platform three steps above the floor. The Captain was hunched low over some papers and he was trying to use a pencil. As they watched him, the pencil slipped from his hand, rolled across the desktop and off the edge, and dropped onto the floor. A policeman hurried forward, picked up the pencil, and handed it to the Captain. The Captain thanked him and started to write again, but somehow he couldn't move the pencil across the paper and finally he put it down and sat there staring at the paper.

"You see?" Pertnoy murmured.

Taggert didn't reply. He stood there watching the Captain. Then very slowly his head turned and he gazed along the rows of crowded benches, the Puerto Rican rioters on the other side of the room, the American rioters on this side, and the policemen standing stiff and tense and waiting for more to happen. They stood there lined up in the middle of the bloodstained floor, all of them holding night sticks and gripping them very tightly.

"You see?" Pertnoy said. "You get it now?"

Taggert gazed again at the Captain. For some moments Taggert didn't say anything. Then very quietly he said, "You want me to tell him?"

Pertnoy's smile became dim and dimmer and then faded altogether and he said, "Do you want to?"

"Well, someone's got to tell him."

"All right," Pertnoy said. "You tell him."

Taggert took a deep breath. He turned and walked very slowly toward the big high desk. Whitey watched him as he approached the platform, saw him mounting the steps, heard the distinct clicking of his heels on the first step and the second and the third. There were other sounds in the room but Whitey didn't hear them. He was watching Lieutenant Taggert moving across the platform to the desk and bending over to whisper in the Captain's ear. The Captain's head was low and he was staring at the paper on the desk. Taggert went on whispering and Whitey saw the Captain gradually raising his head and sitting up very straight, rigid in a metallic sort of way, as though he were something activated by a lever. Then the Captain said something that Whitey couldn't hear and Taggert's reply was also inaudible but his arm was stretched out and his finger pointed at Whitey.

The Captain got up from the desk chair. He walked across the platform, moving like a sleepwalker except that his arms were stiff at his sides. He came down off the platform and there was nothing on his face but the flesh and yet it didn't seem like flesh, it was more like something made of ice and rock. He was headed on a diagonal going toward Whitey and it was like watching the slow approach of gaping jaws or a steam roller or anything at all that could mangle and finish off whatever it touched.

Whitey stood there not breathing. He saw the Captain coming closer. Then closer. He saw the dead-white face of Captain Kinnard coming in very close, some ten feet away, then seven feet away, and he wondered if it made sense just to stand still and wait for it to happen. He decided it didn't make the least bit of sense and he edged away from Lieutenant Pertnoy, not thinking about Pertnoy or Pertnoy's gun or the guns of the policemen. He was thinking about the big hands of the Captain and telling himself to move and move fast.

He moved. He moved very fast. The only thought in his brain was the idea of fleeing from the big hands of the Captain. He was running, not knowing where he was going, not particularly caring, just so long as it took him away from the Captain. He heard someone shouting, "Get him!" and then another voice, and he saw the policemen coming toward him.

In the same moment he heard a lot of shouting in Spanish from the other side the room. He caught a flash of the Puerto Ricans leaping up from the benches and hurling themselves toward the opened door that led to the street. The policemen stopped and stared and for a split second they didn't seem to know what to do. In that instant the American rioters got the exit notion and jumped up and started looking for exits. A moment later the room was boiling with men running in all directions, bumping into each other, fighting to break free of each other to reach the doors and windows, the policemen grabbing at them and trying to hold on, or else using the night sticks to break it up that way, but there was no breaking it up, there was no stopping it, not even when Lieutenant Taggert reached for his shoulder holster and drew his revolver and fired a warning shot. He fired another shot at the ceiling and then decided to really use the gun. He fired at one of the Puerto Ricans and the man went down with a bullet in the kneecap.

That should have stopped it. But all it did was increase the action, the prisoners accelerating their efforts to get through the doorways and windows. Lieutenant Taggert fired again and a big Ukrainian-American was hit in the abdomen and now some of the policemen had drawn their guns and were shooting. One of them hit a Puerto Rican in the shoulder. Another put a bullet through the thigh of an Irish-American who was caught in a traffic jam at the front door. Then another policeman took aim at the crowd trying to get through the front door and changed his mind and aimed his gun for a longer-range shot, pointing the gun toward the large window behind the desk platform on the far side of the room. The window was open and Whitey was climbing through.

The policeman shot and missed and fired again and the .38

slug punctured the window sill an inch away from Whitey's ribs. Whitey threw a sad-eyed, scared-rabbit glance backward at the seething room and saw all of it in a flashing instant that showed convulsive, tumultuous activity. It was a very busy room. The noise was terribly loud, a cracking-up noise that sounded like the end of everything. In the same instant that he glimpsed the frenzied action, Whitey saw the two men who were not taking part in the action, just standing on the side lines and watching it. The two men were Lieutenant Pertnoy and Captain Kinnard.

The Lieutenant stood in the corridor doorway and he had his hands in his trousers pockets. One side of his mouth was curved up, but it wasn't a smile; it was sort of quizzical, like the expression of a man looking at a blackboard and studying a mathematical equation. A few feet away from the Lieutenant the bulky shoulders of Captain Kinnard were limp and the Captain's arms hung loosely and he was shaking his head very slowly. His eyes were half closed and his mouth sagged. He was slumped there against the wall like a fighter on the ropes getting hit and hit again and not allowed to fall.

Whitey saw all of that but couldn't see more of it because now there was another shot and the bullet split the glass of the raised window above his head. He decided he wasn't traveling fast enough, and instead of climbing through the window and then climbing down, he dived through, going headfirst and then twisting in the air, twisting hard to bring his legs down. He landed on his side on the gravel driveway some ten feet below the window. He rested there with his eyes closed, wondering whether he had a broken hip. He felt it and it wasn't broken and he told himself to get up. He got up and started to walk. At first he walked slowly and with a limp. Then he limped faster. The injured hip gave him a lot of pain, but it was more flesh burn than bone hurt, and maybe if he didn't think about the pain he wouldn't need to limp. He stopped thinking about the pain and stopped limping and started to run.

He ran. He picked up speed and told himself he needed more and then he was really sprinting.

5

IT WAS three minutes later and they were chasing him down an alley off Clayton Street. Then it was five minutes later and he was in another alley four blocks east of Clayton. He was moving east and coming out of the alley and running across River Street. They came running after him and he went twenty yards going south on River, then ducked into a very narrow alley and headed east again in the thick blackness of the Hellhole, going toward the river and telling himself it might work out all right if he could reach the river. Along the water front there were a lot of places where he could hide. And maybe later he could sneak onto one of the ships. But that was for later. Much later. Right now the river was a long way off. And the law was very near. And he was very tired.

He heard them coming down the alley and he hopped a fence, getting over it before their flashlights could find him. Then across the back yard and over another fence. Then a third fence, and a fourth, with the back yards very small and piles of wood stacked here and there for fuel in the wooden shacks, just enough space for the firewood and the garbage can and the outside toilet. It was a matter of running zigzag to get to the next fence. He knew the next fence would be the last because now he was really all in. He got there and climbed over the fence and fell on his back. There was a dragging, weak clanking sound like the useless noise of stripped gears, and he knew it came from inside his chest. He had the feeling that all the flesh inside him was stripped and burned out. But it was nice to rest there flat on his back. They'd be coming soon and maybe when they saw what shape he was in they'd take him to a hospital instead of returning him to the station house. That would be a break. He closed his eyes and dragged the wonderful air into his lungs and waited for them to come.

But they didn't come. Several minutes passed and they didn't come. There was no sound and no reflection of flashlights. He reasoned they were still headed east, they probably figured it wouldn't be these back yards and their man was trying for the river. That meant their search would be concentrated along the water front. He decided they'd be busy there for the rest of the night and he might as well go to sleep here. His arm curled under his head and he closed his eyes.

The wind from the river was very cold but he was too tired to feel it. It took him less than a minute to fall asleep. An hour later he opened his eyes and a light hit him in the face. It was a flickering light and it had nothing to do with the back yard. He told himself he was still asleep. But then he opened his eyes again and realized he was really awake and this wasn't the back yard.

It was the interior of the wooden shack. He was resting under some blankets on a narrow cot against the wall. The other furniture was a three-legged stool and a two-legged table with the other two sides supported on wooden fruit boxes. The flickering light came from a candle in a small holder on the table. Along the walls there were rows of gallon jugs containing colorless liquid. On the table there was a bottle half filled with the colorless liquid, and alongside the bottle there was an empty water glass. There was only one door in the room and Whitey knew that what he'd thought was the back yard was really the front yard. So this place had no back yard; in the back it was just another alley and then more wooden shacks. He knew it because now he was fully awake and able to think fairly clearly, able to judge the distance he'd covered from the station house to here. This was strictly seven-dollars-a-month territory. This was the Afro-American section of the Hellhole.

The door opened and a colored man came in. The colored man was as dark as the emery strip of a match book. He was around five-nine and couldn't have weighed more than 115 at the most. There was no hair on his head and there weren't many wrinkles on his face and it was impossible to tell how old he was. He wore rimless spectacles and a woman's fur coat made of squirrel.

Whitey was sitting up in the cot and looking at the woman's fur coat.

"Don't get the wrong notion," the colored man said. He fingered the squirrel collar. "I just wear this to keep warm. I'm an old man and I can't take cold weather. Gotta have this fur on me to keep the chill away."

The colored man had several chunks of firewood tucked under his arm and he moved slowly across the room and put the wood in a small old-fashioned furnace that had a crooked handmade outlet going up through the ceiling. For some moments the colored man was busy with the furnace and then he closed the lid and walked to the three-legged stool and sat down. He had his back to Whitey and all he did was sit there, not moving, not saying anything.

It went on like that for the better part of a minute. There was a certain deliberateness in the way the colored man sat there motionless with his back to the man in the cot. It was as though the colored man were experimenting with the man in the cot, waiting to see what the man would do while he had his back turned.

Whitey caught the drift of it. "You don't hafta test me," he said. "I'm straight."

"Yiz?" the colored man said. He still had his back turned. "How do I know?"

"You musta thought so, or you wouldn't have brought me in here."

"I brought you in cause you were out there freezing. You were half froze when I dragged you in. Just as stiff as a carrot in an icebox."

Whitey didn't say anything. He was thinking about the colored man's accent. There was some South in it, but not much. It was mostly New England. Some of the words were clipped and the edges polished and it was like the highly cultured voice of someone on a lecture platform. Other words were spoken in the nasal twang of a Vermont farm hand. Then at longer spaced intervals there'd be a word or two from 'way down deep in Mississippi. It was as though the colored man weren't quite sure where he'd come from. Or maybe he was continually reminding himself of all the places he'd seen, all the accents he'd heard. Whitey had the feeling that the colored man was very old and had been to a lot of places.

"I hadda go out to use the toilet," the colored man said. "I saw you out there flat on the ground and I didn't like that, I didn't like that at all."

"Did it scare you?" Whitey said.

"No," the colored man said. "I never get scared." He was

quiet for a long moment. And then, very slowly, "But some-times I get curious."

Whitey waited for the colored man to turn on the stool and face him. The colored man didn't move from his position fac-ing the table.

"You wanna leave now?" the colored man said.

"I'd like to stay here for a while. That is, if you'll let me."

"I'm thinking about it," the colored man said. There was another long pause. And then, again very slowly, "You wanna help me decide?"

"If I can."

"I guess you can." The colored man turned on the stool and looked at Whitey and said, "All you gotta do is tell me the truth."

"All right."

"You sure it's all right? You sure it won't hurt you to tell the truth?"

"It might," Whitey said.

"But you're willing to take a chance?"

Whitey shrugged. "I got no choice."

"That ain't the way I see it. I'm prone to think you might try to bluff me."

"No, I wouldn't do that."

"You mean you couldn't do that." The colored man took off his rimless spectacles and leaned forward just a little, his eyes glinting bright yellow, like topaz. There was a certain see-all, know-all power coming from the topaz eyes and shooting into Whitey's head. And the colored man said, "I want you to know it in front. No use trying to bluff me. Ain't a living ass in this world can bluff Jones Jarvis."

Whitey nodded in agreement. It was a slow nod and he meant it. He had the feeling that the colored man was not bragging or exaggerating, but merely stating a fact.

"Jones Jarvis," the colored man said. "Once when I had a phone they'd get it wrong in the book and list me under Jones. Did that year after year and finally I got tired telling them to change it. Got rid of the phone. Man has a right to have his name printed correct. It's Jones first and then Jarvis. The name is Jones Jarvis."

"Jones Jarvis," Whitey said.

"That's right. That's absolutely correct. I like everything to be correct. Exactly in line. It's gotta be that way or there ain't no use talking. So now I want to hear your name."

"They call me Whitey."

"You see, now? You're pulling away from it, you're not telling me correct. I want your real name."

Whitey winced slightly. He told himself it was seven years since he'd used his real name. All the reasons why he'd stopped using it came back to him and hammered at his head and he winced harder. In the instant that his eyes were closed he saw the short and very wide and very long-armed man with the bright-green cap and black-and-purple plaid lumber jacket. Just for that instant, and that was all. And then his eyes were open and he was looking at Jones Jarvis. He heard himself saying, "My name is Eugene Lindell."

The colored man sat motionless for some moments and then very slowly raised his head and looked up at the ceiling. "I know that name," he said.

Whitey didn't say anything.

The colored man went on squinting up at the ceiling. "I'm sure I know that name," he said. "I'll be a sonofabitch if I ain't heard that name before."

Then it was quiet and Whitey waited and wondered whether the colored man would remember. The colored man was trying hard to remember, snapping his fingers as though he thought the sound of it would bring back the memory.

Finally the colored man looked at Whitey and said, "Tell me something. We ever meet before?"

"No," Whitey said.

The topaz eyes were narrow. "You sure about that?"

Whitey nodded.

"Well, anyway," the colored man said, "I know that name. I swear I've heard it someplace. Or let's see now, maybe I read about it someplace." He was looking past Whitey. He raised a wrinkled finger to his chin. "Let's see," he murmured aloud to himself. "Let's see if we can hit this."

"It ain't important," Whitey said. Something in the way he said it caused Jones Jarvis to look at him, and he added offhandedly, "At least, it ain't important now."

The topaz eyes narrowed again. "Was it important then?"

Whitey looked at the floor.

"Want me to skip it?" the colored man said.

Whitey went on looking at the floor. He nodded very slowly.

"All right," Jones Jarvis said. "We'll skip it. Whatever happened to you long ago ain't none of my business. Only questions I'm privileged to ask are about tonight. I wanna know what you were doing on my property."

"Hiding," Whitey said.

"From who?"

"Police."

"I figured that," Jones said. And then, for the first time, he showed a smile. "Can always tell when a man is hot, even when he's freezing. I took one look and you were hot, really hot."

Whitey pulled his legs from under the blanket and lowered them over the side of the bed. He smiled back at Jones and said, "I'm still hot. I'm hot as hell."

"Don't I know it?" Jones said. "I'm taking your temperature right now. Using two thermometers." And he pointed to his own eyes. Then, leaning back a little, with the squirrel coat unbuttoned to show the toothpick build attired in pale-green flannel pajamas, crossing one skinny leg over the other and clasping his knees, he said conversationally, "Tell me about it."

"It happened about an hour ago," Whitey said. "Or maybe ninety minutes. I'm not really sure."

"Let's check that," Jones said. "I always like to be sure of the time." He reached into a pocket of the squirrel coat and took out a large pocket watch and looked at the dial. "It's one-twenty-six A.M.," he murmured. "That help you any?"

Whitey knew he was still under close scrutiny and technical appraisal. He realized that one wrong answer would lose him this hiding place that he needed very badly. The topaz eyes told him to get his answers exactly correct.

He said, "Closest I can come is a little after midnight. Let's say twelve-ten." He smiled openly and truthfully. "That's really the best I can do."

"All right," Jones said. He put the watch back in his pocket. "Where were you at twelve-ten?"

"On a side street not far from here."

"How far?"

"I'd say a coupla blocks."

"What were you doing?" Jones asked.

"Taking a walk."

"Is that all?"

"No," Whitey said. But he couldn't take it past that. He knew he couldn't make mention of the man he'd been following, the man who wore a bright-green cap and a black-and-purple plaid lumber jacket. If he started talking about it he'd be going away from tonight, going in reverse, going back seven years, and it would get very involved. It would be like opening a tomb in his mind and seeing a part of himself that had suffered and died and wanted to stay dead and buried.

Yet somehow he could feel it straining to come alive again, as he'd felt it earlier tonight when he'd seen the very short, very wide man who wore the bright-green cap. He could feel the tugging, the grinding, the burning of a deep pain that tightened his mouth and showed in his eyes.

And the pain was there in his cracked-whisper voice as he said, "I won't say what I was doing on that street. It's got nothing to do with why I'm hiding from the law."

Jones Jarvis was quiet for some moments. He was studying the pain-racked eyes of the small white-haired man. When Jones finally spoke, his voice was very soft and almost tender. Jones said, "All right, Eugene. We'll let it ride."

"But I want you to believe me. I'm giving it to you straight."

"Yes," Jones said. "That's the impression I get. Even though it's kind of blurry at the edges."

"It'll have to stay that way. I can't trim it down any closer."

"I guess you can't," Jones said. "But all the same, you got me sidetracked. You tell me it was past midnight and you're out for a stroll. In the Hellhole. You're just taking a stroll down here in the Hellhole. Where no man in his right mind walks alone after midnight. Unless he's looking to get hurt. Or do some hurting."

"I said I can't tell you—"

"All right, Eugene, all right." Jones smiled soothingly. "Let's leave it at that. Go on, take it from there."

Whitey took it from there and told the rest of it just as it had happened. He said it matter-of-factly, looking levelly at the old man, who sat there on the three-legged stool looking at him and into him and nodding slowly at intervals. When it was finished, he leaned back on the cot, resting on his elbows, waiting for the old man either to accept the story or to start looking for loopholes in it.

Jones Jarvis did not indicate whether he was buying it or doubting it or wondering how to take it. It seemed that Jones was thinking about something else. Now his eyes were aimed past Whitey, like lenses fixed for a wider-range focus.

Finally Jones shook his head very slowly and said, "I feel sorry for the Captain."

"If he ever gets hold of me," Whitey said, "I'll feel damn sorry for myself."

"He's really got his hands full," Jones said.

Whitey shrugged. "I don't care what he's got in his hands. Just so long as it ain't me."

But Jones was thinking above that and far beyond that. "I've lived in this neighborhood a good many years," he said. "It's always been exactly what they call it, a hellhole. But lately it's been worse than that. Like a furnace that can't hold the fire and all the flames are shooting out. It puts a certain smell in the air. Sometimes I walk outside at night and I can smell it. The smell of men hating each other. The rotten stink of race riot."

Whitey was only half listening. He was concentrating on the necessity of remaining hidden from the law. He wondered whether the old man would allow him to stay here for a day or two.

But the old man was thinking about the race riots and saying, "It's a pity. It's a terrible pity. I wonder what started it."

Whitey looked around at the four walls of the small wooden shack. The boards were loose and splintered and in places the wood was decaying. But somehow the walls seemed very secure and there was the comfortable feeling of safety. It was nice to sit here on the cot with the four walls around him and he hoped he'd be permitted to stay for a while.

Then he heard the old man saying, "What do you think started it?"

He looked at the old man. "Started what?"

"These riots. These race riots."

"Damned if I know," Whitey said without interest. And then, shrugging, "Anyway, it don't concern me."

"No?"

"Why should it? I got no ax to grind."

Jones Jarvis took off the rimless spectacles. His naked eyes, narrowed and glinting, drilled into the face of the small white-haired man and he said, "You sure?"

"Absolutely," Whitey answered. It was an emphatic word and he tried to say it with emphasis. But it didn't come out that way. It came out rather weakly.

He heard the old man saying, "Every man has an ax to grind. Whether he knows it or not."

Whitey didn't say anything.

"I've been on this earth a long time," Jones Jarvis said. "I'm eighty-six. That makes me too old to grind the ax. But the Lord knows I did it when I was younger. Did it with all the strength in my body. And don't think I wasn't scared when I did it. So scared I wanted to turn and run and hide in the woods. Much safer that way. Much healthier. But there's some things more important to a man than his health. So I stayed there and saw them coming to grab me and I didn't move and when they got in real close I looked them straight in the eye. I talked back to them and said I hadn't touched that white girl and I gave them the facts to prove it. They moved in closer and I pulled the blade from my pocket and showed it to them. And I told them to come on, come on, come and get me. They stood there and saw that blade in my hand. Then one of them said, 'You swear to it, Jones? You swear you didn't do it? On your mother's life?' I looked at this man who had the rope in his hand all ready for me and I said, 'How'd you like to kiss my black ass?' So then all they did was turn and walk away. I waited until they were gone, then made for the woods, and later that day I hopped a freight going north. But it wasn't no scared weasel running away. It was a man. It was a man going on a trip."

Whitey was looking at the floor. He was frowning slightly and his mouth scarcely moved as he said, "All right, you've made your point. You're a man. And I'm just a scared weasel."

"You really believe that? You want it that way?"

"Sure," Whitey said. He looked up. "Sure. Why not?" Again it sounded weak and he told himself he didn't care how weak it sounded. He put a very weak grin on his lips and he said loosely and lazily, "I lost my spinal column a good many years ago.

There ain't no surgery can put it back. Even if there was, I wouldn't want it. I like it better this way. More comfortable."

"No," Jones said. "You're telling a fib and you know it."

Whitey widened the grin. He said joshingly, "How can you tell?"

"Never mind," Jones said. "I can tell, that's all. It shows."

"What shows?" The grin began to fade. He pointed to his shaggy mop of prematurely white hair. "This?"

"That's part of it," Jones murmured. "And your eyes. And the way your mouth sets. And something else." He leaned forward and let the pause come in and drift for a long moment, and then he said, "Your voice."

"Huh?"

"Your voice," Jones said. "The way you can't talk above a whisper. As if you got a rupture in your throat. As if it's all torn apart in there."

Again Whitey looked at the floor. The grin was gone now and he didn't know what was on his face. He opened his mouth to say something and he tried to get the sound past his lips and nothing came out.

"Or maybe it ain't the throat," the old man said. "Maybe it's the heart."

"It's the throat," Whitey said.

"Maybe it's both."

Whitey lowered his head and put his hand to his eyes and pressed hard. He was trying to deepen the blackness of the dark screen that ought to be very black because it was only his closed eyelids, but something was projected on it and he was forced to look and see. It was a memory he didn't want to see and his hand pressed harder against his closed eyes. On the screen it showed clearly and vividly, and he thought: Now, that's queer, it oughta be foggy. After all, it's an old-time film, it's seven years old.

He heard Jones Jarvis saying, "I'm prone to think that maybe it's both. Ruined throat. Broken heart."

"Let it ride," Whitey mumbled. He still had his hand pressed hard to his eyes. "For Christ's sake, let it ride."

"Eugene Lindell," the old man said.

"No."

"Eugene Lindell."

"No. Don't—"

"Eugene Lindell." And then the loud crisp sound of snapping fingers. And the old man saying, "Now I get it. It's been coming slowly and now it's really hit me and I got it. Eugene Lindell."

"Please don't."

But the old man had it started. And he had to go on with it. And he said aloud to himself, "First time I heard that name I was listening to the radio. The announcer said, 'And now the lad with the million-dollar voice. Here he is, folks, Gene Lindell, singing—' "

"Stop it," Whitey choked.

"Singing—"

"Will you stop it?"

"Singing from 'way up high on the moon and 'way down deep in the sea. High and low and high again, and it was a voice that made you high when you heard it, happy high and sad high, and you hadda close your eyes, you didn't wanna see a goddamn thing, just sit there and listen to that singing. You knew you'd never heard a voice like that in all your born days. And then them bobby-soxers started yelling and screaming and you felt like doing the same. That voice did things to you, went into you so deep it made you get the feeling you hadda come out of yourself and fly up and away from where your feet were planted. So next day I walked into a music store and all the loot I'd saved that week was shoved across the counter. 'Gene Lindell,' I said. 'Gimme his records.' The clerk said, 'Sorry, mister. We're sold out.' A few days later I tried again, and this time he had just one in stock. I took it home and played it and played it, and for weeks I went on playing that record and the jitterbugs would come in and forget to chew their bubble gum, only thing they could do was stand there with their mouths open and get hit between the eyes with that voice. They'd forget to move their feet. They were jitterbugs but they couldn't jitter because that voice took hold of them and paralyzed them. That was what it did. It was that kind of voice."

Whitey was sitting bent very low on the edge of the cot. He had both hands covering his face. It seemed he was trying to shut himself away from the living world.

But he could hear the old man saying, "You had it, Gene. You really had it."

He took his hands away from his face. He looked at the old man and smiled pleadingly, pathetically. His cracked-whisper voice was scarcely audible. "Why don't you stop it? What do you want from me?"

"Just a simple answer," Jones Jarvis said. He had leaned back and now he leaned forward again. "Tell me," he said. "How did you lose it? What happened to you?"

The smile widened and stiffened and then he had it aimed past the old man, his eyes glazed and fixed on nothing in particular. It all added up to a sort of crazy grimace.

"Won't you tell me?" the old man asked very softly and gently. And then, plaintively, "I think I got a right to know. After all, I was one of your fans."

Whitey sat there and tried to look at the old man. But he couldn't look. And he couldn't get the grimace off his face. He was trying very hard but he couldn't do anything but just sit there and stare at nothing.

Jones watched him for some moments. Then Jones's expression became clinical and he said, "Maybe you could use a drink."

Whitey tried to nod. But he couldn't move his head. It felt very heavy and sort of crushed, as though steel clamps were attached to his temples and pressing against his brain.

Jones got up from the three-legged stool and moved toward the row of gallon jugs filled with colorless liquid. He picked up a jug, took it to the table, and began pouring the liquid into the half-filled bottle. He poured until the bottle was completely full. Then he put the jug back in its place among the others. He set it down very carefully, moved some of the other jugs to get them exactly in line along the wall, then nodded approvingly like a show-window expert satisfied with the display.

"It's high-grade merchandise," Jones said, as though he were talking to a potential customer. But his tone was sort of forced. He was trying to get Whitey's mind away from Whitey. He made a stiff-armed gesture, pointing to the gallon jugs, and went on: "I manufacture it myself. Know everything that goes in it, and I guarantee it's a hundred per cent pure, it's really high-grade. Just alcohol and water, but the way it's mixed is what gives it the charge. So it ain't no ordinary shake-up. It's a first class brand of goathead. Real fine goathead. The finest goddamn goathead ever made in any cellar."

He glanced at Whitey, hoping for a comment or any reaction at all. But there was nothing. Whitey just sat there with his glazed eyes staring fixedly at empty space, the wide-smile grimace now wider and crazier, 'way out there in left field, very far away from Jones Jarvis and the goathead and everything.

The old man gave it another try. He pointed to a hinged arrangement on the floor that indicated a floor door and he said, "That goes down to the cellar. All day long I'm down there making it, mixing it, tasting it so's I'll be sure it's just right. Sometimes it tastes so good I forget to come upstairs. Wake up a day later and wonder what the hell happened. But never sick. With Jones Jarvis' goathead it just ain't possible to get sick. That junk they sell in the stores can make a man sick as hell, he'll pay two, three, three-and-a-half a pint and wind up paying five to get his stomach pumped out. But that won't happen when he drinks my brand. No matter how much he drinks, he'll never get sick. And it sells for only six bits a pint.

"That's value, man, that's real value," he went on, trying very hard to get Whitey's mind away from Whitey. "Them big whisky people oughta be ashamed of themselves, charging what they do for that stuff they advertise. They give it a fancy name and a fancy label, with pretty pictures in the magazines, a big-shot businessman sitting there in the big fine room with all the books and a couple of high-priced hunting dogs and he's holding the glass and saying it's real good whisky and he drinks it and you oughta drink it too. What he should do is come here and buy a bottle of Jones Jarvis' goathead. He'd never touch that other junk again. He'd—"

Whitey was getting up from the cot. As he lifted himself to his feet, the wide-smile grimace began to fade from his face. His eyes gradually lost the glazed staring-at-nothing look and the stiffness was gone from his lips. It was a slow change and he went through it quietly and calmly, and finally he stood there completely relaxed.

Then he moved toward the door.

"Where you going?" Jones said.

"Out."

"But where?"

"Station house."

The old man moved quickly to insert himself between Whitey and the door. "No," the old man said. "Don't do that."

Whitey smiled mildly and politely and waited for the old man to get away from the door.

"Listen," the old man said. "Listen, Gene—"

"Yes?" he murmured very politely.

"Stay here," the old man said. "Stay here and have a drink."

"No, thanks. Thanks very much."

"Come on, have a drink," the old man said. He gestured toward the filled bottle on the table. "There it is. Right there. Waiting for you."

"No," he said. "But thanks anyway. Thanks a lot."

"You mean you don't drink?" the old man asked. His eyes tried to pull Whitey's eyes away from the door. He was trying to make it a conversation about drinking.

"Yes," Whitey said. "I drink. I do a lot of drinking. I drink all the time."

"Sure you do." Jones Jarvis smiled companionably, as one drinker to another. "Come on, let's have a shot."

Whitey smiled back and shook his head very slowly.

"Come on, Gene. It'll do you good. You know you want a drink."

"No," Whitey said, wanting a drink very badly, his mouth and throat and belly begging for the colorless liquid in the bottle on the table just a few steps away.

"Just one," the old man said. He moved quickly to the table, pulled the cap off the bottle, and brought the bottle to Whitey. "I want you to taste this goathead."

"No," Whitey said. He was looking past the old man, at the door. "I'm going back to the station house."

The old man stood there between Whitey and the door. For some moments he looked at Whitey's face. Then he looked down at the bottle of goathead. He lifted the bottle to his mouth and took a quick swallow. As it went down and burned and hit like a blockbuster hitting the target, his body vibrated and his old man's head snapped forward and back and forward again. "Goddamn," he said, speaking to the bottle. "You're bad, man. You're a bad sonofabitch."

Whitey reached past the old man and put his hand on the doorknob.

"Don't," the old man said. His hand came down very gently on Whitey's arm. "Please, Gene. Please don't."

"Why not?" He kept his hand closed on the doorknob. He was looking at the door and saying, "What else is there to do?"

"Stay here."

"And wait for them to find me?" He smiled sadly, resignedly. "They're gonna find me sooner or later."

"Not if you hide. Not if you wait for a chance to run."

"They'd get me anyway," he said. "They're bound to get me, no matter what I do. When they're looking for a cop-killer, they never stop looking."

"But you're not a cop-killer," Jones said. His hand tightened on Whitey's arm. "Use your brains, man. Don't let yourself go haywire. You know you didn't do it. You gotta remember you didn't do it. If you go back to that station house, it's just like signing a confession. Like walking into the butcher shop and putting yourself on the meat block."

The sadness went out of the smile and it became a dry grin. Whitey was thinking of the Captain. In his mind he saw the Captain attired in a bloodstained butcher's apron. He saw the cleaver raised and coming down, but somehow he didn't care, maybe it was all for the best. What the hell, he should have been out of it a long time ago. No use continuing the masquerade. He said to himself: The truth is, buddy, you really don't give a damn, you'd just as soon be out of it.

He heard Jones Jarvis saying, "Or maybe you just don't care."

Whitey winced. He looked at the old man's topaz eyes, peering inside his brain.

Jones said, "You gotta care. You gotta drill it into yourself you got something to live for."

"Like what?" he asked in the cracked whisper that always reminded him it was a matter of no hope, no soap, nothing at all.

But the old man was still in there trying. And saying, "Like looking for an answer. No matter what the question is, there's always an answer."

"Sure," he agreed, grinning again. "In this case, it's strictly zero."

"It's never zero," the old man said. "Not while you're able to breathe."

"I'm tired of breathing." As he said it, it sounded funny to him, and he widened the grin.

"It's a goddamn shame," the old man said. He loosened his grip on Whitey's arm. He looked down at the bottle in his hand, then gazed down past the bottle to focus on the splintered shabby boards of the floor. He spoke to the floor, saying, "My fault. It's all my fault. I couldn't keep my big mouth shut. I couldn't leave it where it was, with him sitting there on the cot, man named Whitey just sitting there cooling himself and getting comfortable. I hadda open up my goddamn mouth and talk about Gene Lindell, the singer."

Whitey held onto the grin. "Don't let it bother you, Jones."

Jones went on talking to the floor. It was as though Whitey had already walked out of the shack. "Now he's going back to that station house and the Captain'll tear him to shreds. Really go to work on him, that's for sure. And it's my fault. It's all my fault."

"It ain't no such thing," Whitey said. He put his hand on the old man's shoulder. "It's just the way things are stacked up, that's all. You mustn't feel bad about it. Maybe all they'll do is throw me in a cell."

"I wouldn't bet on that," the old man said. He lifted his gaze from the floor and looked at Whitey. "Not even with fifty-to-one odds. Or make it a hundred-to-one and I still wouldn't take it. That Thirty-seventh Precinct is a madhouse. It's these race riots, getting worse and worse, and now the riots really score and a cop from the Thirty-seventh gets put in the cemetery. And that does it, man, that really does it. That flips the Captain's lid, and I'm prone to say right now he's just about ready for a strait jacket."

Whitey shrugged. "Maybe he's wearing it already."

"No," the old man said. "They don't put strait jackets on police captains." And then abruptly and somewhat frantically he gripped Whitey's wrists. "Don't go back there, Gene. Please. Don't go back."

Whitey shrugged again. It was a slow shrug and it told the old man that Eugene Lindell was headed for the station house. The old man's hands went limp and fell away from Whitey's wrists. Whitey turned the doorknob and opened the door and walked out of the shack.

6

IT WAS like walking inside an overturned barrel that revolved slowly and wouldn't let him get anywhere. There were no window lights and no lampposts, as though all electric bulbs were conspiring to put him in the dark and get him lost. It was the same with the sky. There was no moon at all. It was hiding behind thick clouds that wouldn't allow the glow to come through. The sky was starless and pitch-black.

The only light that showed was the yellow face of the City Hall clock, very high up there about a mile and a half to the north of the Hellhole. The hands pointed to one-forty-five. But he wasn't interested in the time element. He wished that the lit-up face of the City Hall clock could throw a stronger light so he could see where he was going.

He was really lost. There were too many intersecting alleys and narrow, twisting streets to confuse him and take him into more alleys. He was trying to find River Street, so that he could get his bearings and go on from there to Clayton and then to the station house. But in the darkness his sense of direction was confused. And the maze of alleys was like a circular stairway going down and putting him deeper and deeper into the Hellhole.

One wrong turn had done it. When he'd walked out of the wooden shack he'd gone left instead of right, and after that it was right turn instead of left, then south instead of north, east instead of west. He might have used the City Hall clock as a point of reference, except that it wasn't there all the time. It played tricks on him and vanished behind the tenement rooftops. Then it showed again and he'd use it for a while until there'd be a dead-end street or alley and he'd have to go back and start all over. Finally the clock was hidden altogether and he couldn't see anything but black sky and black walls and the dark alleys that were taking him nowhere.

It went on like that and it got him annoyed. Then very much annoyed. Then it struck him sort of funny. As though the Hellhole were using him to joke around with the law. The

Hellhole was getting clever and cute with the Thirty-seventh District. Like saying to the Captain: This stupid bastard wants to give himself up, but you don't get him that easy. We'll let him outta here when we're good and ready.

Whitey laughed without sound. It was really as though the Hellhole were pulling the Captain's leg. Or sticking in another needle. Ever so gently. To let the Captain know that law enforcement was not welcome in this neighborhood, that all honest cops were enemies and the dark alleys were friendly to all renegades. With extra hospitality for cop-killers. Nosirree, the Hellhole said to Captain Kinnard of the Thirty-seventh District, this is our boy Whitey and we won't letcha have him. Not yet, anyway. But don't worry, Captain, don't get your bowels in an uproar, it ain't even two o'clock and maybe you'll have him before morning.

It wasn't anyone's voice and yet Whitey could almost hear it talking. He began to have the feeling that a lot was going to happen before morning.

The feeling grew in him and he tried to make it go away but it stayed there and went on growing. He was walking slowly down a very narrow alley and seeing the darkness ahead, just the darkness, nothing else. Or maybe there was something down there that he could see but didn't want to see. Maybe he was trying not to look at it. He blinked hard and told himself it wasn't really there.

Then he blinked again and focused hard and he knew it was there.

He saw the faint glow pouring thinly from a kitchen window, floating out across the alley and showing the color and the shape of the moving figure.

Bright green. That was the cap. Black and purple. That was the plaid lumber jacket. The shape was very short and very wide, with extremely long arms.

Hello, Whitey said without sound. Hello again.

He stood motionless and saw the short wide man standing there in the back yard under the dimly lit kitchen window. The distance between himself and the man was some forty yards and he couldn't see clearly what the man was doing. It seemed that the man wasn't doing anything. Then Whitey noticed the tiny moving form at the man's feet. It was a gray kitten lapping at the contents of a saucer.

The glow from the window showed the short wide man stooping over to pet the kitten. The kitten went on with its meal and the man knelt beside it and seemed to be talking to it. Presently the kitten was finished with the meal and the man picked it up with one hand, fondled it with the other, held its furry face to his cheek to let it know it had a friend in this world. The kitten accepted the petting and Whitey could hear the sound of its contented meow. The man put it down and gently patted its head. It meowed again, wanting more petting. The man turned away and moved across the back yard under the glow from the kitchen window, opening the kitchen door and entering the house.

Whitey moved automatically. He wasn't sure what he was thinking as he walked down the alley toward the lighted window. He tried to tell himself it didn't make sense to move in this direction, just as it hadn't made sense to follow the man when he'd seen him earlier tonight on Skid Row. It just didn't make sense at all.

It had no connection with now. It was strictly a matter of past history. Something from 'way back there, seven years ago. There was no good reason for going back. And every damn good reason to stay away from it, not let it take him back.

Check it, he said to himself. Stop walking and check it and forget about it. Let it rest where it is. For Christ's sake, bury it, will you?

But the lighted window said no. The lighted window was a magnet, pulling him closer. He moved on down the alley, his feet walking forward and his brain swimming backward through a sea of time. It was a dark sea, much darker than the alley. The tide was slow and there were no waves, just tiny ripples that murmured very softly. Telling him all about yesterday. Telling him that yesterday could never really be discarded, it was always a part of now. There was just no way to get rid of it. No way to push it aside or throw it into an ash can, or dig a hole and bury it. For all buried memories were nothing more than slow-motion boomerangs, taking their own sweet time to come back. This one had taken seven years.

He went on down the alley and came to a loose-nailed fence with most of the posts missing. He gazed across the small back yard, seeing through the kitchen window a still-life painting of some empty plates and cups stacked on a sink. The background was faded gray wallpaper, torn here and there, some of the plaster showing. Then some life crept into the painting, but it wasn't much, just one of the smaller residents of the Hellhole, a water roach moving slowly along the edge of the sink.

He stood there waiting for more life to appear in the kitchen. Nothing appeared and there was no sound from inside the house. It was a small two-story wooden house, very old and with a don't-care look about it. Typical Hellhole real estate. On either side it was separated from the adjoining dwellings by not more than a few inches of empty air. In addition to the kitchen window there was the back door and one dark window on the second floor and then there was a very small cellar window with no glass in it, and he thought: They're not living very high these days. Looks like business ain't been so good.

Just then someone came into the kitchen. It was the short wide man. He had taken off the bright-green cap and the lumber jacket and he stood there at the sink pouring himself a glass of water. He filled the glass to the brim, jerked it to his mouth, and drained it in one long gulp. Then he put down the glass, turned slowly so that Whitey saw him in profile, and began a meditative scratching along the top of his head.

His head was completely bald. It glistened white and there were seams in it from stitched scars and it was like a polished volleyball. He had very small ears and the one that showed was somewhat mashed. His nose was badly mashed, almost completely disorganized, so that it was hardly a nose at all. His lips were very thick and the lower lip was puffed at the corner. Also, his jaw was out of line, as though it had been fractured more than once. It was hard to tell his age, but Whitey knew he was at least fifty.

Whitey stood some fifteen feet away from the kitchen window, his hands resting on the back-yard fence, his eyes focused on the man in the kitchen, his lips saying without sound, Hello, Chop.

And then someone else appeared in there. A big woman. She was very big. Really huge. Around five-eleven and weighing over three hundred. Built like a tree trunk, no shape at all except the straight-up-and-down of no breasts, no belly, no rear. She was in her middle thirties and looked about the same as she'd looked seven years ago. Same bobbed hair, with the neck shaved high and the mud-brown hair cut very close to the sides of her head. Same tiny eyes pushed into the fat meat of her face like tiny pins in a cushion. Same creases on her thick neck and along the sides of her big hooked nose. Same great big ugly girl named Bertha.

Hello, Whitey said without sound. Hello, Bertha.

He watched the two of them in there in the kitchen. They were talking. The window was closed and he couldn't hear what they were saying. He saw Chop taking another drink of water, then moving to the side to make room for Bertha at the sink. Bertha turned on the faucet and started to wash the dishes. She washed them without soap and used her hand for a dishrag. Chop walked out of the kitchen and Bertha continued to wash the dishes. She paused for a moment to light a cigarette, and while she was lighting it another face appeared in profile in the window.

It was a man wearing a bathrobe and smoking a cigar. The man was in his middle forties, sort of flabby and out of condition but not really unattractive. He was a six-footer and weighed around 190, and if it hadn't been for the paunch it would have been a fairly nice build. He had all his hair and it was a thick crop, dark brown, parted on the side and flowing back in long loose waves. His features were pleasantly shaped and balanced and wholesomely masculine. The cigar looked very appropriate in his mouth. His appearance summed up was that of a medium-successful businessman.

Whitey looked at the six-footer in there in the kitchen. Without sound Whitey said, Hello, Sharkey.

Then his hands were tighter on the top of the wooden fence. He was waiting for another face to appear in the window. He told himself he'd seen three of them and that made it three fourths of what he'd come here to see. Or maybe the three he'd seen were nothing more than preliminaries leading to the windup. If that fourth face showed, it would really be the windup. And he'd paid a lot for his ringside seat. He'd paid plenty. The ticket of admission was a stack of calendars. Seven calendars.

He went on waiting for the fourth face to appear in the window. And he said to himself: All you want is a look-see, that's all, you just wanna get a glimpse of her.

Just a glimpse. Just a chance to look at her again after all these years. He thought: What a chance, buddy, what a chance to let it hit you between the eyes and cut through you and eat your heart out. If you had one grain of brains you'd get the hell away from here.

But he stayed there at the fence, grabbing at the chance, just as he'd grabbed at it when he'd seen Chop walking past the hash house on Skid Row; when he'd followed Chop down River Street, with his thoughts not on Chop, but only on Chop's destination, the long-shot bet that wherever it was, whatever it was, she might be there and he could peer through a window and get a look at her.

And while he waited, all other factors drifted away. He forgot where he was. The locale didn't matter in the least. Instead of a kitchen window in a Hellhole dwelling it might be any old window in any old Main Line mansion. Or Irish castle. Or Chinese pagoda. It might be the eyepiece of a telescope aimed at the moon. He stood there focusing with his eyes burning hard like dry ice getting harder. With his mind pulled away from all current events involving the Skid Row bum named Whitey, the captain named Kinnard, the detective lieutenants named Pertnoy and Taggert, the old man named Jones Jarvis, who'd come out with the cosmic conclusion, "Every man has an ax to grind."

But cosmic conclusions and current events had no connection with the kitchen window. In the blackness of the night it was the only thing that showed, the only thing that mattered. It was the chance to get a glimpse of her.

He went on waiting. The window showed Sharkey smoking his cigar and having a quiet discussion with Bertha. Then Sharkey walked out of the kitchen and Bertha resumed washing the dishes. She worked very slowly, and once she stopped to light another cigarette, then stopped again to scratch herself under her arms. Some minutes later she was finished with the dishes and finished with the cigarette. She threw the stub in the sink and reached up toward the wall switch.

No, Whitey said without sound. Don't put that light out.

But Bertha was walking out of the kitchen and her thick finger flicked the switch. So then it was just an unlighted window that showed black nothing.

Well, Whitey thought. That's it. The show's over. But you didn't see what you came to see and you oughta get your money back. Or get a rain check and come back tomorrow night.

But he knew there'd be no rain check for tomorrow night. By then he'd be in the grip of the law and locked up in a little room with barred windows. Or in a bed in a white room with his face all bandaged, a pulpy mess resulting from the two big fists of Captain Kinnard. Or maybe the Captain's fists would take it all the way, and Pertnoy's mention of a trip to the morgue would be no exaggeration.

At any rate, there'd be no show tomorrow night. No second chance to visit this house and take a look through the kitchen window and get a glimpse of her.

His brain came back to current events. This man here was just a Skid Row bum named Whitey, just a punching bag for the slugger named Kid Fate. So what the hell, he thought, it's easier to take the slugging than to wait and think about it.

He told himself to start walking and find his way back to the station house.

He let his hands slide off the fence. He started to turn away and took one step going away and came to a rigid halt.

The kitchen window was lighted again.

He looked. He saw her.

He saw a woman in her late twenties. She was about five-four and very slim, almost skinny except for the sinuous lines that twisted and coiled, flowing warm-thin-sirupy under gray-green velvet that matched the color of her eyes. Her hair was a shade lighter than bronze and she had it brushed straight back, covering her ears. Her features were thin and her skin was pale and she was certainly not pretty. But it was an exciting face. It was terribly exciting because it radiated something that a man couldn't see with his eyes but could definitely feel in his bloodstream.

Hello, he said without sound. Hello, Celia.

He stood there sinking into yesterday, going down deeper and deeper and finally arriving 'way down there at the very beginning. . . .

*

The beginning was the orphanage, the day he'd won first prize in the singing contest. Someone told someone about how this kid could sing. Then that someone told someone else. Eventually some papers were signed and his legal guardian was a third-rate orchestra leader who paid him thirty-five a week. He was seventeen at the time and had the idea he was a very lucky boy, getting all that money for merely doing what he enjoyed doing most of all. No matter what songs they gave him to sing, he sang with gladness and fervor and a certain rapture that really melted them. It finally melted the orchestra leader, who told him he was too good for this league and belonged up there in the big time. The orchestra leader gave up the orchestra and became the personal manager of Gene Lindell.

When Gene Lindell was twenty-three, he was making around four hundred a week.

A few years later Gene Lindell was making close to a thousand a week and they were saying he'd soon hit the gold mine, the dazzling bonanza of naming his own price. Of course, the big thing was his voice, but his looks had a lot to do with it, the females really went for his looks. They went for his small lean frame, which was somehow more of a nerve-tingler than the muscle-bound chunks of aggressive male, the dime-a-dozen baritones with too much oil in their hair and in their smiles. There was no oil in Gene's pale-gold hair, and his smile was as pure and natural as a sunny morning. It was the kind of smile that told them he was the genuine material, everything coming from the heart. So they couldn't just say he was "cute" or "nifty" or "keen." They really couldn't say anything; all they could do was sigh and want to touch him and tenderly take his head to their bosoms, to mother him. There were thousands upon thousands of them wanting to do that, and some of them put it in writing in their fan letters. There were some who took it further than sending a fan letter, and managed to make physical contact, and these included certain ladies from the Broadway stage, from café society and horsey-set society, from the model agencies and small-town beauty contests. And there were a few who were really expert in their line, veteran professionals from high-priced call houses, the hundred-dollar-a-session ladies who never gave it for free, but when Gene pulled out his wallet they wouldn't hear of such a thing. You wonderful boy, they said, and walked out very happy, as though he'd just given them a gift they'd never forget.

But with all of these ladies it was only once, it was never more than a night of having fun. He didn't need to fluff them off next morning when they asked for another date; they seemed to realize he wasn't in the market for anything serious. Or if he was, they couldn't provide it, because this was no ordinary male and it would take something very special to really reach him in there deep.

When it finally reached him it went in very deep and took hold of him and spun him around and made him dizzy. And it was very odd, the way it happened, it was almost silly. At first he couldn't believe it. He tried to tell himself it was impossible. But the only thing impossible was getting away from it. There was no way to get away from it.

He'd been invited to a stag party given by a big name in the entertainment field. He didn't like these smokers because he didn't go in for filth and he told his manager he wasn't going. His manager said it was important that he attend, you can't brush off these big shots, in this game it's all a matter of getting in solid with the right people. So finally he gave in and went to the smoker and it was a lavish affair with the best of food and drink and the comedians knocking themselves out. Gradually the evening became dirty and they showed certain motion pictures imported from France. It was weird stuff and it became very weird and presently it was the kind of cinema that made Gene somewhat sick in the stomach. But he couldn't walk out. It would be more embarrassing to walk out than to sit there and watch it.

They finished the movies and the stage was lit up and the girls came on. The man sitting next to him said, "Now you're gonna see something." He tried not to see it, tried to look down at his coffee cup and finally managed to focus on the cup and keep his eyes aimed there, away from the ugliness taking place on the stage. The all-male audience shrieked encouragement to the all-female cast that came out in pairs, then in trios, finally in quartets performing stunts that made the onlookers shriek louder. But all at once there was no shrieking, no sound at all, not even from the musicians up front. He wondered what was happening, and he looked up.

He saw her walking across the stage. That was all she was doing. Just walking.

She wore a gray-green long-sleeved high-necked dress of velvet. He saw the gray-green eyes and the bronze hair, saw them very clearly because he had a special-guest seat at the front-row table.

He heard the master of ceremonies announcing from the wing, "This—is—Celia."

Then the music started, and she began to dance. The music was very soft, on the languid side, and the dance was a slow mixture of something from Burma and something from Arabia and something far away from any place on earth.

It wasn't a strip tease. All her clothes stayed on, and there was nothing vulgar or even suggestive in the motions of her body. It went high above that, far beyond that, it was a performance that had no connection with matters of the flesh.

The audience didn't make a sound.

He wasn't conscious of the soundless audience. He wasn't conscious of anything except a certain feeling he'd never had before, a feeling he couldn't begin to analyze because his brain was unable to function. He was dizzy and getting dizzier.

She finished the dance and walked off the stage. He heard some applause, a vague sound that didn't mean anything because they didn't understand what they were applauding. Certainly it wasn't the kind of applause that called for an encore. They wouldn't be able to take an encore. She'd done enough to them already. They hadn't come here to be immobilized, to be made to feel like worms crawling at the feet of something they didn't dare to touch or think of touching. They stirred restlessly, anxious to forget what they had seen, impatient for the next number, wanting it to be very raw and smutty and ugly to get them back to earth again.

Two girls came onto the stage. One of them wore masculine attire and the other was entirely naked. Gene didn't see them. He was up from the table and going somewhere and not knowing where but knowing he had to get there. He was in a corridor, then another corridor, then seeing Celia walking out of a dressing room and toward the stage door. He said hello and she stopped and looked at him.

He smiled and said, "I hope you don't mind."

She frowned slightly. "Mind what?"

So then he came closer and said, "I wanted to see you again. Just had to get another look at you."

She let go of the frown and smiled dimly. "Well, that's all right," she said. "That happens sometimes." She leaned her head to the side and said, "Aren't you Gene Lindell?" He nodded, and wondered what to say next, and heard her saying, "It won't be easy, Gene. You better not start."

It was a fair warning aimed at herself as well as at him. It was a warning they both ignored. There was really nothing they could do about it. They went out through the stage door and minutes later they were in a cab and the driver was saying, "Where to?"

Gene was looking at her and saying, "Just drive."

The cab moved slowly through downtown traffic. Gene went on looking at her. The cab got past the heavy traffic and headed toward the big municipal park. Gene tried to speak and he couldn't speak and he heard her saying, "We shouldn't have started. Now I think it's too late." The cab was moving along the wide avenue of the parkway, going deeper into the black quiet of the park, and she was saying, "It's like this. There's a man. He's crazy jealous."

"I bet," he said.

"Look," she said. "What're we gonna do?"

"I don't know."

"Oh, God," she said. "Good God."

"Is it that bad?"

She looked at him. "You know how bad it is."

"Yeah," he said. "I know."

She gazed past him, out through the cab window, at the black lacework of trees and shrubs sliding backward, going very fast. "Tell you what," she said. "Better take me home. Let's forget it, huh?"

"No," he said. "I can't."

"I'll tell the driver," she said. She leaned forward to give the driver her home address. Her mouth opened and nothing came out of her mouth. She fell back in the seat and shook her head slowly and mumbled to herself, "It's no use."

The cab was moving very slowly on a narrow road that bordered a winding creek.

"It's getting worse," she said. "I can feel it getting worse."

"I'm sorry," he said.

"You are? Then do something about it." Her voice was low and quivering. "For heaven's sake, do something."

"I don't know what to do."

"You're just gonna sit there? Not even gonna touch me?"

"If I touch you," he said, "I'll really go nuts."

"You're nuts already. We're both nuts." She took a deep straining breath, as though fighting for air. "I've heard them tell about things like this, the way it happens so fast, but I never believed it."

"Me neither," he said.

"All right, Gene." Her voice changed, rising an octave to a medium pitch, level and cool and trying to stay that way as she said, "Let's get it over with. We'll find a room somewhere."

"No."

"We gotta do it that way. This way it's miserable, it's grief."

"And that way?"

"Well, that's fun, that's having a good time."

"I'm not looking for a good time."

"I wish you were," she said, and her voice dropped again. "I wish that's all it amounted to. Maybe if we went to a room and got it over with—"

"Celia," he said.

"Yes."

"Listen, Celia—"

"Yes? Yes?"

"I—" He saw the driver glancing backward and he said sharply, "Watch the road, will you? You wanna put us in the creek?"

Celia gave a little laugh. "The creek," she said. "We're in the creek already. Up the creek."

"No," he said. "It'll be all right. It's got to be all right. We'll think of something."

"Will we? I got my doubts. I got very serious doubts about that. The way I see it, mister, we're miles and miles up the creek and it's gonna be rough getting back."

"I don't want to get back. I want it to be like this."

"You see?" She laughed again, brokenly, almost despairingly. "That's what I mean. You can't stop it and I can't stop it and it's really awful now."

"Yes," he admitted. "It sure is."

She took another deep breath, braced herself for an effort, then leaned forward again and managed to give the driver an address. Twenty minutes later they arrived at the address, a row house in a somewhat shabby neighborhood. He opened the door and she got out. He started to follow her and she shook her head. He sat there in the cab looking at her and she looked past him, past the walls of the houses on the other side of the street as she told him her telephone number.

On the following day he phoned and a man answered. He pretended he'd called a wrong number. A few hours later he called again. This time it was Celia and he knew the man was there because she said it was the wrong number. Late in the afternoon he tried again and she was there alone. She gave him the address of a taproom downtown and said she'd be there around midnight.

It was a sad-looking place on the fringe of Skid Row, mostly ten-cent-beer customers. He arrived at eleven-fifty and took a booth and ordered ginger ale. It had to be ginger ale because he never used alcohol. He sat there drinking the ginger ale but not tasting it, waiting for her to show. Twenty minutes passed, and forty minutes. He had the glass to his lips when he saw her coming in and the ginger ale in his mouth was liquid fire going down. The sight of her was really combustible.

At the same time it was softly cool, like floating in a pool of lily water. The sum of it was dizziness, and as she sat down in the booth facing him, he had no idea this was a booth in a taproom; he had the notion it was someplace very high above the clouds.

They sat there talking. She ordered double straights of gin with a water chaser. She did most of the talking and she was trying to tell him why they couldn't go on with this.

For one thing, she said, he'd get his name loused up if he got involved with her. There was a big career in show business ahead of him, she said, and already he was in the public eye, he couldn't afford to muddy his reputation. It would really be mud, she explained, because she was a bum from 'way back and she had a jail record for prostitution and all her life she'd been mixed up with small-time pimps and small-time thugs and ex-cons. Her first husband had been a second-story man shot and killed by a house owner, and that made her a widow when she was seventeen. Then came the prostitution and a ninety-day stretch and then more prostitution and a longer stretch. So then she was finished with the prostitution and tried to play it clean and got married again. This second one was a truck driver who seemed all right in the beginning but it turned out he was really an expert hijacker specializing in liquor jobs. They finally busted him to make him a three-time loser and send him up for fifteen to thirty. It was too long for him and one day in the prison laundry he drank from a bottle of bleach and died giggling. While she was wearing black she met the one she had now. It was a common-law arrangement and his name was Sharkey.

"This Sharkey," she said, "he ain't so bad. At least, he tries his best to make me comfortable. Another thing, he don't shove me around like the others did. First man I ever lived with who never gave me a black eye. So that's something, anyway. But all the same, I ain't kidding myself about Sharkey. I know he's meaner than the others. Much meaner. It hasn't come out yet, but I know it's there. It sorta shows when he smiles real soft and tells me how much he trusts me. As if to say that if I ever disappoint him, he won't be able to take it and he'll do something crazy. That kind of meanness. That's the worst kind. Soft and quiet on the outside, and on the inside really crazy.

"These stag-party jobs I do," she went on, "if Sharkey was making a dollar he wouldn't let me do it. But it brings in an average of a C note a week and we really need the cash, Sharkey's accustomed to living high and he don't know how to budget. He used to be a big man in the rackets and he got in bad with the bosses, not bad enough to get himself bumped, but enough to be told he wasn't needed any more. Since then he's been mooching around and looking for an angle and every once in a while he gets hold of something. Like a bootleg setup. Or numbers. Or girls. But it never amounts to anything, it always gets messed up before it can build. I've tried to tell him it's no use, all these operations are strictly syndicate and an independent don't stand a chance. So then he smiles real soft and says nice and sweet, 'You do your dancing, Celia, let me run the business.' And that always gives me a laugh. The business. Some business! He hasn't made a dime in two years."

She shrugged. "I don't know. Maybe if he didn't have me, he could concentrate and promote something and make himself some decent money. He's got the brains for it. I mean something legitimate like handling talent or selling used cars. On that order. But no, he's got me and he wants me to have the best and his hands are itching for important money. The damn fool, last month he went out and borrowed three hundred dollars from God knows who, just to buy me a birthday present. Sooner or later I'll hafta pawn it so he can pay the guy he borrowed it from. Well, that ain't nothing new. That always happens when I get a present from Sharkey."

She shrugged again. "I don't know, maybe one of these days he'll find that angle he's looking for. He says it's around somewhere, all he's gotta do is find it. Lately he's been getting too anxious and sorta jumpy and I'm afraid he's headed for some genuine aggravation. He's hooked up with a couple of strong-arm specialists, a husband-and-wife team that make a business of putting people in the hospital. Or maybe putting them away altogether. Anyway, it makes me nervous, because they're living in the house with us and in the morning when I'm in bed I hear them in the next room, the three of them, Sharkey and Chop and Bertha, having their daily conference. I can't ever hear what they're saying, but I think I know what it's leading up to. When it's a strong-arm routine, it's either extortion or protection racket or a collection agency for clients who want blood instead of money. I don't know why I'm telling you all this. It's got nothing to do with you and me."

"Look," he said. "If it concerns you, it concerns me."

She smiled down at the empty shot glass. "You hear that?" she murmured to the glass.

"Listen, Celia—"

"I know what you're going to say." She looked at him, looked deep into him. "I know everything you want to tell me."

"But listen—"

"No," she said. "It won't work. There's no way you can take me away from him. He just won't let you do it. If you try, he's gonna hurt you. He's gonna hurt you bad."

"I don't care."

"I know you don't. But you would if you could use your brains. That's what I'm trying to do. That's why I'm drinking so much gin. To steady myself and think straight. At least one of us has to think straight."

"Want another drink?"

"Yeah," she said. "Better buy me a pint. Then maybe I can think real straight. Maybe I'll be able to walk out on you."

"No," he said. "You won't be able to do that."

"I'm gonna try." She pointed across the room, at the bartender. "Go on, tell the man to sell you a bottle. I'm gonna give this a real try."

He bought a pint of gin. And she tried. She tried very hard. At one point she said, "Well, here's where I get off," but somehow she couldn't leave the booth. Then later she managed to get up from the booth and gazed past him and said, "Nice to have met you, and so forth," and turned away and started toward the door. She made it halfway to the door and came back to the booth and said slowly and solemnly, "You bastard, you." She sat down and lifted the half-empty bottle to her mouth and took a long quivering gulp. She went on with the drinking, taking it fast and then much too fast and finally she passed out.

When she was able to sit up he phoned for a cab. She said she didn't want to leave, she wanted to drink some more. She said it would be nice if she could really knock herself out and stay that way for a week, so then she wouldn't be able to see him. Maybe that would do it, she said, with her eyes saying that nothing could do it, nothing could keep her away from him.

He put her in the cab and they arranged for the same time, same place tomorrow night.

So then it was tomorrow night. It was a succession of tomorrow nights in the booth in the taproom with ginger ale for him and gin for her. Sitting there facing each other and not touching each other, and it was three weeks of that, just that, just sitting there together until closing time, when he'd put her in a cab and watch the cab going away.

Then on Tuesday of the fourth week she said she couldn't take this much longer and if they didn't find themselves a room somewhere, she'd have convulsions or something.

He didn't say anything, but when the cab arrived to take her home, he climbed in with her. He said to the driver, "Take us somewhere."

The driver took them to a cheap hotel that paid certain cabbies a small commission.

In the bed with her it was dark but somehow blazing like the core of a shooting star. It was going 'way out past all space and all time.

"Lemme tell you something," she said afterward. "I gotta spoil it now. I gotta get dressed and scram outta here."

"No."

"But I gotta," she breathed into his mouth. "It's risky enough already. I don't wanna make it worse."

"All right," he said.

"Please." She touched his arm. "Don't get sore."

"I'm not sore," he said. He was sitting up in the bed. He spoke thickly, falteringly. "It's just that I hate to see you leave."

"I know," she said. "I hate it too."

Then in the darkness of the room she was out of the bed. He heard the rustling of fabric as she began to put on her clothes. The sound was difficult to take. She was getting dressed to walk out of here and it was really very difficult to take.

"Celia—"

"Yes?"

"Let's go away."

"What?" she said. "What's that?"

"We'll go away." His voice throbbed. "It's the only thing we can do."

"But—"

"Look," he cut in quickly. "I know it's wrong. It's giving him a raw deal, it's sorta like larceny. But that's aside from the issue. We just gotta do it, that's all."

For a long moment she didn't speak. And then, very quietly, "What do you want me to do?"

"Write him a note. Pack some things. We'll fix a time and you'll meet me at the train station."

There was another long quiet. He waited, not breathing, and then he heard her saying, "All right. When?"

They arranged the hour. It would be late afternoon. She

finished dressing and there was no further talk and then she walked out of the room and he tried to go to sleep. But he couldn't sleep and already he was counting the minutes until he'd see her again. On a small table near the bed there was a lamp and he switched it on and glanced at his wrist watch. The dial said four-forty. He'd be meeting her at the station in approximately twelve hours. He thought, Twelve times sixty makes it seven hundred and twenty minutes, that's a long time.

He lit a cigarette and tried to think in practical terms of what must be done in the next twelve hours. It would be a busy twelve hours because he'd have to cancel several bookings. He was listed for night-club engagements and guest appearances on several radio shows and a large recording company had him scheduled for some platters. All these bookings were very important, especially the radio and the recordings. His manager would start hopping around and yelling that they couldn't afford these cancellations, there was too much money involved, and another factor, a bigger factor, he hadn't yet reached big-name status and he wasn't sufficiently important to walk out on these contracts.

But, he said to himself, you're sufficiently mad about her to walk out on contracts and manager and everything, if it comes to that. You don't really care if it comes to that. You don't care about anything except her.

As it turned out, the cancellations were handled smoothly and there were no negative reactions. He told his manager that he was very tired and needed a rest and had to go away for at least a month. His manager nodded understandingly and patted him on the shoulder and said, "You got the right idea, Gene. Your health comes first. So what's it gonna be? Florida?"

He said he wasn't sure. He told his manager that he'd send a postcard just to keep in touch. But there mustn't be any publicity, he was really very tired and he just wanted to get away from people for a while. His manager promised to keep it quiet. His manager said, "Leave everything to me. Just have yourself a nice vacation and get plenty of sun. And for crissake stay out of drafts, don't come back with a sore throat."

They smiled and shook hands. The cab was waiting and he climbed in and set his suitcase on the floor. He settled back in the seat and the cab went into gear and moved away from the curb. He looked through the window and saw his manager waving good-by. He waved back and then the cab turned a corner and began to work its way through the heavy downtown traffic.

At the railroad station he was in the waiting room and the big clock said five-fifty. He wondered what was keeping her. Then the clock said six-ten and he wondered if he should make a phone call. When the clock said six-twenty he got up from the bench and moved toward a phone booth.

He was in the phone booth, putting the coin in the slot, then starting to dial, and then for some unaccountable reason his finger wouldn't move the dial. It happened in the instant before he turned and looked and saw the man outside the booth.

The man was smiling at him. The man was a six-footer wearing a dark-brown beaver and a camel's-hair overcoat and smoking a cigar. The man had pleasant features and he was smiling softly and good-naturedly.

He'd never seen this man before, but without thinking about it, or trying to think, he knew it was Sharkey.

He opened the door of the booth and said, "Well? What is it?"

"Can we talk?"

"Sure." He stepped out of the booth. Well, he thought, here it comes. He told himself to take it calm and cool. Or at least try. His voice was steady as he said, "I guess it's better this way. She tell you about it?"

"No," Sharkey said. He widened the smile just a little. "I hadda find out for myself."

He gazed past Sharkey and he saw some people getting up from the benches and walking out of the waiting room. They were headed toward the stairway leading up to the platform. In a few minutes they'd be getting aboard the six-thirty southbound express. He thought of the two empty seats and it gave him an empty feeling inside.

Then he looked at Sharkey. "All right," he said. "I'm listening."

Sharkey took a slow easy pull at the cigar. The smoke seeped from the corners of his lips. He said, "Coupla weeks ago. I got to thinking about it. She was staying out too late. A few times

I checked with the stag parties and they said she'd left the place hours ago.

"I didn't ask her about it," Sharkey went on. "I just waited for her to tell me. Well, you know how it is, you get tired of waiting. So one night I followed her."

It was quiet for some moments and Sharkey pulled easily at the cigar, sort of guiding the smoke as it came out of his mouth. The smoke drifted lazily between them.

Then Sharkey said, "Next night I followed her again. And every night from then on." He shook his head slowly. "It wasn't fun, believe me. I was hoping it would end so I could check it off and forget about it. But every night there she is, meeting you in the taproom. And there I am, sitting in a rented car parked across the street.

"So you see it cost me money. Six bucks a night for the car. And a nickel for the newspaper to hold in front of my face."

"Why'd you do it that way? Why didn't you come into the taproom?"

Sharkey shrugged. "It would have been an argument. I don't like arguments. It always gives me indigestion."

From the platform upstairs there was the sound of the train coming in.

He heard Sharkey saying, "Well, that's the way it was. I'd be sitting there in the car and then I'd see you putting her in the cab. And the cab going away and you standing on the corner. Then I'd put the car in gear and step on the gas to get home before she did."

The sound of the train was louder, coming closer, and then there was the squealing sound of the train drawing to a stop at the platform.

And Sharkey was saying, "Every night the same routine. Until last night. When you got in the cab with her. And I knew I had to follow the cab.

"I swear I didn't want to follow that cab. I knew where it would go. Some cheap hotel with a clerk who doesn't ask questions. So that's the way it was. I'm in the car and it's parked near the hotel and I'm waiting an hour and then another hour and more hours. Finally she comes out and gets in a cab. When she comes home, I'm in bed. Today I told her I'd be away on business. I watch the house and I see her walking out with a hatbox and a suitcase. So then it's another cab and I'm in the rented car and there's a couple people with me."

"Chop and Bertha?"

"Yeah." Sharkey's eyebrows went up just a trifle. "She tell you about them?"

He nodded.

"Well," Sharkey said, taking another easy pull at the cigar, "it figures. I guess she told you everything."

Then from upstairs along the platform there was the sound of the train moving away and gathering steam.

"We stopped her when she got out of the cab," Sharkey said. He laughed softly, amiably. "She's some girl, that Celia. She didn't even blink. I told her to get in the car with Chop and Bertha and she said, 'O.K., Boss.' She always calls me Boss."

The train was going away. He tried to tell himself there'd be another train. He begged himself to believe there'd soon be another train and they'd be on it. But the sound of the departing train was a good-by sound, like music fading out, saying, No more, no more.

"They took her home," Sharkey said. "I knew you'd be here in the waiting room and it was time for you and me to talk."

He looked at the cigar in Sharkey's mouth. It was coming apart and he knew it was a cheap cigar. Then he looked at the camel's-hair coat that must have cost over a hundred when it was new but now it was very old and wouldn't bring fifteen in a secondhand store. The same applied to the brown beaver. The band was tattered and the crown was dull from loss of fibers. Without seeing inside Sharkey's wallet, he knew it contained one-dollar bills or maybe none at all. For some vague reason he felt like treating Sharkey to something. He heard himself saying, "I'm gonna have dinner. Join me?"

"All right," Sharkey said.

They walked into the station restaurant and took a table. There was a wine list and Sharkey ordered double bourbon straight and a water chaser. The bourbon was a bonded brand costing eighty cents a shot. Then Sharkey ordered a four-fifty T bone.

He said, "Make it two," and the waitress wrote it down and walked away from the table. He looked at Sharkey and said, "I'd have a drink with you, except I don't drink."

"It's better not to," Sharkey said. "I don't use it much my-self. Not on an empty stomach, anyway. It don't pay to drink too much on an empty stomach."

"I wonder why they do it," he said.

"Do what?"

"Drink themselves half crazy."

"You mean," Sharkey murmured, "the way she does?"

He didn't say anything. He wasn't looking at Sharkey.

"I'll tell you," Sharkey said. "She don't get crazy from it. Fact is, it does her a lot of good. She needs it."

"Why?" And now he looked directly at Sharkey. "Why does she need it?"

"Problems," Sharkey said.

"You think she'll do a lot of drinking now?"

Sharkey put his large hands flat on the tablecloth and looked down at his thick fingers. "What do you think?"

"I think she'll do an awful lot of drinking."

"For a while, anyway," Sharkey said. He went on looking down at his fingers. "Let's say a few days. A week at the most."

"Longer than a week," he said. "You know it'll be longer than a week."

"Maybe." Sharkey nodded slowly. "Maybe an entire month. Maybe six months." He looked up, showing the soft easy smile. "Maybe she'll stay drunk for a year."

"And then into next year. And the next."

"Well," Sharkey said, "that's up to her." He leaned back and hooked his arm over the back of the chair. "Tell ya the truth, I don't care if she stays drunk the rest of her life. Just so long as she stays with me."

"What if she gets sick?"

"I'll take care of her."

"What I mean is, really sick. I mean—"

"Look, I'll put it this way," Sharkey said, his smile very gentle, his voice soft and soothing. "My main interest in life is taking care of her. It's the only real enjoyment I get. I just wanna take care of her. If she was in a wheel chair I'd spend all my time wheeling her around. If she was flat on her back I'd stay in the room with her day and night. You get the general idea?"

"Yes," he said. "I get it."

Sharkey took the mangled cigar from his mouth and put it

in the ash tray. He sighed softly and said, "It's a queer thing. I used to be a cake of ice when it came to women. I mean, they were all right to play with, but aside from that I wasn't in the market. Sure, I got married a couple of times, but only so's I'd have it ready for me when I came home. In each case it wasn't any deeper than the mattress. The first one turns out to be a nympho and I pay her off and send her to Nevada. The next number is all right in the beginning, but then she develops a weakness for rumba teachers and I hafta throw her out. Then this one comes along and I take one look and it's like falling off a cliff with nothing underneath, just falling and falling. All the time falling."

The double bourbon arrived and Sharkey shot it down and ordered another. Then he had a third, and he was on the fourth when he laughed apologetically and said, "Look at me, the man who says he don't drink on an empty stomach."

"Go on and drink. Drink all you want."

Sharkey went on laughing lightly. "You wanna get me drunk?"

"No, it isn't that."

"I think I know what it is," Sharkey said. "You feel that you owe me the drinks, the steak dinner. Sure, that's what it is, you just feel that you owe me something."

"Maybe," he said, and he was staring past Sharkey. "I'm not really sure."

"Well, anyway," Sharkey smiled, "I'll have another drink."

Sharkey was on the seventh double bourbon when the waitress brought the T bones. The steaks were large and prime and he watched Sharkey tackling the plate with considerable appetite. His own appetite was less than zero and he tried a few bites and couldn't go on with it. He pushed his plate aside and lit a cigarette, and it was quiet at the table except for the sound of Sharkey's knife and fork working methodically on the T bone, Sharkey with seven double bourbons in him but not the least bit drunk, doing a thorough job on the steak and French fries, doing it medium fast and with reasonable etiquette and finally lifting the napkin to his lips and saying, "Goddamn, that was good."

He smiled sadly. "I'm glad you enjoyed it."

"What about yours? Something wrong with yours?"

"No," he said. "I'm just not hungry."

Sharkey nodded slowly and understandingly and somewhat sympathetically. The waitress came to the table and asked if they would like dessert. Sharkey told her to bring a pot of coffee and another double bourbon. Then Sharkey grinned at him and said, "It ain't often I get a treat like this. I might as well take advantage of it."

He didn't say anything. He went on smiling sadly.

"Another thing," Sharkey said. "Maybe I'll get my name in the columns. I'm having dinner with a celebrity."

"I'm not a celebrity."

"Well, maybe not yet. But you're getting there. You're really getting there. I heard you on the radio last week. The disc jockey played three of your records, one right after another. They never do that except with the solid talent."

It was a genuine compliment and he started to murmur thanks. But it wouldn't come out. His hands gripped the edge of the table and he said, "Listen, Sharkey—"

And Sharkey went on quickly: "You're a cinch to hit the top brackets. I can tell. It's like at the races when I look at a horse and I just know it's gotta come in. So it's—"

"Listen," he said, not loudly but aiming it, shooting it. And then, sending in the clincher, "I want her."

Then it was quiet. Sharkey was looking down at the table. He had a technical expression in his eyes, like a dealer studying all the cards face up.

"I want her." Now it was louder. And it quivered. "I can't give her up. Just can't do without her."

Sharkey went on looking at the table. His lips scarcely moved as he said, "You know something? I think we're in trouble."

Then quietly again, and feeling very friendly toward Sharkey but wishing Sharkey didn't exist, he said, "I'm gonna take her."

"Goddamn." As if the cards on the table showed a sorry mess. "We're in real trouble."

"I've gotta have her and I'm gonna have her, that's all."

Sharkey looked up. The technical expression went out of his eyes and the only thing in his eyes was sadness. It was sincere sadness and his voice was gloomy as he said, "It's a goddamn shame."

"Well, anyway, now you know. You know what I'm gonna do."

"Yeah," Sharkey said. "I know. I wish you hadn't told me."

The rest of it was rapid and blurred and there was no thought, no plan, no logic in the pattern of getting up and leaving Sharkey sitting there at the table. He lunged toward the waitress and jammed a twenty-dollar bill into her hand. He ran out of the restaurant, leaving his hat and coat on the hanger, his suitcase forgotten, everything forgotten in the rush to get out of there and get into a cab. The only symbols in his brain were the four numbers of the address where she lived with Sharkey and Chop and Bertha, and what he had to do was erase those numbers, take her out of there, take her far away and make sure they'd never carry her back.

As he entered the cab and gave the address to the driver, he didn't feel the winter cold, he didn't notice the evening blackness, and of course he paid no attention to the telephone wires stretched high above the street, glimmering silver against the darkness. If he had focused on the wires, if he'd been able to think clearly and with a reasonable amount of arithmetic, he would have known what was happening up there at this very instant. He would have known that the wires were carrying Sharkey's voice from a phone booth to the address where the cab was headed.

When he arrived there, they were waiting for him, ready for him. The short wide man opened the door for him and he walked in and then the short wide man moved in close behind him and swung a blackjack and knocked him unconscious. The big woman who weighed more than three hundred was smiling down at him and then she picked him up from the floor and carried him as if he were a child. Or as if she were a child carrying a rag doll. The smile on her face was childlike, and while she carried him down the cellar stairs she purred, "You pretty little boy. You're so cute."

He heard the voice but he didn't know what it was saying. He had a feeling of being carried but there was no way to look and make sure. It seemed there was a thick spike planted in his skull, cutting off all communication between one side of him and the other.

At intervals he could hear her saying, "Really cute."

And then the voice of the short wide man: "Why don'tcha kiss him? Go on, kiss him."

She laughed and said, "Should I? Well, maybe I will, while I got the chance."

He wasn't sure that the big woman was kissing him, he couldn't feel anything on his face except the pressure of some gushy substance, tons of it, as if a carload of jelly had fallen on him.

Then for a long time there was nothing.

When he heard the voices again, Sharkey's voice was included and Sharkey was saying, "Make sure he don't come back."

"You mean finish him?" It was the woman.

"No," Sharkey said. "That's out. Don't do that."

"Why not?" It was Chop. "It's easier that way. All we gotta do is—"

"Please keep quiet and listen to me." The soft gentle voice of Sharkey. "All I want is a guarantee that he don't come back."

"That's gonna be complicated," the woman said.

"It's complicated already," Sharkey said. "It's so goddamn complicated it's making me sick."

"I think we oughta finish him," Chop said. "We could do it right here in the cellar."

"Hell, no," the woman said. "I been working all day cleaning up this place. I don't want it messed up."

"It wouldn't be no mess," Chop told her. "What we do is put him in the furnace."

"Not in one piece," she said. "He wouldn't fit. We'd have to cut him up and that needs a meat cleaver. It means I'll hafta use a scrubbing brush for at least an hour. It's eight-fifteen now and I wanna be upstairs when Bob Hope comes on."

"He ain't on tonight," Chop said. "It's tomorrow night."

"Don't tell me," she said. "I know when he comes on."

"I'm telling you it's tomorrow night."

The woman spoke loudly. "You stupid sonofabitch, you don't even know what day it is."

"Don't shout at me, Bertha. You don't hafta shout at me."

"I wouldn't hafta shout if you weren't so stupid."

"That's another thing I don't like," Chop said. "I don't like when you call me stupid."

"I'll call you stupid whenever you're stupid. All right?"

"Now look, Bertha—"

"Drop it," Sharkey cut in. His voice was low and thoughtful.

"Here's what I want you to do. You'll carry him outta here. Put him in the car and take him away from town."

"In the country?" Chop asked.

"Yes," Sharkey said patiently. "Someplace in the country. Say like twenty, thirty miles out of town."

"Like in the woods?" Chop asked.

"No." It was Bertha again. "We'll find a place where there's a crowd. So they can stand and watch while we do it. We'll sell tickets."

"Lay off me," Chop mumbled.

"Please," Sharkey said. "Please, the two of you. Keep quiet and listen carefully. You'll get him off on a side road someplace. Now check this, I want it clearly understood you're not to finish him. All you do is convince him. He's gotta be convinced. You see what I mean?"

"You mean really convinced?" Chop asked.

"Yes," Sharkey said.

"Goddamnit," the woman said. "Thirty miles out in the country. Now I'm gonna miss Bob Hope."

They carried him out of the house and put him in the rented car. Some twenty minutes later he started to regain consciousness. Then it was forty minutes and he was able to focus and realize what was happening. He was sitting in the back of the car with Bertha. He saw Chop sitting up front behind the wheel. The car was moving very fast on a bumpy road. They were passing through open countryside and there were some lighted windows here and there, but not many. Then minutes later it was another road, much narrower, and more trees and higher grass and no lighted windows.

He sat up straighter. He reached slowly for the door handle and Bertha saw him doing it. She grabbed a handful of his hair and her other hand was a big fist banging him hard on the cheek just under the eye. He went on trying for the door and she hit him again in the same place. He wondered if his cheekbone were broken. It really felt broken. While he thought about it he kept going for the door handle and Bertha kept pulling his hair and hitting him in the face. The car slowed down and Chop said, "What's the matter back there?"

"Keep driving," Bertha said.

"What's he doing?"

"He's trying to open the door," Bertha said. She used her fist again.

"You want the blackjack?" Chop asked.

"No," Bertha said. "I don't need the blackjack. You just keep driving. I'll take care of this."

She smashed her fist into the battered cheek, then aimed for the mouth and shot the right hand short and straight and he felt the teeth coming out of his gums. He could feel the two teeth rolling along his tongue. He spat them out and tried to turn his head to look at Bertha but he couldn't move his head because she was still pulling his hair. His scalp hurt worse than his cheek and his mouth, and he thought: It can't be a woman, it's like something made of iron.

Just then she hit him again and it was really like getting hit with a sledge hammer. She had all of her weight behind the blow and he took the full force of over three hundred pounds of hard-packed beef. It knocked several more teeth out of his mouth and it broke his jaw. He started to pass out and tried to hold on and managed to hold on. He collected everything he had and put it in his left arm and swung his left arm but it didn't go anywhere. It was just a feeble gesture that tagged empty air.

"Well, whaddya know," Bertha said. "He tried to hit me."

"Quit batting him around," Chop said. "You keep it up like that, you're gonna finish him. Sharkey gave instructions not to finish him."

"I won't finish him," Bertha said. "But I'm sorta disappointed. I thought he was a gentleman. A gentleman don't raise his hand to a lady."

"What's he doing now?"

"He ain't doing anything."

"Then leave him alone."

"Sure," she said. "I'll leave him alone. Just one more lick to keep him quiet."

She sent her fist to his head and it crashed against his temple and again he was unconscious.

When he came to, the car had stopped and they were dragging him out of the car. He was spitting blood and teeth and shreds of flesh from his torn mouth. They lifted him to his feet and walked him away from the car. It was a muddy clearing that sloped downward from some trees. A few times he slipped in the mud and they picked him up and tightened their hold on him to keep him from falling again. They walked him some fifty yards going down to where the clearing ended against a wall of thick trees. Then they turned him around so that he faced them, his back pressing against the jagged bark of a tree.

They had him placed so that he stood in the glow of the car's headlights. The car was about sixty yards away but the bright beam was on and it hit him hard in the eyes. He blinked. He tried to look away from the headlights. The headlights seemed to reach out like burning fingers going into his eyes and he blinked again.

"All right," Chop said. "Let's get started."

Chop was wearing a lumber jacket zipped up to his collar. He zipped it halfway down to loosen it. Then he loosened the sleeves and rolled them up just a little. He reached to the rear pocket of his trousers and took out the blackjack.

"Wait," Bertha said. "I wanna talk to him."

"Talk?" Chop looked at her. "Whatcha gonna talk about?"

"I want him to know why."

"He knows why."

"I wanna make sure he knows," Bertha said.

She moved toward him where he stood slumped against the tree. Her massive bulk blotted out the glare of the headlights and he was thankful for that. But then her face came closer and he saw the big hooked nose and the tiny eyes. It wasn't an easy face to look at. He preferred the burning force of the headlights.

She said, "You get the idea?"

He didn't say anything. It wasn't because he refused to answer. His mouth and jaw hurt terribly and would hurt worse if he tried to talk.

"Answer me," Bertha said.

He told himself to give her an answer. But somehow he couldn't open his mouth. She stepped back and hauled off and punched him in the stomach. He went to his knees. She picked him up and pushed him back against the tree.

"You're gonna answer me," she said.

Chop moved in. "Lemme handle him."

"No," she said. "I'm doing this. He's gonna answer."

"For Crissake," Chop said. "How can he talk if he can't move his jaw?"

"He can move it. He's just stubborn, that's all. Stubborn and cute. Real cute."

He saw she was going to hit him again. He tried to fall away from it but her arm was faster and he took it again in the stomach. And then again. She was in real close, and he sagged against her. She hooked one arm around him and used the other arm to keep banging him in the stomach.

It went on like that for some moments. When she stopped punching him it was as though the punches were still coming and forcing his stomach out through his spine and into the tree. She had him pressed hard against the tree and it seemed as if the tree were eating away at his stomach.

"Now listen," Bertha said. "Listen careful and try to understand. That girl belongs to Sharkey."

He shook his head.

"No?" Bertha said. "You won't agree on that?"

"No," he managed to say.

Bertha took a deep breath. She looked at Chop. She said, "You hear? He ain't convinced."

"I'll convince him," Chop said.

"No, I'll do it. I know just what it needs. Gimme the blackjack."

"Now be careful," Chop said, handing her the blackjack. "Remember what Sharkey told us."

"Don't worry." She hefted the blackjack, holding it in her right hand, then slapping it gently against the palm of her left hand.

"Well, all right," Chop said. "But just be sure you don't finish him."

She took another deep breath. He saw her raising the blackjack. There was no way to get away from the blackjack and he didn't bother to try. The leather-covered cudgel came in from the side and hit him in the ribs. There was the sound of bones breaking and his mouth opened automatically and he let out a dry dragging sob.

"Convinced?" Bertha said.

He sobbed again. "No."

"All right," Bertha said. "We'll break a couple more. Let's see what that does."

The blackjack came in very hard. He could feel more bones breaking and he heard himself sobbing. He said to himself: What's the matter with you? Why don't you give in?

"Convinced now?" Bertha said.

"No."

She hit him again, a roundhouse swing that sent the blackjack crashing into his hip joint.

"Now?" she said.

"No."

She stepped back, looking him up and down, like a craftsman examining a partially completed work. Her tongue was out and wetting her lower lip and then she swung again and the blackjack hammered the injured hip joint.

"Well?" she said. "Well?"

He shook his head.

Bertha aimed the blackjack at his hip joint again. Chop walked in and touched her arm and said, "That ain't the place to hit him. You gotta hit him where it does real damage."

"Like where?"

"There," Chop said, his finger pointing. "Try it there."

Bertha stepped back again. She took careful aim, her arm going back very slowly. He stood there waiting to take it. He didn't know what was holding him up, maybe it was the tree, or maybe he was just curious and wanted to find out how much he could take. Whatever it was, it caused him to smile.

Bertha saw the smile. She saw it showing through the blood and the wreckage of his face. She frowned and slowly lowered the blackjack and said to him, "You know what? I think you're crazy."

"Sure he's crazy," Chop said. "He's gotta be crazy to take it and want more."

"Why?" Bertha wanted to know. She moved toward him, and said objectively, "What's the matter with you? What makes you so crazy?"

He gazed past Bertha, past Chop, past the trees and the darkness and everything. He heard himself saying, "Celia."

Then it was quiet. Bertha and Chop looked at each other.

His eyes came back to them and he smiled again and said, "I know you don't get it. Maybe I don't get it, either."

"It don't make sense," Bertha said.

"I know." He shrugged and went on smiling.

"Now look," Bertha said. She had a two-handed hold on the blackjack, gripping it at both ends. "I'm gonna give it one more try. I'm gonna tell you what you'll get if you don't give in. You're gonna get ruined, sonny. It's gonna be the throat."

She reached out and her finger gently nudged his throat. "There," she said. "Right there. So you'll wind up with a busted phonograph. And that would really be the pay-off, wouldn't it? Sharkey told us you're a famous singer, night clubs and radio and your records selling by the carloads. It figures you don't wanna lose all that."

He stared at the blackjack. It looked very efficient. It was definitely a capable tool in the hands of a professional.

"He looks sorta convinced," Chop said.

"I'll know when he tells me." She put her face close to the bloody, broken face and said, "Come on. Tell me. You gonna stay away from her? You swear on your life you'll stay away from her?"

He said to himself: All right now, Gene, enough is enough, you've taken too much already, you'll hafta give in, you'll hafta say it like they want you to say it.

The blackjack was waiting.

He said to the blackjack, "Well, you almost did it. But not quite."

"What's that?" Bertha said.

"It's no sale."

"That final?"

"Final."

And then he heard Chop saying, "My God." Saying it very slowly in an awed voice, and adding, "What these dumb bastards will do for a jane."

As he heard it, he saw the blackjack coming. It came like something alive, a gleaming black demon going for his throat. It smashed into his throat and he felt the destruction boiling in there, he could almost see the foaming bubbles of purple matter getting split apart.

The blackjack hit him again. And then again. Bertha swung it the fourth time but her aim was too high and the blackjack caught him on the side of the skull.

He went down, falling flat and then going out and 'way out.

And in the instant before he went over the edge, he thought: Well, anyway, that's all for now.

Then it was late the next morning and some country boys played hookey from school and went out hunting for rabbits. At first they thought he was dead. But then he rolled his bulging eyes. He had to tell them with his eyes because he didn't have a voice.

He was in the hospital for nine weeks. There were times when they didn't think he'd make it. Too much traumatic shock, they said, and then of course there was the internal bleeding, the brain concussion, the complications resulting from an excess of broken bones. But the worst damage was in the throat. They said it was a "comminuted fracture of the larynx" and they told him it was urgent that he shouldn't try to talk.

When he was able to sit up, they gave him a pencil and a pad of paper so he could make his wants known to the nurses. One day the law came and wanted to know what happened and he wrote on the pad, "Can't remember."

"Come on," the law said. "Tell us who did it."

He shook his head. He pointed to what he'd written on the pad.

Next day the law tried again. But he wouldn't give them anything. He didn't want the law brought into it. He told himself he wasn't sore at anybody. The only thing he wanted was to see her again. He was certain that any day now, any hour, she'd be visiting the hospital. It had been a front-page story, so of course she knew all about it. And now that he was allowed to have visitors, she'd certainly be coming. With the pencil and paper he asked the nurses, "Did Celia phone?" They said no. He kept asking and they kept saying no. So then it began to hit him. Not even a phone call. Not even an inquiry as to how he was doing.

He'd sit there in the bed looking at the other visitors. His manager. Or the radio people. Or the night-club people. They gabbed and chattered and he had no idea what they were saying. He'd stare past the blurred curtain of their faces and he'd think, Why? Why didn't she come to me? Why?

But he went on waiting. And hoping. Waking up each morning to start a day of looking at the white door and begging it to open and let her come in. Or handing the written question to the nurses. "Did she phone?" With his eyes pleading for a yes, and their faces sort of gloomy as they gave him a no.

Then it was the ninth week and one night he opened his eyes and looked up at the black ceiling. He had a feeling it was trying to tell him something. He didn't want to be told and he tried to go back to sleep. But he went on looking at the ceiling. And it seemed to be lowering, it was coming toward him, a huge black convincer, the business end of a blackjack so big that it blotted out everything else.

He spoke to it, saying without sound, All right, Mac. You win. I'm convinced.

As he said it, he could feel his spinal column turning to jelly. But it didn't bother him. In a way it was almost pleasant, really soothing and sort of cozy. On his face there was a lazy smile, just a trifle on the slap-happy side, and it stayed there as he fell asleep.

It was there in the morning when he heard the doctor saying, "You're going home today."

The smile widened. But not because he was glad to hear the news. It was just his way of saying, So what?

"I want to see you in a few days," the doctor said. He was a very expensive throat specialist who'd been called in by the manager. He said, "You've made excellent progress and I'm reasonably sure you'll soon regain your voice."

So what? So who cares?

The doctor went on: "Of course, we mustn't be overly optimistic. I'll put it this way: It's a fairly good prognosis. About fifty-fifty. In all these cases the healing process is rather slow. There's a gradual thickening and induration of the vocal cords, resulting in subsequent ability to produce sound. A certain amount of hoarseness, and quite naturally the volume is decreased. What I'm getting at, Mr. Lindell, it's all a matter of hoping for the best. I mean—your singing career—"

He wasn't listening.

And although he kept his appointment with the doctor, and kept all the appointments in the weeks and months that followed, he paid very little attention to the healing campaign. He went to the doctor's office because there was no other place to go. It was costing a lot of money, but of course that didn't matter, for the simple reason that nothing mattered. His manager took him around to keep him in contact with the right names, the well-fed faces in the elegant offices of big-time show business, and they were very nice to him, very kind, very encouraging. They said he'd soon be up there again, making a sensational comeback. His reply was the lazy smile that said, Thanks a lot, but it's strictly from nowhere, I just don't give a damn.

They began to see that he didn't give a damn and gradually they lost interest in him. It took a longer time for the manager to lose interest, but when it happened it was definite. The manager said bluntly, "Look, Gene. I've tried. God knows I've tried. But I can't help a man who don't wanna be helped. It's plain as day that you don't really care."

A shrug. And the lazy smile.

"Well, I'm sorry, Gene. Fact is, I got other clients need my attention. I'm afraid we gotta call it quits."

A slow nod. The lazy smile. The limp hand extended. His manager took it and patted him on the shoulder regretfully.

"Good luck, Gene."

As he walked out of the manager's office he passed a wall mirror and it showed him that his hair was turning white. But of course that didn't matter, either.

It was on the fourth floor, but he didn't take the elevator going down. For some reason the stairway seemed like a better idea. He walked down the stairs very slowly, enjoying the feeling of going down one step at a time, lower and lower, nice and easy, no effort at all.

One step at a time. He stopped going to the doctor. He started gambling. He was able to announce his bets in a very weak whisper. Then it became a louder whisper as the larynx continued to heal. And finally it was a cracked hoarse whisper that spoke every night at the dice tables or the card tables, with the lazy smile always there, the hair getting whiter, the eyes getting duller. And the cards and dice eating into his bank account, bringing it down from sixteen thousand to fourteen to eleven to eight and always going down. Some nights he'd get 'way ahead but he'd sit there and make stupid bets and manage to lose it all, and then more. One night it was five-card stud and he bet several thousand on his two pair against a very evident three queens. As he walked out with an empty wallet, he heard their comments drifting through the hall.

"Can't figure that one. He plays like he wants to lose."

"Sure. I've seen a lotta them that way. It's a certain condition they get in."

"Whaddya mean? What condition?"

"Like suicide. Doing it slow."

"Slow-motion suicide." And then, with a chuckle, "That's a new one."

"All right, ante up. Let's raise it a hundred."

He went back the next night and dropped another roll. It went on that way, and on one occasion he dropped forty-seven hundred dollars. The following day he walked into the bank and took out what was left. It amounted to a little over seven hundred. That afternoon he decided it was time to start with alcohol. He'd never tried alcohol, and he was curious as to what it would do.

It did plenty. It took him a few thousand feet above the rooftops, then dropped him with a thud, and the windup was an alley with a couple of muggers rolling him for every cent.

So then it had to be employment. He got a job washing dishes. But he wasn't thinking in terms of rent money or food money. He liked the idea of alcohol; it was a very pleasant beverage. He began spending most of his weekly earnings on whisky. As the months passed he needed more whisky, and more, and still more.

Going down. One step at a time.

He was fired from so many jobs that he lost count. He was picked up for drunkenness and tossed into cells where other booze hounds were sleeping it off. It reached the point that it always reaches when there isn't sufficient cash for whisky. He started to drink wine.

And from there it was only a few steps down to Skid Row.

On Skid Row it was a bed for fifty cents a night or any old floor where he happened to fall. Or else it was a free mattress in the alcoholic ward of whichever hospital had available space. No matter where it was, he'd be waking up at five-thirty and wanting more wine.

Twenty-nine cents for a bottle of muscatel. It was the outstanding value in the universe. There was no better way of killing time.

But sometimes he didn't have the twenty-nine cents, or any sum near it, and when that happened he'd go for anything that was offered. It might be homemade rotgut or something made from dandelions or ruined plums handed out free at the waterfront fruit market. It might be the liquid flame that they sold in Chinatown for a dime a jar. They made it from rice and it was colorless and had no smell, but going down the throat it was relentless and when it hit the belly it was merciless. And then of course there was the canned heat, strained through a dirty rag or a chunk of stale bread. And the bay rum. And on one very thirsty night, a really difficult night, there was a long delightful drink from a bottle of shoe polish.

Through winter and summer and winter again.

Through all the gray Novembers of getting up early to distribute circulars door to door. It had to be that kind of job. It didn't take much thinking. It paid two dollars a day, and sometimes three dollars when the weather was bad and the pavements were icy. On some mornings the sign was out, "No Work Today" and if the sign stayed there for three days in succession it was a financial catastrophe; it meant a long cold wait in the soup lines.

And sometimes he'd go lower than the soup lines, much lower than that, lower than any graph could indicate.

He'd stand in a shadowed doorway with his palm out.

"Got a nickel, buddy?"

The cold stare. "What for?"

He'd always reply with the lazy smile. "I'm kinda thirsty."

"Well, at least you're honest about it."

"That's right, mister." With the coin dropping into his palm. "It's the best policy."

But at other moments it was the worst policy and they'd look at him with disdain and disgust and walk away.

Or else they'd take the trouble to say, "Why don't you wise up?"

Or "Nothing doing. I don't give people money to poison themselves."

Or the sour voice of a blasphemer saying, "Tell you what. You go ask Jesus. He'll never fail you."

Then another Samaritan and another nickel. And finally, with fifteen cents in his hand, he'd go looking for Bones and Phillips. They'd pool their resources and make a beeline for the nearest joint that sold the bottled ecstasy.

It was the only ecstasy they sought.

But every now and then the other kind would come his way, a Tenderloin slut just slumping along and looking for company. It would be like a meeting of two mongrels in the street, no preliminaries necessary. Her bleary eyes would say, I need it tonight, I need it something awful.

He'd look at the shapeless chunk of female wreckage. No matter who she was, she'd be shapeless. If she didn't weigh much, she'd be a string bean. If she carried a lot of poundage, her body would resemble a barrel. The women of Skid Row had lost their figures long ago, along with their hopes and their yearnings. But the juice was still there, and every now and then it churned and bubbled and they had to announce their gender.

His eyes would say, All right, Lola.

Lola, Scotch-Portuguese-Cherokee. Or it would be Sally, of Polish-Peruvian ancestry. Or chinless Lucy, descended from Wales and Norway and certain ports on the shores of Arabia. And others whose prebirth histories went back to various ports along various shores. From anyplace at all where long dead sailors and drifters had met the long dead great-great-grand-mothers. So now the result was the walking debris, walking with Whitey toward the dusty hovel where the stuffing was spilling from the mattress.

At any rate, he'd think, it's a mattress, it's better than a cold floor.

Then in the dark it would happen as it happens with the animals. Nothing to say, nothing to think about, just doing it because one was male and the other was female. And it was preferable to being alone.

Yet somehow it was ecstasy, a sort of rummage-sale brand, but ecstasy nonetheless. For one spasmodic moment it took him away from River Street and sent him sailing up into cloud-land. And even though the clouds were gray, it was nice to be so high above the Skid Row roofs. He'd hear a sigh, and that was nice, too.

Later she'd say, "You wanna sleep here?"

"Might as well."

"All right. Good night, Whitey."

"Good night."

He'd fall asleep very fast. It was easy to fall asleep because there was nothing to occupy the mind. But at five-thirty in the morning he'd be wide awake and telling himself he needed a drink.

Why?

Then automatically it would come, the lazy smile. And he'd say to himself: Quit asking, bud. You know why.

It never went further than that. He'd get up from the mattress and walk out. He'd hit the street and join the early-morning parade that moved in no special direction, the dreary assemblage of stumble bums going this way and that way and getting nowhere.

From November to November. And on and on through all the gray Novembers.

Seven Novembers.

He stood there in the alley and his thoughts returned to now. He gazed across the back yard and through the kitchen window and saw the gray-green eyes and the bronze hair, the face and the body, the living cause of it all.

He wasn't sure what he was thinking or feeling. Whatever it was, there was too much of it, a mixture of uncertain contradictions that choked the channels of his brain. His mental mechanism was like a flooded carburetor.

But finally he managed a single thought, pushing it through the maze to make it objective and practical, saying to himself: All right, you've had it, you've seen her, and now it's time to get moving.

He told his legs to move, to backtrack down the alley and resume the march that would take him back to the station house.

And that'll do it, he thought. That'll really finish it, make it final and complete, so the Thirty-seventh District is the end of the road, it's the cashier's desk where you'll get the pay-off, the last installment of what you've earned.

You've really earned it, he thought. You've played a losing

game and actually enjoyed the idea of losing, almost like them freaks who get their kicks when they're banged around. You've heard tell about that type, the ones who pay the girls to burn them with lit matches, or put on high-heeled shoes and step on their faces. That kind of weird business. And it's always the same question. What makes them that way? But you never took the trouble to figure the answer. What the hell, it was their private worry, it didn't concern you.

Not much it didn't. So now you're getting to see. You're in that same bracket, buddy. You're one of them less-than-nothings who like the taste of being hurt. That makes you lower than the mice and the roaches. At least they try to save their skins, they got a normal outlook. But you, you're just a clown that ain't funny. And that's a sad picture, that's the saddest picture of all. Like on the outside it's the stupid crazy smile and inside it's a gloomy place where all they play is the blues.

He frowned. It was a solemn frown and he was saying to himself: It's high time you made some changes.

Like what? he asked himself.

He was searching for an answer and not looking at the kitchen window. His eyes aimed downward through the fence posts and all he saw was the rutted black earth of the back yard. The only sound was the purring of the kitten on the doorstep. Then another sound flowed in and at first he didn't hear it. The sound was cautious and very slow and creeping, coming down the narrow alley, coming toward him, stalking him, the way leopards stalk their supper. They were only a few feet away when he heard them and he looked up and sideways and saw the coffee-colored faces of two Puerto Ricans.

One of them carried a knife. It was a large ripple-edged bread knife. The other Puerto Rican was armed with a beer bottle that had its neck broken off.

He wasn't looking at the knife or the jagged-edged bottle. He was watching their eyes. Their eyes were dull, showing no emotion, only purpose, and he knew they were moving in to kill him.

7

H E TOLD himself he wasn't quite ready to be killed. His brain snatched at ideas and found one that seemed plausible. The lazy smile came onto his lips and he said, "Got a cigarette?"

It stopped them for just a moment. They looked at each other. The one with the knife was medium-sized and in his early twenties. He wore a bandage around his forehead and it was bloodstained and there was a wide gash of dried blood under his nose, slanting down past the corner of his mouth. The other Puerto Rican was about five-three and very skinny. He looked to be in his middle thirties and there were ribbons of baldness showing through his slicked-down jet-black hair. His left eye was puffed and almost closed and under it the cheekbone was swollen and shiny purple.

"Please," Whitey said. "I need a cigarette."

Again it stopped them. They didn't know what to make of it. The taller one came in very close to Whitey and held the knife up in front of his eyes and said, "You see thees? You know what thees is for?"

Whitey went on smiling past the blade. "You ain't even got a cigarette?"

"You keed me? You make fun?"

"I'm dying for a smoke," Whitey said.

"You dying, period," the little one said. He spoke with a less pronounced accent than the other Puerto Rican. "You gonna die right now, you know that?"

"Die?" Whitey told himself to blink a few times. "What for?"

"For damn good reason," the little one said. "You hate Puerto Ricans, we hate you. You want us dead, we want you dead."

"Me?" Whitey pointed to himself. "You mean me?"

"Yes, you," the little one said. "You're one of them."

"One of what? Whatcha talking about?"

"Hoodlum gang," the taller one said. "*Americano* sonsabeeches. Make trouble for us. Start riots. So what eet is, we fight you. We fight you to the end. You hear?"

Whitey shrugged. "I ain't fighting nobody. Crissake, I'm in trouble enough as it is."

"Trouble?" The little one moved in closer. His eyes narrowed. "What you mean? What trouble?"

"Police," Whitey said. "They're looking for me." He shrugged again. "They claim I killed a policeman."

"Yes?" The little one looked Whitey up and down. "You did that, eh? That makes me interested, you know? I think I know you from someplace." He nudged the broken bottle against Whitey's chest. "Keep talking."

"They took me to the station house," Whitey said. "I—"

"Wait," the little one interrupted. "What station house?"

"Thirty-seventh District."

"On Clayton Street? Captain Kinnard?"

"Yes," Whitey said.

The little one turned to the other Puerto Rican and said something in Spanish. Then he faced Whitey and his eyes were very narrow. "Tell me. When this happen?"

"Tonight," Whitey said.

Again the little one looked at his partner and spoke in Spanish. He spoke rapidly and somewhat excitedly and then he turned back to Whitey and said, "All right, we check this. We check it real careful. What happens at the station house?"

"It was jammed," Whitey said. "They'd brought in a flock of prisoners and everything was all bolixed up. I saw the Captain giving them the treatment and it was bad, it was plenty bad. What I mean, he was really doing damage, he was like a wild man. So I figured it was no place for anyone charged with killing a cop. I took a long chance and busted loose. The idea caught on and there was one hell of a commotion. Everyone was running for the doors and windows and—"

"All right," the little one said. He was smiling thinly. "It checks O.K. I wanted to be sure it was you."

"You were there?" Whitey asked.

"Yes," the little one said. "And him too." He pointed to the other Puerto Rican, who nodded, grinning. "We get nice greetings from the Captain. Very nice greetings." He indicated his puffed-up eye and bruised cheek. The taller Puerto Rican fingered the bloody gash running from nose to chin. They both grinned widely as they stood there displaying their injuries, and the little one said, "This Captain Kinnard, he hits very hard."

Whitey nodded. "I saw the way he hits."

"And that's why you run, eh? You don't want him to hit you?"

"That's it," Whitey said. "That's the general idea."

The little one laughed. "You do smart thing to run. Is no make sense to stay there and get hit. You don't run, you get hurt. So you run. You run away from station house." He laughed louder; it really tickled him. "Very smart," he said. "Much brains."

"It didn't take much thinking," Whitey said. "It was all down here," and he pointed to his legs.

"Yes," the little one said. "You tell them to move, they move." He laughed again. "I remember you now. Little white-haired bum who stands with detective on other side of room. Then the Captain, he comes walking slow, and you see him coming closer and you say to your feet, Come on, boys, move. So then you take off, you start to walk, and then you walk faster, and then you run. So we get same idea. We run too. We go out the door and down the street and the cops make chase but we get away."

"We damn sure get away," the taller Puerto Rican said, and he laughed loudly. "The cops, they look so funny. They jump up and down, they don't know what to do."

The little one was suddenly serious. He gave Whitey a side-ward look and said, "You know something, man? I think you did us a good favor. If not for you, we no get away."

"Well," Whitey said, "I'm glad you made it, anyway."

"You mean this? You are really glad?"

"Sure," Whitey said, "It ain't a healthy place, that station house. I like to see people staying healthy."

"What people?" The little one's eyes were narrow again.

"All people," Whitey said.

"Even the Puerto Ricans?"

"Of course," Whitey said. "Why not?"

"You don't hate Puerto Ricans?"

"I don't hate anybody."

"You sure about that?"

"Absolutely," Whitey said. "Why should I hate the Puerto Ricans?"

"Listen to me, mister. Listen careful, now. There is many Americans no like Puerto Ricans. Why they not like us? They say we dirty, we rotten. They say we steal and make trouble and jump on their women. They call us rats and snakes and all names like that. And then they come in gangs, they use clubs and split our heads wide open, we get our teeth knocked out, we get broken arms and legs, and some of us get killed. You think we gonna take that? You think we are damn fools?"

"I don't think anything," Whitey said. "It ain't for me to say who's right and who's wrong."

"You mean you are not interested? You don't care?"

Whitey smiled dimly. "You want the truth, don't you?"

"It better be the truth."

"All right," Whitey said. "Here's the way it is. If I said I cared, I'd be a goddamn liar. I don't give a damn what goes on here in the Hellhole. What happens in this neighborhood ain't none of my business."

"You don't live here?"

"No."

"Then where? Where you from?"

"Tenderloin."

"That is what I thought," the little one said. "You look like Tenderloin bum. In the eyes it shows, that look, that don't-give-a-damn look. But something else I see. Something under that look. It is what?"

Whitey didn't say anything.

"It is what?" the little one repeated. "You give it to me straight, mister. What you doing here?"

"Like I told you," Whitey said, "I'm running from the heat. I'm looking for a place to hide."

The little one was quiet for some moments. Then he turned to the other Puerto Rican and said something in Spanish. They commenced a rapid conversation in Spanish and it went on like that for the better part of a minute. Finally the little one looked at Whitey and said, "You sure you tell the truth?"

Whitey nodded.

"I don't know," the little one said. He looked down at the

broken bottle in his hand, his eyes centered on the jagged edge. "I am not so sure."

"Add it up," Whitey said. "You saw it with your own eyes. You saw me running out of the station house. So it figures I'm hot and I'm looking for a hideout."

There was another flow of quiet. The light pouring from the kitchen window came slanting down across the back yard to make a pool of vague yellow glow in the narrow alley. It showed the thoughtful, doubtful frown on the face of the little Puerto Rican. The taller Puerto Rican was not frowning, not appearing thoughtful or dubious or in any way affected by the issue. His face was blank and his eyes were focused on Whitey's belly, the knife in his hand pointed at the same spot. His attitude was purely functional, like a poultry-market laborer getting set to kill a chicken.

Then the taller Puerto Rican said something in Spanish and took a slow step forward. The little one blocked him with an outswept arm and said, "No."

"*Sí*," the taller one said. He was very anxious to start using the knife.

"No," the little one said. He pushed his partner backward. He looked at Whitey and spoke quietly and slowly. "I tell you something, man. You lucky for now. But maybe only for now. We take you to boss and hear what he says."

"Boss?" Whitey asked.

"Sure, we got boss." The little one smiled thinly. "This riot thing is big fight, man. Is like real war. You know how is with soldiers? The soldiers, they need leader. We got leader."

The little one made a gesture telling Whitey to turn and start walking. Whitey turned, and in doing so he caught a glimpse of the kitchen window. It was dark now and it had no importance, no meaning at all. It was just like all the other dark windows, and he thought: Well, anyway, it was interesting while it lasted.

Then he was walking slowly, with the Puerto Ricans walking behind him. The alley was very narrow and they had to move along in single file. For a moment he played with the idea of running. But he knew they could run just as fast, or faster. He felt sort of sorry for them, not pity really, just sorry they were having such a rough time.

8

A T THE end of the alley there was a narrow cobblestoned street and they crossed it and went down another alley that had no paving and was mostly mud and stones. All the dwellings were wood, or sheet-metal roofed with tar paper. In the back yards there were a lot of cats and some dogs and he could hear them busily engaged in looking for food or romance or argument. There was no loud barking or meowing, just the scuffling and the scurrying, the convulsive squirming and the sound of furry bodies rolling around. At intervals he saw large rats darting between the fence posts. The rats were very large. He told himself he'd never seen them that big. He saw two of them leaping down from a fence and going after a cat. The cat was not yet full grown and it wasn't quite sure what it should do. As it hesitated, the rats pounced on it, but then a larger cat lunged in and the rats scampered away.

The alley extended for three blocks and gave way to a vacant lot heaped with rubbish and garbage and animal excrement. They moved along the edge of the lot, going east toward the river, and now he could see the lights along the water front, the lamps in the warehouses, and here and there the lighted portholes of freighters and tankers. With the little Puerto Rican giving directions, they skirted a lumberyard and another vacant lot and a wide area filled with scrap metal, going north now and entering a network of winding alleys that sloped downward and then up and then down again. The dwellings here were very old, with the wooden walls splintered and some of them partially caved in, and there were large gaps where there wasn't any wall at all. The wind whistled shrilly coming in from the river and racing through the gaps in the walls. Most of the dwellings were two-story structures, and he wondered what was keeping them upright. They looked very weak and flimsy, sort of leaning over and just about ready to go.

He felt a hand on his shoulder and he stopped and heard the little one saying, "In here."

It was one of the two-story houses. It didn't have a doorstep and there was no glass in the first-story windows. The windows were stuffed with cardboard and newspapers to keep the wind out. Along the base of the front wall there were jagged holes where rats had gnawed through the wood. The wood looked easy for the teeth of the rats; it had long ago lost its hardness and resistance, it was more like the pulpy fungus-mushy substance of rotted trees.

The taller Puerto Rican stood close to Whitey while the little one stepped up to the door. The little one hit the heel of his palm against the wood, hit three times and waited, hit again and waited, and then hit very hard with the back of his hand, the wood creaking and groaning from the impact of his knuckles.

From inside the house there was a query in Spanish.

"*Soy yo, Luis,*" the little one said. "*Luis y Carlos.*"

"*Cómo?*"

"*Luis.*" The little one spoke louder. "*Luis, digo!*"

"*Qué pasa?*"

"Goddamnit," the little one said. Then he shouted something in Spanish. After that, in English, "Come on, you dumb bastard, open the door."

The door opened. The man in the doorway was very old and wore a torn overcoat and tattered gloves and had a muffler wrapped tightly over his chin. He was shivering and his thin lips were more blue-gray than red. He made an impatient and somewhat frantic gesture, telling them to come inside so he could close the door and shut out the cold.

Luis entered the house. Carlos shoved Whitey and followed him in. From one of the back rooms there was the glow of lighted candles. The flickering light came into this room and showed some people sleeping on the floor. There was no furniture except for a chair that was used for a table. On the chair Whitey saw an empty wine bottle and some unused candles and the melted wax from previous candles.

They went into the next room and there were more people sleeping on the floor. Several of them had blankets and the others were covered with assorted burlap bags and old carpets. A few were covered with newspaper. Whitey saw there were a lot of children sleeping close together, their arms flung over one another, their legs drawn up close to their bellies. He saw a very short, very fat woman sleeping flat on her back. Her mouth was open and she was snoring loudly. With one arm she held a sleeping infant, and her other arm provided a pillow for a two-year-old. There were several mothers holding their children while they slept. It was not a large room, but there were many sleepers on the floor. He saw it was really crowded in here, and as he walked behind Luis he stepped carefully to avoid treading on them. Luis and Carlos walked with less care, ignoring the fretful mutterings as their feet made contact with chins and shoulders and outstretched arms.

Then there was a stairway with some of the steps missing, and other steps sagging as he climbed behind Luis, with Carlos following. On the steps and along the walls there were a great many roaches and bugs, moving slowly and contentedly in the dim light coming down from the second floor.

The light on the second floor was from a single candle placed on a window sill. Also, some light was showing through cracks in a door at the far end of the hall. They went down the hall and Luis opened the door. Several men were standing in the room and talking quietly in Spanish. A few men were seated on wooden boxes arranged along the walls. In the center of the room there was a pile of baseball bats, broken bottles, lengths of lead pipe, and a varied assortment of bread knives, butcher knives, switchblades, and meat cleavers. As the men talked they gestured toward the collection of weapons. It appeared they were having a problem with the weapons. They were deeply concerned with the problem, but when they saw Whitey they stopped talking. They stared questioningly at Luis and Carlos.

It went on like that and there was no sound in the room. Then one of the men moved slowly toward Luis and said something in Spanish. The man was pointing to Whitey and wanting to know who he was and what he was doing here. Luis began to talk rapidly, addressing the man as Gerardo. It was obvious he had much respect for the man, because he kept saying "Gerardo" in the way that overly humble people who talk to doctors keep saying "Doctor," starting or ending each phrase with "Doctor." While Luis talked, Gerardo wore a detached gaze that gave the impression that he wasn't listening. And when Luis was finished, Gerardo didn't bother to comment. He was looking at the pile-up of weapons on the floor. He said in English, "Is not enough meat cleavers. Little knives no good. We need more meat cleavers."

"I get some," Luis said.

"You?" Gerardo looked directly at Luis. "You go out and find meat cleavers?"

"Sure," Luis said eagerly. "I do it now, Gerardo. I go right now. You say O.K., Gerardo?"

Gerardo said very quietly, "I send you out for meat cleavers, maybe you bring back something else. Maybe you bring another gringo."

There was a laugh from Carlos. The other Puerto Ricans laughed also. They did it hesitantly at first, and then it really struck them funny and there was much laughter in the room.

"Shut up," Gerardo said to them. And instantly they stopped laughing. But Carlos couldn't check it completely and he was grinning open-mouthed. Gerardo looked at Carlos and said, "Is not funny."

Carlos got rid of the grin.

"Is for sure not funny," Gerardo said. Again he was looking at Luis. "Is more sad, I think. Is very sad my men they always make mistakes."

"I—" Luis was swallowing hard. "Leesen, Gerardo—"

"You keep quiet now," Gerardo said. "You do smart thing, you keep quiet."

Luis swallowed very hard and looked down at the floor.

Gerardo turned to Whitey and said, "They bring you here, they make mistake."

"Not me," Carlos said quickly. "Eet wasn't my idea. I tell Luis we have this man in alley, we kill him there. Luis he say no."

"Bad mistake," Gerardo went on, as though Carlos weren't there. "Very bad." He nodded slowly and solemnly. The single bulb that dangled on a wire from the ceiling was directly over his head and the glow was focused on him, high-lighting his features. He was an exceptionally good-looking man in his middle thirties. His build was lean and nicely balanced and he stood about five-nine. He featured a thick crop of heavily greased straight combed black hair, and every hair was in place. It was evident he gave much attention to his scalp. Also, his eyebrows were neatly trimmed, and his face looked cleaner than the other faces.

But that was the only difference. His clothing was just as tattered and shabby as the rags they wore. He was wearing a very old overcoat that looked about ready to come apart. At one time it had been camel's-hair but now it was only a weary jumble of loose yellow threads. He saw Whitey looking at the overcoat and he said, "Is nice? You like it?"

"Yes," Whitey said. "It's a very nice coat."

"Is very expensive," Gerardo said. "Is genuine camel's-hair."

Whitey nodded. He started to say something, and then, whatever it was, he lost track of it, and he stood there looking blankly at Gerardo's overcoat.

Gerardo frowned slightly. "Why you do this? Why you look at the coat?"

Whitey didn't say anything. He wondered why he was staring at the camel's-hair coat. He tried to look away but the coat wouldn't let him turn his head. He told himself it was just a piece of castoff clothing that the Puerto Rican had lifted from a rubbish can. That's all it is, he insisted to himself.

He went on staring at it.

Gerardo took a step toward him. "Here," Gerardo said quietly, "I give you a better look."

The camel's-hair coat was very close to his eyes and he blinked hard.

"What is it?" Gerardo asked. "What this thing with coat?"

"I don't know," Whitey said. He was telling the truth. He really didn't know why he was doing it, staring at the ragged garment as though it had some meaning, some importance. Of course there was a reason, there had to be a reason. Well, he thought, maybe it'll come, but right now you're nowhere near it. Just then Carlos laughed again.

Gerardo looked at Carlos and said, "*Qué hay?* What is funny now?"

Carlos was laughing loudly and pointing to Whitey. "He likes coat. He wants you to take it off and geeve it to him."

"You think so?" Gerardo murmured. "You think that is what he wants?"

"Sure." Carlos was shaking with laughter. "Thees is crazy

man here. In alley he sees we come to kill him, he pay no mind to that. He ask if we got cigarette. Now we bring him here to kill him and he wants your overcoat."

The other Puerto Ricans were grinning.

Gerardo had a calculating look on his face. He turned to Whitey and his eyes drilled into Whitey's eyes. He said, "Maybe Carlos is wrong. Maybe you not crazy like he thinks."

Whitey stared at the loose threads of the camel's-hair overcoat.

He heard Gerardo saying, "In school, long ago, I study the numbers. *La matemática*. They teach me one and one it equals two. And two and two it equals four. And four and four—you see? I learn to add the numbers. Is what I'm doing now."

Carlos had stopped laughing. His face was solemn and he said emphatically, "Four and four is ten."

"No," Gerardo said. He wasn't smiling. "Is not ten. Is eight. Is always eight."

Carlos shrugged. "No matter to me."

"That is right," Gerardo said. "No matter to you, because you no can add the numbers. So you stay away from numbers, you leave that to me. I do all thinking here, all adding up the score."

"Yes," Carlos agreed quickly. "Yes, Gerardo."

Gerardo looked at Luis. "And you? What you say?"

Luis blinked a few times. Then he nodded slowly.

"Not enough," Gerardo murmured. "Say it with the mouth."

"You do all thinking," Luis said. "You the boss."

"Always," Gerardo said. "Always the boss."

"Yes." Luis nodded again. "Sure. Always. You top man, Gerardo. You the leader."

"And good leader, too," Gerardo said. "I no make mistakes. But my men, they make mistakes sometimes. They no do like I say." He turned to Whitey and his tone was mild and conversational. "My men, they sometimes give me a headache. They make me sick sometimes. Is no easy job to be leader of these men."

Carlos opened his mouth to say something.

"Close it," Gerardo said. "Keep it closed." And then he looked at the other Puerto Ricans. "Keep quiet, everybody. No move around. Just stand and listen."

They stood quietly, stiffly, fully attentive.

Gerardo said, "I tell you now what I tell you many times before. This house is secret place. Is headquarters. Is what is called center of operations. So then is understood we no take chances they find us here. They find us here, they wipe us out. We finished."

"We fight them," one of the Puerto Ricans said. "We fight until we die."

"You like to die?" Gerardo asked quietly. "You think it is a happy business?"

"I think we should stop waiting," the man said. "Let them find us here. Let them come. Is better that way. We have show-down battle and get it ended once and for all."

"You are brave man, Chávez."

The man stood there with his spine erect and his head held high and he was gazing upward like someone paying allegiance to a banner.

"Yes," Gerardo said. "You are very brave. You are also very stupid."

The man winced. His chin sagged.

"You are a goddamn fool, Chávez. You need examination of the brain. We no make fight to die. We fight to win, to teach gringos a lesson they no forget. To make them understand we no get pushed around, we no get kicked in face. They treat us like animals, we strike back like animals. But not like clumsy jackass with nothing inside the head. Instead, we hide and wait, we sharpen our teeth, we make our plans very careful. When time is right, we jump on them, we make big riot and they run away."

"They no run away tonight," the man said. He looked sullen.

"Tonight was bad luck," Gerardo told him. "We make good plans but they get break when cops come."

The man's face remained sullen. "Other times was bad luck too. Always something happens."

"You saying it is my fault?" Gerardo asked mildly.

The man didn't reply.

"Say it, Chávez. You can say it. Go on, say it."

Chávez took a deep breath. He was a medium-sized but strongly built man in his middle forties. His eyes aimed past

Gerardo and he said quietly, "I no like these riots in street. Is no way for men to fight. Is not respectable."

"Respectable?" Gerardo murmured. He allowed himself the slightest trace of a smile. "What you mean, Chávez?"

Chávez looked directly at Gerardo and said, "I am respectable man. Very poor in the pockets but not lacking in good manners, clean life. I no drink too much or use dope or—"

"So," Gerardo cut in. The smile was fading. "So what are you trying to say?"

"I am not a bum in the streets," Chávez said. "I am working man with family. I come here from San Juan with my wife and seven children. Much trouble finding job, getting place to live. Is here a bad neighborhood with roughnecks, hoodlums, thugs. For reason we not know, they hate *puertorriqueños*, they make trouble. So then we do the same. We come out on River Street and give them plenty bad business, much commotion. The police they come and we run back here to hiding place. But I no like to hide. Why should I hide? Better I should make announcement, I should give hoodlums my address, say to them, 'Now you know where I live, you want to get me you know where to come, I wait for you, I fight you with all my strength.'"

"And then," Gerardo murmured, "they come in a mob. They break down the door and—"

"They no break it down. I open it for them."

"And they walk in. They smash your head. Maybe they kill you."

"At least I die fighting in house where I live. I die respectable."

Gerardo was silent for some moments. He gazed at the faces of the other Puerto Ricans. Some of them were nodding in solemn agreement with Chávez. These were the older men. The younger ones were frowning thoughtfully. And a few, both young and old, had nothing in their eyes. They hadn't been affected by what Chávez had said; they were waiting for Gerardo to react so they could mirror his reaction.

Finally Gerardo said, "I tell you something, Chávez. Maybe you die respectable this minute. Maybe I kill you."

Chávez stood stiffly. Again he was staring past Gerardo. He didn't say anything.

"Yes," Gerardo said. "Maybe I do it. Is my privilege, you know.

I am leader here. Like general of army. Like captain of ship. I have full right to stop rebellion."

"I no make rebellion," Chávez said. "I only make statement."

Gerardo smiled again. It was a twisted smile. He said, "Sometimes is very expensive to make statements."

And then he took the bread knife from Carlos's hand. He ran his finger along the blade.

Chávez looked at the knife. In his eyes there was more sadness than worry. The sadness deepened his voice as he said, "You would do this, Gerardo? You would put me in the grave?"

"I am thinking about it," Gerardo said. He went on running his finger along the blade. "I am thinking maybe you are not useful now. Like broken wheel. Keeps other wheels from moving."

Chávez took a very deep breath and held it. He stood there waiting to be stabbed.

Gerardo stabbed him. It was more slash than stab, and the knife went in fairly deep, going into the shoulder and ripping down along the arm to the elbow. Then Gerardo stepped back and the knife slashed wide with the blade cutting a deep gash across the forehead of Chávez. "*Ai, Jesús*," Chávez moaned, and Gerardo cut him again, slicing his cheek, the blood spurting from a slanting gash that started under the cheekbone and ended at the mouth.

Chávez fell to his knees. He had one hand pressed against his carved cheek and with his other hand he was trying to stop the flow of blood from his forehead and his upper arm. His hand made a rapid blurry motion going from forehead to shoulder and back to forehead. He was getting a lot of blood all over himself and there was much blood on the floor.

Gerardo was looking at Carlos and saying, "This is good knife, you know? I think I will keep it."

"Sure." Carlos nodded eagerly. "You keep it, boss. Is present from me."

"Thank you," Gerardo said politely. He wiped the dripping blade on his sleeve. And then, gesturing with the blade to indicate the bleeding man, "Take him out of here. Take him downstairs, give him some water. Make bandages."

A few of the older men came forward and lifted Chávez from the floor. And as they stood him upright he fainted. They carried him out of the room.

Gerardo looked at the blood on the floor. "Statements," he said. "My famous fighters, all they do is make statements and mistakes."

The Puerto Ricans were quiet. Some of them were staring at the knife in Gerardo's hand. Most of them were trying not to look at the knife.

Gerardo studied their faces. He said, "Do I hear further talk? Is anyone else like to make statements?"

The men kept their mouths shut tightly.

"All right, then," Gerardo said. "So now we finished with making statements. Now I deal with man who make mistake."

He turned his head slowly and looked directly at Luis.

Luis opened his mouth just a little. Then his face was like that of a child forcing down some castor oil. He swallowed very hard.

"I say it now like I say it many times before," Gerardo said. "I say this is important secret place and you no bring gringos here. There is chance gringo gets away. And then what?"

Luis swallowed hard again. He put his hands in his trousers pockets and took them out and put them in again.

Gerardo pointed at Whitey and said to Luis, "You see this man? You see what he has on his face?"

"On his face?" Luis mumbled, his lips twitching nervously.

"Yes," Gerardo said. "On his face."

"Is just a face," Luis said. He managed a slight shrug. "Like any other face."

Gerardo nodded slowly. "Yes, very true. Like any face that has eyes and mouth. You see what is? You understand what I mean?"

Luis blinked several times. He shook his head vaguely.

"All right, I tell you," Gerardo said. "With the eyes he see. With the mouth he talks."

"But—"

"You hear what I say, Luis? With the mouth he talks."

Carlos let out a murmuring laugh and said, "This gringo no talk. We make sure he no get away."

Moving quickly, Carlos reached toward the pile of weapons on the floor and selected a meat cleaver.

Gerardo smiled. "And now you fix him?"

"Sure," Carlos said. "I fix thees bastard so he no talk."

Carlos raised the meat cleaver above his shoulder and started walking slowly toward Whitey.

9

"NO," GERARDO SAID. He motioned Carlos to stay away from Whitey.

"But why?" Carlos frowned puzzledly. "Is easy to do it. Is very simple job."

"And then?" Gerardo murmured.

Carlos shrugged. "Get rid of body."

"How? Where?"

Carlos shrugged again. "Dig hole. Bury him. Or maybe throw him in river. No trouble."

"Plenty trouble," Gerardo said. "No place to dig outside this house. Ground too hard. Big stones. Too much cement. Is softer ground on empty lot. But empty lot too far away."

"Not so far, Gerardo." Carlos was very anxious to get started with the meat cleaver. "We carry body there in a few minutes."

"In a few minutes much can happen," Gerardo said. "Is many police in this area. Maybe they see we carry something. They get curious, you know? The police, they are very curious people."

"Maybe—" Carlos was stumped for a moment. He tried again, saying, "Maybe is better the river. Is much closer the river."

"Is not close enough," Gerardo said. "The river is three blocks away."

Carlos looked disappointed. Then all at once his eyes lit up and he said eagerly, "Listen, Gerardo. I have answer to problem. We kill him and keep him here."

"Here? In this house?"

"Sure," Carlos said. "We put him in closet. We put him under bed. Plenty of places to put him."

Gerardo was thoughtful for a moment. Then he shook his head.

"But why not?" Carlos asked.

"Dead body make smell," Gerardo said. "Is enough stink in this house without more stink."

"It no have stink," Carlos persisted. "We steal perfume from dime store. We—"

"Oh, shut up," Gerardo said wearily. "You sometimes talk like damn fool." And then, slowly and emphatically, "Is no good to kill him here. Is much risk. Would not be risk if we had plumbing. Easy that way. Down the drain. In pieces cut him up and put it down the drain. But we no have plumbing. I think of that when I tell you many times, you kill a gringo, you do it in gringo section of Hellhole."

Carlos slowly lowered the meat cleaver. He tossed it onto the pile of weapons in the center of the floor.

During the conversation between Gerardo and Carlos, it had been difficult for Whitey to breathe. For the past several moments he'd been holding his breath. Now he let it out and it came out fast.

But he knew the relief was only temporary. He was watching Gerardo's face and focusing on Gerardo's eyes. He saw what was in Gerardo's eyes and again he had trouble breathing. His chest felt tight and it seemed his lungs were out of commission.

Gerardo turned to Luis and said, "You see what bad mistake you have made? You bring him here and now we have big problem."

Luis wet his lips. He didn't say anything. He was looking at the knife in Gerardo's hand.

"Big serious problem," Gerardo said. "And all because you no listen to what I say. I think maybe I teach you something, Luis. I teach you to listen."

Gerardo took a step toward Luis. He'd been holding the knife loosely and now his fingers tightened on the handle.

"Gerardo—" Luis was barely able to produce sound. His eyes widened as he saw the blade coming closer. And then in a frenzy of trying to prevent himself from getting cut, he gasped, "No problem, Gerardo." His arm trembled as he pointed to Whitey. "No problem with this man. This man friend."

"Friend?" Gerardo was in the midst of taking another step toward Luis. He stopped and murmured, "You make joke, Luis? This gringo here, you call him a friend?"

"Is many gringos no hate Puerto Ricans," Luis said.

Gerardo smiled. He folded his arms. "So," he said with thin

sarcasm. "So now we hear speech. Go ahead, Luis. Make speech."

"This man," Luis began, speaking slowly and carefully, working hard to choose the right words, "he is very good friend of Puerto Ricans. He do us big favor tonight. In station house he play trick on cops and is much excitement and we make escape. Me and Carlos and other Puerto Ricans run out the door. We make good getaway. And so you see, Gerardo. If not for this man, we still there in station house and then we go to prison."

Gerardo turned slowly and looked at Whitey. "Is true?"

Whitey nodded.

"You were arrested in riot?" Gerardo asked.

"No," Whitey said. "I wasn't mixed up in the riot. I ain't been in any of these riots."

"Why were you arrested?"

"They said I—" He thought about the dead policeman. It occurred to him that maybe he had a chance now. There was no friendship between these men and the Thirty-seventh District. It was possible that Gerardo would be favorably impressed with a cop-killer. "Well, I might as well tell you. I killed a policeman."

"You did what?"

"He killed a cop," Luis said. "You hear what he tells you? He no fight the Puerto Ricans. Only thing he do is kill a cop."

"Be quiet," Gerardo told Luis. "I let this man talk for himself." He went on looking at Whitey. "Tell me, now. About this cop. When you kill him?"

"Tonight," Whitey said.

"Where?"

"In an alley."

"What alley?" Gerardo's eyes were getting narrow. "I am adding the numbers again, mister. I am listening to you very careful. Be sure you give me the right numbers so is adding up so everything fits. Maybe it winds up you get a break, after all. If this is all true what you say, is possible you live to be old man. If not true, is gonna be very bad. I no like to be played for fool. I take you for a walk somewhere and you die slow. Is not pleasant to die slow. Sometimes it hurts so much you go crazy before you die."

"I get the idea," Whitey said. He told himself to stay as close to the truth as possible. "It was an alley not far from here."

"In this neighborhood? In Hellhole?"

"That's right."

"Give me location," Gerardo said. "I want location of alley."

"I can't remember exactly."

"You can't?" Gerardo murmured. "I think you can. A man kills someone, he remembers the exact location."

"I ain't familiar with this neighborhood," Whitey said. "I don't live around here. There's so many alleys—"

"All right, we'll forget the alley. We'll come back to it later. So now we talk about the cop. What happens with the cop? How you kill him?"

"I hit him on the head."

Gerardo was quiet for a long moment. Then, scarcely moving his lips, "With what?"

With what? Whitey asked himself. In his mind he saw the dying policeman, the wet red seeping through the scalp, and shiny streams of it flowing down the cop's face. Well, it needed something heavy to crack a skull that badly, so maybe the weapon was a brick, or a hammer, or then again it could have been a baseball bat.

"Baseball bat," Whitey said.

Gerardo looked at the collection of knives and lead pipes and baseball bats resting in a heap in the center of the floor. "Now tell me," he said. "Where you get the baseball bat?"

"I found it in the alley," Whitey said. He waited for Gerardo to ask another question. Gerardo was smiling at him. There was something in the smile that told him to keep talking. Or maybe it wasn't that kind of smile. Maybe he'd loused it up already and further talk was useless. He gazed past Gerardo's smiling lips and begged himself to keep talking, to make it clear and brief and fully logical. He said, "The cop was chasing me. I tried to rob a store and the job went haywire and this cop was chasing me down the alley. So then I tripped and fell and he closed in on me. I looked for something to hit him with and I saw the baseball bat. It was busted, it was broken off at the handle. I got a grip on it and when he grabbed for me I let him have it and it cracked his head wide open. Before

I could get away there were other cops moving in. They put cuffs on me and took me to the station house."

He told himself it sounded all right. He wondered if Gerardo thought it sounded all right.

He heard Gerardo saying, "You tell me more about this cop. What he look like?"

"He had gray hair," Whitey said. "Well, anyway, it was mostly gray. He was sort of beefy, and he looked around forty-five or so. Or maybe older. It was hard to tell, there was so much blood on his face."

"All right," Gerardo interrupted. "Is enough about the cop. So now we come back to alley where it happen. You give me location of alley."

"I told you, I can't remember."

"Is important that you remember. Is very important."

"Well—" Whitey frowned and bit his lip. He wasn't trying to remember the location of the alley. He told himself he damn well knew the location. And it would be nice if he could also know what Gerardo was getting at. He was trying very hard to figure what Gerardo had in mind.

"Come on," Gerardo said. "Is no good this stalling. I no like stalling."

"The alley . . ." He hesitated. He wondered why he hesitated.

"Come on," Gerardo said. "Quick now. Where this alley is?"

"Near River Street." And then, as he said it, he had the feeling it was an error to be truthful about the location.

But Gerardo seemed satisfied. Gerardo was nodding slowly and saying, "We getting closer now. Is very good." He turned and looked at the other Puerto Ricans. He gave them a pleasant smile and held it for some moments while he went on nodding. Finally, still looking at the Puerto Ricans, he said to Whitey, "Now tell me, mister. This alley, it is east or west of River?"

"East," Whitey said. But to himself, without sound: What goes on here? What the hell is he building? Maybe you should have said west instead of east. Well, you can fix that if you want to. You can still give him a false location. Trouble is, you don't know what to give him. Hell, you're sure having a bad time tonight. And all because you had to see her again. All right, let's not start with that. You've had enough of that. What you hafta do now is think in terms of staying alive. Maybe if you use your brains you can save your ass. All right, then, what's it gonna be? You gonna switch the location of the alley? Come on, make up your mind, the man's waiting. I think the best thing is to play it straight with the geography. He wants the exact location of the alley and you better give him what he wants. But why does he want it? Oh, well, the hell with it, you'll hafta take your chances and give it to him.

Gerardo was saying, "How far, mister? How far east of River Street?"

"One block," he said. "Make it the middle of the block. It's a very narrow alley and it's off a little side street."

Gerardo started to laugh. It wasn't much of a sound, it was almost no sound at all.

"Yes," Gerardo said. And then he laughed just a bit louder. "Is very funny, you know?"

"What's funny?" Whitey murmured.

"Is same alley," Gerardo laughed. "Same policeman."

"What?" Whitey said. He blinked several times. "What are you talking about?"

Gerardo didn't answer. Now he was laughing loudly. The other Puerto Ricans had no idea why he was laughing and they looked at one another. A few were frowning puzzledly. And some were trying to get with it, grinning and looking foolish and uncertain. The ones who were fanatically loyal to Gerardo were imitating his laughter. Carlos was laughing the loudest and holding his sides and choking on his forced guffaws as he wondered what all this comedy was about.

Suddenly Gerardo stopped laughing. Then all the laughing stopped and they waited for Gerardo to speak. He was in no hurry to speak, and for some moments all he did was run his finger along the edge of the bread knife in his hand.

Whitey looked at the knife. He looked at the tattered and scraggly fabric of Gerardo's camel's-hair overcoat. He thought: It's funny about the coat. And the knife is funny, too. Yes, everything here is very funny. It's just as funny as rain coming down on a graveyard.

Then Gerardo was saying, "You tell good story, mister. Very

much truth in it. But not truth enough. Not hardly truth enough."

Whitey took a deep breath. He held it.

"You no kill policeman," Gerardo said.

Oh, Whitey said without sound. Oh, God. God Almighty.

"Because," Gerardo said very slowly, "I know who kill policeman. Name of killer is Gerardo."

10

THEN IT was quiet in the room and it was a thick quiet that came in layers, falling on Whitey and giving him the feeling that he was being smothered by it.

He heard Gerardo saying, "You want to say something?"

He shook his head.

"Is very sensible," Gerardo said. "You say nothing because there is nothing you can say."

"Gerardo—" It was Carlos. "You really kill the cop?"

Gerardo nodded. His tone was matter-of-fact as he said, "It was during the riot. He grabbed me from the back. He not see what I hold in my hand. I think it was a hammer. Maybe a monkey-wrench. I no remember for sure. Only thing I remember is how I hit him. I hit him on head real hard."

"Good," Carlos said. "I no like cops. Is with cops like cowboys in movie pictures say about Indians. Best policeman is dead policeman."

"This one was stupid policeman," Gerardo said.

"All policemen, they are stupid," Carlos said.

"No," Gerardo murmured. "Not all."

"They are stupid like jackass," Carlos insisted.

Gerardo looked at him and said, "Your mouth, it is always busy. Why you have such a busy mouth?"

"I only say—"

"You say nothing." Gerardo spoke very quietly. "You talk and talk and what comes out is nothing."

"All right," Carlos said. "All right. All right."

Gerardo looked at the other Puerto Ricans. "Listen careful now. Is what I'm saying very important. I go out now with gringo. I take him for a walk. I come back in fifteen, twenty minutes, maybe half an hour. You wait here. You no go outside for any reason. You stay inside so outside it's quiet, so me and gringo we go for nice quiet walk. You understand?"

They nodded.

Gerardo looked at Whitey. "Come on, mister. We go now. You walk in front of me."

736

Whitey moved slowly toward the door. One of the Puerto Ricans opened the door. Gerardo stepped in close behind Whitey and said, "I give you advice, mister. You try to run, I throw the knife. With throwing a knife I am first-rank expert. You don't believe it, you try me out."

"I believe it," Whitey said.

They were approaching the doorway and Carlos came up to Gerardo and said, "Look, boss, I have idea. I think is best you throw him in river. No trace."

Gerardo smiled at Carlos. "Is that your idea?"

Carlos nodded vigorously.

"And you think it is good idea?"

"Sure," Carlos said. "Is best to throw him in river with something heavy tied to feet so he stays down. And then they no find him."

"But I want them to find him," Gerardo said.

"What?" Carlos said. "What you mean?"

Gerardo smiled widely now. He was very much amused at Carlos. He said, "Is much luck for me when they find him. Is much luck for all of us."

Carlos frowned. "I do not understand."

"Because you are an idiot," Gerardo said affectionately. He turned to the other Puerto Ricans. "You see what is my plan? You know why I want them to find him?"

They stared blankly at Gerardo.

"Well, then," Gerardo said, "I explain, and maybe you learn something and you see how I use the brains." He paused to make it impressive, and went on: "The police, they are wanting this man here they think is cop-killer. And while they look for him they no close the case. So in meantime is possible they get information somewhere and they find out cop-killer is Gerardo."

"Is bad if that happen," someone said.

"But it will not happen," Gerardo said. "I make sure it will not happen. They will find dead body of cop-killer and then everything is all right. Case is closed."

"*Bueno*," someone said with admiration. "*Muy bueno.*"

"You clever, boss," another one said. "You real clever."

"For sure," Carlos said loudly. "Is nobody clever like Gerardo."

Some of the men were grinning to show their fondness and praise and worship for the leader. Gerardo winked at them and they winked back. But there were others who looked at one another with solemn disapproval of what was happening. Luis was looking at Whitey and his eyes were dismal, saying without sound, Is not fair, is goddamn shame.

"Is time to go," Gerardo said to Whitey. He gave him a gentle shove toward the doorway. Whitey walked out of the room and Gerardo stayed close behind him going down the hall to the stairs.

They went down the stairs and through the rooms where the women and children and older people were sleeping on the floor. Gerardo opened the front door and they walked out together, Gerardo now moving close at his side so that their shoulders touched.

"Slow and easy, now," Gerardo said softly. "Is just a couple friends going out for a walk. So we walk nice and slow and peaceful. O.K.?"

Whitey didn't answer. He was looking down at Gerardo's right arm. There was nothing in Gerardo's hand, and he thought: Where's he got the knife? But then he took a closer look and he saw the tip of the shiny blade projecting from the ragged sleeve of the camel's-hair overcoat.

They walked slowly through the labyrinth of winding alleys. It was very cold and the wind rushing down the alleys was a mean, wet wind that yowled like something alive and going berserk. He wanted to pull up the collar of his coat but he didn't want to move his arms because maybe Gerardo would get the wrong idea. He kept his hands in his pockets and wished he could pull up the collar of his coat. He told himself it was too damn cold out here. Yeah, he said dryly to himself, you're in a fine position to worry about the weather. Where you're going, there ain't gonna be no weather.

But it would be nice if he could have a drink. One final drink. Anything at all, just so it had some sock in it. Maybe a shot of that goathead, that stuff manufactured by Jones Jarvis. That would taste real good right now. Well, no matter what it was, it would taste good. Even if it was antifreeze, it would taste good. He'd heard of them drinking antifreeze and going blind or getting a fast ride to the morgue, but if some of it was offered to him now, he'd grab it. Sure he'd grab it, and drink it, and what would he have to lose? At least he'd get that one last jolt before the curtain came down.

Goddamn, he said to himself, you're sure a sucker for liquid refreshment. But you ain't alone in that, you sure got plenty of company there. I wonder what Bones and Phillips are doing. They still sitting on the pavement in front of that flophouse? They sure were thirsty. That empty bottle wasn't easy to look at. Well, maybe they put their heads together and figured something out, and got their hands on another bottle. That would be good news. Maybe someone dropped a dollar bill in the street and they picked it up. Yeah, sure. Fat chance. Like the chance you got now. All right, don't start that routine. That ain't gonna help. Well, as far as that's concerned, nothing's gonna help.

Now they were away from the alleys and moving across the flat wide area on which were heaps of scrap metal. They were going toward the lumberyard and they were at the edge of the yard when Gerardo stopped and looked at him.

He thought: Well, here it is. It happens now.

But nothing happened just then. Gerardo was frowning slightly and saying aloud to himself, "No, this not the place. We go farther."

"Yeah," Whitey said. "The farther, the better."

"Shut up," Gerardo said. "I do some thinking. I choose the right spot."

"Let's go to City Hall."

"I said shut up."

"Why should I?" Whitey asked. He wondered why he was doing this. He grinned at Gerardo and said, "Come on, let's walk to City Hall. You can do it there. If you want them to find my body, they're sure to find it in City Hall."

"Goddamn you," Gerardo said. "You gonna shut up?"

"Go to hell," Whitey said. He told himself it was a silly thing to say. But he liked the sound of it. He knew he was grinning widely and he heard himself saying, "Go to hell, Gerardo."

"So?" Gerardo murmured thoughtfully. "So is gonna be like this?"

Whitey shrugged. He sent the grin past Gerardo and he said to the empty air, "How's about a drink? I could sure use a drink."

"What? What you say?"

"A drink." He went on grinning past Gerardo. "I need a drink."

Gerardo mixed a frown with a thin smile. "I think maybe Carlos was right. Maybe you really crazy."

"Let's go somewhere and get a drink."

"All right," Gerardo said, humoring him. "I take you somewhere and we have nice party."

"With girls?"

"Sure. Plenty girls. Very pretty. Real angels."

Then Gerardo nudged him and they were walking again. They came out of the lumberyard and onto the vacant lot. They moved along the edge of the lot and he kept saying he needed a drink but now Gerardo didn't answer. Gerardo was studying the terrain and not liking it. So then they continued along the north boundary of the lot, then went down along the west boundary and past the south boundary, entering a long alley that had no paving and consisted mostly of loose stones and thick mud.

He remembered walking through this alley with Carlos and Luis, and he knew the next thing would be the narrow cobblestoned street. He recalled seeing a lamppost where the alley met the street, and even now he could see the dim glow far down there. He thought: That's where it's gonna happen. He'll give it to you there, right there under that lamppost.

Now Gerardo was walking behind him. He told himself this was a very long alley. He wished it were longer. He saw the glow of the street light coming closer. And then it was very close and he saw the glow reflected on the cobblestones of the narrow street.

Thirty seconds, he estimated. We'll be there in thirty seconds and then it's all over.

Or make it twenty seconds. Or fifteen. So right about now you can start counting them off and predict your future. You know just how long you've got to live. Fifteen seconds . . . fourteen . . . thirteen . . . You oughta be a fortuneteller, you're really good at this. Eleven . . . ten . . . nine . . .

eight . . . We're almost there, just a few more steps, a few more seconds. Five . . . four . . . three . . .

They were coming out of the alley.

"All right," Gerardo said. "Stop here."

He stopped. He was under the glow of the street light, standing there on the cobblestones with his back to Gerardo. In his brain he could see the knife emerging from the sleeve of the camel's-hair overcoat, and Gerardo's fingers getting a grip on the handle.

He heard himself saying, "You can't do it here."

"No?" Gerardo murmured. "Why not?"

He turned very slowly and faced Gerardo and said, "You can't do it anyplace. You just can't do it, that's all."

Gerardo was holding the knife with the blade pointed at Whitey's stomach. He was waiting for Whitey to take a step backward or sideways.

Whitey didn't move. He said, "That's a heavy overcoat you're wearing. Another thing, it's too big for you. It's much too big."

"You think it makes me clumsy? Slows me down?"

"No," Whitey said. "That ain't what I'm thinking. It's just that I'm wondering about the coat. It ain't no cheap article."

Gerardo smiled but it was an uncertain smile and his voice quivered slightly as he said, "Why you talk about coat now? You talking just to gain time?"

"It's camel's-hair," Whitey said. "Genuine camel's-hair."

"So?" Gerardo was trying to see inside Whitey's head. "So what is connection here? What is business with camel's-hair?"

Whitey didn't say anything. He was looking at the overcoat.

Gerardo blinked several times. He was impatient to get busy with the knife, but this matter of the overcoat made him very curious and somewhat worried. He was remembering the way Whitey had stared at the overcoat when they were in the room upstairs. He wondered why this little white-haired bum was able to stall him, to give him a feeling of indecision and confusion. He knew it showed in his eyes and he tried to get it out of his eyes but it stayed there.

And Whitey saw it. Whitey said, "Let's talk about the coat. Where'd you get it?"

"Is make any difference?" Gerardo worked the words through his teeth, his lips stiff.

"Someone give it to you?" Whitey asked.

"Yes." It was a hissing sound. "Yes. So what?"

"Tell me something," Whitey said conversationally. "Who gave it to you?"

For an instant Gerardo's eyes were wide and he was staring past Whitey. In the next instant Whitey kicked him in the groin.

Gerardo let out a choked scream and as he fell backward he was trying to double up. Whitey came in close and kicked him again.

The knife fell out of Gerardo's hand. It hit the cobblestones and bounced and hit again and came down in some stagnant milky water in the gutter. Gerardo was on his knees, trying to hurl himself at the knife, but all he could do was crawl. Whitey moved in between Gerardo and the milky water, made a grab at the knife, and almost had it when Gerardo snatched blindly at his ankle, found him, held him, gripped him hard, and pulled him down. Then very quickly, forgetting the pain in the groin, Gerardo threw a clenched right hand at Whitey's face and caught him on the jaw and Whitey fell over on his side. He told himself he'd been hit very hard and he wondered if he could get up. As he tried to get up, he saw Gerardo crawling again, making another try for the knife.

He managed to get up. He leaped at Gerardo and his shoulder made contact with Gerardo's ribs. They went down together and rolled over and kept rolling with Gerardo's hands going for his throat. He butted Gerardo in the face and broke Gerardo's nose. Gerardo went on grabbing for his throat and now they were rolling over and over in the milky water. It was slimy, greasy water and now it became streaked with red dripping from Gerardo's smashed nose. Whitey told himself this party was getting very sloppy. He was on his back now and he felt Gerardo's fingers closing on his throat. He reached up and took a handful of Gerardo's hair and started to rip the hair from Gerardo's scalp. Gerardo gasped and groaned and let go of his throat. He held onto the handful of hair and kept on pulling and some blood streamed down Gerardo's forehead. But Gerardo was still on top of him and again going for his throat and he knew the important thing was to get out from under. He wondered if he had the strength to roll them over again, told himself to stop wondering and start working, and then he let go of Gerardo's hair and heaved very hard. They went over and for a moment he was on top of Gerardo but they kept rolling and then Gerardo was on top of him. He heaved again and they went on rolling and suddenly Gerardo pulled free and stood up. Gerardo aimed a kick at his face and missed and caught him in the chest. Gerardo circled him and aimed another kick. He rolled away and got to his knees and then got to his feet and now Gerardo came at him with fists.

He slipped away from a roundhouse right hand trying for his head, ducked to avoid a short left hook, stepped back and them came inside another left hook and shot a short right to Gerardo's belly. Gerardo was past feeling it and wouldn't give ground and countered mechanically with another left hook that caught Whitey on the temple and staggered him. Gerardo moved in, completely mechanical now, measuring him very carefully with a right hand, then throwing the right, shooting it in a straight streaking path going from the shoulder. It hit Whitey's chin and it was like falling a few hundred feet and landing on the chin, or something like that, or maybe like getting smashed on the chin with a crowbar. Well, he thought as he went down, it was a cute session while you were in it but you're not in it now. He really made good with that one.

Whitey was down and flat on his back and his eyes were closed. He tried to open his eyes and they wouldn't open. He could feel Gerardo coming toward him. He knew Gerardo was taking his own sweet time, there was no need to hurry things now. Damn it, he said to himself, you're paralyzed, you're really paralyzed, and all he's gotta do is move in and finish the job. Maybe he's finished it already and you're 'way out there off the rim of the world. It sure feels that way, it feels like the world is someplace else and you're nowhere. Or maybe you're somewhere in between, I mean in between the dark and the light, not really out of it altogether, because you know you're still breathing. And your brain's working, so you know you're still conscious. Well, that's something, anyway. All right, what's the good of that? It's only for a short time. How short? Or how long? What's he waiting for? What the hell is he waiting for?

Just then Whitey was able to open his eyes. He saw Gerardo

standing a few feet away and looking down at him. Or rather, Gerardo was looking at the arm stretched sideways with the hand in the milky water and resting on the handle of the knife.

Whitey's fingers closed around the handle. He thought: The bastard wasn't taking any chances, he thought you were trying to suck him in, pretending you were out cold. Pretending, hell. You had no idea the knife was there, right there under your palm. Well, it's there, all right. You have it now and he knows you have it and he can't decide what to do. If he decides to move in, it's gonna be lousy for you, because you're in no shape for more action. You won't be doing much with the knife, you can hardly move your arm. I sure hope he don't move in. Look at his face. He's trying to make up his mind. Look at his eyes popping out, staring at the knife. Well, come on, Gerardo, hurry up and decide, it's gotta be one thing or the other. But I wish you'd decide to take a walk. I'd really appreciate that.

Gerardo opened his mouth just a little and showed his teeth. He took a hesitant step toward Whitey.

Whitey tightened his grip on the knife handle. He was half sitting, braced on his elbows. He grinned at Gerardo and said, "Come on. Come on. Whatcha waiting for?"

It was a difficult problem for Gerardo. He was wondering if he had enough strength left to take the knife away from Whitey. He had serious doubts about that because there was a lot of pain in his groin and his head was throbbing and his arms were very tired. He felt sick and weak and he was terribly unhappy about his smashed nose. But he was anxious to get at that knife. He told himself to give it a try. He took another step forward.

Whitey sat up straighter, not knowing how he was able to do it. And then somehow he managed to get to his feet.

Gerardo turned and ran.

11

WHITEY STOOD there with the knife in his hand. He watched Gerardo running away from him, the ragged camel's-hair coat flapping in the wind. He saw Gerardo crossing the cobblestoned street and aiming at the alley on the other side. There was something acutely purposeful in the way Gerardo headed toward the alley. Whitey saw him stumble and fall and get up and go lunging at the alley.

As Gerardo darted into the alley, it occurred to Whitey that he ought to cross the street and take a look. He was wondering why the Puerto Rican had selected that alley. It didn't make sense for Gerardo to go in that direction; it was the opposite direction from where he ought to be going. It stood to reason that Gerardo should be running north, toward home, or east, toward the river, for an all-out getaway. And there he was, running south.

There he was, running down the alley. Whitey stood at the alley entrance and watched the camel's-hair coat showing yellow down there in the darkness. In the thick black of half past three in the morning, the camel's-hair coat was a distinct yellow, almost luminous. Whitey frowned and thought: That coat. And now this alley. I wonder if—

He wasn't sure what he was wondering. Whatever it was, his brain lost track of it, like a hand groping vainly in thick fog, not knowing what it was groping for, but knowing there was something.

Whitey entered the alley. He walked slowly, staying close to the back-yard fences, telling himself that he didn't want to be seen. He was focusing on the moving yellow of the camel's-hair coat some forty yards away.

Then the distance was about fifty yards, but he could still see it clearly. He saw Gerardo coming to a stop, fumbling with a fence gate and not able to get it open, and then climbing over the fence.

Whitey walked faster now, but quietly, sort of Indian fashion, coming down on his toes, his body crouched. He saw the camel's-hair coat going across the back yard and then up on the kitchen doorstep.

And then Gerardo was banging on the door.

"Open it," Gerardo yelled. "Hurry!"

Whitey came to a stop. He crouched very low, peering through the gaps between the fence posts. He watched Gerardo banging both fists against the back door.

"Is me," the Puerto Rican yelled. "Is me—Gerardo."

And his fists hit the door harder. He was looking down the alley to see if he was being followed.

Whitey moved forward very quietly and carefully. He knew Gerardo hadn't seen him. He told himself to keep it this way, quiet and careful, slow and easy, don't let anything happen to spoil it. And now, as he came closer to the house, he could feel a tightness inside himself. He was gripped with a sense of expectancy that pushed aside the throbbing in his jaw where Gerardo's right hand had landed.

He heard Gerardo banging on the door and wailing, "For crissake, hurry! Let me in!"

And then, very near the house, he took another look through the fence posts. The kitchen light was on and he saw Gerardo waiting for the door to open.

The door opened and Gerardo went in very fast, barging past the man who stood in the doorway. In the instant before the door closed, Whitey got a clear frontal view of the man's face.

It was the man who'd given away a very old and tattered camel's-hair coat. There was nothing generous in the giving, because the coat had been worn out seven years ago, when Whitey had seen it in the railroad station, unbuttoned and falling loosely from the heavy shoulders of Sharkey.

All right, Whitey said to himself. So what's the connection?

Or maybe it's nothing, he thought. Maybe it's just one of them situations where Gerardo does odd jobs around the house, like taking care of the furnace, hauling out the ashes. So it's a very cold November and he ain't got no overcoat and Sharkey gives him the camel's-hair.

But no. You know there's more to it than that. Your chum Gerardo hit that back door like he belonged in that house, not like a handy man who works there part time, more like a member of the family, or let's make it just a bit deeper than that. Let's make it he's maybe a member of the organization.

What organization? What are you building here with thinking about an organization? And another thing, what's it matter to you what it is? It ain't none of your affair.

It ain't?

The hell it ain't. You're on the wanted list for killing a cop, you might as well remember that. You damn well better remember that. And while you're at it, remember the Captain, and what he'll be inclined to do when he lays his hands on you. Of course, the man he really wants is Gerardo, but he doesn't know that. The thing is, you know it. You know how the cop died and what did it and who did it. You heard Gerardo tell it from his own mouth. So there's your cop-killer and he's in that house and you got plenty reason to be gandering that house.

But it's sorta weird, you know? It's weird because she's in there and—

All right, forget that. Or at least try to think you can forget it. What you hafta do now is concentrate on Gerardo. You gotta figure some way to get him out of that house, to get him up the steps and through the front door of the Thirty-seventh District, to have him say to the Captain what he said to you.

Yeah, that's gonna be easy to manage. Very easy. Like trying to tear down a brick wall with your bare hands. Or your front teeth. Or your head.

Your head. Start using it. Start adding up the numbers. Like our boy Gerardo says, *la matemática*, two and two is four and so forth, except in this case it's more on the order of algebra, where you got some unknown quantities. All right, you never took much algebra, so it's gotta be mostly guesswork, or maybe like the science guys who get their answers with the slow but sure procedure of try this and try that and keep on trying until it fits together. I think you got enough brains for that. Anyway, hope so. But it ain't no cinch to use the brains right now. That wallop he fetched you on the jaw was no patty-cake handout, it's got you sorta blocked upstairs, your skull feels like it's all jammed up with putty. Well, anyway, let's try. Let's see if we can do some thinking here.

Well, begin with Gerardo. Or no, that's doing it ass-backwards. It's you that's gotta talk to the Captain, and when you tell him the deal you can't begin with Gerardo, because sure as hell that ain't where it begins. So where does it begin?

The race riots?

No, you can't start with that. In regard to that, you know from nothing. Or wait a minute here. Wait just a minute. It's the race riots that's got the Captain all screwed up and blowing his top. If you could give him something on the riots, it would help your case, maybe. At least it would quiet him down so's he'd give you a chance to get your point across.

All right, then, figure it. What is it with these race riots? What started the fuss? My God, now we're exploring in the field of racial aggravations, some-kind-of-ology, and you ain't geared for that, that just ain't your department. But hold it right there. Don't let it get away. Thing to do is take it from another angle. Like in case it ain't only a matter of race, it's more than gangs of riled-up local citizens fighting riled-up Puerto Ricans, it's maybe a situation where the race hate is secondary, where something else is the important issue.

Something else. Like what? Like— Easy, now, don't stretch it too far, you gotta know what you're aiming at. Better take it on a short-range basis and— But no, goddamnit, it's strictly from long range, it's from 'way out there, 'way back. It's from seven years ago.

It's from that night you sat with her in the taproom and she was talking about Sharkey and she said, "He's been mooching around and looking for an angle," and went on to tell about certain projects that didn't pay off, and then she said, "Maybe one of these days he'll find that angle he's looking for."

All right, all right, I think you got something here. Stay with it now.

Keep remembering. That night, that taproom, and you sat there with her in that booth, you looked at her face and you thought—

Well, the hell with what you thought. The hell with what you felt. That ain't what you're remembering now. You gotta stay with this race-riot business, the big question you gotta answer to pull yourself out of this jam you're in, this cop-killing rap. So don't go off the track. Only things you gotta remember are the words that came out of her mouth, the statements she made about Sharkey. Like when she said that Sharkey was certain he'd someday get the bright idea that would haul in the heavy cash. The way she'd put it, "He says it's around somewhere, all he's gotta do is find it."

Find it where?

Find it here? In the Hellhole?

Look. Let's understand something. I think you're on the track and it figures to be the right track, but just about here is where it stops. I mean, it stops here because your brain just can't take it any farther. Only way to keep it going is with the eyes, the ears. You get the point? You see what the next move is?

Wanna take the chance?

All right. But it's a lead-pipe cinch you're asking for grief. The way you gotta do it is the hard way, there just ain't no other way. It's gonna be getting information from Sharkey, with Sharkey not knowing he's giving it out. So first it's this fence, and then it's the back yard, and finally it's the house.

Well, let's get started. What's the delay? Why you standing here? And why you grinning? How come it all of a sudden hits you comical? It ain't the least bit comical, unless you're thinking of Chop and Bertha and when they had you in the woods, what they did to you, the way they made it plain, no two ways about it, really giving it to you to get you convinced.

But here we are again. And they didn't convince you after all.

12

H E CLIMBED over the fence and moved slowly, very quietly, across the back yard. He was focusing on the cellar window that had no glass in it.

The opening was stingy and he had to worm his way through. He went in legs first, his feet probing for support as he arched his back, his hands clutching the upper side of the window, his torso squirming, pushing past the splintered frame. Then, as he went through and down, his feet found a narrow shelf. From there it was just a short drop to the cellar floor.

There was no light in the cellar. He took a few steps and bumped into the side of a coal bin. A few more steps and his knees came up against the pile of coal. He groped in his pockets, searching for a match. There were no matches and he wondered how he could get past the coal without making noise. It was a lot of coal, and if he tried to crawl over it, the chunks would give way and there'd be considerable noise. The important thing now was quiet. It had to be handled with a maximum of quiet.

He backed away from the pile of coal, then moved parallel with it, got past the wooden wall of the bin, inched his way forward, and hit another obstruction. It felt like an ash can. He touched it and it was metal and he knew it was an ash can. And then another ash can. And still another. He decided the best way to get past the row of ash cans was to get down on all fours and do it by inches.

Crawling, using his forehead to feel what was in front of him, he kept bumping very lightly against the ash cans. He was moving sideways and then there were no more ash cans and again he went forward, still crawling. He kept on that way, going toward the middle of the cellar, gradually feeling the heat coming from the furnace, and then seeing the thin ribbon of bright orange glow that showed through a crack in the furnace door. He crawled toward it, thinking: Maybe we'll find something to light up and use for a torch.

Coming closer to the furnace, he reached out, felt for the handle of the furnace door, found it, and worked it slowly and very carefully. With very little noise the furnace door came open. The orange glow flowed out and showed him the floor surrounding the furnace. He saw a used safety match and got his fingers on it, put it in the furnace to get it lit, and thought: Well, now we can find the stairs.

The flaming match showed something that postponed the stairs.

It was a neatly laid-out row of brand-new baseball bats. And knives, all sorts of knives. In the instant that he sighted it, he thought of the similar but sloppier collection he'd seen in the Puerto Rican meeting place. Then, frowning, staring at the bats and knives, he noticed something else. It was a stack of small wooden boxes, say a dozen of them. The ones on top displayed labels and he came closer, peering past the flare of the match, and saw the printed words: "Handle with care—.38 caliber."

For another instant he looked at the cartridge boxes. And then he saw the glint of metal near the boxes, the glinting barrels and butts of several brand-new revolvers.

Well, now, he said without sound. Well, now.

The burning match was dying fast and he held it higher to find the stairway. The glow showed the stairway off to the right and he checked the distance and then blew out the match. Now he was on his feet and moving lightly toward the stairway, telling himself to do as it said on the cartridge boxes, to handle these stairs with care.

Sure enough, it was a very old flight of stairs, and when he hit the first step it creaked. He crouched low, using his hands on the higher steps, going up monkey style and distributing his weight between the steps to lessen the creaking.

He was halfway up the steps when the mouse came running down.

Or rather, it came falling down, it must have been blind or sick, or maybe one of them lunatic mice that just can't do things in a sensible way. Its tiny furry shape hit him full in the face and instinctively it fought for a hold with its legs. He locked his lips to hold back the startled yell and heard the mouse giving its own outcry of shock. It squeaked as loud as it could, decided this was not the place for it to be, and leaped off.

Whitey shook his head slowly and thought: That almost did it.

He rested there a few moments, trying to forget the feeling of the mouse dancing on his face. He said to himself: Let's disregard these minor issues, you got more stairs to climb, keep climbing.

So then it was the next step going up. And the next. And as he climbed it was like the very slow and precise action of thread passing through the eye of a needle. His head was down and he was watching the barely visible edges of the steps, gray-black against the blackness. Then gradually the steps were tinged with a faint amber glow and he knew it was light coming from the first floor. He raised his head and saw the yellow seeping through the crack in the door at the top of the stairs. The door was maybe five steps ahead. He tightened his mouth just a little, and thought: Careful, now, don't get excited, please don't get excited.

A moment passed. It was a very long moment and he felt it pressing hard on him as he negotiated the next step. The feeling of anxiety was a set of clamps getting him in the belly and squeezing like some practical joker carrying the joke too far.

Or maybe he was the joker, and not a very good one, at that. A first-rate joker never took himself seriously and it was everything for laughs. For instance, that on-and-off comedian who worked from the Thirty-seventh District, that detective lieutenant, that Pertnoy. Now, if it was Pertnoy going up these stairs, it would be a breeze, nothing to it, the man would be grinning and having himself a grand time. On the other hand, if it was Lieutenant Whatsisname, the fashion plate, name starts with D or T—oh, yes, Taggert—well, if it was Taggert climbing up these cellar steps, he'd be strictly business, absolutely a machine, except maybe it would bother him that his clothes were getting dirty. He's sure a sucker for the haberdashers and the tailors, that Taggert. And for barbershops, too. Guess it's always the same routine when he sits himself in the chair. You can hear him saying, "The works, Dominic." But why's it gotta be Dominic? Not all barbers are Italians. Like with Poles, not all coal miners are Poles. You know, Phillips was a coal miner, and Phillips is— As if it makes any difference what he is. As if race has anything to do with it. Yeah, go try and tell that to the Puerto Ricans. People call them Puerto Ricans and right away they're branded like with an iron and given a low road to travel, the lousiest places to live, like that house where you saw them jam-packed sleeping on a cold floor. But you saw some damn fine quality in that house. That Chávez. He was really something, that Chávez. And Luis, too. Luis almost got himself slashed bloody going to bat for you.

Say, come to think of it, you have been having yourself a time tonight, you've come across some real personalities. Take, for example, that Jones Jarvis. If conditions were different it could be Admiral Jarvis, U.S.N. And you know he could do the job, you know damn well he could do it. So it figures it's mostly a matter of conditions. Sure it is. Take Captain Kinnard and put him in charge of a nursery, he'd be like melted butter and them kids would run all over him. But how do you know that? Well, you just know it, that's all. It's that way with some people; you take one look at them and later when you think about it, it hits you and you know. Or sometimes you get hit right away. You ought to know about that, when it comes to that you're an old campaigner. That first time you saw her, the way it hit you. And the way it's been coming back tonight, hitting you, hitting you. All right, for Christ's sake, cut it out. But I wonder if Firpo is still alive and sometimes at night he wakes up and remembers the way Dempsey hit him.

He went up another step and it brought him to the top of the stairs. He stood against the door and his hand drifted to the knob. His fingers tested the give of the knob and at first it wouldn't give, not soundlessly, anyway. He tried it again and felt it turning. A little more, and still more, and then there was the faint noise, more feathery than metallic, of the latch coming free. And now very carefully, working it by fractions of inches, he opened the door.

It showed him the lit-up kitchen. There was no one in the kitchen. But he could hear voices coming from the next room, and there was the clinking of glasses on a wooden table.

He had the door opened not quite two inches. There was the scraping of a chair and then someone was coming into the kitchen. He gave a slight pull on the door to make it appear closed. For some moments there was activity in the kitchen, the sound of a running faucet, glass tinkling against the sink. He heard Chop shouting from the next room, "Not from the sink! There's cold water in the icebox." And in the kitchen the icebox was being opened and he heard Bertha's voice saying, "The bottle's empty." A pause, and then from the next room it was Sharkey's voice: "We got any beer?" and Bertha replying, "It's all gone," and Chop again, "There's some in the cellar."

Whitey closed his eyes. Without sound he said: Goddamn it.

He heard Chop yelling, "We got some quart bottles down there. Go down and bring up a few."

Then Bertha's footsteps were coming toward the door.

He thought: Some people have it nice, they can travel anywhere they wanna go. But you, you can't travel anywhere, you can't go down the steps, and when the door opens you can't get behind it because it don't open in, it opens out. You're gonna be right here when it opens, right here at the top of the stairs where there ain't no room to move around, so this looks to be the windup.

Then he realized the footsteps had stopped. He heard Bertha shouting, "Go get the beer yourself. I ain't no waitress."

Chop yelled, "What is it, a big deal?"

"Get it yourself. Run your own errands."

"You goddamn lazy—"

"Aw, go break a leg."

"Lazy elephant, she won't even—"

"Make it both legs," Bertha yapped at Chop. "I'm tired of you giving me orders. All day long I'm running up and down the steps. This morning you were—"

"I was sick this morning."

"You're gonna be sick tonight if you don't lay off me."

Whitey heard Bertha's footsteps going out of the kitchen. In the next room the argument continued between Bertha and Chop and finally Sharkey cut in with "All right, the hell with the beer. We'll drink what we got here."

There was more tinkling of glasses. And then he heard them talking but now their voices were low and he couldn't make out what they were saying. Again he worked on the door and got it open a few inches. Then a few more inches, and he was straining to hear, gradually getting it.

Sharkey was saying, "Go on, Gerardo. Have another drink."

"I no need—"

"Sure you do." Sharkey's voice was soft and soothing. "We'll make this the bracer."

There was the sound of liquor splashing into a glass. Whatever it was, there was a lot of it going into the glass.

"Drink it down," Sharkey said. "Go on, Gerardo, get it all down."

"But I—"

And then loudly, from Bertha, "You hear what Sharkey says? You do what he says."

"Is too much whisky," Gerardo complained. "I no—"

"Yes, you will," Bertha shouted. "You'll drink it or I'll hold your nose and force it down."

"Why you do me like this?" Gerardo whined.

"Like what?" It was Chop and he was laughing dryly. "You're lucky, Gerardo. You're lucky Bertha ain't giving you lumps."

"I got lumps already," Gerardo said. Then, drinking the whisky, he gasped, went on drinking it, gasped again. There was the sound of the glass coming down on the table, and Gerardo saying, "Enough lumps I get tonight. Look at lumps. Look at my nose."

"It looks busted," Sharkey said.

"All smashed up," the Puerto Rican wailed. "Was perfect nose and now look at it."

"Finish what's in the glass," Bertha said.

"But I can't—"

"Drink it all up," she said. "Drink it up, Gerardo."

"Please—"

"You'll drink it if I hold your nose," Bertha said. "And then you'll really have a nose to worry about."

Then again there was the sound of the glass, the gurgling and gulping as Gerardo forced it down, and the bitter rasping, the gasping.

"Very good," Bertha said. "Not a drop in the glass. But you got some on your chin. I'll wipe it off."

Whitey heard the sound of a backhand crack across the mouth, then louder with the open palm, then very loud with the backhand again. He heard a chair toppling, and a thud, and he knew that Gerardo was on the floor.

He heard Gerardo whimpering, sobbing, "I no understand."

"It's instruction," Bertha said. "You're getting instruction, Gerardo. You gotta learn to do what Sharkey says."

"My mouth!"

Whitey visualized Gerardo's mouth. He knew it was a sad-looking mouth right now. It had received the full force of Bertha's tree-trunk arm, with over three hundred pounds of hard-packed beef behind Bertha's oversized hand. Whitey said to himself: You know how it feels, you had a taste of it, a big taste, and—

He heard Bertha saying, "It's like baseball, Gerardo. You catch on? It's like baseball and Sharkey's the manager and you gotta do what he says."

And Chop said, "It ain't sand-lot ball, Gerardo. It's big-league action and you gotta watch the signals very careful. When you're safe on third you don't take any chances. You don't try for home plate unless you get the signal."

"I come here because—"

"Because you got scared," Bertha said. "You're not supposed to get scared." And then, to Sharkey, "Should I give our boy more instruction?"

There was no reply from Sharkey.

Whitey heard the terribly loud sound of another open-handed wallop, then the thud as Gerardo went back against a wall, bounced away, fell forward toward the table to get it again from Bertha's hand, and again, and then really getting it and starting to cry like a baby.

Poor bastard, Whitey thought. He heard the noise of Gerardo getting it and yowling now with the pain of it. He felt sort of sorry for Gerardo, and yet he was thinking: If Chávez could see it, if Luis could see it, they'd find it interesting, very interesting.

Just then, through the sound of the blows, through Gerardo's yowls and pleas, he heard the voice of Celia.

He heard Celia saying, "What are you doing, Bertha? What are you doing to him?"

"What's—" Bertha grunted, her arm swinging, her hand making contact with the battered, swollen face. "What's it look like?"

Celia's voice was calm. "You keep that up and he won't have a face."

"But he'll have brains," Bertha said. Then another grunt, another wallop, an animal scream from Gerardo, and Bertha saying, "You see what I'm doing? I'm putting brains in his head."

Gerardo was crying out, blubbering, talking in Spanish.

"You calling me names?" Bertha asked. "You cursing me?"

Sharkey said, "All right, Bertha. Leave him alone."

"Was he cursing me? I'd like to know if he was cursing me."

"He wasn't cursing you," Sharkey said. "Let go of him. Let him sit down. I wanna talk to him."

"You think he'll hear you?" It was Celia. "Look at his ears."

And again the dry laugh from Chop, and Chop saying, "The left one ain't so bad."

"But look at him," Celia said. "Look at his face. God Almighty. Give him some water. Give him something."

"I think—" It was Gerardo and he'd stopped crying. He spoke quietly and solemnly. "I think I die now."

"You won't die," Bertha said. "You'll sit there and listen to Sharkey."

"Wait," Sharkey said. "Give him a napkin. He's dripping blood all over the table."

Bertha said, "Where we keep the napkins?"

"I no want napkin," Gerardo said. "I want I should bleed more. I want I should die."

Whitey heard the sound of a cabinet drawer being opened. After that the sounds were minor and he knew they were taking time to stop the flow of blood from Gerardo's face. He wondered how long it would take to get Gerardo out of the fog. It was more or less evident that Sharkey wanted Gerardo's full attention. Whitey hoped it wouldn't take too long to bring Gerardo back to clear thinking. It was getting somewhat difficult, standing here and not making a sound. It was definitely uncomfortable because there wasn't much space here at the top of the cellar stairs. He told himself to quit complaining, all he had to do was stand still and listen. And yet it wasn't easy. He wanted to move around, make some noise, do something, anything, and it sure as hell wasn't easy to stand here like some Buffalo Bill in a wax museum.

He heard Gerardo talking dully, dazedly, in Spanish.

And Chop was saying, "Hey, this ain't so good. He's in bad shape. His eyes—"

"I'll bring him out of it," Bertha said. "Here. Let me—"

"You keep away from him," Sharkey said quietly. "You've done enough already."

"All I wanna do is—"

"No," Sharkey said. "Stay away from him. Stay the hell away from him."

"Whatsa matter?" Bertha asked. "Whatcha getting peeved about?"

"Oh, he ain't peeved." It was Celia again. "He likes the way you work. Don't you, Sharkey? Go on, Sharkey, tell her. Tell her how much you admire her work."

Bertha's voice said, "You still here?"

"Yes," Celia said slowly and distinctly, "I'm still here."

"I wonder why," Bertha said.

"Me too." Celia said it very slowly. "I always wonder about that."

"You got a problem, honey," Bertha said. "You oughta do something about it."

"No." And then a long pause. "There ain't nothing I can do about it."

"Oh, don't say that." Bertha's voice was gentle but sour, soft yet sneering, and dripping with sarcasm. "You can always take a walk, you know."

"Can I? Let's hear what Sharkey says. How about it, Sharkey? Can I take a walk?"

"Drop it," Sharkey said.

Bertha said, "She's asking a question, Sharkey. She wants to know if she can take a walk."

"I said drop it." Sharkey's voice was low and tight. "The two of you, drop it."

"I guess he don't want me to go for a walk," Celia said.

"Yeah," Bertha said. "That's the way it figures."

"Well, anyway, I asked him. You satisfied, Bertha?"

"Sure, honey. I'm always satisfied. I feel very satisfied right now."

"That's nice," Celia said.

"And how is it with you?" Bertha asked, with each word aimed like a jab. "Are you satisfied?"

"I hafta go to the bathroom," Celia said.

Bertha spoke to Sharkey. "You hear what she says? She has to go to the bathroom. She got your permission?"

"I better make a run for the bathroom," Celia said. "I don't wanna throw up in here."

Whitey heard Celia's footsteps running out of the adjoining room. He heard Sharkey muttering to Bertha, "What's the matter with you? Why don't you leave her alone?"

"She started it," Bertha said.

"You'd do me a favor if you'd leave her alone."

"But she's always starting, Sharkey. She's always making remarks."

Gerardo was still mumbling in Spanish. And Chop was saying, "Maybe if we give him smelling salts—"

Bertha said, "I don't like when she makes remarks. I don't like it and I don't hafta take it."

"Then do like I do. Let her talk. Don't listen to her."

"You kidding? Come off it, Sharkey. You know you're always tuned in. You take in everything she says."

"It goes in one ear and—"

"And stays inside," Bertha said. "Deep inside. I watch your face sometimes when she says them things to you, little things, but it's like little knives, and I see you getting cut. Real deep."

Chop again: "We got any smelling salts?"

"Like earlier tonight," Bertha went on, "she makes with the routine about maybe if you'd see a specialist—"

"All right," Sharkey interrupted quickly. "Let it fade, Bertha. I don't wanna hear no more about it."

But Bertha had it going and she couldn't stop it and she said, "Not a heart specialist, either. Not a brain specialist. She meant something else. I know what she meant. It's bedroom trouble. You can't give her nothing in the bedroom. Only thing you do in the bed is sleep."

Then it was quiet. Whitey waited for Sharkey to say something. But the quiet went on. It was a dismal quiet, like the stillness of a stagnant pool. He could almost feel the staleness of it, as though the adjoining room were a sickroom and the air was thick with decay.

Finally Chop said, "I think we got smelling salts in the—"

"He don't need smelling salts," Sharkey said quietly. "He's coming around."

"Sure he is," Bertha said. "How you doing, Gerardo?"

"Very nice." Gerardo spoke as though he had glue in his mouth. "I am doing very nice."

"Want a cigarette?" Bertha asked.

"All right," Gerardo said. "I smoke a cigarette. Then everything is fine. Cigarette fixes everything."

Whitey heard the sound of a match being struck. He heard Gerardo saying, "Is question I have, maybe you can answer. How can I smoke when there is no mouth?"

"You can smoke," Bertha said. "Go on, smoke. And quit singing the blues. It ain't as bad as you make it."

"How you know? Is not your face banged up. Is mine. You no can say how it feels."

Whitey heard Chop laughing and saying, "That's right, Gerardo. Tell her."

"I no tell her anything. I say more, she hit me again."

Sharkey said, "That's using your head, Gerardo. I think you're getting with it now."

"Not hardly," Bertha said. "If you're gonna talk to him, Sharkey, you'll hafta make it later. He ain't ready to listen."

"I listen," Gerardo said. "I just sit here and listen. What else for me to do?"

"You see, Sharkey?" she said. "He just ain't ready yet. Look at him. He can't pay attention to you. He's too burned up at me."

"No," Gerardo said. "I no burn up at you, Bertha. I just afraid of you, that's all."

"You are?" Bertha sounded pleased. "Well, now, that's good. That's the way it should be."

But then Sharkey was saying, "You think so, Bertha? I don't think so. I don't want it that way."

"Why not?" Bertha asked. "He's gotta be made to understand—"

"Sure, I know," Sharkey cut in softly. "But I don't want him all scared and nervous and upset. He's got important work to do. Ain't that right, Gerardo?"

There was no reply from Gerardo.

"Come on, Gerardo. Get with it." The voice of Sharkey was velvety, soothing, very gentle. "Look at me. And listen, Will you do that? Will you listen careful?"

Whitey stood motionless at the top of the cellar stairs with his head bent forward slightly in the three-inch gap of opened door between stairway and kitchen. Without sound he was saying to Sharkey: All right, Mac, we'll listen very careful. We ain't gonna miss a word.

13

H E HEARD the velvety voice of Sharkey saying, "First thing, Gerardo, I wanna get it across again, like when I told you this was a big-time operation and every move hadda be handled with style. With making sure it's perfect timing. And above all, keeping cool. You remember, I said the important thing is to keep cool."

"I try very hard to—"

"It ain't a matter of trying, Gerardo. I didn't tell you to try. I said keep cool, period."

"Yes. Keep cool. Yes. But—"

"Another thing I made clear, the schedule. I said we gotta stick to the schedule. I meant stick to it no matter what happens. So let's have a look at what you did. You messed up the schedule and almost messed up everything."

"Sometime comes bad luck. If comes bad luck is maybe not my fault."

"You weren't due here until tomorrow night. You know what's fixed for tomorrow night and how we got it figured. It's the big move. The big left hook. We're hoping it's the knockout punch so then we go out and celebrate. You listening, Gerardo? I'm talking about tomorrow night."

"I understand about tomorrow night. But—"

"But nothing." And now Sharkey sounded as though he were trying hard to keep his voice down, keep it gentle and very patient. He said, "Look, Gerardo. See if you can get this. It ain't no ordinary action, it's a full-dress show, and we're in it deep. In this kind of job there's no such thing as excuses."

"Is maybe excuse when—"

"No, Gerardo. Believe me. There's no excuse at all for what you did tonight. Making all that noise outside. Running in here like a wild man. All that commotion. What if the cops were around?"

"Was no police."

"But suppose there was? Suppose they got curious and came in to ask questions? And then they're taking a look around.

They're looking in the cellar. They're seeing what's down there—"

"Sharkey, please. Tonight was emergency. I no have time to think."

"Think? I never told you to think. All I told you was what to do. And what not to do."

"Yes. You right, Sharkey. Is very stupid what I do tonight. But you no give me chance to explain about emergency. Was bad emergency. Was—"

"I don't care what it was. I'm not interested. I asked you if it was heat and you said no, so that checks it off. As long as it wasn't heat, it ain't important, and we're not gonna worry about it. Only thing worries me is this caper you pulled. I wanna be sure it won't happen again."

"But sometimes is coming an emergency and—"

"God give me strength." Then a long pause. And then, almost pleadingly, "Listen, Gerardo, you gotta understand we can't afford these mistakes. There's too much on the table to let it slip off. To lose it now, when we're so close to getting it."

"Get what?" Gerardo asked. "You never tell me what we get."

"Sure I told you. I made a promise. I said like this, I said if it paid off you'd wind up with a fat wallet."

"How fat?" Gerardo sounded different now. He sounded as though he'd abruptly forgotten his bleeding, swollen face and was thinking in practical terms. "How much money you give me?"

"Well, let's see now. It's all a matter of—"

"I tell you something," Gerardo cut in quickly. "This job I am doing for you, Sharkey, like you say, it is big-time business. Takes much time. Much trouble. And much risk. Is no easy work for me to do."

"Well, sure. We both know that. I told you in the beginning it wouldn't be easy."

"In beginning you tell me I will get much money. But you no say how much. And all these weeks I work for you, I wonder sometimes, I feel in my pockets and there is nothing. The nickels and dimes you give me, they go fast, Sharkey."

"How you fixed now? You need some cash? I'll give you—"

"Two bits? Four bits? No, Sharkey. Is no good this way."

"For Christ's sake—"

"Is no way to do business. I make big special job for you and you pay me off in little bits."

Sharkey took a deep breath. "Look, you don't get the drift. This small change ain't your pay envelope. It's just to keep you going until the loot comes in."

"How much loot? I like to hear numbers."

"If I told you how much, you wouldn't believe me."

"Take chance. Tell me anyway."

"I can tell you like this. It's gonna be important money. Heavy cash."

"Is nice to think about," Gerardo said. "But tonight for supper I eat one piece stale bread and two bananas."

"You hear him, Sharkey?" It was Bertha. "You got labor trouble."

"Keep quiet," Sharkey told her. Then again he was talking to Gerardo. "If things go right tomorrow night, you'll soon be living like a prince. It's gonna be real gold rolling in, in wagonloads, and you're due for a thick slice. I wasn't just talking when I said you'd be a partner."

"Partner." Gerardo said it very slowly, rolling the "r's," biting hard on the "t." And then with a grunt, saying it aloud to himself, "Fine partner."

"I know what's wrong here." It was Bertha again. "I didn't hit him hard enough."

"Will you please keep quiet?" Sharkey said. Then, to the Puerto Rican, "All right, let's have it. What's the major complaint?"

"You say I am partner," Gerardo said. "Now I ask you something. Partner in what?"

"In what? You kidding? You know what. I told you—"

"You told me what my job is. But you no make clear what business we are in."

There was no reply from Sharkey.

And Gerardo went on: "You say we make much money but you no say how. I think is maybe good idea you put all cards on table. Is better partnership that way."

Then quiet again. Nothing from Sharkey. It went on like that for some moments. And then there was the sound of Sharkey's footsteps pacing the floor.

Whitey listened to the footsteps going back and forth. He

thought: It's like on the radio when you tune in late and you only hear part of the game, and some of these announcers, they won't tell you the score, it drives you bughouse waiting to hear the score.

Just then he heard Gerardo saying, "Is not fair, Sharkey. Why you no tell me? Maybe you think I will know too much? I will open my mouth?"

"You might." It was Bertha.

"And if I did, I would be a fool," Gerardo said. "Would be like putting knife in my own throat."

"You know it too?" Bertha said.

"Yes, I know it," Gerardo replied solemnly. And then, sort of sad and hurt, "Another thing I know. From very beginning I play straight game with you people. I do what Sharkey tells me to do. I follow orders, no matter what. Five weeks ago—"

"Skip it," Sharkey said. "I know what orders I gave you. I know you carried them out. You don't need to remind me."

"Is maybe better if I remind you." And then, saying it slowly, distinctly, "Five weeks ago you tell me to start race riot."

Well, now, Whitey said without sound. That's interesting. That's very interesting.

And he heard Gerardo saying, "So I do what you tell me. On River Street I see an American girl and I follow her. Then I jump on her, I beat her up, I take off her dress. She runs away screaming and then Americans they come and chase me. I get way from them, I tell Puerto Ricans that Americans chase me for no reason. Just like you tell me to do, I make loud speech that Americans hate Puerto Ricans and give us rough time and we must fight back.

"So then it starts. I get Carlos and some others and we go to River Street and make noise, break windows, throw bottles and bricks at gringos. Is nice riot that night. And later that week is another riot, bigger crowd, many people getting hurt. And then more riots with some getting killed, and each time is me who leads the Puerto Ricans into fight, is me who takes chance with my life. Is me who—"

"All right, all right," Sharkey said, and he sounded impatient. "I know what chances you took. It ain't as if I'm forgetting. I'm not fluffing you off."

"Of course not." Gerardo gave a little dry laugh. "You are in no position to fluff me off. You need me tomorrow night when we have biggest riot. With guns."

Sharkey's voice was somewhat tight. "You trying to make a point?"

"What you think?"

Sharkey didn't answer.

And Gerardo said, "You smart man, Sharkey. Very smart. I learn much from you. So now I am smart too."

"Don't get too smart." It was Bertha again.

Gerardo gave another dry laugh. "I get just smart enough to know is my turn now, my turn to deal the cards."

"You're talking too much," Bertha said.

"Let him talk," Sharkey murmured tightly. "I like to hear him talk."

"No," Gerardo said. "Is you who do the talking, Sharkey. Is time for you to make the explaining. Is like this: You tell me reason for riots. Deep inside reason. All details. Is best you tell me everything."

"And if I don't?"

"Then is nothing happen tomorrow night. No riot."

Chop said, "Well, I'll be a—"

Bertha breathed, "If this ain't the limit!"

And Chop again: "He's got you, Sharkey. He's got you over a barrel."

"Yeah, it looks that way," Sharkey said mildly. There was a shrug in his voice. And then he laughed lightly and good-naturedly and said, "All right, Gerardo. Here's the setup."

Then Sharkey was explaining it. He spoke matter-of-factly and there were no pauses, no stumbling over the phrases. It was medium-slow tempo, it came out easily, and Whitey thought: This ain't no made-up story, he's giving Gerardo the true picture.

It was a picture of the Hellhole. Sharkey said the Hellhole was the goal he'd been seeking for a long time. He said the Hellhole was the only territory not covered by the big opera-tors and sure as hell they'd missed a juicy bet when they'd overlooked this neighborhood. As it stood now, it was jam-packed with independent hustlers and scufflers who were al-ways getting in each other's way, with the law always on their tails and giving them a bad time. What the Hellhole needed was the establishment of a system, an organization, and for sure it needed a controlling hand.

Sharkey said he intended to take over the Hellhole. The way he had it figured, he'd soon be in charge of all activities—the gambling joints, the numbers banks, the sale of bootleg whisky and weed and capsules, and of course the whore houses. It would all be handled from one desk, one filing cabinet, and it would follow the general pattern of big-time merchandising.

The most important angle was the law. The layout he had in mind would require an arrangement with the law, a definite mutual-benefit agreement wherein the law would work closely with the organization. In return for a slice of the profits, the law would guarantee full cooperation; there would be no trouble, no raids, no squad cars cruising around and scaring away the customers. He said he'd already arranged for that, he'd made a deal with a certain party who was now a detective lieutenant and campaigning for promotion.

"This certain party," Sharkey said, "he wants to wear a captain's badge. He wants to be captain of the Thirty-seventh District."

It was quiet for a moment.

Then Sharkey said, "The captain they got now is due to be tossed out. It figures he's gonna be tossed because he's losing his grip on the neighborhood. He's going crazy trying to stop these race riots."

More quiet. And Whitey could feel it sinking in.

He heard Sharkey saying, "You get the drift?"

Yeah, Whitey said without sound. Yeah, we're getting it.

"I played around with a hundred ideas before I hit on the riots," Sharkey said. "I hadda give him something that he couldn't handle."

"*Bueno*," Gerardo murmured. "I begin to understand. Is seeming like good setup."

"Yes. I think it's pretty good," Sharkey said. "I don't see how it can miss. This party I'm dealing with is next in line for the captaincy. Each time there's a riot he comes closer to getting it. As soon as he gets it, we're in business."

"*Magnifico*," Gerardo said. And he laughed lightly and

admiringly. "Is everything fits in place. Your man takes over Thirty-seventh and this gives you green light and you take over Hellhole."

"That's it," Sharkey said. "But remember, the light ain't green yet. I'm hoping it turns green tomorrow night."

"It will," Gerardo said eagerly. "You count on me, Sharkey. I guarantee big riot."

"It's gotta be more than that. It's gotta be a shooting war. If it happens the way I want it to happen, they'll blow their tops in City Hall, they'll throw him out of that station house and put my man in. I get the wire they been playing with the idea these past couple weeks, so all it needs now is a final explosion."

"I produce," Gerardo said. "I come through for you."

"And for yourself, too. Once we get started, you'll be drawing a heavy salary. You do a good job tomorrow night and you'll wind up with a penthouse."

After that the talk became technical and it concerned the use of a pushcart. Gerardo was saying it would be best to use a pushcart for the transfer of the guns and ammunition to the Puerto Rican section. He said they had plenty of baseball bats and knives but they could use some meat cleavers. Sharkey asked how many meat cleavers and Gerardo estimated ten would be enough. Sharkey wondered aloud if the pushcart would be all right. Maybe they ought to do it the way they'd done it before, hiring a horse and wagon and covering the weapons with rags and papers. Gerardo said that the last time he'd had some trouble with the horse and he'd feel more secure with a pushcart. Sharkey said O.K., it would be a pushcart, and Gerardo could come for it early tomorrow night.

They went on talking but now Whitey didn't hear. He was making his way very carefully and quietly down the cellar steps.

14

Now it was easier in the cellar and he didn't need to crawl. Some moonlight came in through the opened window and he went toward it, passing the furnace and the ash cans, telling himself to take his time getting past the coal bin. He was getting near the window and it would be a damn shame if he hit the coal pile now and they heard it upstairs. It would certainly be a damn shame, and yet he wasn't thinking about himself. He was thinking about the neighborhood and what it was in for tomorrow night. But maybe he could stop it from happening. Well, he hoped so. He'd give it a try. He had to make good on the try, he couldn't let it happen.

He thought: Maybe what you oughta do is forget the window right now and do something about them guns and cartridge boxes. If you could hide them someplace—but no, that would take too long, and where the hell could you hide them, anyway? And another thing, there's a chance you'd make noise and you better forget about the guns. But you can't forget what the guns can do. Like your friend Sharkey says, he wants real hell on River Street, and like Gerardo said, he means to produce. That Gerardo. He's one for the books, all right. What kind of books? Maybe the history books. Yes, in a way it's on the order of history. That is, if you wanna start drawing parallels. I guess a lot of history is made by the sell-out artists, like Benedict Arnold and so forth. But he'd get worse than Arnold got if them Puerto Ricans found out what he was doing. For instance, if Chávez found out. Or if Luis found out. They'd give it to him, all right, they'd give it to him slow. Maybe for an entire day. Maybe a couple of days. Maybe they'd keep him alive for a week like it used to be in olden times when they'd cut off the fingers one by one and then start on the toes and— Or maybe with fire, like it says in the history books. There you go again with the history books. Say, what's all this with history?

Well, it sorta follows a pattern, I guess. Whaddya mean, you guess? Who are you to guess? Who are you to think about

history? You better get your mind on that window. You better
hurry up and climb through and get outta here.

Wait now, not so fast. Remember, no noise. Do it careful.
Nice and easy, watch your step, you'll hafta feel for a foothold
to reach that window.

Benedict Arnold Gerardo. And what would you call Sharkey?
What name in history applies to Sharkey? Well, there was more
than one expert in that particular field. I mean the field of
going for the big loot by getting some suckers to start a war.
In Africa it was the English always doing business with some
tribal chief and everything nice and friendly until they had it
fixed the way they wanted and then good-by chief. So sooner
or later it's good-by Gerardo, with Chop and Bertha taking
him out for a stroll or a ride. Well, they all get it sooner or
later, if that helps your feelings any. But it doesn't. Because
your feelings got nothing to do with this. You're strictly from
Western Union, all you're doing here is delivering a message.
You're taking it to the Thirty-seventh District and hoping
they'll do something with it.

Yeah. You're hoping. As if there's the slightest possible
chance you can sell all this to the Captain.

Let's say there's one chance in a thousand.

And on the other side of it there's every chance you'll get
your brains knocked out, your face mashed in, your name
checked off the list marked "wanted" and placed on that other
list of "cases closed" or something on that order.

Of course, there's the water front. There's them ships. They'll
be sailing a long ways off from here. Why, you sonofabitch,
you. If you don't drop that line of thought—

All right, all right, it's dropped. We're on our way to the
station house. Our merry way. Crazy, like the man says. One
chance in a thousand. And that makes it comical. Well, so it's
comical. But even so, it seems right. Somehow it seems right.

He was climbing through the window.

Then he was in the back yard and climbing over the fence.
He went down the narrow alley, came to the cobblestoned
street, and turned west. He walked four blocks west to Clayton
and saw the one-story brick structure with the frosted-glass
lamps on either side of the entrance. The lamps were like eyes
coming closer. And the entrance with its opened doors was

like an open mouth all set to swallow him. He moved slowly toward the station house, and he thought: You could walk right past it and go back to Skid Row, where there ain't no worries at all.

But Skid Row was a long ways off. It was just a few blocks away and yet it was a long ways off. It was a land of boozed-up dreams where nothing mattered, where nothing special happened, like on the moon. There was no use trying for the moon and it was the same no-dice with Skid Row. Both places were off limits and the boundary line was the station house.

He went up the stone steps, went past the frosted-glass lamps, then through the opened doorway and into the roll room, where the benches were empty except for a wino sleeping flat on his back. A blue-shirted attendant was sweeping the floor. On the wall the clock showed four-twenty. From the corridor on the other side of the room there was twangy chatter coming in from car radios.

He crossed the roll room to the corridor, and walked down the corridor past the door marked "House Sergeant" and the door marked "Detectives" and toward the door marked "Captain." He opened the door and entered the office and saw Captain Kinnard sitting at a desk, bent over with his head on his folded arms. On the desk there was a whisky bottle, three quarters full. On the floor beside the desk there was another bottle and it was empty.

Whitey coughed to get the attention of the Captain.

The Captain raised his head and looked at Whitey. Then he shut his eyes tightly. He opened his eyes and took another look. His mouth opened and closed, then opened very wide as he leaped up from the desk, hurling himself across the room with his fist shooting from the shoulder and smashing against Whitey's jaw. Whitey went sailing through the opened doorway and landed sitting down in the corridor.

The door marked "Detectives" had opened and Lieutenants Pertnoy and Taggert were standing in the corridor. They were staring at the Captain and the Captain was pointing at the small white-haired man sitting on the floor.

"Look at this," the Captain said. "Look what we got here."

"Well, now," Lieutenant Taggert said.

"Who brought him in?" Pertnoy asked.

The Captain had no answer. All he had was a tightly clamped mouth and a mixture of flame and ice in his eyes as he moved toward Whitey. He aimed a kick at Whitey's ribs. Whitey didn't move, and the heavy shoe made contact with Whitey's side. As Whitey fell over on his face, the Captain kicked him again. The Captain was making noises like an animal and stepping back to ready another kick.

Whitey looked up at Captain Kinnard and said, "How's it feel?"

The Captain blinked. He took another step backward.

"Does it hurt?" Whitey asked.

The Captain blinked again. His mouth was open but he couldn't say anything.

"I hope it don't hurt too much," Whitey said.

Taggert looked at Pertnoy and said, "I know what this one needs. A strait jacket. Listen to him talking to himself."

"No," Whitey said. He sat up slowly. "I'm talking to the Captain."

"Really?" Taggert murmured. His expression was clinical, and he leaned over with his hands on his knees, like a nerve specialist talking to a patient. "I think you got it twisted. You didn't kick him. He kicked you."

Whitey smiled dimly. "That the way you see it? I don't see it that way. I think he kicked himself."

Taggert straightened and frowned at Pertnoy. The Captain was staring at Whitey. For a few moments it was very quiet in the corridor. The only sound was the muffled noise coming from the roll room, where the wino was snoring and the attendant was sweeping the floor.

Whitey was aiming the smile at nothing in particular and saying, "You ready, Captain?"

"Ready for what?" The Captain's voice was choked.

"For the news," Whitey said. "For the morning extra edition."

"You're the morning extra," the Captain said. He was trying not to tremble as he looked at Whitey. "I got the headline right in front of me."

You ain't just kidding, Whitey said without sound, and he thought: He's got the headline standing there where it's one of these lieutenants who's hungry for a captain's badge and

itching for the big loot that comes in when Sharkey makes this
station house the branch office of Sharkey and Company. So
it's either Pertnoy or Taggert. But which one? You can't flip
your finger and say eeny, meeny, miney, mo. It's gotta be arithmetic. It's two minus one equals one. That's what's gotta be
done here, it's strictly a matter of subtraction. But how do we
go about it?

He sat there on the corridor floor and heard the Captain
saying, "Get up."

He looked at the Captain's big fists and told himself he was
in no hurry to get up.

"Get up, killer," the Captain said. "Get up so I can knock
you down again."

Whitey's eyes moved up from the Captain's fists to focus on
the Captain's face. It was the color of milk. Poor sick bastard,
Whitey thought, and he wanted to perform some brotherly act
like giving the Captain a soft pillow for his splitting head. But
sometimes, he knew, you gotta knock them out before you can
help them. Like when they're going under in deep water and
sure as hell this one is going under. What you'll hafta do is hit
him with a left hook, give it to him dead center between the
eyes. So don't wait, don't think about it, just give it to him.

"You're dying," Whitey said to the Captain. "You're a dying
man."

The Captain closed his eyes and kept them closed for a long
moment.

"And nobody cares," Whitey said, knowing it was a very
hard left hook, seeing the Captain reeling with the impact, although actually the Captain was motionless.

Whitey hooked him again. "You're all alone," Whitey said.
"You ain't got a friend in the world, not even that whisky bottle
I saw on your desk. It can't give you no lift because you're too
far down."

The Captain's eyes were wide open and staring past Whitey,
past Taggert and Pertnoy, aiming all the way down the corridor, going on across the roll room and out the door, going on
and on and away from everything.

It's working, Whitey thought. I think it's working.

But then he couldn't be too sure because now the Captain

looked at him again. There was a moment of knowing it was touch and go, it was gonna be this or that, and the Captain would either lunge at him and rip him apart or take hold of the other prisoner who wore a blue shirt and a captain's badge.

The Captain turned away from Whitey and walked with his head down, his arms limp at his sides as he entered his office.

15

WHITEY REMAINED sitting on the corridor floor. He looked up at the two detectives and saw they were watching the opened doorway of the Captain's office. No sound was coming from the office and it went on like that for the better part of a minute. Then there was the sound of glass on wood, the whisky bottle on the desktop, the bottle lifted and lowered and lifted again, the glass bottom tapping on the wood as the drinker played with the bottle and fought with it, fighting against the idea of another drink.

The glass hit hard on the wood and Whitey heard the ice-cold voice of the Captain: "All right, I'm ready for him now. Bring him in."

Whitey stood up. Followed closely by the two detectives, he moved toward the office. In the doorway he turned and looked at the two detectives. He saw the light-brown pompadour and clean-shaven face of Taggert, saw Taggert's carefully knotted tie and expensively tailored Oxford-gray suit and the semiglossy black Scotch-grain shoes. He thought: This tells you exactly nothing. And his eyes went to Pertnoy, taking in the flat-brushed pale-blond hair, the gray sort-of-poolroom complexion, the slim physique attired in flannel that needed pressing. Then up again to Pertnoy's face to check the notion that this man was on the cute side, cute with a cue stick or a deck of cards. But it was just a notion so far.

He heard the Captain telling him to sit down. The Captain spoke flatly, pointing to a chair at the side of the desk. Whitey seated himself, his arms crossed in his lap, his eyes looking directly at the Captain.

"Start talking," the Captain said.

Whitey told himself to forget there were others in the room. The two detectives were standing near the desk and he knew they were there, but now he had to talk as though they weren't there, and he said, "Nobody brought me in. I came in on my own two feet."

"Your conscience?" the Captain said. And he managed a trace of a smile.

"No," Whitey said. "It ain't conscience. It's information."

"I don't think so," the Captain murmured. "I think you're gonna tell me a fairy tale. Or something from Ripley."

"Ripley always backed it up," Whitey said.

"Can you?"

"I think so. It depends."

"On what?"

"On you, Captain." And then, making it a gamble, "It depends on how much brains you got left."

Captain Kinnard started to lose the smile. His lips strained to hold it, managed to hold it, and then went farther than that and made it wider, almost a pleasant smile. He nodded slowly as though admitting that the prisoner had made a point. He said, "I think there's still some tools upstairs. Keep talking."

"Here's item one. I didn't kill the policeman."

The Captain didn't say anything.

"Item two. I know who did it."

And he waited for the Captain to say something. The Captain remained silent and went on smiling at him.

He returned the smile and said, "You ready for item three?"

The Captain nodded again.

"Item three is the clincher," Whitey said. "The riots." The Captain shivered as though he'd been pushed into icy water. He sat there with his hands sliding across the desktop, searching for the edge so he could grip it.

Whitey said, "The riots are a put-up job."

For some moments the only sound was three men breathing. The Captain wasn't breathing.

Then Whitey said, "It's an organization. The man who killed the cop is working for them. They're racket people and they wanna take over the neighborhood."

Another pause. Whitey told himself it was all timing now and he had to get it timed just right.

He said, "They can't take over while you're in this station house. They're trying to get you out."

And another pause. And the Captain saying, "Go on, mister. I'm listening."

"They have it figured you can't be bought, you can't be bumped, they ain't in no position to put pills in your coffee. So they're doing it the slow way. Slow but sure. And when it comes, it'll come from City Hall. They know you're slated to go if you can't stop these race riots."

The Captain looked down at his hands. His hands gripped the edge of the desk. He said very quietly, "Where'd you get this?"

"I can take you there," Whitey said.

"And then what? What can you show me? Can you show me something that proves what you're saying?"

Whitey nodded. "It's in the cellar," he said. "They got a big show arranged for tomorrow night. The way they got it planned, it's gonna be the biggest of all. This time they're looking for the pay-off, and if you look in the cellar you'll see they're not playing. They got guns stacked there."

The Captain raised his head and for a long moment he gazed at Whitey. Then, getting up very slowly, he said, "All right, let's you and me go for a ride."

Whitey didn't move.

"Come on," the Captain said.

But Whitey sat there, knowing he had to swing it now, it had to be complete or it wasn't any good. He looked at the two detective lieutenants and wished he could see inside their heads so he could point his finger at one instead of two. His finger was indicating both of them and he was saying, "I want these men to come along." The Captain was halfway to the door. He stopped and looked at Whitey and said, "Why?"

"For my protection," Whitey said. He smiled at Captain Kinnard. "For yours, too."

"How come?"

"Just in case you blow your top again."

"You think I'm that bad off?"

"Yes," Whitey said. "I'm scared to be alone with you."

But his eyes were saying something different, begging the Captain to understand, to add some number and arrive at a total.

The Captain looked at the two detective lieutenants. For some moments the Captain didn't say anything. And then, his voice toneless, "All right, we'll make it a foursome."

Whitey got up from the chair.

The four of them walked out of the room.

On the instrument panel of the black-and-orange squad car the clock showed four-forty. The speedometer showed twenty miles per hour. The Captain was driving and he had to drive slowly because they were on River Street and this section of the street was hard on tires. There were a lot of bumps and deep chuckholes. From curb to curb the street was littered with overturned ash cans, fruit boxes, and broken glass, the tokens of the action that had taken place earlier tonight. The car's headlights put a bright polish on the asphalt ribboned with bloodstains.

Whitey sat beside the Captain. In the rear-view mirror he saw the two detectives in the back seat. Pertnoy was smoking a cigarette and Taggert was leaning back comfortably with his arms folded.

"Where do I turn?" the Captain asked.

"Next block. You go left," Whitey said.

They hit one of the ash cans and it made a clatter as it rolled toward the curb. Whitey focused on the rear-view mirror and saw that Pertnoy was finished with the cigarette, and now he was busy with something else. Whatever it was, it sounded metallic. Then it made an efficient clicking sound and Whitey knew it was a revolver and Pertnoy was loading it. The rear-view mirror showed a vague smile on Pertnoy's face.

Whitey turned and looked directly at Pertnoy. The detective went on smiling and inserting clips in the automatic. He saw Whitey looking at him and he widened the smile just a little and said, "You ever get hit with one of these?"

"No," Whitey said.

"It don't shoot water," Pertnoy said.

"I guess not." Whitey returned Pertnoy's smile. Then it occurred to him that he was paying too much attention to Pertnoy. He got rid of the smile and looked at Taggert and said, "You better load up, too."

"Mine's loaded already," Taggert said.

"Naturally," Pertnoy murmured.

Taggert looked at Pertnoy. "What do you mean, naturally?"

Pertnoy pointed to Taggert and said to Whitey, "He's a former boy scout. He's always prepared."

"And you're always funny," Taggert said. "You're always very funny."

"Cut it out," the Captain told them.

"You ought to be in vaudeville," Taggert said to Pertnoy. "You'd be a big hit."

"I don't think so," Pertnoy said. "I don't care much for the spotlight."

"Meaning what?" Taggert's voice was stiff.

"Meaning nothing," Pertnoy said mildly. "Unless it means something to you. Does it mean something to you?"

"No," Taggert said. "Why should it?"

Pertnoy shrugged. He didn't say anything.

The squad car had turned left and it was moving very slowly on the narrow street. The street was extremely narrow and on both sides the tires scraped the curbs. The car bumped lightly on the cobblestones. Whitey was still facing the back seat and he saw Pertnoy replacing the loaded revolver in the shoulder holster. He was doing it very slowly and carefully, smiling while he did it. Taggert was watching him. There was no expression on Taggert's face. But it seemed he was aching to say something to Pertnoy. His mouth opened and closed and opened again.

And then, not looking at Taggert, but letting the smile drift sideways toward him, Pertnoy said, "Go on, say it. I don't mind if you say it."

"I don't like working with you," Taggert said. "I never liked working with you."

"When they feel that way," Pertnoy said aloud to himself, "they oughta quit."

"I been thinking," Taggert said. "I have a definite desire to punch you in the mouth."

"Now look," the Captain said. "I won't have this." He was trying to concentrate on the wheel and the accelerator. The car was creeping along at five miles per hour and every few moments the front tires got jammed against the curbs and the Captain had to put it in reverse and straighten the wheels. Now it was quiet in the back seat but the quiet was colder and deeper than the talking and the Captain said to them, "I said

stop it and I mean stop it. And you." He spoke to Whitey.
"You face front. You wanna look at something, look at the
windshield."

Whitey turned and faced the windshield and his eyes were
aimed at the rear-view mirror. He saw Pertnoy lighting another
cigarette. Taggert was sitting up straight and rigid, breathing
somewhat heavily and looking at Pertnoy.

"Because I know," Taggert blurted, and it was like someone
throwing up curdled milk. "You think I don't know, but I do.
I got it from good authority you're a long ways off center."

"Really?" Pertnoy sipped lightly at the cigarette.

"Yes, really. The comedy is just a front. Actually you're
nothing but a freak."

"Is that what they call it?" Pertnoy murmured.

"Yes. Because that's what it is. You're a freak, Pertnoy. You
hear what I'm saying? You're just a freak."

"All right, if you want it that way," Pertnoy said.

"You men gonna stop it?" the Captain shot at them.

"This one isn't a man," Taggert said. "This one belongs in a
sideshow. I'm told he likes to be locked in dark closets. Once a
week he gives a local whore ten dollars to tie his wrists and
bind his eyes and put him in the closet for an hour."

"An hour and a half," Pertnoy corrected.

"You hear that?" Taggert said it very loudly, as though he
stood on a platform facing a large audience. "He ain't even
ashamed."

"What goes on here?" the Captain wanted to know. "What
kind of talk is this?"

Whitey pointed toward the windshield. "Down there, Captain. You park near that street lamp."

Pertnoy was saying, "In the final analysis we're all in the
same boat. We're all ashamed of something."

"That's right, get witty again," Taggert said. "Cover it up
with a gag."

"No gag, Taggert. It's fundamental truth. With me it's because I do the kind of work that makes a lot of people unhappy.
Some of them don't deserve it and that puts things off balance.
So once a week I let her put me in the closet and maybe that
gets it balanced. At any rate, it helps to—"

"You're a liar," Taggert interrupted. "That ain't the reason.

The reason is pleasure. That's the only way you can get your pleasure."

"And you?" Pertnoy purred. "What's your weakness?"

"I—"

"You'll answer him later," the Captain said. He was switching off the ignition and pulling up on the brake. They were parked near the street lamp and the Captain opened the door on Whitey's side and told Whitey to climb out. The Captain followed close behind him and then the two detectives joined them, the four of them walking now toward the street lamp, walking abreast on the cobblestones until they reached the alley.

Whitey pointed to the alley entrance on the right and they started down the alley with Whitey and the Captain in front, Whitey looking at the houses and telling himself he'd recognize the house when they came to it. He saw a flashlight in the Captain's hand but it wasn't lighted; there was enough moonlight here to let them see where they were going.

They were walking slowly in close formation, his shoulders rubbing against the Captain's shoulders and the footsteps of the two detectives very close on his heels. There was no talk. But one of the detectives was beginning to breathe somewhat heavily. Whitey could hear it, and he thought: I'd like to turn and look at them and see which one it is, that heavy breathing puts the finger on him, he's worried plenty right now and every step we take he gets worried more. Well, we'll soon be there. We're getting there, all right. What's he gonna do when we get there? What can he do? Well, that's his problem. It's quite a problem. Maybe he'll make a run for it before we arrive. But no, he wouldn't do that. He knows he can't run from bullets. He knows. But there's your house, Captain, there it is with the cellar window with no glass in it, saying, Everybody welcome, come on in and get warm.

He touched the Captain's arm and pointed to the house. Then he turned and looked at the two detectives. Whichever one of them had been breathing heavily, he had stopped now; they both breathed at the normal rate and their eyes showed nothing. They were watching the Captain, who was working on the rusty latch of the fence gate.

The Captain worked on it very carefully and it made hardly

any noise as he pulled it free. The gate swung open and the four of them walked across the back yard.

And then they stood at the cellar window and the Captain was looking at Whitey.

"The guns," the Captain said. "Where are they stashed?"

"On the floor. Near the furnace."

The Captain turned to the two detectives. "This won't take long," he said. "All it needs is a look."

"You going in alone?" It was Pertnoy.

The Captain nodded very slowly.

"Be careful," Pertnoy said.

The Captain turned and faced the cellar window. He crouched low and began to climb through. He had a hard time getting through. At first it seemed that his thick body was too wide for the window frame. He twisted and squirmed and got one shoulder through, then squirmed some more and got stuck and they watched him reaching up above his head, trying to get a hold on something for leverage. He found it and went on squirming his way in. Altogether it took him more than a minute to get in. They could hear him moving around in there and they saw the reflected glow of his flashlight pouring out in tiny splashes of bright yellow. It went on that way for some moments and then there was no light at all, and Whitey knew that the Captain was on the other side of the coal bin.

He heard Pertnoy saying, "How do you feel?"

"Me?" He faced Pertnoy. "I feel all right."

"You're not worried?"

"No," Whitey said.

"And you?" Pertnoy said to Taggert.

Taggert didn't say anything. His lips were clamped tightly and he was staring at the cellar window.

Pertnoy said, "You look plenty worried, Lieutenant."

"Leave me alone," Taggert said. He sounded as though he were talking to himself.

"You wanna spill it?" Pertnoy murmured.

Taggert glanced at Pertnoy and then at Whitey. He blinked a few times and let out a cough and followed it with a louder cough.

"You trying something?" Pertnoy asked gently, somewhat

sadly. Then, with a gesture toward the house, "You'll need more noise than that to tip them off."

Whitey looked at the face of Detective Lieutenant Taggert. The eyes were glazed and it seemed the skin was stretched to the cracking point. He wondered if Taggert was really cracking up and in the next moment he was sure of it because he saw Taggert going for the shoulder holster.

"Oh, for Christ's sake," Pertnoy said wearily.

Taggert had the revolver in his hand and it was pointed at Pertnoy's chest.

"You freak bastard," Taggert said, and Whitey knew it was sick talk, it was persecution stuff, the way they talk to the attendants and the visitors when they're very sick. "I won't let you laugh at me."

"I only laugh when it's funny," Pertnoy said. There was real pity in his voice.

But it didn't reach Taggert. It seemed that nothing could reach Taggert now. He began to sob like a child, and what came out of his mouth was a kindergarten complaint. "You—you're always picking on me. Just—just because I get my shaves in barbershops. And get my suits custom-made. And wear expensive shoes. What's—what's wrong with that?"

Pertnoy didn't reply. It was as though he realized he couldn't make contact with Taggert.

"And," Taggert choked on it, "that mirror I put up on the wall. In the office. That tickled you, didn't it? You had a lot of fun with that mirror. You thought it was so comical I like to look at myself."

"You need that mirror now," Pertnoy said. His voice was like a dash of cold water, trying to bring Taggert out of it. "You ought to see yourself now."

"I—" Taggert blinked several times. He turned his head slowly and looked at the house. He said very quietly, "How'd you know I was in with them?"

"Just a notion I had," Pertnoy said. "I guess it was growing on me. A lot of little things, but I couldn't put them together. You listening?"

Taggert nodded solemnly. He came a step closer to Pertnoy and he had the gun just a few inches away from Pertnoy's chest.

Pertnoy wasn't looking at the gun. He was saying, "In the car, when we were driving here. When you called me a pervert. As if you just had to get it out. As if you'd been holding it back for a long time and you had that one last chance to get it out."

"But it didn't hurt you." Taggert was sobbing again. "It didn't even move you."

Pertnoy shrugged. He looked at Whitey and shrugged again.

"I wonder—" Taggert blubbered. "I wonder if this can move you," and he pulled the trigger.

16

PERTNOY WENT down with a bullet in his lung and before he hit the ground another bullet went into his abdomen. Taggert walked toward him to shoot him again and Whitey came in from the side and made a grab for Taggert's wrist. Taggert turned and shot at Whitey and missed. Then Taggert aimed again at Whitey but just then a bullet came from the cellar window and went into Taggert's shoulder.

Whitey had thrown himself to the ground, and as he rolled over he caught a glimpse of the cellar window. He saw Captain Kinnard pointing the gun at Taggert. He heard the Captain saying, "Here I am, Taggert. Right here."

But as the Captain said it, a light was switched on in the cellar, and someone was shooting at the Captain. Then the Captain wasn't there at the window and Whitey heard a lot of shooting going on in the cellar. He told himself to forget the cellar and concentrate on Taggert. As he turned his head, he saw Taggert clutching the injured shoulder with the arm hanging limply, the hand straining to hold onto the gun. Taggert was backing away from Pertnoy, who had pulled himself up to a sitting position and taken out his revolver. Pertnoy was biting hard on his lip, biting so hard that blood came seeping out. It was bright blood and it mixed with the frothy blood that welled up from his throat and gushed out of his mouth. The front of Pertnoy's jacket was covered with blood pouring down from the wound in his chest, and from his punctured middle the blood spurted and streamed over his trousers. But the revolver in Pertnoy's hand was fairly steady and he had it aimed at Taggert. Whitey saw Taggert lifting the bad arm and aiming at Pertnoy's stomach. He heard Pertnoy saying, "This is silly."

Taggert shot first, but before the bullet went in, Pertnoy was able to pull the trigger. A red-black hole showed on Taggert's forehead and he was instantly dead. Pertnoy was sitting there and then sagging sideways, finally resting face down.

Whitey moved toward Pertnoy to see if he could do something for him. He knew it was a stupid thought, there really wasn't anything he could do. As he knelt beside Pertnoy, he heard the sound of the back door. He turned and saw them coming out. It was Chop and Bertha and Gerardo. They came out running. Whitey saw a gun in Chop's hand. Chop took a shot at Whitey and the bullet went into Pertnoy's face. Whitey reached for Pertnoy's revolver, telling himself he'd never handled one before, and wondering what he could do with it. He saw Chop taking aim at him and he decided the only thing to do with a gun was pull the trigger. He pulled it and the bullet went past Chop and past Bertha and hit Gerardo in the thigh. He pulled it again and saw Chop dropping the gun and hopping around, holding onto his hand.

Bertha went for the gun and Whitey shot at her and missed and caught Gerardo in the knee. Gerardo was sitting with his legs crossed and he was screeching. Chop was running back into the house. Bertha stood there frowning down at Chop's gun on the ground. Then she frowned at Whitey, and then at the gun again. She was trying to make up her mind. Whitey aimed at her immense bulk and said, "You move and you're dead."

She looked at him and said quietly, "You mean you'd hit a lady?"

He didn't know how to answer that. He saw her walking toward him. He told himself it was a female and he didn't like the idea of hurting a female. He said to himself: How stupid can you get? She walked in closer and he knew it would be very stupid if he didn't shoot her. Of course, both of them were acting stupid. The only thing that wasn't stupid was the gun. It felt solid and capable in his hand and he told himself to use it. Now Bertha was in very close and he begged himself to shoot her. He shot at her and missed and knew he'd missed purposely.

"Sucker," she said, and swung her right arm with all her weight behind it. Her big fist put the impact of more than three hundred pounds against his jaw. A few stars came down and flared in his eyes and through his eyes and then he was out of it.

*

In the station house the clock on the roll-room wall showed ten minutes past five. The roll room was crowded with policemen. The wino who'd been sleeping on the bench was still asleep. On the same bench Whitey sat leaning back with his head against the wall. He had an ice bag pressed to his jaw. He told himself the cops were very considerate to let him use the ice bag. It sure helped. But a drink would help more. He wished he had a drink in front of him.

"How you doing?"

He looked up. It was Captain Kinnard.

"I guess I'll make it," Whitey said. He took the ice bag away from his swollen jaw. He touched his jaw and winced slightly. Then he shrugged and placed the ice bag on the bench beside him.

"You wanna go now?" the Captain asked.

"Is it all right?"

The Captain nodded. "You're clear. We got a confession from your friend Gerardo."

Whitey stood up. For some moments he was quiet. And then, not looking at the Captain, "Only Gerardo?"

"The others got away."

"What?"

"I said they got away. They had a car and they got away."

"Oh," Whitey said. He was staring at the floor.

"What's the matter?" the Captain said.

He shook his head slowly. "Nothing."

"Well, anyway," the Captain said, "we put them out of business. There won't be no more riots, that's for sure."

Whitey wasn't listening. He was thinking about her. In his mind he could see the gray-green eyes and the lighter-than-bronze hair, and he said to himself: You didn't even get a chance to talk to her. And if you'd had the chance? What then? What could be said? Not a damn thing more than hello again and good-by again. Because she'd never leave Sharkey. She can't leave Sharkey. If she tries to leave him, he puts the hook on her and drags her back. She knows she can't skip out on him. So that's the way it is. She's hooked, that's all. Maybe she wants to be hooked, whether she knows it or not. After all, that's the only life she knows, and without it she's nowhere.

Like you're nowhere without a drink. And sure as hell you need one now. All right, stop carrying on. At least you had another look at her. You had that, anyway. So you ought to be satisfied. All right, you're satisfied. You feel great. But where can I get a drink?

He heard the Captain saying, "You look knocked out. If you want to, you can sleep here."

"No," he said. "But I could use a bracer. I'm kinda thirsty."

The Captain nodded toward the corridor. "Go in my office. It's on the desk. Take it with you."

Whitey smiled. "Thanks, Captain."

"No," the Captain said. He didn't smile. "I'm saying thanks. Thanks a million, mister."

Whitey walked across the roll room and down the corridor and into the Captain's office. It was there on the desk, the whisky bottle three quarters full. He picked it up and held it under his coat as he walked out the side door of the station house.

It was very cold outside and he walked fast to get some circulation in his legs. After a while he stopped and uncapped the bottle and drank, and a few minutes later he drank again. It felt fine going down. On River Street, headed north toward Skid Row, he stopped and took a big drink. Then he looked at the bottle. It was about half filled. He wondered where he could find Bones and Phillips. They ought to be somewhere around.

Then he was on Skid Row and he found them in the all-night eatery across the street from the flophouse. They were seated at the counter near the window. Of course, they weren't eating anything; the hash house never handed out free meals. They were just sitting there at the counter.

Whitey tapped on the window. Bones and Phillips looked up. They came hurrying out of the hash house and Phillips said loudly, "We been worried to death. Where the hell you been?"

"I took a walk," Whitey said.

"He took a walk," Bones told Phillips. "He keeps us sitting up all night and he says he just took a walk."

"Look at his face," Phillips said. "He's all banged up."

Whitey shrugged and didn't say anything. Bones came in

close to Whitey and sniffed a few times. Then Bones looked sideways at Phillips and said quietly, "I'll be a sonofabitch, he scored for the booze."

Whitey smiled and reached under his coat and took out the bottle.

The three of them walked across the street. They sat down on the pavement with their backs against the wall of the flophouse. The pavement was terribly cold and the wet wind from the river came blasting into their faces. But it didn't bother them. They sat there passing the bottle around, and there was nothing that could bother them, nothing at all.

CHRONOLOGY

NOTE ON THE TEXTS

NOTES

Chronology

1917   Born David Loeb Goodis in Philadelphia on March 2, the oldest child of William Goodis, co-owner of a news dealership on the southeast corner of 2nd and Chestnut Streets, and Mollie (Halpern) Goodis. (William Goodis was born in Russia in 1882, emigrating with his mother, Rebecca, around 1890. He will later become a cotton yarn salesman, working for Globe Dye Works and the William Goodis Co. Mollie was born in Pennsylvania in 1895 of Russian émigré parents.) At time of Goodis's birth, family resides with William's mother at 870 North 6th Street, but will live for most of his childhood and adolescence at 4758 North 10th Street, in the middle-class Logan neighborhood.

1920   Brother Jerome Goodis born (exact date of birth unknown). He will die from meningitis around age three.

1923   Brother Herbert Goodis born.

1923–29   Attends General David Bell Birney Elementary School.

1929–31   Attends Jay Cooke Jr. Middle School, where he meets Paul Garabedian, who will remain a lifelong friend.

1935   Graduates from Simon Gratz High School in Philadelphia, where he edits the student newspaper, *Spotlight*, joins the track and swimming teams, and serves as President of Gratz Student Association. Gives valedictorian speech, "Youth Looks at Peace."

1938   Graduates from Temple University with degree in Journalism, and works briefly for a Philadelphia advertising agency. At Temple, Goodis writes for student paper, *News*, and contributes cartoons to student magazine, *The Owl*. (Will later claim he worked during this period on an unpublished, lost novel, *The Ignited*, though existence of this book may be one of the deadpan fabrications in which Goodis occasionally indulged in interviews or author notes: "The title was prophetic. Eventually I threw it in the furnace.")

1939   First novel *Retreat from Oblivion* is published by Dutton.
         Goodis moves to New York City, where he lives in Green-
         wich Village and the Upper West Side. Starts to write for
         pulp magazines, including *Wings, Battle Birds, Fighting Aces,
         The Lone Eagle, Gangland Detective Stories, True Gangster
         Stories, Detective Fiction Weekly, 10 Story Western, Air War,
         New Detective Magazine, Double-Action Detective, Popular
         Sports Magazine, Sinister Stories, Thrilling Western, Dime
         Western, Captain Combat, G-Men Detective,* and *Dime De-
         tective,* among others. His stories appear under his own
         name (or rarely as Dave Goodis) and probably also under
         various pseudonyms, including Lance Kermit, Logan C.
         Claybourne, Ray. P. Shotwell, and David Crewe. (In keeping
         with standard pulp publishing practices, these pseudonyms
         likely served additionally as recurrent "house pseudonyms"
         for other writers in the magazines where Goodis's stories
         frequently appeared, the pseudonyms in some cases pre-
         dating his own initial appearances, making a thorough ac-
         counting of his magazine writing impossible. Goodis will
         continue to publish in pulp magazines at least into 1947,
         and perhaps through the early-to-mid-1950s. Goodis main-
         tained that he published writing under seven names, and
         estimated that in the early 1940s he wrote over five million
         words in five years.)

1940–45 In New York Goodis also writes for radio programs includ-
         ing "House of Mystery," "Superman," and "Hop Harri-
         gan," for the latter of which he is ultimately Script Editor
         and an associate producer. When in Philadelphia, Goodis
         maintains an association with the Neighborhood Players,
         where he works alongside actress Grayson Hall (Shirley
         Grossman), who will remain his close friend for many
         years. Philadelphia and New Jersey friends include Paul
         Garabedian, Frank Ford (also known as Ed Felbin), Jane
         Melgin (later Jane Fried), Irving "Bud" Fried, Joe Schor,
         Monroe Schwartz, Leonard Cobrin, Dick Levy, Stanton
         Cooper, Ruth Burnat (later Ruth Norkin and Ruth Wend-
         kos), Dick Levy, Phyllis Schulman, Marvin and Omi Yollin,
         and Herb Gross.

1942   During a short stay in Los Angeles, Goodis works on treat-
         ment, "Destination Unknown," for Universal. Visits Mexico,
         and is particularly enamored by the bullfights in Tijuana.

1943   On October 17, Goodis marries Elaine Astor (1917–1986),

formerly of Philadelphia, at the Ohev Shalom Congrega-
tion, in Los Angeles.

1945   In December Warner Brothers acquires film rights to his
novel *Dark Passage* for $25,000. Elaine Astor Goodis files
for divorce in Philadelphia.

1946   Following serialization in *The Saturday Evening Post, Dark
Passage* is published by Julian Messner. Warner Brothers
signs Goodis to a term contract for an initial year plus five
options for renewal. His starting salary is $750.00 a week,
with 5 step-increases that ultimately would raise his salary
to $2,000 a week. Contract specifies a six-month annual
working period at Warner Brothers, with six months off to
write fiction, and Goodis will spend part of each year in
Los Angeles and Philadelphia. Publishes story, "Caravan to
Tarim," in *Colliers* (October 26). Goodis and wife divorce.

1947   Release of Warner Brothers film of *Dark Passage*, directed
and written by Delmer Daves, and starring Humphrey Bo-
gart and Lauren Bacall. Publication of novels *Nightfall*
(Julian Messner) and *Behold This Woman* (Appleton). With
James Gunn, writes screenplay for Warner Brothers film *The
Unfaithful*, based on W. Somerset Maugham story "The
Letter," directed by Vincent Sherman. At Warner Brothers
Goodis also works on story treatments and scripts, "Within
These Gates," "Somewhere in the City," "The Fall of Valor,"
"The Persian Cat," and "Up Till Now." Comments on
"Black Dahlia" murder case for *Los Angeles Evening Herald
Express* (February 6). In early April, visits Boston with Del-
mer Daves, producer Jerry Wald, and art director Leo Kuter,
scouting locations at historic sites for "Up Till Now," sup-
posedly completing the film treatment on the train from
Hollywood to Boston. ("Up Till Now," Daves remarks, "is
aimed at giving people a look at themselves and their heritage. We want to show people what the Founding Fathers
gave us to live up to and we want to analyze the Declaration
of Independence and the Constitution in terms of personal
problems today." The film will not be made, but Goodis will
recast elements of the work for his 1954 novel, *The Blonde on
the Street Corner*.) Goodis directs "amateur theatricals" in
Los Angeles for the Vermont Players of the Sinai Young
Peoples' League, including productions of Noel Coward's
Fumed Oak and Walter MacQuade's *Exclusive Model* at the
Sinai Temple at West 4th Street and New Hampshire. During

his periods in Hollywood, Goodis variously sleeps on the sofas of friends (including lawyer Allan Norkin, to whom he pays $4.00 a week), resides at the rundown Oban Hotel, or rents an apartment at the elegant Hollywood Tower Apartments. Norkin recalled Goodis receiving phone calls from Ann Sheridan, Lizabeth Scott, and Lauren Bacall. Goodis becomes friendly with screenwriter Samuel Fuller, who many years later will adapt and direct a film based on his 1954 novel *Street of No Return*. When in Philadelphia, Goodis lives with his parents and brother. In Hollywood, Goodis develops a reputation for personal eccentricity and practical jokes.

1948 Works on story treatment "Of Missing Persons" for Warner Brothers, which grants him rights to publish the work as a novel. His Warner Brothers activities conclude in June.

1949–50 Goodis is hired by producer Monte Proser to adapt Jon Edgar Webb's prison novel, *Four Steps to the Wall*, for a film, and in writing the screenplay he apparently retains only the original names of characters, creating his own story. While working on the script, Goodis lives at the Crown Hill Hotel, a Los Angeles flophouse, although he apparently is earning $1,000 a week from Proser. Disappointed by Goodis's reshaping of his novel, Webb takes over adaptation of *Four Steps to the Wall*. Goodis stops dividing his year between Los Angeles and Philadelphia, and returns to Philadelphia to reside with his parents and brother, now living (since the early 1940s) at 6305 North 11th Street in the East Oak Lane neighborhood. Gallimard publishes first French translation of Goodis, *Cauchemar* (*Dark Passage*), in the Série Blême. (His writing will attract growing interest among European aficionados of crime fiction.) Philadelphia haunts over the coming years will include Club Harlem, the Blue Note, the Blue Horizon (for boxing matches), and Superior Billiards. Because of *Dark Passage* and his stint in Hollywood, Goodis would remain something of a Philadelphia semi-celebrity, and the occasional subject of newspaper gossip columns ("David Goodis, author of "Dark Passage," out funning Club Harlem-way, squiring fine-framed and 'tractive sepia misses.")

1950 Publishes novel *Of Missing Persons*. Broadcast of *Sure As Fate* (CBS), television production of *Nightfall*, directed by Yul Brynner.

1951   Gold Medal publishes novel *Cassidy's Girl*; it is a paperback original, like all of his subsequent novels. Broadcast of *Studio One* (CBS) television production of *Nightfall*, directed by John Peyser. Around this time Goodis starts relationship with artist Selma Hortense Burke, which will last until 1956.

1952   Publishes novels *Street of the Lost* (Gold Medal) and *Of Tender Sin* (Gold Medal). Broadcast of *Lux Video Theater* (CBS) episode, "Ceylon Treasure," based on forthcoming Goodis story "The Blue Sweetheart," directed by Buzz Kulik, with Ronald Long, Audrey Meadows, and Edmond O'Brien.

1953   Publishes novels *The Moon in the Gutter* (Gold Medal) and *The Burglar* (Lion). Publishes stories in *Manhunt*, "The Blue Sweetheart" (April), "Professional Man" (October), and "Black Pudding" (December).

1954   Publishes novels *The Blonde on the Street Corner* (Lion), *Black Friday* (Lion), and *Street of No Return* (Gold Medal).

1955   Publishes novel *The Wounded and the Slain* (Gold Medal), the Jamaican setting reflecting Goodis's trip there. Writes screenplay for film version of *The Burglar*, directed by Paul Wendkos and featuring Dan Duryea, Jayne Mansfield, Martha Vickers, Stewart Bradley, Peter Capell, and Mickey Shaughnessy; the film is shot on location in Philadelphia during the summer, but release is delayed. Release of *Seccion Desparecidos* or *Section des disparus*, Argentinian/French film based on *Of Missing Persons*, directed by Pierre Chenal.

1956   Publishes novel *Down There* (Gold Medal). Broadcast of *Lux Video Theater* episode, "The Unfaithful," based on 1947 Warner Brothers film written by Goodis and James Gunn, directed by Earl Eby, with Jan Sterling.

1957   Publishes novel *Fire in the Flesh* (Gold Medal). Release of *Nightfall*, film directed by Jacques Tourneur, with Aldo Ray, Brian Keith, Anne Bancroft, Jocelyn Brando, Frank Albertson, and Rudy Bond; and of *The Burglar*, following Jayne Mansfield's success in *The Girl Can't Help It* and *The Wayward Bus*.

1958   Publishes story "The Plunge" in *Mike Shayne Mystery Magazine* (October).

1960   Release of *Tirez sur le pianist (Shoot the Piano Player)*, film directed by François Truffaut based on *Down There*, with Charles Aznavour, Marie Dubois, and Nicole Berger. Goodis meets Truffaut in New York. Grove Press reissues the novel under the title *Shoot the Piano Player*, with an enthusiastic blurb by Henry Miller: "Truffaut's film was so good I had doubts the book could equal it. I have just read the novel and I think it is even better than the film." Broadcast of episode of *Bourbon Street Beat* (ABC), "False Identity," based on *Of Missing Persons*, directed by William J. Hole, Jr. Dick Carroll, Goodis's editor at Gold Medal, dies, and Carroll's successor, Knox Burger, is less hospitable to his fiction.

1961   Publishes novel *Night Squad* (Gold Medal), the last book to be published during Goodis's lifetime.

1963   Writes teleplay, "An Out for Oscar," based on a novel by Henry Kane, for *The Alfred Hitchcock Hour*. Goodis's father dies. Herbert Goodis is confined to Norristown State Hospital for severe psychiatric problems.

1965   Publishes story, "The Sweet Taste," in *Manhunt* (January). Goodis initiates lawsuit against United Artists Television, Inc. and ABC claiming that the television show "The Fugitive" (1963–1967) infringed on copyright of his novel *Dark Passage*.

1966   Goodis's mother dies, and he is briefly hospitalized at the Philadelphia Psychiatric Center (later known as the Belmont Center for Comprehensive Treatment). According to his friend Monroe Schwartz, Goodis is mugged leaving Linton's Restaurant on North Broad Street, and hit on the head when he refuses to surrender his wallet, the episode leaving him weak, frail, and with a chronically bloodshot right eye. Goodis also informs members of his family that he has a "coronary condition." Between illnesses he gives two depositions in New York for lawsuit involving "The Fugitive" and *Dark Passage*. (In 1970 Federal District Court will dismiss complaint about "The Fugitive" against United Artists Television, Inc. on grounds that since Goodis had published installments of *Dark Passage* in *The Saturday Evening Post* without a copyright notice appearing in the magazine, the work was in the public domain. Goodis Estate appeals, and Court of Appeals reverses lower court decision, remanding case for trial. In 1972 Goodis Estate accepts $12,000 in full settlement of lawsuit against United Artists Television.) Jean-Luc Godard includes character named David Goodis (played by Yves Afonso) in *Made in U.S.A.*

1967   David Goodis dies at the Albert Einstein Medical Center in Philadelphia on January 7. Death certificate lists "cerebral vascular accident" as cause of death. Funeral on January 10, at Rosenberg's Raphael-Sacks Funeral Home, and burial in Roosevelt Memorial Park. Goodis wills his personal effects and the bulk of his $220,000 estate in trust for his brother Herbert, along with $30,000 to "our faithful family employee" Camelia Edmonds. Novel *Somebody's Done For* published posthumously by Banner.

Note on the Texts

This volume contains five novels by David Goodis: *Dark Passage* (1946), *Nightfall* (1947), *The Burglar* (1953), *The Moon in the Gutter* (1953), and *Street of No Return* (1954).

Goodis's second novel, *Dark Passage*, was published eight years after his first, *Retreat from Oblivion* (1939). In the interim he had devoted himself to writing prolifically for pulp magazines and radio. *Dark Passage* was originally serialized in *The Saturday Evening Post* (July 20–September 7, 1946); Warner Brothers purchased movie rights even before the novel was serialized. *Dark Passage* was published in hardcover by Julian Messner (New York, 1946). A second edition, tied to the 1947 release of the film version starring Humphrey Bogart and Lauren Bacall, was published in the same year by World (Cleveland). A hardcover edition appeared in England from Heinemann (London, 1947). In 1948 an American paperback was published by Dell (New York) in their "map-back" series devoted chiefly to crime novels. The text published here is that of the 1946 Julian Messner edition.

Nightfall was also published by Julian Messner, in 1947, and in England by Heinemann in 1948. It was reprinted in paperback by Lion Books (New York) under the title *The Dark Chase* in 1953; Lion issued the book again in 1956 under the restored title *Nightfall* to coincide with the release of the Columbia film version. The text published here is that of the 1947 Julian Messner edition.

Starting with *Cassidy's Girl* in 1951, all of Goodis's novels were published as paperback originals. *The Burglar* was published in February 1953 by Lion Books, whose editor-in-chief was Arnold Hano. The text published here is that of the 1953 Lion edition.

Gold Medal, a paperback imprint of Fawcett, published *The Moon in the Gutter* in November 1953, the fourth Goodis novel to appear from the house under the editorship of Richard Carroll. The text published here is that of the 1953 Gold Medal edition.

Street of No Return, another Gold Medal title, appeared in September 1954. A second Gold Medal edition, textually identical but with a different cover appeared in 1961. The text published here is that of the 1954 Gold Medal edition.

This volume presents the texts of the original printings and typescripts chosen for inclusion here, but it does not attempt to reproduce nontextual features of their typographic design. The texts are presented without change, except for the correction of typographical errors. Spelling, punctuation, and capitalization are often expressive features and are not altered, even when inconsistent or irregular. The following is a list of typographical errors corrected, cited by page and line number: 4.7, tary; 30.15, patched her; 36.32, wrapping; 55.28, beside; 65.6, street; 87.23, Maybe; 122.26, Amercan; 147.13, Parry's; 153.30, State Park; 206.34, a extremely; 211.2, worth while; 215.10, that,'; 227.35, slipt; 242.2, hand.; 270.19, windup; 276.27, me?'; 283.33, more.; 288.31, Vanning; 289.19, right.; 290.21, approximeately; 290.37, button beside; 313.29, said.¶; 316.1, Isn't is,; 320.21, Frazer; 320.29, cigarete; 324.20, smile "I'm; 330.7, of a; 330.19, shoved; 333.1, frabric; 334.12, youself; 362.10, three forty; 362.18, gray; 394.23–24, of quaking; 403.25, Ciy look; 405.28, though Baylock; 443.24, with gun.; 451.25, Charlie; 458.10–11, pitch black; 485.4, solemly.; 489.27, tonight?"; 497.21, Ukranians; 499.11, safe,; 503.4, poor; 510.13, door step; 515.29, internationally minded; 516.1, asked; 516.10, this his; 540.11, said "I; 543.15, newpaper.; 543.29, same from; 550.8, was "Of; 560.20, "what; 569.10, said.; 570.37, told me; 571.25, tall bony; 574.20, Street the; 575.3, Channing the; 588.6, it."; 590.2, matter of fact; 596.22, anwer; 608.19, he heard; 612.17, it.; 615.22, watcha; 642.9, Scotch grain; 651.10–11, Of maybe; 679.35, his eyes.; 680.24, no no; 687.4, shrugged,; 689.17, Its; 693.18–19, saying.; 696.34, have here; 716.17, "All right."; 718.15, hesistated; 750.10, is was; 753.40, made it; 754.9, "Goddam; 786.19, Whitney.

Notes

In the notes below, the reference numbers denote page and line of the present volume; the line count includes titles and headings but not blank lines. No note is made for material found in standard reference works. For additional information and references to other studies, see Philippe Garnier, *Goodis: La Vie en Noir et Blanc* (Paris: Editions du Seuil, 1984); David Goodis, *Black Friday & Selected Stories*, ed. with introduction by Adrian Wooton (London: Serpent's Tail, 2006); David Goodis, *Street of No Return*, introduction by Robert Polito (Lakewood, Colorado: Millipede Press, 2007); Woody Haut, *Pulp Culture: Hardboiled Fiction and the Cold War* (London: Serpent's Tail, 1995); Geoffrey O'Brien, *Hardboiled America: Lurid Paperbacks and the Masters of Noir* (2nd edition, New York: Da Capo, 1997); James Sallis, *Difficult Lives: Jim Thompson—David Goodis—Chester Himes* (New York: Gryphon Books, 1993); and *David Goodis: To a Pulp*, written and directed by Larry Withers (On Air Video, 2010). A range of material relating to Goodis can be found at www.davidgoodis.com. The editor would like to thank the Philadelphia Historical Society, the Free Library of Philadelphia, and especially Lou Boxer for his generosity and insight.

DARK PASSAGE

29.25–27 *Every Tub . . . Out the Window*] Recordings by the Count Basie Orchestra; all were released on the Decca label, 1937–38, with the exception of "Lester Leaps In" (featuring Lester Young), which was released by Columbia in 1939.

35.18 *Shorty George*] Recorded by Count Basie for Decca in November 1938.

36.18 Buck Clayton] Wilbur "Buck" Clayton (1911–1991), trumpet player for the Count Basie Orchestra, 1937–43.

45.14 *Holiday for Strings*] Instrumental hit (1944) by David Rose and His Orchestra.

49.17–18 Is your trip really necessary?] Variations of the phrase were used by the American and British governments as slogans during World War II.

104.35 *Sent for You Yesterday And Here You Come Today*] Count Basie recording, featuring Jimmy Rushing as vocalist, recorded in February 1938.

176.2 Kasserine Pass] Site of a battle fought in Tunisia in February 1943, in which American troops were routed by German forces commanded by Erwin Rommel.

NIGHTFALL

199.19   Jimmy Kelly's]   Cabaret, formerly a speakeasy, at 181 Sullivan Street in Greenwich Village, billed as "The Montmartre of New York."

202.9   The Book of Knowledge]   Multivolume series originally published in England in 1908 as *The Children's Encyclopedia*, and in the United States as *The Book of Knowledge* from 1912.

202.11   Horney and Menninger]   Karen Horney (1885–1952), German-American neo-Freudian psychoanalyst, author of *The Neurotic Personality of Our Time* (1937) and *New Ways in Psychoanalysis* (1939); Karl Menninger (1893–1990), American psychiatrist, founder of the Menninger Clinic in Topeka, Kansas, and author of *Man Against Himself* (1938) and other works.

229.38   Noro Morales]   Norosbaldo Morales (1912–1964), Puerto Rican pianist and bandleader; his hit rumba recordings included "Serenata Ritmica" (1942).

246.33   Rover Boy]   The Rover Boys were protagonists of a long series of boys' adventure novels beginning with *The Rover Boys at School* (1899).

264.20–21   Charlie Chaplin . . . the Klondike]   In *The Gold Rush* (1925).

264.25   listening to Bob Hope]   Bob Hope appeared on NBC radio's *The Pepsodent Show Starring Bob Hope* from 1938 to 1948; under different names the show continued broadcasting until 1955.

265.8   Theodore's]   French restaurant formerly located at 4 East 56th Street.

290.18   Governor Winthrop desk]   Slanted-top desk of eighteenth-century origin, named for Governor John Winthrop, seventeenth-century governor of the Massachusetts Bay Colony.

295.36   Van Johnson]   Movie star (1916–2008) whose films included *A Guy Named Joe* (1943) and *Week-End at the Waldorf* (1943).

THE BURGLAR

357.19   Guy Lombardo]   Canadian-American bandleader (1902–1977), associated from 1924 onwards with his band The Royal Canadians.

366.36–367.2   Betty Grable . . . Dick Haymes]   Grable and Haymes co-starred in the Technicolor musicals *Diamond Horseshoe* (1945) and *The Shocking Miss Pilgrim* (1947).

369.2–3   the library, the big one on the Parkway]   The Parkway Central Library at 1901 Vine Street, which opened in 1927.

THE MOON IN THE GUTTER

524.11   Marin]   John Marin (1870–1953), American artist best known as a landscape painter in oils.

STREET OF NO RETURN

621.36   Tenderloin]   Philadelphia red-light district centered on Vine Street
from 8th to 11th streets.

649.22 Jeffries]   James J. Jeffries (1875–1953), world heavyweight champion
from 1899 to 1905. He came out of retirement in 1910 to contend unsuccess-
fully with Jack Johnson.

698.28   when Bob Hope comes on]   See note 264.25.

753.25–26   Firpo . . . Dempsey]   World   heavyweight   champion   Jack
Dempsey defeated Argentinian challenger Luis Ángel Firpo on September 14,
1923, at the Polo Grounds in New York.

776.5   Ripley]   Robert Ripley (1890–1949), creator of the newspaper series *Ripley's Believe It or Not!*, dedicated to odd and exotic information, which
evolved subsequently into radio and television programs.

THE LIBRARY OF AMERICA SERIES

The Library of America fosters appreciation and pride in America's literary heritage by publishing, and keeping permanently in print, authoritative editions of America's best and most significant writing. An independent nonprofit organization, it was founded in 1979 with seed funding from the National Endowment for the Humanities and the Ford Foundation.

To subscribe to the series or to order individual copies, please visit www.loa.org or call (800) 964.5778.

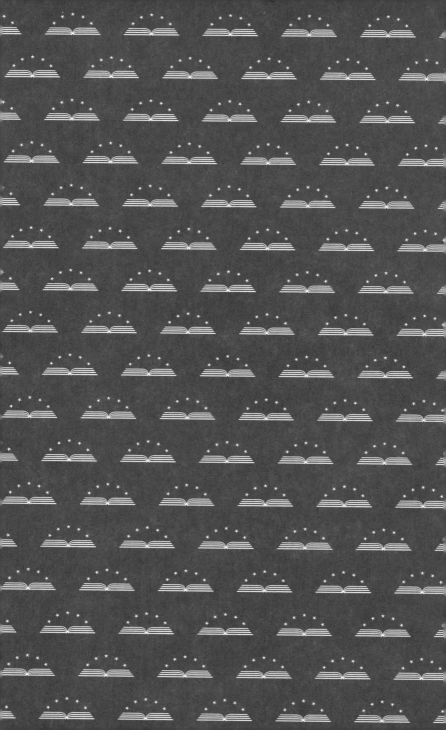